*For Meimei*

# the submissive spy

# The Submissive Spy

## Author's Note

Since the collapse of the Soviet Union in 1990-91, various locations in the former USSR have changed in spelling, most notably Kiev has now become Kyiv, and Odessa has become Odesa. Similarly, St Petersburg was known as Leningrad. I have endeavoured to retain these and other such changes in the form they were in 1977.

*   *   *

# PRELUDE – ANDREAS
# Azerbaijan, February 1975

*Presto*

# PROLOGUE – The Means

The shoreline lay in darkness to the east of the rutted road – which daylight would reveal as a flat, featureless beachscape washed by the brown-grey waters of the Caspian Sea. Emerging from the blackness ahead of the rattling Trabant were the first lights of Astara, a small, nondescript town whose sole claim to fame was its location straddling the border between the Azerbaijan Soviet Socialist Republic and Iran. The actual boundary was defined by the Astarachay River – a narrow, meandering watercourse that flowed through the middle of Astara and established the location of the border facilities in the northern and southern portions of the town.

The man driving the Trabant wore a heavy leather overcoat and matching cap against the cold. The car's passenger window didn't shut properly and the heater was not working. The battered vehicle carried no markings, nor did the driver wear a uniform that would have indicated he was with the intelligence service of any of the Eastern Bloc countries.

Andreas Meyer was a long way from his home in East Germany, and had no intention of troubling the border guards on this cold February night. It had started to rain, water flicking through the gap at the top of the passenger window, making the chill in the car even more unpleasant – but at least it kept him awake. It had been a four-hour drive down the Caspian coast from the anonymous warehouse in Azerbaijan's capital, Baku, where he had collected the four wooden crates that now sat in the boot and on the back seat. Like the heater, the car radio had long since ceased to function and Meyer had been left to his own thoughts for the drive along the flat coastal plain, where towns were few and far between.

He did not normally have time for reflection, since – until this latest diversion – his days were typically filled with analysis and decisions concerning his operatives and their marks. Now, in the noisy, wet darkness, contemplation was permissible, and came more easily.

Andrea Meyer was a child of the Second World War – the son of a Luftwaffe pilot and a young woman named Elke Stein, a machinist in the Heinkel manufacturing plant in Rostock, on the Baltic coast. Meyer's father had been killed over England in 1942, and though his mother had re-married to a co-worker named Hans Fischer, two years later, Meyer had clung to the surname on his birth certificate, even though his mother had become Elke Fischer. His father would always be an unknown but heroic figure – a bomber pilot fighting for the Fatherland – of whom the young Andreas would always be proud.

There had been another child – a second son for Elke and a younger step-brother for Andreas – born in 1944, before Hans Fischer had also perished in a bombing raid on the factory soon after the birth. Elke Fischer had raised the two boys through the hellish final years of the war and the traumatic post-war years, following the Red Army's takeover of eastern Germany and the creation of the German Democratic Republic – East Germany – in 1949.

By the time Andreas Meyer was old enough for compulsory military service, reconstruction of the country was underway, though the East would always lag behind the West. Meyer had at once taken to the order and intent of the NVA – the National People's Army – and saw in it a career opportunity, for the NVA was a priority in Cold War East Germany. Conscientious, loyal and ambitious recruits looking beyond compulsory service were soon sought out by their officers.

It had been fourteen years since the raw twenty-year-old Lieutenant Meyer had supervised the installation of barbed wire and rough blockwork along Berlin's Ebert Strasse in the dark hours of 13 August 1961. That Sunday morning was still vividly etched in his memory – the arc lights, the Volkspolizei, the armoured vehicles, and a gut-churning nervousness of everything coming unstuck in a flashpoint conflict between Soviet and Allied troops. There was no doubt in Meyer's mind that the erection of the wall to bar subversion against the countries of the Socialist Bloc had been successful. Successful, that was, save for the fact that Lina, his girlfriend at the time, had a week later abruptly left him to make her way to West Berlin, before the weak spots in the wall were gradually closed off. She had been Meyer's first love, and held a special place in his memory for that reason. None of the women passing through his life since then had brought the same innocence and intense passion of youth. She had flaming red hair and voluptuous breasts, and her betrayal still rankled him, even after all the years.

Nearing his destination, Meyer looked for a solitary ruined house that would indicate a gravel road leading westward off the main road, a kilometre short of Astara. Just when he thought he had missed it and would end up driving into the town, he saw the outline of the derelict building in the rain-blurred headlights, along with the side road just past it. The tyres crunched on to gravel as he turned off the tarmac and headed inland into the blackness. His Soviet Army map showed a narrow plain between the Caspian and the steep Talyshskiye mountains that rose over two thousand metres to peaks that would shine white with snow after sunrise. The map was largely redundant, for this was the third time he had made this trip. Meyer was a prudent man and he kept the map in case of emergency.

He looked at his watch. The luminous hands showed a little after 2 am; he was on schedule for the meeting with the Iranians. Meyer was a full *Oberst* – Colonel – of the *Hauptverwaltung Aufklärung*, the East German

Intelligence Service, known as the HVA, and had many contacts and resources at his disposal for clandestine operations. Had he wished, he could have delegated this exercise, but the operation had now become highly personal for him.

At 34, he had a reputation as a rising star of the Stasi – the Ministry of State Security. He was a protégé of powerful people not merely in the higher echelons of the HVA but also the Soviet Intelligence Service, the KGB. Three years previously, as a major, Meyer had spent twenty months seconded to the KGB First Chief Directorate in Moscow, and had finished his stint fluent in Russian. More significantly, he had been taken into the confidence of the KGB strategists who had come to rely on liaison with their East German counterparts for better access to western technological and political secrets. During that time with the 8th Department, he had visited the Caucasus region – the Socialist Republics of Georgia, Armenia and Azerbaijan – and was now familiar with the borders of Russia's ancient enemy Turkey, and the USSR's neighbour, Iran.

In most other circumstances, Meyer would have considered himself too senior to be involved with field ops, but this particular operation had originated directly from Moscow, and as such bypassed his immediate ministerial superiors. For a plan which could have world-changing consequences, Meyer could not contemplate delegating control of the crates to an unknown subordinate. He had enough influence to take leave from his office in East Berlin's Normannen Strasse, with his superiors made aware that such 'leave' was at the behest of powers beyond the East German border. That same prestige had facilitated the availability of the two crates of Czech-made Cemtex explosive and the two boxes of Rocket Propelled Grenades from the Soviet military warehouse in Baku, along with his 'transport', with no questions asked.

As the gravel road deteriorated into a muddy, rutted track barely visible in the bouncing headlight beams, Meyer returned to the part of his mind where the map of a Soviet-dominated world lay unfurled. His actions this night would be a further step – maybe not such a small one – in securing access to the warm waters of the Persian Gulf for the Eastern Bloc. Sometime in the not-too-distant future there would be a government in Iran that would be sympathetic to the Soviets, and this operation would expedite that transition.

Following that change in government, another in a series of cooperative infrastructure projects would be commenced. A heavy gauge railway between Baku in Azerbaijan and the Persian Gulf would provide land access to a Soviet fleet and give secure passage to Middle Eastern oil, while controlling the Gulf. The USSR's own vast resources would be supplemented by those of an Iran with a head of state receptive to the socialist assistance on offer from

Moscow. Iran would move from being merely within Moscow's "sphere of influence" to become a full member of the Eastern Bloc, bringing with it a wealth of oil and gas, as well as control of the energy heart of the world – the Persian Gulf. The 1973 energy crisis and skyrocketing oil prices would prove to be merely the first wave of price hikes undermining the dependent industry of the capitalist West.

Meyer's Iran involvement had begun a year after his return from Moscow to East Berlin. Success begat success, and his time in Moscow within the Soviet State Intelligence apparatus had brought with it a warm recommendation as to Major Meyer's reliable socialist inclinations and strategic foresight. The reward had been two years with the HVA in Bonn, West Germany's ad hoc capital since 1949, wherein lay the embassies of other western nations and which had become a happy hunting ground for HVA operatives working for the Soviets. To most westerners, East Germans and West Germans were indistinguishable, East Germans thus having a most valuable attribute over their Russian counterparts. The coveted posting to Bonn had come with a comfortable apartment, access to western currency and a living standard well ahead of East Berlin.

Meyer had shown his efficiency and zealousness in setting up a series of honeytraps using East German female operatives known as *inoffizieller Mitarbeiter*, or "unofficial employees". He had a remarkable flair for the work – an ability to provide the appropriate temptation and to judge the right moment to snare a hapless victim with the threat of exposure of their peccadillo. As controlling officer of a number of *inoffizieller Mitarbeiter*, it had provided him a unique insight into the sexual depravity of the west and its morally corrupt politicians in particular. It had also shown off the full skillset of Karla Graf. That had been a whole new experience.

Meyer was not a prudish man, and the extremes of his job left him unsurprised by most things in life. Karla Graf, however, lately divorced from his younger step-brother, Konrad, had proven a revelation in both Meyer's personal and professional lives. He had pulled strings to have her brought to Bonn – to a lifestyle significantly better than in Berlin, though with her family remaining under close and overt observation by the Stasi. Karla's skills in devising and executing honeytraps had brought kudos to both of them, though naturally it was only Meyer's version of the truth that went into his reports. Even those versions had drawn raised eyebrows from his priggish superiors, which he had used to further emphasize the degeneracy of the western society in Bonn. He smiled at the thought of Karla. It was a shame she was a lesbian.

While Meyer had exercised his devious skills in Bonn, within the back rooms of the Soviet and East German planners, long term and large scale strategies had moved ponderously but inexorably onward.  Within the First Chief Directorate in Moscow's Dzerzhinsky Square, the name of Andreas Meyer had resurfaced, with the recollection of the zealous officer from East Berlin who had shown initiative and insight in his time with the KGB's 8th Department, two years before.  Meyer's increased exposure to western diplomats and politicians as a "liaison officer" in Bonn, his fluency in Russian and English, and his understanding of Soviet strategies were now seen as appropriate for the role of an "industrial representative" in Iran.  He would be based in Tehran to promote the industrial capabilities and the competitive terms offered by the Eastern Bloc countries to the rapidly expanding oil-based economy of Shah Mohammad Reza Pahlavi.

The posting had also brought about his promotion to Lieutenant Colonel and Commercial Attaché at the new East German Embassy in the elegant suburb of Elahiyeh, along with a substantial expense account for the role within Tehran society.  A year of establishing contacts and setting up supply networks for the underground communist Tudeh Party of Iran had been on track for rebellion of the people, until disaster had struck.

Fresh from their success winning the 1974 Asian Games Final, the Iranian football team had moved on to the world stage as an acknowledged force, and the profile of the team was sufficient to attract competition from Eastern Bloc nations, including East Germany.  It had been Meyer's vision to utilise an Aeroflot Tupolev aircraft chartered to carry the East German team and officials to Tehran for a friendly match in Aryamehr Stadium.  The visit was to last five days – time enough for the German team to acclimatise to Tehran's weather and elevation – with the plane remaining in the low-security apron near the freight hangars.

Money had changed hands and security had been bypassed.  Four nights after their arrival, on the night of the game, the cache of small arms, RPG's, hand grenades, explosives and ammunition would be off-loaded from the plane's hold into an unmarked and unlit van driven by members of the Tudeh.

Like this night beside the Caspian, it had been raining, which Meyer had taken as a good omen at the time, concealing the presence of the van and his opening of the hold.  Since that night, however, rain now made him nervous, through the sudden materialisation of half a dozen police cars and plain clothes security out of the airport darkness.

Meyer had gone over the debacle a thousand times in his head.  Somehow there had been a leak – something he had eventually attributed to the British and their MI6.  He could not be sure if it was at the Tehran end or the East Berlin loading point, though he suspected it was the latter.  In the confusion and shouting and violent arrests under the rain-curtained headlights, he had seen the man he recognised from the British Embassy, standing discreetly in the background, beside an Iranian colonel.

The consequences had set them back months, including his own humiliating recall ahead of a likely expulsion as *persona non grata*. He had blamed it on the British, and there had been several denunciations and arrests at Schönefeld Airport that had apparently vindicated this allegation. The embarrassing matter had been hushed up at diplomatic level, with relations not helped by the German footballers winning three – nil in an ill-tempered match.

If Meyer had held a grudge against the British before that night – not least through the wartime death of his father – it was an enmity that was re-doubled after the sight of the Englishman on the airport tarmac. All the HVA intelligence had concluded that this man was MI6, and was clearly in the pocket of the Shah and his secret police, the Savak. With the loss of the weapons, Meyer had been forced to regroup and undertake several trips down the Caspian coast to smuggle the remaining munitions across the wild and mountainous border by horseback.

Now, as he drove along the rough trail into the border foothills, his eyes straining through the drizzling rain for a signal, the moment for lighting the touch paper of rebellion was approaching. As usual, there would be no specific meeting point, merely somewhere along this, the only road in the area. When the torch beam abruptly flashed from a dark smudge of trees to his left, he slowed and the Trabant stuttered to a noisy halt. The flashlight moved up to the car and Meyer turned on the small interior rooflight to show himself. He left the engine running and the headlights on as he opened the driver's door, pulling his leather cap down firmly against the wind. Even under the thick coat he was stiff and cold as he climbed out of the car. The wind carried with it the icy edge of snow higher in the mountains, driving the rain against his unshaven cheeks.

The dim lights of the torch and the car revealed glimpses of two men of around thirty wearing sheep's wool cloaks against the weather, their bodies lean and hard from a harsh outdoor life. Under their heavy beards, their expressions were impassive. Both men had Soviet Kalashnikov rifles that had likely been obtained as part of one of many such cross-border transactions. They were both known to Meyer by sight, though he did not know their names. It was merely business as usual. Meyer suspected there were further horsemen hidden beyond the small ring of light.

There was no need for codes or identification, for their communication system was basic but reliable. These men were smugglers, transporting anything and everything that might turn a profit between the communist and ostensibly atheist government of Azerbaijan and the liberal Muslim monarchy of Iran. They did not inquire as to what they might be transporting, provided the price was right and there was a guaranteed buyer at the end of their route through the mountains. In this case the four wooden crates, each the size of a suitcase, were easily secured to the two pack horses standing beside the other two animals. Each crate was sealed with metal straps, patches of clean wood standing out where the Czech and Cyrillic markings once stencilled on the wood had been sanded off. Two of the crates contained Czech-made Cemtex explosive, while the others carried eight Bulgarian-produced versions of the RPG-7 grenade launcher.

In less than five minutes the transfer was complete and Meyer slammed the boot lid closed, giving it a second thump to make it engage properly. He did not shake hands or speak, for the less they saw of his features the better. Then the men and horses were gone, vanished into the windy wet night, and Meyer returned to the comparative warmth of the car for the long cold drive back to Baku. In the mind's eye of Colonel Andreas Meyer, the snowball had been launched down the slope, set to gather mass and speed until it was unstoppable.

\*     \*     \*

# OVERTURE – LEILA

# Tehran, April 1975

*Doloroso*

# CHAPTER 1 – Motive

Ahmad Zia-Zarfi turned away from the freshly dug plot in Section 33 of the Behesht-e Zahra cemetery. Nearby, in the yellow sandy earth were eight other graves, placed so closely it was barely possible to walk between them. The men were now reunited in death, their lives taken from them supposedly in the act of escaping from a prison minibus, though everyone knew they had been executed by Savak on the high hills above Evin Prison.

Ahmad was nineteen, tall and slim, eight years younger than his brother Hassan, martyred for the cause, whose body now lay at peace with Allah between the lines of straggly pine trees in the largest cemetery in Tehran. For years, Hassan had forbidden his younger brother to follow him into the outlawed Tudeh Party of Iran, in their fight against the Shah's regime. Should anything happen to Hassan, somebody had to care for their parents. Hassan had foreseen the inevitable, and after years of writing clandestine books and essays, his leftist views had brought his downfall and three years of imprisonment. He'd been allowed no meaningful representation at trial, nor any appeal process once the sentence of fifteen years had been handed down. Instead, there had been long periods of savage beating and torture that had left Hassan hospitalised for days at a time. His comrades had been rounded up, one by one, whether from Hassan's incoherent, agonised ramblings, or through the web of other arrests spreading like ripples in a pool. The foul basement cells of Evin Prison, on the northern outskirts of Tehran, was full of the victims of the *Sazman-e Etelaat Va Amniat Keshvar*, the Organization of Intelligence and Security of the Country, where electrodes, hot grills, acid and brute force torture were *di rigueur.* "Savak" was a word spoken in whispers, a fearsome entity beset by horrific stories that made people glance over their shoulders and stare at others with suspicion.

Ahmad had admired his brother, had wanted to emulate him in the fight against the corrupt Pahlavi regime. The Tudeh had long been illegal, but even the alternative opposition parties had now been banned. Less than two months previously, the *New Iran, People,* and *Pan-Iranist* parties had been banned, the Shah ordering the establishment of a single new one – the Resurrectionist Party. "Anyone who does not like this system can get his passport and leave the country," the Shah had declared. Except that Hassan and his eight comrades would never have that opportunity, for somebody had decided their presence was still prejudicial to the government, irrespective of the new party system, and they had been taken away to be gunned down on a lonely hillside. That was when Ahmad had disregarded his brother's command and had pledged his own life in revenge.

*

The black tie event at Niavaran Palace was an extravagant affair, in keeping with the Shah's lavish spectacles. Mohammad Reza, Monarch of the House of Pahlavi, was resplendent in his Commander-in-Chief dress uniform, the white jacket adorned with gold braid, a sky-blue sash, and a dozen dazzling medals spangling his chest. At fifty-six, the silver-haired King of Kings and Light of the Aryans, wore the gold-encrusted epaulettes, collar and cuffs with dignity and gravitas, outshining the Empress Farah in her exquisite but simple emerald green gown. She was the taller of the royal couple, for he had always been attracted to tall women, and at nineteen years his junior, his second wife had fulfilled his expectation of a male heir while capturing the hearts of the people with her beauty. Together they made a powerful couple, backed up by others of the Pahlavi family.

The gathering at Niavaran Palace had been a who's-who of the rich and powerful of Tehran society, including ambassadors and wealthy foreign nationals, all eager to consolidate favour with the progressive regime and its growing investment in oil and infrastructure. Iran had become a powerhouse in the Middle East, with growing oil revenues and a willingness to spend these on its military, causing a feeding frenzy that attracted western arms magnates and governments in a diplomatic rush. An invitation to a Niavaran Palace cocktail party meant a glittering soiree of embassy and industry overlords, mixed with the purveyors and operators of intelligence networks in the role of embassy "attaches".

Circulating just beyond the main spotlights of the great ballroom in the palace were the movers and shakers of the Shah's retinue, not least his twin sister Princess Ashraf, and his younger brother Ali Reza, together with the other seven half-brothers and -sisters who shared the vast family wealth and success. However, it was the Shah's half-sister Princess Fatemeh who many considered to be the power behind Mohammad Reza. Astute and refined, Fatemeh had married at eighteen but had been instrumental in promoting the rights of Iranian women, and had been amongst the first important women to cease wearing the traditional veil. She had contributed three children to the extended royal family, amongst whom was Leila Khatami. At twenty-five, the beautiful Leila was also the Shah's favourite niece.

Leila was petite, her glossy ebony hair now swept back beneath a diamond tiara, her slender body encased in a form-fitting silver sheath that seemed to outshine the other women in the great ballroom. She had graced the cover of Vogue and was a customer of the fashion houses of Milan and Paris, turning heads even in the simple act of entering a restaurant. Men were captivated by her lithe, easy walk and her figure that promised another adventure beyond that already on display. They were drawn in by her flashing smile, the flounce of her hair as it brushed her shoulders, the intimacy of her gaze when it fell on them, as though there was a shared secret. Even women – her competitors in everything from prestige to partners to society profile – reluctantly acknowledged her beauty and the unexpected humility that gained her respect and admiration from the royal court and its followers. However, few of the Shah's retinue knew of the nature and depth of Leila's discreet relationship.

From the mezzanine balcony encircling the airy space above the ballroom floor, onlookers could gaze down on the circulating guests while they held their own private discussions. Such observers would have seen the handsome Englishman whose arm was firmly linked with Princess Leila's.

The Englishman was a dozen years older than Leila, tall and urbane. Unlike many in the room, he wore civilian clothes rather than uniform, as though non-military attire disavowed connection with the armed forces. His thick, shadow-black hair was trimmed to leave neat sideboards, and his skin glowed from the recent cut-throat shave at the open-air barber in Jomhouri Avenue. He carried himself with confidence, his blue eyes genial and smiling amongst the other guests – an equal number of whom appeared to know both him and his royal companion.

They had met six months previously at an embassy function, where he had captured the attention of the reserved Leila, who – in taking a fancy to him – had determined to draw him from his cloak of apparent social reticence – or was it secrecy? In fact, the opposite had happened, and Leila Khatami had all but disappeared from public view, ensnared by the man she now adored and who had revealed unknown inner longings within her.

Had such balcony observers asked, they would have been told that the man was an economic and political analyst with the ear of the Shah, and his association with the Shah's niece was both noticed and approved in the westernised Imperial Court. The man's superiors in the British Embassy also looked on with benign smugness, as though the burgeoning relationship was their own doing, though they remained ignorant of the details. Now, at the crowning point in the Tehran social calendar, he was seen as an elegant cat burglar, opening doors and making just the right sort of contacts.

*

It was gone two in the morning when the limousine dropped the chic couple off at the three-storey house on Fereshteh Street after the palace party. Soon the light came on in the first floor room, which in daylight had views over the extensive gardens of the nearby Turkish Embassy and beyond, as far as the snow-clad Elburz Mountains marching across the northern skyline. It was an affluent suburb, home to the wealthy, to diplomats, and to the influential upper classes of Tehran society.

An hour later, facing the tall french doors leading on to the balcony, Leila Khatami stood naked, her arms raised above her head. Eight turns of white sashcord held her bound wrists together, cinched by a further turn, the trailing cord leading over a steel hook embedded in the high moulded ceiling, then descending to a cleat hidden behind the drapes. The drapes were wide open, the french doors ajar, letting the warm night air drift into the room. Leila's legs were spread, the balls of her feet supported on two concrete blocks half a metre apart – just sufficient in size to prevent her touching the floor if she chose to step off them.

The room was empty of furniture, save a low chest of drawers against the back wall, and lit only by two wall sconces, casting symmetrical shadows behind the restrained figure. Her ebony hair was now in a pony tail to her shoulder blades, the rope that stretched her arms upwards also lifting her small breasts so that they jutted provocatively, the nipples hard and protruding like fingertips. Her body was athletic, the taut muscles outlined by her enforced position. Small runnels of perspiration slid down her flanks and soaked into the coarse concrete blocks.

At that moment the room was silent, save for her ragged breathing and the occasional tinkle of two small bells, fastened to her nipples by steel clamps. Every few seconds her thighs would tremble with the strain of her pose, the tremors activating the bells. She tried to turn her head, to see if the man – her man – was behind her, but the rigidity of her arms forced her head down towards the floor, and she could not determine if he was standing watching her, or if he had slipped out of the room.

She wanted him desperately – wanted him inside her, wanted him to finish what he'd started, as his hands had teased her to the edge of a climax, then retreated, leaving her to contemplate what was to come and to beg him for gratification.

Leila Khatami squirmed in her bonds, making the bells on her nipples jingle again. The smooth skin of her buttocks was striated with red marks from a flogger, and she could feel the hot glow rising from the fired-up nerve ends. Sometimes he would flog her legs, obliging her to wear pants or long skirts for several days afterwards, until the marks had disappeared. But each time, the stimulation and pain of the riding crop or the flogger would end in a rapturous ecstasy which continued to surprise her, and she had come to associate the torment as a prelude to a hazy nirvana that came with the bondage and the enforced vulnerability. Like a drug, the more she received, the more she wanted, astonishing herself at her desire for this forbidden and unashamedly hedonistic pleasure.

Now he was back. There came the faint whisper of cologne, the gentle breathing as he moved close to her. Hands stroked her glowing buttocks, then the figure moved in front of her, blocking the window, his strong face half in shadow. He had removed his shirt, exposing a well-muscled chest with an attractive growth of dark hair. Standing on the concrete blocks, she almost matched his height, so that she needn't tilt her head to kiss him. His hand moved between her legs, fingers touching the mixture of sweat and juices in the dark space of her groin. She caught her breath at the faint, barely discernible caress and leaned forward, seeking a kiss. Their lips met, his tongue slipping between them the way she wished his penis would do between the lips of her pussy. She arched her body towards him, wanting to press her breasts against his body, to suffer the sharp twinge from the nipple clamps, bringing her alive with the mix of pleasure and pain.

His hand was firmer now, cupping her mons, a finger easing between the slippery labia. She strained against the rope holding her wrists, again trying to arch forward, the balls of her feet perched on the edges of the blocks. She was unable to advance, but still sought some resistance, something on which to force herself to provide satisfaction. His finger moved inside her, just a little, and she thought she might be on the road to the promised paradise. She wanted to seize his cock, to devour it, to feast on the sensation of it moving within her, but again she was denied.

'Please,' she whispered. 'Please, Sir.' She spoke Farsi, her voice husky with her desire. 'I want you…'

The man appeared to consider her words.

'What will you do for me if I agree to your demand?' His response was also in Farsi, assertive and sufficiently fluent that on first hearing a local might not realise the speaker was foreign.

'I'll do whatever you command, Sir. Whatever pleases you.'

'But you'll do that in any case, my darling…' A suggestion of amusement lingered in his voice. 'You're bound and helpless – you have no choice. Is this the best you can offer?'

Leila was silent. He always manipulated her like this and she had yet to find an answer for his hypothetical bargaining. Her power had been removed from her, her decision-making capacity tossed aside in a way at once both frustrating and liberating. She had placed her very life in his hands, for he could walk from the room and leave her to starve, her calls for help inaudible beyond the thick walls of the empty house.

In trusting him with her life, she knew he would never harm her beyond those limits that defined their game, the limits which drove her to new heights with every scenario, every role-play they enacted, every act done to her. The uncertainty of what would happen each time was a drug - an unexpected new torment each time driving her to greater depths of passion and forcing her to admit she had never loved a man so much. Oh Allah, she wanted him in her so much at that moment!

But he was gone. Her failure to answer satisfactorily had prolonged her desire and made more protracted the time until she would be satisfied. But how much sweeter that would be!

Somewhere behind her there was faint movement. She could still feel where his finger had stimulated her, triggering new juices and driving her crazy. She wondered what would be coming next. Would it be another bout with the flogger, or something more pleasurable? Or would he just leave her, to let her imagination run wild, conjuring in her mind all manner of painful and pleasurable acts?

She thought she heard a movement. Was he retrieving an implement of torment from the drawers, or was he leaving the room? No, please not the latter!

Outside, a hundred metres away on a low knoll, from where he had been watching the activities on the first floor through binoculars, Ahmad Zia-Zarfi jumped as the white Volkswagen beetle packed with Cemtex exploded in front of the house, hiding the street in a ball of flame and smoke. In the first second of the explosion a hail of shattered glass blasted through the room on the first floor – moments before the façade of the building gave way and the front of the house crumbled and toppled into the street.

Ahmad smiled with the knowledge that his brother was finally avenged.

*   *   *

# FIRST MOVEMENT - AYSHA

## Overland, June 1977

*Andante, con amore*

# CHAPTER 2 – Khajuraho

It was a place, from a thousand years earlier in time, that would remain etched in Lily Maddison's mind. It had been a concoction for the senses, a moment which made a connection with India in the early morning stillness and the soft, ethereal sunlight which she was to learn were evocative hallmarks of the Indian landscape.

It had been a week since they'd left the comfortable warmth of Kathmandu, descending to the stifling heat of the Indo-Gangetic Plain, riding out the last days until the monsoon arrived to bring blessed relief.

Khajuraho lay on the southern edge of the great plain, its temples an ornate monument to a culture celebrating love and sex in glorious excess. The Sundowners bus had arrived early in the morning to explore the temples, set in the deserted expanse of desiccated, straw-coloured lawns. After barely a week on the subcontinent, Lily had learned that the peacefulness at this hour – save in this instance for the loud cries of itinerant peacocks patrolling the temple grounds – was unusual for the country. But now at 9 am, the heat was building into another oppressive day which would suck the travellers' energy as the hours wore on.

The half dozen temples were scattered through the parkland like wedding-cake structures rising into the clear morning sky. Her fellow travellers on the bus were blessedly subdued as they followed the brown gravel pathway to the first of the shrines towering above a sprinkling of ancient trees.

The group moved ahead, so that Lily's first exposure to the stone carvings covering the temple exteriors was out of earshot of the remainder of her group. Only her new roommate, Aysha, had been with her. The pair had gazed at the carvings with unconcealed fascination, beguiled by the exquisite detail of the erotic carvings and the sexual poses. It would have been easy to joke about the athleticism of the buxom, nude women and the well-endowed men, but mockery seemed inappropriate.

\*

Lily Maddison had enjoyed two days in Kathmandu before the Sundowners bus set out for London. She wandered the narrow alleyways amidst the ancient overhanging wooden buildings that looked as though they could fall into the street at any moment. Lily's senses had been assaulted by the spice markets, the street stalls and the effluent lingering in open drains. She explored Freak Street, where vestiges of the sixties hippies culture still lingered, though none of the hashish shops mentioned in her Lonely Planet guide had survived. The buffalo burger at Aunt Jane's Place – another Lonely

Planet recommendation – was delicious, while Durbar Square and its temples had captured her heart, along with the white-bearded old swami who anointed her with a yellow bindi mark on the forehead.

'All people have a third inner eye,' he had told her solemnly. 'The third eye focuses inward towards God, to keep him at the centre of your thoughts.' He had blessed her and held her hands clasped in his long enough for Lily to feel special.

It was Lily's first solo trip from New Zealand. At twenty-two, she was a naïve backpacker wide-eyed at the sights around every turn. Her grey eyes and warm, open expression made stout Nepalese women want to take her home for a meal and to introduce her to their sons. The wavy auburn hair falling to her shoulders and her pale complexion stood out amongst the dark-skinned, black-haired locals in a way that hawkers loved, and her innocent transit along a thronged street was like a young giraffe wandering through hunting dog territory. For Lily, being totally on her own was as much an event as the exoticism and novelty of the Kathmandu itself.

As evening fell on the first night in the modest Blue Star Hotel, Lily thought she could make out the faint outline of distant mountains through the heat haze along the northern horizon. An unexplained shiver ran through her, a sense of something vast lurking just beyond the edge of her perception, at once both exciting and eerie.

The following evening was the pre-departure meeting, and Lily tried to quell her nervousness as to how she would fit with a random bus-load of other young people. Rebuking herself for overthinking her appearance she had headed down to the first meeting with her fellow travellers. She wore no make-up, nor did she even carry any in her suitcase. Her skin was smooth and her fingernails cut close, with tiny calluses on her left hand fingertips the legacy of years learning the cello. To modestly celebrate this achievement, Lily wore a pale yellow tee-shirt embellished with 'Mellow Cello' in small letters over her breast, alongside a silhouette of the instrument. The tee-shirt showed off her curves, and attracted several glances from other overlanders while the denim skirt revealed sufficient smooth thigh to also draw attention.

Lily had first encountered Aysha Newton as they found themselves sardined together in the tiny lift. At first glance Lily had taken her for one of the locals, for Aysha's ebony hair, pale coffee skin and delicate cheek bones showed little clarity of parentage except some exotic Eurasian mixture, but at two inches taller than Lily's five-foot-nine, Aysha's lean frame stood out from the smaller Indians and Nepalese. She wore black-rimmed glasses that gave her a vaguely studious air and highlighted deep brown eyes.

A rainbow-coloured bandana barely tamed the abandoned flurry of hair cascading to her shoulders. The faded khaki tee-shirt, patched maroon dungarees and flip-flops were accompanied by a faint aroma of sandalwood in the close confines of the lift. She had accessorised with a rawhide necklace of colourful beads which gave a bohemian look, aided by a silver ring in the left nostril. Lily thought she looked like a refugee from a hippy community.

In the hotel foyer two dozen people milled uncertainly, eyeing those they did not know, weighing them up as travel companions – comrades they would spend the next three months with in the greatest adventure of their young lives. Accents were Commonwealth – broad Australian vowels, the flat Kiwi intonation and a variety of dialects from the Old Country – save for a handful of west coast Americans. The shyness of some merged with underlying excitement and the beginnings of youthful bravado.

Lily and Aysha found themselves sitting next to each other on a worn sofa as the meeting began, and they had continued talking after the details of the route – the conditions, hazards, insurance, and all things guaranteed to affect a three-month voyage halfway around the world – had been raised. To Lily, Aysha Newton stood out from the others through her reserve amidst the boisterousness. Lily was intrigued, for she sensed that Aysha's apparent aloofness was not all it appeared, and that the young woman was biding her time in sizing up her travel companions.

Lily and Aysha had soon singled each other out as prospective roommates after the initial nights in cheap segregated dormitory rooms. Perhaps sensing like minds, they sat together on the first day in the yellow Ford bus with 'Sundowners Adventure Travel' emblazoned on the side, as the road twisted and turned downwards from Kathmandu to Pokhara, a Fleetwood Mac tape loud on the sound system. The Great Overland Journey to London had begun.

In Pokhara, their last night in Nepal, the group had awakened to a sunrise lighting up the spectacular snow-capped pyramid of Machapuchare, before they left the great white wall of the Himalayas behind them. Lily had been surprisingly relaxed on the narrow and winding descent through the Pokhara Valley, and the exhilarating sight of the Annapurna range marching white-toothed across the sky lifted her heart. She felt a kinship with the mountains, and wished she could stay longer, get closer, but they left Pokhara to continue their descent to a languid backwater border crossing. Here, as the males kicked a soccer ball around a dusty car park, the bus and its passengers were stamped into India.

Lily and Aysha had quickly settled into life on the road, to the heat, dust, questionable food, unreliable plumbing, incessant noise and the unremitting presence of people. Stillness prevailed only at sunrise, broken by roosters and restless dogs and the rumble of donkeys and bullocks, before being overwhelmed by rising traffic noise.

# the submissive spy

Compared to their respective urban comforts of Auckland and Brisbane, the new way of life was not easy for Lily and Aysha. The remnants of their own culture travelled with them – twenty-seven other westerners all with different expectations and travelling experience. Cliques had soon developed – the two married couples, the half-dozen testosteroned males determined to sample all the local beers, and the four Californian girls travelling together. The rest were left to define themselves and seek like-minded company, with the expectation that sooner or later more intimate relationships would develop.

Twenty-nine passengers and forty-four seats allowed a degree of separation or sharing, and it wasn't long before the rear seats were staked out as the territory of the Aussie lads, where the occasional mooning of passing vehicles could be achieved more readily through the rear window, or hangovers eased without the need to engage in refined conversation. Further forward, the marrieds, the Americans, and the solos distanced themselves from the rear rowdiness and began to prise out the motivations and life stories of their fellow travellers.

The driver, a laconic Australian named Craig, and the courier Wayne – also Australian – had done the overland trip several times. Opinion was that Craig – dark-haired, moustached and lean – would not have to seek out female company before the trip had gone far. He was nicknamed 'Budgie', supposedly because he drove a big yellow bus, but all manner of rumours would circulate during the trip. He was content to manage the bus and leave the interaction with the passengers to the bearded, long-haired Wayne, a more outgoing character from Sydney. Both appeared sufficiently competent to raise no concerns with the passengers, and to assert their rights to join the "boys' club" when not on the move.

On the fourth night, in the comparative luxury of a one-star Benares hotel, the overland trip had moved a notch up the accommodation ladder as the travellers were provided with double rooms, albeit with a shared squat toilet at the end of the corridor. There was a tiny balcony barely big enough for two folding chairs, where Lily Maddison and Aysha Newton had spent half the night sharing life stories and had bonded overlooking a sea of flat concrete roofs.

It was their second night in the spiritual capital of India – a city where Hindus came to die in the belief that it would free them from the endless cycle of reincarnation. That morning the group had embarked on a sunrise boat trip along the Ganges, watching the pilgrims bathe in the waters of the holy river, and to see the ritual cremations taking place on the stone ghats leading down to the water. The sun had been loath to contribute to the scene, providing only a hazy light over the jumbled yellow-brown stone walls and buildings, rising in staggered layers above the crowded steps. The overlanders travelled in two open wooden boats, drifting on the refuse-laden waters, barely a stone's throw from the funereal activity, where family members prepared the pyres and touched off the final passing rite.

Lily saw a young woman standing alone – a white-shawled, statue-like figure, watching as the first flames licked at the stacked cords under a flower-draped figure. Around her was scattered the ash, garlands and detritus of previous cremations, cursorily cleaned up by the untouchables who managed the location. Something in her posture, in her stillness, made Lily's heart lurch. Was she bidding farewell to a husband, child, or mother?

It had been four years since Lily's mother's coffin had vanished behind the curtains at the crematorium, amidst consoling murmurs from the gathering of people around her. Grace Maddison was gone, taken by a heart attack that left Lily and her father, Peter, to return to the emptiness of a house now devoid of the warmth and laughter of Lily's closest confidant. Lily had just started university, while her father had been largely based in the capital, Wellington, as an elected Member of Parliament. Peter Maddison's recent promotion to Minister of Overseas Trade had been well received by his colleagues and his absence from Lily's life as well as that of her mother made Lily withdraw into herself.

The brief experiment of bringing Peter's older sister Jean to live with Lily had failed, and Lily had found a student flat where she could live in her now private, shuttered world. The university's old Music School practice rooms had become Lily's second home, and despite her efforts, the gulf between her and her father had widened merely through geographical separation. Lily found solace for her loss in the practice rooms with their high widows and polished floors looking out over Albert Park, and it was here that she communed with the ghosts of the old masters, whose melodies moved her in a way that she had not experienced until her mother's death. With just the companionship of her cello, she felt the anguish of Elgar, the intensity of Brahms, the consolation of Bach, in a refuge from the distractions of the world.

Seeing the grief on the edge of the holy river had brought occluded feelings rushing back to Lily – emotions that she had never shared with others, even her father. This dreamlike setting had caught her unawares and pried open a door that had been firmly locked for a long time. Even her relationship with boyfriend Robert had not exposed the grief hidden beyond that door, for Robert had never been curious of human emotions. That was why he'd ended up in law school, Lily had once reckoned.

For once the more vociferant members of the group had been silent as their boat had drifted on the grey current past the melancholy scene of birth and death that had been repeated for centuries. Lily had wiped away the tears sliding down her cheeks and hoped nobody had noticed, before banishing her resurgent grief in the gaudy temples and teeming market alleys that occupied the remainder of the day.

That night, on the balcony, Lily was again wearing her Mellow Cello tee-shirt, the incessant humidity now showing sweat stains under her armpits and breasts. Opposite her, Aysha pushed a damp lock of hair back behind her ear as they did a delicate dance around their reasons for the journey. Lily had seen the hardback journal which was always in the bus seat pocket in front of Aysha, and in which she was regularly scribbling random notes or observations, and could not help asking about it.

Aysha took a gulp of her beer and gazed down on the narrow alleyway below them. She wore a black tank top and frayed denim shorts, her long legs stretched out and ankle-crossed. She was three years older than Lily, and made Lily feel a novice in their daily new experiences.

'Oh, it's just observations and stuff.'

'Observations? Of what?'

'People. Things that happen. Thoughts that come out of nowhere. One day they'll appear in the Great Novel. That's with capital letters, by the way.'

'You're going to be an author?'

Aysha shrugged, as though unwilling to admit such an implausible thing. 'What would *you* like to be, Lily, if you didn't have to work for a living - with the definition of work being anything you *don't* like doing? Something to do with that cello tee-shirt, I'm guessing.'

'Yes, okay – a fair cop.' Lily leaned back in the rickety chair and stared out over the mass of close-packed buildings of night-time Benares. It was all a bit surreal, just as the question was. With an effort, she applied herself to articulating her dream, though it was one she'd barely acknowledged to herself. 'I'd be travelling the world playing my cello with the great symphony orchestras in Berlin, Amsterdam, London… wherever. Jesus, that sounds so idealistic… Fairy tale stuff.' Lily took another swig on her can of Fosters and put it on the tiles beside her chair. She sighed. 'So, in the fairy tale, I'm going to go to the Albert Hall, to the Proms. Get a cello gig somewhere. That would be brilliant.'

'Well I'm going to write the Great Novel.'

'About…?'

'People. Other than that sharply defined subject, not much of a clue. But I figure at least part of it will have to be written in a garret in Paris – because that's what one does.' Aysha smiled – a flash of teeth in the dim light seeping from their room. 'Except I'll be using a typewriter, not a quill pen. I want to write another Brave New World, another Fahrenheit 451, or Animal Farm.'

Lily had studied a couple of these at school. 'Pretty political,' she said non-committally, not knowing what those politics might be for Aysha and how much of a crusader she might be. Lily herself was completely apolitical, and since the death of her mother had found solace in fiction about far-off places.

"Yeah. Sometimes you think all the good causes have been winkled out and written about, then some new movement will rise up somewhere. Some of them are instigated by events, some by something more fundamental – hunger, war, religion, whatever. You just have to look for protest.'

'You a protester?'

'Hell yeah. Vietnam, Apartheid, legal abortion, free university, equal pay – no shortage of causes in Oz in the last few years. Carried my share of banners; got my share of beatings. Melbourne, Sydney, Brisbane – gotta support the sisters, sister.' She grinned. Lily felt the true innocent, for she had never been near a protest. Coming from a household where her father had transitioned from a bank manager to a conservative politician, there had been only one viewpoint for discussion, mirrored in New Zealand's illiberal news coverage.

'So… Are you expecting stuff along the way?'

'Stuff?'

'You know, causes that might spring up.'

'Sure, why not? India's only a few months out of a state of emergency. Pakistan's only had a handful of years under civilian government since the fifties. Afghanistan is unstable, the Shah of Iran is on shaky ground… And we haven't even got to the Soviets yet.' Aysha grinned. Again, Lily felt wholly inadequate in her limited world view.

'How do you learn all this?' she asked.

'Read the papers, watch the news, go to libraries, hang out with the wrong people in the wrong pubs and parties.'

'Australia sounds very cosmopolitan.'

'The big cities are – though Queensland is a bit behind the times. They don't bother with this political bullshit unless it affects the price of beef.'

'How would the others on this trip answer your question – about ideal "occupation"?'

'I guess you've seen me scribbling. Yeah – spoilt for choice, but lots of blank canvas. Half the bus hasn't a frigging clue. They've never even been out of Oz before.'

'You?'

Aysha laughed. 'Sure. World traveller, me. My ex and I went to Bali for two weeks. That was an eye-opener.'

'Why?'

'Seeing how the Balinese live, and seeing the stupidity and ignorance of my own people – including myself.'

'How so?'

'Near got caught smoking dope. Scared the shit out of me.'

'Really?' Lily had never touched a reefer in her life. 'You don't look like a druggie.' She said so in jest, but realised how it sounded. Then she thought that perhaps Aysha *did* look like one. The beads, the rings, the bandanna in a big sunny Woodstock field, pot smoke drifting on the breeze. 'Sorry – I didn't mean...' She blushed.

Aysha laughed. 'There's an awful lot about me you don't know, Lily,' she said, but offered nothing more. 'But the other tourists in Bali?' Aysha continued, warming to her theme. 'Ignorance of culture, disrespect for the locals, can't spend a night away from the bars. It just goes on. And that's just Bali. Take Singapore. Long-haired guys turn up there and find they're barred from entering unless they get a haircut. It may be prudish and fucked up, but at the end of the day it's the Singaporeans' country and you have to abide by their rules. Some Aussies are too ignorant to find out or understand this. And the place has a mandatory death penalty for drug trafficking, for fuck's sake? I see those idiots at the back of our bus and I seriously wonder if we'll all make it to London.'

Lily was silent. It was a sobering thought and likely one that at least some of them had never considered. They had been lectured on it at the pre-departure meeting, how drug-taking and misbehaviour would not be tolerated, not least because it could affect the entire group, and be severely punished under local laws. "You do *not* want to sample a prison in India or Iran," Wayne had told them seriously. Lily was not sure whether it had sunk in.

'Look, we're all young,' Aysha continued, with a worldliness Lily found comforting. 'Half of us don't know what we want in life or where we're going, other than Earl's Court, and we've no freaking idea what will happen then. We're looking to find ourselves, or find... something. We don't think long term. Most of us will make a shitload of mistakes before some sense gets into our heads.'

'That's very pragmatic. You sound like you've made one or two mistakes yourself...'

'You got that right, girl.' Aysha paused and looked away, as though reminded of something distasteful. Lily wondered if she'd hit a nerve as Aysha changed the subject. 'But this is *your* first time away from EnZed. Is it what you thought?'

'I suppose so. But it's always the small stuff which catches you out.'

'You're so right,' murmured Aysha. 'The small stuff, and the stuff you never saw coming, until it kicks you in the arse, runs over you and disappears in a cloud of dust, leaving you wondering what the fuck just happened.'

\*

Lily was still admiring a pair of round-breasted, hour-glassed stone females engaged in an intimate and complicated sexual pose when Aysha said:

'Did you know that the word "kama" – as in "Kama Sutra" – can mean "desire", "wish", "longing", "sex" or "love"? It's such a fantastic word… And a "sutra" is a rule, or an observation. They come from Sanskrit.'

'You speak Sanskrit?' Lily asked, amazed.

'Nah - just a few words,' Aysha said casually. 'Indian heritage and all that. You pick up a few things in the course of all the family gatherings. Some of it sticks, in spite of everything.'

'But how Indian is your surname? Newton?' Lily asked. It was something that hadn't come up in the conversation of the previous night.

'The Indian stuff comes from Mum's side. Dad's as Aussie as they come. "Newton". A good, strong Olde English surname.'

Aysha shaded her eyes and stared up at the multitude of life-sized statues intertwined in coital positions. 'Can you imagine what the culture must have been like, if they could dedicate the time and expense to replicate these things to show off to the world?'

'Pretty energetic poses,' Lily murmured.

'That's our Indian blood.' Aysha grinned. 'And you see those two?' She pointed to a pair of women deeply preoccupied with each other's well-defined breasts and labia. 'Clearly, if the men won't come to the party, the girls make out with each other. Who'd have thought gay women would have been so accepted a thousand years ago?' Then she'd asked, innocently enough: 'Don't you wish you could do that?'

Lily's thoughts had been miles away, a mixture of wonder at the athleticism of these women, and also the perfection of their breasts and bodies – at least in the eyes of the sculptor. She felt her cheeks redden.

'Uhh…' She didn't know how to answer, nor to respond to the light touch on her shoulder. Aysha did not meet her gaze but continued to stare at the pantheon of figures towering above them.

'I really like this place,' Aysha said. 'Can you take a photo of me, Lily?'

Aysha pulled a folding Polaroid camera out of her daypack and showed Lily how it opened, revealing the clever bellows-like interior.

'It's really simple,' she said. 'You look through here, hold it steady, and press the red button down till the film comes out. Then you grab it and put it in your pocket, or somewhere dark. Fifteen minutes – Bob's your uncle.'

'Handy for places like this where you can't drop it into the chemist for processing,' Lily observed.

'Sure. Also handy if you've been taking photos of … intimate things. When you don't want your roll of film processed by your friendly local chemist – the one who's known your family since you were knee-high.'

'You do a lot of that? Photographing intimate things?'

Aysha shrugged and smiled. 'Take one of me in front of this wall. I like the backdrop.'

Lily did as she was asked, positioning Aysha just to the side of the two women in their athletic pose, then holding the red button down for a second as the camera whirred and the thick square of film slid out the front. She grabbed it and passed it to Aysha, who tucked it inside her journal and slipped it into her pack.

*   *   *

# CHAPTER 3 – Agra

There had been an unacknowledged tension between the Aysha and Lily during the fortnight following the Khajuraho temples as they had crossed the shimmering dusty plains of India, along congested, white-knuckled highways to Agra and the Taj Mahal. The monsoon continued to threaten but would not break, leaving people drained of energy and desperate for relieving rain.

In that time Aysha had been gently subtle in suggesting to Lily that their sharing a room could be other than platonic. Lily had started to see the hard side of Aysha – the side as tough and uncompromising as a biker's Moll. Lily suspected it to be – if not a complete guise – at least a cloak for something that she did not want to reveal.

Aysha had been persistent, despite casual attempts by Lily to underscore the solidity of her relationship with her boyfriend Robert. Aysha herself had been a little less casual, in suggesting that Robert might be more interested in his career pathway to a senior associate in his law firm, and the two girls had relentlessly teased each other about partners left behind, and the reasons for that.

Aysha had broken up with her girlfriend – insisting it was amicable – simply because Aysha wanted to travel and Joanne did not. Lily hadn't been convinced, and finally extracted a confession that the breakup was far more conflicted than merely having different life goals. The pair had drunk too much Fosters beer in the seedy Agra hotel bar, away from the prying eyes of the rest of the group.

There had finally been a drunken, teary confession from Aysha concerning an infidelity by her partner, which turned out – or so Lily thought then – to be the real motivation to travel to London on a demanding overland journey. Travelling halfway around the world, with its daily challenges and distractions was Aysha's attempt to create a forgettery, and to then lock that facility away in a deep chamber. Lily's perseverance had found the entrance to the chamber, and her compassion had unlocked the door to the forgettery.

The confession had escalated into the cathartic, as though Aysha had to rid herself of the baggage to move on. It had taken the alcohol, the heat and Lily's patience to extract the hurt that Aysha still felt after a four-year relationship had fallen in a heap, to leave the rawness that still overlaid Aysha's psyche, however much she pretended resilience. However, revealing as the confession had been, Lily's instinct told her Aysha was still hiding something more.

Lily and Aysha had come a further step closer that night, Lily supporting an inarticulate Aysha as they climbed the stairs to their room. The air conditioner was on the blink, and their sweat-smudged clothes had clung to them. The tepid water in the shower had been a dribble that was not worth the effort, so they had lain together in their underwear on one of the hard single beds for the night, as Aysha sniffled through a series of drink-released admissions, as much anger as loss. Curled up next to her friend, her arms wrapped around Aysha's lithe body, Lily did her best to ignore her own physical stirrings, brought on by the warm touch of female flesh and the closeness of the Agra night beyond the open window.

The next day they had visited the Taj Mahal. Away from the rest of the group, they sat side by side in a corner of the gardens and gazed at the great building, conscious something had changed between them, that Lily was closer to a secret Aysha had told no other.

Lily felt as though a soft hand slipped over her in the under-tree shade, as the crowds of people drifted past. The gorgeous building was a mausoleum, built for a dead princess of centuries past, then entombing the emperor himself, seventeen years later. Lily could not shake off a feeling of sorrow lingering in the garden, despite the millions of people who had visited the memorial over three centuries and countless empires. She wondered if the melancholy lay with the location or within herself. After her experience at the Benares ghats, she sensed the presence of her mother again and the recurring sadness, bringing with it an awareness of mortality in her life. But for Lily and Aysha as travelling companions, the great marble-white monument would come to signify the burial of Aysha's own past relationship, and with it the need to progress onward in time and place.

Aysha had continued to tease Lily in subtle ways and ways not so subtle. Lily could not miss the desire in Aysha, and thought she detected barely-concealed passion everywhere – true or imagined. The dropping of a towel wrap, a touch, the angle of Aysha's exposed neck – all registered with Lily, though her friend took each gesture no further. And with each instance, Lily began to question her own feelings towards the Aussie girl, and along with that, her commitment to Robert.

*

At twenty-three, Robert Petrie was a year older than Lily, and they had been together for over two years. Her father had clearly hoped something significant was going to come from the relationship. Blond, tall and lean, Robert had excelled both at school and at Auckland University, where an honours degree in law had seen him snapped up by a leading legal firm, a successful career likely assured and unsurprising to anyone.

Lily and Robert had met at university and the relationship had grown slowly. Neither was in a hurry – Lily through her natural reticence, and Robert in his all-consuming academic focus. Their initial physical fascination in each other had settled down as they completed their degrees in the routine of semesters, study and final exams. Against the preciseness of Robert's contract law, Lily had finished the abstract subtleties of her Bachelor of Music and a post-graduate diploma, before the first career decisions were upon them.

A week after her final exam, Robert had taken Lily to an expensive restaurant to celebrate the end of her studies. It had also been an opportunity to demonstrate his newfound affluence as a bonafide legal firm employee, with the novelty of a decent and regular income after years of student penury. Robert had proudly worn his best suit, presented Lily with a corsage and had complained that their table was too near the kitchen. Lily, her hair falling loose to a black satin blouse, emerald-patterned skirt and black boots, had sensed tension in Robert but tried to ignore it. Something was coming, she thought.

Robert had presented her with a gold choker chain she had later worn on her flight out of Auckland, and Lily had divined the gift and the evening was maybe a prelude for proposal. If it had been, the impetus had died in the candlelight overlooking Auckland Harbour, when Lily finally articulated the thoughts in her own mind – the desire to visit the great concert halls of Europe and to experience the magic of legendary orchestras and conductors. Somewhere in the back of that plan was the intention to further her own career in such hallowed places, but the idea as yet had no substance.

The argument had arisen after a second bottle of ostentatiously expensive champagne had been ordered by Robert, when his own latent expectations had surfaced, involving moving in together and the possibility of something more parental.

In the course of their relationship they had discussed the importance of children, though without specific reference to their own future together. Lily had seen several of her acquaintances become young mothers, and the possible loss of her freedom and potential had frightened her. She was ambivalent towards producing a family, for she saw her musical career as yet barely started and her creativity untapped. This had been overlooked or ignored by Robert, who envisaged a small clan of offspring, and with Lily's focus now past exams, he had seen this evening as an opportunity to cement their future plans together.

The release of Lily's mind from the pressure of university had left a sudden void, which had been unexpectedly filled in a chance visit to a travel agent and the collection of several overland travel brochures. Her imagination had been fired, and the assumptions that Robert had shown concerning her wants and her future, made her realise in a flash of insight that they were not on a common course but rather, the proverbial ships passing in the night.

The champagne had done neither any favours by way of rational explanation, but had at least opened the windows on their respective balcony views.  The evening had ended unhappily with Robert returning alone to his new apartment, while Lily's taxi had taken her back to the old Mount Eden house she shared with three fellow students, and a tearful download on the shoulder of one of them.

It had been the beginning of the end, the parting of ways.  Far from being of idle interest, the travel brochures had taken on real purpose.  Now, in the heart of the subcontinent, each day she was being taken further from her home and its comfortable security, into some unknown but increasingly exotic future.  As she and Aysha came upon each new spectacular marvel, Robert's presumptive arrogance had grown in her mind along with realisation of a bullet she had unwittingly dodged.

*   *   *

# CHAPTER 4 – New Delhi

In New Delhi the sky had become ominously dark and the air crackled with the imminence of rain. The mood of people had also changed, and the two girls could feel the tension like an audience waiting for the curtain to go up. The temperature was dropping and it seemed harder to breathe.

In the bustling precinct of Connaught Place, Aysha steered Lily away from the gem shops promising cheap prices and guaranteed return for anybody on-selling their wares in London.

'How much do you know about gemstones, Lily?'

'Not much.'

'*How* much?'

'Nothing.'

'Right. Shiny pretty things. Let's avoid the rip off and go get you some mail,' Aysha told her firmly.

They had made their way to the GPO, where at the Post Restante counter bustling with backpackers and hippies, the harassed official had handed over two letters for Lily – one from her father and one from Robert. It was the first mail stop of the trip, and Lily was eagerly looking forward to catching up with home.

'You going to check for mail?' she asked Aysha, standing in the line beside her.

'No point. Nobody has my itinerary. Nobody'll be writing.' She added dismissively: 'Saves me time and money on postcards.'

They had barely moved away from the counter when an audible sigh drifted through the assembly of people and an undertone of chatter began. They stepped outside to the covered colonnade to see the first fat drops of rain splattering and steaming on the asphalt, filling the air with the sweet scent of wet concrete footpath. Pedestrians were half-heartedly seeking shelter, with many standing to receive the bounty now being provided from the heavens after months of searing sun.

'Guess we're going to get a little damp,' Aysha said. 'I've got a plastic bag in my daypack if you want to protect your letters.'

The hotel was barely half a kilometre away, and there was nothing for it but to get wet. Traffic slowed to a crawl and nobody appeared to care or be in a hurry as the coolness gave wonderful relief. After nearly ten days of suffocating sultriness, the girls had taken to wearing simple wrap-around skirts and going braless under their tee-shirts, and it had seemed that the locals had not even the energy to care, much less take notice. Now they suddenly realised their vulnerability, as the deluge unleashed on them in the heart of Delhi.

31

They sprinted between covered portions of the footpath, under overhanging awnings and colonnades, but it was only a few minutes before they were soaked through, skirts clinging to thighs and breasts outlined under the thin cotton. At each point of shelter, the footpaths were crowded with people, content to watch and enjoy the rain without rushing out into it. The young males in these crowds found new energy, and considered the sight of two foreign women dashing through the downpour to be equally as stimulating, as the cooling effect of the water had made the girls' nipples push against the taut wet fabric.

Aysha and Lily found unwelcome hands groping and touching them, and they became increasingly skittish. Waiting beyond their final dash across the road to the Metro Hotel's awning, a dozen young men were crowded on the narrow footpath, and it was here Lily tripped on the kerb, sprawling on to her knees. Young men stooped to "help" her, but most were intent on anything except providing assistance. Hands groped her breasts and rolled her on to her back in the midst of a scrum of dark bodies, a ring of harassing faces closing in above her, sharp unintelligible insults egging each other on. Fingers plucked at her tee-shirt, her wrap-around and she panicked, trying to kick out but hampered by the wet skirt. Delayed through dodging traffic, Aysha was seconds behind in the sprint, and saw her friend disappear into the melee.

She arrived with furious arms wrenching the bunched bodies out of the way. The young men turned to meet this attack, then saw the wrathful dark haired young woman who might have been one of their own, except for her provocative clothing, as outrageous as the foreigner at their feet. Aysha's black tresses clung to her scalp, her pale blue tee-shirt and maroon skirt plastered to her skin and leaving nothing to the imagination. Her breasts were heaving, nipples aroused from the cold and exertion, but also in fury. Eyes blazing at the crowd – a tigress finding her cub threatened – she dared them to attack.

Unnerved, the men moved back from where Lily lay on the ground, save for one young man in dark trousers and a white shirt who might have been a student, but who had not seen the danger coming at him from behind. Intent on the fallen foreign woman in the offensive outfit, he had resolved to punish this behaviour for its effect on hot-blooded males with no other outlet for their hormones. He was bent over Lily, pawing at her breasts when a female foot caught him hard in the testicles and he fell on top of her, castrato-screaming and clutching at his groin.

There was a confused flurry of limbs as Lily thrust him away and Aysha tugged her to her feet, before they barged their way through to the hotel entry door. The crowd surged uncertainly in their wake - some men angry, some amused, either at the fate of the women or that of their comrade.

The noise and bravado subsided with the closing of the door, and an anxious old man behind the desk eventually got them their key after goggling at them, until Aysha barked something in Hindi. They dripped their way up the stairs to the sanctuary of Room 105 where Aysha grabbed a towel for herself before pushing Lily into the bathroom.

'You have a hot shower, babe. Take all the time you want.'

That evening, they sat in the bar of the Metro, Lily re-reading her letters and Aysha flicking through a week-old Time magazine making its way round the bus. Still shaken by the events of the afternoon, Lily finished the ragged scrawly script that was her father's news of faraway Auckland and political Wellington, and Robert's single page of untidy scribble which told her little.

'News from the front?' Aysha asked, raising an eyebrow as Lily put Robert's letter back in the flimsy airmail envelope. Lily shrugged.

'Apparently not much is happening there. But they were written only a week after I left.'

Aysha sighed and took a swig of her Kingfisher beer. 'Families are over-rated. They say blood is thicker than water – but then, so is soup. Make of that what you will.' Lily laughed. 'And I suppose Robert is missing you desperately?'

Lily frowned and said nothing - enough to indicate that perhaps there was less desperation than might have been hoped for.

Aysha put her hand on Lily's arm. 'He'll come round. It might just take a few weeks. He'll get tired of playing with himself.'

'Thanks for the romantic support, Aysh,' Lily said wryly. 'I need another beer. My shout.' Lily touched Aysha's arm: 'And thanks again for today. You were pretty amazing.'

'Much as I'm proud of my Indian heritage, the men here give me the shits even worse than elsewhere. And I don't like seeing my friends getting hurt.'

'I *wasn't* hurt,' Lily said.

'You could've been. If we'd been in another part of town who knows what might have happened.'

As the evening wore on over several more bottles of Kingfisher, Lily discovered the real story behind Aysha's comment about not giving her itinerary to anyone.

'I said I come from Brisbane,' Aysha told Lily. 'That's sort of true, but Mum and Dad live in Sydney. I left home when I was fifteen. "Ran away" would be a better way of putting it. Hitched a ride to Brisbane as soon as I had enough money from odd jobs after school.'

It was now dark and smoke-filled in the corner where they sat on a bench with a small glass-ringed table sporting four empty beer bottles. The place was largely the domain of European backpackers, and as two attractive females they'd had to fend off several advances by what Aysha disparagingly called Romeo Wannabes.

She downed her beer and ordered two more. She was ahead of Lily in the drinking stakes, but Lily suspected there was more Aysha needed to get out, and the beer was again proving effective.

'I know I talked about Indian family gatherings and stuff,' Aysha said. 'Sure, we have a family culture, but it's a family culture only when it aligns with the parents' wishes. You know about arranged marriages?' Lily nodded. 'Well, believe me, the custom's still alive and kicking in Western Sydney, though perhaps not as blatant as it might be. Dad's a total wimp and would do anything Mum said. Mum wanted grandkids and as eldest offspring I was first in line to bestow this honour on the family.

'Of course everything went sour. Mum found out *why* I'd been resisting all her attempts to match me up. *"Mrs Patel's boy Sunil is an accountant, Aysha. We should invite them over..."* She mimicked what Lily took to be her mother's voice, with a wobble of the head and undisguised virulence. 'When she learned the real reason I was dodging her match-making was because I liked other girls – and that there was bugger-all chance of any grandchildren exiting from my loins – that was pretty much the end of it. There'd be no wedding with three hundred people and no welcoming any accountants or doctors into the family, and there would have to be explanations and excuses for me to the rest of the community. Which made me persona non grata, so as soon as I turned fifteen, I was out of there, reproduction obligations officially passed to my sister. As I said – hitched to Brissie, worked at what I could, then teachers training college and primary school. End of story.'

'And Joanne?'

'Oh yeah. Met her at training college. Cheating bitch.' Aysha's anger slowly changed and she looked away from Lily, staring into the smoky distance as tears filled her eyes. 'Fuck,' she said quietly.

Lily put her arm round her friend and Aysha's tears slid down her cheeks. She brushed them aside, tucking her black hair behind her ears and sniffling. 'Fuck I hate this feeling.'

'What's your sister's name?' Lily asked gently. 'How old is she?'

'Nisha - four years younger than me. So now – at twenty-one – she's happily married to a stockbroker after a humungously expensive wedding, and she's also the mother of two boys.'

'So... I'm guessing she's flavour of the month and your mum is a doting grandmother...'

'You got that right,' said Aysha, unable to hide her bitterness. 'Aunty Aysha is probably never mentioned. Doesn't have to be – out of sight, out of mind.'

'Do they know you're overseas?'

Aysha turned to Lily and put her hand on Lily's arm. 'Lily, honey, I haven't had word from my parents for the best part of five years. I've only heard of things through an occasional Christmas card from Nisha. Mind you, I might have been a bit hard to find... But I didn't even get an invite to the wedding... Mum would have been behind that.'

'Well, for what it's worth, *I'm* here.'

'I know - and I appreciate you listening to my tale of woe. But I still need another beer.'

*　　*　　*

# CHAPTER 5 – Srinagar

They had driven past the grey, monsoon-soaked British monuments of Delhi, before turning north, into the pine-forested Himalayan foothills, which merged into distant white-fanged teeth cutting across the skyline. The twisting road was narrow, their passage slowed as they got caught up with military convoys making their way into the area disputed with Pakistan.

Lily knew a little of her family history, and had listened as a child as her mother had told her of her Scottish ancestry, and her great uncle Hamish Buchanan. In 1910, as a surveyor, he had joined the India Office – the British government department charged with oversight of the most populous of the Empire's territories. He had been charged with mapping some of the areas they were now travelling through – the northwest frontier that was then an ill-defined, vulnerable zone of influence for both Great Britain and Russia.

Lily gazed up at the steep wooded slopes disappearing above her eyeline, and tried to imagine the place at the turn of the century, a lonely dominion inhabited by isolated tribes, connected by trails and pathways that became impassable under winter snowfalls. Her great uncle might have passed up this very valley at the head of a donkey train laden with survey gear and provisions for many months. As she had in Nepal, she sensed an affinity with the mountains, forests and untamed backwoods. She now understood why some of the great composers like Grieg and Sibelius could write music the way they did. The loneliness of the valley made her wish for her cello and the chance to hide away and immerse herself, for she realised how much she was missing her music. One day she might come to a place like this, rent a remote mountain cabin and just compose. But there was another thought hiding in plain sight, she now realised, harking back to a question that Aysha had posed back in Benares – what profession would she follow if money and opportunity were no obstacles.

The rugged landscape and the high passes did more than inspire music within her soul – they stirred something older and more fundamental: a need to explore, to follow the paths of travellers past. It was great uncle Hamish's fault, she decided, smiling inwardly. He must have been a dreamer, too. Perhaps not brought up on the great travel stories of James Mitchener, E.M.Forster, Hemingway and Kipling, but simply enamoured of the high passes and blank spaces on maps. Lily had never before acknowledged such thoughts. She had never even been camping, let alone developed a love of the outdoors. With her mother's death, Lily's hopes and dreams had existed with her favourite composers in the music practice rooms, without considering the real existence and the possibility of exploring some of those faraway places.

# the submissive spy

On this trip she had found a new love of geography and maps, and had taken to studying her map of the Indian Subcontinent, tracking their daily progress and occasionally interrogating Budgie the driver as to the exact route they had taken. She had fingered the single red line on the map showing the road leading north to Srinagar. It paralleled vast white-coloured crinkles where the western end of the Himalayas crushed up against the jagged Karakorams, which in turn squashed into the Hindu Kush – the 'Hindu Killers' – that marched westward across the top of Pakistan into the heart of Afghanistan. Lily's dreams were starting to crystallise, and she found them made up of lonely wind-swept trails, of frigid temperatures and vistas that encompassed half of the earth, where the wind mourned lost travellers and uncompleted journeys. In these uncharted heights the human race was reduced to something meaningless, and Lily somehow felt she had experienced this before.

'What is it, Lily?' Aysha's voice floated in on her thoughts. 'You're miles away.'

'Actually, I'm not – rather, years away, but still right here.'

'Explain.'

'My great uncle Hamish was a surveyor in these parts, back at the turn of the century.'

'Really?'

'I don't know much. Our family's not big on round-the-fire family stories. He came out to India around 1910, while my grandmother and her brother were younger and emigrated to New Zealand with my great grandparents a year or two later. He was old enough to do his own thing, I guess.'

'What happened to him?'

'I think he died when Pakistan split from India. He'd have been... maybe late fifties by then.'

'So he lived most of his life here?' Aysha was delighted. 'Hey, you may have some Indian rellies – some long lost cousins!'

Lily shrugged. 'Maybe.'

'It's not that bad. Bonking the natives has been one of the benefits since Alexander the Great came through here with his Greek boys two thousand years ago. That's why you still see the odd blond head and blue eyes. Have you noticed?' Lily nodded, still taking in the slightly unsettling idea of an unknown branch of the family going its own way for the last few decades.

'I wonder if they'd be Muslims or Hindus?' Aysha mused, clearly taken with the concept, even if it was just to wind up her friend.

'Or Presbyterians,' Lily countered.

It began to rain as their warm bus climbed higher into the mountains. The rain here was light and misty, unlike the monsoon downpours they left

37

behind on the plain. Lily sat back and retreated again into her weird, unexpected reverie, now embellished with the unsought possibility of an entire Indian branch of her family. Thanks Aysha.

The rain was finally left behind as they reached the cool air of the Vale of Kashmir – the fabled mountains of Kipling and the British Raj – and the serenity of Srinagar and Dal Lake, its edges fringed with ornate wooden houseboats. For centuries the ruling powers had come to Kashmir, beginning with the Moghuls nearly four centuries before, seeking respite from the cruel summers on the Indian plains. A ban on foreign ownership of land had led to the use of moored houseboats, made from local cedar pine, which did not have associated property holdings.

The houseboats were a Srinagar icon, with the Sundowners group splitting into six or eight people per boat in twin bedrooms, serviced by an obliging houseboy and cook who lived on the adjacent kitchen boat. Lily's and Aysha's boat, which they shared with the four American girls, was called the Blue Jay, and was accessed from the water by a wooden staircase at the prow. The houseboat was of dark wood with carved sliding doors and deep woven carpets that were the local speciality, while the beds came with soft piles of blankets to stave off the cold mountain nights.

During the day they were visited by *shikaras* – one-man gondola-like boats – peddling tissues, fruit, sweets and cigarettes, accompanied by a shrill chant advertising their wares.

The girls were enchanted, and the following day – with lunches packed by the houseboy – they had set out to climb high into the hills above the lake. Dressed in new tee-shirts and wrap-around skirts they'd bought in a Jammu bazaar, and their hair pulled back in ponytails, they took a *shikara* which dropped them at the foot of a forested slope. A beaten path led into the forest and soon they were climbing through the trees, breathing cold air infused with the scent of deodar and balsam. By noon they had reached a high vantage point where they spread their jackets and managed a makeshift picnic on a grassy knoll amongst fir trees. Below them, the lines of moored houseboats looked like toys, lined up in the forest-fringed blue water amongst the lakeside gardens.

Most of their food eaten, the pair laid back together on the grass, giving them the view without effort. There was a silence for a while, and Lily sensed a tension in Aysha – a presage of something to come, like the first breeze signalling a distant change in the weather.

'How cool is this?' Lily said, dry-mouthed. Aysha didn't answer, but raised herself on her elbow and leaning over, dropped her lips in a brief and gentle kiss. Lily's eyes opened wide, but she made no move to resist, nor did her mouth respond. Aysha lifted her head and smiled, then slid her hand slowly down over Lily's right breast under the tee-shirt. She let it rest for a short while, feeling the warm flesh and the slowly stiffening nipple. She was delighted at the effect, watching a matching little bump appear on the bulge on the left side.

Lily turned her head slightly to look up at her friend. It was the moment when all the allusions and gentle flirting in the weeks since the erotic temples came to a head. This was to be the moment Aysha's seduction culminated – something she'd seen coming but had tried to ignore, for all the complications it suddenly brought into her life.

Lily had never fancied other women – at least, not that she'd admit to herself. Until Auckland Airport was dwindling beneath the wings, Robert Petrie had been the focus of her love life – a solid bet for an acceptable future. Robert would be a provider, a keeper, someone to underpin Lily the musician in whatever she wanted to do with her life – until maternity took its proper pride of place and the subject of grandchildren was raised. Lily had no doubt as to what would be expected by the families. Robert would do his bit. His bedroom performance was adequate, if not spectacular. He would be late home from the office when the dictates of a solid career path required, but after all, Lily would have the children...

The myriad tiny doubts and heretical thoughts lurking at the edge of Lily's mind for the last fortnight finally coalesced into the first ideals of rebellious reason. It was not an issue of whether she was really gay, or bi, or whatever. She simply fancied Aysha, with her smooth Eurasian skin and dark eyes, and the intense, slightly discomfiting, predatory looks she sent in Lily's direction. For all her reluctantly revealed emotional vulnerability, Aysha was still strong and fearless. In brief and enticing glimpses between bed and bath in the rooms they had shared along the way, Aysha shown both her openness and her naked body.

But Auckland was a million miles away now. They were in their own bubble that was the Sundowners bus and the odd group of fellow travellers, experiencing the same daily cultural disconnects. Parents and boyfriends were no longer factors in this intimate little dalliance – for that was how Lily suddenly saw it. It would be an uncomplicated fling which would come to nothing, but which she found herself unable to resist, for she had seen in Aysha things Robert had never offered, not the least being equality in thought and acceptance of who she was. Aysha had shown an equanimity and sense of humour in coping with the small inconveniences which had recently become regular events, and Lily was daily more appreciative of this, and the fact they had each other to lean on.

It was a movement without conscious decision that saw her bring her left arm across to pull Aysha's head down so their lips could meet again. This time the dark-haired girl barely supported herself, and Lily felt Aysha's breasts now pressing against her own.

Aysha's lips were full and warm, her breath and tongue fresh from the apples that had finished their lunch. Lily was struck by how pleasant the experience was, compared to the often clumsy and half-focussed making out that was Robert's trademark. Her already swollen nipples had abruptly become very hard, almost painful, and she was aware of two similar hard pebbles pressing down into her chest.

Aysha's fingers were now in her hair, as her own breath came faster. Aysha's hair smelt like apple blossom, or perhaps the surrounding air had just become more intoxicating. It was as though – with a decision made – Lily had leapt off a high waterfall, taking a plunge where the consequences did not matter, sensing a safe pool in the distance below. Whether she would ever have seen herself making out with another female a year ago was now irrelevant and inconsequential. Aysha was not some generic sign of Lily's sexuality. Aysha was Aysha, a lithe, intense woman who at that moment was pushing Lily's buttons in a way she had never experienced.

The blood rushed to her cheeks, her breasts, her loins. She thought she heard a moan, and wasn't sure whether it was herself or Aysha. It didn't matter. Aysha gently took Lily's lower lip in her teeth and nibbled, at the same time as her hand began to slide down Lily's stomach, then lower. The hand pressed into the folds of the skirt between Lily's legs, and she wriggled slightly to part them further. Fingers insinuated themselves deeper into the cleft, forced down by the weight of Aysha's own pelvis. Lily moved her head aside, just to take in more air, and it was then the small noise registered, forcing her to open her eyes from the faraway world which she had been entering.

Sitting five metres away, where the long grass merged into the trees, were two small barefoot boys, one holding a goat on a tether. The boys were perhaps brothers, aged about six or seven, dark-skinned with brown eyes wide with interest. They wore ragged shorts and tee-shirts and regarded the Indian-looking foreign woman forcing herself on top of the paler one like an audience waiting to see how a soap episode will end.

Aysha sensed her friend's sudden change in attitude and the stiffening of her body, and looked up, then rolled to one side. Lily's cheeks flushed even more as they instinctively moved to smooth down their clothing.

'Uhh... Namaste,' said Aysha, the first to recover. Lily looked at her friend and – in contrast to her own embarrassment – saw Aysha doing her best not to laugh out loud.

'Namaste,' said the bigger of the two boys. Both parties regarded each other for a moment, which gave Lily time to change an embarrassing moment into a merely awkward one. The older boy then said something, addressing a clearly serious query to Aysha with a wobble of his head.

Aysha replied in what Lily had come to recognise as basic Hindi, the equivalent of her own schoolgirl French. Aysha had previously denied any real knowledge of her mother's tongue, but it had become evident to Lily that she was merely being modest, as her elemental grasp of Hindi had been on display through several visits to bazaars and markets.

Aysha had told her the problem with having Indian blood and being a tourist meant everybody assumed you were fluent, and they immediately gravitated to her as a conduit for anything and everything they were selling. Now, though, there was a gentle back and forth as Aysha apparently explained to the boys what two western women were actually doing in the long grass when they thought they were alone.

'I think it's time we were going back,' said Aysha, standing up and looking at her watch. 'We've got an hour until we meet the *shikara-wallah*, though I'm sure he'll wait for us.' She brushed bits of seed and grass off her skirt and they began to stuff the detritus of their meal back into their day packs. 'And I suspect we'll have company back to the lakeside,' she added, with an inclination of her head towards the two serious faces watching them.

That night, the others of the group on their houseboat accepted an invitation to a party in a nearby houseboat. With the serendipity which sometimes happens on a journey, the four Americans had met and befriended an American brother and sister globe-trotting with their parents in two Land Rovers. They were leaving Srinagar after a two-week stay and were throwing a party on their houseboat. In the generosity of spirit which sometimes accompanies expatriates, the entire Sundowners group had been invited to one of the biggest and most ostentatious of houseboats on Dal Lake. With a knowing look at each other, Aysha and Lily had politely declined to join them, and had waved to the two *shikaras* which ferried their comrades a half kilometre along the canal to Party Central. It wasn't long before the laughter and shouts of revelry began to drift through the still night air to Lily and Aysha on the covered balcony of the Blue Jay.

They had bought a small bottle of a whiskey called Solan Number One from a *shikara-wallah* hawking alcohol and cigarettes, and on tasting the liquor, Aysha considered it 'not bad'. Lily was not a whiskey drinker, but allowed herself to be persuaded to partake, and with the coming of darkness over the lake, Lily and Aysha had succumbed to the alcohol and had curled up in the cushions on the benches, overseen by the dim illumination of a hanging kerosene lantern. The white-coated houseboy had rustled up some naan, rice and rogan josh, and the two foreign women had contentedly eaten and drunk to the accompaniment of the quiet slapping of water against the hull.

During the remainder of the afternoon neither had referred to their adventure in the forest, as they had sought out the dingy post office, where they'd supervised the stamps being stuck on to Lily's postcards and actually franked by the teller, thus ensuring they were not removed for resale. As they meandered through the back alleys of the old city, Lily's mind was still reliving the feel of Aysha's body against hers, trying to ignore the distractions of the quaint overhanging roofs and the open sacks of unidentifiable spices and vegetables in shop doorways.

Now, as the whiskey and food lured them into a comfortable languor beneath a blanket, Lily felt a security she had never known with Robert. She lay curled up with her head on Aysha's lap, letting the whiskey warm her inside while the gentle touch of Aysha's hands gave a pleasant presence, folded across her chest.

'You never told me what you said to the boys today,' Lily murmured contentedly.

Aysha laughed softly. 'It was awkward, wasn't it. You do realise homosexuality is illegal here? We were breaking the law – or might have been about to…'

'What you mean 'we', Indian girl? I was on the receiving end…'

'Yes, you were fighting me off with all your strength, weren't you. I forgot. The boys saved you from a fate worse than death.' Lily could hear the smile in the semi-darkness. The whiskey was going to her head. She'd had time to reflect on what might have been up in the forest, and now reckoned it was simply nature's way of postponing a big event for a nicer location.

'So – what did you tell them?'

'Well, I couldn't exactly claim sisterly love, could I? Not you and I – unless we have something seriously weird in our genetics or the milkman was involved.'

'We could be *step*-sisters.'

'My Hindi and a couple of seven-year-old boys are never going to have an understanding of that, are they? Really, Lily! Next thing you'll expect me to give them a lecture on the birds and bees – Australasian lesbian version. No, even at that age they're like all men – talk to them instead about how old they are, whose goat is it, where they live and are they old enough to go to school, and they'll likely overlook what the two foreign women were up to. That was my artful plan.'

'You're amazing,' said Lily, and meant it.

'Not bad for a primary school teacher. Hey – I'm used to dealing with kids. I know how they think.'

'Kids… men… not all that different…' Lily placed her hands over the top of Aysha's, under the blanket and gave them a gentle squeeze. Somewhere further up the canal a series of skyrockets shot into the air, leaving arcing silver trails, followed by a series of sharp bangs.

'See what we're missing out on?' Lily said. 'The group's having all the fun.'

'Maybe we just need to ignite a few fireworks of our own,' Aysha said with mock innocence. Lily felt her heart miss a beat, and her breathing tightened. This time there would be no small boys to interrupt things.

In the fragrant closeness of the wood-panelled bedroom, behind thick curtains and a flimsy hook-and-eye lock on the sliding door, Lily watched Aysha undress, shedding her clothes and tossing them across one of the single beds. The low wattage bulb gave her pale coffee skin a lustrous glow, and for the first time Lily could appreciate the beauty of her friend beyond the momentary teasing slip of a concealing towel. With her trademark bandanna gone, Aysha's lustrous black hair dropped in a flurry to her shoulders. She ran her hands through it and shook it in an absent way, then struck a pose in front of where Lily sat on the second bed. Lily gazed at the small breasts, the flat stomach and the black thatch between Aysha's thighs, and felt herself blush. Nervously she glanced at the door, wondering if there was a small crack through which the staff could ogle at young women visitors.

Aysha smiled at her and held out her hands to take Lily's, gently pulling her to her feet and embracing her. Aysha's arms slipped down to grasp the bottom of Lily's tee-shirt and pull it up over her head, followed swiftly by a practised unclipping of her bra. Lily's ponytail came undone and her hair cascaded softly on to the bare skin of her back and shoulders. Free of the constriction of clothing, Lily's breasts were super-sensitive and the cool air in the cabin made her nipples come erect.

She was proud of her breasts, in a modest way. They were not over-large, and needed no support, projecting like two neat half-mangoes, adorned with small pink areolae now surrounding flint-hard nipples pointing like fingertips. The only blemish that had been to Lily's despair was the fingernail-sized wine-coloured birthmark on her left breast, over her heart. There were, in fact two marks – a larger one and a smaller one below it. Both were in the shape of drops, as though somebody had spilt some red wine on her flesh.

Aysha's fingertips brushed over the marks, her gaze looking questioningly at Lily, who avoided eye contact.

'These are so lovely,' Aysha whispered. 'Nobody else has teardrops on their boob – at least nobody I know... God, you're gorgeous, Lily Maddison...'

Before Lily realised it, Aysha's head had bent and her tongue – wet and warm – was making little circles around the hardened buds that were her nipples, with forays over her birthmark. Lily groaned with pleasure, closing her eyes and wrapping her arms around Aysha's nakedness. Aysha lifted her head and kissed Lily's throat and then her lips, pulling her close so their breasts pressed together.

Any inhibitions Lily had stored up until then disappeared in a slow passage of caressing hands and lips seeking out erogenous zones. Whatever had been left in the reluctance-and-shyness department was quashed by the whiskey. Lily did not recall how she became fully naked, nor how Aysha intuited Lily's most sensitive spots on the back of her neck, her nipples and the inside of her thighs, as they fell gracefully on to the bed. Aysha's finger-touch across Lily's skin was like static electricity, raising her hairs in a tactile prickling as though in a thunder storm. Aysha's head slipped between Lily's legs, her lips moving through the triangle of burnished fluff, her tongue probing deeply as her fingers slid over the smooth flesh of Lily's thighs.

Lily had no idea how tense she had become in the last week, aware of Aysha's advances and their likely outcome. Now, accepting the moment had finally arrived and there was no need for inhibition, it was as though a switch had been flicked, a dam gate opened. Aysha straightened up, pressing the full length of her body against Lily, breast to breast, stomach to stomach, thighs intertwined. Lily gasped as fingers invaded her most private parts, stimulating nerve ends and releasing endorphins, finding the place which had so often eluded Robert. Her back arched and Aysha bit lightly on an exposed nipple, bringing Lily back to the present with a spark of pain just before the wave could be released on to the dam spillway. Then the fingers were gone from her loins, leaving her perched on the crest of a tsunami that was building strength. The fingers reappeared on Lily's breasts, tweaking, twisting and squeezing her nipples, making her whole body tense with the fire and the joy of the touch. She had never realised how the small shocks of pain could at once both stall and enhance the pleasure, and she found herself wanting Aysha's fingers back inside her.

She tried to push Aysha's hand down, to find its home in their intertwined bushes, but now Aysha was on top of her, straddling her stomach, her feet pinning and holding Lily's thighs apart. Lily was taken aback as Aysha grabbed her wrists and held her in a position of surrender, bending down to kiss Lily deeply on the mouth and to suck and bite her nipples. Lily bucked, overtaken by the urgent need for release, but Aysha was not easily dissuaded from her task, which clearly was to drive Lily to the heights of frustration. It was an art only a woman could practise on another, teasing and fondling with well-honed skill.

Only when Aysha could lick the sweat from Lily's breasts as she struggled – not very hard – to break the grip on her wrists, did Aysha change her position and slide one leg between Lily's, her thigh now forced against Lily's mons, grinding hard in a way that made Lily jerk. Aysha knew her charge was almost ready, and abruptly released her wrists. As one hand shot down to Lily's pussy, so did the other one close over Lily's mouth. Aysha's body became taut as she pinned the other girl, her fingers sending shock waves into Lily's groin. Lily bucked and grunted under Aysha's weight, aware things were now beyond her control, and she was at the mercy of the other. This was revealed in a moment of lucidity, accepting of the loss of control and the instant freedom with it. She gave up trying to stop that which she desired the most, as the pleasure waves crashed over the wall and she arched her back again, crying out into the palm covering her mouth.

Lily had forsaken privacy, dignity and control, and only later recognised this state as something Robert had never achieved in her. Lily's sense of decorum, of her awareness of her surrounds and the thinness of the cabin walls were lost in the moment when she almost bit Aysha's palm, as it stifled cries which might have brought the houseboy running. Somewhere in the distance there were more fireworks going off, but nothing like the ones Lily was experiencing, and for the New Zealand girl everything finally merged into one big explosion.

Aysha finally removed her hands long enough to let Lily breathe, and for her gasping to come under control. Lily wrapped her arms around Aysha and held her as tightly as she could, trying to calm her own racing heart. Eyes screwed shut, she panted into the mass of black blossom-smelling hair, aware of the tiny grunts coming from her throat and runnels of sweat – or were they tears? – on her cheeks.

Only Aysha heard the return of the four American girls sharing the houseboat with them, a couple of hours later, as the Americans did their best to tiptoe down the narrow passageway past the lovers' cabin. Aysha lay in the darkness, listening to whispered voices mellow with alcohol and the prospect of bed. Beside her Lily lay asleep, contentedly snuffling and murmuring to some visitor in her dreams, her arm draped across Aysha's breasts. Lily's slightly clumsy and inexpert fingers, feeling their way around another woman for the first time had done enough to warm Aysha's own sensitive parts and generate a discreet climax that – if not exactly rocking the houseboat – had elicited an unexpected gasp of pleasure. Aysha smiled to herself, for the first time sharing her friend's contentedness.

While the party-goers slept late the next morning, Lily and Aysha ate a breakfast of omelette and fresh fruit on the boat veranda, before summoning a *shikara-wallah* for a trip through the floating gardens. The *shikara* had a wide seat for two under an aft-sloping overhead shade, which gave them privacy from the old man with the paddle behind them. Mister Razdan was a small, genial fellow flaunting wrinkles and white hair, who had been taking tourists for many decades. Including the expression 'yes please' in most of his sentences, he smiled a lot and waggled his head, but had the awareness to leave the two young foreign women to enjoy the boat ride without a running commentary.

The sun was starting to warm the day, raising shivers of mist from the glassy surface of the water. Lily and Aysha slowly became more awake with the morning, as they snuggled together under a rug. It was an idyllic setting – enough to limit their conversation, for they both felt sated from the night and the leisurely breakfast. Mister Razdan seemed to have a set route, and they were content to absorb the calls of the waterfowl and the stillness hanging over the weeping willows and poplars lining the water's edge. Beyond them rose the nearby mountains, basking grey-green under a cloudless azure sky.

The warmth of the morning sun was soporific, and they flagged down a tea-wallah, samovar mounted on his little boat, to briefly take tea, the two boats sitting side by side in a setting they would probably never encounter again.

'God, if the rest of the trip is as good as this...' Lily said languidly, as they moved off again. 'I could ride this boat forever.'

'Make our little man an offer and he'll probably accept,' said Aysha. 'The trip *will* get harder. We're still at the enthusiasm stage. Wait till you get a bad case of the runs...'

'Oh don't say that, Aysh...' A silence crept over them, broken only by the rhythmic dip of the oar in the water and a distant calling cry of a merchant.

'Why did you pick this particular trip?' Lily asked.

'Because I knew you'd be on it.'

'Oh ha ha. Really.'

'It was the next one off the rank.'

'Seriously? You didn't look at the routes, the costs, the timing?'

'Nah. Just wanted to get out of Brisbane. End of school term, relationship gone to shit. Just needed to get away. Decided to go to London, but thought I'd see a bit of the world along the way. Picked the next trip – it was this one, going wherever this one goes.'

Lily laughed. 'You're funny.'

'Why? I suppose you did all that stuff – looking at timing and routes and shit.'

'Maybe.'

'So why this one – and don't say you knew I'd be on it.'

'Because it goes behind the Iron Curtain.'

'What? Really? You specifically *want* to go behind the Iron Curtain?'

'We're all doing it, whether we want to or not on this trip, dumbass,' said Lily. 'I think most people are pretty fascinated by the idea.'

'Including you?'

'I want to see what it's like. I love the music so much.'

'What music? Oh, yeah, you and your cello.' Then, sensing the serious tone in Lily's voice: 'You miss it, don't you...'

'Uh-huh. I know we have those tapes in the bus, but that's about it. I don't mind top ten stuff or those compilation tapes, but I'd kill to go to a good concert. I'm determined to see one in Russia – Moscow or maybe Kiev. I guess it depends on which day we get to be there, but I've read that the classical scene is amazing.'

'And your choice of music would be...?'

'There's bound to be some Tchaikovsky playing somewhere... Rachmaninov, Borodin, Rimsky-Korsakov, Mussorgsky... there are so many.'

'Funny about the Russians, isn't it... They're happy to impose their rigid government on others, but as a people they have a collective soul that has to be free.'

Lily sat up and looked at her friend. This was a viewpoint she hadn't seen coming.

'Never took you for a philosopher,' she said.

'I like reading,' Aysha told her. 'I guess your music is my literature. God, I loved War and Peace! I've read it three times. I wish I could write like Tolstoy.'

'Don't write like a Russian. Russian stories never have happy endings. It's something in their soul that precludes happiness.'

'You're right. But their sadness and stoicism are always so well articulated.'

'And how is *your* novel going?'

'You've seen my book.'

'Seen it. Haven't read it.'

'Maybe it's a little bit novel – ideas, plots... Mainly it's the outlet for all the voices and ideas in my head.'

'*You* have to set them down in words. *I* have to set mine to music... kind of a nice symmetry, don't you think?'

'Mmmm,' Aysha sighed, watching a waterfowl drift past.

'I'd like to come back here one day. Hire a houseboat and just write music. Sit on the veranda and watch the world go by. No complications.'

'A modern day equivalent of the poet in the garret in Paris. How romantic.' Lily couldn't tell whether Aysha was making fun of her or not. 'You'd get the runs and the plumbing would fail. You're not tough enough for that,' Aysha teased.

'I still feel something for this place, Aysh. Not just here in Srinagar, but these mountains. Pakistan over that way, China over there...'

'You're doing the Greta Garbo thing again.'

'What?'

'*I vant to be alone…* All very well until the tanks start rolling and the shelling starts. Pick somewhere a little more stable, please.'

Lily ignored the cynicism. 'Seriously. Isn't that something you'd like? Can you imagine this place in winter? Snow everywhere. I wonder if the lake freezes?' She turned her head to speak across the high seat back.

'Mister Razdan, does the lake freeze in winter?'

Mister Razdan grinned, showing perfect teeth, and waggled his head, a gesture which Lily had yet to fully understand. 'Oh yes – small, small.' He held up his hand and waggled it with the thumb and fingers close together. 'Very nice, yes please,' he opined. 'All year good for visit.'

'We should make a commitment,' Lily said firmly to Aysha. 'We should come back here together for three months – within five years. After we've got our artistic directions sorted.'

'Artistic directions?'

'You know… I'll have three sonatas under my belt and be working on a symphony, and you'll be into chapter eighty-three of your Great Novel. You'll notice I used capitals for those two words,' she added with a smile.

Aysha pulled her close and kissed her lightly. 'Not sure I'm real good on commitments.'

'There's a first time for everything.'

'Like last night?'

Lily felt herself colouring. From their time of awakening, dressing and taking breakfast, they had not spoken of the passion of the night. Lily's conservative family upbringing had never been an environment for free expression of emotions. Her parents had met in their late thirties in England, and the arrival of Lily when Grace Maddison was 38 had been into a 1950's New Zealand society deeply entrenched in post-war orthodoxy.

The country had fought alongside Britain, which at Lily's birth still accounted for nearly two thirds of its exports and imports. New Zealand had suffered the highest ratio of per capita deaths amongst the Commonwealth nations, underlining the ties with the mother country and the perception visitors had of a little Britain on the opposite side of the world, clinging to British health, education and religious views. Some things were not talked about, and Lily's upbringing in a relatively affluent family had seen her shaped by conservative mores.

Peter and Grace Maddison belonged to a generation which had lived through two world wars, the Great Depression, rationing, and the sacrifices and hardships arising from all of these. Lily had arrived at a time when she would experience the first of the new social order in the world - the advent of Rock and Roll, Flower Power and the Pill, all of which were alien and incomprehensible to Lily's parents, no matter how much they tried to understand and identify with their daughter.

Lily's cherished relationship with her mother remained distanced by age and her mother's involvement with Peter's political interests, leaving Lily largely to her own devices, consorting with her own age group and absorbing their equally uninformed but enthusiastic life advice. New Zealand's isolation and limited news exposure had done little to promote Lily's openness with her peers, and despite her attractiveness, her years at university had been dominated by her studies. Everything in Lily's upbringing now seemed incredibly 'conventional', if not genuinely repressed.

Both Lily and Robert had struggled to open up to each other, and the arrival of Aysha seemed to show the world to Lily through a new set of eyes. She was beginning to see the similarities between herself and Robert, and to realise that the concept of 'birds of a feather' was not necessarily a healthy thing.

Lily tried to respond but the words wouldn't form themselves. Aysha patted her hand on top of the blanket over their knees.

'I know. First time with a girl,' she said, her voice low enough to be inaudible to Mister Razdan at the stern of the boat. 'Confusing, isn't it. But good, yes?'

Lily nodded, not making eye contact.

'So now you're wondering if you're a lesbian,' Aysha said with the primness of a school mistress. 'Everything you thought and practised has been given a shakeup. Honey, it's not a big deal. We had some good sex. We'll have some more. You'll still fancy men, I promise you – though perhaps none of the dorks on our bus.' Lily smiled now.

'It was lovely, Ash. Thank you. Nothing like Robert and I ever did.'

'But you did orgasm – with Robert, I mean?'

'Uh... yes, I guess.'

'Honey, if you're guessing, then you probably didn't.'

'It's just that last night – with you – it was all different, you know?'

'Female fingers know the spots like no male, Sweetie,' said Aysha.

'Can't argue with that,' Lily smiled. Robert had never been much into foreplay, never mind anything else. 'But what you did...'

'You mean holding you down? Hand over mouth?'

Lily nodded, not trusting herself to speak of an aspect she suddenly realised had been more significant than the same sex experience itself.

'Ahhh...' Aysha's smile broadened and her expression took on the knowing look of one who has had her suspicions just confirmed.

'Tell me if this is close to the mark, Lily... You were reacting to my advances. It was nice. Those lovely warm feelings coming up from your pussy. You were wondering what you should be doing in return, how you

might reciprocate… Distractions from the real thing. Then suddenly you actually *didn't have* a choice. Your wrists were held down, you had me on top of you, and all thoughts of what you might do disappeared under your inability to do *anything*. You'd lost control, Sweetheart. Lost the ability to make choices, lost the ability to react in any other way than your restrained physical limits. That would be me on top of you – my leg between yours.'
Lily felt her cheeks flush at the recollection of those moments.

'Loss of control means acceptance of your circumstances and everything flowing from that. You release the need to worry about those things and bring yourself fully into the moment. It's a moment of selfishness, if you like, and accepting that is not a bad thing. Your climax showed that. You tried to shout out, but couldn't, and all that energy then went to other receptive places. I'm betting you weren't a screamer with Robert, though…'

'No…' admitted Lily. 'Too inhibited I guess.' She gave an embarrassed smile. 'Always seemed to be people in the next room…'

'Didn't seem a problem last night,' Aysha observed. 'If I hadn't shut you up I think you'd have shouted the boat down.'

'Oh Aysh…'

'It's okay, Honey. Really. The fact you didn't know what you were doing or were in no position to do what you wanted were the things which took you over the edge. It's like jumping off a diving board – you just say "Fuck it!", close your eyes and nature takes its course.'

'And… was it good for you?' Lily asked shyly. 'You seemed to be doing all the work.'

Aysha grinned – porcelain against chiselled lips. 'I know it sounds one-sided, but I actually get off on doing what I did.'

'What – being on top?'

'Being in control.'

Lily was quiet for a while, giving in to the slow passage of the boat, the unhurried ripples in their wake. So much of the night had been like nothing in her life until that point, and she felt embarrassed she had surrendered so totally. Her yielding of self-control had been willing, and her reward had been unexpected in its intensity.

'Don't over-think things, Lily,' said Aysha gently. 'We had sex. You enjoyed it. I enjoyed it. You don't have to dive down a Freudian rabbit hole.'

Lily laughed. 'You're right – and I was trying to do just that. Too much introspection - that's me.'

'I know, Honey. "Am I doing the right thing?" "What will she think?" Nothing wrong in looking out for the other person, but for fuck's sake you're allowed to indulge *yourself* now and again. And that includes this lovely spot. Who wouldn't want a little joy as icing on the cake in a place like this?'

'So we're agreed, then?'

'What?'

'Come back in five years and we'll take the music and literature world by storm, living on a houseboat together?'

Aysha giggled. 'Oh all right.'

They half-paddled, half-drifted through a series of backwaters where numbers of boats had congregated to trade fruit and vegetables. Some vessels arrived piled high with tomatoes, watermelons, aubergines, cucumbers and lotus, while others served as floating general stores. The pair watched the bustle and genial bargaining from a distance, pleased not to be hassled, able to observe people going about their ordinary business.

They had agreed to go with the flow and let Mister Razdan take them for as much of the day as necessary to see the sights. Simply sitting on the placid water of the lake and letting the world go past was as delightful as they could want. At Mr Razdan's suggestion, they crossed the lake to a palace amongst the trees.

He guided the *shikara* alongside a dozen others where people were alighting at a concrete pier, and helped the girls off.

'This place called Shalimar Bagh,' he said, his head moving like a toy dog in a car. 'Built by Emperor Jehangir for his wife. They come here in summer by elephant train. Called 'Abode of Love.' He stretched out the syllables.

'Awww...' Aysha looked at Lily, who pretended to look at the other visitors. 'That's so lovely. Isn't it Lily? 'The Abooode of Love'.' Aysha touched her friend on the arm.

'Stop it,' murmured Lily under her breath, now studying her shoes.

'I wait here. You take all time you want, yes please. Then I take you for lunch.'

They spent a pleasant hour dawdling amongst fountains, pools and ornate pavilions, debating how romantic the Indian Moghul emperors had been when it came to catering for their partners, then deciding they had probably been wimps and that it had been the mothers-in-law who were pulling the strings behind the scenes.

Mister Razdan was waiting for them when they returned and helped them into the *shikara*.

'Fifteen minutes, yes please,' he grinned. 'My friend has very good restaurant.'

The restaurant was a converted houseboat, with a few customers enjoying the open-sided dining room stretching for half the length of the boat. They climbed up the entry steps, and were shown to a table by the owner.

Mister Razdan then disappeared with him to evidently accept payment in kind for delivering two clients to the establishment.

The girls looked through the English menu and made their choices. Unsurprisingly, they over-ordered, and sated themselves on mutton *aab gosht* and sweet *modur pulao*, along with naan, fried lotus and eggplant. As they sat back, Mister Razdan appeared, accompanied by the owner.

'Good?' the boatman inquired.

The girls rolled their eyes and clasped their stomachs. 'So much!' said Lily.

'*Kitana achchha!* So much!' Aysha said. The men were clearly impressed with her Hindi, and the owner said something to Mister Razdan.

'He say come up for *phirni* and hookah,' the boatman translated, pointing to a steep flight of stairs leading to the roof of the houseboat. Lily looked mystified but Aysha simply nudged her to follow the two men. They were ushered upstairs to a small table under an umbrella. If their view from downstairs had been idyllic, that from the roof was even better.

'What are we having now?' Lily whispered. 'I'm so full!'

'Not sure about the *phirni*, but I'll happily go for a hookah,' said Aysha as they settled into two large rattan cane chairs with soft cushions.

'What's a hookah?'

'Oh my dear innocent darling,' said Aysha with exaggerated concern. 'Watch and learn.'

A young boy of eleven or twelve appeared with what they learned was the *phirni*.

'Very famous,' he told them, putting down a full dessert bowl on the table along with two smaller bowls and spoons. His English was better than the owner's. 'Made from rice, milk, saffron, cardamon, fruit. Very good.'

It looked a little like the rice pudding Lily's mother had made every Sunday along with the traditional roast dinner when Lily was young. Lily tasted it and pronounced it sweet and edible, before serving one of the smaller bowls to her friend. They had barely cleaned their plates when the young boy was back, this time with two cups of coffee, albeit nothing like they were used to.

'A bit different from Nescafe,' said Lily, cautiously tasting the pinkish liquid.

'They use rose petals, I think. And I can taste masala spices.'

The boy returned a final time, this time carrying a tall ornate vase-like jar which he placed on the ground between them. He took a piece of glowing charcoal from a covered steel pot and placed it on a perforated screen on the small bowl at the top, then passed the long rubber tube and mouthpiece to Aysha.

'He recognises a user when he sees one,' she murmured, sucking hard and watching the coal glow as the airflow bubbled through the water in the glass base. She exhaled a thin stream of smoke. 'Oh God, that's good!' she breathed, her eyes closed. 'I'd forgotten just *how* good. Apple?' she inquired of the lad. He nodded, clearly pleased to see a customer with experience in the use of the device.

Aysha drew in another long breath, held the smoke in, then pursed her lips in an 'O' to exhale the plume. 'I've died and gone to heaven. Maybe a rum and coke would finish me off, but I'm pretty well there right now...' She passed the mouthpiece to Lily, who shook her head.

'Come on, Lily,' Aysha told her. 'You've had your first sex with a woman, your first *phirni*, now it's time to have your first smoke. This thing was invented in India. You have an obligation to try it.' Aysha waved the mouthpiece in front of Lily, who took it reluctantly. 'Tastes like apple – they mix it in with the tobacco. Go *on!*'

Lily sucked hesitantly on the plastic mouthpiece, coughed and tried to return it. Aysha put up her hand.

'No... do it *properly*. A good suck so you can taste the apple, into your lungs and out slowly. Then just relax and breathe...' After another coughing fit, Lily began to get it, and laughed at a straight plume of smoke. 'It's not about the content of the smoke, Lily. It's about the act, the relaxing, the sharing, the appreciation of time and place...'

They sat for another hour, as the sun began to drop in the sky and the apple and tobacco mix was finally exhausted. It was a time to savour the crystal blue of the lake and sky, to watch the *shikaras* idle past, barely making a ripple, and committing to the Great Novel and to the Srinagar Symphony. Lily knew she would never lack inspiration in this place.

Aysha showed the hookah boy how to hold the polaroid camera and press the red button, and after one aborted effort they ended up with a passable record of the pair of them sitting comfortably either side of the hookah, with the serene Dal Lake behind them. Lily had come to learn that Aysha took photos but rarely, for the polaroid film was too expensive and precious to waste on anything but significant moments, and Lily admired her friend's ability to discern what these were.

Neither had any inkling where Aysha's photographic judgement was ultimately to lead them.

Mister Razdan dropped them at the markets where they idled their way through narrow alleys, buying a kaftan for Lily and several fine silk scarves for Aysha, before watching the world pass from the comfort of a local chai house.

After dinner that night, they had retreated to their cabin, while the four American girls had continued talking on the veranda of the houseboat. Lily was again nervous, unsure how to behave now that she and Aysha had spent their first night together as lovers in the same bed. The day was etched in her mind, a day of clear skies and languorous feelings of well-being, gratitude, excitement, and new adventures. It had been such a sublime day she was scared of anything which might now spoil a perfect experience. Aysha sensed her tension and hugged her reassuringly.

The cabin was a comfortable temperature, after the warmth of the sun on the boat all day. The monsoon did not much affect Srinagar and they had just sampled it at its summer best. Aysha moved a small carved bedside table to the middle of the floor and placed a pillow on it, lighting a candle beside the bed and turning off the main overhead light. The illumination within the room became at once warm, flickering and intimate.

'Sit down here, Lily,' said Aysha gently, motioning her to the table with the pillow. Not understanding where this was going, Lily did as she was told, looking questioningly at her friend, trusting but puzzled. Aysha made a point of locking the sliding door, then stood in front of her and took her face in both hands.

'Lily, Honey, I'm going to do something which I hope you'll enjoy. I want you to tell me if anything becomes too much. I sensed something in you last night, something which I'm not sure you realise you have. I'm going to try a little experiment. It won't hurt, and I think you'll enjoy it. I hope so. Do you trust me?'

Surprised by the question, Lily said: 'Of course,' as though it was the stupidest thing she had heard all day. This was the woman who had rescued her from the men in Delhi, who had taught her to smoke a hookah pipe and who had aroused her in a lustful passion.

'Good.' Aysha looked at her intently, staring into Lily's eyes. 'Because more than anything else, whatever happens, this is about trust. If you don't trust, you cannot relax, and you cannot commit yourself to my care. I want you to surrender, Lily, to give yourself into my care. Yes?'

'Uh... yes,' said Lily, still not understanding where this was going.

Aysha moved behind her and produced one of the silk scarves she had bought that afternoon, tying it securely over Lily's eyes and ensuring it was snug.

'Now, you need do no more than sit there, darling Lily, until I tell you otherwise. No noise, no talk.'

Lily sat in her now darkened world. She sensed Aysha was seated on the bed behind her, for as she focussed on sounds around her, she thought she could detect the sound of Aysha's breathing. Somewhere in the distance came the faint murmur of the voices from the veranda, but otherwise the houseboat was silent save for occasional lapping of the water and quiet creaking of the ancient timbers.

Five minutes passed before Lily felt Aysha's hands on her shoulders.

'Lift your arms, Lily. Straight up.'

Lily did so, and felt her tee-shirt pulled gently over her head, followed moments later by her bra. Then there was silence again. Unused to nudity in quite such an obvious form, Lily felt her vulnerability as cool air drifted over her exposed skin. She realised Aysha was either blowing over her flesh or softly fanning her with something. The movement of air made her nipples tighten and pucker, and she went to cover them with her hands, but Aysha firmly took them and placed them back where they rested on her thighs.

'No,' she said. 'You do *not* move unless you're told. You must trust. You will not *do* – you will be *done to.*'

The darkness sharpened Lily's sense of smell, now taking in the burning wax and the exotic cedar wood fragrance she had hitherto barely noticed. Somewhere in her mind they coalesced to take her to a new and faraway place, maybe an oriental palace, built by an emperor for his princess.

Something soft slid over her shoulder and curved around her neck. It felt exquisite – perhaps another silk scarf. It fluttered across her breasts, delicately touching her nipples with the gentleness of fairy floss. Lily shuddered, and her nipples grew harder, suddenly filled with an ache that needed attention, but she could not touch them herself – that was the rule.

Then the soft thing was gone, replaced by something sharp and hard, maybe a knife edge, maybe scissors. It was cold and unyielding, the edge slowly sliding down her left breast then up her right one. Her breathing quickened, the intakes and exhalations making her top lip feel cool, the sound of her breath now dominating her hearing. The object turned around, and suddenly it was the steel point poking into her skin, coarse needle points in her areoles, and in the most tender part, the nipples themselves. She was about to open her mouth in an involuntary gasp when a finger was laid over her lips and she stifled the sound rising in her throat.

'Stand,' said the voice, which sounded like Aysha's but different in tone.

Lily slowly got to her feet and remained motionless while her wraparound skirt was undone and disappeared into the darkness. A pair of hands moved her ankles apart, then she was left there again, the unspoken inference being to remain motionless. Again she heard her own breathing, trying to work out where Aysha was, and what was going to happen next.

Nothing did happen for several minutes. Lily's imagination began to conjure up all sorts of possibilities, each worse than the last. She imagined the bite of a cane across her bare legs, and the unexpectedness of these images left her bewildered, and she began to tremble. Then a hand was on her arm, gentling her, soothing, shushing. She quietened, like a young filly in its first encounter with an unknown trainer. Trust. It was all about trust.

Hands slipped through the waist of her panties and they slid down her thighs to her ankles, before disappearing in the blackness. More minutes, standing, sensing, hearing, smelling, but no sight, no touch. Then a body was behind her. Arms moved slowly to encircle her, warm hands covering her breasts, thumbs and forefingers tweaking flinty nipples. This time she could not help herself and her breath exhaled, half groan, half sigh. Two other rock-hard points pressed into her back, followed by the soft fullness of breasts as the arms pressed her own into her sides.

Aysha's hot breath drifted past Lily's ears, as the encircling arms slid across the firmness of her stomach to the tangle of hair at her groin. A finger slid inside her, meeting no resistance, only a welcoming slipperiness. A second finger, from the opposite hand, also entered, and the exploration of Lily's secret garden began, alternating from deep probing to withdrawal and pressure on the tiny sensitive nub at the top of her labia.

The hands were skilled, arousing each spot to the point where Lily thought she could take no more without response. Finally, her tormentor succeeded, and Lily involuntarily bent at the waist with a gasp, her hands flying to arrest the impossible torture. But the questing hands were gone, and her own hands were slapped away from where she wanted to provide some relief and comfort, to bring about what was being denied.

The warmth of Aysha pressed against her back was gone. She was alone again, standing motionless in her black world, wondering what was about to happen next.

She sensed movement in front of her, a breath of air across her nipples, then the hot wetness of lips, teeth and tongue over them, sucking and gently biting. Lily made to ward off these wonderful, terrible sensations with her hands, but Aysha had gripped her wrists and held them at her sides. This time Lily could not suppress a groan, and heard her breathing switch from nose to panting mouth.

Then Aysha was kneeling, still gripping Lily's wrists, as Lily struggled not to jerk back from the mouth now buried in her bush.

'Ohhh...' she gasped as Aysha's tongue continued on the secret spots where her fingers had performed the overture. Aysha's arms slipped around Lily's clenched buttocks, pulling her into her mouth, while Lily, her hands now free, endeavoured feebly to disengage Aysha's head from where it was seemingly attached by suction. Instead, she found herself moving the dark mass of hair in time with the little bends to her knees and the unconscious rocking which became faster and faster, until with a sudden rush she was in that far off emperor's palace, a wonderful, fairytale place filled with shining lights and exploding stars, and vibrating with a distant voice softly grunting 'uuh-uuh-uuh...'

Then: 'Lily – stop it! Be quiet!'

The wonderful spasms of pleasure abruptly ceased from her loins as Aysha disengaged. 'Lily!' the voice hissed. 'You will make no sound! If you want to climax, you will not utter a single noise unless I say so. Do you understand?' Aysha's voice brooked no argument or resistance. Lily's blindfolded head nodded emphatically and the heavenly feelings erupted again. Then she could resist no longer, for the dam was breaking. Lily's whole body stiffened, her back arching, her fingers fiercely gripping Aysha's hair. Aware of the warning she had been given, sound froze in Lily's throat, finally making its way to the outside as a choking snort, as she tried to suppress the exhalation of joy and to breathe at the same time.

Then she was bent over, hugging the kneeling figure and panting as though she had run for a bus. The emperor's palace drifted into the darkness and Lily subsided into enveloping arms.

*     *     *

# CHAPTER 6 – Jammu

The bond between Lily and Aysha changed irrevocably after Srinagar. The yellow Sundowners bus carried them back down the twisting road through the cool forests to the monsoonal heat and bustle of Jammu. It was a long day, again made more protracted by the presence of military convoys heading into Kashmir. Relations between India and Pakistan – never good – were strained to the limit, and Lily had overheard a driver-courier conversation concerning the border they had to cross, and whether it was still open.

The monsoon rain began again as they reached the Jammu foothills. Lily and Aysha had talked little, resting instead in a contented silence which occasionally yielded the gentle touch of a hand laid over the other's. In the window seat, Lily watched the pine trees drift past as they descended from the mountains, her mind trying to process all that had taken place in Srinagar.

She felt she was walking along a narrow path in the mist, with guilt and betrayal lurking in the depths to one side, her very sexuality in question on the other. Ahead lay the unknown, but it was preceded by the present, with delicious smells and sounds in the mist which tantalisingly teased her of more to come.

Lily smiled to herself. In the night just passed she had undergone the experience of total surrender to another, and the effort of trust it required. It had been a lesson in the joys of the flesh, but went beyond that in the promise of something more, something as much emotional as hedonistic. Aysha's dominance had surprised Lily but not dismayed her. She had felt comfortable, relieved in a way she had never experienced before. She was minded of the yin-yang symbol – the light and dark halves of a circle, divided by a curved line. She thought of them as two commas, fitting together perfectly to form that circle in a way which just seemed right.

Thus far, Aysha had appeared to expect little in return, though Lily had done her best in her exhausted state to reciprocate. But to Lily it seemed that Aysha's very dominance was as fulfilling to the Aussie girl as any sexual climax, though Lily secretly challenged herself to test this theory.

Whatever Aysha's sexual skills, whatever heights she had taken Lily to, there was the hint of a more complete Elysian future for them, which Lily was not prepared to ignore. The thought made her smile again, and she realised that whatever had transpired to date, it had made her happier than she had been for... years.

Two days later, on 26 June, they had crossed the Indian side of the border at Amritsar, and after a tense wait of several hours, they had been allowed into Pakistan. It was a country which only thirty years previously had materialised out of the partitioning of India in the largest mass migration in history, involving the relocation of over ten million people. The country had been ruled by the military for almost half the period since Partition, and now, after six years of civil rule and an election only months previously, the place was teetering under an increasingly unstable political system.

'I won't sugar-coat things,' Wayne had told them in their daily briefing. 'We'll push ahead with our schedule, but the place is a powder keg at the moment, and anything could happen. Borders could close, martial law could be introduced. It's volatile as hell. We might have to make a run for it, but until such time as alarm bells start ringing, we stick to Plan A.

'On a more down-to-earth note, remember that this is a Moslem country. During the Partition, many Moslems in India moved here, and most non-Moslems moved out. That was the theory, but it cost millions of lives. If you haven't worked it out, there's no love lost between India and Pakistan, as you saw at the border. You'll also see that men vastly outnumber women on the streets,' he told them through the bus mic. 'And they all seem to be just standing around, picking their teeth and doing bugger-all. Which means they have time to get up to mischief. We'll probably be okay until we get to Peshawar – last stop before Afghanistan.

'That place is a bloody wild west town. If you have to walk the streets, do so in groups. Girls, don't go out alone, take a guy with you. Not that we're bodyguards, but there are weird propriety issues here, to do with honour. Women have been killed for all manner of stuff that would make your hair stand on end. And whatever you do, dress conservatively. No shorts – male or female. Girls cover up as much as possible, though no need for scarves. Cover shoulders and legs, everyone. Oh, and no show of public affection – even married couples. Just not worth it.

'And more bad news, folks. In April this year, the government banned the sale of alcohol, so don't expect to get rat-arsed, you guys at the back.' There was a chorus of protest and suggestions that maybe they could fly over Pakistan. 'Better learn to enjoy a cup of tea.' There were several boos.

'I hope we won't have any political trouble, but the place is jumpy as hell. We almost didn't get through today. Pakistani politics is volatile at the best of times. Now both parties are ready to go at each other, and we don't want to be in the middle. However, we have a nice drive up to Swat Valley and two days to soak up the sun, so let's make the most of that.'

Aysha waved her hand.

'Aysha?'

'So... if you are the authorities, and a bus load of young unmarried men and women come into your country, and you can't have unmarrieds cohabiting with each other, then you have to segregate them, right? But you can't have women sleeping with other women, or men with men, for fear that they might do something unnatural… Does this mean we each get our own room to maintain propriety?'

The others laughed and Wayne grinned. 'They're not big on logic here - sorry. Looks like you're stuck with sharing. Wanna change partners?' The inference was unsubtle.

Aysha looked at Wayne as though sizing him up. 'Nah. I'll pass. Guess I'll just have to make do…'

Wayne shrugged, clearly not offended. 'Your choice,' he said.

\*     \*     \*

# CHAPTER 7 – Swat

The day after the Sundowners bus crossed into Pakistan was a Friday – declared by the government as the first of the new Sharia system instituted to replace Sunday as the traditional day of rest. Political observers saw it as a sign of increasing instability and indicative of worse to come.

After nights in Lahore and Rawalpindi, it took two days driving slowly up into the mountains to reach Swat Valley. Though they now shared a bed – when it was big enough, or if a pair of single beds could be made to touch – Lily and Aysha had not had sex since Srinagar. Although she did not voice it, Lily was confused, though accepting of Aysha's claim that the long days travelling wore her out. The days were indeed tiring, initially hot in Lahore, then catching the tail of the monsoon, before they climbed into the foothills of the Hindu Kush.

They had slipped into an unconscious convention that Aysha had the window seat for much of the city driving and Lily for the country and mountains. Had she expressly thought about it, Lily might have noted the copious notes Aysha took in the tumult that characterised the urban subcontinent, and the apparent disinterest that followed as they moved into the more recent transition to the less-populated foothills. She, by contrast, was less settled in the municipal chaos, and more at peace with the bucolic hill villages. Leaving behind the populated sprawl of the Punjab lowlands, she felt her spirits begin to lift with every metre of altitude.

Ahead of them, the great Hindu Kush range swept in from Afghanistan to collide with the Pamirs and the Karakorams, with Swat Valley an arrowhead penetrating this meeting of mountains. The bus pushed northwards along the narrow, pot-holed road, dodging huge gaudily-painted trucks bedecked with tassels and piled high with passengers and baggage. Lily found herself obsessively tracking their route on her map, as the mountains closed in. As they neared their destination, she nudged Aysha and pointed to a red line on the reverse-folded map on her knees.

'What?'

'See this road here?' Aysha adjusted her glasses and moved to better see the map. 'This is where we are. This is where we'll be tonight.'

'And?'

'Well… if you continue north on this road, you'll see it changes from a continuous red line to a dotted one. See how the mountains close in even more? You keep going, over this high pass into the Chitral Valley, and then you go further along the track. You finally come to this skinny bit of land here. This is Afghanistan – a weird bit that sticks out like a panhandle from here in the west right across to meet up with China in the east. It pokes out between the Soviet Union in the north and Pakistan in the south, just like a tongue separating upper and lower lips.'

'Huh-huh,' said Aysha slowly, sensing a strange tone on Lily's explanation. They had learnt to decipher the contours and colourings on the map sufficiently to gauge the sort of terrain that was shown, and she could immediately imagine what this little corridor of land would be like – a narrow desolate valley beset by high mountains, most likely barren and devoid of life, save for an occasional camel caravan picking its way between borders that had never been acknowledged by any who trod those lonely places. Lily wore a faraway expression.

'You wanna go there, huh?' Aysha said softly, as though in sympathy, albeit for an unachievable fantasy.

Lily was a long time in answering, staring at the mountains rising around them.

'Sometimes I kind of feel I've already been there, Aysh.' Lily's voice was a whisper. 'Maybe it's great uncle Hamish and his genes again. Maybe it goes back further. I just sense that isolation, that emptiness. I suppose most people would run a mile from it. I can see a camel caravan plodding towards a distant pass. I want to find the music for it. Maybe that's a movement for the Srinagar Symphony. Maybe it's bigger than just Srinagar. Maybe it's the Karakoram Symphony...'

The Serena Hotel was snuggled in a green valley with hidden passes to Afghanistan and China in the clouded heights above, where Alexander the Great and contemporaries of Marco Polo had passed in bygone days. After a succession of mediocre hotels with missing towels, missing hot water and malfunctioning plumbing and electrical fittings, the Serena was a joy. Built during the British Raj, before Pakistan had become a nation, the two-storey U-shaped building was fronted with lawns and rose gardens, the bedroom doors opening on to a wide tiled veranda running full length, scattered with heavy cushioned chairs begging for bookworms to curl up and enjoy them.

The rooms were large and airy, the houseboys plentiful and willing to take on the washing of dusty, travel-stained clothes at minimal cost.

'I like this place,' Lily declared, sitting on one of the large beds in their upstairs room.

'It's cool,' Aysha agreed. 'I can see Rudyard Kipling in here, or the British civil servants up from Rawalpindi in the summer.'

She put on an upper class British accent: 'Dahling, isn't this place just su-u-per! We should meet with Agnes and Mabel and have some G-and-T over bridge!'

Lily matched her tone: 'Yes, and after that we can have rampant sex on the front lawn with those adorable houseboys!'

'And housegirls!' They fell about laughing.

They sat comfortably beside each other in the large armchairs outside their bedroom, while some of the group played a noisy game of volleyball on the lawn below. Lily was writing some postcards they had picked up in Lahore, while Aysha jotted industriously in her hard-back journal. There had been another two letters from Lily's father at the Lahore Poste Restante, and one more from Robert. Some of Lily's early postcards had reached their destination as reported by her father, while Robert's news had taken a decided backward step in both information and emotion.

She sat silently for a while, trying to get back to the mood they had first experienced there, the exhilaration of travelling in the footsteps of famous people in such an exotic place, but the feeling had passed. The sun was setting and they would soon be called for dinner. The boys would be peeved – no booze and only a television in the lounge, probably only showing Pakistani TV.

'Aysh?'

'Mmm, yes Honey?' Aysha did not look up from her journal.

'Why haven't we had sex since Srinagar? That was so amazing… Are you really that tired?'

Aysha lifted her head and smoothed a lock of hair behind her ear. They had visited a Lahore bazaar the previous day and both had bought salwar kameezes – the local Pakistani fashion comprising a tunic reaching to the knees over matching loose trousers. Lily's had been a pale olive, Aysha's a deep emerald green, and she was now wearing this as a change from her usual western garb, and Lily thought she looked very beautiful.

It was the first time Lily had seen the outfit outside of the shop, and she had blurted the question about their sleeping habits after five minutes feasting her eyes on her friend's casual elegance. Lily thought Aysha had no right to look as gorgeous as she did, and she dearly wanted to get up close and personal with what lay under the clothes. Nothing Lily had experienced before had been remotely comparable to the nights in the houseboat, and – notwithstanding Aysha's slightly weird, if hugely erotic slant on their activities – Lily wanted more. Too much time in her own thoughts on the bus had left her decidedly horny, in a way that – if she was honest – thoughts of Robert had never done.

Aysha had drawn her knees up under her, and now laid down her journal. She reached across the gap between the chairs and laid her hand on Lily's.

'Sweetheart, sometimes the absence of things can make their return even more pleasurable. "Absence makes the heart grow fonder?" Is that the way with Robert now? Do you miss him even more? Was his letter nice?'

Lily's silence said it all. Then she countered: 'But when one thing is replaced by another, and that thing is taken away…'

63

'Ohhh, Lily, don't sound so miserable...' Aysha's tone was meant to cheer her up. 'I promise we'll do something very special tonight. I was just waiting for the right time and place.'

'You make it sound like you have everything planned...' Lily tried not to let petulance creep into her voice, though Aysha's words excited her very core. 'And *I* want to do something... to you...'

'*To* me?' Aysha mimed surprise, like a mother hearing a request from a five-year-old wanting to make breakfast on Mother's Day.

'You've been giving me pleasure without letting me return it...' Lily's voice dropped to a whisper, though the length of the balcony was empty of other guests.

'We'll see, Lily. We'll see.' Aysha's tone intimated that some things had to come to pass first – things which would be played out on her terms. Only then would Lily get to put her own plan into effect, if she were even capable.

A buffet dinner was held in the dining room for the group, for there were no other restaurants nearby, save for the village half a kilometre down the road. Lily toyed with her food, mainly because her stomach was full of butterflies at Aysha's inferred surprise – that they would do 'something special'. She couldn't wait to slip away from the gathering, but clearly Aysha was in no hurry, if only to drag out Lily's suspense. Lily at once loved and hated her for this.

By the time they returned to their room after dinner, Lily was stifling her impatience and trying not to appear like a child waiting to open birthday presents.

'Go and take a shower, Lily,' Aysha said, though not unkindly. 'You're like a cat in heat.'

Chastened, Lily did as she was told, wondering why, as a twenty-two-year-old woman, she was obedient to her friend in this unquestioning way. She stripped off, enjoying the hot water which had been at best intermittent in their last few hotels, and wondering if Aysha would be joining her.

'And don't use all the hot water,' came her friend's voice around the door, as if to clarify Lily's unspoken thought.

When Lily emerged, coyly holding a towel around her upper body, she found the room illuminated only by a dim bedside light. Aysha was still dressed, and approached Lily unhurriedly. Lily stopped where she was, not knowing what was expected, and yielded when Aysha embraced her, kissing her deeply. Lily felt her body relax, accepting that this was going to be nothing extreme – that Aysha was not going to pull some strange rabbit out of the sexual hat - but that it would also be 'something special'.

She closed her eyes and explored Aysha's lips with her own, hardly noticing the towel as it dropped to the floor and her breasts were pressed against Aysha's. Warmth flooded her body – tiny trembles of expectation, which stopped abruptly as Aysha pulled back and pushed her on to the bed. Lily sat down involuntarily, noticing for the first time that the duvet had been removed and a collection of silk scarves lay on the sheet. She uttered a small gasp as her heart did a flip and the butterflies returned.

'Stay,' said Aysha. She picked up a scarf and in seconds Lily was deprived of sight, sitting meekly on the edge of the bed as Aysha tied the scarf over her eyes and behind her head. Aysha's hands fluttered over the naked girl's body, briefly touching breasts, thighs, stomach. Lily's nipples pricked up, stimulated by a brief draft of air Lily guessed came from Aysha's lips. She felt fingers on the nubs, toying with them and making them harder still, before Aysha ordered her:

'On your back, Lily, knees bent. Remember – *trust*. Okay?'

'Yes.' Her voice came out of a throat suddenly dry, making the sound barely a whisper. Lily licked her lips and swallowed. Uncertainty reared up.

Clarity came first in the form of a silk scarf tied firmly around her left wrist, before it was pulled down beside her left ankle and firmly bound to the bent leg. A minute later Lily's right wrist had been bound to that ankle and she found herself utterly helpless on her back, barely able to move. She mentally qualified that lack of movement, when she discovered the one option she did have was to open her legs widely, like a butterfly opening its wings, as Aysha pushed her knees apart with almost no effort.

Lily realised then her complete vulnerability. She tried to move her hands, her wrists, but each had been secured firmly, crossing the outside of the ankle. She could not find any knots, and had little wiggle room. Aysha held Lily's legs apart and gently stroked her mons with her fingertips. Lily gasped and could not suppress a little moan of pleasure. Every part of her now was open and receptive, with the discovery there was nothing she could do about her situation. The pressure on her labia increased, and the fingers slipped inside her. She was wet, and she knew it. She had been thinking about whatever might lie in store for her for hours, inventing vague scenarios which lacked detail available from any previous experience.

Aysha tweaked Lily's nipple and kissed her hard. Lily squirmed, her breath coming faster, then everything stopped, and Aysha was gone. Lily heard the bathroom door open and close, then the sound of a running shower. Shit. She was hot to trot and Aysha had just done a runner on her! Lily rolled about, tugging at her bonds, but they were unyielding. She rolled on to her side, and found her legs then pulled backwards, changing the position. She rolled again and with a short struggle wound up on her stomach, her wrist-ankle binding turning into a hogtie, her heels resting against her buttocks, breasts pressed into the mattress.

Lily grunted, her frustration increased by the flexibility of her tie yet the unrelenting restraint to her limbs. Aysha had started something in her loins, teasing and lighting fires Lily now wanted to stoke. She could not get her hands anywhere near her pussy, and trying to grind it into the mattress was ineffective. Lily swore under her breath at the simplicity yet functionality of the tie. She listened to the sound of the shower, waiting for its diminution and the prospect of Aysha's return, warm, soaped, eager…

It was evident Aysha was in no hurry and knew the absence of haste would rile her prisoner further. Finally Lily heard the door open, soft footsteps on the tiles and a hand resting on her exposed buttocks, which then slipped between her thighs.

'Mmmmn,' Aysha said. 'We should market you as a heat source. You could fry an egg down there…' She pushed Lily on to her side and then her back again, with more gratuitous groping which made Lily whine in frustration.

'What?' asked Aysha, her tone impatient.

'Can we… can you…' Lily stuttered weakly, not quite knowing how to ask Aysha to just stick her fingers, her lips, any fucking thing in there and finish what she'd started. Lily didn't know the protocol for asking a desperate release when she had the bargaining leverage of a gnat.

The hands were abruptly gone from Lily's body and Aysha told her: 'Lily, you're not in a position to ask favours. Seriously, there is no reason I shouldn't leave you tied up all night. You'll be perfectly safe, because I'll be right beside you. Oh I might wind you up a little, stir the pot, so to speak. Imagine how you'll be after eight hours of that? Oh yes, *that* would make you whine and complain, wouldn't it? No need to turn the heater on. No need for the duvet. Lily Maddison, the new energy source to save mankind is doing all the heating.' Aysha chuckled. 'That actually sounds a lot of fun. I think we'll do that, Honey. I'll just lie down beside you to keep you company.'

She pushed Lily on her side and Lily felt the duvet retrieved and pulled over her, with Aysha crawling underneath it to lie facing her.

'Please, Aysh…'

'Please what? What do you want, Lily? Tell me.'

'I want… you to make me cum…'

'Really? And what do I get, Lily Maddison? I seem to be doing all the work around her. You just lie around and let people have their way with you. God, you're such a slut.' Fingers grabbed Lily's nipples and twisted them. Lily yelped and jerked ineffectually at her bonds. 'You have lovely nipples, Lily. You could poke someone's eye out if you weren't careful. I could hang a washing line between them.' She squeezed them and Lily whimpered.

'I really do think they are a danger, Lily. I think we should do something – like health and safety stuff, you know? Like those traffic cones they use to warn motorists of potholes. Now what could we do in this instance...?'

Aysha's feigned puzzlement was evident, but Lily had no way of anticipating the next development until there was a biting grip on each flinty nub. She gasped and squealed and was about to cry out further when a hand clamped over her mouth.

'No, Lily. No noise. I'm going to take my hand away. If you squeal or carry on, I swear I'll gag you. Understand? You going to be quiet?' Lily had seen none of this coming, and over and above the bite on her nipples from what she assumed were plastic clothes pegs, the threat of some sort of gag was a sobering thought. She nodded her head.

'Uh-huh.'

'Good.' Aysha's voice was sweet and reasonable. 'Just breathe, sweetheart. Slowly and surely. The pain will ease. Breathe through it.' Lily's breasts rose and fell, the clothes pegs tugging gently and catching on the duvet – or was it Aysha's fingers tweaking and flicking them? Lily bit her lip and the initial sharp pain settled. She found the ardour in her loins had also eased, though she was not sure which was worse – pain and less frustration, or pure, full-on, unfulfilled loin-lust.

Lily's breathing became less ragged and for several minutes Aysha simply lay with her, not touching, but letting Lily's body become calmer, adjusting to the restraints and the feel of the pegs holding her sensitive flesh. Lily's mind did not rest, however, and continued to imagine all manner of possibilities which the arrival of the pegs had just initiated.

'You okay now, Honey?' Aysha gently asked at length.

'Uh-huh,' Lily whispered, her mouth again dry.

'Good. Now I want you to understand the situation. You may have worked out you're not going anywhere, not doing anything I don't allow. Conversely, anything I *do* require from you should be undertaken with enthusiasm. Understand?' Lily nodded. 'Sorry? I didn't hear that.'

'Yes, Aysha.'

'Good. Now it seems to me that in our recent encounters you've done quite well for yourself, and *I've* been the one doing all the work. Now, here you are wanting to get yourself off again, with no suggestion of perhaps showing a little gratitude in return. Never mind. I won't bother examining your lack of thanks and your clearly selfish motives. Rather, I will avail myself of that pretty mouth of yours until I decide you have adequately atoned for your selfishness. If you perform well, we'll see about your own satisfaction.'

# the submissive spy

The duvet was thrown off again and Lily was pushed on to her back. She had a momentary vision in her head of herself, pegged nipples pointing up like two rockets about to take off. Then Aysha was on her, kneeling over her face with a warm soapy fragrance that suddenly pressed down on to her. Lips closed on lips, but of a different sort, and Lily found her tongue sucking and probing between Aysha's labia, sucking intermittent breaths through her nostrils when she could. Aysha sighed, leaning forward, resting her upper body between Lily's bent, bound legs, her own tongue teasing at Lily's furry mound when it pleased her. Aysha knew she could finish Lily off, but concluded not unreasonably that she deserved a full service herself, and contented herself with occasionally taking a clothes peg and tugging it, to see if she could put her prisoner off stride.

Lily worked furiously, in part wanting to show Aysha what she could do, to repay her, but also to earn more of Aysha's own ministrations. Lily had learned enough of what could be done to a vagina by another woman, from her experience in Srinagar, along with her own self-driven efforts in Robert's absence. This time, Lily's fingers were unavailable. She sensed the pressure of Aysha on her face and knew she was getting through. Beyond the flicking of tongue and the wetness of labia against her cheeks, she could hear her friend's breathing speeding up, her body beginning to rock in time with her efforts. Her tongue found Aysha's little nub hidden in the delicious folds of flesh, and unearthed it enough for the hardness of her teeth to stimulate it. Aysha jumped at this sudden intrusion in her most intimate place, then pressed harder. Her breath was now underlain with a series of low pants, becoming groans.

Then the rush came through Aysha's body, all semblance of support gone, her loins crushing Lily's mouth, stifling her breath and her own gasps, as with a last effort Lily bit and sucked while Aysha ground down then bucked, as the final spasms took her. Somewhere in the midst of blood rushing to brains and loins, there was a stifled cry, then a series of shudders from the girl on top as she collapsed on to Lily.

Lily could hear gasping, though she was not sure who was voicing it. In the distance someone was saying 'fuck-fuck-fuck...' as Lily managed to free her mouth and nose from Aysha's slippery flesh. Nothing else happened for several minutes, between the two exhausted bodies. Finally Aysha heaved herself up and disappeared to the bathroom, leaving Lily still trapped and wearing the pegs.

When Aysha reappeared, she pulled up the duvet again and slipped in beside Lily.

'Fuck, girl. Where did you learn that? My, my... Sorry, I gotta rest, Sweetie, really...'

'But...' Lily bit her lip, knowing she was still in no position to bargain. 'Could you please take the pegs off...'

'I don't know, Honey... I think they keep you from getting too excited. Really. They'll settle down during the night. Your nips, I mean. They'll ache a bit, but you'll fall asleep, believe me. Especially after that effort.'

'No, Aysh, please... I can't last all night like this... I'll start to scream, I know I will...'

'So I'll just have to gag you – like I said...'

Lily felt the tears starting to creep out of the corners of her eyes. This was not what she had envisaged. She didn't know if she could go on with it. Deep inside she had a desperate desire to please Aysha, to make her proud, to lock in the likelihood of doing this again, but not on such stark and brutal terms...

Then she felt the tears being brushed aside, Aysha's lips on her eyelids, her cheeks, her mouth.

'Shush, Darling, only teasing. You are *so* easy to wind up! Hold your breath for an instant...' Lily did as she was told and felt the pressure slowly released from her nipples. There was a brief pain as the blood flowed back, then Aysha's lips were on top of the nipples, licking and soothing, nuzzling the pain into pleasure, before her voice came in a whisper next to Lily's ear.

'It's all right, Sweetheart. I'm not going to leave you tied up all night.' Then: 'Not yet, anyway. Maybe one day, when you ask for it. Because now you've had a taste and the thought is going to worm its way into your brain. Soon, when we're driving the long and boring roads between here and London, you'll think of this moment. You'll wonder what it'll be like to be bound all night, helpless and open to every whim I might have – good and evil.'

Lily could hear the warmth and pleasure in Aysha's voice as she painted a deliberately tantalizing picture. 'You'll start to imagine all sorts of things being done to you. You see, Lily, what I'm doing now is planting a seed which can't be dug up. However many times you cut off the new stalk and pretend you never had such lewd and pornographic thoughts in your head, that seed will regenerate underground and pop up again. No amount of weedkiller can stop these things now they're in your mind. Your brain will feed on them, grow with them and invent new and more devious ways to harvest them. I'm sorry, Lily. You'll remember this night as the one where I ruined your life forever, where I sent you down a one-way street when you were only looking for directions...'

The silence hung between them, Lily still trapped in her immovable dark world, taking in Aysha's words with relish and comfort, though not realising the far-reaching import of then. The future was far away. Always would be.

She'd had no time to process the significance of what Aysha was saying. That would come later, over the next few weeks of travel. What mattered right then was that Lily's bound legs were parted and Aysha's face was nuzzling her pussy, initiating sudden waves of pleasure from Lily's already-engorged loins. What happened next was fast and furious, an assault by Aysha on Lily's defenceless parts, like a Mongol horde sweeping through a helpless town. Lily was whisked away, back to the emperor's palace and a dark but beautiful world of bliss. It was the same place she had been transported to in Srinagar, standing blindfolded and naked in the houseboat. This time, however, as the intensity crashed over her and she climaxed, there was neither let-up nor possible response available to her.

Aysha registered the shock and shudder within her charge. She felt the tugging of Lily's arms and legs against the bonds, but made no effort to stop her attention to Lily's pussy. For her part, Lily now realised the true significance of those bonds, of the extra layer of intensity the restraint gave to Aysha's actions. Lily could not push her friend away, could not deflect that incessant tongue starting another onslaught, could not stop her own gearbox shifting into overdrive. She tried to wriggle away, to close her legs, but Aysha was far too strong and was positioned to control her prisoner.

'No...no... oh God!' Another climax burst through Lily's defences, her brain an explosion of lights, her loins bucking against the mouth and lips which would not stop. She knew a third orgasm was on the way but did not think she could survive it. She was becoming weaker, her breath more ragged, her voice distant and incoherent. She felt herself fading, losing the strength to resist, sliding into some dark abyss, when out of nowhere a slippery finger insinuated itself into her anus and she bucked like a wild thing.

'No, no!' she gasped again, though the lack of conviction behind the protest was evident. Lily had never experienced anal before, and the surprise itself was as potent as the finger. Lily had no time to consider whether it was something she wanted or liked, for it simply became another part of the battering on the fortress doors. As more fingers penetrated her front passage and the rear one probed deeper, Lily struggled violently and finally gave in with a series of stifled cries turning into a protracted moan, leaving her a snorting mess as the invaders were withdrawn and Aysha again retreated to the bathroom.

By the time she returned, Lily was trying to curl up foetally, but her bonds had turned the position into a hogtie again. Aysha undid the scarves and watched fondly as Lily lay on her side, her hands clasped together between her legs, still panting as her breath slowly came under control. Aysha pulled up the duvet and slid in beside her, turning off the light.

'Good night, my darling Lily,' she whispered.

In the bright sunlight of the mountain valley the next day, Lily and Aysha walked down to the nearby village. The side trip to Swat was intended as a relaxing pause in the westward journey. It was a last tranquil break before the rigors of Afghanistan, Iran and Turkey - a hiatus to be savoured to recharge energies. The girls wore their salwar kameezes, set off with silk scarves draped back over their shoulders, their hair pulled into ponytails.

The world seemed glorious to Lily under the clear sky, as they passed fields of maize, interspersed with poppies, though they had passed their flowering stage. Aysha saw her gaze and they stopped at the edge of the gravel road.

'Are they...' Lily started to ask.

'Yep. Opium poppies.'

'Wow.'

Aysha squatted beside one, cupping the egg-like seed pod between her fingers. 'See these little vertical slits here?' She indicated brown lines on the green skin. 'That's raw opium coming out.' Lily was suitably impressed as they walked on to the village.

'How come you know about that?'

Aysha shrugged. 'You read stuff. Opium's part of our culture in India, though for some reason we don't have such addiction problems. It's very medicinal – we use it for everything from pain relief to scorpion bites, as dispensed by the medicine men.'

'How come your culture is now Indian?' Lily teased. 'One moment you're from Brisbane - or is it West Sydney – and the next you lay claim as a Bombay native?'

Aysha recognised a wind-up when she saw one. 'Can't all be White Anglo-Saxon Protestants. Someone has to put a little colour in a monochrome world.'

They entered the small town lying at the junction with the gravel road to their hotel. The place was interesting, in a basic, not-very-clean sort of way. Dogs lazed in the sun near an open-air butchers shop, where several skinned carcases of goats or sheep hung under an awning. Various off-cuts – recognisable and unrecognisable – sat in enamel bowls on a counter.

'God, I hope our meals don't come from here,' Lily said, as a small girl vainly fanned at the flies, her big eyes following the two foreigners as they walked past.

The main street was a hundred metres of small shops selling fruit, fabrics, and general goods, interspersed with a motor cycle mechanic and several dubious-looking outlets which might have been pharmacies. They found a small bakery that doubled as a chai-shop, with three plastic tables and chairs under a canopy, set back from and above the street. From here they could watch the passage of people and vehicles, and gaze over the corrugated iron rooftops down the valley.

A tantalising aroma drifted out from the shop and a white-bearded man in a flat hat smiled and waved to them to be seated at one of the rickety tables. Before long, tea had been made and a plate with several spiral-like pastries and another of samosas had been placed before them. Aysha leaned back in the chair and gazed down at the torpid street scene.

'God, how amazing is this. Just one thing missing, though...'

'You want a hookah, don't you.'

Aysha smiled. 'Am I that obvious, or are you just being super-perceptive?' She waved to the elderly man and made an inquiry. The man had little English, but clearly understood the word 'hookah', and nodded agreeably. A minute later a young lad appeared with a battered metal hookah and began preparing the pipe. He offered them a choice from several grubby packets of indeterminate contents. Aysha sniffed at them and selected one, and the boy loaded the bowl with some of the contents before vanishing again, to reappear with some embers from the baker's oven.

Aysha sucked hard and the coal glowed with the airflow. She let out a stream of smoke and coughed briefly.

'Wow. A little different from Srinagar,' she said with a smile, waving away the last of the smoke from her eyes.

'What was the choice?' Lily asked.

'Erm... your choice of full blown tobacco, unknown, dodgy unknown... and one which might have some apple or other fruit mixed in.'

'So you got the fruit?'

'Ahhh... no. Dodgy unknown. Have a drag.' Lily dubiously took the carved wooden holder at the end of the tube and wiped the metal mouthpiece. 'Scared of getting Aysha germs?'

'No – scared of getting whatever the male population of this place have.'

'A bit late for Aysha germs, anyway, after last night,' she smirked.

Lily sucked in a lungful and coughed. 'Ooo... Strong! Seriously, what's in it?'

'It is a precocious little number, isn't it? I'd say it's from the south side of Swat, vintage 1977, likely June, probably last Wednesday,' said Aysha.

Now priding herself on at least being close to Aysha's coolness in smoking a hookah, Lily took another drag and blew out a plume. 'It may be strong, but at least it's rough,' she opined. Then her eyes became momentarily unfocussed. 'Shit, Aysha, what is in this?'

'Tobacco, and probably a fair portion of hash. The tobacco makes it burn better.'

'What? We're smoking hash? Fuck!' Lily was aghast.

'I do love it when you talk dirty,' said Aysha. 'Just relax and have another pull.'

'But it's probably against the law...'

'Oh lighten up, Lily!' Aysha was impatient. 'Who's going to arrest you here? You expect to see a couple of cop cars with blue and white checks screech to a halt and a dozen constables all called Khan take you away in handcuffs? Or is that just another fantasy I have yet to arrange for you?' Aysha laughed, and Lily smiled at the mental image. 'Jesus, Lily, every man and his dog smokes the stuff here. It's what the men do when they can't be bothered with sex, and what they probably do before and after it as well.'

Lily took another drag on the mouthpiece and held the smoke inside her, slowly exhaling and feeling the creeping release of her anxiety, though whether through Aysha's logic or the hookah's contents, she couldn't tell. But she felt better.

'I can't believe I'm smoking hash in Pakistan! Dad and Robert would have conniptions!'

'Of course,' Aysha agreed laconically. 'Because you were always brought up the right way. Right school, good university, right match with somebody with a dick.'

Ordinarily Lily would have taken offense, but now it didn't seem important. What was becoming more important were the colours of the Coca Cola sign on the shop on the other side of the street. Lily could see the rust coming through the sign, and how it was taking away from the impact of the picture of the liquid in the bottle.

The owner appeared again, a questioning look on his face and beamed when the girls nodded and smiled their approval.

'Music?' he asked. It seemed as though nothing was too much trouble, for he reappeared with a battered boom box, the power cord for which was just long enough for it to sit on the concrete slab at the doorway entrance. He showed them several cassettes, mostly Pakistani but one of Saturday Night Fever and one by the Eagles. Moments later 'Hotel California' was drifting out into the street.

> 'Such a lovely place
> Such a lovely face;
> Plenty of room at the Hotel California
> Any time of year
> You can find it here.'

'My god, how fucking amazing is this,' said Aysha, crossing her legs and inhaling deeply.

She decided the scene warranted a picture, and the polaroid camera came out of her daypack, with the baker persuaded to assist. The result was a picture of the two semi-stoned travellers, arms intertwined, smiles expressing their contentment with the world, in a ramshackle bakery in the wilds of north Pakistan.

'Here are Aysha and Lily, glowing in the aftermath of rampant sex in a country where it's illegal, sucking down dodgy smokes and with fields of opium in the background. Just like home,' Aysha said, after the photo had developed in the darkness of her journal, then reappeared for scrutiny.

'Like home? Really?' Lily was still fooled by Aysha's sense of humour. Her friend was worldly and made Lily feel like an innocent. For Lily's first time abroad she had travelled straight to the prim exoticism of Singapore, then Kathmandu, without even a sample of Australia just across the Tasman. 'You get some of that in Queensland?'

'Shit no.' Aysha laughed. 'Well, there's certainly been a bit of rampant sex, but the story goes that when you're flying from Sydney to Brisbane, the pilot comes on the intercom and tells you to 'put you watches back one hour and twenty years'. Not exactly liberal, Brisbane. But Sydney was okay – apart from certain family aspects, about which we shall say no more. At least there's the Cross.'

'The Cross?'

'King's Cross. Jeez, Lily, don't they teach you anything in New Zealand?'

'Evidently not. Not about King's Cross, anyway.'

'Sydney's finest inner city suburb, source of any vice you wish to name, and home to the finest cops money can buy.'

'Oh. You mean like a red light district?'

'Uh… yeah. At least you've heard of those. You got such a thing in Kiwiland?'

'Ha! Our illustrious prime minister is slightly more conservative than Genghis Khan. Liberal sex is not high on his agenda. Probably no sex of any sort… Damn – now I can't stop seeing him naked… Eeeww!' Lily dissolved in giggles.

'Well, at least we have that in common – in Queensland, I mean. Our beloved premier is just to the right of Atilla the Hun in *his* views. You want sex mags in Brisbane, better be prepared to get them mail order from the Cross - and hide them under your bed, 'cos the puritans are in power. Woe betide if you're a guy and fancy another guy. If you're not just beaten up by the cops as a warning, be prepared for some jail time. But the irony is that any bloke convicted of buggery and sent to jail is probably going to ask for an extended sentence,' Aysha snorted with a grin.

'What about us girls?' Lily asked, intrigued. 'Were you and Joanne breaking the law?'

'Oh, we're legally okay. Doing rude things to your girlfriend isn't criminal. Of course, you'll still be abused by the cops and shunned by much of society, but it's better than being a gay guy and getting thrown into jail.'

Lily took a bite of the spiral pastry. 'Mmmn, this is really good. Sort of sugary, like a heavy doughnut mix, with some almonds thrown in. I'm hungry!' She sipped her milky tea. 'So... all that stuff we did last night... Where on earth did that come from?'

Aysha eyed her over the hookah with an expression stopping just short of pity, reserved for a city girl to bestow on her unsophisticated cousin from the back blocks.

'Have you never done anything like that with Robert? With a few scarves, a tie or two, maybe? Fluffy handcuffs?'

'God no! Robert comes from a good family.' Aysha found this hugely amusing and Lily smiled at the ridiculousness of her own words.

'It's not a *bad* thing, Lily. You're not some sort of deviant if you admit to liking something a little different.'

'That's *quite a lot* different.'

'But did you like it?'

'No, it was fucking awful.'

'What?' Aysha looked at her askance, and Lily was unable to maintain a grim expression.

She felt herself blushing. 'I've never done anything like that, Aysh... Well, you sort of started it up in Srinagar, but I didn't expect... I mean, I didn't think it could go...'

'Further?'

'Uh huh.'

Aysha sat back and offered the pipe to Lily.

'Ever been to those movies where the heroine is bound to a bed and about to be ravished by the villain? You know - the hero's on his way, but in the meantime the girl is gagged and struggling to get free whilst trying to resist the bad guy's evil intentions?' Lily nodded. 'Ever seen those American detective magazine covers? Same thing. Wonder Woman? Oh my! She was my heroine! Then there's the chick tied up in some basement cellar, maybe chained to the wall? "Oh woe is me!" Ever felt anything looking at that? A little frisson of excitement? Something catching inside that makes you wonder what she's feeling, and maybe the hero needn't hurry?'

'Uh... I don't know...' The question and the images were so out of the blue that Lily hadn't got her thoughts in order. Yes, she had seen these moments in "literature" and on the screen, and... She paused. 'Maybe,' she finally admitted.

'I knew it,' said Aysha, though with more than a hint of smugness. 'You're a natural, Lily.'

'A natural what?'

'A natural submissive.'

'Oh,' said Lily blankly.

'Honey, do they even have sex shops in New Zealand?' Lily was not sure if Aysha was exasperated or merely baffled at her innocence.

'Of course they do. Well, in Auckland there are a few, along K-Road...'

'Ever been in one?'

'Once,' she admitted, as though it was a bad thing – probably the opposite of what Aysha hoped for.

'Was it exciting?'

'Uh... I think so. I was a bit drunk at the time, with some university friends. But I think it was really pretty tame.'

'So you weren't with Robert?'

'God no! He'd run a mile to avoid being seen entering one of those shops. Auckland's a small place. Reputations need to be protected.'

Aysha sighed. 'Well, at least I have my baseline now.'

'What does that mean?'

Aysha smiled warmly but stayed silent. Lily thought her friend's expression was almost one of gratitude, perhaps for what the universe had delivered to her, or what she had been smart enough to identify and claim for herself. Lily liked it, all the same. In the confusion of the smoke, she wondered if she now loved Aysha, in the sense beyond the physical...

Lily was in no doubt that in a little baker's shop in the foothills of the Hindu Kush, something had happened in her life, and this moment would always remain with her. It was a second in time when she felt her allegiances shift across a frail bridge from Robert to Aysha. Then a thought occurred to her.

'Aysh... what happened with Joanne? How long had you been together?'

'Five years – close to.'

'Was she a submissive?'

'Yes.'

'Like me?'

'No, not like you, Lily. At least not to this point.'

'How so?'

Aysha took another lungful of the hookah and stared out down the valley, as though thinking how to explain something complex.

'This is so complicated, Honey. I don't want to overwhelm you at the start of your journey.'

'Try me.'

'Well... Jo was a pain slut.'

'A pain slut?'

'She was submissive, but needed pain to climax.'

'Really?' Lily was stunned. 'You can climax from pain? That's...'

'Sick? Bizarre? Perverted? One woman's perversion is another woman's orgasm, Sweetie. That's the simple fact. It doesn't matter how straight or modest a person is, I guarantee if you dig deep enough you'll find some weird obsession they'll ultimately admit to. I may not be the most orthodox in the sexual world, Lily, but I've learned enough to know that whatever ludicrous activity or desire you can think up, someone will have an obsession about it. If you love ballroom dancing or collecting stamps, you find others who are likewise inclined. That's the light side. On the dark side exactly the same thing applies, it's just that finding like-minded individuals is that much harder and more risky. You risk reputations, relationships and even your freedom. Joanne and I somehow found ourselves out of an initially uncomplicated encounter. Once you've got *that* far, things can happen very fast in the privacy of your own bedroom.

'We found we complimented each other. I liked to be in control. I liked to think up stuff for her. I liked to fuck with her mind, as much as her body.'

'Was it a nice body?'

'*I* thought so. It worked for me. That said, just for the record, yours is even nicer.' Her smile was gentle now, as though trying to balance what had gone before with not scaring off her new best friend. 'Jo would never win a Miss Australia, but she made up for that with character and stamina.'

'Stamina?'

'Uh-huh. I guess you need more context. Jo had a massive fixation with bondage. She absolutely loved it. Being restrained was her passion, but it was so much more than the restraint itself. I met her at training college but she dropped out and ended up working for a PR company. Smart move, smart girl. It was a high pressure job, lots of decisions. She was like the female equivalent of an alpha male running the show. A born leader, you might think. Until I told her to go and fetch the riding crop... or the cuffs... or the rope. Then she just went to jelly.

'A big part of the experience for her was giving up control – handing over power and forsaking that until such time as she was released. It was as if part of her mind could then just shut down, leaving behind all the day-to-day shit and just be physically in the moment. Somebody else – me – was making the decisions. As long as Jo trusted me to have her back, she would be mine to do as I pleased with.'

'And what *did* you do?' Lily asked, agog.

'Pretty much anything and everything. You see, Honey, going down this road isn't like missionary sex. Oh sure, we've seen those temples at Khajuraho, and there are a lot of ways to stick a dick into your vagina and have a jolly good orgasm. And there are variations involving mouths, fingers and carved objects. So far so good. But you reach the end of the road fairly soon.

'Go down the bondage road and you still have all of that, but overlaid with a million other variations, from tight restraint, long-term restraint, predicament stuff, role play, chastity, pain, punishment, you name it.' Aysha laughed. 'There's so much to explore, and each of these little genres will depend on a person's tastes and proclivities. You know, you can learn another person's normal tastes in a night, but go down this road and you're forever experimenting and refining.

'Here – you look like you need another drag.' She passed the mouthpiece to Lily. 'Long and short of it was that we rented a small Queenslander for a year, together. It was scheduled for refurbishment and was kinda decrepit. You know what a Queenslander is, right?'

'Someone from Queensland?'

Aysha rolled her eyes. 'It's a house, Sweetie, built on timber piles to let the air flow underneath. This one was pretty rundown, and nobody minded a few more eyebolts in the walls – convenient places to lock a chain to... We were only limited by our imaginations, the hardware store and our salaries - mine was meagre; Jo's was pretty good. We built a small cell for Jo downstairs where she could be locked up, and of course there was plenty of scope upstairs as well.'

'You said she was a pain slut?'

'Ohhh yes...' The knowing, recollecting smile. 'I'd never come across such a thing before I met her, either. I don't think even she realised it until I got a bit heavy with a cane one time.'

'A cane? What, you were beating her with a cane?'

'Lily, Darling, stay with the story, please. Handing over control means just that. Absolute trust that your partner will have your back, and ultimately do no permanent harm.'

'*Permanent* harm?'

'Okay, I can see this is doing your head in. Let's give you a scenario – a Joanne special. We'll combine it with something called predicament bondage, in bondage slang. Imagine a chair – just an ordinary dining chair, no arms, straight back. Except the seat is a hard sheet of ply with a bunch of heavy nails hammered in so that the heads stand up about an inch, and spaced an inch apart. Kinda like the old bed of nails trick but without the really sharp bits. Let me tell you, it's pretty uncomfortable to sit with your naked arse on this chair. Do-able, but not for too long. Okay, imagine your ankles are tied to the chair legs, and the chair is fixed to the floor. Let's tie your wrists together in front of you and attach them to a rope which goes through a pulley overhead, which is tied to a bucket of water. When you stand up with your arms above you, the bucket rests on the floor. It's a change from having to sit on that horrible seat with the load on your arms. So standing up is preferable, right? Except that you have a couple of cords tied to your nipples, which are in turn attached to a couple of lead sinkers. When you stand up, the load comes on them as they're lifted off the floor. Get the picture now? See the predicament?'

'My God!' said Lily, trying to envisage the nails on her backside, the strain on her arms and the tugging on her breasts and nipples. 'It sounds horrendous!'

'So imagine you've been left alone and you're trying to deal with all these different things. Your mind is fantasizing what might still be in store for you, how long it might last, how painful – or pleasurable – it might be. Your own imaginings may well be worse than reality. In short, you may be your own worst enemy.

'Let's say you're blindfolded – I know how you love *that*.' Lily avoided her eye. 'Everything becomes ten times worse. You sense someone's presence but don't know what they're carrying, what they're armed with, when something's going to happen. Your sensitivity and expectation are heightened. You anticipate something is going to occur but can't determine where and when. Inevitably, when it does happen, you weren't expecting it and it's a shock.

'You don't see someone come in and shove a vibrator or fingers between your legs. Distracting, yes? A surge of pleasure amongst all that pulling and tugging of sensitive bits. More vibrator, taking you away. Then a sudden pain across your arse as a flogger comes out of nowhere. The balance now is between pleasure and pain, and we know the way most people would go. But the impact of the flogger heightens sensitivity and in most cases makes a pleasurable reward that much more intense. Except with Joanne. We found it was the opposite. Oh yes, she liked her pleasure, but ultimately it was the pain that pushed her over the edge for the most intense orgasm. Jo would be shouting the house down in ecstasy as her pussy was whipped.'

'No!'

'Yes. Truly. She was one of a kind, our Jo. Or so I thought. I actually found out pain sluts are not that rare, but strangely it doesn't seem to be something discussed over the dinner table. Jo herself didn't realise until we got hot and heavy one day, and the penny dropped for both of us.'

Lily was shaking her head, but something deep inside her was telling her not to miss a word of this lurid exposé which would have done credit to a racy Sunday newspaper.

'And what happened to you and Joanne?' Lily asked.

A hard edge came into Aysha's voice. 'I'd been away on a school camp, supervising some kids on a farm visit. It was the start of school holidays, but the weather had turned to shit and we'd called the thing off after the tents got smashed, so I'd come home a day earlier. Arrived to find a strange car parked outside. Went upstairs to find the television on but nobody around – until I discovered this chick I'd never met before hiding under the bed. We had words, shall we say. I know how to handle myself, and she left the house with a black eye, a broken nose and a damaged manicure.

'Jo was nowhere to be found – at least not upstairs. Remember I said we'd built a cell under the house? It seems what *I* gave to her was not enough, and while I was away this chicky had been providing a little extra punishment on the side.'

Lily covered her open mouth with her hands and stared wide-eyed.

'Well, I was pretty pissed off when I went downstairs. Dear Jo was chained up naked in the cell, which I might say, is pretty well soundproofed with thick walls. She had a vibrator locked in place and the door was bolted on the outside. Her hands were bound behind her back and she had a number of clothes pegs on her tits. In short, between the pleasure and pain, she was having a whale of a time, expecting to see chicky-babe return when she'd done with watching my tv and drinking my beer. Well, that was it. You'll only betray me once, Lily. I don't react well.'

'So what did you do?' Lily's question was a cliff-hanging whisper.

'I literally lost it, sweetheart. I kept her in there for three days. That was how long it took me to send my resignation in for what was a shitty school posting anyway, and get an ticket to Kathmandu and on this trip.'

'Seriously? My God! You just up and left?'

'Yep. Took out my savings, closed my bank account, and left Joanne to find the remaining rent money. Bus to the airport with the bitch still chained up in her little cell.'

'No! How did she get free?'

'You learn a lot about improvisation in bondageland, Lily. In particular, those into self-bondage have to dream up ways to get free when they don't have a nice helpful lover or housemate to do it for them. I learned that from Jo, who was a... solo practitioner, shall we say, before I came along. The favourite method is the ice block. You freeze a block of ice around a key. When the ice melts, the key is available. You can hang the ice up to stop any interference with it. The bigger the ice block, the longer you have to wait.

'I reckon in this case, with the ice block the size of a small bucket – limited by what I could fit in the freezer – dear Jo would have been staring at those drips for the better part of a day. Well, not exactly staring, since she was blindfolded, so she would just have to imagine how fast – or slow – it was melting. She could sit underneath it and catch the drops in her mouth if she was thirsty. You can't be more considerate than that to your prisoner, can you? But ultimately, she would have been wondering how big the ice was, and how many more hours would she have to sit there before she could unlock herself and get the vibrator out.'

'Wow. You really are evil!' Lily's enhanced imagination had now been etched with a picture which suddenly made her loins wet.

'I know. Just remember that before you run off with somebody else who promises you the world, Lily darling.'

\* \* \*

# CHAPTER 8 – Afghanistan

They descended from the mountains to Peshawar, which proved every bit as wild west as Wayne had promised. Here they'd stopped briefly to check out the gunsmiths' shops where any form of hand-held armament could be replicated, and where in the next street they could visit the 'International Hashish Store' – or one of many others with less imposing titles. Lily showed only a cursory interest, and found herself impatient to be on the road again, where the long hours of driving lulled her mind and let her drift through subliminal doors, into sexual corridors previously either unknown or taboo, their keys now revealed through Aysha's intriguing narratives.

From Peshawar it had been a short drive to the Khyber Pass border crossing into Afghanistan. Here the features of the locals changed from sub-continental to the melting-pot mixture of Pashtun and Tajiks, infused with a two-thousand-year-old sprinkling of the blue-eyed progeny of Alexander. This was the harsh, uncompromising country that had come to be known as the Graveyard of Empires, where both Russian and British armies had succumbed to centuries of uncompromising resistance of the Afghans.

They were stamped into Afghanistan without incident, passing under a fortress-like gateway with the sign beside it stating "Foreigners not to go off Jamrud-Torkam Road unless specially permitted". Lily felt an unexpected shiver of excitement, for in the romantic recesses of her mind Afghanistan was a mystical place, akin to Tibet, though she could not have articulated why this might be.

'We're in dodgy territory again,' Wayne had explained to them. 'They have a president who overthrew the monarchy four years ago, and who seems to be cosying up to the Soviets. We've had reports of sporadic anti-government demonstrations and arrests of the opposition. Normally this sort of stuff doesn't affect us directly until they start closing borders, when it all goes to hell in a handbasket. So let's hope we continue being lucky.'

The garish Pakistani trucks with their mirrors and tassels were now replaced by battered pickups, crammed to overflowing with wild-looking turbaned men, clinging to the outside. They wound their way up a series of hairpins in the deep shadow of the Khyber Pass, the grey-black rock utterly devoid of vegetation. It was an engineering marvel, and it did not take much to see the potential for ambush on any attacking or retreating force. As though to underline the volatility of the region, two days after crossing the border, they were to learn that the Pakistani military had staged a coup and closed the border. They had made it through just in time.

In Kabul they revelled in the exotic mix of faces transported from the pages of Sinbad and the Arabian Nights. Grey hills rose around their hotel, their summits stark and barren, the lower reaches strewn with mud-roofed houses that seemed to be a throwback from the previous century. The hotel was basic, dormitory-style, and after settling in they had wandered down the iconic Chicken Street, window shopping the stores displaying Afghan lambswool coats, hashish, and gorgeous lapis lazuli jewellery. Aysha had spent hours scribbling in her journal.

Afghanistan left an indelible impression on Lily if only through the intense clarity of the air and the azure skies as backdrops to dun brown mountain ranges from horizon to horizon. Alternating with the forbidden thoughts elicited by Aysha, was the evolution of the Karakoram Symphony. The sublime surroundings of the Dal Lake were now behind her, supplanted by the harsh clarity of the Afghan vistas, the exoticism of the people and the timelessness of the culture. Lily found herself humming chords, little melodies which she jotted as best she could in a notebook. The grandness of the country got to her – the huge skies and panoramas which made her feel insignificant.

She had read James Mitchener's novel *Caravans* the previous year, and it had seized her imagination. The high passes of the Hindu Kush, the gathering of tribes, the isolation and grandeur of the scenery now came rushing back each time she scanned the jagged horizon, and each time they passed a camel train heading who-knew-where. The colourfully-garbed tribes accompanying these caravans had been trading this way for centuries, long before the colonial powers had tried to annex the country, building their roads and bridges and trying to spread their ideologies. The tribes had continued to travel, bedding down in the mudbrick caravanserais, the ruins of which still appeared at intervals alongside the road.

Lily the dreamer was captivated, and for a while her visions of being bound and in Aysha's power were again supplanted by dreams of being on camel-back, winding high into the treeless valleys and across passes to high pastures and ancient trading places. Moments like these made her wonder fleetingly about past lives, and whether there might be some distant experience embedded in her subconscious or her genes that stirred such feelings as though they were real memories.

Borodin's "*In the Steppes of Central Asia*" flitted through her head repeatedly, with its gentle opening oboe and horn calls, merging into the slow passage of the camel caravans across the grassy steppe, in the shadow of great snow-capped mountains. Alexander Borodin had composed the piece nearly a century previously, and it was known as a "*tableau vivant*" – a living picture. It was one of Lily's favourite pieces, even though it was not for the cello. Now she was seeing this living picture at the road's edge, and something connected with her. The musical build-up came slowly, as in Lily's mind the caravan wended its way up a long trail to the hidden pass, cresting it finally to the climactic expanse of a myriad valleys and icy ranges beyond, the moment when the hairs on her neck stood up with the intensity of the music, and goose bumps broke out on her skin. She resolved to somehow put this passing land into music, into what would become the Maddison Caravan Cello Concerto. Might as well aim high.

They thrummed south from Kabul, skirting the Hindu Kush mountain range as it fanned out into the centre of the country, driving all day on a Soviet-made concrete highway which provided no let-up in road noise. Lily occasionally scrawled notes as impressions and chords flipped through her brain, while Aysha's own notebook was never far from her side. One part of Lily wanted to read it, but the other did not.

The hotels were as basic as it got, with ineffective plumbing and dormitory rooms. Kandahar came and went, as they turned northwest. They halted near noon at an almost deserted Soviet-built hotel, their lowered voices echoing in the bland, cavernous dining room as they sampled the equally bland menu. Later in the afternoon they stopped to swim in a shallow, ice-cold glacial river, which woke them from the torpor of the long straight road. Lily and Aysha dozed in adjacent seats, feeling the effects of questionable food and unsettled stomachs. Lily watched the sun climb on one side of the bus and fall on the other, as they rumbled towards Iran. When she was not mentally toying with notes and chords in her head, Lily's thoughts invariably returned to the revelations both of what she had experienced and what Aysha had told her in Swat. Aysha had left Lily alone with her thoughts several times during that night, and those very thoughts had been Lily's worst enemy at the time. Now, in the monotony of long distance driving, they returned and took her away from the feel of the veloured seatback and the dusty window with its ageless landscapes.

Aysha had not only lit new fires in Lily's mind, but had stoked them further with her story of her breakup with Joanne. It had been so visual that the conjured up images now lingered, and in turn triggered her own recollections of the bonds at her wrists and ankles, the darkness under the blindfold, and the utter powerlessness in response to Aysha's lips and fingers. Some days were long and tiring; some days the thoughts just made Lily hot for Aysha's touch, only to find it was another dormitory hotel at day's end, or else Aysha was not in the mood, or so she said.

Lily began to think her friend was tormenting her, having provided Lily with a sexual experience beyond anything Robert had come close to. Lily had decided it was likely she had never had a true orgasm with Robert, for she could not recall anything as intense as Aysha had elicited. Lily became convinced Aysha was dangling this sexual apogee in front of her like a carrot to a donkey, then taking pleasure in keeping it just beyond Lily's reach. She was starting to understand the mind games Aysha was bringing to the relationship – which manifested themselves as much outside the bedroom as within it. It did nothing to lower Lily's libido, and the shared dormitory rooms likewise offered no opportunity for any relief. Aysha sensed Lily's frustration without her having to voice it, and soothed her ardour with the promise of "something" when they reached Tehran – their first two-night stop since Kabul, where a double room was promised.

\*   \*   \*

# CHAPTER 9 - Iran

There had been another briefing from Wayne as they prepared to cross into Iran, where Mohammed Reza Shah reigned as "King of Kings", "Light of the Aryans" and "Commander-in-Chief", according to Lily's Lonely Planet guide. The briefing was more of a warning, and was followed by a roadside inspection of the bus by courier and driver. Budgie lay on his back in the dust and checked underneath the vehicle, for it was common for locals to plant drugs on through-transport, retrieving them at the other end of the journey. Wayne suggested to his charges that anything incriminating be dumped right there in the bushes if there was even the remotest chance of it leading to a filthy cell in Tehran's notorious Evin Prison. After two hours of chaos leaving the Afghan border, they travelled a mile across no-man's land to face a three-hour search by Iranian customs with a fearsome reputation for drug detection.

In Iran the promise of two nights in the same room – just the two of them – had materialised, and Lily had been like a cat on hot bricks. They had arrived in Tehran in late afternoon, after their first experience of suicidal Iranian driving on a hair-raising road from the Caspian Sea through the Elburz Mountains.

The Arman Hotel was situated near the bazaar, towards the south side of the great polluted metropolis that was Tehran. The hotel was nothing special, though a cut above the basics of Afghanistan, and the streets were lively and filled with crazy honking traffic. Aysha had insisted on getting their washing organised with the hotel laundry, then making their way several blocks to the Post Restante with Lily to collect her mail. This time there had been nothing from Robert, but two letters from her father.

Lily had read them cursorily, distracted and on edge from Aysha's sexual promise two days before. News from home could be savoured in due course, in the monotony of a long distance drive, with postcards to be written later.

In what was left of the day they had wandered around Toopkhaneh Square – in actuality a giant rectangle that seemed to function as an exhaust-fumed transport hub for taxis and buses – exploring shop windows and enjoying what they saw as the most modern cityscape since leaving Kathmandu. They opted for an early dinner and found a window table in a small restaurant in Ferdowsi Street, just off the square, where they could watch the western-suited men and chic women pass by. The place exuded progress, despite what Lily had read of the activities of the Shah's secret police. The reality was that anything happening outside the bubble that was Lily and Aysha was irrelevant, and Lily couldn't wait to get back to the hotel.

'Eat up your stew, Lily,' said Aysha, as though to one of her primary school classes, while finishing the last of her *kabob koobideh*.

'Yes Miss Newton.'

'No lip from you young lady. You'll eat because you'll need your strength,' Aysha added in an undertone.

Lily looked around at the other diners. They were few, for it was only a little after six pm, and it seemed most Iranians were given to later dining. At the nearest table a middle-aged moustached businessman and his wife engaged in their own earnest conversation. They were seated far enough away for Aysha to give Lily her next lesson in what to expect.

'We need to talk about a few things, Lily,' said Aysha.

'Oh? That sounds ominous.'

'It's important, not ominous. Your life might depend on it.' Lily looked up from her stew, which she was finding very tasty – a tangy, citrusy slow-cooked mix of lamb and herbs, with steamed rice as a side.

'You may recall – if you can get past the bunch of orgasms you were experiencing – that you were somewhat restrained during our last performance – in the literal sense. Your *reactions* weren't restrained in any way, shape or form, I might add. My point is, supposing you suddenly decided you were having a heart attack, or you couldn't feel your hand because the blood flow had been cut off? You'd tell me, right? Because I wouldn't know otherwise. But if we get a little deeper into this, particularly if we try a little corporal punishment, then you may find you need a Safeword.'

'A what?'

'A Safeword – something you can yell out and whatever I'm doing, everything will come to a screeching halt.'

'Why don't I just tell you?'

Aysha pushed her glasses up her forehead into her hair, and gazed at Lily with a new intensity. The rearrangement of the glasses made her cheekbones more prominent and Lily again was taken by her exotic beauty.

'Because, my dear Lily, in the throes of passion, you may find yourself screaming "No! No! No!" when you're in the mind and role of a slave girl begging for mercy, but in actuality you're lapping up your punishment. For "No", read "Yes". It can get very confusing. A Safeword is a word or phrase that bears no relation to whatever is happening to you at that moment, and it'll stick out like dog's balls to me.'

'What sort of thing are we talking about?'

'I'm going to suggest the same as I used with Joanne – not because you remind me of her, or I want to be reminded of her, but because I'm attuned to it. So if – for whatever reason – the going gets too tough and you can't take it anymore, or if there is a real problem, you shout out "Happy Birthday!" and I'll stop immediately. Is that clear?'

'Sure.'

'But it comes with a caveat.  Be *very, very sure* of your need,' she said sternly.  'For example, you may find yourself on the receiving end of something other than a beating.  There are so many things I could oblige you to do.  If it turns out you're just a bit overwrought and haven't reached any sort of limit, or there is no real emergency, either you will be denied future pleasure for a long, long time until you're dying of frustration, or else the punishment will be doubled.  Comprendo?'

'Uh-huh.'

'Comprendo?' Aysha glared at her.

'Yes, Aysh.'

'This is serious, Lily.  This is about trust – again.  You have to trust me, and be willing to push your boundaries.  You need to trust that I recognise these and can decide how far we *do* push them.  Just because something hurts a bit doesn't mean you're going to be scarred for life, or that you'll die.  I won't let either of those things happen to you. But the pain may mean that – when the pleasure part follows – you'll get further into orbit than you've ever been before.'

'So... are you going to beat me?'

'I don't know, Sweetie,' said Aysha with a sly smile.  'And if I did, I wouldn't tell you, anyway.  It's not something you need to know, only to wonder about...'

Lily felt the butterflies reassemble in her stomach along with an unfamiliar wetness in her loins.  She didn't know whether this was the thought of being beaten, and if so, was it fear or desire?

'Oh, and another thing, if I decide you need to be gagged because you're getting a little boisterous or out of control, the same thing applies with a Safeword.  You simply *hum* the "Happy Birthday" tune - since you won't be able to enunciate very well.'  Aysha gave her a lascivious grin from across the table.  'Think you can focus enough to manage that?'

'Uhh... I guess.'

Lily's butterflies took flight.

They were about to leave when there was a commotion in the street outside, as a young man wearing a suit and a white collarless shirt came sprinting between the pedestrians and burst through the doors of the restaurant.  Diners looked up as he dodged past their tables, evidently looking for a way out the back.  Moments later two bearded men dashed through the doors after the fugitive, who had got no further than the door to the kitchen, where he slipped on greasy tiles.  The two men were on top of him, trying to pin him to the ground when a young woman in a long gown and hijab headscarf entered the restaurant in the wake of the two men, screaming at them. She rushed at where they were trying to subdue the young man. It did not take much to understand the body language to realise the fugitive and the young woman were somehow related, for she flew at his attackers, beating them with flailing fists.

The diners appeared frozen in a background tableau, knives and forks poised as the action unfolded around them in a matter of seconds. Aysha and Lily were stunned by the unexpectedness and violence. The shouts and screams of the protagonists were unanswered by those at the tables, and a third man now entered, grabbing the girl and pulling her roughly away from where the two bearded men had handcuffed their prey. The third man slapped the girl hard across the face, and Aysha began to rise from her seat, clearly intending to intervene, until the moustached businessman at the nearby table caught her eye and waggled a finger at her.

'No!' he hissed. 'Savak!'

Aysha knew enough of the feared secret police to lower herself reluctantly back to her chair, watching as the young man and woman were dragged out of the restaurant to an unmarked van that had appeared in the street, where they were bundled inside as people cleared a path for them. Then it was as if nothing had happened, like wet pavements drying under the sun. Other diners looked briefly at their fellow clientele, then resumed their eating. The businessman avoided Aysha's eye and concentrated on his meal. Aysha met Lily's gaze and they grasped hands across the table, the shock of the spectacle beginning to set in.

They each had a vodka before leaving the restaurant, enjoying alcohol for the first time since India, but the incident had unsettled them. It was only with an effort that they turned their thoughts again to the evening of pleasure they had promised themselves, and then the butterflies that had momentarily deserted Lily returned.

Freshly washed and smelling of Lifebuoy soap, Lily found herself naked, spreadeagled and bound to the single bed in their hotel room, the curtains drawn against the Tehran night and the apartment blocks opposite. Aysha had used the long silk scarves again, and Lily's arms were now pulled to the upper two corners of the bed, her ankles to the lower two. Aysha had tied her loosely, and had then begun to tickle her, learning in the process that Lily had sensitive feet, ribs and armpits.

Aysha had discarded her own clothes save bra and panties, and with her black-rimmed glasses framing her luminous eyes, Lily acknowledged how seductive her roommate looked in the light of a single bedside lamp. Looking at the Eurasian girl, Lily realised how horny she was in her bound state, and how much she just wanted Aysha to get on with it.

Aysha sat on the edge of the bed and began to stroke the soles of Lily's feet. Lily tried to move them out of reach, and began to giggle and squeal each time Aysha ran a fingernail down the arch of her feet. With each wriggle, Aysha tightened the scarves a little, until Lily found herself stretched out with no slack left and only able to twist her feet from side to side. Aysha picked up one of Lily's sneakers and slowly extracted the shoelace.

'What are you doing?' Lily ventured, her mouth dry.

Aysha ignored the question and concentrated on tying one end of the shoelace around the big toe on Lily's right foot, then tautly securing the other end to the big left toe. Suddenly even the small movement was gone from her feet. With the aloofness of a surgeon working on a patient, Aysha produced a small pocket knife from her suitcase and opened the blade, running the point down the sole of Lily's foot. Lily tried to jerk away and uttered a small shriek. Aysha stopped and looked severely at her captive over the top of her glasses, making small tutting noises.

'I did warn you about this, Lily,' she said, cooly producing a further scarf, making Lily wonder how many she had. 'I told you if you started carrying on, you'd get gagged.'

'But I –' Lily started to say, when Aysha squeezed a nipple. 'Ow!'

Aysha appeared not to have heard the slightly sullen tone, for she was intent on rolling one of Lily's socks into a small ball and wrapping it within a knot tied in the middle of the scarf.

'Open wide.'

'What? No, you can't do this... Please...'

Aysha's left hand gripped Lily's nose, sealing off her air supply, and the moment her mouth opened, the knotted ball was stuffed in. Aysha released Lily's nose and lifted her head, winding two turns of the scarf around and tying it at the back.

Lily had never had anything like this done to her, and fought the wad jammed in her mouth. She tried to force it out with her tongue, but to no avail. She realised with sudden clarity that Aysha knew how to make a decent gag and how to install it to best silence her victim.

'Going to behave, now?' Lily glared at her, then as Aysha took her nipple between thumb and forefinger and began to gently roll it, she grunted meekly. It had all been over in less than a minute. Lily Maddison had succumbed willingly, with the most token of resistance.

Aysha sat back to look at her handiwork, smoothing an errant lock of chestnut hair away from Lily's brow. She smiled and uttered a soft chuckle. To Lily it sounded predatory, and the very thought made her wet.

Aysha leaned forward and kissed Lily's nipples, tweaking and licking them until they stood like two tiny watchtowers guarding their fortress hillocks. Her fingers stroked the mounds, hands then caressing Lily's stomach, down through the soft auburn curls to her loins. Lily stiffened, straining against her bonds as Aysha's fingers slipped into the wet cleft. A gasp came from beneath the gag – a kind of soft grunt, overlain by an increase in breathing.

'Nice?' inquired Aysha softly. Lily nodded. 'Want more?' More nodding. 'Too bad.' Then the fingers were gone, brushing the inside of her thighs that were almost as sensitive. Lily stifled a snort of frustration.

Aysha stood up and walked over to where her jeans lay on the bed, picked them up and slid the thin leather belt out of the loops, then returned to stand over the spreadeagled form on the bed.

'I think it's time we found out whether you have the makings of a pain slut,' Aysha said casually. 'What do you think, Lily? A little warm up between your legs? A little flogging of those darling nipples of yours?' Lily shook her head and made garbled noises through the gag.

'No? Oh, but I was really looking forward to it...' Aysha sounded like a child whose ice cream has been taken away. 'All right, I'll give you a choice. You understand I really shouldn't. You won't get many choices with me in the future, Lily Maddison, but in this one case – because I'm feeling charitable, I'll offer you a heads-or-tails option. God, I'm so generous!' She fished out a coin from her jeans. 'Look – ten rials. The Shah on one side, the lion on the other – heads and tails. The choice you have is this: accept a flogging now, or we flip a coin. Heads you'll get the flogging anyway, but perhaps worse than you might have got it had you chosen it first, and tails will be an unknown fate. Might be better than a flogging, might be worse. Who knows? Oh, *I* do, that's right. *I* know.' She grinned at the helpless girl. 'So, missy, what's it to be? The belt now, or the coin toss?' She held the belt in one hand and the coin between the fingers of the other. 'Show me.'

Lily's head was in a whirl. She was horny enough to set the sheets on fire but Aysha kept just prodding the fires rather than dumping petrol on them to let them burn out. She wondered what it would be like to be whipped? Did it really make the pleasure afterwards even better? Should she risk the coin? But the belt looked hard and painful. But what was the alternative, the unknown fate? She was reminded of the Dirty Harry movie: "Do ya feel lucky, punk?" Could it be worse than a whipping?

Lily turned her head slightly to eye the coin, and grunted.

'Coin toss?' Lily nodded.

'Okay. So be it, Lily darling. I love a girl who can take a risk.' She leaned over, mouth close to Lily's ear. 'Remember, no going back now. Heads it's the belt, tails its... the other...' she whispered.

She straightened up and flipped the coin. Lily felt it land on her stomach. Aysha picked it up and showed Lily the side with the lion on it. 'Be brave, Lily,' she said. 'There are things worse than a whipping... maybe... Or maybe they're better. Who would know?'

Aysha burrowed in her case again and pulled out a further scarf.

'Last one, Sweetie. They weigh nothing, take up no room, but god, they can be fun! Don't you think so?' she asked, as Lily's world went dark.

Lily lay there, blind, silent and bound, her hearing heightened, trying to work out what Aysha was doing in occasional movements about the room, a visit to the small cramped bathroom, then silence. She reasoned that her captor was letting her stew, letting her mind race ahead, imagining the worst things that could happen to her. The uncertainty only made things worse, and Lily tugged gently on the ties at wrist and ankle, but found no slack. Aysha knew her business. Lily chewed on the wad in her mouth but her cheeks remained distended and the gag was going nowhere.

She lost track of time. Her thoughts did nothing to calm her, and once when Aysha came from nowhere to run her fingers between Lily's legs, she jerked and moaned. Then the hand was gone and Lily groaned inwardly. How long was this torture going to last? Maybe this was the alternative to the whipping – death by a thousand cuts... or caresses.

More time to think... then Aysha was back, seated on the bed, hip to hip with the helpless girl.

'Okay darling Lily, here comes your punishment. Or maybe it's not? I wonder? Remember, Safeword – if you want to use it, you'd better be *really, really* sure. Life or death. Okay?'

In her dark world, Lily nodded.

There came a clicking sound Lily at once recognised as scissors, and suddenly a hand grabbed her pubic hair, fingers entwining and tugging. There was a coarse grating feel, as the scissors cropped a handful. God, Aysha was cutting her pubes!

'Don't struggle, Lily, otherwise you'll get the whip as well. Ever been whipped on a naked pussy?' A laugh. 'No, of course you haven't, my innocent little darling. You haven't been whipped at all... Have you ever been shaven down there? Well?' Reluctantly, Lily shook her head.

'Well you're now about to have another new life experience. How about that! You'll love it, trust me.' Lily was not in a position to argue that they were *her* pubes and only she should be doing anything with them. Nor could she point out that Aysha's own thatch was intact. She suspected this plan had been Aysha's intention all along. She had not actually seen the fall of the coin on her stomach – only what Aysha had chosen to show her. Bitch.

The fingers and scissors continued methodically, and Lily felt even more exposed, if that was possible. Finally, something persuaded her brain to accept her fate, and to lie back and enjoy somebody else doing her personal grooming. The clipping of the scissors stopped and Lily sensed a draft of air from Aysha's lips waft over her mons. Then there was the touch of warm water and a gentle soaping, followed by a razor. Lily was apprehensive, afraid a nick or cut could curtail their sex – which she was starting to think about as being likely enhanced. But Aysha had done this before, and the razor and soap were tactile and exciting in their own right. Lily knew she could only yield, only surrender to Aysha's skills. No amount of mmmphing into the gag – short of humming the birthday tune – would stop the process.

Then there came the cool rinsing of the soap and the soft patting dry.

'My God, what an adorable little pussy,' Aysha said. 'So neat and folded in, just a tidy little cleft without the frills. We were so right to clean things up, here, Lily. You have no right to hide this little treasure away.'

There came the sound of feet traipsing to the bathroom, running water, and a return. Then Aysha's face was between Lily's legs, her lips kissing and sucking on the sensitised opening. Whether it was having been shaved, or the anticipation of an unknown torment, Lily sensed the end of the drama and felt herself hot and wet under Aysha's ministrations. She tried to close her legs, to trap Aysha's head between them, but her ankles were tied too far apart. Aysha was taking no prisoners now and Lily had no defences to offer. The gate to her garden had been stripped of its camouflage and Aysha's lips burrowed between Lily's labia, then sought the delicious nub that made Lily arch her back and strain futilely against her bonds. It was as though all of Lily's half-hidden thoughts and desires over the past week – fruits of long imaginative hours in the bus – now came rushing to the fore in a headlong, past-caring deluge. Then somebody was screaming, grunting, trying to enunciate while trying to fight off her 'assailant', then yielding to the rush of blood and juices between her legs, radiating like a hot cloud through her body.

Lily spent the rest of the night in Aysha's arms, discovering – when she was finally *compos mentis* – that in the time Lily had been held blind and silent, Aysha had shaved her own sex, and Lily was finally able to give her friend some of the joy she'd had forced on herself, though without the restraints. For Lily, another milestone had passed in their relationship, though she did not quite know how to interpret it. Each time Aysha had subdued her, Lily had learnt more about trust and commitment. She was beginning to accept that a commitment to the Eurasian girl in a way she had never experienced before, but also that Aysha was committing herself to Lily. She fell asleep in a state of blissful exhaustion.

A short distance along Ferdowsi street from the restaurant the pair had dined in lay the Central Bank of Iran. The following morning the group of overlanders had filed between machine gun-toting guards down the wide marble stairs and through the steel door of a massive vault where the Iran

National Jewels were on display. To the young people from the suburbs of Sydney, Auckland, Bristol and San Francisco, it was like nothing they had ever seen, yet like every cinematic pirate's treasure cave. Except the glistening jewels were real. There was the great Peacock Throne – a construction more like a raised sleeping platform than a chair – its gold-covered exterior studded with twenty-five thousand gems. Nearby were glass cases of diamond-encrusted crowns and tiaras, sceptres, golden belts, bejewelled swords, shields and daggers, and caskets full of loose rubies, emeralds and sapphires piled up like boiled sweets.

The awed, muted exclamations echoed in the marble-lined room, as they examined the legends of some of the massive jewels, whose history stretched back centuries to their origins in India, the collection enlarged through the Persian ruling dynasties. There was the largest pink diamond in the world, the Daria-i-Noor – the Ocean of Light – and several others the size of small eggs.

They wandered from case to case, as if in a museum. There seemed to be little by way of guards or attendants in the vault itself and they had the place almost to themselves. There was a huge globe entirely covered with jewels in the rubied outlines of continents and islands - in some instances small countries were a single jewel – amidst oceans of emeralds. Perhaps under orders, or else a whim, the globe's creator had England, France and Iran covered in diamonds.

'Glad we didn't go gem shopping in Delhi?' Aysha whispered to Lily. 'This place would kind of devalue anything we had.'

'I'd be tempted to bin them on the way out,' Lily giggled.

The National Jewels was the highlight of the day, and with a free afternoon, Lily and Aysha found themselves in the huge Tehran Bazaar, not far from their hotel. After the excess of the jewels it was a pleasant time to meander and inspect the metalwork, pottery and carpet shops, all of whom would offer tea to the two young women in a gesture of simple courtesy, clearly not expecting a sale. They even found a wine shop where they bought a bottle of Shiraz.

'Since we'll have a night there, we might as well sample the real thing,' Aysha had decided, putting the absurdly cheap purchase in her shoulder bag.

It was late afternoon when they emerged from the bazaar and headed at a leisurely pace back towards their hotel. After a circuitous and unplanned route, they emerged on Ferdowsi Street again, north of Toopkhaneh Square and their hotel. Their arrival on the main street was presaged by a loud clamour, and from their side street they saw a procession of people moving south on the main street towards the square. They emerged a few moments after the last of the procession had passed, before turning to follow the tail end.

'Should we be doing this?' asked Lily in a low voice. 'It looks like a protest march – there are banners up ahead.' The crowd stretched several hundred metres ahead of them, chants drifting back from the densest part of the gathering.

'Relax, Lily,' said Aysha. 'I've been on dozens of protest marches.'

'But we shouldn't get involved,' Lily insisted. 'We don't even know what they're protesting about.'

'Nobody bothers foreigners,' Aysha assured her. 'We're just tourists.'

'What's that smell?' Lily asked suddenly as they ambled along at the rear. There were several loud bangs in the distance and a faint white mist could be seen above the banners. Lily began to cough as her throat suddenly constricted.

'Oh shit – tear gas!' This time there was no bravado in Aysha's voice, only the recollection of previous incidents. Fifty metres ahead of them the chanting turned to disordered panic as the procession came to an abrupt halt and began to scatter. Screams and shouts carried on the breeze while the demonstrators began running towards them, faces twisted in fear.

Lily was rooted to the spot, for she had never experienced such a thing. Aysha grabbed her wrist and tugged her to start running back the way they had come. The mostly young protesters quickly overtook them, and Aysha pulled Lily into a doorway, to let the protesters pass. The two of them were, after all, merely tourists. Whiffs of tear gas caught in their throats, but mostly seemed to have dissipated with distance and the breeze. It was still enough to make their eyes water and catch in their throats as they shrank back into the doorway. Shouts and yells accompanied the panicked running feet and Aysha peeked around the corner, expecting to see a mass of uniformed riot police pursuing the protestors. Instead, there were a few dozen men in plain clothes, in a clearly coordinated attack on the slowest of the crowd. Many of the men had batons and were being followed at a crawl by a number of black vans. The slowest of the demonstrators were being picked off, beaten and manhandled into the vehicles.

There was no mistaking Aysha's alarm as she turned back to Lily, reached past her and tried the door, which seemed to be the entry to some apartments. It was locked. Again, Aysha grabbed Lily's wrist and they pushed out into the mayhem.

They had taken only a few steps when a weight came on Lily's small daypack and the sudden load caused her to stumble, pulling her free from Aysha. At once there were milling bodies separating the pair, and Lily felt a blow to her temple that sent her sprawling to the pavement. In a haze of pain she felt someone trying to drag her by her backpack the way they had come. It was a swarthy moustached man in a dark jacket and pants, his eyes angry. She tried to get to her feet but the momentum of the man's pulling made this impossible and her knees scraped across the concrete. She cried out in protest, but her English made no difference to the furiosity of the man who shouted something unintelligible at her.

Terrified, Lily struggled to resist, and was barely aware of the sudden movement that came from the crowd, accompanied by the sound of glass breaking and a red liquid spraying, before the man went down and Aysha was hauling her to her feet. There was a moment of pandemonium, then Lily and Aysha were dragged out of the mob, but this time into a shop entrance, through a door, closing down the crowd noise.

A slender young man with the beginnings of facial hair had shut the door behind them, and they found themselves in a narrow arcade-like corridor running deep into the building, with small shops on both sides. The place was deserted, as though the locals had expected such an event and closed early. Beside the street entry was an open door into a tailor's shop. An elderly man with thinning hair and a silver beard said something to them that they could not understand, before the youth intervened.

'You must come with us, quickly!'

Lily was still reeling from the blow to the head and her impact with the ground, but Aysha knew a friendly, concerned voice when she heard one. Street smarts had taught her to recognise friend from foe when the moment arose. She looked quickly at Lily, noting the blood starting to trickle from a small wound just below her hairline and saw the ugly grazes to her knees, but decided they were not life threatening. The older man was already closing and locking the tailor's shop door.

'This way,' urged the young man, leading them down the dimly-lit passageway, before they took a side corridor that led into a maze of smaller offshoots. After a minute they reached a bare concrete stairwell and climbed two floors, the youth leading, followed by Aysha holding Lily's hand, and the other man at the rear.

The upper floors were evidently modest apartments. The corridors were clean and was no graffiti, but there was a dinginess about the place that marked it as less than well-off. They stopped and the older man unlocked a pale green door with the number 207 on it, standing aside to let the two women in.

The apartment was tiny – a living room that merged into a kitchen alcove and a curtained-off bed – and smelt vaguely of old clothes and stale cooking. It was clean and tidy, however, with a small television on a table and a window that looked out into a dim light well.

'My name is Arash,' said the young man. 'This is my grandfather, Farhad. Please, sit down.' He gestured to a small two-seater sofa, the only furniture aside from the small table and two wooden-backed chairs. 'I think you are tourists, yes? You speak English?'

'Yes, thank you so much! My name is Aysha – this is Lily...' She turned her attention to Lily and held her face in her hands, looking at the cut to her temple and trying to assess the damage.

Arash and Farhad had a brief conversation before the elder man disappeared out the front door.

'You are lucky,' said Arash. 'That was a demonstration against the Shah that you were caught up in. Those men who tried to catch you were Savak. You know Savak? Secret police. You must stay here until it is quiet. Where is your hotel?'

'The Arman.'

'Oh yes.' He smiled for the first time, running a hand through unruly black hair. Aysha guessed he was sixteen or seventeen, wearing jeans and a black tee-shirt. 'We can reach the Arman through the back streets, though they might be looking for you.'

'Looking for us?' Lily spoke for the first time, her voice stuttery and hesitant.

Arash moved to the kitchen alcove and opened a small refrigerator, taking out a plastic bottle of water, which he poured into two mismatching glasses, handing them to Lily and Aysha.

'Aysha hit the man who tried to hold you. Did you not see it?' he said. 'I saw it right outside our shop – my grandfather's shop.'

Lily turned to her friend. 'You did what?' She was aghast.

'Sorry. I busted the bottle of Shiraz on his head.'

'Fuck!'

'Sorry. The wine probably wasn't a very good year – not at the price we paid for it.' Aysha tried to smile, but the shock of the events was starting to set in, as she tried to keep her hand steady while sipping from the glass. Her concern took over. 'You okay, Sweetie?'

Lily was about to reply when the door opened and Fahad reappeared, this time with a middle-aged woman in tow, carrying a large handbag.

'This is Darya,' said Arash, looking vaguely relieved that someone older was now able to take over the care of the two female foreigners. 'She lives on the next floor and works in a pharmacy near here. She will help with your injuries.'

The woman smiled reassuringly at the two girls. She was stocky but attractive, her black hair cut in a bob to her jawline, wearing a dark blue uniform that suggested she had recently returned from work.

'English?' she asked.

'New Zealand,' said Aysha, pointing to Lily, then 'Australian', pointing to herself.

'Ah. You are welcome. I am so sorry you had to experience this.' Her English was fluent and precise, if accented. She knelt on the worn carpet to examine Lily, then opened her bag, revealing a compact miscellany of first aid supplies. She had the calm sureness of one used to managing a situation and dealing with traumatised people. Arash and Farhad stood back and watched as she cleaned the gash to Lily's temple where a large lump had now formed, then did the same to the lacerations to her knees. Lily dutifully answered as the woman asked whether she felt dizzy or whether the light bothered her, of if she felt sick. Lily gave her name, the city they were in, and the day of the week, and Darya pronounced that she did not think there was any major concussion, though she gave Lily some Panadol tablets. Finally she stood up.

'You will probably have a headache for the next day or so, based on that lump, but you should be okay.' She turned to Aysha. 'Did you really hit a Savak man?' There was genuine admiration in her voice.

'He was attacking my friend,' said Aysha simply. 'You don't do that to me.'

'You hit him with a bottle of wine? Really?'

Aysha nodded.

Darya said something to Farhad, who ducked into the alcove and produced a further miscellany of glasses and a dark green bottle of dubious-looking origin, with a picture of a dog on the label. Farhad poured shots into four glasses and was about to pour a fifth when Darya waved her finger and said something to him.

'Lily must not have alcohol until she is better,' she told Aysha, as though to Lily's guardian. '*We* can all drink to her health, though,' she smiled.

Aysha sniffed it cautiously. 'What is it?'

'It's called *araq-e sagi*. Persian vodka.' She held up her glass. 'In Iran we say "Salamati!"'

Aysha downed the shot with the expertise of a pro, but could not help herself coughing as the fiery liquid caught in her throat. She saw Lily smile for the first time in a while, and grinned back.

'Out of practice,' Aysha admitted.

'It's made from raisins – around 50% proof,' said Darya off-handedly, apparently unaffected by the drink. She turned to Arash and said something to him. There was a brief conversation and the young man left the apartment, closing the door behind him.

Darya and Farhad took the two wooden chairs and the man poured another round of araq.

'You were lucky,' said Darya. 'The Shah's police are not well liked around here. Evidently the feeling is mutual.'

'We are very grateful to Arash and Farhad,' said Aysha. 'Please convey our thanks to him for getting us out of the street.'

'And to you, for your help,' Lily added. Then she asked, her voice still shaky: 'Why were they protesting?'

'Many things. Too much change, too quickly. Not enough change. The economy has done well, but the Shah has become a dictator. His fabulous wealth is at the expense of our nation. Have you been to Persepolis yet?'

'We'll be there in a couple of days,' Aysha said.

'Six years ago, to celebrate two and a half thousand years of the Persian monarchy, the Shah decided to throw the world's biggest party there. They built this huge tent city, each tent fit for a head of state, complete with direct telephones and telex. They had monarchs and presidents from almost sixty countries – all in this desert city that only lasted for a week. They brought in mature trees and fifty thousand birds, but almost all of them died – trees and birds – in the harsh climate. There were massive parades and equally massive security forces and of course all these men needed somewhere to eat and sleep. Everything was flown in and built from scratch. There was catering by Maxims of Paris. And you know what? The Iranian people were not invited to attend their own celebration. It was the world's biggest and most expensive party for the Shah to show off, with none of his subjects present. The Shah has done much good for this country, but it has gone to his head. Now the people are getting fed up with it, and Savak are having to become more and more powerful to keep control of the people.' Darya translated briefly for Farhad.

'What about other countries?' Aysha asked, a subject Lily had learned was dear to her political heart. 'Wasn't the CIA messing around here in the fifties?'

'Of course. We have oil. The United States wants it. The Soviets want it. Everybody wants to be our friends – and to deny us friendship with others. A few months ago the Shah banned all political parties except a new one he set up himself. Farhad used to belong to a party called the Tudeh.' Darya paused and said something to the man, who became animated and there was a brief discussion – enough for his passion on the subject to be evident.

'It was a nationalist party that was banned in 1949, but went underground. It tried to avert the CIA coup which toppled our prime minister and re-asserted control by the Shah. Farhad himself was imprisoned and tortured in the sixties.' She nodded at the man, who appeared to understand the subject of conversation and suddenly seemed older than he probably was. 'Many of the protesters today are probably part of the Tudeh, even though it officially doesn't exist.'

Lily tried to understand what it would be like to live in a society with immense natural wealth, but still be run in a way that people could be snatched off the street by secret police, and everyday folk such as these lived in fear of them, as they had seen the previous night.

Aysha told Darya of their experience in the restaurant, and she translated for Farhad, who rolled his eyes and elicited an expression of disgust.

'You have been unlucky,' she said with a half-smile. 'It is not so common, really. You have come at the end of university holidays, when the students are restless and have nothing better to do than protest – so they do. Bad timing. I hope you do not take away a bad impression of our country. Tell me where you have been and where you are going.'

The mood eased as Aysha and Lily told Darya and Farhad their experiences and outlined the remainder of their route. Farhad was amazed that two young women could do such a trip, but Darya gave them a motherly smile. Arash reappeared with several packages of steaming food, which were spread out on the table – flat bread, cheeses and kebabs – and Aysha and Lily yielded to the hospitality and their hunger.

After night had fallen, Darya fetched a long skirt and headscarf for Lily to cover her legs and chestnut hair, when they ventured outside. 'Not a modesty thing, you understand. We Iranians consider ourselves very fashionable – much like westerners. We just don't want to attract too much attention.

'You –' she said to Aysha, '– you could almost be Persian.' She touched Aysha's black hair and smooth neck admiringly. 'You are okay in jeans – I don't think you need to cover up. But Lily – too European. Still beautiful, yes, but in a different way – so we hide her lovely hair and legs. I hope you were not seen dealing to that Savak scum. I hope it was all overlooked in the confusion, but we must still be careful. Perhaps the pig will be too embarrassed at being taken down by a woman,' she chuckled. 'They will not bother three women together, I think, but we will go by the back alleys to your hotel.'

The streets were eerily quiet when they made the journey to the Arman Hotel. They had avoided Ferdowsi Street and made a large detour without incident around Toopkhaneh Square, with Aysha and Lily seeing imagined stalkers lurking in every corner shadow. Finally, in the brightly lit but dowdy hotel reception Darya hugged them both and waited while Lily removed the headscarf and slipped out of the long skirt.

'I wish you all happiness for the rest of your trip. You are very good for each other,' she said, as she slipped out the door with a smile.

Lily looked at Aysha, who gawked back. 'Is it that obvious?'

They left the madness of Tehran traffic, Lily and Aysha flaunting a low-key air of contentment which predictably went unnoticed on the bus. A few relationships had developed on the trip so far, but Aysha and Lily's had slipped under the radar – save for the perspicuity of Darya. Early on – in separate instances – they had made it clear to several males in the group that they were not on the market for a dalliance, due to commitments at home, and this was accepted. Now nobody seemed interested in looking too closely at what might have been otherwise a platonic friendship developing in seats 14A and 14B.

They told nobody of the protest and their rescue. Noone noticed the bruising on Lily's temple, which she covered with deft hair placement. They had slept close that night, grateful to have got away from what might have turned into a horror show, but still nervous that some anonymous government thugs would take it on themselves to check out foreigner-frequented hotels, or a bright yellow Sundowners bus taking the main road south.

Their worries proved groundless, and Lily could now read the letters from home again, filling in the missing details, the 'between the lines' information that was not articulated, most significantly being the absence of any word from Robert. Lily's relationship with Aysha had been gnawing at her conscience whenever she thought of the two years she had spent with her boyfriend. They had been comfortable times, as the pair had gone to classical concerts and followed the conventions that pleased both families. Comfortable times, but – compared to the stimulating and intriguing experiences that came with the Aysha Package – 'comfortable' did not cut it anymore. Building a snowman was a pale substitute for downhill skiing.

Her father's letters – initially touching on Robert's missing her – now avoided all mention of Robert. Lily surmised that this was not through her father wanting to spare her feelings, but rather because she suspected there was now little – if any – contact between him and Robert. It had been seven weeks since she had left Robert and her father at Auckland Airport, and the implication was that Robert was either not missing her, or had found someone else already. The thought should have cut her to the quick, but in this new life with Aysha by her side, every day brought some new discovery, some new experience, whether in the daylight hours of travel or the darkened hours of strange bedrooms in strange towns, with the unfamiliar but intoxicating feel of another woman's body next to hers, the smoothness of breasts, of softly-haired arms and gentle lips touching her own.

They followed the ancient trade route southwards, tracing empires that had risen and fallen over the millennia, leaving behind strange and often eerie ruins and statues as a legacy to their passing. Most of the Sundowners travellers had little knowledge of either the history or geography of the places they passed through or the sites they visited, other than to add to a collection of instamatic photos they would get developed when they arrived at Earl's Court. Of more importance was to suss out the local beers and bars, and snatch whatever sleep they could in the bus seats.

Lily had studied neither history nor geography to any extent, but she had read widely, and through her reading, peripheral knowledge had kicked in by osmosis. Through Tolstoy she had learned of the Napoleonic Wars and the sentimental pessimism buried within the Russian people that had inspired the great poets, composers and authors of that land. She'd read enough Kipling to find all manner of triggers as she passed through the exotic lands that had once been a solid red colour on the map of the world. Herman Hesse, Jules Verne, H.G. Wells and Joseph Conrad had been reliable library companions, opening her eyes to new wonders of real and imagined worlds. Then had come the great twentieth century populists in Mitchener, Clavell and Graham Greene which left her dreaming of different cultures in exotic lands, in the idealised world of the young.

Now, in the ruins of Persepolis, the gardens of the Moghuls or some ancient, half-collapsed roadside caravanserai, Lily felt herself touched by these people who had gone before, in a way she could not explain to herself, never mind to Aysha. One day, she vowed, she would capture these moments in her music. Maybe by then the primal feelings lingering at the edge of her awareness would have shown themselves and their ancestry in a little more detail. For now, she would have the hours of watching the deserts, mountains and towns thrum past her window, letting her thoughts and daydreams fall where they would, materialising into something more solid or simply vanishing into dust.

The bus drove south across the edge of the Great Salt Desert – hundreds of miles of flat white salt where no rain ever fell. The country merged into a sameness of low arid hills, bare and brown, with mountains hidden in the hazy distance. This leg of the journey was another detour, sampling the great civilisations of the Persian Empire and the Islamic Golden Age. On a sun-parched plain near the city of Shiraz, they found the ruins of Persepolis, once the pinnacle of the Persian Empire, destroyed by Alexander the Great, but – according to Darya – resurrected by the Shah in the greatest, most extravagant party of the century.

Lily was entranced by the vividly carved reliefs adorning wall after wall, showing the representatives of subject nations bringing gifts to the Persian King Darius the Great. The bearded king, with his tight curls and crown reminded Lily of pictures she had seen at primary school, when they had studied the Iliad – the story of the Greeks and Trojans. She saw, too, amongst the gifts of gold and cattle and exotic animals, female slaves, their wrists chained, brought into the presence of the mighty Darius and his Queen Phaedymia. Lily tried to imagine being a simple country girl captured and brought before such wealth and power.

She had somehow lost Aysha in the ruins, and found a small patch of shade in a wall niche, beneath tall columns that towered into the translucent sky. The group had the site to themselves, for it was remote and off the beaten track for most tourists. Overlooked by the cliff tombs of long-dead Persian kings, Lily felt the strange energies of the place, the sense that she had possibly been there before – brought against her will. The thought lay in a back corner of her mind, triggered by the undefined familiarity of some of the carvings, as though she had passed them many times in the course of her work. It was not an oppressive feeling, but one of routine and drudgery, broken with brief moments of happiness. It was also unsettling, she realised, as she suddenly missed Aysha.

She rose and moved out into the bright sunlit, shading her eyes to search for Aysha's willowy form, spotting her near a great entrance flanked by winged bulls with human heads. Lily ran to her friend, who saw her coming in time to hug her, then decided such a public display of affection was not appropriate for either the group or the location. They broke apart, embarrassed, and Lily smiled. It was the expression of a person who has momentarily lost, then found her best friend, lover, or partner, and at an instant when the world has just been put right.

'You okay?' asked Aysha. She sensed something was off with Lily.

'Yeah. Had a little flashback.'

'A flashback?'

'That's what I call them. Strange. I don't know how to explain it, just that I've been here before. Same energies. Little fleeting things in my mind that I can't put my finger on or define. Like people you see out of the corner of your eye, but turn your head and there's nobody there...'

'But it's passed?' Lily nodded.

'Okay, I want to take your picture here.' Aysha had the polaroid camera out of her daypack. 'Look – just there, against the wall carvings.' Lily did as she was told, posing a little self-consciously in her pale pink blouse and denim skirt against the sun-polished figures etched in stone over two thousand years before. The shutter clicked and a minute later the camera spat out the blank picture, which Aysha secreted in her pocket until the outline and then the details came into being. Lily looked over Aysha's shoulder and saw the composition of the photo – the diminutive human female in front of the rows of bound slaves being presented to the great Persian king.

Lily and Aysha indulged in enormous banana and watermelon milkshakes in the bazaars of Isfahan and Shiraz, their relationship becoming closer as they shared intimacy on more regularly. It would not have been surprising to anybody in the know why the pair slept so much during the long desert crossings, not least after their return overnighter in Tehran, before they again turned westward, heading for Turkey.

By a coincidence they had been given their old room in the Tehran hotel, and they had visited the same restaurant prior to retiring, though with an unstated anxiety lest something else befall them.

'Iran is becoming my favourite place,' said Lily over yet another sweet watermelon shake as they waited for their dinner to appear. Banishing recent memories of the place, she now wanted to touch Aysha, to hold her hand over the table, to be able to demonstrate to the world they were in a relationship, but she dared not, for it could offend the locals.

'Why's that, Lily?' asked Aysha, disingenuously.

Aysha made no secret she enjoyed teasing Lily and cajoling her to pursue the submissive role, but such was her skill in this that Lily was content, for Aysha had never taken advantage of it. After what Lily called the 'Shaving Ceremony', their love-making had been more equal, and Lily had begun to feel more comfortable in being able to extract more response from Aysha.

Their meals arrived, giving Lily the opportunity to ignore the question and ask one of her own.

'Aysh, tell me one thing. Do you get off more in *controlling* me, or letting me make love to you?'

Aysha looked up from pulling some naan apart, and pushed her glasses up on her forehead. Lily had learned that this was Aysha wanting to impart something serious. She loved the gesture because it showed off the Eurasian girl's brown eyes so much that Lily wanted to dive into them. She knew that Aysha was giving weight to her answer.

'That's a pretty heavy question for dinner,' said Aysha. Lily knew she was stalling.

'So give me a heavy answer. Come on.'

'Sweetie, trying to explain something like this isn't easy. It's like trying to explain to a man what loving a woman is like for me. There are some things you can never appreciate unless you're that way inclined. A man will never understand what a woman feels when she's loving another woman. Similarly, if you don't understand *control*, and all the excitement which comes with that, then my explanation will be difficult. Control and love – the act of love-making – aren't mutually exclusive, Lily. Sometimes I want more of one than the other. Sometimes – if I get it right – they complement each other perfectly. One leads to the other and the evening ends in a rapture that only someone of my proclivities will really understand.

'You, on the other hand – you're starting to realise the joy you obtain in your mind from entrusting yourself into my care. It's a giving of yourself – an act which makes you feel good both from the abdication from responsibility and from the gift of that control to me – someone who loves and appreciates it. It's Yin and Yang, Lily. That's what we do. That's why it works when two people like us find each other. There's no greater gift than handing your life to somebody else to care for, even if it's only for a short time. That we both experience the same end result – the pleasure of a climax – is the ying-yang miracle.'

When they reached their room Lily knew there was another experience awaiting her, and her intuition was enough to believe it was that which she dreaded. Aysha had led her to the brink of being flogged, on the night of the Shave, and it had been at once terrifying and thrilling, like driving a car too close to the cliff edge, glimpsing the drop, then pulling away at the last minute. Now there was no doubt in Lily's mind that her initiation was about to commence, and the butterflies were back.

Lily was also beginning to understand the seemingly endless variations-on-a-theme that dwelt in the bondage world, layer-upon-layer over the basic coupling. The positions, the punishments, the potential for teasing and tormenting – physical, mental and emotional – all were ingredients that could make up a unique recipe on any given occasion, limited only by resources on hand and the ingenuity of the players.

This time Lily found herself on all fours, kneeling across the bed on her forearms, her wrists bound by the ubiquitous scarves to one side of the bedframe, her ankles to the opposite side. Lily was very conscious of her raised backside and the target it must present. Aysha had gagged her again, and Lily found the wadded ball now stuffed in her mouth a little easier to deal with than the previous time. She supposed every new experience would gradually become familiar, and something to be desired or feared to a greater or lesser degree with that familiarity.

Her position now made her feel like a pet of some sort, unable to move as Aysha sat beside her on the bed, stroking her neck.

'Do you know, Lily, I think one of the most beautiful parts of a woman's anatomy is actually this little hollow in the small of your back.' Aysha's fingertips slid down Lily's spine, coming to rest in the small of her back. 'There's such a lovely curve here, especially in a nice romantic half-light. I could just gaze at this forever.' She leaned over and touched the spot with her lips, kissing it so gently that Lily couldn't suppress a shiver shooting through her body. Aysha was naked as well, and the taut flesh of a breast brushed Lily's flank during the kiss. Then Aysha's hands moved beneath Lily, sliding over her breasts as they hung in their full natural shape. The hands had no need to coax the nipples in this instance, for they had become erect as the first turns of the scarves had been wrapped around her wrists. The analogy to a pet seemed to be reinforced by the thought of Pavlov's dog. In her case, it was now the sight of scarves that excited her and made her loins damp in anticipation.

This time Aysha had refrained from a blindfold, and this meant that Lily had to frequently turn her head to see what was about to happen. Aysha was in no hurry, though the belt had reappeared and had been draped over Lily's neck with the instruction that she was not to cause it to fall.

Compliance would not have been difficult had Aysha not then run her hands over much of Lily's body, teasing and tickling just enough to make Lily jittery, without directly arousing her further. The belt had begun to slip, however. Lily could feel it, and reckoned Aysha had placed it in a lopsided way so that there would only ever be one outcome. By the time Aysha dug her nails into the soles of Lily's feet, causing her to jerk violently, the belt was already sliding off.

'Oh... Lily...' Aysha's voice dripped with false disappointment. 'One small thing I asked of you, and you couldn't even do that...'

For some reason Lily felt genuine remorse she had failed to carry out the task to please her overseer. Only later would she realise how deeply she had slipped into their game – the little tasks Aysha set for her, and which Lily willed herself to achieve. It was this commitment to please the woman commanding her that for Lily was the ultimate indicator of her submissiveness. There were no caveats, for both realised there was no need. Both were in the same place, and Aysha knew what could and would be do-able for her new submissive.

In the low light of the bedside lamp, Lily watched Aysha's graceful arm drop to the floor to retrieve the belt, and she knew the moment had arrived as Aysha disappeared behind her. She tensed, expecting a searing pain. Instead, the blindfold finally appeared and her world turned into a dark realm of fantasies waiting to emerge.

When first contact came, it was a soft slapping of the doubled over belt against the back of her thighs – flap-flap, forehand and backhand, slowly tattooing its way from just above the knee up to the buttocks. One leg, then the other, creating a warm glow. There followed more blows down the back of her calves and on the soles of her feet. Then it was the turn of her buttocks, the blows a little harder now, striking the taut skin with a soft 'crack'. Lily could not see the change of colour of her skin, from pale ivory to warm crimson, enhanced as the impacts stopped briefly for Aysha to rub her hands over the areas, stirring the blood flow and nerve endings and suddenly adding several painful hand-slaps which left darker palm-prints.

Lily grunted into her gag, instinctively tugging on the bonds holding her wrists and ankles, but there was no give. The belt came back with more enthusiasm, and Lily began to utter a little grunt with each strike. Her bottom was being thoroughly warmed up, and she was taken by surprise when Aysha's skilled wrist action abruptly turned through ninety degrees and the belt flipped between Lily's legs, taking her squarely on her shaven mons.

Lily jerked and cried out into the gag, but it was a muffled noise barely audible above the Tehran traffic below their window. Thwack! Another line of fire across her most sensitive parts. Lily yelled again, waggling her buttocks and trying to somehow avoid the next blow, but there was no respite from Aysha's expert marksmanship. Lily was starting to buck and strain at her bonds, her stifled voice merging into moans behind the gag. More strikes, variations on the theme, as the tip of the belt landed on the puckered rosebud of Lily's anus, sparking a new level of struggle. Lily was going frantic, not sure whether to move forward or sideways to try to disrupt the terrible accuracy of the belt as it flicked between her thighs.

Now she was making garbled noises of pleading, though the idea of using her Safeword never even entered her head. Somewhere along the way she had been transported to a slave harem, where as a recalcitrant slave she was receiving a punishment which she really did not deserve. It had not been her fault, but she was taking the rap as decreed by the queen, simply because she had no say in the matter.

Aysha slowed the tattoo, leaving several seconds between each strike, letting Lily try to anticipate the blow, to savour whether the pain was more or less than expected.

Lily had been anticipating another blow which never came. Instead a hand slipped between her buttocks, between her labia, fingers sliding effortlessly inside her, revealing wetness and sensitivity that Lily had only been dimly aware of beyond the flogging itself. Suddenly she realised just how aroused she was, how sensitive were her pussy and clit.

Aysha's penetration needed little effort to inflame the slave, who now – instead of trying to avoid the punishment – pushed back with an unbridled lack of decorum which clearly indicated her guilt. It took only moments for a rush of juices to her loins to leave Lily trying to clench the hand in place, to hump it like the unworthy slave girl she was, in front of her fellow slaves and any of the nobles who had ventured to the punishment square. There was a muffled scream which Lily thought might have been herself, trying to make herself heard through the soaking wad of material jammed in her mouth. Then the hand was gone, leaving her head down, eyes closed, snorting and panting, her limbs trembling like a racehorse.

If Lily had thought her misdeeds within the palace would be assuaged with a single punishment, the opposite proved to be the case. The fierce cut of the whip was again striking vulnerable soft flesh, and she was shuddering and bucking once more, before the hand was there again, invading and demanding another offering, taking her energies as penance for her wrongdoings. But this time there was a further expiation required, as the focus moved from her vagina to her back passage, and while the invasion of the first continued, one finger, then a second, slid into Lily's vulnerable arsehole. It was only the second time Lily had been violated in such a way, but her bound limbs left her helpless to resist. She realised at that moment how much offense she had caused the queen, and how much she owed her as penance, and the double invasion seemed only appropriate. But the second intrusion came in concert with the first, and in a flash of insight Lily realised it was not a penance she was paying the queen, but rather a demonstration of loyalty, and the punishment was turning to reward.

Lily pushed back with all her strength, feeling the resistance of the fingers as they drove deeper into both orifices, the collection of nerve endings aroused by the sting of the slave whip now reacting with a massive surge of pleasure. Lily lost awareness of the crowd of watchers around the small square. She lost awareness of the hardness of the flagstones, the catcalls of the audience, the hard, satisfied gaze of the queen, watching from her balcony. There was only the fullness, the excitation within her loins, and the enormous effort to articulate the orgasm through something filling her mouth, before she collapsed on her haunches into an unmoving Child's Pose in a Tehran hotel room.

*    *    *

# CHAPTER 10 – Turkey

The crossing of the border into Turkey seemed to signal another stage in so many things. Coming only two days after Tehran and the other-worldly fantasy that had occurred in Lily's mind, it appeared to her that the last piece of a jigsaw had slotted into place. Whatever she'd had going with Robert, it was over, and she owed no allegiance to anything that had occurred back home. The experience of the flogging and the climax that followed had left Lily in awe of Aysha, and – in her mind – had cemented her devotion to the older girl. Whether this devotion was actual *love*, well, there were a few long days in the bus to figure that one out, along with opening the door to new passageways in her mind which might stem from such a conclusion.

The drive to the Turkish border took five hours from the city of Tabriz and another frustrating dormitory-style room. It had been a celibate night for Lily, and though her bed lay within touching distance of Aysha's, it was also within touching distance of one of the Californians on the other side. Lily convinced herself that a night away from temptation was probably not a bad thing, though in the bus she curled up against Aysha like a cat who has missed her mistress.

They could not discuss these most intimate of feelings on the bus, for there were too many ears close by. Lily was forced to hold her tongue for a night and a day as she tried to process the latest strange and wonderful experience that Aysha had visited on her. The beating was something she had feared, though she managed not to chicken out before she had been gagged and it all became too late, under threat of worse punishment if she uttered the Safeword. The flogging with the belt had been painful, but not as much as Lily had imagined, and the exquisite pleasure that had followed... Lily had been transported to distant places like nothing Aysha had done before. Dear God, how had she been satisfied with simple missionary sex before this?

The relinquishing of control lay behind all of this, Lily realised – yet another, overarching nuance in this new sexual order. It was as much in her mind as in her body – the total surrender to somebody else's intentions. But since the initial forays, this last encounter with the flogging had taken things up a further notch, messing with Lily's thoughts as much as with her endorphins. The slave fantasy had seemingly come from nowhere, although it was possible the amazing carvings at Persepolis had set off whatever fold of brain conjured up dreams and nightmares.

Lily had climaxed twice more that night – more than she'd ever done before. Each time it had been spurred on by the slash of the belt, the pinch of clothes pegs on her nipples and the utter, utter helplessness and inability to resist either the pain or the overwhelming cascade of pleasure that left her gasping, snorting, and way beyond caring.

Aysha had called her a slut – albeit with a smile when she said it. Lily stared out the window at the last few miles of Iran, and wondered if she really was a slut. What did that even mean? She felt it should be a bad thing – demeaning – but it also gave her a warm feeling inside, like discovering something missing, and which she now knew to be appropriate.

She wondered how long she had really had this urge to surrender to someone like Aysha. Was it Aysha as a person who had unearthed this side of Lily, or was it something subliminal or genetic that had always been there, just suppressed by her conventional upbringing? The lasting feeling from the night had been one of completeness, of discovering a new side of herself, recognising it, and being comfortable with it. It was like being able to share a deep secret with a close friend – finally finding someone trustworthy who would understand and recognise the reality. Perhaps this was what gay people felt when they came out of the closet and were accepted by their peers. This made Lily's thoughts turn to her own sexuality, and question whether she had really ever liked men. She thought of Robert, and decided that yes, she could still make love to him if he popped up in some parallel universe, but it would be a lovemaking session like he had never experienced before – this time with her evil twin. Lily reflected on some of the males on the bus. Intellect aside, she thought several were spunky enough she could share a bed with them. Lily realised she was blessed with the choice of both sexes, and decided that having such a choice was, in fact, very freaking cool.

The weather had turned gloomy as they passed hundreds of transcontinental trucks lined up at the bottlenecked Turkish border. Lily reckoned it must have taken days for a truck to cross. Along with the change in the weather the countryside had turned green, with running streams and copses of birch, beech and poplar. Two hours at the border had been tolerable, especially after the group discovered the duty-free shop, emerging with sufficient whiskey and cigarettes to see them through to Istanbul.

In Turkey the food changed as well, with familiar soft fresh bread, and many stews and soups appropriate to the cold rain now falling. Food remained high on the discussion list, and the longing for things recognizable from home was a common theme in the bus. It was the first tangible indication they were approaching Europe, leaving behind the Persians and encountering the Turks, where misogynist culture at least went through the motions of politeness to female travellers.

Snuggled up in the bus away from the wet, Lily and Aysha watched the snow cap of Mount Ararat slide along the northern horizon. For several days they continued westward to Goreme Valley, in the heart of Anatolia and the chance to rest for two nights, as they explored the Buried City. Lily had been re-reading Lord of the Rings, and found it difficult to dissociate the damp greenness of Turkey from her mental picture of Middle Earth, as their route took them almost to the snowline amidst mist-shrouded mountains.

Reaching the geographical centre of Turkey also turned out to be the point at which the group ditched hotels for camping grounds and tents, entailing a further change to the relationship. Aysha and Lily found themselves without the soundproofing and privacy afforded by four solid walls, nor the space and opportunity provided by a mattress and bedframe. They mastered the pitching of their two-person tent, along with the low camp beds they were now to sleep on, but they were not happy about it. According to the itinerary they would be camping the rest of the way to London, save only for Istanbul and Athens.

While she had known the journey was part hotel and part camping, Lily had not been concerned about the amount of either when she booked. That was, until the relationship with Aysha had developed to the point where every day Lily could barely wait until they were in the seclusion of a hotel room.

In the week they had travelled across Turkey, Lily had continued to sort things in her head, as she watched the towns and forests slide past. Now beyond the sexual wonderment Aysha had introduced her to, Lily began to look beyond the journey, to their arrival in London and what that might mean. She was besotted with Aysha, and the feeling appeared to be mutual. The pair found little to argue about, and if there was any trivial disagreement, Lily was firmly told what the solution was going to be, which she accepted without rancour. Even this outcome endeared her to Aysha and her dominance.

But while the appearance of tents was a frustrating inconvenience, it signalled their arrival at the edge of the Mediterranean Sea, and a burst of glorious warm weather. The girls gawked at the remains of civilisations that had once inhabited the coastline - a trail of ruined castles and fortifications seemingly at every headland and harbour. These were not famous structures like Windsor Castle or the Persepolis ruins, but were strongholds barely documented, much less maintained or administered by the authorities. They were crumbling, overgrown walls and turrets built by the Romans, the Crusaders, the Greeks or the Phoenicians, still standing after a millennium or two and disregarded by locals who had better things to be concerned with.

Lily found them fascinating, and dragged Aysha into any nearby ruins when they stopped for lunch or settled into the camping ground. There was no shortage of opportunity, and the pair also found it was not difficult to be alone, particularly now they were passing through a country where Fosters and Tuborg beer were readily available for the drinkers at the camping ground store or in the villages where they shopped for lunch.

A series of camps followed along the southern Turkish coast, the weather hot enough to allow changing into swimsuits as soon as the tents had been pitched and luggage off-loaded.  For Lily, seeing Aysha in a deep green bikini with a matching sarong, was like turning a new chapter page in a book.  Though she loved – and had explored – every inch of Aysha's body, the nakedness had always been in a low-lit hotel room.  Now she got to gaze on her partner's all-but-naked body in the bright sunlit warmth of the beach, or whatever rocky crag passed for access to the water.  Sans bohemian clothes, Aysha's tall, willowy frame showed off her pale coffee skin and glossy hair, her glasses looking oddly out of place with her figure.  Her bikini was conservative in the vital areas, and her height made her look more athletic than Junoesque, while still attracting admiring glances from much of the group.

Lily's black and white swimsuit was equally eye-catching.  Three inches shorter than Aysha, Lily did not have the svelteness that showed Aysha's muscles to perfection, though she was endowed with fuller breasts, of which Aysha had made no secret of her envy.  Aysha had played with them for long periods, driving Lily wild as she had struggled in her bonds, helpless to disengage the insistent fingers that just would not stop.  Lily's breasts had been a source of joy for Aysha, and her ability to rouse Lily to heights then send her crashing down with judicious placement of clothes pegs had brought the pair closer every time they played.

It did not take much for the males of the group to amuse themselves with alcohol or kicking a ball at these camping spots.  Lily and Aysha, by contrast, were periodic absentees and learned there were new ways to make out – now amongst nature, rather than with scarves in hotel rooms.  It had become common knowledge that Lily and Aysha were an item, and the belated revelation amongst the males had caused several unkind remarks, most of which had to do with what a 'waste' such a relationship was.  These had been ignored, and to their credit, some of the women had shamed the guys with a few choice come-backs concerning their own male prowess, or lack of it.

For their part, Lily and Aysha found the prospect of someone discovering them outside, *in flagrante delicto*, to be exciting, though they did not go out of their way to tempt fate.  The memory of the two small boys in the forest above Dal Lake was still in the back of their minds, and they contented themselves with secluded spots in the long grass, overlooking a trail or with a spectacular view.

The change to their lovemaking pattern brought with it the smells and sounds of the outdoors, the views over the crystal clear sea, the breeze through the trees and the smell of herbs and flowers now in full bloom.  Much as Lily loved this, she still found herself longing for the imposition of bonds at the hands of Aysha, and the control exerted over her, and admitted such to

Aysha one afternoon when they had made an early stop at the coastal camping ground at Side.

Their tent pitched, they had changed into swimsuits and with their towels and day packs had walked a kilometre along the pearl white beach to where a trail led off up to barely visible grey stone ruins of a castle on a headland. Lily had taken a picture of Aysha with the ruined castle in the background, and had pleaded for the picture as a keepsake, once the image appeared after the backpack developing period. She was gratified to see the product of her photographic skills – Aysha tall and lithe, hands on hips, her expression of mild amusement.

They had chosen this quiet spot for a swim, and had emerged from the gentle waves with hair dripping and bodies glistening, swimsuit and bikini doing little to conceal their best attributes. They ran up the beach to the edge of the grass where they had dropped their bags, and grabbed their towels. Aysha could not resist grabbing Lily's nipple where it pushed hard and erect with the cold water against the taut lycra of her swimsuit.

'Come here, slave,' she whispered in a tone that made Lily's knees weak. Aysha pulled the younger girl against her and they embraced, wet breasts on wet breasts. Aysha's tongue slid deeply into Lily's mouth and made her shudder, the lingering coldness of the swim now replaced by warmth flooding her loins.

Aysha was stronger than Lily, though the latter had rarely, if ever, put up any resistance to Aysha's advances. This time she succumbed to Aysha unexpectedly pushing her on to her stomach on her towel, intrigued that they were still on the edge of the open – though still deserted – beach. Lily did not know where this "attack" was going, and put up little resistance as her breasts were pressed into the sand with Aysha sitting on top of her. She had thought it to be fun, possibly a little forerunner to some more hot and heavy making out, when Aysha had grabbed a wrist and the familiar tightness of a scarf had materialised around it. Lily was in no position to resist as her other wrist was grabbed, and Aysha began binding one crossed over the other behind her.

'No! Aysh! What are you doing? Not here! People will see!' Lily pleaded softly, her face turned to one side in the sand. She tried vainly to struggle, but she had no chance. Her bound wrists made her arms useless and hindered her movements when Aysha climbed off her, deliberately letting her hand linger between Lily's legs.

'Let me go, please, Aysh…' Lily tried to turn on the charm, the "little girl look" which sometimes worked and made Aysha go soft. Lily looked down the beach but saw nobody whose presence could be used to justify her freedom. 'Aysh, you can't do this… What if we're caught?'

'You already are caught, my darling Lily,' Aysha said with a wicked smile. 'Now get up and let's see if this trail leads to the fairy castle.'

'But -'

'Don't make me gag you, Lily. I have several more scarves in the daypack. Then you really will be embarrassed if someone comes along.'

Aysha dusted the sand off Lily's front with far more vigour than was necessary, and with particular attention to Lily's breasts and crotch.

'We don't want sand in these private places, do we, Lily?'

'No, Aysh,' whispered Lily, head hung, conscious of the magic the other girl's hands and fingers were already starting to work. Aysha arranged Lily's towel around her shoulders so that it hung down sufficiently to hide the bound hands, then grabbed the daypack and pushed Lily up the trail away from the beach.

Lily's heart was racing, in part because of the possibility of encountering someone while in her present state of restraint, and in part because of what terrible – wonderful – thing Aysha might have in store for her. Aysha had shown herself to be a master of inventiveness, able to not only utilise anything handy, but to create imaginative positions that exposed Lily in ways she never saw coming. Now they were heading up to a bush-clad hillside where neither had been before, and Aysha's powers for adaptation and creativity would be at the fore.

As they climbed higher, and the outline of crumbling stone bulwarks began to show through the trees, the trail divided. Lily was becoming more apprehensive, but a part of her mind demanded that she proceed, that she was a prisoner without rights, subject to the will of her captor without recourse to mercy. 'Trust, Lily,' said a voice in her head.

At a nudge from Aysha, now carrying a short stick, Lily took the left, less distinct pathway, then paused for a moment. Sunlight momentarily blinded her, and in the back of her mind she was surprised Aysha did not shove her onwards.

Lily's sudden stop was outside of her normal submissiveness, her willingness to follow Aysha's commands, and there was no reason for it other than that something had come over Lily – something inherent in the time and place, within the stone ruins which only now emerged out of the trees and undergrowth. Aysha waited for a full ten seconds, before Lily abruptly began to move forward again.

The shift in mood which came over Lily had begun the first time Aysha had bound her immovably, in the hotel room in Swat, where the strangeness of being restrained had also invoked something familiar. The feel of bonds at wrist and ankle had awakened something long dormant within Lily Maddison's psyche, and this latest instance was the more intense for its happening in the outdoors. Lily's eyes were cast down, her bare legs feeling the swish and swipe of bushes and long grass as she pushed along the overgrown path. Behind her, her captor goaded her with a spear, prodding her forward through the great door which led into the inner sanctum of the castle.

Lily's vision blurred. Noises entered her head as though other people were here, half-seen, at the periphery of her vision. She did not understand what the voices were saying. They spoke a language different from hers, their sounds harsh but distant whispers. She half-turned to try for a better look at these people watching her, but there was a further poke from behind and she continued to move forward. She was, after all, a prisoner. Her parents had warned her not to wander too far, but in foraging for shellfish she had overlooked the presence of the castle and had been captured by the soldiers.

She was pushed through a low, collapsing stone doorway which led to an overgrown courtyard open to the sky. On the seaward side the wall had crumbled, giving glimpses of the sparkling blue Mediterranean, disappearing to the base of the cliff below. There were fractured flagstones beneath her feet, broken by the small trees amidst tangled undergrowth. It seemed the place had been unvisited for years.

Lily stopped, unbidden. Hands grasped her roughly and pushed her against the trunk of a beech sapling. Something appeared in front of her face – a cloth of some sort, which was bound over her eyes. Another piece of fabric was tied around her waist, trapping her bound wrists against the rough bark of the tree, and securing her firmly in place. The fabric was knotted at her stomach and the tails pulled tightly down between her thighs, before being tied again behind the trunk.

Lily tried to say something, to ask what was happening, what was to become of her, but she could not enunciate her question. This was what she had expected – a yet-to-be-determined fate for a mere peasant girl. The shoulder straps of her dress were pulled down, exposing her breasts to the cool air of the shadowed courtyard. Crude hands tweaked her nipples and she gasped at the roughhouse treatment, though she was not in the least surprised. Somehow the hands felt good, and she wanted them to continue, but then they were gone.

She was alone, now, alone but for the unseen figures lurking in the corners of the courtyard, watching her. There would be whispers as to her fate. Somewhere there was the sound of a horse's hooves on cobblestones, the clink of armour and the creak of a drawn cart. Lily's breath came faster, and she thrust against the tightness of the fabric drawn down over her stomach and between her thighs, tethering her to the tree trunk. The ties were secure, and felt good, felt stimulating, arousing.

Lily strained at her bindings, tugging against the tree, but finding no slack, only the persistent pressure immobilising her hands and compressing her loins. The noises faded, and Lily wondered if she was alone. The recollection of the hands was strangely comforting, and she now wished they were back, regardless of what fate they may have in store for her. She pressed outward again, feeling the bindings sliding wetly over her labia, exciting her.

Somewhere in that excitation, the need for decorum and the awareness of her location slipped from her mind, with the warmth of the distraction from between her thighs. She found that with a little effort, she could create a gentle rhythm against the bonds, stimulating and arousing a sudden blaze of pleasure. Was she now a public spectacle - a brazen whore pleasuring herself for the amusement of the castle folk? Or was it something worse – evidence of her guilt and irredeemable proof which would warrant a further and final punishment?

Lily didn't care, now. The bonds were her means of pleasure and only served to exacerbate the tide rising in her loins until she could resist no longer, succumbing to the falling barricades and surrendering to advancing forces. Lily bucked and heaved at her restraints, suddenly finding a hand clamped over her mouth as the waves of ecstasy shuddered through her body and she finally slumped against the tree.

Then the hand was gone, and so was the blindfold. She straightened, blinking in the shadowy light, uncertain of where she was, though there was no mistaking the warm, post-coital feeling flooding through her. She looked around as best she could, bringing herself back to whatever reality had brought her there, feeling the bindings still at her wrists, waist and pussy, and in a flash wondering where Aysha was. She tried to turn her head but the tree trunk made it difficult to see properly. A bead of sweat rolled down her cheek and she realised the top of her swimsuit had been pulled down, exposing her breasts to anybody walking into this little ruined courtyard.

'Aysha? Where are you?'

There was no answer. A faint zephyr made the leaves whisper and hardened her nipples again. A shiver ran down her spine, a sudden irrational sense of abandonment. Here she was, bound to a tree miles from anywhere in a ruined Turkish castle, panting like a slut who had just got herself off, but now coming down to the vulnerability of her situation. She called out again.

'Aysha? Stop fucking about and let me go.'

Lily swore under her breath, tugging again at her bonds, as though something might have inexplicably loosened since her last effort, seconds before.

'Not funny, Aysh!' she said, but the tumbledown stone walls ignored her plea. Lily's initial indignation and anger subsided as a wave of exhaustion swept over her, as though she had undergone a long and arduous interrogation which was now over and done with. She hung her head, listening to the blood in her ears and the open-mouthed panting of her breath.

Aysha was just playing with her. She would be around here somewhere. Close by. Trust, Lily. She eased herself upright, willing herself to relax. Trust, Lily.

Ten minutes passed with just the faintest soughing of leaves to break the silence. Lily felt the warmth return to her loins, looking down to see that the tails of the scarf had embedded themselves through the thin lycra of her swimsuit deep between her labia. She wondered how loud she had been? Everything was hazy. She was hot and thirsty, and did not want to set off another uncontrolled orgasm. Aysha was just taking the piss now, teasing her and showing her up. How long was she expected to stay here on display?

A twig cracked behind her – behind one of the crumbling stone walls. All thought of another climax disappeared from Lily's brain as her heart skipped a beat at the realisation of her situation. What if it wasn't Aysha? What if it was some dirty Turkish farm boy who stumbled on a half-naked western woman bound to a tree? Fuck!

'Aysha?' That's right, draw attention to yourself, Lily. Aysha knows where you are. You don't have to advertise your plight to anybody else who doesn't!

The noise turned to footsteps crunching on leaves and dried twigs behind her. She tried to crane her neck as a pair of hands slipped from behind the tree and closed around her neck.

'Did you enjoy your little fantasy, my darling?' Aysha asked sweetly.

*

As they turned inland to the hot springs of Pammukale, the weather held fine and Aysha and Lily settled into the routine of pitching tents, taking their turn at buying food and cooking, and sneaking in a chance to make love whenever they could find privacy.

The incident in the Crusader castle had become a watershed for both of them, for Lily had found herself overwhelmed in the post-orgasm descent, collapsing into tears on Aysha's shoulder as they arrived back at the edge of the beach. She had tried to explain how the place had affected her, how she felt she had somehow slipped into a different time, but it had come out garbled and barely coherent. Her experience had been overlaid with the hurt at being left bound to the tree, and her relief when Aysha had appeared. In her confused state Lily had held Aysha and as the tears had dried she had whispered:

'Aysha, I love you so much...'

'And I love you, too, my darling Lily...'

In the quiet moments away from the others they had discussed Lily's epiphany at the castle, and it was only on reflection that Lily started to see a pattern which had become more prevalent as they had travelled westwards, and through some strange phenomenon had been triggered – or at least made more vividly accessible – when Lily had found herself a bound prisoner.

Sitting on a campsite wall at sunset, Lily felt like a child trying to explain something complicated to a big sister. 'There's something between you and me, Aysha, which acts as a conduit. I don't know why. It's like... as we've got to know and experience each other, the bond has become stronger. Then suddenly when you tied me up, that connection seemed to take on this weird familiarity. It was like I'd known bondage before. It was unknown, yet familiar... Fuck. I'm not making sense. Sorry.' Lily stared moodily at the flaming ball of the sun just touching the horizon. 'It was like I'd been here before.'

'At the castle?'

'Maybe not there specifically, but in that time.'

'What, like a past life?'

'Uh... I don't know. Maybe like whatever conjures up an extreme form of déjà vu. I almost saw people. Heard them.'

'It wasn't just you slipping into Lily's fantasyland?' There was no teasing in Aysha's voice.

'No. Not this time. Maybe back on the bed – that first time you beat me... Maybe there *was* fantasy there. We'd come from Persepolis after all, and that affected me, too. But maybe what I thought was fantasy there actually wasn't?' Lily hugged herself and watched the sun disappearing. 'This is so hard to explain. I just felt somehow... at home... when you first tied me. Like I'd experienced this before, like it was right and proper that I be treated like this, like *you* had been here before as well... I guess the first stop in London will be the Funny Farm.'

'Why? Didn't you enjoy it?'

'Oh, you know I did! You know I loved every minute of it...'

'But can you accept that freely, or do you have to now start looking for reasons and excuses for what you see as aberrant behaviour?'

Lily shrugged.

'You're over-thinking things again, Honey. Look, let's not make a big deal of this. You've admitted you love submitting to my evil intentions, and there's no denying I love doing rude things to you. Why not let it be? If you have a few fantasies along the way, let's not try to analyse them. Just be grateful! There's plenty more in my armoury. I'm only just getting started, my love. Does that thought excite you?'

'My God, yes!'

'Sweetheart, we'll have to make do as best we can with this whole camping thing. Who'd have thought when we signed up for a little spot of camping that it'd be the most frustrating time of our lives?' She laughed, tossing her hair back and showing sparkling teeth.

'And we can get a flat together, in London?' Lily asked again. 'You're sure that's what you want?' Aysha could spot Lily's insecurity and need for reassurance, and had no hesitation in such confirmation.

'Of course, my darling. We'll both end up as barmaids in the local pub – they love Aussies and Kiwis because we work our arses off to make travel money. We may not be long term workers, but while we're there, they think we're the bee's knees. Common knowledge.'

Lily took heart from this confident prediction, and slid her arm through Aysha's. The older girl bent her head and they held a long kiss.

'Jeez, you're gorgeous,' said Aysha. 'I want to just bundle you up in a sack and keep you under my pillow.'

\*

The next few days flew by, with blurred passages through the ruins of Ephesus and Troy, before they were on a small vehicular ferry across the Dardanelles and stepping foot on to European soil for the first time in their lives.

A visit to the battlefields and cemeteries of Gallipoli was a rite of passage for any Antipodean making the overland pilgrimage to the Motherland. In low but ironic tones, Aysha had opined:

'Don't you think it's weird that Australia and New Zealand revere Anzac Day, yet we're celebrating an instance where we invaded a foreign country at the behest of our master – Great Britain – and got our butts kicked into the bargain? A pretty bizarre choice, in my humble opinion.'

Lily did not respond. For many of the Sundowners group there were personal reasons for the visit, looking for the graves of young relatives who had perished on the beaches or in the surrounding hills in the abortive invasion sixty-two years previously. Lily's mother had told her of great uncle Arthur – Lily's grandmother's younger brother, who had emigrated to New Zealand with her in 1910 – who had fought and died on the peninsula. His brother Hamish had made the wiser choice to become a surveyor in British India.

The Sundowners bus had parked at the Chunuk Bair New Zealand cemetery and the travellers had slowly fanned out to look at the perfectly tended grave sites, planted with roses and lavender. In the wild fields beyond, spills of red poppies stood out in the grass below the pine trees.

Lily did not know much about Gallipoli, other than that Anzac Day was venerated on both sides of the Tasman, and it was this war engagement that had formed such a bond between the two countries as their soldiers fought side by side. She was not expecting the solemnity and heartbreak of the place to wash over her like a tidal wave as she took her first tentative steps across the lawn to the rows of engraved concrete headstones overlooking the distant sea.

Lily lost all sense of time and place, so overwhelmed was she. She was hardly conscious of the tears streaming down her cheeks as she walked between row after row of New Zealand fallen, anguish and heartache welling up inside her. Aysha saw the tears and slipped her arm through Lily's, though the latter was barely aware of her friend.

Lily stopped suddenly, beside a headstone and knelt down, touching it with her fingers. Aysha read the inscription:

PRIVATE ARTHUR BUCHANAN
WELLINGTON INFANTRY REGIMENT
19 MAY 1915    AGE 19
HE DIED A MAN & CLOSED HIS LIFE'S BRIEF DAY
ERE IT HAD SCARCE BEGUN

Lily was whispering something under her breath which Aysha could not hear, her hand resting on the gravestone. She stayed there for several minutes, almost as though she was conversing with someone. Aysha felt her own tears flowing, not knowing why, then Lily was standing, hugging her.

'What is it, Sweetie?' Aysha asked softly.

'This is my great uncle…' Lily sniffed.

'Buchanan?'

'My mum's family name. His brother was Hamish – the one I told you about in India. Our menfolk were travellers…'

Aysha didn't know what to say. Lily was done, and sat down on the stone steps of the great marble-faced memorial to watch the other Sundowners make their way slowly along the lines of graves. Even the rowdy back-seaters were subdued by the place. Aysha sat beside her friend.

'He was only nineteen,' said Lily in a small voice. 'Christ, what did *we* know at nineteen? What would he have known about this place in 1915? Would we do that today?'

'Ask those who were in Vietnam,' said Aysha.

'Yeah, I guess you're right. Some things never change. That's my great uncle,' she repeated. 'He brought me here. Just to let me know he's okay…' Her eyes welled over with tears again and she tucked her head down on Aysha's shoulder.

# the submissive spy

\* \* \*

# CHAPTER 11 – Istanbul

It seemed that every event they shared brought the two young women closer, as they learned more about each other and themselves, and a minute apart from the other was a minute not shared. A half-day drive took them to Istanbul and a cheap hotel with a view over the nearby Blue Mosque. By a quirk of organisation – though in truth it was Aysha slipping Wayne two half-bottles of scotch – Aysha and Lily found themselves in a twin room, while some of the other females were relegated to rooms with multiple beds. Aysha figured one of the bottles would end up with the booking clerk, and one with the courier, for she wanted Istanbul to be special.

The hotel was in the old quarter, a cheap-and-cheerful hangover from colonial days, often used by overland companies. Their room had an old-fashioned run-down charm, with a parquet floor, random furniture and a view of the six minarets of the Blue Mosque rising into the evening sky like rockets ready for blast off. Lily was entranced, as she bounced on one of the creaky wooden beds.

The city was a fascinating blur Lily would never forget, without any of the déjà vu effects that had ambushed her previously. Their time had been spent in the Grand Bazaar, on ferry boats and in the great mosques. Lily loved the Blue Mosque, with its glittering hanging lights and the warmth of the vast red carpets calling out to be knelt on.

They visited Post Restante, unsurprised to find just two letters from Lily's father, then managed to get lost in the wonderland of the Bazaar, with its vaulted brick ceilings and Aladdin's caves of carpets, jewellery, porcelain, spices and metalwork. They drank endless cups of mint tea and used all their feminine wiles on an old white-bearded proprietor who at least pretended to be taken in by their beauty, before they bought two silver Turkish puzzle rings. The rings came in four interlocking pieces, and the old man showed the pair how to manipulate them so they cleverly came together to form an intricate whole. The girls were delighted when they finally mastered the technique, and could put them on each other's fingers. There was an awkward moment when Lily asked:

'Which finger should we put them on?'

'Would you be happy with third finger right hand?' Aysha asked gently. Lily nodded, and inexplicably became choked up as she slid one ring on Aysha's finger, then received the other on her own. A tear escaped her eye and she kissed Aysha lightly. The old man beamed and ordered more mint tea.

They hung out in the Pudding Shop, a favourite overlander pit-stop, reading the bulletin board with its pinned requests for rides to India, or offering space in a Combi or Landrover to distant parts. There were pleas for information on missing travellers, a family member, or a lover – whose disappearance might have been accidental or wilful. They were welcomed into the local hookah houses and restaurants, reaching their room after one too many *rakis* and collapsing in a laughing heap on the bed.

Istanbul was the climax to the trip thus far, and it seemed to Aysha and Lily that they had never been happier. For their third and final night they had vowed to dress up – as much as their meagre suitcases of clothes allowed.

Aysha wore her salwar kameez with a silver scarf draped back over her shoulders, her ebony hair worn up, while Lily had produced a light blue halter-neck dress with a narrow waist that flared loosely to her knees.

'Is this too daring?' she had asked Aysha.

'It's lovely, Sweetie, but you have to wear a bra under it. I can't be responsible for half the male population of Istanbul wanting to see those beautiful boobs in more detail.'

Lily undid the halter and slipped on a strapless bra that would not show, then deliberated: 'I still feel like there's too much skin.'

Aysha moved behind her and fluffed out Lily's hair. It had grown longer as the trip progressed and now the chestnut tresses covered much of her shoulders. 'You look good enough to eat. In fact, I think I'll pass on my dessert tonight so I can do just that. We're not going too far. I'm sure we can do that without causing offence.'

The night was warm and still, as they passed through the down-at-heel marble-floored lobby and waved to the young man behind the desk, who gazed at the two western women with undisguised longing – or lust.

They walked only a short distance to a restaurant they had spotted during the day, tempted by the menu displayed in the window, to be captured by the enthusiastic young waiter standing in the doorway competing for customers with neighbouring establishments. They were shown to a small table in a dimly-lit corner, and it wasn't long before the restaurant filled with locals and the noise level cloaked their own conversation. Under the young man's close attention they dined on *meze*, *dolma* and *Lüfer* – a blue fish from the Bosporus – lubricated with *raki*.

Aysha had seen Lily under the influence of alcohol, and knew she let her guard down easily for a period before she became uncoordinated and inarticulate. Aysha reckoned there was a little way to go before the lack of coordination set in, when she placed her hand over Lily's. Lily looked up, sensing something a little less light-hearted than the happy tone of their conversation to that point.

'Sweetie, there's something I'd like to talk to you about...'

'Oh... is this a "we need to talk" moment?' Lily tried to make light, then said: 'Should I be worried?'

'No, of course not. I hope just the opposite. But you need to listen to me and understand some things. This is important.'

Lily sensed the seriousness in Aysha's voice and seemed to pull herself back from the blithe path of banter she had been following.

'Lily, back in Oz, there is a community of people who think like I do – like *we* do – who get off on bondage, discipline, all that sort of stuff. It's a bit underground – certainly in Queensland. It's mainly hetero, but there's queer stuff as well. Once you get into the community there seems to be more tolerance for us non-conformists.

'Many of them – male-female or same sex – like to formalise their relationship, where one person is dominant and the other submissive. Like master and slave – or mistress and slave. You'll have noticed I may have referred to you as my slave, sometimes. Yes?'

Lily nodded.

'Does that bother you?'

'No.'

'And that's because you're smart enough to know that it's a term of endearment, most of all. Relationships come in all shapes and forms – this much I've worked out in talking to some of these people. It's all very secretive, particularly in Brizzie. There are little gatherings in people's houses…'

'You make it sound like witches gathering in covens!'

'Well… in Brisbane it kind of has to be that way. Being queer is bad enough. Being queer and into bondage is enough to get you into the loony bin – after the cops have given you a hard time and probably shown you what real bondage is about, without a Safeword. You have that problem in Kiwiland?'

'God, Aysh, I wouldn't have a clue. Nobody I know has ever mentioned it. We're all properly brought up. There's nothing like that – or if there is it's all behind closed doors.'

'So all this has been a revelation?'

'You know that! I never knew I could feel like this Aysh, honestly. It's weird when you tell me there are lots more people out there who like this stuff.'

'There were some fetish magazines around in the fifties and sixties - all underground stuff, but it resonated, you know? People realised they were not alone in these proclivities. It was a wonderful shock for some of us when we came across our first bondage magazine. So, little communities appeared, but you had to be in the know. The culture developed, and some aspects became more mainstream, including this master-slave thing. Sorry, this sounds like I'm giving a lecture. I'm just trying to put things into context. This whole subject is so broad, Sweetie. Everybody does things differently within a relationship. We all have our little foibles, our boundaries, or weaknesses. You figure out what turns you on and what you go to sleep obsessing about.

'My long-winded point is –' she smiled and squeezed Lily's hand 'that a mistress-slave relationship – because that's what we're talking about here – can take many forms. Some people love the concept of being a slave twenty-four/seven. Others go down the bondage path every now and again, while living as partners, but with opposite roles. Whatever form it takes, they often acknowledge it with a ceremony, called 'collaring'. It's like becoming engaged, except that a collar is placed on the submissive, rather than exchanging rings, and they pledge their love and commitment to each other.'

The inference was not lost on Lily, who looked at the seriousness in Aysha's face. For the first time that Lily could remember, Aysha looked hesitant, as though sounding out Lily's reaction and hoping for the right response. As though to break a tension, she caught the waiter's eye and ordered coffee for them.

'Lily, I'd like you to think about formalising what we have. For me it's a way of showing you I will always care for you when you're under my control – and, of course, when you aren't. It will show that you trust me, that we respect each other's boundaries. It's also showing that I... love you, Lily.'

Aysha looked away, staring into the distance, her eyes wet, as though the waiter needed to reappear to stop the display of weakness. There was a long silence that Aysha thought would never end, when Lily squeezed her hand and whispered:

'I'd like that. Very much.'

When the time came to return to the hotel, Lily was laughing on Aysha's arm, a mood that continued as they made their way up to the fourth floor of their hotel in the ancient clanking open-sided elevator in the centre of the stairwell. They had been approached by a young girl selling flowers outside the restaurant, and Aysha had bought Lily a red rose. Lily had been overwhelmed by the tenderness with which Aysha gave it to her, and the gentle kiss accompanying it. In her tipsy state her emotions had overflowed along with the tears of happiness, as they had returned to the hotel.

Inside the room, Lily fell on the bed, giggling from more *raki*, as though everything she or Aysha said was the height of wit. She was un-resisting when Aysha turned her on her front and quickly bound her wrists behind her. That was when the laughter died to occasional giggles, as she became pliant in Aysha's hands, the first inklings of what lay before her starting to cast an air of sobriety over her senses.

The start of roleplay was a big turn-on to Aysha, and she loved springing such surprises on Lily. As the overland journey had progressed and they had grown to understand each other, Aysha had been able to push Lily's buttons more and more specifically, and to mess with her mind as much as her body. She had learned Lily's vulnerabilities, her likes and dislikes, and the things against which she found herself utterly helpless. For Aysha, planning was as much fun as implementing, and she had vowed that this would be a special night Lily would never forget.

The moment the scarf was bound over Lily's eyes, her inebriation level seemed to lower, as her world became dark. Her mind and body were now competing between the drink that had gone before and the unknown fears and anticipation of what were undoubtedly still to come. Like a young horse, the blindfold had at once calmed Lily, but also meant she could not see what her captor now had in store for her.

Aysha sat her on the end of the bed and bound her ankles, legs apart, to the two bed legs, sensing the apprehensive trembling in Lily's muscles. Blindfolded, bound hand and foot, Lily's head turned this way and that, once again trying to follow the movements of the other woman in the room, wondering what devious delight was to follow – what combination of pain and pleasure. Lily whetted her lips as the halter button was undone behind her neck and the top of her dress fell forward. Seconds later her bra was gone, and Aysha's hands were gently cradling Lily's breasts, now exposed to the night air drifting through the window, and supplemented by soft lips teasing the rapidly enlarging nipples and stroking the teardrop birthmarks. Lily's breathing became shallower and faster. She heard Aysha's words overlain with a serious and commanding tone that sent a shiver down her spine. This was not Aysha the tender, wooing lover but Aysha the dominating controlling figure.

'Lily, you're no use to me drunk. I need you to sober up and to reflect on your situation. I have some business to carry out, and I'll leave you here to decide which world you will be inhabiting by the time I return. I expect to find you sitting here obediently, exactly as I leave you. It's dark, there will be no housekeeping around but I'll leave the "Do Not Disturb" sign on the door. I want your full concentration on what you do and where you go next. Do you understand?'

'Yes.'

'Tonight it will be 'yes, Ma'am'. Comprendo?'

'Yes... Ma'am.'

'Very good. But I don't trust leaving you to your own sordid little daydreams, Lily Maddison, so I need to ensure compliance.' Lily wondered what Aysha was getting up to, as she heard some rustling and movement of the heavy armchair nearby. Then came the bite of clothes pegs, one on each nipple. She gasped. The grip was firm, not fierce, but with the potential to become sharper in time. Certainly it had got her attention.

'Lean forward,' Aysha ordered, and Lily felt a slight tug on the clothes pegs as she did so. She made to lean backwards again and found that she could not – not without the pegs tightening on her nipples. Aysha had somehow tied them to something – probably the chair.

'Ow,' she breathed.

'You know I do nothing without a reason,' Aysha told her softly, her voice just in front of Lily's face, suggesting the older girl was kneeling beside her. 'Those pegs will focus your mind, meaning that you will sober up over however long it takes for me to do my errand. I suspect they will also take you away to whatever fantasy steps into the breach. Now I have one other thing to do. Open your mouth, Lily.'

'But Aysh – don't gag me – I –'

The slap on her cheek was unexpected and shocked Lily into silence.

'What did I say about tonight's form of address?' There was a fierceness in Aysha's whisper next to Lily's ear.

'I must call you... Ma'am.'

'Good. And what do you think you're doing telling me what I can and can't do? Lily Maddison, you're a prisoner, a slave, a submissive who's surrendered all form of control to me. I'll do with your body and mind what I decide, without contribution from you. Comprendo?'

Lily hung her head.

'Yes, Ma'am,' she said quietly.

'Very well. Now open your mouth.' Lily did as she was told, but instead of feeling the bulk of a wadded cloth stuffed roughly between her teeth, she felt the stem of the rose placed across her tongue.

'Close.' Lily gently closed her mouth on the rose now between her lips. Aysha's voice was now different – warm and loving, in a way that made Lily want to cry again. 'Lily, this rose is a gag, of sorts. It represents how much I love you – how much I've grown to love you more than anyone else in my life. It's a gift of my love to you to safeguard until I return. I know things may get a little painful while I'm gone –' she plucked at the string securing the clothes pegs, making Lily grunt softly – 'but love is never easy. There will always be hard times – but you can get through them, and I will always return, and things will always be easier then. I hope you still have this rose in your mouth when I return, Lily. Consider it a little test for you. If it's still here, it'll be an indication of your own love, my darling slave. And when I do return, I will have some more gifts for you...'

Then she was gone, the door clicking shut and locking behind her. Lily sat on the bed, bound and gagged by the one she loved like no other.

In Lily's darkened world the bonds at her wrists and ankles, bite of the pegs on her nipples and the feel of the rose stem between her teeth held her immovable. There was no way in the world Lily was going to drop the rose, even if she had to eat the damned thing. Aysha had given it to her as a symbol of love, and Lily had no choice but to respond in the only way possible for her. Regardless of whether the slowly growing pain at the tips of her breasts was meant to distract her, to make her forget her purpose, that was not going to happen. If it became too much, forcing her to articulate her suffering, then such articulation would only be through clenched teeth.

Lily had been waylaid, ambushed, captured in so many ways. Now she was being tested, her ankles and wrists secured in a way both familiar and oddly comforting, as though a badge of rank, albeit that her rank was that of a lowly peasant girl. The coldness of the flagstones on which she sat could not distract her from the task of fealty that the queen had imposed on her, testing her further with the slowly growing pain in her nipples. In the darkened dungeon Lily had no sense of time. She had been here before, confined, tormented, but ultimately rewarded by one of the many owners who had seen her as their property. Today it was the queen, the true ruler of the castle in which she was imprisoned. Everybody knew the queen was the power behind the throne, dominating her husband as much as she did the lowly peasant girl, whose wish was merely to discreetly satisfy the queen's desires, in the times when the king was away.

Lily knew the queen's predilection lay with the female sex, and that nights with the king were avoided where possible. The begetting of two sons early in her marriage as a child bride had been sufficient to satisfy the hereditary requirements for the king. He was thereafter free to pursue his own agenda with the page boys or the army. Much as Lily loved these secret encounters with the queen, she also feared discovery by either of the queen's two sons, who were now of marriageable age and had the run of the castle and the serving staff. There was no way she would be found in this deep dungeon where the queen had left her. The princes were not given to traipsing these dark corridors, but... Should she be found, she would be helpless to resist whatever might be done to her... Despite the slowly growing pain in her nipples, Lily's crotch was wet. She squirmed, feeling alternate tugs on each clothes peg, but finding the movement only served to increase her wetness. How long would she be left here before her guardian returned?

Occasional little jolts of pain began to shoot through her nipples. She supposed she might dislodge the fiendish devices with a sharp pull backwards, but she might also merely pull along whatever they were anchored to, making the whole agony even worse. She decided to forgo that option, at least until the pain got unbearable. But that might mean dropping the rose, as she surrendered to the pain... No, she could not allow that...

She had lost all track of time. Only the throbbing in her nipples kept her focussed. Where was Aysha? Where was her queen? The effects of the *raki* had long since disappeared and Lily sat still, only her breathing evident, making the two clothes pegs rise and fall against the string holding them. There was a rattle at the door.

'House-keeping!'

What? Aysha had said she'd put out the "Do Not Disturb" sign! Oh God! Lily's heart shot into top gear. She tried to articulate a protest, but could not bring herself to drop the stem from her mouth, instead making garbled mumbles in response, as the key turned and the door creaked open. Lily clamped her legs together in anticipation of an accident.

'Dio mio!' said the husky female voice. Whether it was that Lily registered that the words were in Italian rather than Turkish, or that she recognised Aysha's voice, the wave of relief flooded over her and it was this that almost caused her to lose the rose. Then Aysha was on her knees beside her, tenderly taking back the rose while Lily sniffled and her eyes leaked into the scarf.

Neither said anything, for the spell was still powerful. Aysha removed the clothes pegs gently, allowing the blood to return to the tortured nubs and kissing them gently as Lily had little intakes of breath. Aysha's hands lifted the bound girl to her feet. It was a relief for Lily just to change position, but she knew more was to come, and did not wish to give cause for a worse punishment than that which she thought would likely be ahead.

She was right in her anticipation, for hardly had the rose and the pegs been removed than the familiar gag was embedded between her jaws and her dress and panties were pulled down below her knees. A sharp pain came slashing across her thighs. The implement was some form of leather flogger, she thought. It was not the belt that Aysha had used before, but was no less effective as it beat a cadence up and down her spread thighs and into her crotch. It continued across her stomach, making its way up to her breasts. She held her breath as Aysha paused, Lily's mind anticipating a strike to left or right breast. When it came, it was worse than she expected, and she found herself grunting into the gag with each strike. Her nipples – already sore – were super sensitive and the flogger made her jump and twist to try to avoid the blows. But she could not see where Aysha stood, nor the timing of the coming impact. Occasionally Aysha would stop for a few seconds, as Lily tried to pre-empt the blow with a twist. Aysha would wait until Lily realised the blow was not coming where and when she had thought, and her body would uncurl, trembling with the anticipation of a strike somewhere else.

Thwack! Grunt! Thwack! Grunt!

Aysha switched to Lily's rear, paddling her backside as Lily tried to protect her butt with her bound hands. It was a game of cat and mouse, where the mouse was blind and the cat always won. The blows flicked between her legs, splaying out over her mons and making Lily yelp and moan into the gag.

As her labia became engorged with the stimulation, Lily felt her wetness rising towards orgasm just from the stimulating pain. She knew she would not get there just from that, and so did Aysha. When the assault stopped abruptly, Lily bent over, sucking in lungfuls of air to the accompaniment of rapid grunting. Aysha's hand slipped between Lily's legs, and that in itself had almost been enough to send Lily over the edge. Aysha's hand came back wet, her fingers now running along Lily's top lip, leaving the smell of sex and desire in their wake.

There was a short pause, filled with odd scratching and scraping noises Lily could not make head or tail of. Once again she realised Aysha was letting Lily's mind go off to a place of imagined future torment - which might or might not eventuate. The mental torture Aysha put her through was frequently worse than the real thing.

Lily was expecting the hand to reappear between her thighs, sampling the moisture and sensitivity of the engorged lips. She was unprepared for the sensation of fingers opening her vagina and the feel of something smooth and hard entering her passage. She gasped at the fullness of it and the way it slid in easily against her juices. It was large enough to make her moan into the gag, stifling the first snort, then giving into those subsequent, as the object began to move in and out. Dear god, it *was* large – larger than anything Robert had managed – filling her and sparking a new onslaught of dopamine and oxytocin.

Somewhere in the distance a voice said: 'Hold that, Lily Maddison! Do *not* let that slip out!' Lily did not question the command but clamped her thighs and abdominal muscles as tightly as she could, clasping the intruder inside her as though her life depended on it. A quiet descended on the room, broken by dull intermittent traffic noises drifting in on the warm night air through the open window.

She felt a slight movement of the object, the first vestiges of slippage, and tried to clench it tighter, but the way her ankles were tied to the bed legs meant she could not bring her feet closer.

'Lily!' the voice said sharply, as though sensing her weakening hold. Desperately Lily redoubled her efforts, her vaginal muscles trembling with the need to grip the thing, but at the same time wanting to savour its presence and again feel the movement of it inside her.

A minute passed, then maybe two – Lily was focussed only on the invader, and her need to not let it drop, lest she displease the disembodied voice and attract consequences. She did not know how she had ended up like this. One of the princes had somehow found her, and she was helpless to resist as he now thrust inside her again, pressing his body against hers, overpowering the feeble struggling against her bonds. He was large, driving, initiating all the responses she could not control, so intense were the waves of pleasure washing up from her loins. Lily twisted and turned, but his manhood plunged deeper. Lily felt the bonds at her wrists and ankles, as she strained to pull her legs together. The words of protest she tried to enunciate turned to savage grunts and then to muffled cries of insuperable pleasure as the wetness of her passage exploded and she bent over in surrender.

Then the intruder was gone, and before Lily had a chance to catch her breath, Aysha's hot lips were into her crevice and seeking out her clit. Lily tried to articulate 'No! No more!', but the sound came out like 'Nnn! Nnnmm!' Lily's brain had closed the passage door leading to the emergency room armed with the Safeword, and had she possessed the presence to analyse her predicament, she might have concluded that this was not, in fact, a life-threatening situation.

As Lily climaxed again, Aysha gripped her naked buttocks and sucked furiously until Lily's trembling legs gave way and she collapsed on the bed, like – as Lily later reckoned – a sated harlot devoid of any vestige of shame.

Lily recovered her strength a short while later, finding herself naked but unfettered. She sat up.

'Jesus.' Her voice was hoarse and she drank greedily from a bottle of water beside the bed. 'What did you do to me, Aysha Newton?'

'I fucked you over, little slave.' Aysha's tone was warm and loving. 'It's amazing what you can get in a Turkish bazaar at nine o'clock at night. Sorry I took so long...'

'Don't try that Italian chambermaid thing again. I nearly crapped myself.'

'I'm sure Esmeralda or Maria has encountered stranger things in her work,' Aysha grinned.

'What, stranger than a naked woman bound, gagged, blindfolded and tethered by her nips? What kind of world do these chambermaids live in? I'll apply for a job!'

'You were only *half*-naked, in any case. Your dress was only at half-mast.'

'Oh, of course. That makes it all right and much more acceptable to our Catholic lady from Naples.'

'I think we'd be more likely to meet Fatima from Ankara, but I can't do a Turkish accent.'

'Oh yes – that would be much better. Muslim women are so much more liberal than staunch Catholic senoras.'

'Soooo... you okay?'

'Oh dear god, Aysh. Are you trying to kill me? I was off in some other universe, getting beaten and fucked by some prince, I think.'

'Was it good, for you?'

'My god! Yes, yes and yes! You are amazing... or he was... or something was... What did you do to me?'

Aysha let go a sly smile. 'You know how I've always told you about improvisation? Meet Mister Carrot!' She flourished a large carrot that bore the unmistakable evidence of sculpting into a circumcised penis, now encased in a condom. 'You can still buy anything in the bazaar, even at this hour. It's like a medieval seven-eleven.'

Lily burst out laughing. 'Prince Carrot, you were wonderful! Now I think we need a cigarette... And you bought a flogger? What were you beating me with?'

Aysha held up a fly whisk made of thin strips of leather attached to a short handle. She slapped it down on her hand. 'I figured this would do the job.'

'God – did it! Got me to the space station before the docking vessel even took off!'

Aysha sat on the bed beside Lily and put her arm around her, kissing her gently on the mouth and then harder, before Lily broke away.

'I... I'm sorry Aysh. I don't think I could go another round.'

'It's okay. But I want to tell you I am so proud of you. I know those pegs must have hurt, but you still had that rose in your mouth.'

Lily's eyes misted. 'I was never going to drop that, Aysha... Truly.'

'I know. And I love you for that. But I have something else for you. Bit of a shopping spree of sorts.' She picked up a flimsy pink plastic bag and pulled out a thin black object, which Lily saw was a collar.

Aysha did not look at Lily's eyes. Rather, she seemed to search for the right words.

'Look, you know what we talked about over dinner – all that collaring stuff. I know this is sudden, and I'm not going to make a big formal deal out of it.' Lily thought it was the first time she had seen Aysha as anything but confident and sure of herself. 'I wanted to give this to you now. This is not cementing a commitment between us. It's too soon for you to have even thought about such a thing. But it is something I want to do, just to put my side on the table. This doesn't signify that you belong to me Lily, that you are my slave. It shows that when you wear this, you are submitting to me, and that I am obligated to look after your well-being, to protect you, and to care for you. That I will also love you goes without saying.'

Aysha took out the thin black collar with a small copper plate the size of a fingertip riveted to it. On the tiny plate was etched an emblem – a fleur-de-lys – the three-leaved symbol of the lily flower.

Lily stared at it, then looked up at Aysha. Her lips were dry.

'I... I don't know what to say... I mean, I love this, I love what you've told me, and I'll always treasure it... I don't know what to say in response other than that I love you so much, Aysha...' Tears rolled down Lily's cheeks and she saw Aysha was crying as well.

Lily let Aysha buckle the collar at the back of her neck, feeling the snugness at her throat and the warm feeling of belonging it gave her. She was now Aysha's even if Aysha was reluctant to ask for that. Whether worn or not, the collar was a now symbol of their relationship, of its definition and its promise.

Lily had never been happier.

\*    \*    \*

# CHAPTER 12 – Greece

They had taken four days to get to Athens – four days of impatience for Lily as each night she lay with Aysha in their tent, listening to the slow breathing from the camp bed beside her. Outside the night silence was broken by snoring from nearby tents, and the odd soft passage of footsteps of someone on a night mission to the bathroom block. Voices carried a long way, either from those staying up late drinking and shooting the breeze, or those conveying intimate gossip in the faux privacy of their tent. Athens would be the last of the hotels on the trip and for Lily it couldn't come soon enough. She was sure Aysha was testing her resolve, tweaking her sexual frustration level like shaking an opened bottle of fizzy drink with a finger over the top.

The drive along the Aegean coast had taken them to two beachside camping grounds, where too much sangria and retsina had been drunk by the group, in between swimming, sun, and crowds of holidaymakers on the sand. It was nearing peak summer holidays, and while Lily found the crowds irksome, and the teasing standoffishness of Aysha maddening, she was nevertheless deliriously happy. She felt she had been given the keys to the sweetshop, but after sampling some heavenly delights she now discovered she couldn't reach the shelves on her own. Aysha merely watched with folded arms and a wicked smile.

Lily had become obsessed with her collar, wanting to wear it all the time, but Aysha had forbidden this, saying it was not intended for such. Rather, it was of special significance and would only attract unwanted attention from the back-seat brigade. Aysha did her best to conceal her concern that Lily had not grasped the import of the collar, and the significance it could have once they were in a settled environment.

'I don't want it to look like you belong to me, Lily.'

'Oh, but I *do*, Aysh.' Lily said, her gaze reinforcing her words. 'I'm sorry, but I think most of the bus has already worked that out.'

Aysha smiled ruefully and silently agreed. But there was no need to make it any more obvious than it already was. At this stage of their relationship the collar was for special occasions. Their day-to-day interactions were so varied that there was no such thing as a 'normal' day – one without external stimulus to keep the relationship fresh.

Lily grasped the need for routine in their relationship. They were sleeping in a new place almost every night, eating different food and living out of their suitcases. Such adventures laid bare any underlying character weakness, but did not prepare them for the daily drudgery of real life that must commence at the end of the trip.

While Aysha promised there would be a surprise in Athens, it did not stop the pair of them making out, en route. At Platamon they had walked to the ruins of a fourteenth century castle on an adjacent headland, finding the place deserted enough to explore each other's bodies.

Lily still found it hard to believe how horny she had become, for her relationship with Robert had never stirred her to such arousal. The variants Aysha had shown her, and the responses these had generated within Lily's body had surprised them both. Aysha had assured Lily they had barely begun what would be an adventurous journey into Bondageland, and Lily had found a childish impatience, awaiting each treat from the sweet shop.

After the two seaside camps they continued south into the Parnassus mountains to Delphi, where after bending tent pegs in the rocky ground trying to erect their tent, Aysha and Lily had sat on a low rock wall at the camping ground as the sun set. Someone had put a Pink Floyd tape on in the bus, letting the cool tones of "Wish You Were Here" drift out through the open door. As darkness came, the two girls had held hands and worked their way through a bottle of the local Moschofilero wine, followed by several glasses of ouzo. The moment was not lost on them, and as the wine disappeared so too did their conversation. It was an evening where music, location and a strange sense of the past imposed on them. With the last light disappearing, a near full moon had risen, illuminating the view over the valley, the small village and the distant Gulf of Corinth. The iconic chords slid through the night:

*"Remember when you were young...*
*You shone like the Sun*
*Shine on, you crazy diamond..."*

Lily and Aysha rocked slowly with the music, each taking in the moment, somewhere in their beings recognising that this song would forever be associated with a slightly alcoholic night at a camping ground in Greece. They had kissed – long, lingering anise-flavoured kisses that needed no words, teeth nibbling lips, tongues probing, the scent of pine trees and shampoo filling their senses.

Lily's heart was fit to burst, and back in their tent she had tried her best to take advantage of Aysha, but had fallen asleep fully clothed on her camp bed, and had been grumpy on the journey into Athens the next day.

\*

Athens had been a series of scorching plazas, alleyways and marble stone buildings exuding the fierce reflected heat of the sun. They discovered that many businesses were closed by 3pm, and then learned the sound and light show at the Acropolis was not performed on either side of the full moon.

They had seen the ruins by moonlight, however, retreating to the Plaka for an evening of bouzouki music, moussaka, and over-priced drinks, before finding their way back to the Hotel Florida.

This time Lily was not going to take no for an answer, and Aysha had to issue stern instructions for Lily to undress, fetch her collar and kneel before her. Lily did so, failing to control her nervousness in the slight trembling of her body. Suddenly the whirring of the air-conditioner poking through the wall seemed intrusive, the tiled floor cold and hard beneath her knees, as she knelt in front of Aysha, presenting the thin black collar on up-turned palms. The cold air had made her nipples betray her again, though this was only part of the reason they now stood erect and hard.

Anticipation had run riot in Lily's mind since Istanbul. She had fallen asleep each night imagining the feel of ropes binding her limbs, of being unable to resist the pain and pleasure being delivered to her body, being unable to protest, unable to see where the next touch was coming from. Once she had woken in the middle of the night to find herself wet in the aftermath of a dream she could not quite remember, but which left her feeling warm and exhausted. She wondered if she'd cried out in her sleep, but had not been brave enough to ask Aysha the next morning, though the Aussie girl had smiled enigmatically at her for no reason.

Lily had thought about the significance of the collar, and wanted it more than anything. She could not envisage how it might function in a normal working-day relationship, but such a thing was too far ahead for her to even think about. Lily was living in the moment, unable to get enough of Aysha and of being her... slave... bitch... did a name even matter? She felt secure and safe in whatever Aysha had in store for her. Trust, Lily – always trust.

Aysha waited several seconds before accepting the offering and lifting the collar from Lily's hands. She slid the collar behind Lily's neck under the mass of chestnut hair, before pulling the two ends together at Lily's throat and lifting her gently to her feet, one hand brushing the erect nipples enough to make Lily shudder. Aysha buckled the collar snugly and pulled a small steel padlock from her pocket, holding it in front of Lily's eyes.

'Do you have any objection, Lily Maddison?'

'No, Aysha,' said Lily, her throat dry.

'You accept that you will obey my commands until such time as this collar is removed?'

'Yes, Aysha.'

'You accept that I shall not impose unreasonable undertakings, but those I do impose are to be done with promptness and without reservation.'

'Yes Aysha.'

Aysha looked deep into Lily's eyes, her finger hooked under the collar, pulling Lily's lips closer to her.

'Do you trust me, Lily?'

'Yes, Aysha...' Aysha was momentarily focussed on the little lock, and Lily felt the snick as it locked the collar in place, and the unexplainable thrill it triggered.

'You will remain collared until I decide otherwise. Do you understand?'

'Yes, Aysha. Thank you, Aysha...'

Aysha took Lily's face in her hands and kissed her deeply. Lily was not sure how to respond – whether it was appropriate for a naked slave to take her mistress in a passionate embrace, but decided against it, though returning the kiss without body contact was so hard.

Aysha broke away and looked pleased, the tip of her tongue flicking over her lips as though savouring the taste of her slave.

'Tonight I have something special in store for you, Lily. Consider it a test of your commitment. And it will be a test, believe me, although I think you will ultimately enjoy it. Do you think you're up for it? Are you willing to prove yourself?'

Lily's stomach turned over with excitement and goosebumps shivered on to her skin.

'Yes, Aysha.'

'Good. Now you need to make yourself presentable. Go wash your face, put some lippy on, go to the loo.'

'Are we going out?' It was gone eleven o'clock, and Lily had been expecting bed to be the next stop. Lily did not know whether to be excited or whether there was some devious twist yet to be played out, for Aysha's craftiness had showed up many times since they had been together.

'Yes we are, now do as you're told!'

Ten minutes later Lily emerged from the bathroom, to be immediately blindfolded by Aysha. Lily's knees went weak again. The blindfold always got her, always started ridiculous thoughts and ideas that she could not stop, and which were inevitably wildly off the mark.

Aysha bound Lily's wrists in front of her with another scarf, then guided her to the bathroom door. Lily could not see the piece of cord tied to the door handle on the far side, which stretched up over the top of the door, now to be tied to Lily's wrist bonds, hauling her wrists above her head where Aysha knotted the cord. Lily now discovered how vulnerable she was, made so in a trice by Aysha with a single pull of the cord, immobilising her hands out of reach and securing her facing the now-closed door. Lily's breathing increased, and though she tried to keep things under control, the light brush of Aysha's fingertips down her flanks, between her legs, then up her stomach and over her breasts did nothing to maintain Lily's composure.

Lily could not see Aysha take a coat hanger from the closet. It was made of wire, with a piece of wooden dowel pinned between the ends of the wire, and it took Aysha only seconds to extract the dowel, giving her a short cane which swished softly when she waved it.

'Lily, darling, I have a new experience for you. It will be painful, but it will also be brief. It will be the first part of your test, and possibly the worst – unless you decide you enjoy it,' she chuckled. 'I want you to show me that you can control your reactions – that you can remain silent to please me. Do you think you can do that?'

'I… I don't know, Aysha…'

'That's the wrong answer, Lily.' There was now a firmness in Aysha's voice. 'I want some positivity in your reply. There's always the possibility that if you do *not* stay silent, the punishment may be lengthened and administered with you gagged. Perhaps *that* is sufficient motivation. Now do you think you can do this for me, Lily?'

'I… yes, Aysha.'

Aysha picked up the fly swat she had bought in Istanbul and began to lightly flick Lily's buttocks, bringing a warm red blush to the surface. She upped the tempo for ten seconds, beating harder, then stopping abruptly.

'This is not your test, Lily, you understand? This is merely a little appetiser, designed to warm you up for the main course, to prepare your lovely – Lilywhite – skin for the real thing.' Aysha ran her hands over Lily's buttocks, squeezing them enough to detect a faint intake of breath from the bound girl. 'Now I will deliver the true test, Lily. There will be three strokes. They will not be soft – because you know I'm not a soft person – and you will make no noise. Is that clear?'

'Yes Aysha.' Lily tried to suppress her trembling, wrapping her fingers around the cord holding her wrists high up the door.

When the first impact of the wooden dowel struck Lily's naked flesh the pain was like nothing she had experienced before. She jerked and just managed to suppress a grunt as the searing pain shot across the creamy flesh, leaving a deep red mark on each buttock. Her breath turned to a series of snorts as Aysha paused, to allow the pain to settle, and to rub her palm over the silky flesh. Then came the second strike, an inch below the first but otherwise matching in severity. Lily caught herself in mid-whine, her eyes screwed up under the blindfold, struggling not to cry out. This time there was no pause and the third stroke followed almost immediately, below the second.

Lily moaned between tightly pursed lips, feeling tears well out between closed eyelids. Aysha rubbed the six matching marks, the first ones starting to turn bruise blue, then slid her fingers between Lily's legs, finding her cleft moist at the entry and deeply slick inside as they penetrated. Lily groaned with a mixture of pain and pleasure, now distracted from the agony burning into her skin. Aysha turned her victim around to face her and kissed her again, lingering with her tongue and stroking her breasts. Lily whimpered.

'That's my darling, my brave Lily. You did so well, Sweetie… that's all the pain – I'm proud of you. Just let it settle down…'

Lily sensed Aysha move away and heard some noises that indicated Aysha was up to whatever was the next step of this… initiation. Lily had begun to think of it as an initiation, though had she reflected sufficiently, she would have acknowledged the pattern of learning that started in Srinagar. *Each step* had been an initiation of sorts. She listened to the rustling and scraping noises as Aysha moved, sat, did something else, and Lily imagined all manner of terrible possibilities.

She learned the next stage of her education five minutes later, as Aysha wrapped a length of the thin clothesline around Lily's waist and tied it snugly at her navel, with the two cord tails hanging down her legs. Aysha turned her round to face the door again and reached between her legs to grasp the tails.

'Spread your legs, Lily,' Aysha ordered quietly. 'Relax,' she added, sensing Lily was like a young filly about to feel her first bridle.

Aysha's fingers ran through Lily's labia, then paused, slick with oil, at Lily's butthole, pressing at the puckered entry enough to lubricate it. Lily tensed and suddenly felt something nuzzling her pussy lips, sliding in on the slipperiness. It was large, but not so large to be uncomfortable. Lily felt the cords pulled, holding the intruder wedged inside her, just before a second invader nosed against her rosebud. She tensed, resenting its presence, then registering Aysha's whispering, soothing, in her ear.

'Don't clench, Lily, just push pack a little, just a little, like you're having a crap.' Lily felt the head of the object push past her sphincter, opening it, wider, then wider. She caught her breath as there was a sudden pain and then the fullness as the object was inside her – mostly. The base of it nestled between her cheeks, also held there by the twin cords.

'Breathe, Lily,' said Aysha, and Lily realised she'd been holding her breath. She exhaled with a groan that might have been pleasure, but which was certainly something she'd never experienced. Aysha pulled the cords tighter, running them up to the waist cord in the small of Lily's back and knotting them there. She slipped her fingers under the cord and tested the tension on the two objects now embedded firmly in Lily's holes. Lily let out a small gasp.

'Nice,' said Aysha. 'You'll soon get used to them.'

A minute later Aysha was standing behind Lily again, this time obliging her to lift one leg, then the other, and Lily found her halter-neck dress being pulled up and buttoned at the back of her neck. Aysha arranged it demurely with gratuitous handling of each breast.

'What are you doing?' Lily asked, as it slowly dawned on her. 'Surely we're not going *out*? With…these… inside me? Aysha…'

'Shush, Lily. Hold steady while I undo the cord from your wrists.' Lily stood while Aysha undid the cord, then the scarves and finally the blindfold. Lily wiped a tear away with the scarf and looked at Aysha, muted horror on her face.

'I can't go out like this…'

'Of course you can, Honey. I'll be with you all the time. We'll go for a little wander, find a bar, have a drink or two, then come back and see what lies in wait for you then.'

'But…'

'Lily! Need I remind you of the commitment you made only half an hour ago?' Lily hung her head and could not bring herself to speak. 'Now, put on your shoes – those mules look good with that dress. You'll be a real eyecatcher.'

Reluctantly Lily pulled out the fawn-coloured cork-soled mules which added two inches to her height, then made to sit on the bed to put them on, realising as she did so how everything tightened between her legs and things slid deeper inside her. Instead, she dropped the shoes on the floor and knelt on one knee to do up the buckle of one, grunting with the effort as the fullness inside grew more intense. Things were moving in unexpected ways.

She buckled up the other shoe and stood up, smoothing down her dress as far as it would go, unable to hide several inches of thigh and aware of the absence of any form of underwear. That thought alone made her redden.

Aysha pre-empted any remark. 'Go brush your hair and we're out of here. Hurry up, Lily!'

While brushing her hair in front of the small bathroom mirror, she had lifted her dress and inspected the damage to her body. Across her butt cheeks were three blue bruised impact lines that still smarted and were tender to the touch. With some contorting and touching with her fingers, she realised that Aysha had played the carrot trick again, and that Lily was now wearing a dildo and a plug fashioned from carrots, each encased in a condom, each with a hole in the base through which the cords secured it in place. God, how devious was this woman! Things were happening so fast! Lily played with the intruders, wiggling them and trying to extract them, but they were too large and too deep to remove without cutting the cords, and Lily was starting to get used to them, so much so that removal might not be her first choice.

But going outside, with no underwear and impaled by two obscene devices like this! Perhaps an instance of someone glimpsing them might not be the worst outcome. What if they began to excite her? She was already deciding she rather liked the fullness of them… What if she got herself off? What if she actually couldn't resist them?

'Lily! Get your sweet arse out here…'

Aysha allowed Lily time on the stairs from their room on the second floor. There was no elevator in the hotel, and with each step Lily felt the objects move inside her in a way she was starting to find stimulating. By the time they had reached the narrow street, the plugs had set up a smooth rhythm which got easier as Lily's juices increased. They walked a couple of blocks to find a small local taverna with a couple of vacant bar stools.

'Sit,' Aysha ordered, locking eyes with Lily. Gingerly, Lily eased herself on to the stool, feeling the intruders penetrate deeper, then the pain as her striated buttocks made contact with the stool.

'Aahhh...' Lily groaned under her breath, sucking up the strange and exciting sensations from her loins. Oh dear god...

They were barely halfway through the first glass of *raki* when two young Americans asked if they could join them. They were around Lily's age, clean-cut, and the taller one – Pete – ostentatiously tried to use an American Express credit card to pay for drinks, only to be told the taverna did not do credit cards. Neither Aysha nor Lily had ever owned a credit card, and the splashy gesture was not wasted on them. They both found it hilarious, though kept straight faces, while Pete explained that he and his companion Kevin were Peace Corps volunteers, on their way to Afghanistan, by way of a short sojourn in Europe. They were impressed to hear that Lily and Aysha had passed through Kabul, and quizzed them on the place.

Lily sensed the pair eyeing them up, and wondering – should the hypothetic situation arise – who would make a move on whom. Lily let Aysha do much of the talking, and was shocked to see her lay her hand on Pete's thigh after the second round of *raki*. The young men had been unsteady before their arrival at the bar, and after the *raki* things went downhill. Pete attempted to kiss Aysha, but had been sidestepped with the ease of one who is used to being hit on, and has all the defences she needs. Aysha stood up, then with expert timing and showmanship, gave Lily a deep throat kiss which left the two volunteers speechless in their wake, as the young women headed back to the hotel, trying not to laugh openly.

Having been restlessly seated on the stool for half an hour, Lily was glad to be on her feet again, but she now found that even in that time things had been working down below. Obviously sensing something, Aysha detoured up several flights of stone steps, with the predicted effect, causing Lily to stop abruptly.

'I... I...' She thrust her hands into the fold in her dress between her legs. She did not know whether to sit down or stand, for the warmth being generated in her loins was pushing her to the edge. The lane was dark and deserted but Aysha was having none of it.

'Lily – don't you dare!' She gripped Lily by the shoulders. 'As long as you wear that collar, you're mine, and you will not climax without my permission! Do you understand?'

'Uh... yes, Aysha...'

'If you feel something coming on, you will ask: "May I please climax, Aysha?" Yes?'

'Yes... Aysha.'

'You may climax only if it pleases me. If I tell you "no, you may not", then you'd better get a hold of yourself or things will be bad for you afterwards. Are we clear?'

Chastened by the severity of the instruction, Lily gulped and nodded.

'Well?'

Lily closed her eyes and leaned against the stair railing, sensing forces building inside her, deep between her legs.

'May I please climax, Aysha?' she asked in a small voice.

'No, Lily, you may not. Get a hold of yourself. This is not about your weakness of the flesh. I don't care how horny and excited you are, you will climax when *I* decide, and not before. I'm prepared to wait a minute or two for you to get some control, but then we'll be off. I'm *not* prepared to stand around watching you hump yourself stupid like a bitch in heat.' Aysha folded her arms and stood glaring at her charge as Lily tried to make her thoughts focus on anything except the rising heat in her groin.

Finally Lily made a move to go on, and managed to stay in control until they were within sight of the hotel, when the last of a further set of steps brought the issue to a head.

'No, Lily!' was Aysha's response again, but it fell on deaf ears, as Lily promptly sat on the last step, her back against the wall and her hands deep between her legs. Had there been any passers-by just then, there would have been little doubt just what was happening to the young woman in the halter-neck dress, but Lily would not have cared, for the plugs inside her had done their job and she could take no more. With a series of grunts and moans she jerked and jammed her hands hard into her groin as the wonderful wave washed over her. Lily was not loud, but her vocabulary was unbecoming for an ex-prefect of Epsom Girls Grammar School, and her English teacher Mrs Thomas would have been both upset and disappointed.

Lily had lost track of where she was, sitting on a hard stone step grinding a large carrot into her vagina and loving every second of it as all that had been building for the last hour came to the fore, and she slumped, exhausted, her legs drawn up, uncaring of any exposed flesh on display.

Aysha was unimpressed. When Lily finally regained coherence, Aysha hauled her to her feet and marched her the rest of the way to the hotel and up the stairs to the second floor. Lily stumbled into the room and made no move as Aysha removed the halter-neck and shoes.

'Go to the loo! With all that *raki*, you need to – it's your last chance.'

'But how…?'

'Go!'

Lily found she could still urinate with the big carrot in place. It was not pretty, but she was past caring. She felt warm and sated, and shuffled back to the bedroom. Aysha was in an unforgiving mood, at once binding Lily's hands behind her, palm to palm, and gagging her with a wadded scarf tied in place. Then she forced her on to the bed, removing her shoes, and binding her ankles.

'You'll be sorry, now, Lily. I'm disappointed in you. I thought you were stronger than that. I thought your word meant more than that. I thought *I* meant more than that!'

Lily didn't try to reply, though a tear slipped from the corner of her eye. She lay on her side facing the wall as Aysha undressed and spooned up behind her, draping her arm around the bound girl. Lily knew she was in deep trouble, but could do nothing about it. They die was cast, and she would have to take whatever punishment was given.

Fundamental to Lily's punishment was her mind, which Aysha knew only too well. Nothing Aysha could say or do would equal what went on in Lily's mind as she looked back on the events of the last few hours. Lily was slowly coming to her senses sufficiently to realise what she had done, and how she had failed the big test. The guilt took hold and she began to envisage all manner of punishments that Aysha might inflict, ranging from withdrawing her collar to some form of severe beating.

Aysha knew exactly what Lily would be thinking, and decided the very act of the guilty conscience was going to be enough. Aysha had merely to keep Lily awake, to keep her mind furiously analysing her failures, for the punishment to be effective without Aysha lifting a finger. The placement of two clothes pegs on Lily's nipples was sufficient to keep her conscious and focussed, while Aysha drifted off to sleep, her slow, sad breathing the final blow to Lily's pride as she lay in the darkness.

Somewhere during the night the pegs had come off, though the carrot plugs remained in place and Aysha had woken long enough to play with them, using the small amount of slack in the cords to slide them in and out, sensing the build-up within Lily as her inevitable fantasies took her away in the darkness. Only this time, the fantasies did not materialise, and while Lily tried to make herself comfortable, squirming from one side to the other, she was unable to bring things to a head herself. Occasionally, if Lily thought herself approaching an orgasm, Aysha would twist and squeeze Lily's nipples sufficiently for her to yelp into the drool-soaked gag while the lusted-for feelings of pleasure were driven away. Somewhere, in between Lily trying to climax and Aysha provoking it then driving it away, the pair finally fell asleep together.

The sun was streaming in when Lily awoke, her hands and feet still bound, her loins engorged with a strange fullness – the reason for which Lily only remembered as the *raki*-fuelled fuzziness drifted away. Her mouth tasted foul and she chewed disconsolately on the soaked wad of material between her teeth. She struggled to turn on to her other side, so she could face Aysha. One wrist had gone numb and her feet had become tangled in the sheet. Aysha was watching her when she finally completed the manoeuvre, and raised herself on one elbow to study her captive.

'You remember what you did, last night?'

Lily could not look her in the eye. 'Uh huh. I-hrrry.'

Aysha reached into the auburn hair and untied the gag.

'Did you say you're sorry, or you're horny?' she demanded.

It was one of the rare occasions when Lily could read her companion, and did not miss the glint of Aysha's eye.

'Uh... both...?'

The last day in Athens passed in a drawn-out morning of love-making, Lily finally with her limbs free and unencumbered. The events of the night had left both girls limp and languid, now slipping into a dreamy day with the "Do Not Disturb" sign on the door and sunbeams streaming through the open window. The rising heat of the stone-clad city aroused both girls like cats awakening from a nap on a sunny ledge.

Still collared, Lily lay in Aysha's arms and acknowledged her failure, pleading for forgiveness, which was freely given.

'I can't believe I was so randy at the instigation of two carrots,' she muttered, aghast at her own behaviour.

'It wasn't merely two carrots, my darling Lily,' said Aysha contentedly, stretching out a languorous arm to gently stroke the birthmark on Lily's breast. 'You got the literal "carrot-and-stick" treatment. How is your lovely bottom this morning?'

'Bruised. Sore.'

'It'll pass,' Aysha opined. 'It's important you have something to remind you of the night, of your... lapse.'

'I'm so sorry, Aysha,' Lily mumbled for the umpteenth time. She was not sure whether her mortification was driven by her failure in self-control or by the fact that it was instigated by a vegetable.

'No more apologies, Honey. I think we've established you're a little slut who will stop at nothing when it comes to self-gratification, even if it means doing it in a public place like a cat in heat.'

'Please don't remind me, Aysh...' Lily buried her head in the pillow. 'I've said I was sorry...'

'Yes, you have, Sweetie. Multiple times. No need for more remorse. I have accepted your apologies, but they will not absolve you of future training and punishment, but that may be a little way off. Part of your punishment will be to think about what I will do to you next. Knowing you, your thoughts will be more guilt-filled and contrite than anything I can dream up.'

'You do dream up some pretty weird stuff though, Aysh.'

Aysha smiled at the ceiling. 'Yes, I do, don't I. I wouldn't want to be in the shoes of any slave in my care... Now get your pretty head under the sheets and see what you can do to warm me up a little.'

They made time to take in the Acropolis and the Agora, but Aysha claimed the heat was making her dizzy, and they retired to the hotel after an early dinner, ready for the two-day drive to the Bulgarian border. Lily had tried to be interested in the view from the Acropolis, and they had persuaded another tourist to take a polaroid of them standing in front of the Parthenon, but neither of their hearts was in it. Lily did her best to imagine what the place must have been like over two thousand years before, but the number of tourists and the heat both distracted her, and she had been unable to make the connection as she had with the nameless castles in Turkey and the quiet ruins of Persepolis.

\*

They had slept most of the journey from Athens back to the beach-side camping ground at Platamon, where it had rained and cast a depressing air that split the campers into the bar-frequenters and the tent-dwellers. Lily had almost got over her debacle in Athens, having reconciled herself to the fact that whatever the outcome, she was still the wearer of Aysha's collar, and still had the extraordinary experience of Athens to warm her heart, even if it would forever remain a shared embarrassment between them.

Over the previous month each hotel stop had proven a new intimate adventure for Lily, as she became a more enlightened acolyte under Aysha's wing. Now, as they approached the Iron Curtain, there would be no more hotels and – Lily suspected – the laid-back travel routine would be different, though she did not know how. In the back of her mind the great political amalgamation that was the Communist Bloc now lay like a grim creature waiting to engulf them.

# the submissive spy

The crossing into Bulgaria – the parting of the Iron Curtain – turned out to be a super-efficient exercise, and they found themselves in a green and wild landscape, though without the snow-caps of Turkey. Aysha again slept much of the way, claiming it was probably just the time of the month, although a little runnel of concern had reared up in Lily's mind, for she had not seen her friend suffer any form of illness in the nine weeks they had been together. This compared with others on the trip who had been persistently laid low by everything from food poisoning to hangovers.

Sofia, the capital, had proved interesting, if not in the severe, Big Brother way that they were half expecting. Little English was spoken, and while making the mandatory money exchange had proven problematic, the place seemed pleasant enough. As they did a city tour on their second day, Sofia had impressed them with its cleanliness, the ridiculous absence of traffic, and the reticence and uncertainty of the population when faced with a busload of very casually-clothed westerners.

Lily had done the city tour without Aysha, who professed to have a bug and a slight temperature, opting to curl up in her sleeping bag in the tent, claiming she'd be better after a day or two in bed.

The reality of the overland journey was that days in bed were not an option in many cases, and Lily fretted for her friend as they travelled into Romania for two nights at a camping ground, sited in a shady oak forest on the outskirts of Bucharest. The city had suffered badly from an earthquake earlier that year, and everywhere they went on the city tour here, they saw giant props supporting buildings scarred by the effects of the quake. Again, Aysha had forgone the tour, leaving Lily to tell her that in Lily's view the Romanians were much friendlier and more laid-back, and that there were a few more things to buy with the obligatory money change. As they had done in Bulgaria, the group was treated with a cultural evening, although Lily attended it only after a severe talking to by Aysha saying Lily was not to miss out on things just because Aysha was tired and wanted to sleep.

But Lily had observed that it was more than just fatigue affecting her friend, if Aysha's more frequent trips to the toilet were anything to go by, and she had admitted to throwing up more than once. Lily wanted her to see a doctor, but Aysha refused, though making a conciliatory offer that she'd consider it if there was still a problem when they crossed into the Soviet Union. There, at least, they would have an Intourist guide for the ten-day passage through to Poland. Lily did not see what difference that made, but acceded to Aysha's request. The next day they reached the border, at the appointed time and place, to be admitted to the largest country in the world, under the all-encompassing power of Leonid Brezhnev and the KGB. Though she could not explain it, Lily was unable to shake off a feeling of foreboding.

# the submissive spy

* * *

# CHAPTER 13 – The Iron Curtain

It was a grey, overcast morning threatening rain when they left the Sofia campsite. At the front of the bus, Wayne took the microphone for the usual day's briefing.

'Glad to see you've all scrubbed up properly,' he said. 'I can't impress enough the importance of conducting ourselves correctly at this border. Only Iran is on a par with this one.' He had stressed the previous day that they were to dress respectfully and be on their best behaviour, and the group had complied, refraining from outrageous tee-shirts and skimpy tops. 'The other thing about this place that makes it a little special is that we will have a local Intourist guide with us the whole time. Intourist is the Soviet Tourist Agency, responsible for all the bookings and itineraries of travellers. Our guide – her name is Ludmila – will be responsible for us. But here's the catch. I haven't travelled with Ludmila before, but chances are she is probably KGB. For the uninitiated, that's the "Committee for State Security".' He paused for effect, noting a number of mildly surprised expressions. 'It's something we've learned over the years of travelling through here. Do *not* ask her about it. Don't do anything to embarrass either her or yourselves, and be aware of what you're talking about in her earshot. That said, there's no need to be paranoid or stand-offish. I've been through here three times and I've never had any issues – yet. They just like to keep an eye on things and not have us wandering around unattended.'

They reached the Prut River, the border between Romania and the Soviet Union – or more specifically, the Moldavian Soviet Socialist Republic, a small and insignificant republic within the USSR. The Romanian border officials provided a smooth exit from their country and the yellow Sundowners bus crossed the steel bridge over the river near its discharge into the Black Sea. Lily looked up the river on the Soviet side, noting an occasional watch tower standing above the trees lining the river bank. On the eastern side of the river they pulled into a fenced compound, stopping inside a cavernous drive-through shed. The walls and roof were of unlined, khaki-coloured corrugated iron, adorned with a series of political posters featuring rugged male and female workers against symbolic backdrops of industry and farmland. To one side a small complex of concrete block offices within the shed housed the bureaucracy required for admission of people into the country. A large poster of Leonid Brezhnev in a navy suit bedecked with medals watched benevolently over the workings of the border guards. A banner stretched across the end of the building with the dates "1917 – 1977" beneath some presumed exhortative slogan.

The travellers disembarked and emptied the bus, placing their luggage on long stainless steel benches outside the offices, along with the tents and camping gear. For the next three hours they watched and opened their luggage for examination, as the customs officials scrutinised their belongings for pornographic or counter-revolutionary material or any items that – according to a notice on the wall in English, French and German – might be considered "politically and economically harmful to the USSR". The list of forbidden imports included "army weapons and ammunition, pornographic pictures, printed matter, clichés, negatives, films, manuscripts drawings and similar articles".

Lily and Aysha stood off to the side, waiting uneasily as sniffer dogs examined all the camping gear, then the line of suitcases. The mood was quiet amongst the travellers. Even the least astute of the back seat brigade recognised this was not the place to make jokes. In their dark grey uniforms and caps with over-sized crowns, most of the customs officers appeared to have some fluency in English, but not in sense of humour. The travellers had been warned about this; warned also that on departure, any travel diaries and journals might be scrutinised for derogatory passages about the USSR.

A cold breeze funnelled through the shed, as the overlanders queued up for entry stamps in their passports, then again at a single window to purchase roubles, needing to declare the full amount of foreign currency and travellers' cheques in their possession. In the same breath as he exhorted them not to mention Aleksandr Solzhenitsyn, Wayne had counselled them to ensure they got receipts for any and all exchanges, since these would be checked against currency in their possession as they exited. It was a cheerless introduction to the country as they slowly repacked, and reboarded the bus.

Across the road from the border complex they pulled into a small café and picked up their Intourist guide, Ludmilla, who would accompany them on their passage through the USSR to the border with Poland. Ludmilla – or Luda, as she offered as a simplification – had been born in Odessa, their first stop in the Soviet Union. She was slim and pretty with blonde hair wrapped in a plait around her head, but came over as aloof to the faces staring back at her from the rows of bus seats. She spoke clearly into the microphone but with a strong accent, telling the group that she had been to university in Odessa, providing the first of the vast repository of statistics that in her eyes – or the eyes of her scriptwriter – would define her country.

Like the border officers, Luda appeared to have taken note of the official embargo on a sense of humour, and as the rain began to fall, she retreated to the front seat and contented herself with providing directions to the driver.

Lily listened to their guide, wondering if she really was KGB. Lily did not read spy novels, but she knew a little about the KGB, and pretty much all of that was not the stuff to put in an advertising brochure. Lily had read Solzhenitsyn's novella *One Day in the Life of Ivan Denisovich* and it was enough to suggest that the Committee for State Security had a lot to answer for. She looked at Luda, not many years older than Lily, and wondered just how a person could be a part of such an organisation. An unexpected chill ran down her back.

Lily had given the window seat to Aysha, as she had done for the last few days, allowing the older girl a chance to place a sweater against the window to cushion her head as she dozed. Lily was becoming more worried about her friend with each day, as Aysha showed no signs of returning to her normal mellow self. She decided to broach the subject with Wayne, when they reached Odessa. In the interim, the rain-soaked flatlands of the Black Sea coast slid past, green and monotonous. Somewhere along the way they passed into the Ukrainian Soviet Socialist Republic, though the pictures of Brezhnev and the exhorting production posters – if that's what they were – continued in the same vein.

The road was of concrete, like the ones they had travelled on in Afghanistan – noisy and tedious from the joints in the slabs. They passed through several small towns of unimaginative grey blocks of flats and shop frontages devoid of content advertising. Many had partially white-washed windows, as though to conceal the wares from prospective customers.

They reached Odessa late in the day, passing more of the ubiquitous bland apartment blocks, and a population singularly incurious of the yellow bus. In contrast to the Romanians, the locals rarely responded to a wave or a smile from the tourists. The fashion, too, was different, for the Romanians had exhibited a degree of colour and style in their dress, but now this had faded to greys and browns, with a marked absence of young women in the streets.

Luda was providing all the information she thought they needed to know about Odessa – that it had a population of over nine hundred thousand, had 16 technical colleges and twenty-three technical training centres, and more than seventy thousand students, making it the fifth largest educational centre in the Soviet Union. At the end of the long wet day, the information was received in silence.

The campsite was on the edge of a forest just before they reached the city proper – the grass long and the showers without hot water. There was a cafeteria offering an assortment of foods, dispensed by unsmiling women in white coats with chef-like hats who spoke no English. Lily had pitched the tent by herself, set up the camp beds and carried both suitcases to their usual position at the head of the beds, before getting Aysha on to her bed. Lily dined with the others in the restaurant and brought borsht and bread to Aysha, who managed to eat most of it, but only at Lily's insistence, before curling up in her sleeping bag.

She sought out Wayne, and found him working through expenses at a vacant table in the cafeteria. The place was noisy, since the darkness and rain had driven most campers indoors, and now had them engaged in games of cards, reading or drinking beer. Wayne had a bottle of Baltika beer beside him, and looked up when Lily pulled out a chair and sat down. She had long ago decided the job of a courier called for enormous patience – with local officials, local cultures and the travellers themselves – and she wouldn't have done the job for anything. With his thin beard and rough good looks, Wayne was competent and made the most of the perks of the job, not least being the availability of a tent partner of the opposite sex, his current being one of the American girls.

'What's up, Lily?'

'Nothing to do with bad food or cold water,' she told him with a slight smile. 'I'm sure you've had plenty of that.'

He grinned wryly. 'Wouldn't expect it from you two, anyway,' he said, an what she took as an awkward acknowledgement of the fact she and Aysha were typically uncomplaining. The reality was that they'd had very little real interaction with Wayne during the course of the trip. He put down his pen. 'Wanna beer?'

Lily shook her head. Wayne sensed this was not a social call. The two young women kept themselves to themselves unless something of real concern arose.

'Aysha's not well.' He was at once attentive.

'How so?'

'She's been really tired, not eating, throwing up a bit... I think some diarrhoea... a bit of fever...'

'How long for?'

'Since Athens, I think.'

'Not some 24-hour food poisoning thing, then.'

She shook her head. She figured Wayne would have seen and experienced his fair share of illnesses over several overland trips.

'She's been resisting going to the doctor. Likes to be strong, you know?' Lily was having trouble concealing her concern, now that she was sitting with someone other than Aysha for the first time. 'She keeps insisting she'll get over it, but she doesn't seem to be improving.'

Wayne thought for a minute, then consulted a lever-arch folder on top of his papers, flicking through pages and sections delineated by orderly coloured tabs. 'Divided by country and cities along the route,' he explained, as he alighted on the particular page. 'These are our notes, and they're always being added to by other couriers and drivers, so that our experiences are shared.' He skimmed his finger down the page and flicked it over to read the other side. 'Do you think it can wait until Kiev? Kiev is twice the size of this place and has a couple of private hospitals that the foreign community use, according to these notes. We have a tour of Odessa tomorrow, then we're in Kiev the day after. I'd be happier having her looked at there, if possible.'

'Uh... sure. Whatever you think.'

'If there's a sudden change, we'll do something here, but I think Kiev will have a better facility, honestly. We'll have an additional local guide there.' Lily stood up. 'Talk to me at breakfast tomorrow, unless anything changes drastically, okay?'

'Sure.'

Aysha insisted she just wanted to sleep the next morning, which Lily relayed to Wayne, and the group set out for the city tour of Odessa. They saw the two sides of the Soviet Union, despite Luda's emphasis on the modernness of the city – the department store, the railway station and the trams. In Lily's eyes the script was all about the twentieth century, in an ironic comparison with the west, where historic architecture was preserved. Here, beyond the Soviet showpieces lay the cold grey apartment blocks and the continued absence of vehicular traffic. Lily also saw many uniforms, both military and police, and a large number of young people also, though she could not work out if these were school uniforms or youth groups.

Queues were ubiquitous, often starting at 5am, though Luda seemed to see nothing unusual in this, and queuing for lunch in a cafeteria was part of their experience. Lily ended up with macaroni, some sort of mince in a batter case, together with rock cakes and apple juice. It was no wonder the locals were solidly built, she thought.

Luda pointed out a Dollar Store, where goods could be purchased in US dollars – fridges, cameras, even cars. Wayne had told them that a black market existed for US dollars which could get three to four times the official rate, offered by locals wanting to take advantage of the Dollar Store. Luda evidently did not see the irony.

Despite the interminable facts and figures Luda threw at them, her personality was starting to come to the fore, as the travellers expressed their interest in more mundane aspects like free medical care and nominal student rental. The limited range of goods in shops was something Luda evidently considered normal.

The wide streets and nineteenth century architecture of the old parts of the city only went so far, Lily reckoned. Beyond downtown everything seemed dirty, coated with a layer of dust and mud, the drabness of the Stalinist architecture, the clothes, the streets and the very people themselves. Lily had been worried about Aysha, but when she returned in early afternoon, the dreary character of the city had rubbed off and she found she already disliked the country. The sun came out briefly and the two girls sat outside the tent as Lily recounted her observations. Faced with two weeks before they emerged from the Eastern Bloc into West Germany, Lily could barely contain her misgivings.

'We're leaving early tomorrow,' she told Aysha. 'We'll be in Kiev just after lunch, and Wayne said we'll get you to a doctor – and don't argue! This has gone on long enough.'

Aysha nodded her defeat, smiling wanly and putting her hand on Lily's.

The drive to Kiev was long and monotonous, a grey, overcast day that brought its mood to Lily and Aysha. The Ukraine was the bread basket of the Soviet Union, fought over across the centuries for its grain fields and more lately its oil. They watched the passing fields of wheat stretching from horizon to horizon – when the road was not actually lined with trees. In these stretches, to suspicious foreigners it was as though something was being deliberately hidden behind the double rows of trees. There were a few 'knife and fork' signs supposedly indicating a traveller's restaurant, but none seemed to be open, and they had to resort to snacks. The mood was not helped when they were flagged down by traffic police in one of many small observation boxes along the way, where Luda was advised they had taken a wrong turning and were not permitted to be on this road. It was a major loss of face for her, as they were obliged to backtrack twenty kilometres to a junction to take a different route.

They eventually arrived at the large Kiev camp site in early afternoon, with many of the group visiting the cafeteria before bothering putting up tents. The site was busy with other travellers, including many Germans, whom Lily assumed would be from the Eastern part of that country. It was here they collected their local Kiev guide, a slight woman of about thirty called Natasha with a cheerful smile, her mousy hair cut like a man's.

After a brief lunch, the bus headed into central Kiev, carrying Lily, Aysha, Luda, Natasha, Wayne and the driver, Craig. As they moved through the outer suburbs of Kiev, Lily took in more dreary blocks of multi-storied apartments, which Natasha called *khrushchevka,* and of which she appeared inordinately proud – the validation of her country's modernisation in housing its people. Coming from green, suburban Auckland, Lily found the sight simply depressing.

Near the centre of the city the architecture changed, with larger, older buildings, wider streets and glimpses of golden domes amid forested areas overlooking a broad river. They pulled into a car park outside a two-storey building looking as though it was built in the time of the Tsars, painted in white and baby blue with ornate plaster lintels and columns guarding the entrance.

'Once was palace for when Tsars visited Kiev,' Natasha explained. 'Now is people's health clinic. Behind is Vatutin Hospital, named for General

Vatutin who was hero of Great Patriotic War here in Kiev. Biggest in Kiev - built in 1954. Has six hundred and twenty-five beds, many operating theatres.'

Lily looked at the eight storey edifice of brutal architecture looming over the blue and white elegance in front. It did not seem like a welcoming institution for healing.

Inside the clinic, they waited barely ten minutes in a hospital-green waiting room devoid of decoration save for several exhortative posters obviously relating to health, and the need to work together for the benefit of the nation. Two doors led off the waiting room, to the left and right, each signposted by a series of directions in Cyrillic characters, with occasional numbers. Lily had never felt so helpless at not even being able to read, let alone pronounce the words.

There were a dozen other people waiting placidly on hard wooden seats, as Natasha spoke earnestly with a solid woman in a white uniform behind an opaque sliding window. Lily could sense the unaccommodating response from the window, then insistence from Natasha.

Craig and Luda had remained in the car park with the bus, while Wayne had accompanied the three women. Now Lily sat holding Aysha's hand. Aysha had been tired and uncommunicative, as though finally admitting defeat in coming to the clinic. Lily found the whole scene surreal, sitting in this waiting room listening to the strange accents of a language she could not understand. The words sounded strangely beautiful, soft and slurry to an ear brought up on English, French and German.

The other visitors stared incuriously at the foreigners, then ignored them. The window closed, then opened again after a minute, revealing a different woman, who might have been a manager of some sort. Again, there was a discussion with Natasha, and the woman leaned her head through the window to look at Wayne, Lily and Aysha, before seeming to nod in agreement with Natasha.

A few minutes later a white-coated, middle-aged woman with greying hair tucked into a bucket-like white hat appeared through one of the doors. She spoke to Natasha, who came over to where the three travellers sat. Lily sensed that as foreigners they were receiving priority treatment, as a demonstration of the efficiency of the Socialist Republic, but she was not complaining. Natasha asked Lily:

'You are her friend, yes?'

'Yes. I want to come with her when she is examined.'

Natasha translated for the white-clad woman, who shrugged.

'Okay. This is doctor – she will do examination. I think maybe you wait here, Wayne, yes?'

'I'll go wait in the bus with the others,' said Wayne. 'You'll stay with Aysha and Lily?'

'Of course.'

The three women followed the doctor through the door and along an antiseptic-smelling corridor into a small internal room with two metal chairs, an examination table, a washbasin, and a small writing desk and swivel seat. Underneath an official-looking notice Lily could not understand, a small bedside table carried a stainless steel sphygmomanometer and cuff in an open tray. Natasha gestured to the girls to be seated, while she remained standing as the doctor soaped and washed her hands. Natasha took Aysha's passport and translated for the doctor as she made notes on a form attached to a clipboard.

Through Natasha, the doctor asked about symptoms. Aysha was lethargic and disinterested, so Lily gave her version of the things she knew about, and the time line. As Aysha sat placidly, the doctor took her blood pressure and temperature, her expression giving away nothing as she scribbled results on the clipboard and asked more specific questions. Did she have joint pain? Stomach pain? Was she vomiting? Aysha answered in a monotone, which in itself made Lily anxious, for Aysha's very spirit normally came out in her cadence, her forthrightness.

The doctor said something, which Natasha translated as: 'Please take off your clothes.'

Aysha began to disrobe, not caring that at least one of those present was neither her friend nor a doctor. Lily watched the slowness of her movements, noted the dark shadows under her eyes. Her meekness was so out of character it made Lily want to cry.

There were no hooks on which to put her clothes, so Lily took them and draped them neatly on Aysha's chair. Aysha removed her shoes and socks ending up standing in her bra and panties. Though it was summer, the room was cool, but Aysha's face was flushed.

The doctor said something – clearly indicating the last of the clothing should be removed, regardless of whether there were others present. Her manner was brusque, as though foreigners could expect no better treatment than the last *babushka* she had seen. Aysha seemed not to mind, or more to the point could not summon the strength to object, and moments later stood naked. Lily felt guilty as her loins stirred, aroused by the svelteness of Aysha's body. The light in the small room was harsh, so different from the gloom of their tent or the ill-lit hotel rooms where they had embraced, illuminating every hair and tiny mole on Aysha's body. It also showed the complete absence of hair at Aysha's shaven crotch, which did not go unnoticed by the two Russian women. But Lily missed the inner glow that

Aysha normally radiated, that manifested itself in her sharp observations and her confidence.

The doctor examined Aysha, palpating her body as she stood, then lay down on the examination table. She gestured for Aysha to remove her glasses and looked into Aysha's eyes and mouth, then examined her fingers and toes, before palpating her torso and listening to her breathing with a stethoscope.

The doctor gestured to Aysha to put her clothes on and commenced a long conversation with Natasha, whose expression was serious. She turned to Lily.

'The doctor thinks your friend has hepatitis. So now I ask about you. You are sharing a tent with Aysha?'

'Yes.'

'You are close to her, yes? Closest person in group?'

'Yes.' There was no need for translation. The doctor then asked a further question.

'Are you lovers?'

Lily was taken aback and for a moment did not know what to say. She didn't know whether such a thing was legal in the Soviet Union, and what bad path it might lead down. Natasha saw her confusion and smiled gently, putting a hand on Lily's arm.

'Doctor asks for medical reason. We do not care what you do in private. But if you are lovers, you are at higher risk, no? Please tell me truth.'

Lily nodded. 'Yes.' Her voice was a whisper. She did not know what hepatitis meant by way of symptoms and treatment and where this whole thing was going.

'You must let doctor examine you, too, Lily. You are person most likely to also contract disease. You have been sharing tent, food, all sorts of things.'

Lily submitted to the thermometer and the sphygmomanometer cuff tight on her bicep, as the doctor listened to the sound of her blood, peered in her eyes then at her fingernails.

'Please undress for doctor.'

Lily felt her hands shaking. The focus of the whole examination had turned on her with no warning. What if she had this disease too? As she undid her denim shirt she found herself thinking of any recent instances of the runs she had noticed. Had she had any other symptoms like Aysha's? She stepped out of her skirt and sandals and was momentarily self-conscious as the doctor waved impatiently at her to remove her underwear.

Lily was more uncomfortable than Aysha, standing naked before the three of them, and covered her pubis as best she could. The doctor ignored her modesty and palpated her body thoroughly. Lily wasn't sure if there was a disapproving cluck of the tongue as Lily was also obliged to reveal her hairless crotch, but the seriousness of the situation dominated her thoughts and fears.

There was a discussion between Natasha and the doctor, who left the room.

'Doctor thinks maybe you are okay, Lily, but you must both have urine and blood tests to confirm. Whole bus will also need to take tests. We will organise these now for you two, plus people outside on bus. Nurse will come to take blood and give you things for urine test. I will go to talk to Wayne. You get dressed now. Okay?'

'Sure,' said Lily, as Natasha left the room. As she pulled on her clothes, Lily realised she had not asked about the implications of hepatitis, and what it might mean. What was the treatment? Things had happened so quickly she had missed the opportunity to ask.

Lily sat next to Aysha. 'You okay?'

'Just really tired, Sweetie. Feel like shit, really. I could sleep for a week. Bit nauseous. Joints feel like I have the flu – you know, achy? My back especially.'

'Your eyes are yellow,' Lily said quietly. 'I hadn't noticed before. Must be the glasses.' Aysha nodded.

'What do you think they'll do?'

'Dunno. I've no idea what the treatment is. But we have to confirm it first, I guess.'

A nurse of about their own age appeared – blonde, capped, with a badge likely proclaiming her name in the unreadable alphabet. She carried the clipboard the doctor had used and said something they did not understand, but the friendly gesture to follow her was evident. She took them further down the corridor to a white-tiled room with a number of cabinets and gestured to a metal chair on one side of a small table. Aysha sat down.

The nurse pronounced Aysha's name tentatively from the clipboard and smiled at Aysha's acknowledgement, motioning her to roll up her sleeve, before wrapping a rubber tube around Aysha's bicep and tapping for the vein. She produced a glass hypodermic with stainless steel grips and took out a needle from a drawer, fitting it to the syringe, before expertly taking a blood sample from Aysha's arm. This went into a test tube with a stopper and the nurse copied the details from the clipboard.

'Li-ly?' she asked, reading from the second page.

Lily swapped with Ayesha and a second syringe and needle were produced from the drawer and the process was repeated. The nurse then took two small jars from one of the cabinets and wrote labels on them, ensuring she gave the right jar to the right person. She gestured for them to follow her down the corridor again, to a door with a sign outside it, holding it open to indicate the toilet stalls inside. By mime she indicated filling the jars halfway, screwing the top back on, and returning to the room they had just left.

The girls entered the washroom – gloomy in the light of flickering fluorescent tubes. It had exposed water pipes above the half dozen wash basins on one tiled wall, opposite six toilet stalls. The place reeked of disinfectant and looked as though it had seen little maintenance over many decades of strenuous use. The untiled wall sections needed painting and the concrete floor bore a history of unknown stains.

The girls tentatively inspected the stalls separated by tiled walls, selecting two of the least objectionable ones – the only ones with any paper in the dispensers – and eventually completed their task, washing their hands thoroughly with a single piece of grey soap before returning to the room where the nurse awaited them.

From the blood-sampling room, the nurse escorted them back to the seats the reception area. They sat in silence, watching people come and go, checking in with the lady at the reception window, before sitting down to wait their turn. Lily checked the car park and saw the empty bus, figuring the others were likewise getting examined. It was late in the afternoon when Wayne, Craig, Natasha and Luda appeared with another man, also in a white coat.

Craig and Luda continued to the bus while Wayne sat beside Lily on the bench.

'Lily and Aysha, this is Doctor Fischer. He is from East Germany and speaks good English. He works in the big hospital behind this place.'

Doctor Fischer was in his early thirties, with sandy hair and a moustache and sideboards that stood out as stylish amongst the Russian men in the street. Underneath his white coat he wore jeans and a beige roll-neck sweater. Lily realised it was the first pair of jeans she could recall seeing since they had arrived. She thought he was quite handsome but somehow slightly effeminate. He nodded politely to the girls, but did not offer to shake hands.

'You may call me Konrad,' he said genially. 'I work here on an exchange program with some Russian doctors who work in East Germany, and I think I speak reasonably good English. I'm afraid the news is… well, good and bad. Our examinations are subject to confirmation with the blood and urine tests, but so far we think that only Aysha has contracted the disease.'

'The disease?' asked Lily.

'Yes, we think it's most likely hepatitis – Hepatitis A in all likelihood. It's a very contagious disease – usually picked up through contaminated food and drink, or bad hygiene. You have seen Aysha's symptoms. They could be worse, so perhaps she has been lucky. I think you, Lily, are also lucky in that you don't appear to have caught it, despite close proximity to Aysha.'

Fischer's English was fluent enough to prompt Lily's next question:

'I'm sensing a 'but'...'

Fischer looked at Wayne, who said:

'We can't take Aysha with us in this condition. We are going to have to leave her here.'

'What?'

Fischer stepped in. 'Lily, there is no cure for Hepatitis A except rest and a steady diet – and quarantine. It's affected her liver, and could be serious if she is not given the opportunity to recover quietly.'

'Then I'll stay with her.'

'Sorry, Lily, but it doesn't work that way,' Wayne said. 'Our trip is pre-planned and pre-paid, and all the people on it must be accounted for at each overnight stop, save for emergencies such as this one, where a letter of exemption will be obtained.'

'But she can still travel, surely? Maybe she'll sleep most of the way.' Lily was talking as though Aysha was not even there.

'There are several issues,' Fischer said. 'Firstly, she will put the whole bus at risk through her infection. Everything she touches could leave traces of the disease. She will likely not eat properly, since you are in a different place most days, nor will she get rest. It's a contagious disease and the authorities do not want it being carried right across Russia.'

'But... but... where will she stay?'

'She will have a single room in the hospital next door, and will remain there until she is strong enough and her tests are negative.'

Lily's face fell. 'How long will that take?'

'Minimum a couple of weeks. Maybe longer. We cannot tell precisely. A person may be contagious for up to a month after contracting the disease. The problem is that we don't know when this actually occurred. Symptoms can take anywhere from two to six weeks after exposure, but we have no way to work out what that period is in the case of Aysha. So we have to assume it is the most recent date. She will have to pass time in quarantine then be considered healthy enough to travel.'

'Can't she fly – on to England, I mean?' She could barely control the quaver in her voice.

'She won't get clearance from here and the airline won't accept her. They don't want to expose their passengers to this, for obvious reasons,' said Fischer.

Lily was crying now. She didn't know what to do, as all her arguments had been met with implacable logic.

'But I could stay here...' she repeated.

'There isn't anywhere to stay, honey,' Wayne said. 'You can't stay in this hospital. Aysha will be in isolation, in any case.'

Only then did Aysha put her hand on Lily's shoulder. 'I'll be okay, Sweetheart. It's a hospital, after all. Leave some books from the bus for me.' She did her best to summon up a wan smile.

'Aysha will have to stay here tonight,' Fischer said. 'Wayne and I have discussed this. You can go back to the camping ground and collect Aysha's things. Natasha will go with you, and you can bring them back here. We don't want Aysha to come into contact with any more people. Tomorrow the remaining people on the trip will all have to come in for blood and urine tests, and we will probably have the results of today's tests.'

Lily did her best to control the tears in the bus back to the camping ground. She had been unable to embrace or kiss Aysha goodbye, and no amount of solicitousness from Wayne or the two Russian women could lessen her desolation. Doctor Fischer had taken her aside at the entrance and told her:

'I have contacts in Berlin. I will arrange an address for you to collect letters from Aysha. It is not easy for a quarantine patient to communicate outside, but we will do what we can. We will discuss this further when you come back with her things.'

It was a small consolation, and one which did not really sink into Lily's brain, as she knelt in the tent between the two camp beds, packing Aysha's case. She wore latex gloves that Doctor Fischer had provided, as a precaution against any last-minute infection, and despite cautions, she had taken two polaroids out of Aysha's case – one of her on the beach in Turkey, taken before Lily had been bound to the tree – and one of the pair of them at the Swat tea shop.

She looked at the photos with a sick feeling in her stomach, her heart breaking at this separation, at the thought of her beloved Aysha left alone in a system and country where nobody spoke English. The situation was only saved from a complete catastrophe by the presence of Konrad Fischer and his promise that he would ensure she was well cared for.

It was dark when Lily and Natasha took a taxi to the hospital – the large anonymous block behind the clinic. The streets were quiet, even though rush hour was not long gone. Traffic was minimal and there were few pedestrians, as Lily sat in silence with Natasha in the back seat of the yellow Gaz cab. Lily stared at the shops – if they even were such. She realised again that there was no advertising, no pictures, no logos to announce the goods and services on offer. Everything subsided into a grey, colourless, featureless world that seemed to rub off on to the inhabitants. The strange city with its unreadable signs and the absence of people were dream-like to Lily. She had barely convinced herself that this was happening, that she was leaving behind a tent now devoid of all Aysha's personal things that had made it distinctly *theirs*.

The foyer of the hospital was designed to be spacious and imposing, but in reality it was coldly intimidating with a continued absence of people. Rows of beige vinyl-cushioned benches occupied one side of the lobby, which was dominated by a semi-circular reception station opposite the glass entry doors, staffed by three women in white coats. Lily waited a step away from Natasha as she talked to one of the women in low tones, as though in a church, afraid their voices would carry to the high arching roof.

The woman picked up a telephone receiver and dialled a number, then spoke briefly, before hanging up.

'Doctor Fischer is on his way,' Natasha said. 'He will be here in two minutes. He will take you to see Aysha. I will wait here.' She smiled consolingly. 'Take as long as you like. We Russians are used to waiting for things. I have book.' She pulled a dog-eared paperback from her handbag.

'Thank you,' said Lily.

Konrad Fischer appeared from a bank of elevators opposite the waiting area and walked purposefully across the echoing marble floor. He smiled.

'Hello Lily – nice to see you again. Hello Natasha.'

He spoke briefly with the guide, then turned to Lily. 'Let's go. Here, let me take that.'

He moved to take Aysha's brown leather suitcase, with its stickers from Bali, Singapore and Bangkok on it. Lily only let go of it reluctantly, wanting to keep touching the last tangible link with her lover.

Inside the big bed-sized elevator the doctor pushed the button for the sixth floor.

'The sixth floor contains the isolation ward,' he explained. 'She has a room to herself, because of her illness. I think she is asleep, but we will see. She was very tired, last I saw of her. Don't worry, Lily, she'll get good care here. This is the biggest and best hospital in Kiev. We will discuss things after you have seen her. I need to get more details from you.'

Lily nodded. On the face of it Konrad Fischer seemed a compassionate man. She thought she liked him better for his being German rather than Russian. Somehow a true European upbringing and birthplace were a little closer to her own. She had learned German at school and university, and understood a little about the country – both sides of the Iron Curtain. Complicated though that situation was, it was less impenetrable than the vastness of Russia with its political oversight and alphabet she could not even pronounce.

Fischer led the way out of the lift into a deserted pale green corridor flanked by doors with small windows in them. They passed a nurses' station with a young woman in a white uniform and cap, to whom Fischer spoke briefly. She said something, waving him to proceed.

'The nurse says she is asleep. They may have given her a calming sedative, to settle her down.'

Lily felt her stomach plummet. This might be her last chance to see Aysha, and she didn't want to miss that opportunity, although the rest of the bus would have to return to the clinic in the morning for tests.

They stopped outside room number 617. The door carried an intimidating red laminated sign reading : *Карантин! Не входить!*

Fischer gestured to the sign and said: 'Quarantine – no entry. We should not be going in, but this is an exceptional circumstance. I think we will be okay.'

The bed in which Aysha lay was a narrow, white-painted, iron-framed affair on large rubber castors. The small room had just enough width for the bed, a bedside cabinet and a chair in front of a narrow window, while just inside the door was a tall metal locker. The pale green walls were devoid of decoration save for a laminated sign that might have been a list of directions or regulations. In her twenty-two years, Lily had never entered a hospital in New Zealand, and found the silent sterility daunting and oppressive.

Fischer put the suitcase on the linoleum floor beside the locker and moved to the bed. Aysha lay on her side, face to the wall, her mass of ebony hair pulled in close to her head. He motioned Lily to approach.

'Aysha,' he said softly. There was no movement from the bed. He shook her shoulder gently through the blanket, but there was no response. 'Lily is here for you, Aysha...' The sleeping form did not stir, and Lily felt the tears sliding down her cheeks.

'I'm sorry,' Fischer said. 'She's out of it. I think you will be able to see her tomorrow, perhaps, when the rest of your group come in for their tests.'

'Will you be here, Doctor?'

'Please, call me Konrad. I know we Germans have a reputation for formality – though the Russians are even worse – but some of us younger generation are not so fixated on that. I at least know what it is like to be in a foreign country away from your home. But to answer your question, I will try to be here, yes. You need to understand that I am not Aysha's doctor. Because I speak English I do a lot of... liaison work if there are foreign patients, and Kiev does have a number of foreigners working here.' He put his hands on Lily's shoulders, and she wiped at the tears. 'Come, let's get some tea. I need to take down all the details of you and Aysha. Let's find somewhere to sit and talk.'

'Th-thank you,' Lily whispered, barely controlling her voice. 'You're very kind.'

They retraced their footsteps, past the elevators, collecting a clipboard with some forms from the nurse's station on the way. At the end of the corridor was a small niche with a samovar of hot water standing on a table beside a small trolley with several trays of glasses.

'During the day a *babushka* will constantly bring tea around. The place runs on it,' said Konrad. 'The samovar boils the water – keeps it hot – but you see this pot here?' He pointed to a small pot sitting on top of the samovar. 'This contains *zavarka* – it's like a tea concentrate. You add boiling water to a little of it. Depending how much you use, you get stronger or weaker tea.' He took a small glass, fitted it into a metal holder and poured out a measure of dark liquid from the small pot, before topping it up with steaming hot water from the samovar. He passed the cup to Lily and poured one for himself. 'I will put one lump of sugar in for you, otherwise it will be too bitter.'

'Now – there is a small meeting room in here where we can talk.'

They entered a room across the corridor. It reeked of cigarettes and there were two heavy ashtrays on the yellowing formica table, with burn marks at the table edges. Eight chairs surrounded the table, while a large window looked out over a Kiev nightscape of streetlights and largely deserted roads. On one wall were four posters, of the sort Lily was now starting to see as the only sources of colour in this monochrome world. She looked at them, distracted momentarily from her own unhappiness. Konrad put the clipboard and his teacup on the table and moved beside her to explain the poster Lily was examining. It was emblazoned with the year 1977 at the top and 1917 at the bottom, with stylised, flag-waving marchers in between, beneath a slogan.

'This year is the sixtieth anniversary of the Russian Revolution,' he said. 'There will be many celebrations later in the year. The words here say "Peace, labour, freedom, equality, happiness!".'

Next to it was a poster depicting a smiling female doctor, in white hat and coat with a stethoscope and a bunch of daisies.

'The nation's gratitude to the medical profession,' Konrad said. ' "Thank you for your kindness, your care and our health!".' Lily looked sideways at him, to try to gauge his worldliness and belief in this unsophisticated messaging, but he had moved to the third poster – a collage of broadly smiling workers' heads – a male welder, a female construction worker, a male surgeon and a female labourer. ' "We create happiness when we come to work",' Konrad intoned, and Lily started to sense – if not an aversion, then at least a cynicism in his interpretations.

'I contributed this last one, just to demonstrate our peaceful fraternal relations,' he said, pointing to the final poster on the wall. It showed a scythe cutting large stylised ears of wheat, the handle of the scythe wrapped in the Soviet flag alongside that of East Germany, with a slogan in German and Russian.

'Peace and creativity,' said Lily, reading the German. Konrad turned, not disguising his surprise, nor the smile on his face.

'You speak German?'

'*Ein wenig*,' she answered, suddenly self-conscious. *A little*. 'From school, and some at university. But your English is far better than my German. I won't embarrass myself further.' She felt her cheeks redden.

The moment had broken the ice, and as the pair sat opposite the posters and drank their tea, Lily began to relax a little while Konrad made notes on the clipboard forms.

'Do you mind if I smoke, Lily?'

She shook her head and he extracted a red and white packet, and she saw the word 'Embassy' on it. He noticed her gaze.

'English. Occasionally I cadge cigarettes off travellers. The Russian ones are shit and the East German ones not much better. You smoke?' He offered the packet.

She shook her head again, briefly thinking of the polaroid photo in her shoulder bag showing Aysha and herself smiling contentedly over a hookah at a Swat teashop.

'I need to get some details of you and Lily for our records and so your embassies can be contacted. Aysha is Australian, and you are from New Zealand, yes?' She nodded. 'Australia has no representation outside of Moscow – there is no consulate here in Kiev. So we will go through Moscow and let the embassy know of Aysha's illness. I expect your tour company will advise the embassy as well.

'Perhaps we can start with Aysha's details? I have her passport information, but I would like some contact details for her family, if you know them. Though perhaps I should ask first, what is your relationship with Aysha?'

Aysha felt herself flush. 'Uh... we met on this trip – three months ago.'

'And you have... shared a tent all this time?'

'No. We've come from Kathmandu. There were no camping grounds until Turkey. We shared hotel rooms.' She tried to make it sound innocuous, but concluded that the unsaid implication hung large.

'I don't mean to pry, Lily, but I need to know - to properly understand your relationship and how much involvement you may have if there are any complications.'

'Complications? I don't understand...'

Konrad shrugged. 'If her condition got worse, for any reason. If we need to advise anyone, who would it be? Is there any private information she would not want disclosed to a friend? Are you more than friends, Lily?'

Lily thought Konrad's blue eyes had seen right through her, or else he had talked to the female doctor who had examined them.

Embarrassed, Lily bowed her head, but could not bring herself to say anything.

'Are you lovers, Lily? I am not being judgemental. I know the ways of human beings. I will not be surprised or offended.' His speech was proper, clipped, correct. Somehow it lost any emotion and almost sounded like a translation exercise.

'Yes,' she admitted. Konrad jotted something on the form.

'Am I right to then think you had no secrets from each other?'

'I suppose so. But how can you really know that about someone? How can you know what is secret?' she said, almost to herself.

'How long have you been lovers, Lily?'

'I... Since India... Look, is this important? Do we have to talk about this?'

'I'm sorry, but yes it is important. What other family does she have?'

'She has a younger sister, in Sydney. Her parents live there, but she hasn't been in contact with them for years. I guess you'd call them estranged, if you know that term.'

'Of course.'

'I don't think any of them know she's even left Australia.' She did not mention Joanne, last heard of incarcerated in a cell below their house in Brisbane, waiting for a block of ice to melt. Lily did not expect much interest from that quarter. 'If anything has to be done, I guess I'm like a next-of-kin. Isn't there any way I can stay here with her?'

Konrad shook his head. 'I'm sorry. We've already explained this. Russia is a very regulated country. Most tourists from outside the Eastern Bloc come here on tours with a guide, and they're all booked in advance – guide, accommodation, transport, itinerary. The tourist industry is not very sophisticated here and there are limited approved hotel rooms.'

'I could stay in the camping ground.'

'No, Lily, you couldn't. It would never be permitted. The authorities don't like random foreigners wandering around, never mind hanging about getting in people's way wanting to be with a patient in quarantine. Do you get what I'm saying?' Numbly, Lily nodded. 'All right, so you don't know any of Aysha's family contact details. I'll get those details from her. What about you? You are going to England, yes?'

'Yes.'

'Do you have relatives there? A contact address?'

'No. I'll find a place to live. Lots of Aussies and Kiwis go there. I'm sure it won't be a problem. My mail will be going to New Zealand House – that's our High Commission in London. You can use that. Aysha can use that.' She pulled out a small red address book and read out the address. 'But I must talk to her before then – after I've left Russia, I mean. Can I ring the hospital, here?'

'Maybe, though it would be better to send a letter. She's in quarantine and of course has no phone in her room. And very few people here speak English. It will be difficult to phone.' Lily looked glum.

'But Lily, it may not be as bad as you think. Depending on test results, but it could be as little as two weeks before she recovers sufficiently to travel.'

'Then what?'

'Then she'll fly out – I suppose to England. That will be up to her.'

'Who will organise that?'

'We will organise the flight from here. As to who pays, I don't know the details – not my area. Maybe *we* do, maybe it's insurance, maybe Aysha herself. But of course, all the hospital treatment here is free – courtesy of the workers' paradise.' He smiled, but again Lily sensed there was more behind the smile, and decided to test the water.

'Do you like it here?' she asked. 'In Russia, I mean.'

'Sure, what's not to like?'

'Restrictions, queues for limited goods in the shops, censorship, being careful about what you say, all this poster stuff, travel restrictions…'

'I'm from East Germany. I travel.'

'What if you want to go west?'

'We have the border wall to keep out the capitalist decadence – those who want to destroy the free health and education, and the guaranteed employment.'

'And which way do the guns in the guard towers face?' Her frustration overflowed at a system that was taking control and sucking her friend into it.

Konrad sighed, but with a glimmer of annoyance. 'Lily, I don't want to argue about this. I want to get information which will help Aysha when she is well, and which can go to the authorities who will have to deal with this outside of this hospital.'

Lily took a deep breath. 'You're right. I'm sorry. I'm just upset.'

He put a hand on her arm. 'I understand. And believe me, I know what it's like trying to deal with a faceless organisation. It must be so much worse when you are travelling through and don't speak the language. I'd like to move on, please.

'We were talking about Aysha flying home. This might be only a couple of weeks away. So, to summarise… your tour company will be involved, once the Australian Embassy is notified. Your courier will be advising his office that the bus will be arriving with one less passenger. They will deal with the regulations and diplomatic aspects.

'And you have given me an address for your postal contact in London. Do you not have friends or relatives there?'

'I think my mother had some family in the north of England. I don't have details.'

'What do you do for a living, Lily?' He had stopped writing, and now seemed to be making an effort to make the conversation a little friendlier. He took a long draw on his cigarette and dropped a finger of ash into the ashtray.

'I... I just finished university. I studied music.'

'Oh – you're a musician! What instrument?'

'Cello – and piano.'

'Ah! You must go to the symphony in Moscow – tickets are very cheap. There are many concerts. Whatever you may think of Russians, they are passionate about their music. If you can get into a church to hear a choir, make the most of it.'

'I thought the churches were all closed?'

'Many were, but not all. Many are still used, and the music … ahh… Like nothing else you have ever heard. Will you play in England, in an orchestra?'

'I hope so, but I'm sure it won't be easy getting in. I'll probably work in a bar or office until I can gain entry or pass an exam or whatever I have to do…'

'Are your parents okay with all of this? Solo travel around the world, I mean.'

'Sure. Why not? I'm an adult.' Lily made no reference to the fact that only one parent had been able to kiss her goodbye at the airport.

'What does your father do, Lily?'

'He's a Member of Parliament.'

'Really? That must be very important.' Konrad was clearly impressed. 'I don't know how your system works, but there are surely few better occupations than being an elected representative of the people.'

'We have several political parties,' Lily explained. 'My father belongs to the Nationals – sort of conservatives. He was elected by the people of our electorate in Auckland, and he's now also a cabinet minister. That means he's one of the representatives who also get national responsibilities, you know, like Health, Education and so on.'

'And what position does he hold? He's not your president? I'm not talking to a president's daughter?'

Lily laughed. 'We only have a prime minister. My dad is Minister for Overseas Trade. We live in Auckland while he commutes between Auckland and Wellington, where our parliament is.'

'Well, give me your parents' address, just in case something goes wrong with the London one.'

'Everything will be okay, won't it, Konrad?'

'Of course it will. When do you arrive in London?'

'Twenty-seventh of August.' The date was etched into her brain - the day she and Aysha had talked about, when they would step off the bus in London, ready to take on a new world.

'That's just over two weeks away. Aysha may even be there to meet you when you arrive.' He gave her an encouraging smile. 'All this assumes the tests are okay for everyone tomorrow, and that Aysha gets better quickly from our treatment - which may not be the case, but let's hope so.

Lily pulled out her little address book. 'I must write to Aysha – maybe postcards. Can I write to her here? What is the address?'

'I will give you my address, care of this hospital. It will be easier if things come through me, because she may be moved within the hospital. Give me your notebook – I will write my name and address in Russian for you.'

Konrad wrote in neat Cyrillic script and slid it back to her. Lily studied the words, and could make out a vague similarity in the letters. She saw how Konrad Fischer became *Конрад Фишер,* and while the remainder of the address made little sense to her, she took comfort that she could now at least write to Aysha every day, and hopefully find a post box.

'You can buy stamps and postcards at any Intourist hotel,' Konrad told her, anticipating her thoughts. 'They only cost a few kopeks, and you can post them there. The camping grounds are also Intourist-run, so I think you can also do the same there.'

Lying on her camp bed with one half of the tent empty was unsettling and lonely for Lily as she tried to come to terms with the terrible change in fortune which had befallen her. Perhaps she should have seen it coming, should have made Aysha go to a doctor sooner, but would that have changed anything? The doctor's assessment that Lily herself did not show any symptoms, and would likely not have the disease, was encouraging, though a part of her would have liked to share the sickness and thus have an excuse to stay here with Aysha. But how would that be if they were in separate but adjacent rooms and still unable to converse because of isolation?

And had she raised the issue earlier, would quarantine in Bulgaria or Romania or Odessa have been any better? Lily tossed and turned and batted her doubts and guilt and heartbreak back and forth before she finally fell asleep, having concluded the best she could hope for was that nobody else had caught the disease.

\*

In the malodorous meeting room where he had spoken with Lily the previous night, Doctor Konrad Fischer stood over the table now covered by the neatly laid out contents of Aysha's suitcase. He was confident the young woman was sufficiently sedated to have no awareness of his removal of the case from her room "for security purposes".

It had been three years since Fischer had arrived in Kiev, ostensibly as part of a doctor exchange process. Under these auspices he had dutifully carried out his medical role within the Vatutin Hospital – along with other duties required of him by the KGB, where foreigners were involved. There would never be any doubt as to Konrad Fischer's qualifications and skills, for his training at the Berlin University of Medicine was amongst the best in the Eastern Bloc, and his knowledge had been sought by many of the medical residents at Vatutin. None of his medical colleagues knew that Fischer's role was also as a medical consultant to the Ukraine Committee for State Security – services arranged at the behest of his older step-brother, Andreas Meyer.

Fischer took a deep pull on his cigarette and exhaled to the ceiling. He looked over the array of clothes, and shoes, toiletries, a couple of notebooks, several paperbacks, a few souvenirs and the odd shape of the polaroid camera arranged on the tabletop. He knew they would all have been examined at the border, and he also knew the border guards were not necessarily selected for their high IQ's.

It was not the first examination of foreign belongings that he had done in the hospital. His knowledge of English and German as well as Russian made him exceptionally useful, as did his upbringing in East Germany with its greater proximity to the technology of the West, even if only through television and radio beamed across the border, but unavailable in the Ukraine. Fischer's involvement with foreigners was on both medical and other pretexts. His position as a multi-lingual professional saw him readily trusted by passing tourists or permanent foreign residents obliged to visit the hospital. After Moscow and Leningrad, Kiev was the third largest city in the Soviet Union, its medical facilities often sought by senior officials from the Caucasian and other proximate Soviet republics, as well as satellite countries of the Eastern Bloc. All these visitors were routinely scrutinised by the Ukrainian KGB, many through the legitimate guise of Doctor Konrad Fischer. For the most part, Fischer's non-medical interactions and observations revealed little of relevance to the State, though more than once there had been positive responses from his KGB liaison officer to whom he reported when the need arose. The officer had typically provided little feedback, other than that something might be 'extremely interesting', along with directions for a follow-up 'consult' and a request to focus on some particular issue or other that rarely made sense to him.

Fischer picked up the polaroid camera and examined it. He had seen them before though he had never personally handled one. He had a camera himself – a 35mm high quality Zeiss from the East German Dresden factory, of which he was inordinately proud. The polaroid photos he'd seen in the past were less than impressive when compared to those from his Zeiss.

This sort of work was not enjoyable for Konrad Fischer. Every time he was required to do this – to fill out a report for the Security Committee – the resentment of his step-brother boiled to the surface again, along with an equal antipathy for Fischer's ex-wife, Karla. He had looked back on his circumstances many times since he had arrived in Kiev. The flat he had shared with Karla in East Berlin had not been palatial, but it had been adequate. The goods in the stores there had been basic, but had been supplemented by Karla's visits to the west accompanied by Andreas. By contrast, his accommodation in the Vatutin staff quarters seemed primitive. Though the Vatutin was considered a leading hospital of relatively recent construction, the associated facilities for doctors and nurses in a converted Tsarist-era building nearby were grim, and Fischer was convinced that his brother had chosen this place deliberately.

The antipathy between Andreas and his younger step-brother had existed from their childhood, from their different fathers, different surnames and their very different personalities. They had grown up in a rough, dingey Rostock apartment, their mother managing to keep her factory job while entrusting them to the daily care of the state education system. It was that system which saw Andreas inducted into the NVA as a second lieutenant, at the foot of a tough but well-defined career ladder for anybody with street smarts and without scruples. Andreas had fulfilled both criteria, and after the first two years in uniform he was in no doubt that he had made the right choice, his forthright manner and ruthless ambition quickly becoming noticed as potential assets for the socialist fatherland. Andreas had grown up with the legacy of his Luftwaffe pilot father, proud of his father's sacrifice and disdainful of his mother's betrayal of that memory, when she had married a second time and abandoned the Meyer surname.

Konrad, by comparison, had been the softer, gentler of the pair, gifted with intellect and sensitivity. To the annoyance of his older brother, he had excelled at school such that after his military service he had been granted a place at Charité Medical School in the Soviet Sector of Berlin – something that Andreas never got over. Unlike Andreas, Konrad had adored his mother, while his un-remembered father held no sway in his life.

Towards the end of the sixties, Konrad had returned to the Rostock area to undertake his community general practice obligations, the pay-back for the free tertiary socialist education provided by the State. It was in the Evershagen Medical Centre just outside Rostock that he had first encountered Karla Graf, in the prim white state-standard uniform of the nursing fraternity.

Karla, two years younger than Konrad, was lithe, blonde and attractive enough to make most people consider Konrad a fortunate man. She was vain enough to seek out the underground copies of western magazines with their movie-star covers and Vogue models in the latest Paris fashions, and to do her best to emulate these. The pair had frequented the few underground clubs where western records were played and the more adventurous local pop groups strayed from the State-approved music repertoire advocating socialist principles and mores.

Karla and Konrad had dated, laughed, bonded, got drunk, and discovered secrets about each other. They had become companions around these secrets, taking comfort in the ability of each to share them. and making outrageous plans around them. In 1968 they had married in a small civil ceremony attended only by immediate members of both families, and had moved to East Berlin, where as a married couple they had finally been able to rent a compact one-bedroom apartment in the inner suburb of Mitte.

For the two young people, the East Berlin scene was light-years ahead of the rural backwater of Rostock. However much the authorities tried, the influence from the other side of the wall was pervasive. Visitors still came from West to East Berlin to see relatives, smuggling magazines, books, news and stories of the other side. East Germany was the only communist country where normal western television and radio could be received in its native language, for the GDR authorities had given up attempting to jam signals from the west.

Despite these keenly-viewed glimpses of the west, and despite the relaxation of abortion laws, traditional mores within the majority of GDR society still retained some deeply held beliefs. While pre-marital sex, abortion and unmarried mothers were accepted by a socialist government needing population growth, the people were less tolerant of 'unnatural' same-sex relationships. It had been on one early drunken after-work outing that Karla and Konrad had revealed to the other that they fell squarely into that category, and the career of each would likely be dragged by the anchor labelling them as misfits and degenerates within the socialist plan for the Fatherland. Apartments for single men and women were hard to find, much less for those that preferred their own gender as sexual company, along with the ostracism that came with such an admission. For Karla and Konrad, each with a determination to succeed in their profession, the solution was obvious, and the "marriage" had satisfied any doubts that their families might have had regarding their gender preferences. Their families glowed in the acceptance of convention and the possibility that somewhere soon there would be grandchildren.

Acceptance of all, that is, except Andreas, who had shared a room with his younger step-brother for the whole of their childhood. Andreas had questioned his brother when the wedding had been announced, and had grilled Konrad almost to the point of blows, at which point Konrad – leaner, more sensitive and definitely not a brawler – had fled the room.

The marriage of convenience had become a secret for Andreas, now risen a captain in the State Security Service, commonly known as the Stasi. Along with much other confidential information both from within and outside official Stasi files, Andreas filed this away for the right moment, and while his meetings with his brother were few, he used his access to the official files to monitor the movements of his brother and sister-in-law. Underneath his plan was the festering fact of Andreas's own relationship failures, for in his brief attempts he found himself continually irked by the female demands for emotional bonding beyond the physical consummation. The same dispassionate qualities that fitted Andreas Meyer so well in his job had denied him the satisfaction and prestige of attracting a beautiful woman in the way that his pansy step-brother had managed. Such a waste.

But Andreas loved his work. The Stasi was all-pervasive within East Germany. Full-time officers were posted to all major industrial plants and one tenant in every apartment building was designated as a watchdog reporting to an area representative of the Volkspolizei. Spies reported every relative or friend who stayed the night at another's apartment. Schools, universities, and hospitals were extensively infiltrated. With access to all eight floors of the grimy brown Norman Strasse headquarters, Andreas Meyer soon began to collect information on his too-smart homosexual step-brother, and his attractive lesbian "wife", waiting for the right time to use it.

Looking back, Konrad had no idea how long he and Karla had been under surveillance. What had seemed like a good solution to their mutual "problem" at the end of the sixties had gradually turned sour as the brightly lit reflections of the Berlin beyond the wall had continued to seep into the grey Eastern half of the city. Underground clubs began to appear, offering anything from folk music to mildly erotic dancers. Prostitution had been criminalised in East Germany, but the allure of such in the bright lights of West Berlin, where it remained legal, continued to seep across the divide. Despite Stasi clamp-downs, underground clubs had started down the degenerate western path, and with the arrival of the seventies, almost any predilection could be found in East Berlin, if one knew where to look. Perhaps through his naivety, perhaps just through pressure of work, Konrad had never seen the pathway that Karla had taken.

Notwithstanding their nominal obligations to control prostitution, the Stasi regularly turned a blind eye to such activities, especially when it would lead to greater leverage against both parties engaged in a "transaction". At the same time came the first cracks in the union of convenience between Karla and Konrad, as Karla found more and more reasons to be absent from their flat. This puzzled rather than bothered Konrad, for his own absence was frequent enough, though usually due to work commitments at the hospital. Karla, by contrast, had been steadily reducing her nursing hours, and sleeping late, while refusing to provide any explanation of this to Konrad. The pair maintained separate bank accounts, but Konrad noticed an increase in the clothes within Karla's wardrobe, as well as a change in their nature, though he was not given to questioning his partner, who was becoming increasingly distant and preoccupied.

With hindsight, Konrad had decided he should have seen it coming. He should also have recognised that the bitterness simmering in Andreas's mind would not lessen, and that the absence of contact between them since the wedding would not change that, given his brother's Stasi role.

When an ashen Karla had returned one evening, with Andreas behind her, Konrad's world had collapsed. There had been a sordid explanation by Andreas – a commentary around a high-level local government officer caught with his trousers down in a compromised position in Karla's presence, from which there was no recovery for the participants. The married man's reputation for upright, staunch socialist values was in tatters, and his vulnerability to western pressure meant the end of his job.

That the man's compromising position was in a small rented garage and involved receiving a severe beating at the hands of Karla Graf had been just the bonus that Andreas had hoped for. The garage had been under surveillance by the Stasi for a long time, and in due course there would be numerous other clients of 'Mistress Helga' who would now have to reconsider their careers. 'Mistress Helga' herself had been presented with the choice of continuing her work in the name of the Fatherland, overseen by the Stasi, or a serious period in the notorious Stasi prison on Gensler Strasse. That was when Karla Graf had essentially become property of the Stasi – specifically Captain Andreas Meyer – while her parents had become hostages of the State as collateral for her compliant behaviour. Meyer had gained an asset, an enhanced reputation, and the opportunity to extend his operations further.

The fact that Konrad and Karla were living together as husband and wife, and that Karla was potentially facing serious charges, was all the leverage that Andreas needed to extend his vindictiveness to his step-brother. It would not be difficult for Meyer to link Konrad with the mis-deeds of his bogus "wife" in front of a court, never mind the fraudulent procuring and occupation of an apartment by masquerading as a heterosexual couple. The fallout from such a course of action would be catastrophic for both.

However, Andreas had provided an option that had at least retained his brother's education for the benefit of the socialist bloc, and Konrad had been professionally 'exchanged' with a doctor in Kiev. Such exchanges of professionals were common, seconded to reciprocal institutions, though generally for no more than a year. It had now been three years since the disaster, and the bitterness that had infused Andreas had now seeped into the mind of Konrad Fischer. He had visited East Germany only once in that time, to see his ailing mother, now suffering from cancer, and his helplessness through the tyranny of distance galled him dreadfully. Andreas had been unheeding of Konrad's pleas to return to care for their mother. Andreas was adamant that his brother's penance in Kiev was not yet complete. Konrad was a stool for his brother, an ear to the ground in the heart of the Russian Soviet Socialist Republic and its KGB monitors. Anything Konrad heard, Andreas was to know about it.

As Konrad looked through Aysha's possessions for anything forbidden in the hospital or against other criminal or political regulations, he looked through a small collection of polaroids in a plastic bag. There were pictures of Aysha and Lily together and separate – at Persepolis, on a beach, at some Indian ruins, with castles in the background. There were no photos of sites on their own, only as backgrounds to the two young women. Konrad studied each for a long time, wondering what it would be like to travel freely around the world the way these people could. There was no mistaking the happiness on the girl's faces as they stared into the camera, bare legs, the casual confidence of youth, sometimes laughing in the pleasure of the moment in the sun. It was a different world from the short summer of Kiev and the long dark nights in the hospital singles accommodation.

Konrad picked up the thick hard cover exercise book brimming with a random concoction of Aysha's scribbles, sketches, jottings and occasional pages of deeper rumination. Not for the first time he felt the prickle of guilt at intruding on somebody else's personal and private thoughts, and could not bring himself to do more than flick through the pages. It was only when he got to the back to find a couple of pages had been taped to the cover to create a thin pouch that his curiosity was mildly piqued, and he turned the book upside down to shake the pouch empty.

Konrad Fischer stared at the contents for a long time, examining them closely, his heart beating fast and his mind trying to decided how best he could work this discovery to his advantage. He sat back in a chair and lit another cigarette, staring at the posters on the wall without seeing them. He would place a call to Berlin. It would be a long, awkward, delicate conversation, likely turning into a negotiation. He would sell his idea, cajole his brother and – if necessary – plead. Just possibly, this was his ticket home. Whatever became of Lily and Aysha would simply be unfortunate collateral damage.

\*

The travellers were at the clinic again by nine o'clock the next morning, having been given the news by Wayne that Aysha would not be coming on the remainder of the trip, and that they must all be tested for hepatitis. There were murmurs of sympathy and muted discussions concerning this possible hiccough to the last stage of their long journey, but they duly trooped into the waiting room of the blue and white clinic building.

Konrad Fischer was waiting for them.

'The testing is all arranged,' he told Wayne, Natasha and Lily. 'It will probably take less than an hour. Depends how fast you guys piss and bleed.'

'They're full of piss and they bleed freely,' Wayne assured him.

'By the time you've finished with your donations, we might have the results back from yesterday. If Lily is clear, I think that will be good news – I'm sure the rest will be okay, then. Whatever happens, everyone will be given an injection of gamma globulin, as an extra precaution to lift immunity. In the meantime, while this is happening, I thought Lily could come with me to see Aysha.'

This time, with the day shift on duty and the hospital bustling, they were given access to Aysha only after some grudging discussion with a large woman who appeared to be in charge of the ward, and then she required the pair of them to don gowns, caps and masks. Clearly the quarantine was taken seriously, and the queen of the ward was not about to let any foreigners bypass the rules.

'We're only in here on sufferance,' Konrad said, opening the door to Room 617. 'Normally visitors are not allowed – this is a one-time. There must be no touching or we'll be thrown out. She'll probably be watching through the little window,' he added, indicating the ward matron with an inclination of his head.

In a faded hospital gown, Aysha was sitting up in bed, her glasses pushed up on her forehead, a book open in her lap. She looked up blankly at the two gowned and masked figures.

'Hey Sweetie!' said Lily.

'Lily! Oh my god!' Aysha's features were briefly animated, but became tempered with the reality of what her friend was being forced to do.

Lily sat on the only chair, an arm's length from the bed, glancing furtively over her shoulder to see Konrad standing by the door, and a face observing them from the corridor.

'Sorry, Aysh – I've only got an hour. The rest of the group are being tested in the clinic. I hope I come up negative, otherwise I'll be in the room next door and we'll have to communicate by banging on the wall…' Lily tried to make light of the situation but it was all she could do not to burst into tears.

She told Aysha of their visit the previous night, and the information she had provided to Konrad. Aysha's suitcase was on the floor beside the locker, and her toiletry bag was on the nightstand.

'How are the facilities here?'

'I don't really know,' Aysha grimaced. 'They make me use a bedpan – I guess to keep me in this room and not go spreading the plague to all and sundry. It's a bit demeaning...' she said quietly.

'What did you have for breakfast?'

'Some bread, tea, a piece of cheese, some sort of cereal, like porridge...' Lily sensed Aysha didn't want to be critical of it in front of Konrad or because she didn't want Lily to be any more guilt-ridden than she was already.

Konrad used the awkward moment to try to prompt some further family contact details out of Aysha.

'If anything needs to be done, go through Lily,' she told Konrad. 'As far as I'm concerned, she's the only person who cares, and who I care about. I'm not giving you my parents' address. We have no interest in each other.'

Lily was surprised, and a little flattered, though she would have liked the confidence to have arisen in different circumstances.

Aysha seemed a little more animated than she had been during the last few days of travel. It was as though now that the sickness  – and thus the treatment – had been identified, if that sickness only involved enforced rest, then so be it. Aysha was strong, Lily thought – stronger than her watery-eyed self.

There came a knock on the door and the doctor who had performed the examination appeared and spoke briefly to Konrad, before leaving.

'They have confirmed the results,' Konrad told the two girls. 'Hepatitis A. You have it, Aysha. Lily, you don't. Good news, I think, yes?'

'I guess so,' said Lily. 'If I don't have it, probably none of the others do.'

The time seemed to drag on one hand, as they were both self-conscious with Konrad there, ensuring they did not engage in the forbidden physical contact. Lily so wanted to hold her friend, to whisper in her ear that it would be all right and that she would be back in London in no time, that time would fly past. Lily wanted to let loose her tears on Aysha's shoulder, and she could see Aysha was also struggling, despite her pretence at off-handedness.

Then, as though the time drag had suddenly turned into fast forward mode, Konrad was saying their time was up and they had to return to the group. Lily saw the face was still watching through the doorlight.

'I have to go,' Lily said, standing up, choking, feeling the tears run down her cheeks and soak into the surgical mask. 'I love you, Aysh – so much... I'll meet you off the plane in London...'

Outside the room, Konrad Fischer gave Lily a moment to compose herself.

"Don't worry about Aysha, Lily. I'll make sure the Australian embassy is notified, but Aysha can write to you at an address in West Berlin.'

'But surely she can use the Post Restante there?'

'Maybe, but unfortunately the Soviet postal system is somewhat antiquated – meaning slow. I think you'd be through Berlin before any post from Kiev caught up. This is a special address that uses a diplomatic courier. It is a place belonging to my older brother – Andreas. He's the entrepreneur of the family and decided to move to that side of the wall. Long story, but we have a channel between east and west for... let's say "trade goods". There are many western things that find a market in the east in the Dollar stores and other places. Andreas facilitates this. We have a much faster system than the Soviet Post. I will make sure Aysha can send you letters through Andreas. The building is on Friedrich Strasse. You have heard of Checkpoint Charlie?'

'Yes.'

'Give me your address book.' He took it and found a blank page where he wrote out a name, address and phone number, before passing it back. "Friedrichstrasse 214 – first floor". 'His name is on the door buzzers beside the entrance. I will make sure he is expecting you. When will you cross into West Berlin?'

Lily pulled out a much creased itinerary of their nightly stops, against which she had written dates. 'Twenty-third of August.'

Konrad Fischer smiled and decided to make a further phone call that night.

The tour of Kiev that occupied the rest of the day was a blur to Lily, seen through tears that none of her companions could do anything to assuage. None of the others tested with Lily had proven infected, and it was hoped the remainder of the group would be given a clean bill of health before they departed the next morning.

Lily tagged along with the rest as they visited the Tomb of the Unknown Soldier, guarded by uniformed teenagers with replica rifles, and frequented by bridal parties who laid bouquets of flowers at the tomb. The golden domes of St Sophia and the long queue for lunch were lost on Lily, but she was cheered by Natasha's success with purchasing stamps and postcards for her – one for each day remaining in Russia. Lily did not care what was on the postcards – they seemed to be a mixture of bland photos of buildings and statues – but she now had an opportunity to vicariously share the remainder of the journey with Aysha, to tell her what they were doing each day. She imagined Aysha sticking them on the wall of her room to brighten it up, though she doubted such would actually be allowed.

Then it was back to the lonely tent, and more rain that completed Lily's downcast mood.

*   *   *

# CHAPTER 14 – Moscow

A phone call by Natasha to the clinic the next morning had been all it took to establish that there were no other cases of hepatitis on the bus, based on the test results, and they were at once on the long monotonous drive north to Moscow. Two days of green steppe and birch forests, made more palatable by the reappearance of the sun and finally hot water in the Moscow camping ground.

Wayne had told her he would make contact with Sundowners in London and advise them of Aysha's plight, and they would ensure the relevant protocols would be followed. Lily wrote another postcard and dropped it in the box at the camping ground.

Two days in Moscow disappeared in a succession of visits to Red Square, the Kremlin, and various memorials and a space park. They were approached in the camp by local youths looking to buy their jeans, or anything else re-sellable on the black market. Western jeans were clearly de rigueur in Moscow, and any local able to flaunt such was a trend setter. Entrepreneurial young men were on the lookout for anything western at ridiculous rouble exchange rates, though there were few opportunities to buy Russian goods with these roubles.

When Lily approached Luda to see if there was any chance of going to a symphony concert she was surprised to find the young woman enthusiastic. As in Kiev, they had taken on a local guide, who was responsible for taking the group to the Moscow circus that night – something Luda had seen many times. The one-on-one opportunity to show a westerner the talent and professionalism of a Russian symphony orchestra delighted Luda, not least with Lily paying for the tickets.

Lily had promised herself some Russian music, though she'd been expecting to share it with Aysha. It had to be better than the Moscow circus the others were going to, she decided. The program was Wagner, Shostakovich and Tchaikovsky's Sixth Symphony, preceded by a short ride on a metro system that emerged next to the Tchaikovsky Concert Hall. Mayakovskaya Metro station had been a marvellous experience in itself – a vast perspective of marble floors, inlaid arches and spectacular lighting that would have done credit to the greatest of capitalist nations. The extravagance had continued in the concert hall, the exterior a colonnaded block in the Stalinist Empire style, the inside again sumptuous with marble and chandeliers.

The Wagner and Shostakovich had distracted Lily from her depression, and they had enjoyed cheap champagne and caviar on toast during the interval. But Lily had not been prepared for the symphony, however, for though she knew it well, she had never before heard it while so emotionally charged herself. The last symphony Tchaikovsky had written, it had debuted a week before his death, and now the music overflowed into Lily's mind, dragging her into such depths that before the sad chords of the last movement had slowly faded away, she was openly weeping. Her circumstances, her despair at parting from Aysha came to the fore, and it seemed that Tchaikovsky – on his deathbed – had captured the deepest melancholy of the human soul in a way no words could. Lily felt Pyotr Ilyich was personally caressing her with his music, sharing his final thoughts.

Luda was prescient enough to sit quietly with Lily in the foyer afterwards, watching the audience make their way into the warm Moscow night, while Lily composed herself.

'I think you are perhaps part Russian, Lily,' she said gently. 'Many people are moved to tears by this music. You are not the first to cry in this concert hall.'

'I…I just wish Aysha was here with me…' she whispered. She took a deep breath, striving to control her voice. 'Then we could cry together…'

Two nights later they were in Smolensk, speeding across the western steppe towards what Lily viewed as the real Europe, away from this grey land of grey people. The Smolensk camping ground in turn led to the Minsk camping ground, and at each stop another postcard went into the camp post box. She had briefly written of her meltdown at the concert and said that the symphony was now etched in her mind across Aysha's absence.

Wayne had told Lily that the Australian Embassy in London had been advised Aysha had been left behind in Kiev. By the time they left the Soviet Union, the fact the Australian Embassy in Moscow had been informed and would follow up on Aysha's circumstances was a huge relief to Lily, given there was nothing else she could do.

They had crossed the border into Poland, with prolonged Soviet baggage inspections, though not with the same ferocity as the entry, nor the promised scrutiny of diaries and journals. Clearly they were more interested in revolutionary and subversive contraband being smuggled *into* the country. Likewise, the Red Square Cooperative store offered few forbidden articles for a tourist to exit with.

In Poland, after being waved through the border by laid-back Polish guards, the tourists found they could renew their acquaintance with Coca Cola and some degree of advertising, as well as being able to see the contents of stores through the shop windows. More goods and a better variety of food was available, and while the queues were shorter, hot water in the camping ground remained elusive.

# the submissive spy

Warsaw brought with it the European history she had imagined – the narrow streets of the old town, the cobbled squares and quaint, colourful architecture overlooking the streets. The fact that much of this was either restored or rebuilt entirely was lost on the tourists, who had little concept of the catastrophic waves of invaders that had flowed back and forth these lands for centuries. Only the more recent events – the brutality of the Ghetto Uprising and the transport of Polish Jews through Parwiak Prison – had a direct and powerful effect on Lily, making her visit to the peaceful expanse of Chopin Park more comforting. Lily was still downcast in Aysha's absence, still thinking of her on an hourly basis, wondering how she would be coping in the hospital without any form of external stimulation, and like as not unable to venture much from her little room.

But with each passing day Lily was one step closer to Berlin, where she could pick up letters from Aysha, regardless of how delayed they might be. She did not suppose they would contain much news, but anything connecting the pair would be seized with open arms. The sights of Warsaw – though interesting and at times poignant – were diminished for Lily by the absence of her friend to share them, and she could hardly wait to be moving on.

One final long day, half-dozing across the flat, green Polish landscape, then they were into East Germany, where the post-war restoration seemed to have gone on hold in favour of utilitarian housing blocks. It was a short drive into East Berlin, and even late in the day the mood of the bus was now excited. The Soviet sector of the city was not dissimilar to many of the cities they had seen in Russia, drab and run down, its citizens clad in dowdy grey and brown fashions a decade out of date.

Then the reality of the Berlin Wall was ahead of them, cutting a wide swathe through the city blocks on the eastern side, its approaches protected by parallel barbed wire fences, floodlights, vehicle barriers and observation towers. Bleak East Berlin buildings overlooking the wall had their windows bricked up, watching like ghosts over the death zone in front of the high concrete wall itself.

A year or two before, Lily had seen a movie called "The Spy Who Came In from the Cold" on television. It had starred Richard Burton and was filmed in black and white, and though Berlin and the Wall had seemed remote and untouchable, the film's ending had reduced her to tears, and she had never forgotten the gloom and futility on the eastern side of the wall.

The presence of these skeletal buildings unnerved Lily, as did severe-looking soldiers with sub-machine guns and unfamiliar helmets eyeing the bus warily as it parked inside the first processing area. Here the grey-uniformed officers moved slowly down the bus aisle, examining each passport and matching its owner with the photograph inside. A stern-looking man took Lily's black New Zealand passport and flicked through several pages, then turned back to the photograph, holding it up to compare with Lily's face. Though they had now been through many borders on the trip, the presence of these people always made Lily nervous, and the closeness to western culture just beyond the wall made her more anxious than usual. Surely there could be no hitch this close to the sanctuary of West Berlin? The man seemed to study her for an age, until she finally decided he was mentally undressing yet another decadent young western woman in her tee-shirt and denim shorts. Lily stared back at him, determined not to be intimidated, until he handed back the passport and moved to the next row of seats.

With preliminary passport checks done, the group was shepherded off the bus and told to remove the luggage from the hold. They stood round in the late afternoon sunshine, casting glances at the silhouette of West Berlin a hundred metres away beyond further walls and barriers, while the Aussie lads piled up the tents and camp beds beside the bus. The guards inspected the luggage hold and the interior, and an Alsatian dog with its handler sniffed the whole vehicle. It seemed like the capitalist west was a mirage being dangled just beyond their reach, the likelihood of reaching it diminishing with the prospect of something terrible befalling them in the search.

They were directed inside the long low blockwork building housing the border post administration, where they queued for their passports to be stamped. Despite the warmth of the day, the interior was cold and unwelcoming, the walls scattered with posters proclaiming penalties and warnings, along with several propaganda posters, their German slogans understandable to Lily.

Papers checked, they reloaded the bus with palpable relief, then drove a hundred metres through two concrete-barriered chicanes to a second holding area, where their passports were again checked. Only then could the bus pass through a gap in the thick wall designed to prevent vehicular penetration. Another fifty metres, a red and white barrier, and a small building in the centre of the road with the words "Allied Checkpoint" on a large roof sign. More passport checking, but this time brief and cheerful, the sound of American and British accents, before moving away into the heart of West Berlin.

Lily was surprised at her reaction to the sudden change of the city within the space of half a kilometre. The appearance of advertising billboards, posters, and logos was almost overwhelming, as though they had been transported to an entirely different country. The people were clothed with colour – whether dressed smartly or casually. Flared jeans were abundant, the men wearing open-necked figure-hugging shirts, the women showing off short bohemian skirts and dresses. The place felt alive. The traffic was busy, the footpaths crowded, tables and chairs occupied outside restaurants and konditorei. It was almost dusk - Saturday night in West Berlin, and as the streetlights came on, so too did the garish but wonderful neon signs of capitalism.

Lily eased herself back in her seat, as though a weight had finally been lifted, with the knowledge that the next day she would have word from Aysha. The nightlife of the city swept past her window as they made a slow trek into the British sector then out to the camping ground on the shores of Wannsee Lake in the American zone. Here, after the luxury of a hot shower, Lily sat at the entrance to her tent, listening to the excited talk of others in the darkness around her, with raucous sounds drifting over from the camp bar. For the first time in many weeks she heard other languages and accents she recognised, though she had no desire to engage. For now she simply sat and hugged her knees, wondering what Aysha was doing, and disturbed at a sudden strange feeling that things were not quite right, and that something unexpected lay ahead of her – something foreboding and unsettling. It was the first intimation Lily Maddison had that her world was about to turn upside down.

*   *   *

# INTERMISSION

# Moscow, August 1977

# CHAPTER 15 – Consultation

R oughly a mile from the yellow brick neo-baroque KGB headquarters in Moscow's Dzerzhinsky Square, the modest Australian Embassy stood at a five-way intersection in the Tagansky District. It was a four-storey building built over a hundred years previously in the reign of Tsar Alexander III, and served as embassy and accredited consulate to the fifteen autonomous republics that made up the Union of Soviet Socialist Republics.

Head of Consular Section Graham Parminter sat back in his chair and swivelled to face the window looking down on Podkolokolny Lane. He ran his hand back over his almost bald scalp, as though expecting to find a covering of hair. Most of it had vanished with premature baldness in his thirties, about the time he was ending his provincial rugby playing, accepting with good grace the ribbing from his fellow forwards alongside him in the scrum. Parminter had been big then – tall enough to have presence in the line-out and heavy enough to leave opposition players in his wake when on a charge. The fitness of twenty years ago had been lost through a succession of desk-bound jobs sorting out the misfortunes and mishaps of Australian tourists in Chile, Spain, Greece and now the Soviet Union. It had always been an interesting role, and the ineptitude of his fellow citizens continued to astound – and often embarrass – Parminter, requiring all manner of legal, administrative and diplomatic skills. This latest one that Helen had brought to him seemed just a little different – as was often the case in the USSR.

The woman sitting opposite Parminter's desk was in her mid-fifties. With an unruly shock of grey-streaked ash blonde hair and black-rimmed glasses, Helen Feldman was slightly older than her boss, and the two made a good pairing in a difficult posting. Helen was nominally First Secretary under Parminter, but given that the embassy payroll beneath her comprised only a few locals, Helen was used to having to do much of the donkey work herself. Her parents had been born in the Ukraine at the turn of the century, fleeing the country ahead of the anti-Semitic pogroms of the Russian Civil War. They had reached Australia in 1924, just in time for the birth of their first child, christened 'Alina', but soon anglicised to 'Helen' to suit their new country.

Helen had grown up speaking Ukrainian at home, and English with an Australian accent. She had excelled at languages at the University of Melbourne and found herself as a translator in the Australian diplomatic service in the middle of the Second World War. She loved the work and the embassy pathway that followed it, and her sympathetic but non-nonsense interactions with Aussie expatriates had made her name well-known in consular circles. Her fluency in Russian made the embassy in Moscow a natural fit, and she had been there almost five years, happy in her single apartment two blocks away.

As though puzzled at finding nothing on his head with which to run his hands through, Parminter swivelled back and picked up the smouldering cigarette from the worn ashtray near the edge of the desk, matching one on Helen's side. Both were inveterate smokers – a bond that had seen them through many crises and which guaranteed there were always cartons of Winfield finding their way to the third floor office through a variety of diplomatic means.

'What makes you suspicious?' asked Parminter.

'It was a gut feeling at first,' Helen said. Her voice was sharp and edgy from years of cigarette smoke. 'We got the notification from Australia House on Friday. They'd been notified by Sundowners in London. I phoned the hospital in Kiev, and got all the usual propaganda about how the hospital was taking the best care of her, blah-blah-blah, but as soon as I pushed for a release date, the guy got all cagey. I wanted to talk to Aysha herself, but apparently there is no phone in her room and because she's in quarantine, she can't come to a phone.'

'And this was when?'

'Two days ago.'

'You said it was a gut feeling – at first. Something's changed?'

Helen Feldman pulled on her cigarette and breathed a cloud of smoke up to the high, ornate ceiling. 'The guy I spoke to was East German. Unusual, but not unheard of – they run a lot of exchange programs with the satellite countries. Spoke good English, but he was evasive. Wouldn't commit to anything, uncooperative in either passing a message to or from Aysha. So I spoke to the Brits at Sofiyskaya, to see if they had anything. I at least wanted to know about Hepatitis A – which is what she has – and what the treatment is. I spoke to their tame doc. He said the main issues with hepatitis are the contagiousness and the need to rest with the right diet. The problem with the contagious period is that its duration varies considerably, and it's measured from the time of contracting the disease.'

'Which was when?'

'Well, that's the second problem. We know Aysha had the symptoms when she turned up in Kiev – that was on 12 August. According to this East German doctor, she had likely exhibited symptoms for a week, but could actually have contracted the disease up to five or six weeks earlier. Which would have meant she was past the contagious stage.'

'So what's his position?'

'He says they must take a conservative position and assume the disease has just been contracted recently, and thus she may still be contagious.'

'How long has she been there?'

'What's today?' Helen glanced up at the calendar on the dark panelled wall under the portrait of the Queen. 'Wednesday the 23rd. So she's been there eleven days.  Allowing a few days before her admission as being part of a contagious period, and you've got about three weeks, minimum, since she contracted it.'

'So she's past contagious stage.'

'I think so.  The Brit doc agrees with me.  Should just be a question of whether she is healthy enough to fly.'

'And?'

'Well, this is where it gets interesting.  I had the contagious discussion with the German – his name is Konrad Fischer.  He conceded on the contagiousness – reluctantly, I might add – but insisted Aysha was not well enough to travel.  It all gets a bit vague at that point.  I think I need to get down to Kiev.  There's something not right here.  It's like they're stalling.'

'Have you tracked down her family yet?'

'No – that's another weird thing.  Aysha refused to give any details to the hospital.  Sundowners have none on their records.  I can go back through our passport section but I'm a bit reluctant, given she was adamant in the hospital admission.  I think I need to have a chat with her first.'

\*   \*   \*

# SECOND MOVEMENT - KARLA
# West Berlin, August 1977

*Allegretto, risoluto*

# CHAPTER 16 - Friedrich Strasse

Lily had taken a long time to fall asleep that night, had woken early, showered, and breakfasted in the camp restaurant before most of the other overlanders. They were scheduled for a city tour in the morning, after which they would have the rest of the day as free time, before meeting the bus to return to the camping ground. Lily was hugely impatient to make the rendezvous that would bring her news of Aysha, but was bound to the tour program for their first morning in Berlin.

The Wednesday morning was bright and sunny and she dressed in a pale green sleeveless dress and sandals, unsure exactly who Konrad Fischer's brother was, what he did, and what level of formality she should adopt. She filled in time waiting for the bus's departure, walking along the lake and doing a circuit of the tree-lined camping ground. To the rear of the camp she found a sign saying "You are leaving the American Sector" in English, French, German and Russian – evidence of the precarious position West Berlin still occupied as a walled island in the middle of East Germany. A hundred metres beyond the sign she could see a tall concrete wall topped with barbed wire, and an observation tower, marking the continuation of East Germany beyond. It was a sobering glimpse of the tension that overlay the city, despite its efforts to portray capitalism in its best light.

The city tour took most of the morning – the Olympic Stadium, the Reichstag, and Ploentzee Prison, ending up at the ruined Kaiser Wilhelm Cathedral before they were left to explore on their own. It was the first country since Pakistan in which Lily felt comfortable with the language, and she was saddened at not being able to show this off to Aysha.

The city was bustling, the outdoor restaurant tables overflowing with patrons dining in the warm sun. Lily paid the shops only a cursory glance as she followed her tourist map towards Friedrich Strasse, and the address given to her by Konrad Fischer. However, her attention was caught as she passed a small shopfront where the light was on inside, displaying a selection of stringed instruments – guitars, violins, violas and cellos. The sight of several golden polished cellos at once re-energized Lily's urge to play, which until then had been suppressed by events over the last fortnight. It reminded her that at some stage she must purchase an instrument if she wished to pursue her career in England.

Lily had set aside some money for this purpose, though she had no idea how much a good cello might cost in London. The sign on the window read *"Strauss und Sohn seit 1956"*. Lily peered through the glass at the handful of beautiful instruments on display, noting their prices in Deutschmarks and mentally trying to work out the equivalent in sterling. The more she looked at the instruments, the more she felt her need to play and the emotional outlet it had previously provided for her. It had been over three months since she had last rested a cello against her chest and snugged the body between her knees with the C-peg close to her ear. The feel of the bow and the touch of the polished wood came flooding back in an unexpected rush. She pushed open the door, which caused a discreet bell to tinkle. A friendly-faced man in a dark suit appeared.

'*Kann ich Ihnen helfen?*' Lily wanted to respond in German, but her mind went momentarily blank, and it must have shown on her face. Noting the map in her hand, the man tried again: 'Do you speak English? Can I help you?' He was around thirty, clean shaven and wore round-rimmed glasses.

'I… I was just looking…' Lily said, as though to delay her own sudden longing to go about this place touching all its wares. But it also seemed like a reason to set aside the inexplicable nervousness she felt at the meeting with Konrad Fischer's brother in Friedrich Strasse.

The man smiled, obviously pleased that he had identified Lily correctly. 'Please. Look all you want.'

Lily liked his unassuming approach. What harm could there be? Friedrich Strasse could wait just a little.

The interior was redolent of aged timber, resin and polish, all of which added to Lily's growing desire to feel a cello again.

'My name is Oliver,' the man said. 'This is my father's shop. I think you are a visitor, ja?' His English was accented but fluent, and his pride in the shop and its contents was evident. He held out his hand. 'Nice to meet you. Welcome to Berlin.'

'Lily,' she said, shaking hands.

'You are passing through, Lily? You are from where?'

'From New Zealand – on my way to London.'

'You are a player, Lily?'

'Cello.'

'Ach. Such a lovely instrument. My favourite, in fact, I think. You have one?'

'Back home. But I'll have to buy one in London, when I get there.'

'Ah. Not necessarily.' Oliver led her deeper into the shop. The place was narrow, only a few metres wide, with a wooden counter that ran most of the way. On both walls hung dozens of stringed instruments, the overhead light glinting off the polished surfaces. He stopped in front of a number of cellos.

'You will find cellos in London nearly twice the price of ours,' he said. 'The Eastern Bloc does not have many significant skills, apart from making armaments and causing mischief, but one thing they do well is make musical instruments. East Germany and Czechoslovakia make good violins and cellos. Strange, isn't it? Ironic, ja?' He picked up a cello and handed it to her. Lily cradled it, feeling the familiar weight and form, and the longing to coax a melody from it. 'You have a budget?' Oliver asked, his voice clipped, precise but amiable.

'I... didn't know what they might cost over here,' she said truthfully. 'I can't afford anything fancy.'

'Ours range from about 500 Deutschmarks upwards. That's maybe 130 pounds sterling?'

It was at the upper end of Lily's budget, but the thought of the cost being considerably more in London – along with rental deposits and other setting up costs – got her attention.

'That one – that is Czech. Nothing special, but still good quality. It's not a Tononi or a Goffriller,' he grinned, and she smiled back. The legendary Italians were to cellos what Stradivarius was to violins.

Half an hour passed like a flash, as Lily found herself drawn back into the world she loved, trying out different instruments, listening to their timbre and resonance, savouring the weight of the bow in her hand, the pressure of the strings under her fingers. For a short time the prospective meeting was gone from her mind as she talked to the knowledgeable Oliver and toyed with the finances and logistics of getting such a purchase to London. There were only a few days to go, and she saw no problem with having the cello sit on a vacant seat next to her for the remainder of the trip. It was a twist of fate that had brought her here, a chance to make up for the horrible time of loss behind the Iron Curtain.

Lily made a decision and turned on her charm, finally concluding a deal that would see her in possession of a second hand Czech-made instrument, together with a bow and case for a hundred pounds. No price could be put on the lift she felt in her heart and the purpose it now gave her. Lily was rapt.

The building on Friedrich Strasse was a dull pale grey apartment block with six floors, each with a small recessed balcony. At street level, beside the entry, there was a souvenir store and a shop selling interior décor items. Lily looked up at the first floor apartment, but the windows had lace curtains and she could see no sign of life. She hesitated, not knowing why. Was it anticipation or concern at meeting a new person who had some connection with Aysha, who should bring news – good or bad. What if it was bad?

Resolutely, she crossed the road and saw the list of buzzers in the entry alcove below an intercom. First Floor: ANDREAS MEYER – a new, neatly-typed label that should offer hope, but in reality scattered butterflies of nervousness in her stomach.

She pushed the button and with no questions asked, the latch on the front door clicked. She entered and found herself in a small tiled foyer with a single narrow lift and a set of plain iron-balustraded stairs. The place was bare and bland, giving nothing away as to the nature and status of the inhabitants. Lily climbed the stairs to the first floor, to be met with a further small name card beside the dark varnished door, identical to that beside the buzzer. She was about to knock when the door opened.

'You must be Lily,' he said in slightly accented English. 'I am Andreas Meyer. Please come in.'

Andreas Meyer was around in his mid-thirties, shorter and stockier than his younger step-brother and showing no obvious family resemblance. Wrinkles were beginning to show under his eyes, but his wheat-brown hair was thick and matched a close-cropped bearded jawline. His intense dark eyes and thin lips reflected neither warmth nor unfriendliness, rather the sense of a business meeting about to take place. He appraised Lily with a look which showed a small blue vein pulsing in his temple.

Meyer was dressed in a white open-necked shirt and a brown suit with slight flares. Lily had seen enough of insipid Eastern Bloc fashion to recognise a good cut that was clearly from the western side of the Wall. He shook Lily's hand with a firm grip and led the way down a hallway, turning into a small living room. It smelled musty, with a vague aftertaste of cigarettes.

'Please, have a seat, Lily. I'll fetch my colleague, and we can talk.'

*

The phone call from Kiev, twelve days previously, had been out of the blue. Meyer had received regular entreaties from his brother to be allowed to return, as the health of their mother deteriorated. It had been a year since Konrad had seen his ailing mother, though Meyer himself had not seen her since the marriage "ceremony" of Karla and Konrad eight years previously. He felt no obligation to visit her, although the prospect of her imminent death might prove distracting if family matters and her estate had to be wound up. Perhaps it was something Konrad could be tasked with. He was a doctor, after all, and used to caring for people.

The possibility of softening his position with his step-brother became more real as Meyer had listened to the man – not so much in regard to any relocation concessions, but the possibilities arising from what Konrad had discovered. Three days later the package had arrived, and Meyer had examined the contents with mounting interest, his mind exploring possibilities.

Meyer had spent much of the last five years working with what was known as the Romeo network, in West Germany's capital, Bonn. Strategically located on the Rhine, Bonn was a city of a quarter of a million, chosen as West Germany's de facto capital. It was officially designated as "the temporary seat of the Federal institutions", with the expectation that at some time in the future there might be a unified Germany that could return to the old capital of Berlin. A city of government ministries and foreign embassies, Bonn was also the West German administrative headquarters of NATO. As such, it was a prime target for East German intelligence, whose agents were indistinguishable from their West German compatriots.

In a camp in Belzig, southwest of Berlin, the Stasi had trained many agents known as Romeos, with the specific purpose of forging relationships with the many lonely secretaries in Bonn ministries and embassies. It was a strategy that took years of subtle development, of coaxing and manipulation, as the agents inveigled themselves into the confidence of the women, though stopping short at the idea of marriage. It was known amongst the agents as *Verdammt für das Vaterland, or* "fucking for the Fatherland", and was masterminded from HVA headquarters in East Berlin.

Meyer's involvement with the scheme had come about through exploiting the potential of Karla Graf, after her "husband" – Konrad – had been shipped off to Kiev and their apartment had been given to more worthy occupants. Meyer had participated in many of the aspects of training at Belzig, specifically those reliant on applied psychology and the study of human nature – the ability to engage, observe, seduce and deceive. In addition to the Romeos and more conventional female honeytraps, Meyer saw the possibility for unconventional sexpionage, as it was known. The Stasi had long had an extensive network of watchers in Bonn, identifying positions of responsibility and – often more importantly – those on the periphery with inconspicuous access to the seats of power.

With alcoholic inducement in the bars and clubs of Bonn, a few individuals had been singled out whose proclivities lay outside the sexual norms, and it had been Meyer who had led the exploitation of these weaknesses through the skills of Karla Graf, now his chief operative. It had been easy to set up a well-equipped "play centre" in a small house on the rural north fringe of the city, kitted out with a full range of devices for audio and visual recording, as well those for inflicting pain and pleasure.

The original intent had been blackmail, but Meyer and his "Chief Whip" as he called Karla, had discovered that the sessions with Karla and some of her clients developed into addictive relationships without the need for blackmail, in just the same way as those of the Romeos. Karla had found and trained a number of women – both dominant and submissive – to extend the activities of this sub-network. In most cases the clients were not particular as to who provided the service, provided they were competent, attractive and sensitive to the client's needs. As Karla explained to Meyer, now a full Colonel, a client's needs in the dungeon were unique and individual, and took time to be learned and refined. It was not a whorehouse with a revolving door of employees. The whole exercise had also developed into a lucrative business for those involved and for a country desperately short of foreign exchange.

With the successful but covert entrapment of a couple of high-level officials, more kudos had come to Meyer, and the concept had begun to be expanded beyond West Germany. Six years previously there had been a mass expulsion of KGB agents from Britain, which had almost obliterated the Soviet network there. Two years later, however, East Germany had been officially recognised by the UK, and an official embassy had been set up at 34 Belgrave Square. This had allowed a major increase in the influence of the Stasi, now operating in a de facto KGB role. Meyer's role had expanded again. Then there had been the time in Iran, his involvement with the Tudeh Party, and the ignominious deportation. The unfinished business remained, despite the fact that an explosion had almost killed the British agent responsible for Meyer's failure. For once, his superiors had been sympathetic to their prodigy's bad luck, and had provided him with the opportunity to make amends. Too much planning and work had been put into the Iran operation to let it wither on the vine, and Meyer's motivation was now extremely personal.

Events had abruptly heated up, and Andreas Meyer suddenly found himself with a large number of balls in the air. Unlike the gradual extraction of secrets from the clients at the play centre, matters in Iran and with the exiled forces of the Tudeh based in Paris, were rapidly coming to a head. Meyer had suddenly found himself under extreme pressure from his HVA superiors to ensure that the eyes and ears of MI6 did not prematurely lift the lid from the pot coming to the boil.

Until now, Meyer had trusted the judgement of Karla Graf – her ability to assess the talents and understand the proclivities of her recruits. But something had gone wrong with this latest one in London. Erika Baumann had seemed a good fit, but had turned out to be a mistake. The woman was attractive and there was no doubting her enthusiasm for what the illiberal Meyer still regarded as a perverted sexual lifestyle – and which she seemed able to elicit aplenty in her current position. But the woman had no initiative, nor was their hold on her as secure as with other recruits. Erika Bauman was motivated by money, not by family threat, and Meyer was convinced that as long as she was being paid, she was not inclined to exert herself beyond satisfying her own predilection and that of her employer. The fact that there was no intelligence coming from her placement was a huge concern for Meyer. He now had to make the decision whether to replace her, and if so, with whom? Time was running out.

The arrival of this fresh-faced young New Zealander in the Berlin HVA safe house, in the wake of the package from Konrad, had sparked hope in

Meyer's devious mind, and he received his guest with barely-concealed covetousness.

*

Lily sat in one of the armchairs facing the lace-curtained windows overlooking Friedrich Strasse and looked around, as the background traffic noise drifted into the room. It was gloomy; the worn sofa and two armchairs were of cracked brown leather, with a glass-topped coffee table taking centre stage on the beige shag carpet. A large dresser stood at one end of the room, and next to it a plain-shaded floor lamp that reminded Lily of one in her grandparents' house. It was furniture from two decades ago – formal and prim, left over by previous occupants. Several pictures hung on the walls – bland landscapes which might have come from a second-hand shop. Lily felt the absence of personality in the room even before she registered the lack of knick-knacks or photos.

She had barely seated herself, leaning the cello case against the chair, when Meyer returned, this time accompanied by a stunning blonde woman in her mid-thirties. She was taller than Meyer, dressed in a black silk blouse and a white leather skirt that stopped halfway down her thighs. The long legs emerging from the skirt ended in roman sandals with black straps wrapping her calves almost to her knees. The blouse had short sleeves and a deep cleavage, under a sleeveless white leather waistcoat.

'This is my colleague, Karla Graf,' said Meyer.

Lily stood, taking the woman's offered hand. It was the second time Meyer had used the word "colleague". Lily murmured a greeting, noting the smoothness of the hand but also the strength of the grip. Karla had flaxen blonde hair in a long bob to her shoulders, framing agate blue eyes that locked on to Lily's and did not blink for fully five seconds as their hands remained clasped. Karla radiated coolness and sophistication and Lily had an unnerving sensation of power that almost made her shiver.

'I'm very pleased to meet you, Lily,' said the perfectly outlined crimson lips. Her voice was deep and husky. 'I have been so looking forward to this moment.'

Lily was confused as to what "this moment" was, and exactly who Karla was. The woman gestured to the armchair as she took the adjacent one, while Meyer remained standing. As though to ease Lily's awkwardness at her situation, he began to speak.

'We're glad to see you made it to West Berlin all right, Lily,' he said. 'My brother told me of your circumstances. I hope you didn't have any problems on the way? No border hassles? No more sickness?' Lily shook her head. 'And you are in good health?'

'Yes – thank you.'

He inclined his head towards the newly-polished cello case. 'Have you just bought it?'

'Yes. There's a small shop on Charlotten Strasse that I passed on the way here. I think it is much cheaper here than it will be in London.'

'I know the shop. You are a musician, Lily?' Meyer appeared genuinely interested. 'You have studied at university?'

'Four years at Auckland University.'

'Your favourite composer?'

'Uh… Elgar, Bach… Dvorak.'

Meyer smiled, though Lily got the impression it was not about her choice of composer but for some other reason, particularly since he was looking at Karla when he did so. She wondered if these questions were something other than just pleasantries.

Karla asked: 'What made you decide to come overland? Did you and Aysha travel together?'

It was the first mention of Aysha, and Lily suddenly felt they were heading back to the reason she was there.

'No – we met on the trip. I travelled alone.'

'That's a big decision – to travel half way round the world by yourself.'

Lily shrugged. 'I make my own decisions,' she said.

'You'll be pleased to hear we have some correspondence for you, from your friend Aysha.' For the first time Lily felt a little comforted, that she was in the right place, that things had happened as she had been promised, that she would hear from her friend. She realised how much she had been fretting. Meyer moved to the dresser and opened the top drawer, extracting an envelope, which he passed to Lily. He stepped to one side and turned the floor lamp on, projecting a round pool of light on to the edge of the coffee table closest to her.

Lily was about to ask why there was only one letter, but decided to hold her disappointment until she had read it, when she would perhaps be better informed and her nerves had been quietened.

'We will leave you to read in peace, Lily,' said Karla. 'Would you like a cup of tea? I'm about to make some.' Lily absently nodded her thanks as Karla stood and left the room with Meyer. Lily was alone with the rough envelope in her hands. She realised her fingers were trembling.

\*

Karla Graf had seen many young women slip into the murky world in which she moved, and over the years had managed to suppress any moral scruples she might once have had. Since the first time that Andreas Meyer had exposed her own penchant for the infliction of restraint and pain on willing participants, she had been beholden to him – not merely through his rank and power within the Stasi, although this was by far the most potent weapon he held over her. The Stasi could offer or withhold promotion within a company, could bribe, threaten friends and family, or imprison without reason. Rumour had it that one in every twenty people in the GDR was a Stasi informer, and Karla had seen what Meyer could do with his power.

The other cause of her obligation was more personal. For a short time after her arranged marriage to Konrad Fischer, all had seemed to be progressing well. She and Konrad had congratulated themselves on pulling off a formality that had permitted them to rent an apartment, had brought respectability to their respective families, and now allowed them to pursue their disparate sexual appetites. While Karla and Konrad were the best of friends, the need to keep up appearances had begun to wear, and with the gradual exposure of East Berlin to decadent western magazines and books – and eventually smuggled "accessories" – Karla had undergone an epiphany with the realisation of her true sexual calling.

It had taken a little while to set up the garage in the alley off Bernauer Strasse – a time of the utmost caution, of seeking out and improvising her "furnishings", while working extra shifts to finance this secret venture. Then had come the furtive, surreptitious contacts through coded classified ads, cautious meetings in underground clubs, and word of mouth. "Mistress Helga" had come into being, and along with her persona, and a lucrative increase in income, as a few men within the government bureaucracy found their way to the improvised dungeon. Once vetted, Karla had concerns about none of her clients, for they, as much as she, had everything to lose. She provided a service which was gratefully received, and repeat custom was the norm. She reduced her daytime nursing shifts, invested in further "devices", and developed contacts on the western side of the wall. West Germans were still permitted to visit relatives in the east and smuggling of all manner of things was the norm, often under the cooperative eyes of the border guards.

Karla was still convinced that she could have continued the business undiscovered, had it not been for Meyer's suspicions of his step-brother's sexuality, and unsatisfied doubts as to the legitimacy of the marriage. Karla was an only child, her parents now in their sixties in Rostock, far to the north, but nevertheless now caught in the pervasive Stasi network that guaranteed compliance on her part. Whatever disdain Meyer showed towards her activities and sexualities, he'd had the imagination to see how such an enterprise could work for him. Meyer was astute enough to understand the psychology behind Karla's business and the needs of her customers. However much he despised them, he saw the enormous relief in her clients, once their sexuality had been acknowledged and their needs provided for within Karla's safe private space.   Meyer had the foresight to see how this could be implemented on a much larger scale, for the benefit of the Party.

Karla had become a reluctant partner of Colonel Andreas Meyer, providing her clients with services and experiences which – should they be exposed – would bring down their careers and their families.   The Socialist Unity Party espoused healthy, "normal" sexual practices, and would routinely expose and vilify any unnaturalness.   The apparent depraved nature of these activities was not such that it prevented the Party from training its operatives to use them to their own advantage, however.

Yet such were the uniqueness and intensity of the experiences Karla offered that her clients returned like addicts to an opium den, bringing with them snippets of information, often documents, as part of the deal. Sometimes this information was provided willingly, sometimes requiring a little reminder of their circumstances.   Sometimes the eliciting of information came under a consensual scenario, where the client finally yielded under "torture".   Within the dark role play of the garage, under the heightened levels of adrenalin and dopamine, reality and fantasy often merged, and the seriousness of an act of passing information was lost in the moment.

The initial collapse of her world with the exposure of their "marriage" and the banishment of Konrad had gradually resolved itself into a stimulating and lucrative outlet for Karla, who reluctantly acknowledged that Meyer had all the cards and could do with her what he pleased.   She did, however, recognise her own expertise, and was careful not to groom a successor who might see the larger picture.   Women who were ready to raise or receive the whip – especially if it meant an escape from the drudgery of the East – were not too hard to find.   Those chosen had friends and family who would be put under observation to ensure compliance.   Such an arrangement was *di rigueur* for Meyer, and it usually only took one example to be made to bring participants back in line.

Meyer had eventually given Karla Graf a relatively free hand in recruiting her people, including several years in Bonn, where Karla had become accustomed to the luxuries of the west, although strategic oversight remained firmly with Meyer and HVA headquarters in Berlin.   There had been joint visits to France and to England, to scout for talent and to initiate further *Fetischfallen*, or Fetish traps.   In her heart of hearts, Karla had never gone with the whole Marxist-Leninist thing, nor accepted that the Stasi were truly the "Sword and Shield of the Party", but carried out her work for the buzz that it gave her.   As much as her clients, she, too, was victim of her own success, her own proclivities.

Karla had watched Meyer's understated inquisition of Lily in just a few subtle questions.   He had confirmed that she was cultured, educated, and had sufficient   initiative and resolve to undertake an overland trip on her own.

# the submissive spy

Right then Karla Graf could see exactly where Meyer was heading. The young foreign woman now in the sitting room of the safehouse was just another in the line of people who had walked too close to the trap.

*

Lily turned the envelope over. It was of coarse paper and carried no stamp. Her name and the Friedrich Strasse address was written in block letters in German and Russian on the front. The back of the envelope was blank and sealed, but opened easily under her finger.

There were two pages inside – small lined pages from a notepad. Aysha's neat printing jumped to her eye with a warm familiarity, and the cold surrounds of the room vanished as she began to read.

*My Darling Lily, I don't know what the date is, but it's the day you will have left Kiev. I've been thinking of you sitting in seat 14A looking out the window. I still see your profile against the light, as I've done for so many days on our journey. Of course you'll want to know how I am. Tired as hell. But I can't begrudge the rest. I don't have any problem falling asleep, though no doubt I'll come to hate this little room as I get better. I don't know how long I'll be confined here. I suppose it depends on my blood results and how soon they improve. I'm sorry I put everybody through the testing and of course I hate the fact you've had to go on without me. I'm selfish enough to wish you were here in a bed beside me – or in this one with me, haha. At least then we could rest together. I'm sure the time wouldn't drag the way I expect it to. We've never been stuck for things to talk about.*

*I haven't had a chance to work out the routine of this place – that'll likely take a WHOLE DAY more, so I'm saving that exciting news for the next letter. Konrad said he will collect one from me each day to forward to you. I think maybe he has some sort of diplomatic bag access that will get things through to West Berlin, or maybe it's under the counter. I don't care how it gets there, as long as it does. I suppose they will probably read this – who knows? – so you may notice I'm perhaps not my normal forthright self. All is good, so far. The food is... well hospital food is pretty ordinary the world over, apparently. I have to eat a fat-reduced diet – nothing that puts a strain on my liver. No alcohol – bugger. So I'm not allowed to buy from the cool mobile bar that is wheeled around the ward by a spunky Russian bartender called Ivan for happy hour every night, haha.*

*Thank you for the books you nicked from the bus library. I'm trying to ration them for myself, since there's no tv or any other English language outlet here. I don't know how much time Konrad can spend here, though he's promised to look in each day, just to make sure there are no language problems and to collect a letter each time. Thank god for his presence. This place would drive me nuts otherwise. More nuts than I already am, of course. Mind you, there's still time for that.*

*I miss you so much. I think of you on the bus and try to imagine what you might be doing each day. I'll probably get a little confused as I try to remember our schedule and where you'll be at any time. Serves me right for paying more attention to you than to where we were actually going. But you're worth it! Did I say I miss you? Oh I did. Good. I do. You're the best thing that has happened to me – ever! (Don't even mention Joanne.) I can't wait until we get together in London. I don't know if it will be 2 weeks or four. Konrad is vague and says the recovery varies from person to person, but he says he has advised Moscow and they will inform the embassy first thing tomorrow. (I don't know who 'Moscow' is, and why he couldn't call the embassy directly, but I guess they have more rules here. Not everybody can just call up a foreign embassy, I suppose.)*

*I thanked you for the books. I have to ask – did you take anything from my luggage when you were packing? A few personal things to remember me by? I hope so. Maybe something from my journal? At least I still have that to remember you by. Shame on me for writing so much detail in it, but now I'm so glad I did.*

*I think of you in the tent by yourself. Knowing you, you'll be fretting and depressed – that sounds like I'm pretty into myself, doesn't it? But I know you love me, Lily darling, and you know I would never, ever do anything to harm you. (Well, aside from the odd consensual moment, if you get my drift.) Seriously. I want so much for us to be together when we both get to London via our separate journeys. We must think about the future, not this crap that's been foisted on us at the moment. I can't imagine where you'll be when you read this, but I hope it brings you a little joy that I'm all right and being cared for. I love you so much I can't put it into words. Trust me, Lily. Always trust me.*

*Letter number two tomorrow xxx.*
*Aysha.*

Lily was only aware of her tears when one dripped on to the paper, causing a large blot that smeared the ink. So many thoughts were chasing around in her head. The relief that her friend was all right – albeit merely a day into recovery – was overwhelming. Merely hearing from Aysha had lifted her spirits, as she tried to take in the details in the letter. It had not occurred to Lily that the Soviets might read Aysha's letters. The address on the envelope was not in Aysha's handwriting. Somebody else had written that, meaning Aysha had likely handed the letter to some gowned and masked nurse to put in an uninfected envelope. But Aysha was smart enough not to slag off at a hospital which would decide her release date. So Lily would have to read between the lines.

She wiped her eyes and re-read the letter, more slowly this time. She figured Aysha might have to be a little obscure in some aspects. Yes, she got that the food was "ordinary". But Aysha's allusions to removal of things from her luggage was strange. She had not looked in Aysha's journal. However close the pair were, as far as Lily was concerned, Aysha's journal was off limits. So no, she hadn't removed anything at all, other than two polaroids sitting in a little pocket in the top of the suitcase – the one of them in the Swat teashop and of Aysha on the beach in Turkey. Was Aysha intimating that something had gone missing from her belongings – something she didn't want to raise with Konrad Fischer? And what had she meant about not wanting to do harm to Lily?

Lily's initial euphoria in reading the words from her friend subsided into puzzlement at the vague implications that she couldn't figure out. She sat for a long minute, her brow furrowed, hands holding the letter on her lap, staring but not seeing.

Karla and Meyer reappeared, the former carrying a wooden tray with cups and saucers, a sugar bowl and a small milk jug. She put it on the coffee table and asked:

'How do you take your tea, Lily?'

'Milk... and one lump,' said Lily, noticing the bowl of sugar cubes. There was a pause while Karla poured three cups and handed Lily hers. Lily's hand trembled slightly, enough to make a rattle with the cup as she hastily deposited it on the coffee table.

'Everything okay, Lily?' asked Meyer, remaining standing as Karla resumed her seat in the armchair next to Lily.

'Uh... yes, thank you.'

'Is Aysha all right?'

'Yes. Yes, thank you. But... she said she'd be writing a letter each day... Is this the only one?' Lily looked up at Meyer feeling like a child asking for more birthday presents when she's already been given the best one. Meyer looked at Karla, who gave a slight nod.

'Yes, Lily, there are more letters. But let's just save those for the moment.' Meyer put down his teacup on the dresser and leaned against it, facing her. 'This is a difficult situation to explain to you, Lily, so I'm going to do it a little differently. Before we provide you with the remaining letters, there are some things we want you to look at.'

'Things? I don't understand...'

Meyer opened the dresser drawer again and crossed the room with something clutched in his hand. He bent over the coffee table in front of Lily and in the manner of a man putting down playing cards, he deliberately laid out six polaroid photos side by side in front of Lily, reverse side upwards.

Lily stared in confusion. Each of the photos was inscribed on the back with Aysha's careful handwriting:

'Swat 1-7-77: Lily's 1st tie'

'Tehran 11-7-77: 1st shave'

'Tehran 17-7-77: 1st belt'

'Side: 25-7-77: Lily's castle fantasy'

'Istanbul: 30-7-77: Carrot and stick'

'Athens: 3-8-77: Lily does a double'

Lily's blood ran cold and her stomach seemed to turn over. Her breath suddenly had to be helped on its way, and her mind went into overload, asking questions to which she knew the answers, but which she could not accept. She stared at the backs of the photos, her brain trying to reconstruct the details of those instants, to comprehend that they had been recorded by Aysha and that they were now likely on the table in front of her. She clamped her hands between her thighs, trying to still the sudden trembling that had started, not knowing what to do.

Karla leaned over from her chair and slowly turned over the first photo. The reality of seeing it was worse than Lily had dreamed. A blindfolded Lily lay naked on her back on a bed in the Serena Hotel, the blankets removed, legs bent, her wrists bound to her ankles. The angle was oblique, but with enough of Lily's crotch visible to show she had yet to experience the touch of the razor.

Lily caught her breath, the rush of blood pounding in her ears as Karla turned over the second photo, taken on their first night in the Tehran hotel, where the shaving had taken place. Lily was spreadeagled on her back, tautly secured by the scarves to the corners of the bed, gagged and blindfolded, her pussy now clean and exposed, the razor artfully lying between her legs.

Karla turned the third photo over to show the same bed, the same room, though a week had passed. This time the view was from the rear – a view of Lily on all fours secured across the bed, two scarf knots at the back of her neck, her buttocks adorned with the red outlines of an impacting belt.

Karla's hand moved to the fourth photo.

'No – I don't want to see any more!' The tears broke as Lily looked at the woman.

Karla picked up the photo and held it in front of Lily's face. Lily was blindfolded and bound to a tree in the silent little clearing of the castle above the beach at Side. The top of her swimsuit had been pulled down to expose her breasts, their nipples erect and pointing, the birthmark on the right breast giving away her identity to anybody in the know.

'You look like you're enjoying yourself, Lily,' whispered Karla. 'And what about this one? Dear me!' She picked up the next one. The sound of Istanbul traffic drifting through the window flooded back to Lily, standing with her halter-neck at half mast, ankles bound to the bed legs, wrists secured behind her. Two clothes pegs stood out jauntily from her nipples as she peered sightlessly at the unseen camera, the stem of a red rose clenched in her teeth that she would never allow to fall. Lily moaned, and tried to push the photo away, but strength seemed to have left her arms.

In a quick movement the final photo was in front of her. It was another rear view, this time in Athens – a naked Lily bound with her wrists pulled above her head, their securing rope disappearing over the top of the bathroom door to the handle on the other side. Lily's buttocks each showed the harsh red outlines of three impacts of the clothes hanger stick. She was standing with her legs apart, her body taut, stretched, young muscles showing in a perfectly composed snapshot. Around her waist were two turns of cord, knotted in the small of her back, the tails disappearing between her legs. The head of a large carrot protruded from her anus, the cord passing through a hole in it, en route to a similar intruder in her pussy.

Lily covered her face with her hands, tears of shame coursing down her cheeks. She struggled to breathe, and was surprised to find Karla's comforting hand on her shoulder, stroking her neck and hair. Lily's sobs got mixed up with her breathing and Karla rubbed her back gently.

When she looked up next, Meyer was no longer in the room, but Karla was handing her a clean handkerchief.

'What... why are you doing this to me?' she stammered, unable to process what was happening to her.

'Shhhh...' Karla whispered, as though to a small child who has grazed her knee. 'Catch your breath. Breathe, Lily. All will be explained, but we want you back, present with us. I know – it's a shock. It's a lot to take in – the how's, the why's, the what now...' The husky voice was somehow soothing, suggesting she was on Lily's side, understanding her pain, her shock, wanting to help. 'Here, drink this.' She held a small glass tumbler containing a finger of brown liquid. Lily smelt alcohol and without considering consequences, drained the glass, feeling the hot fire of brandy slide to her stomach. It distracted her enough to allow her to focus, to get her breathing under control, to look up at Karla with tear-blurred eyes and ask huskily again:

'Why?'

\* \* \*

# CHAPTER 17 – Fetischhaus

The olive green Mercedes Benz 300d with the dark tinted windows pulled up outside the Friedrich Strasse flat, where Karla and Lily were waiting. Despite her embarrassment and shame, Lily had subconsciously noted the roles of the two players suddenly controlling her life. Meyer was the boss, Karla was hands-on. Lily was still not processing details, but had gathered enough of her senses together to at least not make a total sook of herself.

At Karla's insistence to be quiet and patient, she had done so, just aware enough that she was giving herself a chance to think more clearly and to try to make sense of things, now that the initial shock was over – or so she thought.

'We're going for a short ride,' Karla had told her. 'Don't worry, we're not kidnapping you. You'll be back in your tent safe and sound tonight, I promise. Trust me, Lily.' There they were – the two words Aysha had always used. The insistence on trust, just before you threw yourself off the ledge hoping the swimming pool was full. Karla's voice had an insistence about it that reminded Lily of her friend, and for some reason she saw fit to acquiesce, perhaps because right then she felt she had not the strength to fight.

At Karla's direction, Lily had brought her new cello with her, and she did as directed – opening the front passenger door and placing it beside the driver, Meyer. She closed the door and climbed into the back seat. Karla followed her, smoothing her leather skirt over her long legs. Meyer did not glance back at the two women.

Karla allowed Lily to settle. 'This will only take ten or fifteen minutes, Lily.'

'Where are we going?' asked Lily dully, trying to set aside the awful last hour and the host of questions now jostling to be asked. Perhaps she could start anew and simply learn what was immediately ahead of her. Lily wanted to push further, but Karla was intimidating.

'We're going to visit a shop a little way from here. I won't pre-empt the surprise, but it will be better than what you have just experienced.' It wouldn't need to be much to do that, Lily thought, trying to quell her anxiety. 'Just relax and enjoy the ride. I won't be answering questions for a little while.' Karla put her hand over Lily's. Lily looked down at the elegant fingers with the long scarlet nails and pulled her hand away.

They rode in silence for ten minutes, Lily only half-seeing the streets and the people going about their business. The photos had brought back so many memories – wonderful memories, if Lily was honest with herself – of experiences in distant hotel rooms, in the privacy of her relationship with Aysha. In every one, Lily had been blindfolded, unable to see Aysha take out the Polaroid and capture Lily in a state of – if not rapture, then well on the way. There had been traffic noises in the background, noises of plumbing, the sound of Lily's blood pounding in her ears, her panting breath as she tried to maintain some sort of composure with each new level of wonder and joy that Aysha took her to. Lily had not recognised the whir of the camera amongst all the stimuli going off in her head. Now she understood what Aysha had alluded to in suggesting something was missing from her luggage.

She should have been angry at what Aysha had done, but she knew that this was not the moment, that certain things had to be played out first.

Meyer dropped them in a small square, after confirming where Lily was to meet the Sundowners bus that evening to return to the camping ground, and that the cello could remain with the car. It was a quiet neighbourhood oasis, amidst low-rise wall-to-wall apartments above a range of street level shops. They crossed the square with its flower beds, trees and park benches, to a small konditorei on the far side, where a line of tables and chairs sat outside the doors.

'I haven't had lunch,' Karla told her, as they seated themselves at a white-clothed table under the awning. 'We were waiting for you. Have you eaten?'

'I'm not hungry,' Lily muttered.

'We'll have *Kaffe und Kuchen*. I'll order for you,' Karla said as a waiter appeared. She rattled off an order too fast for Lily to properly follow and the waiter disappeared inside. Karla eased herself back in her chair and crossed her legs, taking out a pack of cigarettes from her small shoulder bag. Lily noticed the brand was Embassy, the same as Konrad had smoked in Kiev.

'Do you smoke, Lily?' Lily shook her head. Karla pushed a lock of blonde hair back behind her ear and eyed Lily, as though sizing her up for the first time and deciding how the conversation was going to go. Something about the woman unnerved Lily. It was the first time she was able to examine the German woman in good light, and without the tears of shame blurring her vision. Karla Graf wore little make-up – just enough to highlight cheekbones and skin other women would die for. The matching lipstick and nail polish were faultless on top of her clothes which showed style without flashiness. She was calm, poised, letting the world know she was in control and nothing about that would change. There was an unconscious feeling in Lily's mind that Karla had been here before. Intimidating enough for Lily to stay silent despite the profusion of questions fighting to make the head of the queue.

'Are you religious, Lily?'

'No,' said Lily, taken by surprise at the question.

'Really? Were you not brought up in the church, in Auckland? Are you people not Christians? Catholics, maybe?'

Lily was unsettled further, not least by the familiar reference to her home in Auckland, coming from someone whom she had only met an hour ago.

'Uh… we're Presbyterians…'

'Ach. So you do have religious upbringing. That's good.' Karla smiled enigmatically.

'Why?'

Karla shrugged. 'Conservative values start young. I think you are not a wild child. Your parents looked after and provided you with a good upbringing, yes?'

'I suppose so.'

'How did they feel about you going overseas – to Kathmandu, of all places?'

'I guess they trust me.'

'Of course.' Karla took a long pull on her cigarette and exhaled the smoke away from Lily, a satisfied expression on her face. 'You are setting out on a voyage of discovery. Of self-discovery. You are twenty-two, you want to experience the world outside New Zealand. I am thinking life there is pretty dull, yes? Not much to get excited about, not much news of the rest of the world, only what makes the headlines for something really big. You go to high school, maybe get a degree at university, get a job, kids, settle down…'

For the first time Lily noticed the proficiency of Karla's English. There was no mistaking the German accent, but her articulation and grammar could not be faulted. Lily figured some of it must have been learned outside of Germany.

The waiter arrived with two coffees and set them down, followed by two slices of cake – a marbled apple cake and a chocolate gateau. Karla stubbed out her cigarette.

'Which would you like, Lily?' Lily remained silent, not looking the older woman in the eye. 'Lily!' This time she did look up, locking on to the blue eyes and finding herself now unable to look away. 'Lily, you are going to see a lot of me in the near future, and I will tell you this only once.' Her voice was hard. 'Do *not* make me angry. Do as I tell you and life will be good. You do *not* want to cross me. Now eat your cake and stop behaving like a child.'

Lily sipped at her coffee and tasted the gateau. It was delicious. Karla was mollified and smiled encouragingly. Lily felt uncomfortably like a pet which had just performed a trick for its mistress.

'Did you have a boyfriend or a girlfriend at home, Lily?'

Lily blushed. 'A boyfriend,' she admitted, though she then wondered why she had said this, seeing as she had received no letters from Robert for weeks. Perhaps it was just bravado – an attempt to assert herself.

'I thought so. Something tells me you were utterly 'normal' at the start of this trip, yes?'

'Why are you asking me these questions?'

'Because, my dear Lily, I have seen a series of photographs of you, taken – and most conveniently recorded by your obsessive friend – over the space of six weeks. Such a wonderful record!' She smiled. 'Your friend has sussed you from the beginning. I have to hand it to her – she's very good. Ah, I can see you are wondering what I am talking about... Aysha has been *training* you, Lily. You're a submissive, and I can see you are into all sorts of things you never realised. I admire what Aysha has done – so clever. Training a submissive while travelling through third world countries. Quite remarkable. Did you enjoy it, Lily?' Karla paused to sip her coffee, then put down her cup. 'Of course you did. You lapped it up. The photos tell me that. First the feeling of being tied... The shaving... Then your first flogging, the feel of the whip on your bare skin... Anal... And then the... vegetable... What was it Lily?'

'A carrot...' said Lily, lowering her eyes at the thought, the humiliation, but the recollected feeling of fullness and the inevitable outcome. And the longing for more.

'Was there any part you did not like, Lily?' Karla's voice was now low and insistent, a hungry animal seeking out its prey, or an inquisitor seeking the final confession to send his victim to the stake.

'No...' Lily whispered, finally meeting the piercing eyes again, now understanding where all this was going, understanding the nature of the elegant woman sitting across the table from her, and feeling completely out of her depth. Karla Graf had seen right through her, peeling away her layers to expose that which she could not hide.

Karla put down her cup and leant forward, elbows on the table. Lily was momentarily distracted by the cleavage – deep and creamy breasts against white leather and black silk. Then Karla's eyes drew her in again.

'Those photos tell such a story about you, Lily. It is nothing to be ashamed of. That was why I asked of your upbringing. You've discovered there is a whole world outside of your old-fashioned little country, so far away from the rest of the world. You've discovered there's another gender in this world, and you've discovered there is much more than simple straight sex. What fantastic revelations these are, yes? If you have learned nothing about the world through which you've travelled, you have learned these two things, *ja*?' There was no mistaking the fierce enthusiasm in Karla's voice.

'Well, Lily, I am going to show you that you've barely scratched the surface of those revelations, that you've barely stuck your toe in the water - to mix up some of your English metaphors.'

Lily looked down and saw she had finished her coffee and that the gateau plate was empty.

From the café they walked a block to a small group of shops, one of which advertised itself as *Fetischhaus*.

'This is it,' Karla said. Lily gazed in wonder at the sex shop window.

Lily was not a sex shop virgin, for she had once explored such a shop in Auckland's Karangahape Road with some inebriated girlfriends, the result of which was a giggled-at purchase of four vibrators – one for each of them. But in Lily's now-wide eyes the K-Road shop was like comparing a Morris Minor with a Rolls Royce, where the former had no sophistication nor any of the accessories that would make the ride uniquely memorable.

Karla pushed the door and went inside, followed by Lily. For a sunny mid-week afternoon the store was quite busy, the browsing customers being a roughly equal mix of male and female.

A pretty young woman came up to them, greeting Karla with a discreet bob that might have been a curtsey. Lily gaped at the woman, who was about her own age. From the waist up she wore a figure-hugging shiny black costume of rubber or latex, the overhead fluorescent light gleaming on every curve of her body from the bulge of breasts to the narrow wrists. Beneath this eye-catching garb was a matching, clinging skirt which fell to her ankles, but with a central slit almost to her waist, revealing knee-high black pvc boots. She wore little – but expertly applied – makeup, emphasizing full red lips and mascaraed eyes, while a long blonde ponytail stood out against the glistening latex.

Karla said a few words to her and then turned to Lily.

'This is Gisela. She's my assistant in some things. She also works here in the store and gets to try out all the products. It means she can provide excellent customer advice, and she has also become somewhat of an attraction herself. She is on commission, I should add. It's her dream job.' Gisela smiled and nodded to Lily, then disappeared into the bowels of the shop.

Lily was still staring at the outfit that had just vanished from view. She had not known where she was being taken, but had expected nothing like this. This was not some mainstream sex shop with a few lubes and pink dildoes, the odd pair of pink fluffy handcuffs and some ostensibly risqué underwear. Lily gazed around at walls of floggers, whips, canes and restraining harnesses. There were shelves of polystyrene mannequin heads adorned with all manner of leather masks, hoods and elaborate gag harnesses and blindfolds.

'Come, Lily. Let's wander,' said Karla.

They moved slowly down an aisle and found themselves in a section of handcuffs and a variety of steel restraints. The other customers ignored them.

'I'm guessing they don't have much like this in New Zealand, *ja?*'

Lily shook her head dumbly, wondering at the strange thrill creeping through her body. Whatever had transpired in the Friedrich Strasse apartment, this was enough to push it to the back burner. Lily was in the moment, unable to stop herself imagining what an experience would be like with these devices.

'In West Germany we are well known for being sexually progressive, Lily. We are like Holland, I think, and maybe the Danes. But we have very good craftsmen here – people who are skilled in metal, rubber and leather, and who have found a very successful niche market right here. We export all over the world – except to New Zealand, perhaps.' She smiled mischievously, showing perfect teeth behind the cherry-red lips. She took down a pair of stainless steel manacles.

'I think these are your size, Lily,' she said, peering at the sales sticker. 'We will try them on. See if you like them.' Lily was rooted to the spot, staring at the heavy manacles. An allen-key on a loop hung from a hook, evidently to facilitate the customer hands-on experience. Karla used the key to undo the allen screw in one of the manacles, which flipped open.

'Give me your wrist, Lily.' Karla slipped Lily's wrist into the inner curve of the manacle and closed the outer, before screwing the manacle closed. 'You see how that curves to your wrist, Lily? Many handcuffs and manacles are round – like a circle, you know? But your wrist is not. It is a kind of oval, and you see how this fits? Nice and snug. Hard to rotate on your wrist. Comfy, huh? Now give me the other wrist.'

The two manacles were joined by two inches of heavy chain, and Lily watched dumbly as the second bracelet encircled her left wrist and was screwed in place. The steel was cold, shiny and weighed her wrists down. More to the point, they were now locked in front of her. She was captured, imprisoned, a hostage. Her heartbeat rose and her breathing came faster. She felt no trepidation, only excitement, like something was coming to pass which had always been in her stars.

Karla slid the key into her pocket and turned to face her, noting the flush now in Lily's cheeks.

'Okay? I did promise we'd have you back in your tent tonight. We're not about to kidnap you. Well, not unless you want us to...' That teasing smile again.

'They're... pretty,' said Lily tentatively, feeling the heft as she lifted them in front of her face to examine them, sensing the permanence of them. As though reading her thoughts, Karla said:

'Can you imagine what it would be like to wear these for a long time, Lily? To have your movements forever restrained, knowing you cannot escape?' Lily said nothing, but she had been wondering just that. 'Those come off only when I decide. It's not something you need to concern yourself with.' A shiver ran down Lily's spine, the hairs at the nape of her neck standing up – a strange, intoxicating medley of excitement, fear and anticipation.

They examined rows of collars of leather and steel, some decorative, some for posture correction, and some clearly intended to be attached to a wall in a dark and brutal dungeon. There were gags and head harnesses, designed to stifle speech and curtail sight, some in the form of complex hoods denying all sensory input. The smell of new leather permeated the air and Lily's own senses went into overload. She went to feel one of the soft leather hoods and found that both hands had to move together, coping with the unfamiliar limitation and weight of her wrist restraints. She picked up a black hood. It was made of beautifully soft leather and smelt divine. Lily hardly realised she was holding it to her face. Karla took it from her and put it back on the mannequin.

'All in good time, Lily,' she told her firmly, as they moved to a wall titled "*Spielzeit*", which Lily interpreted as "playtime". Evidently the idea of playtime for these customers involved the use of canes, floggers, whips, crops and all manner of implements for impact on the human skin. Karla took down a small flogger from its hook and slapped it against the white leather of her skirt.

'What do you think, Lily? You like?' Lily licked her lips, which had suddenly gone dry, with the memory of an Iranian hotel room many weeks previously, in another world. Karla saw the girl's eyes widen. 'Really?' The red lips parted in a sly smile.

'Do you know the definition of a masochist, Lily?' Lily shook her head. 'A masochist is someone who likes a cold shower every morning. So they have a warm one.' Lily tried to hide a smile. 'I think you are a masochist, too, Lily. Your eyes tell me there are many things here you wish to try out. Your imagination is running wild. Imagination is so important to a bondage relationship. The mistress must have inventiveness to control and devise the punishment, and the slave must have the imagination to multiply the next punishment by ten times in her head. Then you know you have a symbiotic relationship that will satisfy both parties.'

They passed a clothing section, redolent of leather, pvc and rubber, the straightjackets with prices in the hundreds of marks which Lily's overtaxed brain could not convert to pounds. She could happily have spent an hour trying on leather skirts and dresses, while the thigh-high boots made her manacled hands tremble with desire.

They passed shelves of what were called "*Einsätze*" – inserts – and it did not need much translation. Lily gaped at what people evidently pushed inside themselves – or each other, and then, in some cases, attached to electrical sources. They finally came to a long aisle of books and magazines, with beautiful models – male and female – enduring all manner of privations which sparked wetness between Lily's legs. Lily's gaze lingered over the magazines wrapped in clear plastic. Most were in German, though many were in

English, with names like "Hogtie", "Knotty" and "Bondage Classics". The covers depicted women in all manner of restraints and vulnerable positions. Some of the victims were naked, others clad in high shiny boots and tight-fitting leather. Some covers labelled "Bishop" sported exquisitely-drawn bound women in the throes of subjugation.

If Lily had ever been in any doubt of her "calling", that doubt had now been blown away. The most comforting part lay in the epiphany that with this much merchandise on display, such perverted desires – for she still thought of them as such – were harboured by thousands of others. Lily was not alone, and like a secret shared, that understanding was pivotal in her embracing of her fate.

Like a reluctant but obedient child, Lily followed Karla out of the shop into a back stairwell. It led both upwards and downwards, and it was the first floor which was their destination. They emerged into a workshop of sorts, where four men of different ages moved quietly between large tables. They ignored the newcomers, save for one man in his fifties, who recognised and smiled at Karla and murmured a greeting. The smell of leather, rubber and strong glue was heavy in the air from various moulds and leather cutting areas on the workbenches. At one end of the room were shelves with rolls of material ready for cutting, while nearby were racks of garments hanging in various stages of completion.

For Lily they had moved from the sweet shop to the factory making the sweets. Everywhere she looked there were suggestive objects and final products which captivated her. So entranced was she that she had not ventured to ask the reason behind the tour, in part because she feared it might bring the party to an end. Karla was not about to give away secrets, it seemed. She beckoned Lily to a rack where a number of black and white jackets hung.

'Have you ever tried on a straightjacket, Lily? No, of course you haven't. Do they even have those in New Zealand? Do you have mad people there? Probably not. But I think you should try one. These ones are so cool. Come, give me your wrists and I'll take those nasty steel cuffs off. Did you like them?'

'Yes, Karla...' Lily said, trying to keep up with the conversation, the products and her own thoughts. It took only a few moments for the removal of the manacles, then Karla was flicking through the rack of garments. There were straightjackets of black leather and white canvas, and Karla had no hesitation in picking the former.

'Canvas is for role play, Lily. That's when you end up in a real padded cell somewhere for a day or two at a time. That's when we see just how together you are,' she grinned. 'Some asylum doctors are very prone to mis-treating the inmates – if you know what I mean.' Lily was starting to get a good idea. 'I think we'll try a nice leather one. Here – smell this.' She handed Lily a heavy black leather jacket that was a mass of laces, straps and buckles. She sniffed at it, drawn in and captivated by the new leather aroma.

'All right, Lily. No need to have an orgasm just from the smell.' Lily thought she could almost do just that. 'This way.' Lily followed Karla back out the door to the stairwell, and through a second door on the same level. It led into another, smaller, workshop, with a single table and more shelves containing large cardboard boxes. The place was empty of people, its slightly decrepit air suggesting it was a storeroom. Karla took the straightjacket from Lily and opened the jacket to face her. 'Put your arms in – go on, right in, as far as you can.' She wrapped the jacket around to Lily's back and buckled the straps with practised efficiency, before making her prisoner cross her arms in front and pulling the straps around to meet at the rear. Lily felt herself enveloped in the leather, arms hugging herself, unable to move, the collar snug about her neck. Then Karla was folding up the hem of Lily's dress, tucking it under the bottom of the jacket. Lily felt the air around her exposed groin, bringing a rush of embarrassment on her as Karla's fingers brushed the cotton of her panties.

Lily could hardly believe she was now half-naked with a woman she had only met a couple of hours before, one who had subtly controlled her every step of the way, and to whom Lily – in the excitement of a child at the Christmas tree – had offered no resistance. Lily did not know if Santa Claus was going to appear, but his helper was doing a damned good job, a little voice inside her conceded. Karla threaded a vertical strap around Lily's arms at her stomach and pulled the strap between her legs, giving it a firm tug between Lily's buttocks before buckling it in the small of her back.

'There! Nice and secure, Lily?'

Lily tried to move her hands and arms, but they were anchored in place. She wriggled and twisted, but that only made the strap groove between her legs, sending blissful messages radiating out from her loins. Lily spotted a chair beside the table and promptly sat, unwilling to take the chance on her legs suddenly becoming unstable.

Karla looked on with an amused expression, as Lily closed her eyes in an unexpected rush of euphoria, which stopped as Karla's open palm slapped her hard across the cheek. 'Lily! You do not get off without my permission! Do I make myself clear?'

Lily opened her eyes, as though suddenly becoming aware of where she was and who was doing this to her. Her interactions with Aysha came flooding back, and she realised Karla had slipped into a controlling role without any acceptance of such by Lily. There had been no negotiation, just Lily diving impetuously and unashamedly into the shiny objects dangled in front of her, offering new and better experiences than Aysha had been able to give. Lily felt ashamed, like a dog who has been given a new mistress and who accepts the ownership change without a thought, provided the new owner can feed and care for it. Lily was better than that, and the thought of Aysha and her situation brought Lily back to ground.

But Karla was not done. She pulled one of the cardboard boxes from a shelf and put it on the table. 'I know you've been gagged before, Lily. But have you ever had a *real* gag?' Lily had no chance to respond, as a heavy rubber face mask appeared in front of her head. It was the front half of a full head mask, made of stiff red rubber with tiny eye holes as though made with a paper hole punch, as well as for the nostrils. The exterior showed closed, sculpted lips, but the inside of the mouth had a protruding rubber mouth insert like the mouthpieces used by footballers to protect their teeth. Lily saw the mask advancing on her just in time to open her lips to permit the mouthpiece fill her mouth, her upper and lower teeth coming to rest in U-shaped hollows, her tongue pressed down firmly.

Karla's hand held the mask against Lily's face while the rear half was pressed against the back of Lily's head and buckles were done up on each side of her head. Lily wrestled with the intrusion in her mouth. The rubber was snug against her lips and jaw and she could neither open her mouth nor enunciate anything with her tongue subdued by the rubber. She shook her head, suddenly panicking that she could not breathe properly through the small nose holes. She snorted and whined into the rubber, but hands pressed down on her shoulders until she realised she could not move or complain. A voice whispered beside her ear:

'There, now, Lily. Just breathe. Calmly. No panicking. You're quite safe. Trust me, Lily.' There it was again.

Lily had little choice. She made a plaintive hmmming noise. It sounded loud in the tight rubber head-prison, but she didn't know how much sound actually escaped. The pressure on her shoulders vanished, and she sat there, not knowing where Karla had gone, or what was happening. She sucked in lungfuls of air as best she could, getting her breathing and heart rate under control, willing herself to settle down. She could just make out some detail of the room through the tiny eye holes, and when she had finally calmed, she ventured to stand up, nearly stumbling with her limited vision. She turned very slowly. It was like watching the world through two narrow pipes with a very small field of vision.

Finally her eyes landed on Karla. The woman was leaning back against the wall, arms crossed, watching her prisoner and clearly enjoying herself. Lily found her predicament and earlier panic were now replaced by annoyance that she should have fallen into this trap so easily, and that this Karla person was now being entertained at Lily's expense. The assault on Lily's senses had pushed reason back, leaving the baser emotions and sensory stimuli to dominate her attention. Lily wanted to kick Karla, to demand to be let go, but there were too many agreeable feelings coming into her brain which she did not want to stop. The overpowering smell of the rubber, the tightness of the straightjacket and the ominous sliding of the strap between her legs – Lily wanted none of these to end.

She stuttered in short steps to where Karla lounged, watching her, and made an attempt to speak. She tried first to use her tongue, but the attempt died before it could even start. She modified the attempt by making a series of muted nasal grunts which made no sense. Lily was baffled at how her speech had been all but silenced so quickly and effectively. The control Karla now had over her was overwhelming.

'Do you have something you want to say, Lily?'

Lily nodded her head and snorted. Karla's indistinct figure stood up straighter and moved closer, then suddenly Lily's eyesight was gone as some sort of tape was pressed over the two tiny holes.

'Hnnn?' Lily whimpered. That was the end. She could not see where she was, nor enunciate her distress. 'Hrnnn?'

No sound reached her ears under the rubber hood. She was alone in a dark world, the very epitome of helplessness. Karla could walk out of the room right then and leave Lily to be found by the workers when they came back to retrieve supplies. The very thought struck fear into her heart. Karla had seemed rational and reasonable up until that point. Now Lily's worst fears reared up from the dark pit in which they'd been hiding, suppressed by the deluge of strange and delicious feelings which had taken her to new heights – until that moment. Karla had surely known that Lily – like most submissives – was at her most vulnerable when exposed to the doubts and black imagination of her own mind. It did not and would not occur to Lily that her predicament was a test for evidence of that vulnerability.

She froze in her darkness, trying to remember in which direction the chair had been. She remembered the work bench and edged in what she thought was the direction for it. She did not know what else to do. Something hard bumped against her arms clasped across her stomach. It was the bench. She turned to put her back against it and slowly tried to lower herself to the floor as gracefully and carefully as possible, but one of the straps caught on something and she fell on her side with anything but grace. She tried to sit up, but found the straightjacket hampered her movement. Without arms to push against anything, or with which to counterbalance herself, her attempts to sit up were ridiculous and probably hilarious to a watcher. Karla was no doubt watching, and Lily was determined not to give her any satisfaction. But that determination faded, replaced with the realisation Karla was probably already laughing herself silly at the stupid

Kiwi girl who had gotten herself into this position, through her lust for the new and sensuous embrace of something as exciting as a straightjacket.

Lily rolled on to her back, her chest heaving under the leather of the jacket, frustrated and humiliated, not knowing what to do next. The reality was that there was little she *could* do, other than to let her breathing slow and wait for Karla to intervene.

The German woman was there a minute later, kneeling astride Lily's stomach facing her feet, her hands stroking the exposed inside of Lily's thighs, sparking a new round of pleasure creeping through Lily's body, re-igniting what had been momentarily suppressed. Lily tried to resist, to kick out, though she knew it was only a token, and not what she really wanted.

'Stop that, Lily,' said the stern voice somewhere in the distance beyond the rubber helmet. 'Or I'll bind your ankles and leave you here for the night.' Lily was at once still, now just wishing Karla would get on with things. Lily had capitulated on all fronts, and now opened her legs as best she could in the only thing she could offer to her subjugator. Karla saw the movement and stopped for a short interval, as though musing on where to go next. Then Lily felt the tightening of the crotch strap again, and Karla's fingers under it.

God, I must be wet down there, Lily thought, aghast. I'm going off like a dog in heat with this woman I barely know!

The fingers probed deeper and Lily began to squeeze her buttocks, thrusting herself against the weight of the woman on top. God she wanted it so desperately now, and it was on the way, surely…

Then Karla was gone and the pieces of tape were pulled off. Two hard slaps landed against the rubber over her face, and though it barely stung, it distracted Lily sufficiently that the arousal in her loins subsided. Lily whined. It was so unfair. Karla grabbed her by the shoulders and hauled her to her feet.

'All right Lily. That was fun, wasn't it. You're such a slut – I'm surprised, for one so inexperienced. You have submissive genes, I think. But let's go see what's happening in the dungeon.'

'Hnnm?'

'Yes, there's a dungeon here, too. It's a very good little earner on the side. It's rented out to apartment dwellers who don't have the space themselves. *I* have it for today.' Upright, Lily stumbled and felt light-headed as her blood relocated.

Karla stopped and faced her, holding her by the shoulders and looking hard into her eyes. Lily's vision blurred, and it was with relief that she heard Karla's next comment.

'I'm remiss, Lily. I'm sorry. You're not used to any of this, are you? You've not experienced a decent gag before, never mind this nasty rubber hood… Poor *Liebling*…' Karla moved behind Lily and suddenly the buckles at the side of her head were eased, and the two halves came apart. The front half peeled away from her face, extracting the mouthpiece with a wet plop. Lily would have liked to wipe her face but her hands and arms remained immobilised. Karla took Lily's face in her hands, peering intently at her, smoothing her hair and wiping the damp sweat and drool with a small handkerchief, dabbing at the edges of her mouth and eyes. Her concern was touching and made Lily feel grateful, regardless of what she had just experienced.

'Better?'

'Yes. Thank you.' Lily sounded absurdly apologetic, as though she had inconvenienced her captor.

'Good. Come, now. We'll go downstairs to the dungeon. Believe me, Lily, you haven't seen everything yet. You may get to watch somebody else get the treatment. If you learn nothing else, I hope that the one thing you realise today is that your desires are not unique. There are many, many others who seek the same releases you do, who follow the same imaginary paths.'

Karla led the way back to the stairs and they started down. Trapped in the straightjacket Lily was scared they would meet someone else, before realising that everybody else in this place was as twisted as she evidently was, and she should be beyond any embarrassment. They passed the retail store door and continued down to a rusty steel door with a skull and cross bones painted on it, the stairwell here lit only by a single low-wattage bulb. The door opened with a drawn-out creak.

While Karla had warned Lily that she had not yet seen everything, Lily was still unprepared for the cellar of this building. Heaven knew what the place had once been. Perhaps a storeroom, a wine cellar, or maybe a shelter from falling bombs. Now it was a gloomy warren of low-ceilinged cell-like rooms, some with wooden doors, some with barred doors, the walls of spalling plastered brickwork. The place smelt of dust, damp and decay.

They followed a short corridor to a larger, central room, and descended another flight of steps. Here the room was brighter, the walls lit by downlights, displaying a huge range of implements of restraint and pain. There was not the full scope Lily had seen in the shop above, but these were not pristine, either. They had the hallmarks of usage, the traces of wear, of impact.

The effect of a wall of canes, floggers, hoods and gags, as well as the neat coils of rope hanging on hooks was impressive, if not shocking to Lily. This was Lily's first dungeon, other than the fantasy worlds she had begun to inhabit in her head, during her sessions with Aysha. Being in this chamber underneath Berlin was surreal, and Lily squirmed in the straightjacket again, as though to confirm she was really there.

The descent down the last few steps made the open space seem larger, the ceiling higher, with various hooks and pulleys dangling from the concrete slab above. There were already two other people in the dungeon. The first was Gisela, she of the shiny black rubber clothing – an acolyte tasked with looking after a prisoner while the head mistress went about more important business. Gisela was standing beside the second person, a slim young woman in her twenties with copper-coloured hair pulled into a tight ponytail. She stood at the centre of the room, bare feet braced apart by a bar attached to two leather ankle cuffs, her hands secured behind her back and naked as the day she was born.

Lily was busy trying to assimilate her surroundings. The timely presence of the two young women – obviously waiting for the arrival of Karla and Lily – did not register with Lily as being part of a coordinated performance intended to sway a prospective client.

The bound young woman looked at the two new arrivals with large mascaraed blue eyes, her face shiny with sweat beneath a complex gag harness that wedged her mouth open with a red rubber ball on a wide strap. At the top of the head harness was a metal ring, to which a cord was tied that rose to pass over a ceiling hook, before descending to attach to a black object the size of a large, slim flashlight, the lower end of which rested on the concrete floor in front of her.

Karla led the way, followed by Lily, again self-conscious at her dress rolled up under the black leather straightjacket which held her so firmly. They approached the bound prisoner and Karla walked around her, as though inspecting the quality of Gisela's work.

'This is Liezel,' said Karla, as though introducing a pet dog. 'Liezel is a slut generally, but a pain slut in particular.' Lily gazed at the woman, her eyes taking in the small breasts, athletic body and shaven pubes, looking as though her skin had been oiled from head to toe, though Lily suspected it was sweat. Liezel was evidently undecided whether to look frustrated or perhaps contrite and pleading. Lily had not worked out the circumstances of the prisoner, until Karla barked out a command.

Liezel began to squat, to lower her body as far as she could in the limitations of her spread legs. As her head sank downward, the cord began to raise the black object until it came level with her crotch. Lily could now hear the buzzing sound and gleaned that this object – looking not unlike a microphone – was a blunt-headed vibrator. As Liezel reached as low as she could, the vibrator nuzzled her crotch and Liezel shuffled an inch further forward, trying to get more pressure from the object against her clit.

Lily could see the effort the woman was exerting, her legs starting to tremble, her body tense with the struggle. Her eyes closed as she concentrated on getting the device to the exact spot, then tried to hold it there and absorb the blissful vibrations. However it was evident there was not enough weight in the vibrator itself to push her over the edge, and that the squatting effort required was exhausting her, for she had clearly been seeking relief for some while.

With a strangled moan she gave in to the tremors of her thighs and straightened up, trying to release a sob. Lily thought that what she had presumed was sweat on her cheeks might even be tears of frustration and disappointment.

'You see what goes on here, Lily? Dear Liezel has been seeking to climax for a little while, though she knows like a good communist she will never get reward without struggle. It is a very simple little thing that Gisela has rigged up here, don't you think? Have you heard of predicament bondage, Lily?'

'Yes, Karla,' said Lily demurely, not realising that she spoke exactly as she might to Aysha, her avowed Mistress ever since the placement of the collar in Istanbul.

'Excellent!' Karla beamed. 'Your education and value has just gone up a notch. Well done, Lily. You see our little predicament here? Of course you do. Dear Liesel keeps trying to get herself off, but cannot sustain the knee bend, and each time becomes more tired and more frustrated, until such time as I or Gisela take pity on her. Do you think I should put her out of her misery, Lily?'

Lily saw the desperation on the prisoner's face, and took in the faint hmmming sounds coming from behind the rubber ball which might have been pleading of some sort. Fascinated, she watched as a runnel of drool dropped from the gag strap on to Liezel's left breast and slowly found its way past the nipple, following the wet path made by others down her stomach and into the dark cleft between her legs.

'Well, Lily?' Lily didn't know what to say. Liezel looked like she was ready to explode but couldn't reach the detonator.

'Uh... yes, Karla...'

'No, Lily – wrong answer. That's why you'll never be a Domme. You're too soft-hearted. You wave your feelings around as though they're a flag for all to see.' Karla sighed. 'But then, you don't know Liezel, so I have an advantage. No, Liezel wants more...'

Karla moved to a shelf with dozens of accessories laid out like a museum display and selected two objects which Lily could not see clearly. She returned to the bound woman and to the sound of tinkling, fastened a small steel clamp on each nipple, before stepping back to admire her handiwork.

'Come over here and look close, Lily,' Karla ordered. 'These are called clover clamps.' She showed Lily the small metal pincers that attached either side of the nipple with contact points the size of a tiny button. Attached to the free end of each clamp was a little brass bell that now tingged with the smallest movement of their wearer. Karla tugged each one and Liezel groaned, squeezing her eyes closed. Lily was fascinated, caught in two minds at the prospect of the pain versus the chance to wear those evil clips without choice, pinioned as they were by the evil queen.

Liezel's breathing was more ragged, now.

'I can put those close to the nipple – more painful, Lily – or I can set them deeper, to give my darling slave an hour or two to savour the rising agony, as she contemplates what a little shit she's been and how much more punishment she deserves.' Karla laughed. 'These are the moments I do love so much, and – truthfully – these are the moments this little slave loves, too, don't you *Liebling*?' Karla kissed Liezel lightly on the nose, running her fingers over the breasts around the dangling clamps and making the bells jingle. Liezel moaned again and snorted with what might have been pain, pleasure, indignation or any combination.

'But as I said before, Liezel is a pain slut, so don't be fooled by those plaintive noises. This is why we gag her. Liezel is also a shouter, a crier, a complainer. In short, she is a noisy bitch who never knows when to shut up, and when she *does* get what she wants, she tries to shout her pleasure to the world. She will complain but take her medicine, secretly getting cranky if it's withheld.'

Karla moved over to the wall hung with instruments of pain, the sight of which made Lily's heart do flipflops and her stomach turn over. Karla selected a smooth rattan can the thickness of her little finger and flexed it, then swished it through the air. It made a frightening noise and Lily caught a flash of what she could only interpret as fear in Liezel's eyes as she tried to turn her head to see what was to befall her.

Karla said something to Gisela and the black-clad figure hastened to the bound figure and untied the vibrator, before pulling the cord to the back of Liezel and looping it through her bound wrists. She began to haul and moments later Liezel's wrists and arms were dragged vertically away from her body, while her gag harness was also pulled upwards, immobilising her head. Gisela tied off the cord at the wrists, leaving Liezel standing rigidly, barely able to move. Karla swished the cane again, and it was evident why this new position had been imposed. Liezel could not now protect her exposed backside which was to be the target. Liezel whined and tried to turn away from the woman in the white leather with the cane, but to no avail.

Lily was transfixed, in the manner of one watching a lioness approach an antelope caught in a snare, sharing the anticipation and fear. Karla rested the cane against the white buttocks and began to tap gently, moving the stick down the backs of her thighs then up again. She gave a few taps across Liezel's breasts, making the bells tinkle and extracting a few snorts of pain from Liezel. Then it was back to the backside, now a bright red from the multitude of tiny impacts.

But playtime was over – that much was evident. Karla said something and swung the cane hard, the impact sounding shockingly harsh as it landed. Liezel stiffened and uttered a stifled cry. A dark blue mark appeared moments later across each buttock, as Karla struck again. Liezel hopped as best she could, snorting and yowling into the ball, her breathing confused with trying to scream at the same time. A third stroke cut into her flesh and Liezel screamed and bucked as best she could.

In the next seconds Gisela had taken the cane from Karla and swapped it for the vibrator, which Karla now jammed into Liezel's crotch. Liezel's gagged cries went up an notch, as did her struggles, as she jerked and tugged at her bonds, yowling into the rubber ball, her eyes squeezed shut. Gisela gripped her arms from behind while Karla hugged her body, pushing the black vibrator hard into Liezel's pussy as the hapless prisoner humped – and was humped – mercilessly until she hung feebly, grunting and snorting, trying to catch her breath, sweat pooling around her feet.

In watching this drama play out, Lily realised how turned on she was becoming herself. All thoughts of Aysha, of the photos, and her humiliating capitulation to Karla upstairs had vanished in the moment. Lily wanted to be Liezel, to have what she was having. Lily became aware of the urgent need arising from her own loins, where the strap from the straightjacket ran through her crotch, taut against her most sensitive parts. She squirmed, and the movement felt good down there. Under the leather of the jacket her nipples were engorged and hard, but at once both safe from and lacking any chance of being fondled. Lily's body tensed in synch with the other prisoner as the cane strokes were administered and the vibrator applied, and she found herself trying to work the crotch strap deeper, to get some satisfaction, herself. Clearly it would be nothing like Liezel's, for the poor girl now hung limply, offering exhausted but sated moans to the universe.

When Lily registered the approach of Gisela and Karla, she did not know whether to be afraid or grateful. The movements that followed happened quickly and efficiently, as Gisela grabbed a handful of Lily's hair and pulled her head back. Lily opened her mouth to complain, to gasp, to protest, but got barely a squeak out before a rubber ball was forced behind her teeth and its strap buckled snugly behind her head. It was different from the rubber helmet she had experienced upstairs. The ball pried her mouth open, her lips sealed around it. It was large and palpable and she tried vainly to push it out with her tongue. She was in the process of trying to shout when something ground into her crotch and waves of heavenly pleasure exploded out of her pussy.

Karla and Gisela pushed her back against a wall and pinned her there. Lily tried her best to struggle, not because she was threatened, but because it just seemed the right thing to do. It was vain, stupid, pointless, but appropriate to a forced orgasm wrought by these two enemies who held her fate in their hands. Then Lily didn't care anymore. Didn't care that she was in some cellar in Berlin, didn't care that she might be compromised, didn't care about Aysha... All that mattered was the thunder and lightning detonation between her legs amidst the far-off cries of surrender.

*

While Gisela soothed Lily and eventually helped her out of the straightjacket, Karla had returned to the shop above and spoke softly into the telephone behind the counter. Her message was short and to the point.

'She is all we thought and more, Andreas. She is perfect. We must proceed with the plan. I will see you in London.'

*    *    *

# CHAPTER 18 – Der Bunker

Lily lay exhausted in her tent, trying to make sense of a day like no other in her life. The bus ride back to the camping ground had been stressful, if only because she was afraid people might notice the wet stain on her dress where her body had betrayed her big time under the impact of the vibrator and her two 'assailants'. The time spent strapped in the leather straightjacket had left sweat stains under her arms and around her breasts, and she had been obliged to skulk in an alley near where the bus was due to pick them up. Fortunately she had been one of the first to arrive and board when the bus had shown up. Waiting on board was not such a chore with her arms folded and her new cello on her lap.

Now, after a decent wash and a burger at the camp restaurant, she lay in the darkness reliving the most bizarre day of her young life. If only Aysha had been with her to share things, instead of Karla, but then, Aysha was the reason all this had happened in the first place. Aysha and that bloody camera!

She surmised that probably Aysha would have been proud of her, though there would no doubt have been serious competition between she and Karla for who could do the most devious things to Lily Maddison. Lily tried to imagine the outcome if Aysha was let loose in that dungeon…

The day had been an epiphany for Lily, if only because of the realisation of what could be found in this new world, and that she so much wanted to be in it. It excited her beyond all reason, and the knowledge that so many people evidently enjoyed these activities gave her comfort that she was not genetically wired wrongly.

Lily had tasted the Elixir, and she wanted more. Aysha had given her a sip, controlled her intake, rationed the potion in small doses, subtly stoking her addiction, teasing her with stronger measures with a new ingredient each time. What would have happened in London, Lily wondered, if they had reached there without incident?

Then Karla, Goddess of Excess, had arrived, tossing Lily into the very maelstrom whence most of the Elixir originated, with new lessons on its potency and potential. Lily lay on her camp bed and slid her hand down between her legs, still seeming to feel the presence of the crotch strap and the powerful head of the vibrator. A tremor ran through her body, and she blushed at the way she had debased herself in the sin of self-indulgence.

It had been Gisela driving the Mercedes back to the rendezvous with the bus, and in the afterglow of orgasm and the need to hide her debauched activities from the outside world, Lily had almost forgotten to ask about the remainder of Aysha's letters. Karla had assured her she would receive them the next day, the group's last full day in Berlin. They were scheduled for another half-day tour, but Karla had told her she would be collected at 9am at the entrance to the camping ground, for a special day out. Lily had advised Wayne she would not be coming on the tour – that new friends would be taking her out for the day, and again the fires of Lily's over-active imagination had been ignited.

Lily was not sure if she would sleep. What she'd seen and experienced had been enough on their own. Her thoughts of Aysha had been sufficiently assuaged with the expectation of more letters the next day. She had decided that Karla had delayed their handover simply because Lily had been too over-stimulated, though in her mind she had not questioned why she had been given the deluxe treatment in the first place. That was firmly in the too-hard basket, to be kicked around only when Lily had finished re-living and savouring the awful and delectable things done to her that day. Now was not the time for motives, she decided. Aysha had always told her to live in the moment. Alongside the expectation of receiving the rest of Aysha's letters, she had vague hopes that the hugely embarrassing and incriminating polaroids would also be given to her. Ultimately, Karla seemed like a nice person, but worry eked into Lily's mind. Somewhere, just out of sight, something awful was brewing. Lily fought her mind not to speculate, not to imagine the worst outcome. Better to think about the good things of the day...

But the thought would not go away. Aysha had alluded to something missing. She had to mean the photos. Perhaps they had been seized as pornographic material. Well, they *were* just that, but of course she probably couldn't elaborate in the letter. Aysha would be going through a guilt trip of her own with the knowledge that a bunch of Soviet oiks were probably passing polaroids of Lily around the barracks, or auctioning them off, more likely. She shivered with the thought. Aysha likely knew the pictures were gone, and there was nothing she could do about it. She was subtly asking if Lily knew anything, without actually admitting the existence of those terrible photos...

But the photos had passed over the border with Aysha's letter. They were out of Russia, at least, but Lily did not know what was going to happen to them. Pushing away the possibility of something terrible about to befall her, she returned to the feel of that straightjacket, the rubber hood and that mouth-filling, all-silencing rubber ball, and moved her hand slowly down again...

Wearing a modest wrap-around skirt and a pale lilac cotton blouse, Lily had been waiting nearly fifteen minutes when the Mercedes arrived on the dot of 9am. Again it was Gisela behind the wheel with Karla in the rear seat. Lily climbed in beside her, greeting the two women in German. Karla gave a small smile as Lily closed the door behind her. The car did not move. In the gloom brought about by the tinted windows, Lily's eye caught sight of high polished boots, a flash of black-stockinged leg and a black sleeveless leather dress, belted at the waist with a fine silver chain. Karla was the black queen today, her blonde hair wound into a bun with locks dangling at her temples.

'Lily, we are going to do a little role play today. Yesterday you had a little sample of the sort of experiences that lie in the bondage world. It was good, *ja*?'

'Oh yes,' said Lily.

'You were not hurt, and I think you enjoyed yourself. And you were delivered to the bus just like we promised. The same thing will happen today, though we will bring you back here tonight, with the rest of Aysha's letters. Those are the rules. Again, you will need to trust me. I will have some new and wonderful things for you today, Lily, provided you do as you're told. Okay?'

Lily could already feel her mouth going dry and the butterflies reproducing in her stomach at the thought of... who knew what?

She nodded. 'Uh-huh.'

'Good. Give me your hands.'

Not thinking, Lily put out her hands, as though to allow Karla to read her palms.

'Ach. Silly girl,' tutted Karla, turning them palm to palm. She produced a length of cotton sashcord and proceeded to bind Lily's wrists loosely, then looped several turns between them, cinching the main cords snug tight. Lily continued to be astonished at how quickly she could be immobilised.

'Now, Lily, we are going to pretend you have been kidnapped. I suspect this will stimulate your imagination. We will go to a fun place where we will spend the day. Nobody else will be involved this time. Just you and me. Okay?' Lily nodded again.

'In order to kidnap you, I have another hood – much nicer than the rubber one from yesterday. I think you will like it. Turn your head away from me.'

Lily obeyed, and had just time to see something black descend on her head, covering her eyes and pulled down over her nose, mouth and chin, its edges tugged together at the back of her head. It was made of soft, wonderful-smelling leather and felt very comfortable. Firm hands smoothed the leather down over her head and with practised movements began tightening laces that ran down the back. Lily revelled in the covering, as the laces were tied off and fingers did a final check of the alignment of nostril and mouth holes.

The mouth opening was little more than a slit, and Lily received another surprise as Karla's voice murmured 'Open wide, Lily.'

Lily was actually unable to open her mouth much at all, but she felt a smooth cold plate slide through the opening. It was about the size and shape of a flat metal spoon but twice as thick, pressing her tongue down. It was attached to a small steel plate that covered the mouth slit in the leather and curved around outside the mask, held in place by what seemed like a chain on each side, the ends of which were now locked together behind her neck. Lily tried to speak, to enunciate something, but it came out as a garbled, barely audible mumble. Oh my, thought Lily with a thrill. Now I really have been kidnapped!

The car engine started and they moved away from the entrance.

'On the floor!' ordered Karla's voice, and her hands pushed Lily down, head and hands under Karla's legs, her own bent legs on the floor behind the passenger seat. The Mercedes was roomy enough for Lily to lie, now with Karla's boots on her back, pinning her to the floor. As though to complete the scenario Lily's ankles were quickly roped together and she was powerless, bound and gagged in the back of the kidnap vehicle.

Lily savoured her helplessness. She tugged at the bonds at her wrists, but could find no weakness, nor in those at her ankles, the ropes tight on her skin above the straps of her sandals. She decided to shout, to cry for help, for she was being abducted, but could manage no sensible sound around the metal plate holding down her tongue and the hood sealing her mouth shut. Lily's imagination took her away in an instant, the daughter of a business magnate, snatched off the street to be held for ransom.

Lily knew she had an overactive imagination, and could not help herself. The overland journey had been an awakening of so many things for her, not least her sexuality and her realised love of submissive bondage. This in turn had opened doors in that imagination, sufficiently dramatic and yet comforting, such that each revealed stage had often become a 'go to' scene as she drifted off to sleep. She had surprised herself how often she had fallen asleep in her alternative world in the locked and bound clutches of a villain, whence there would be no escape. Had her lascivious desires been so obvious the previous day that Karla had been able to satisfy her with such a simple scene as was now in place?

The car hummed through the traffic, stopping and starting, inducing small bumps and undulations for the prisoner on the floor in the back. Lily tried to squirm into a more comfortable position, but the boots were heavy on her back and were making no allowances for the captive. She lost track of time, caught up in her own daydream and subconsciously distracted by a slow warming of her loins as they lay across the raised transmission hump in the middle of the car floor. She wondered if she could actually squeeze off a discreet climax, for she was becoming more aroused than she had expected. The restraint and the strong scent of leather over her face was doing nothing to calm her.

The car stopped, reversed, and came to a halt with the engine then switched off. Lily, now suddenly aware that they must be at the abductors' hideout, determined to learn all she could through her limited senses. She felt her ankles untied, and she was hauled upright to a sitting position. The door opened and hands grasped her bound wrists, pulling her awkwardly into the open, allowing her questing feet to find the concrete. There came the sound of car doors closing and the vehicle driving away. Lily knew she was alone with her captor. Perhaps she could find a moment to escape, if only she could see what she was doing, and where she might run. Until she had sight, even thinking of a freedom break was pointless.

She tried to raise her bound hands to touch the darkness over her eyes, but there seemed to be a trailing rope attached to the wrist binding, which was now used to tow her along to her unknown fate. Lily tried to listen for noises, sounds which might indicate her whereabouts. Was it near a railway, a road, an airport? She thought she heard birds, but couldn't be sure. Her own breathing and the pulse of blood in her ears under the hood masked most external input. She stumbled along a concrete surface which still seemed to be outdoors – maybe a loading bay – before they slowed and she was made to climb half a dozen steps.

Thereafter the effort to deduce her location was lost in a mishmash of opening doors, passageways and a series of descents of more concrete steps. Her movements were controlled by a strong hand gripping the nape of her neck, forcing her into a bent position, utterly at the mercy of her captor as she lurched forward in her darkened world. Lily was almost lost in her fantasy, trying to suppress the nagging, lurking fear that something was wrong.

They went through another door – heavy steel which closed behind them with an echo Lily heard through the leather hood. Then a further door – one that creaked open but did not slam. An open space, where she was left momentarily, standing in a void which became no clearer through her waving her bound hands about in front of her, trying to ascertain the presence of a wall or furniture.

Her wrists were seized, the trailing rope providing tension once again, but now Lily found her hands being raised, hauled up above her head.

She stood still, her arms above her, not fully stretched out. Her left ankle was grabbed and a leather cuff was buckled around it, her foot pulled out to the side and anchored there. A minute later her right leg was similarly secured, her feet now half a metre apart and the rope on her arms devoid of any slack. The immobility forced on her excited Lily, but the unknown location and the newness of her association with Karla was beginning to sow seeds of doubt in the part of her brain not obsessed with her submissive fantasies of capture and restraint. Karla had shown her a whole new world the previous day which had enthralled Lily and left her craving more. It was easy

226

to convince herself she was now experiencing the encore, but a little voice was banging on a door in her mind, demanding to be heard.

For the moment, she was in a vacuum. No noise, no touch of air against bare legs or arms. The place smelt of bricks, concrete and dust. Underground. Darkness, only the pull of the rope on her wrists above her head and the inability to move her feet together. She tried again to call out, but her tongue remained trapped beneath the plate and only a mumble escaped. She twisted her head, trying to identify any sort of noise from the unknown void around her. For all she knew, she could be spot-lit on centre stage in a great arena, watched by thousands of people. Her imagination was providing no let-up.

Lily shifted her weight, trying to ease the pull on her arms, but to no avail. She had never experienced such a situation and had no idea how long she could last before reality might creep in to spoil her fun.

Out of nowhere a hand slid up the back of her thigh, under the hem of her skirt and between her legs. Fingers slid to her crotch and she squirmed at the touch, before they were gone. Moments later they were back, this time with two hands reaching from behind, sliding past her armpits to fold over her breasts. She had not realised that her nipples had again betrayed her, and if they were not already fully aroused, the unseen touch of finger and thumb brought them to flint-hardness. Lily moaned and tried to push herself against the hands, but the ropes on her arms and legs had no give. Any doubts as to her situation and fate which might have been creeping into her mind now took flight with this tangible torment. Yes, her adventures the previous day were going to be continued. This was Part Two! A soft, contented sigh escaped the hood.

But then the hands were gone, and this time Lily heard the distinct scrape of a chair or maybe a stool, and Karla's voice.

'So, Lily, how does it feel to be kidnapped? Is it as exciting as you thought?' Lily nodded blindly. 'Role playing is such a part of this world. The biggest problem is when the fantasy merges with reality, when you can't tell one from the other. Some people like that.

'But here we are, Lily Maddison, daughter of Grace and Peter Maddison, living at 83 Meadowbank Road, Remuera, Auckland – except when Mister Maddison is in Wellington, in his role as New Zealand's Minister of Overseas Trade.'

The words hung in the air and Lily's stomach dropped, a cold hand clutching at her heart. An involuntary gasp got caught on the steel gag in her mouth and only a whine escaped. Dear God, what had happened? What had she got herself into?

'Have you heard of the *Rote Armee Faction*, Lily? You may know it as the Red Army Faction. Well?'

She nodded again, trembling, gorge rising in her throat, hoping she wouldn't vomit. She'd read an article in a Time magazine in Athens reporting the recent killing of the head of the Dresdner Bank by the Marxist-Leninist urban guerrilla group in West Germany. Was Karla part of this? The article had outlined the capture of some of the founding members five years previously, including Andreas Baader and Ulrike Meinhof, and the terror campaign aimed at forcing the release of various members. Yesterday, during the Berlin city tour, she had seen fliers being handed out by police seeking information on the killing. In a sudden panic Lily heaved on her ropes and tried to twist her body free, uttering a demented howl from beneath the leather hood. They were going to ransom her... Or kill her? Surely a New Zealand Minister would not have much political publicity value for them? But then any publicity was supposedly good publicity...

'What do you think you're worth to your father, Lily? Or your country? Will your people rise up to support you, demanding you be freed? Suddenly the news will spread beyond West Germany. It will become a global issue. Perhaps not so much fun to be a bound hostage now, Lily, *ja*?

'I think maybe you will have a long time to consider this. Nobody knows where you are. Lily Maddison has disappeared in Berlin from a Sundowners overland tour. Coincidentally she has vanished two weeks after her friend was obliged to remain behind in the Soviet Union. How could such bad luck happen to two beautiful young women?' Karla's tone was level, casual, practised. 'We can keep you here for months, Lily, even years. You will never see Aysha again. She will never see you again. Nobody will know whatever happened to Lily Maddison.'

Lily felt the tears flooding her cheeks, soaking into the soft leather of the hood, tasting the saltiness in her mouth. She stifled a sob, desperately willing herself not to choke on the steel gag in her mouth.

A silence descended. Lily tried several times to elicit a response from the air around her, but Karla was either not there or not talking. Lily had left her fantasy world of bondage. The ties at her wrists and ankles were now very real, very solid, holding her in place until it pleased the interests of others to change that. Her brain was awash with thoughts of her father and the possibility she could be held for a ransom. And if that ransom was not paid?

She thought back over recent events, recalling her conversation with Konrad Fischer in the meeting room of the Kiev hospital, where she had provided him with contact details for herself and her parents, and the amused response of the man to her remark that her father was the Minister for Overseas Trade. Save for Aysha, Konrad Fischer was the only person she had told. Even Sundowners didn't know that. So Konrad had told his brother Andreas, who had told Karla. Whatever was happening to her, there was a link between the Soviet Union and East Germany.

They already had the incriminating photos of her, and in an odd way that perturbed Lily even more than the possibility of being held hostage. Somehow abduction resulted in a legitimate victim. Being a bondage slut posing for disgusting photos – that would bring shame and humiliation for herself, her father and friends – was worse. She had brought this on herself.

She was terrified – a prisoner in a strange city with nobody to come looking for her. Tomorrow morning Wayne would find her tent empty and unslept-in as the time came for the bus to leave. Police would be called, but who would find her here in this cellar or dungeon or whatever the hell it was?

More time passed. Lily was struggling to process the possible scenarios when she felt fingers under her skirt again. Oh, no, she did not want that. It was unfair and wasn't going to happen. But again her pussy and breasts were teased and fondled, and again she hated that her youthful body responded unequivocally.

Something cold pressed against her neck. It was heavy and encircling – a steel collar, she decided, feeling the ends meet and hearing the sound of a lock snicking. The cuffs holding her feet apart were removed, and she groaned with relief as slack came into her arms and legs. Whatever was in store for her, it had to be better than being strung up by her wrists, for her hands were turning numb from lack of circulation.

The rope was released and her arms dropped. Another moan from under the hood. She was made to stand with her hands out in front of her, fingers clenched into fists. She did not understand when she felt duct tape being wound around each fist, but soon realised her fingers and thumbs had just become useless. She tried to feel what was attached to her neck, and could roughly discern that the heavy collar was attached to an equally heavy chain. She was trying to understand her new restraints when Karla's voice penetrated the hood.

'Lily! Get on your knees!'

Karla's hands undid the lock holding the metal gag in place and pulled it free through the mouth hole in the hood, then began to undo the laces at the back. Lily's head emerged to find herself underneath a spotlight in a rusty floor-to-ceiling steel cage. She saw her hands were taped into black unusable balls as she unsuccessfully tried to wipe her eyes and face. Karla – standing behind her – slapped her hands down. Lily saw a complex harness of straps appear in front of her face and was reminded of poor Liezel the previous day, not least because of the bright red rubber ball threaded on one of the most prominent straps that was nearing her mouth.

'No! No – no – I – errph!' Karla grabbed a handful of hair and jerked Lily's head back, forcing the ball into her prisoner's mouth. Lily's attempts to hinder the buckling of the straps were met with a sharp slap on the cheek. Lily clamped down on the ball, as straps went up the sides of her nose, over the top of her head to meet with the main gag strap at the nape of her neck. Somehow they all joined up at the back in a maze of buckles that pulled the ball hard into Lily's mouth, effectively stifling her voice.

But at least she could now see.

Karla stood in front of her, leather dress, stockings and polished boots, imperious and wearing an expression far from her amenable manner the previous day. For Lily, that moment epitomised her plight – on her knees, gazing up, pleading silently to this woman now controlling her very existence.

Karla motioned for Lily to raise her still-tied wrists, and undid the cord, leaving Lily with arms free but hands immobilised, before turning without a word and stepping through the cage door, then closing and snicking a large padlock through the bolt. The overhead spotlight had a narrow beam that left the space beyond the cage in darkness, and the black-clad figure disappeared to the sound of a steel door closing with a solid thump.

Lily knelt in the pool of light, looking around at her prison. Steel bars formed three sides of her space – a square the size of a king bed – while the fourth side was a bare brickwork wall. The bars spanned from concrete floor to concrete ceiling, the barred entry grille in the side opposite the brick wall. Lily looked down at her taped fists, and the two-metre chain securing her collar to a waist-high anchor bolt embedded in the brickwork. She pawed at the straps around her head, like an animal trying to dislodge something stuck to its fur, but it was useless. With her taped hands she did not have the ability to undo buckles or to even grip a strap. While part of her saw a cage for an imprisoned princess, another saw a long term cell where a hostage might languish for years. Once the light was turned out, it would be a black nightmarish place, for surely no sound could find its way in from the outside.

With her ears now uncovered, Lily tried to pick up any noise from beyond this underground space, but she could detect nothing. Perhaps there was the drip of water somewhere in the distant basement recesses, the scuttle of a cockroach maybe, but no indication of human life.

Lily could barely discern anything in the darkness beyond the cage perimeter, although she thought she could maybe detect movement. She stood up, feeling the drag of the heavy chain at her neck. As she did so, further downlights came on, one in each corner of the cell. Lily made a startled hmmm exclamation. Half a metre beyond the cage bars on all three sides, was a mirrored wall. Staring back at her beyond the grille was another Lily, clad in matching blouse and wrap-around skirt, bound and chained identically, staring with equally wide eyes.

Lily looked left and right, to see further images of herself, reflecting down a tunnel of cells into the infinite distance. What bizarre scheme was this? Lily looked closer at the main mirrors opposite the brick wall. Something was taped to them. She moved closer, reaching the bars just as the chain at her neck pulled her up. She went to grip the bars but realised she had no workable fingers. She peered through the bars at the objects taped to the mirror, part of which was the back of the door through which Karla had exited.

There were two rows of objects. The top row, she saw, were envelopes like the one she had been given at the apartment – letters from Aysha! The bottom row were the six polaroid photos of Lily at her most compromised. Lily reached out to touch the letters but found they were just beyond her outstretched fist. The enormity and hopelessness of her situation finally came home to her, looking at her failures and unable to reach her strength – Aysha.

Lily Maddison retreated to the brick wall and collapsed on the floor against it, tears dripping on to the dusty concrete, unable to be stopped by impotent black-taped fists. She would have bawled, cried, sobbed, but even that was negated by the dreadful rubber ball now stifling her grief. All around her, dozens of Lilys also cried their hearts out, hugging their knees to their bodies, before all the lights were switched off and impenetrable night descended.

If the previous day had been one of the most exciting and eye-opening days of Lily Maddison's life, the world had surely turned on its head since then. Crouched and chained in pitch darkness, Lily struggled to contain her tears, silently asking the world what she had done to deserve this fate. She was an innocent victim. She had harmed nobody, was guilty of nothing save stupidity in yielding to her own desires. Perhaps, by dint of her youth, she had not realised the extent of this addiction that had lain untouched for the first twenty-two years of her life, until Aysha had opened the door and unleashed those demons.

But Aysha had at least controlled and commanded those demons for the good of both of them. Nobody got hurt; Lily and Aysha bonded and loved each other; the world was a better place. Lily lived out her fantasies, encouraged by her best friend and new lover. "Kidnappings" ended in reconciliation and tenderness, a sharing of feelings and the story that had been running through Lily's mind as she succumbed to the privations of the prisoner. She had confessed to Aysha her deepest reveries – the abductions, the forced sexual encounters, the tortures that ended in climax.

A thought occurred to her, intruding in her misery. It was the image of Aysha jotting down things, recording thoughts and observations in her journal. This was the Aysha who had secretly snapped photos of her in her most vulnerable moments – photos Aysha had kept buried in her suitcase until somebody had searched it at the hospital, seizing them as pornography. Those were pictures. What of the words? Had Aysha written of Lily's confessions?

231

Had someone read her journal? Were those secret thoughts now coming home to roost?

Questions fluttered about like the random flights of released doves – no order, no logic.

The possibility that Karla might be playing on Lily's very specific fantasies began to take on more significance in Lily's mind, and with it, another swing to the likelihood that this might still be an elaborate role play. It did not, however, negate the presence of those six polaroids and the Damoclean sword hanging over her because of them. However much Lily wanted her suffering to be a fantasy come to life, there was no getting away from the menace of those photos.

Gradually Lily calmed, convincing herself that there was nothing she could do right then, other than to adjudicate the battle taking place in her mind, to decide whether Karla represented the forces of good or evil, and if the latter, to what extent Lily's life was about to implode. The silent darkness went on and on. She stood for a few minutes, running her taped fist along the invisible bars, then trying to loosen the gag harness, realising that the rubber ball prevented her trying to peel back the duct tape by using her teeth. She made snorting sounds and mumbled grunts which echoed against the invisible mirrors where the other Lilys lived. Karla had thought it all out, leaving her nowhere to go, no choice but to sit and mentally fight her demons in the dark, feeling the weight of the chain and collar anchoring her to the wall. Lily was learning that there was so much more to bondage and captivity than mere physical shackles, and that deprivation of sight and sound intensified her thoughts.

She thought again of her father and the prospect of a ransom. He would be devastated. She knew her father and how he loved her, even if he was of that conservative generation which was reluctant to show feelings. He was not rich, but he was an honourable man – someone who did his work for the people who had elected him, not for the unspectacular salary of a Member of Parliament. He had always provided for his family, given Lily the best education he could manage. Lily knew little about his financial situation, other than that he drove a modest car, had a modest house and no property investments. Again the tears began to flow.

When the lights snapped on, Lily was still crouched against the wall, hugging her knees. She looked up, expecting to see Karla come through the door concealed by the mirrored wall, but nothing changed. The dozens of mirrored Lilys looked at each other, alone in their company. She stood up, feeling the tug of the chain again, watching the identical figures do the same. Motionless, she waited for something to happen. There was a slight flutter and something dropped from the unseen blackness of the concrete roof, above

232

the lights. It landed with a slap and Lily saw it was another polaroid, face down on the concrete. It must have been pinned there all the time, let loose with an unseen string... Her heart beating furiously, dreading what this next development might be, Lily knelt to pick it up, then found that her taped hands could not do so. She pushed the photo across the floor with her sandal and eventually wedged it against the brick wall sufficiently to flip it over with her foot. She squatted down, staring at the face of Aysha, eyes closed in sleep, on the worn pillow of a Kiev hospital bed.

Lily moaned – a nasal, primeval sound of anguish, of frustration, of helplessness. Aysha's ebony hair was strewn across the pillow, her face turned to one side, her features relaxed and dreaming-soft. Lily had been so caught up in what she may have done to her father, she had forgotten the plight of her lover in a hospital a thousand kilometres to the east. She thought she was all cried out, but the sight of Aysha found fresh reserves, and Lily wept as best she could round the ball in her mouth, her sobs caught up in her efforts to breathe.

Working with her sandalled foot, she eventually managed to lift the photo between the balls that were her fists, and clutch it to her breast. She looked at her reflection beyond the bars, lonely, lost, desolate. Then the door opened and Karla appeared, unlocking the grille and stepping into the cage. Lily sensed Karla was about to order her on to her knees, but the impact of Aysha's photo was so intense she found herself kneeling of her own accord, wanting to plead, to be given the chance to make things right by whatever means possible. She whined, wanting her speech back, and with it the opportunity to beg.

Karla paused, looking at the dusty tear streaks on Lily's face – controller and controlled. Lily bowed her head, almost at the end of her tether, unable to take much more. Karla moved behind her and began to undo the straps around her head. When the ball plopped out of her mouth, Lily's sobs found new strength, and her head dropped almost on to her thighs. She was shuddering and shaking when Karla knelt beside her and put her arm around Lily's trembling shoulders.

Karla was all tenderness, shushing the chained girl like a child, comforting her with the knowledge that things would be all right. Lily subsided into choked sobs, finally getting her breathing under control. Apparently satisfied with her charge, Karla stood up and leaned back casually against the bars of the cage. From a pocket of her dress she produced a lighter and cigarette, inhaling deeply when it caught, sending a smooth plume up to the ceiling.

There was a pause in which Karla regarded Lily, but the kneeling girl still seemed overwhelmed.

'Lily, let me start by telling you a few things. I do *not* work for the Red Army Faction. We have no intention of demanding any ransom for you. I told you that you'd be back in your tent tonight, and so you will. Do you understand what I'm saying?'

Lily looked up with watery eyes, nodding, wanting to believe, and feeling the flood of relief wash through her body. She hiccoughed, and nodded.

'I also promised you would get the rest of Aysha's letters, and you'll be able to read those as you lie on your camp bed tonight. Are we okay so far?' Lily nodded again.

'So we come to what you might call the nub of the matter. We'd like you to do something for us, when you get to London, Lily. It is something you – as a submissive – have shown a particular aptitude for.' Lily raised her head and looked at the aloof, leather-clad woman. With her tall boots and pinned-up blonde hair, Karla was the epitome of female authority. 'Given the circumstances, Lily, and given the unfortunate nature of those photos, I hope this is something you can help us with, *ja?*'

'Uhh... what would I have to do?' asked Lily tremulously.

'We will talk further in London, Lily. I can tell you that you will be well paid for your services, and you'll be provided with accommodation at no cost – something not to be sneezed at in London, you know. It will not be onerous, and you will likely enjoy it. I can also tell you that I will be there with you, to help you along the way.'

Then Karla's voice became harsher. 'So again, are you prepared to help, Lily? We wouldn't want those photos to fall into the wrong hands. I don't think the Sun in London, or the New Zealand Herald would pass up a scandalous story that might result in... who knows? Not to put too fine a point on it, things wouldn't look good for your father or his nice conservative cabinet...'

Lily's whisper was echoed by the other Lilys all watching her. 'All right... I'll do what you ask. Please don't send the photos...'

Now Karla's voice was soft, reasonable. She smiled. 'In light of this understanding we now have, Lily, you will be rewarded. You may put aside your concerns and I'll show you how we take care of our people. Stand up and hold out your hands.'

Lily got awkwardly to her feet, still clutching the photo of the sleeping Aysha. Karla took it and slipped it into her pocket. 'You'll have it back, Lily – don't fret. All of that stuff is over for the day. I want you to relax and enjoy what I have for you? Can you do that?'

'Uh...huh...' Lily snuffled wiping ineffectually at her face. Karla began to unwind the duct tape from Lily's hands, and her fists slowly became fingers, the blood returning with pins and needles. Lily surprised herself when she summoned up the courage to ask:

'Who are you working for? Who would I be working for in London?'

Karla halted her unwinding and looked at her charge, a frown marring her smooth forehead.

'Lily, I made this clear. What we've just talked about – what we've just *agreed* – that is *done* for the day. If you're going to start things all over again, with a load of questions, then I'll gag you and leave you chained up here in the darkness until it's time to go home. Is that what you want?'

Lily shook her head.

'I'm sorry,' she whispered, 'but…'

'Lily! Last chance!'

Another shake, silence.

'Good. Now just be calm.' Karla pulled off the last of the tape and tossed it in a corner. 'Better?'

'Yes… Thank you, Karla.'

'I think we need to educate you a little, too, Lily. I am not your sister, nor your lover. I am the person who will do things to you in the next short while. You will address me as Ma'am. Clear?'

'Yes … Ma'am.'

'Very good. As I said, I intend to do a lot of things with you – *to* you – this afternoon, Lily. Have you been taught about safewords?'

'Yes, Ma'am.'

'And yours is…?'

'Happy Birthday.'

'*Ach*. Not so uncommon. Good. And let me guess: if things get too much for you, and your little tongue can't get around something in your mouth, you may burst into humming that tune?'

'Yes, Ma'am,' said Lily, feeling a little embarrassed.

'Good. Then we understand each other. And you must also know I will not be happy if you resort to it unnecessarily, when you are merely enduring a momentary discomfort. That will end the session. You understand, Lily?'

'Yes, Ma'am.'

'And also, Lily,' Karla added, in a softer tone, 'if you do that, you will be disappointing *me*, because it means I've misjudged you, your tolerance, your desires, and what I might do to fulfil those. I hope that doesn't happen. Now, I am going out for a few minutes to get you something to eat. You are to take your clothes off. I want you naked when I return.'

She did not wait for a response but exited through the grille, clicking the padlock shut behind her, despite the chain still anchoring Lily's neck to the wall.

# the submissive spy

Lily watched the mirrored door close and shook her fingers back and forth, feeling them once again. She hesitated in undressing. This was not Aysha in whose presence she would be naked, but a woman whom she had met only the day before. In the course of the overland journey, Lily had discovered she was not a prude, and the fact that she had been brought to a climax already by this woman should have been enough for her to cast reticence aside. Yet she still hesitated, trying to ignore the logic that told her being chained to the wall was not a good bargaining position. And what about what was being offered? Lily would do her best to push the angst of the morning aside to claim a reward for her body – she hoped – both physically and emotionally. To do this the rules of the game were clear.

Slowly she untied the wrap-around skirt, let it drop to the floor and stepped out of it, followed by her panties, collecting both and placing them, folded on the concrete. She unbuttoned her blouse, shrugging it off, then her bra, placing them on top of the other clothes. Finally she removed her sandals. She looked at herself in the mirror beyond the bars, naked but for the heavy collar at her throat and the trailing chain. There was something primeval about this image, she thought, unable to help admiring herself. Here she was, a prisoner in the purest sense of the word, simply but implacably secured in the bowels of a castle, at the mercy of whoever chose to next enter the cage.

It was the essence of her childhood fairy tales of captured princesses, and which had inexplicably excited her at the time. It was everything helpless and impotent from every fantasy that had slipped through her mind in its less-focussed moments. Now it was reality, and with it came the great unknown, the nameless fate that lay before her, with its bondage, pain and pleasure.

The underground space was warm, and Lily did not shiver. She savoured the moment, running her fingers around the steel collar and tugging futilely at the chain. She ran her fingers over her body, feeling the sensitivity of her thighs and finding her nipples were erect, despite the comfortable temperature. It was not cold air arousing her. What was Karla planning? How on earth had this whole situation arisen in the space of two days in a foreign city she had never been to before?

The mirror door opened again and Karla appeared, with a brown paper bag and a folding chair. Karla entered the cage, set up the chair against the bars and put the bag on the seat, then turned to Lily, her gaze roving over the naked girl. Having almost accepted her nudity in her own mind, Lily suddenly found this scrutiny unsettling, and unconsciously made to cover her groin and breasts as best she could.

'No!' snapped Karla. 'Put your hands down – by your sides, Lily.' Then, more kindly, she went on: 'Don't ever cover up in my presence, Lily. You have a gorgeous young body. Be proud of it. When you wait for me, or unless I require otherwise, in my presence you will stand as you are now. Feet slightly apart, hands by your sides.

Karla took a step closer and ran her fingers over the birthmark on Lily's left breast, letting the touch slide over the semi-erect nipple. Lily tried to suppress a small shudder of pleasure.

'You can see why there will never be any mistaking you in those photos, Lily, even blindfolded and gagged. That birthmark is a giveaway. And it's lovely.' She moved slowly around Lily, her boot heels making soft clicks on the concrete as she straddled Lily's chain. Lily felt the hands with their red fingernails slide down her arms, then her ribs and the narrow indent of her waist, then her thighs. The caress was so soft as to be barely noticeable, but Lily caught her breath as the hairs on her arms stood up.

'Raise your arms, please, Lily – to the sides, horizontal.' Lily complied, and Karla's hands rested in Lily's armpits, fingers brushing the smooth skin where Lily had shaved the day before. There came the gentle pressure of Karla's body against her back, pressing the heaviness of the chain against her spine, leather-clad breasts nudging her shoulder blades. Lily was becoming more aroused by the minute, though there had been no hint of any further restraints. When the scarlet-nailed hands slid around her body to enclose her breasts, Lily sighed, and was unsurprised to find her nipples now rock-hard. Karla played with them, flicking them gently then rolling them between thumb and forefinger. Lily couldn't suppress the shudder and the sudden warmth invading her loins. Karla's hands cupped her breasts as though gently weighing them, testing their heft and firmness, and another sigh escaped Lily's lips. All embarrassment had vanished, and had Lily not been so caught in the moment, she might have felt some small element of guilt at her submission in the hands of a woman other than Aysha. But Lily Maddison had stopped over-thinking things. It was all too complicated, and when the hands finally slid down to her crotch, and the voice behind her warned her to keep her arms outstretched, it was all Lily could do not to crumple at the lightness of the contact.

Then the hands were gone, and Karla stepped into Lily's field of view. 'Arms down, Lily. First appearances are usually right. You have an adorable body. You're lucky. *I'm* lucky, for that matter. *I* get to admire it and play with it. This is going to be such a fun afternoon.' Karla handed the paper bag to Lily. She opened it and saw a wrapped sandwich and a small plastic bottle of water. She looked at Karla, silently seeking approval to eat, for she suddenly realised how hungry she was.

'Yes, Lily, sit down and eat,' said Karla, seating herself on the metal chair. Lily at once sat cross-legged on her little pile of clothes and attacked the contents of the bag, any self-consciousness over her nudity forgotten, at least for the moment.

# the submissive spy

'I want to make this afternoon as enjoyable for you as I can, Lily. To do this, there will be no discussion about this morning, or about London. You will focus solely on your predicament here. And believe me, it is a predicament, for you – as a spy, perhaps a slave, perhaps a captured warrior princess – you are at my mercy. I have some instructions from higher authorities – perhaps a list of confessions they require. Perhaps they want to embarrass you, perhaps break you, make you plead. You won't know the details until you are obliged to comply with my commands. There will be some pain involved, Lily. You must push through that. Nothing pleasurable is received so well as when it follows pain. I suspect you are inclined to pain, Lily, yes?'

Lily swallowed a mouthful and looked up at Karla, one nyloned leg crossed, the high-heeled boot swinging in the air.

'I'm not sure, Ma'am.'

'Yes you are, Lily. I have the photo of the welts on your backside. Clearly you were worked up to that by your lover. I've looked at the dates on the back of the photos. It's obvious you were being introduced to something new each time.'

Lily was silent.

'So, Lily, I repeat my question, with the added comment that further marks were also visible in a later picture. Are you inclined to pain, Lily? Be honest, please.'

'Uh... I guess so, Ma'am.'

'You *guess* so? Oh well, I suppose we'll have to make do with that.' Karla uncrossed her legs and leaned forward, resting on her thighs. 'Lily, there's nothing shameful about this. I know many women who get off on pain. You've obviously accepted that you have this inclination to bondage and discipline. Well, I suspect it's a little more than an inclination.' She smiled. 'More like an obsession, *ja*?' Lily nodded, averting her gaze. 'So, we admit that bit. Then admit you like some *pain*, Lily. This whole thing – there are so many subtleties and nuances in B&D. Everyone likes something different. Thousands of peculiar obsessions – giving *and* receiving. Once you have figured out someone's likes, there's then the question of how hard, how long, or how many times... *Ach*, so many questions, so many roads to follow. Getting to know somebody's true predilections in the world of bondage is very difficult, Lily. It's not a case of just hooking up in a club and a quick fuck shows what you like and who you are. You understand?'

Lily nodded again.

'This is the place I find myself, now, Lily. You are a new canvas for me. A new land to explore. This afternoon is going to be a little reward for you, I hope. You've stumbled into this world and whatever you've seen up to now, it's nothing compared to here on this side of the Berlin Wall, I think. I get

238

that yesterday was an eye-opener for you. That's good. But it was also barely scratching the surface.

'You see this place?' She gestured at the brick wall, the concrete floor and ceiling. 'This is called *'Der Bunker'*. Translates as 'the Vault'. We are under an old factory, which is owned by a friend of mine. It is a relic of the war, which was only thirty years ago, of course. Sometimes there are gatherings here, or in the factory above. There are many rooms and cells here. Sometimes they do bondage shoots here – for the magazines. It is very popular, which again tells you how many people are into this lifestyle. You can rent parts of it for a short term – like an afternoon or a night – or for a longer term, like a week.'

'A week?' Lily was startled. 'What do you do over a week?'

'You'd be surprised how many people harbour abduction fantasies, Lily. Sensory deprivation. They may be chained up here as you are, left in the dark for long periods. This particular room with the mirrors surprises many people, and makes them very conscious of themselves. They can also see themselves in bondage – in chains – and it heightens the experience.'

Lily reflected on this and finished off the last of the water in the bottle.

'What are you going to do to me, Ma'am?'

'I'm going to do many things to you, Lily. But you will not know any of them until they happen. One thing I'm sure about you, is that you have a very vivid imagination. I know that for people like you the *possibility* of something bad happening is often more effective than what actually *does* happen. Thinking and imagining your fate can be just as potent as the real thing. Always the unknown, Lily. Not knowing is always worse than finding out. There are so many things I'd like to do to you, my dear innocent girl, but I have only an afternoon, rather than a month. But I want your memory of Berlin to be unforgettable – however you interpret that word. It will be our first time together. I hope it will not be the last.'

'What do you –'

'Shush, Lily. No questions. Trust, accept, savour. That is all you need to do. Finished your lunch?'

'Yes. Thank you – it was nice.'

'Good. I like a polite submissive. You are well brought up, Lily. Now stand up and face the brick wall.' Lily did as she was told, feeling the heavy collar twist about her throat. 'Hands behind your back, please. These are genuine German Police handcuffs – they have a hinge in the middle, designed to encourage compliance from the wearer.' Cold steel enveloped Lily's right wrist, accompanied by the multiple snap of the closing ratchet, followed by her left wrist, and Lily found herself secured – and compliant.

'Nothing like the sensation of steel against bare skin, is there, Lily,' said Karla. 'Though I suspect you haven't actually experienced much in that way.

Seems to me it was only a few scarves and the odd carrot thrown in,' she smirked. 'Feel what it's like, Lily. Feel the strength, the permanence of steel, with the knowledge you will never get free without a key. You could wander the streets like this and nobody could free you without serious cutting gear. And the same goes for your collar. Steel restraints are indestructible. Some submissives wear them for months, as collars, manacles, or some even more bizarre accessories. I think we'll take the chain and collar with us now. You look very fetching. I could enjoy waking up in my bed and seeing you chained to the opposite wall every morning.' The picture that popped into Lily's mind made her stomach flip, sufficiently for Lily to think she might even enjoy it herself.

Karla unlocked the chain from the wall and aligned her collar so the chain passed down her back and between Lily's legs, allowing Lily to be led along from the front, her cuffed wrists trapped behind her by the chain nuzzling her crotch. Lily glanced at her clothes lying on the floor. Karla saw the look.

'Don't worry about those. You won't be needing them for what I have in mind for you.' She laughed wickedly in a way that made Lily both excited and fearful. 'Come, Lily, let's find a torture chamber which will receive an innocent but recalcitrant young maiden...'

The "torture chamber" looked to be just that. They had walked the length of two low-ceilinged passages, dusty and ill-lit, before opening a steel door into a space as large as a double garage. As had been the case in the dungeon the previous day, one wall was covered with instruments of torture and restraint. Lily figured this was evidently *de rigueur* for dungeon designers, and she now looked at the implements with trepidation. It was exactly as Karla had said – her imagination was running away with her before anything had even happened.

The room was dominated by two solid wooden posts, about ten centimetres square and spaced three metres apart, spanning from concrete floor to ceiling. To one side was a low table-like bench, its top constructed of thick wooden slats and the sides decorated with cleats and u-shaped steel anchor points.

Karla positioned Lily between the two posts and unlocked her collar, removing it and dropping it and the chain in a corner.

'I like the collar, Lily. One day you'll wear one formally, showing your acceptance of a Mistress – or Master. I think you'd like that. It would suit you. And so I have to ask, Lily, before embarking on this trip, did you have a girlfriend in New Zealand?' Then, before Lily could answer, she looked sideways at the handcuffed girl and added: 'No, of course not. Not into scandal, I think. You did say you had a boyfriend?'

'Yes, Ma'am.'

'And you had sex?'

'Yes, Ma'am.'

'Excellent. You know what it's like to feel one of those lovely things inside you, then. Was it good sex, Lily?'

'Uh…' Lily had thought it was good at the time, but all her norms and benchmarks had been thrown out since she had met Aysha. 'I guess.'

'You do a lot of guessing, don't you Lily, when what you really mean is 'no', as in this case, or at best it was 'okay but not take-your-breath-away brilliant'. Am I right?'

'Yes Ma'am,' Lily admitted quietly, like a child caught out.

'So you've drunk at both taps, so to speak. Good.' Karla had taken down a long coil of rope and now knelt beside Lily's right foot, fastening one end of the rope with multiple turns around her ankle. 'Spread your legs, Lily. More.' Lily pushed her feet apart further to twice the width of her hips. Karla ran the rope to the left ankle and wound further turns around it before knotting it, limiting any further leg-spreading, then ran the rope around the left post, back around the right post and finishing with another knot at Lily's right ankle.

'There. I don't think you'll be going anywhere, Lily.' It had taken only a minute, but Lily realised she was already helpless and exposed. Karla stood in front of her and dropped her hand to Lily's groin, caressing her mons then giving her three sharp slaps with cupped palm. The noise was loud in the room and Lily jerked, biting her lip to stop crying out. It was more the suddenness of the impact than the pain.

'Are you a crier, Lily? Will I reduce you to tears easily?'

'I don't really know, Ma'am.'

'No, probably you don't. I suspect you're not.' Karla lifted Lily's chin with her hand. 'I think you can take a lot – or you will do where you're going. Have you ever heard of "sub-space", Lily?'

'No, Ma'am.'

'Ach! I think you have not got to that lesson, yet. But perhaps it is time to explain this thing. Maybe you will even visit there yourself, today.' Lily looked at her curiously, wondering where this was going.

'It's an emotional "place" which some submissives "go to" when they experience high levels of pain or pleasure, Lily. It's like a trance, with some people more inclined or receptive to them than others. Often, those who like pain the most slip into sub-space as a way to deal with it, when your body is releasing a whole load of different hormones. These may give you a "high", if you like.'

'Will *I* go into sub-space?'

'I really don't know, Lily. It's something you'll have to find out for yourself. Sometimes there are triggers which might push you over – like pain on a particular part of your body, or a certain level of pain.'

'How will I know?'

'Oh, you'll know, I think,' Karla smiled. 'This is not something a Dominant can ever tell you. You'll need to have this discussion with other subs. I'm just telling you this "place" exists. You may find yourself suddenly all floaty... things become hazy, perhaps. I don't know. I only hear what subbies tell me.'

'Oh,' said Lily, uncertain whether sub-space was a good thing or not.

While talking, Karla had retrieved two folded lengths of what looked to Lily like thin black rope, which she looked at curiously as Karla returned.

'What's that?' Lily asked, not sure if she should be looking forward to the next stage. It felt oddly exciting standing in the centre of the room, her legs bound apart and her hands locked behind her. She had no choice as to what happened next – that she had accepted. Karla held up the rope in front of Lily and she saw it was a long strip of leather, about twice the thickness of a shoelace.

'What are you going to do with that?' Lily asked, failing to hide her apprehension.

'My, Lily, you are a talker, aren't you. You want to know everything that's going on. Perhaps that's good. You'll learn things. I'll tell you what's going to happen with this – I'm going to bind those lovely tits of yours.'

'What?'

'You'll see. Just be quiet for a bit. Which reminds me – are you a screamer, Lily? I suspect you are.'

'A screamer?'

'Incapable of a quiet orgasm.'

'Maybe.'

'What, girl? Yes or no? Are you a screamer?'

'Yes.'

'Just so I know. I have delicate ear drums.'

'So why are you going to tie my breasts?' Lily asked, a mixture of curiosity with a touch of disquiet.

'Oh Jesus Lily! Because I fucking want to! Okay? Look, I'm going to do a lot of things to you this afternoon for exactly that reason. Now I want to concentrate, and because you're so annoying right now, you're going to get gagged.' Karla put down the hanks of leather strip and went to the wall adorned with the mass of implements, spending a moment in contemplation. She selected a simple gag – a bright red ball slightly smaller than a tennis ball, impaled on a black buckled strap.

'Do you like being gagged, Lily?'

'I'm not sure...' she said, as though admitting it would somehow be bad.

'Yes you are, Lily. You really love it, because you can scream your lungs out and nobody can hear. You can let go those inner restraints, not worry whether parents are listening or whether there are people in the next room. Letting go with your voice is the most primeval thing you can do, at the most pivotal of moments. Open wide.' Lily gingerly opened her mouth and Karla pushed the ball between her teeth. Karla tugged the strap tight at the back of Lily's neck, over her hair, and buckled it firmly.

Karla stood with her hands on her hips in front of Lily as she clamped her jaws down but the ball was solid rubber and had very little give. She tried to articulate something but could barely manage a soft garble. Only when she hummed through her nose was there any sound – albeit incomprehensible – that might attract attention. Lily shook her head and made mmmphing noises, but the futility of the attempt was soon evident. Karla smiled with the expression of a parent who has demonstrated a "told-you-so" moment to a child.

Picking up the leather cord, Karla draped a double length around Lily's neck and down over her breasts, caressing and tweaking the nipples as she did so. Before long, the thongs had encircled Lily's right breast, pulling and tugging it from the half-mango shape into a taut globe with the nipple sprouting like a fingertip. Lily watched with interest, then concern, as her left breast was similarly captured and restrained, and the thongs encircled her torso above and below her breasts, with cinches either side and between them.

Karla stood back to admire her handiwork, her fingers running over the taut flesh. She bent slightly to kiss one extended nipple, tongue licking and teeth nipping. The tension in her flesh and nipple had made things super-sensitive for Lily. She bucked and her breath became ragged as Karla suddenly tugged at the nipple with her teeth. Lily froze and her body quivered until Karla opened her mouth to release the teat.

'God you look yummy,' Karla exclaimed. Lily rolled her eyes helplessly as Karla slipped her hand between Lily's legs again, rubbing her fingers in front of Lily's face. 'See – wet. Slut,' she said conversationally. 'You can't hide your true self here, Lily.'

Karla unlocked the steel handcuffs and buckled a leather cuff around each wrist, locking them in place with small padlocks. Lily looked at the cuffs – heavy black leather with solid D-rings for attachments – and wondered what was next. Karla grabbed a long rope hanging over a pulley at the top of one post and pulled it across to tie it to Lily's right cuff before hauling on the other end. Lily's arm shot up towards the roof. A minute later Lily was standing like a starfish, legs and arms stretched high and wide. It was difficult to imagine a more vulnerable position. Lily's heart began to race as she considered how accessible she now was.

'Subbies' motto, Lily – "It's always better when you can't move".' Karla grinned. 'The only thing missing is your blindfold. If you're going to go on some astral journey, or whatever the fuck it is that you do, you don't want any distractions, I think.' That was it for Lily when a soft leather blindfold was buckled in place over her eyes and she was left to deal with the world of her imagination and all the terrible suffering that lay before her.

The flap of a crop of some sort struck Lily on her backside, followed by another strike, and another – an insistent tattoo across the white mounds of her buttocks, turning them pink with the impacts. At first it was a distraction, then a focus for Lily, as the strikes became harder. They ranged down the back of her legs, then across her back, all the while sensitizing the skin as Lily's breathing became heavier. Then there was a cessation, and hands caressed the taut globes that were her bound breasts, kneading and tweaking her nipples until there was a sudden biting pain on the right, then the left one, as a clamp was released on each.

Lily struggled against the ropes holding her high and wide, and caught her breath as a weight came to hang on each of the clamps, distorting her nipples downwards and making a slight tinkling sound. Lily deduced that her breasts were now sporting small bells. She twisted her torso back and forth and heard the jangle of her new adornments.

Hanging bells like this was a test for witchcraft, and the jangling was a sure sign of guilt. Lily tried to still her movements, to focus, not knowing what was to come next, here in the chamber beneath the Baron's castle. They had brought her here, accusing her of sleeping with the Devil, when in reality she had been lured there by John of Dalkeith, who had never forgiven her for jilting him. Sleeping with the Devil would bring severe punishment, Lily knew, once they had forced a confession out of her...

The flogger cut across her breasts, followed by a series of blows across her stomach. It took some time before her torturer was satisfied most of her body was glowing red from the impact. Lily had managed to keep her composure – until the tails of the flogger slapped upwards between her legs. A snort escaped the gag, and Lily went on to her tiptoes as a series of blows impacted between her legs. She twisted and tugged at the ropes, but there was no escaping the flogger. The blows became harder, then stopped. Lily hung there, trying to sense where her tormentor was in the chamber, wondering what instrument was being selected for infliction of the next stage.

The cane stroke across her already burning buttocks made her yowl into the gag. Another blow an inch lower, and then another. A voice said something about a confession, but Lily was past thinking now, not making sense of references to the Devil and how she was a slave to Beelzebub. She jerked and twitched in her ropes, muscles clenched and body rigid at the impacts. A further impact, at the top of her thighs, then silence. Why would she not confess?

There was a long pause. Lily hung there, her breathing mingled with sobs, runnels of sweat sliding remorselessly down her flanks. She tried to pull herself together, to stop the shaking of her thighs and feet. Somewhere there was a high pitched keening sound that slowly eased, as she got her breathing under control, though there was no stopping the tears seeping from under the blindfold.

Why had she done this? She had known the consequences. She had known that pain and punishment would follow, but young, foolish and reckless, she had transgressed anyway. Was this what she really wanted?

Something thin and whippy caught her across the top of her breasts – a rapid patter of smacks from a thin cane – tap-tap-tap! Her birthmark! The sure sign of a witch! Striking on the same place though not as hard as the varied blows on her buttocks. Bells jangled as Lily swayed and shrieked incoherently in her ropes, biting on the gag in her mouth but articulating no confession which might stop the torture. Then that, too, ceased, and a whole new persecution began, as an object – firm, flexible, the like of which she had never encountered, nuzzled her love tunnel, then forced its way inside. What was this blasphemy, this humiliation? Was this the Devil himself, with whose form she had been accused of copulation? The intruder penetrated deeper. It was large and filling. Her pain was abruptly forgotten by the movement of this beast inside her, and her groan this time was one of pleasure, but the distant bells now tinkled and clanged with a different, insistent rhythm.

Something was happening in her loins, as the Devil or his henchmen thrust into her, a helpless and innocent country lass, given to the forces of darkness and now reliving her fall from grace. It had been worth it at the time, and again, the roiling pleasure flowed through her body like nothing she had ever known in her few years on this earth. She did not care about her fate now. Did not care what further punishment her copulation with the Devil meant, for right then it simply felt so good nothing else mattered. In and out went the Devil's member, taking Lily to a place no amount of pain could reach her in a crescendo of guttural grunts and thrusts as Lily Maddison climaxed in her bonds.

After undoing Lily's ankles, Karla let her down gently to the floor. Lily slumped on to her side, managing to raise a hand to the clamp on her right breast. Her fingers squeezed the handles and with a shot of pain the pincers released and the clamp and bell flipped out of Lily's hand. Only half *compos mentis* and barely aware of where she was, Lily prised the other clamp off, groaning into the ball as the blood flow returned to her tortured nipple. She tried to get the same hand to the buckle at the back of her neck, but found a small lock in place securing it.

'Hhnnn?' she whined.

'Shush, Lily,' came Karla's voice close to her ear. 'You don't get away that easily.'

In her foggy mind, Lily was not sure whether Karla meant the gag strap, or the whole exercise – whatever it was. Ultimately Lily had no choice in the matter. Karla helped her to her feet and they stumbled to what Lily guessed was the wooden slatted table she had seen when she first walked in. Here Lily was made to sit while Karla bound her wrists together behind her, palm to palm. The ropes were snug, not excessively tight, and Lily could not help testing the bonds, finding a small amount of leeway to twist her wrists.

That disappeared when further ropes were slipped around her elbows, inexorably drawing them towards each other.

'Very good, Lily. You are very flexible. Not many people can touch elbows. I'm impressed.'

Lily felt a distant sense of pride, of satisfaction at having pleased Karla, though it was through no effort on her part, merely a quirk of age and genetics. Then she was standing up again, the cool concrete under her bare feet, shuffled round to the end of the table, ankles pushed apart to the width of the table legs. Lily sensed the table was bolted to the floor, for it seemed immovable when she pushed gently against it. Karla bound Lily's ankles to the legs in the parted position, the table edge hard against the back of Lily's thighs.

'Do you know what a strappado is, Lily?'

'Uh-uh...' Lily grunted.

'It was supposedly invented by the Italians, during the Renaissance. You're about to experience it, yourself. There are many variations, some of which would dislocate or break your shoulders, but of course a confession by you will no doubt stop the pain.'

'Huh?' Lily mumbled, turning her head blindly back and forth to try to detect Karla's movements. A rope was slipped between her bound wrists and secured, and Lily Maddison found her arms being slowly elevated behind her. The pull on her wrists was irresistible, and as her hands went up, so too was Lily forced to bend forward at the waist. Everything tightened – the ropes on her wrists, elbows and ankles – and Lily grunted with the stress as she found her head down at waist level and her arms pulled up vertically, at the mercy of her tormentor.

In Lily's dark world the strain on her shoulders began to eat into her resistance. Her bent-over position evidently beckoned to the person with the flogger and Lily was barely able to move when the first impacts began to pepper her already-striated buttocks. It seemed her performance with whatever Devil had been summoned up previously was insufficient to satisfy the authorities holding her prisoner and supposedly seeking her cooperation.

As she swayed and struggled against the flurry of blows on her backside and the tops of her thighs, Lily was rapidly reaching the conclusion that whatever confession they sought from her was secondary to their enjoyment of her misery and humiliation. Her struggles elicited a small degree of movement as she lifted her head to ease the pressure on her shoulders, but even this small yielding was unacceptable for her captors. The bite of the clamps came on her nipples again, and Lily felt the tug of weights on strings pulling her back down. She yielded to the pull, finding the load stopped when the weights touched the floor. The relief to her nipples was replaced by the strain on her arms, as Lily was induced into a simple bondage predicament – ease one pain by replacing it with another.

The Inquisitor was back again, poking and prodding her, flicking at her naked skin with a riding crop, making her jerk at each unseen impact. Surely she had paid her penance now to John of Dalkeith? How much did she have to endure to satisfy the man? Was there hope of rescue from this dungeon?

Things went quiet for what seemed to Lily an interminable time, bent over with the intractable pull on her nipples, the clamps now sending random shockwaves through them which made her snort with the pain. She had decided the pain in her shoulders was only marginally less bad than that of her nipples, and that the less movement she made, the less pain would result. Her Inquisitor had other ideas, however, and seemed not content with the shame and indignity Lily had endured in her previous spreadeagled position. Lily felt the return of the intruder which had previously reduced her to a panting, sweating mess, but this time there was no foreign hand involved in its use. The dong slid slowly inside Lily, then stopped, as though wedged or propped in place. Lily moaned softly, then squirmed and wriggled, seeking out the limits of this member lodged inside her. It did not budge. Rather, Lily's own movements – the sliding of her labia and pussy around the bulging member – had the same effect. In her haze of pain and restraint, the imposition of pleasure led her down a different path, with the realisation she could initiate the pleasure herself.

Lily squirmed some more, but found that as much as her movements had begun to send waves of bliss from her crotch, so too did the same movements send sharp jabs of pain through her nipples and exacerbate the ache in her shoulders. Lily realised she would have to choose between pleasure and pain, and the insistence of the rising thrill coming from between her legs was growing. She began to hear a mounting grunting, which might have been herself, sounding like a wild animal in full rut. The tide of pleasure was spreading with increasing intensity, and suddenly the dam burst, the waves crashing over Lily, swamping the pain that left her screaming into the gag with mostly joy and gratification, heedless of whatever her torturer might still have in store.

Karla allowed Lily to rest for some time on the slatted table, though she removed neither the blindfold nor the gag. Lily moaned and snuffled, and mumbled her gratitude as the elbow ropes were removed and she could stretch out on the wooden slats. Things were blurry, and Lily was a little light headed. The clamps were gone from her nipples, and she had involuntarily tested the gag again when Karla had taken them off, rubbing the tender nipples without mercy, while Lily fought futilely.

After that, Lily succumbed to a perceived exhaustion, content to lie on the table while her ankles were lashed to a pole which kept her legs apart and was suspended at mid-point from a pulley. Lily could not see this, of course, but put up no resistance as her legs were lifted half a metre above the table. She did not care about John of Dalkeith any more. Nothing they could do to her would make her confess. The House of Pain had become a House of Gratification, whose effects had left Lily's system flooded with contentment, such that she just wanted to curl up and go to sleep.

However her tormentor had not finished with her. A heavy semi-circular iron band positioned over her throat was secured to the table top, holding Lily's neck in place, while the rope that had previously dragged her arms up behind her now pulled her wrists to the foot of the table. Compared to what Lily had endured to that point, it was not the worst position, though in her foggy state the fact her legs remained spread and suspended above her did not bode well.

There was more movement and Lily's spread legs were now pulled further, but back towards her head. Lily had ceased to react to what was being done to her, and the immediate exposure of her buttocks and the backs of her thighs was lost on the captive girl. Her upper body was melded to the table, but her lower half now curved in a forced arch over her head.

Lily had lost any sense of modesty in the presence of however many people might be witnessing her torture in the dungeon. In her mind, blurred by the waves of ecstasy which had recently flowed over her, she had heard the word "bastinado", but she did not know what it meant. It sounded ominous, like the "strappado", like something devious that might have been borrowed from foreign inquisitions. Most parts of Lily's body had been subjected to the cane and the flogger over the two sessions, but so far her feet had been inviolate. She did not realise that the soles of the feet were one of the most sensitive parts of the body, and that compared to the buttocks and breasts, the beating of feet had elicited many more confessions from witches.

Lying on the rack, the blood rushing to her head as her legs were raised, Lily had slipped into a foggy space, blood pounding in her ears, her breathing laboured by the contortion forced on her body compressing her stomach and breasts. There had been hands on her bruised buttocks and between her legs, caressing and stroking, trying to re-ignite the passion with which she had betrayed herself before, but this time she would be strong. They would break her with neither pain nor pleasure.

The hands persisted for some time, fingers probing not only into her now-wet pussy but into the tight but exposed rose-bud behind it. She resisted, clamping her buttocks as much as she could, but in her spread-legs position it was hard. She thought she had succeeded in deterring further interference when the fingers then turned to her feet, kneading the soles and the toes. Something light touched her left foot, just in the arch, then a sharp tapping started. It was a thin whippy cane, and the tattoo rapidly became painful. Then the right foot. Lily was struggling now, as the pain began to burn into her brain and she moaned continuously around the ball stuffed in her mouth. She did not know how long she could take this. Yet the thought of capitulation to her torturer and the punishment for her confession which would surely follow drew out her last reserves of resistance.

Somewhere in the distance a voice told her she would have to endure three full strokes to each foot. Surviving these would be deemed sufficient evidence she was not a witch. A hand gripped the big toe of her right foot, pulling it back so as to tense her sole. The impact of the cane made her bite down on the ball as the electric shock seared through her body. The second strike saw her again scream into the gag, convinced she could not endure a third, though her brain refused to issue the confession. When the third blow struck, Lily went into a paroxysm of shaking and struggling against the ropes holding her, a thin keening escaping the gag. But part of her knew she was half-way there, and from somewhere an encouraging voice suggested that there would be pleasures aplenty if she could maintain her stoicism.

Now the dungeon and its inquisitors became more distant, and the first stroke on the sole of her left foot seemed somehow less intense, as though she had passed a mental barrier, approaching the end of the tunnel. The second blow was a distraction, for now she was emerging into a different place, where the third blow was endured with more strength.

It was quiet for a short while, as Lily's body trembled with the stress, then her exposed holes became the focus of her tormentor. Lily struggled again, but this time for different reasons, as a big intruder forced into her love passage stirred up a continuation of the gratification she had recently succumbed to. This time the invader was vibrating, pushing the intensity to a new level, in and out, in and out, with Lily's moans and breathing in concert with it. Lily's hands clenched into fists as she savoured the assault, feeling the rising tide of rapture spreading outwards, flooding her body and overwhelming her senses. She was on the way to a wonderful place, abruptly crashing through a barrier which sent her brain into a place of stars and light, as her body bucked and struggled against the restraints and her strangled voice grunted around the gag.

Her body seemed to relax, as though a mountain had been climbed and she could now rest, sliding into a soft, warm nook which promised quiet and relief from the glorious intensity of everything she had just endured. Except that the intruder was still inside her, vibrating insistently and resisting her contractions to expel it.

No, she could not do this again. She did not have the strength. This was worse than the pain, summoning up energies from her deepest part and expelling them into the ether, albeit through a glorious explosion. But Lily had barely enough to go on, or so she thought. When a second, slightly smaller object nuzzled then penetrated her anus she tried desperately to resist. This was just wrong, something told her brain. But another voice whispered of a half-forgotten moment of penetration with Queen Aysha and the glorious reaction it had produced. In that instant of recollection, of hesitancy, the object slid deep inside her and as she bucked and jerked, so a last wave of euphoria slid over her like a sparkling blanket of stars.

Lily had no idea how long she lay curled up on her side on the slatted table. She was wrapped in a warm blanket, her hands – now freed – thrust between her thighs. Sharp spasms of pleasure continued to randomly spark through her body at intervals, making her twitch and catch her breath.

Karla appeared in her field of vision with her clothes and put them on the bench beside her, then helped her into a sitting position on the edge of the table. Lily's head swam. Exhausting sensations of pleasure, countered by fierce localised pain sites, sent mixed messages to Lily's brain, scrambling the hormones and receptors. Lily did her best to focus, but it was difficult. She wanted to go back to that far-off place where the pleasure waves broke on the beach and washed over her, where even the sharp sting of the cane and flogger added to the rapture.

At Karla's encouragement, she slowly dressed, requiring what she thought was a ridiculous amount of concentration to do up the tie on her skirt and the buttons of her blouse. The car, with Gisela driving, was waiting for them in a weed-strewn asphalt car park outside *Der Bunker*, which turned out to be a cellar under a largely derelict three-story building. Karla spoke little as she sat beside Lily in the rear, during the drive back to the campsite. She clutched a handful of Aysha's letters and the polaroid photo of Aysha asleep in Kiev. The mental stress Lily had endured chained up alone in the dark that morning was now a distant memory, swamped by the intensity of the afternoon torments. Lily could still feel the heat from her backside, sporting numerous striations from the cane, and the tenderness at her breasts and the soles of her feet. She was glad that – albeit in her innocence – she had worn the wrap-around skirt that fell to just below her knees, hiding any stripes which may have landed on the tops of her thighs. She would have to be careful displaying herself in the camp showers, she thought, barely able to stay awake.

Now she was sprawled on her camp bed in the last rays of the long summer evening, the smell of a barbeque somewhere drifting past the tent, her cello case lying forlornly on the empty bed beside her. She had eaten heartily in the camp restaurant as she devoured Aysha's letters with equal ferocity. There were five more in addition to the first which Lily had read the previous day, written and numbered on consecutive days. They decreased in news as Aysha found it hard to find something new to write about, though she made up for that with reminiscences of their experiences together on the trip, up until they had reached the Soviet Union.

Aysha did not mention the naked polaroids of Lily, though her words alluded to a 'mistake' she had made, for which she hoped Lily would forgive her.

*If only you knew*, thought Lily. Aysha's words would have meant little, and could easily have been brushed off had the photos simply been confiscated, but it was clear to Lily that Aysha did not know the real fate of the polaroids. She did not know they now hung over Lily's head and that Lily's very livelihood in London would likely be dictated by them.

Aysha's recollections of their shared moments touched Lily deeply, particularly in her emotional state after the intensity of the day. She wrote a return postcard purchased at the camp shop, but knew as she scribbled her words that she could not tell Aysha what was really happening. Aysha had to be kept at arm's length, quarantined from the mess Lily's life had become. There was to be no risk to Aysha's repatriation as soon as she was well enough.

Lily hoped Aysha would not see the tear-wet spots on the postcard.

\*     \*     \*

# THIRD MOVEMENT - AURELIUS

## London, August 1977

*Andante, con brio*

# CHAPTER 19 – Arrival

L ily stood on the footpath beside her suitcase and cello case, under the awning of a florist shop, as the others of the group retrieved their bags from the hold of the big yellow bus which had been their home for three months and twenty thousand kilometres. It was a moment for saying farewells and lots of hugging, yet many of the group would be sharing the same hostels and dormitories that night, and it was largely the English contingent that were moving on. For the Antipodeans, the big adventure of London and the United Kingdom was just beginning.

It was Sunday morning and raining gently, cloaking the streets in a drab mist which sucked the colour from everything. Tyres swished past and Lily felt very alone. This was not at all what she had expected. The ferry from Brugge to Dover had been devoid of the anticipated excitement. Aysha's absence and the experience of Berlin had stirred Lily's emotions like a mixed broth. On the road to London, where once she had dreamed of a green English countryside populated with bucolic villages centred around small churches, the reality of a grey rainy landscape either side of a motorway had proven an anti-climax.

The depressing greyness had continued through the southern suburbs as they drove to Old Brompton Road in Earl's Court. Now, watching the pile of luggage and their owners gradually disappear amidst frequent hugs and best wishes, she turned her attention to the addresses of nearby cheap hotels and the mud map Sundowners had provided, as a guide for the first night in the greatest city in the western world.

In the few days since Berlin, Lily had found it difficult to focus on the upcoming tasks she would face in finding employment and putting a roof over her head. She had funds for a few weeks, though she had no idea the cost of anything, nor where to even start looking for digs in a city this vast.

At that moment, Lily Maddison was a little overwhelmed by her surroundings. Then a familiar voice came from beside her.

'Hello Lily.' Under an umbrella was Karla Graf, her blonde hair pulled back in a ponytail, wearing a short white pvc raincoat and matching knee-length boots.

The sight of Karla made Lily smile, the memory of her sexual abilities – and Lily's own reactions – came flooding back, unbidden.

'Karla!' The German woman offered a hug, and Lily surprised herself in returning it.

'Surprised to see me?'

'Uh... Yes... I mean...'

'We have a deal, Lily. I told you we would take care of you when you arrived. We will do exactly that. I'm sure everything is new and strange, but don't worry. We'll settle you in. Did you have a good trip from Berlin?'

'Um... yes, thank you.' Lily had so many questions, now that the intimated 'work' was suddenly manifesting itself, and the next stage of her journey seemed to have materialised in the blink of an eye.

'Come. Bring your cases – the car is just around the corner.'

Swallowing her questions, and lugging her suitcase and cello, Lily followed Karla's trim figure down a side street. Here a dark green Triumph 2000 sat at the kerb, and the driver got out as they approached. It was Andreas Meyer, Karla's Berlin colleague. He nodded to Lily, a perfunctory greeting without warmth.

Karla provided no further elaboration as to Meyer's role, after they had climbed into the back. He evidently knew where they were headed and they set off without comment. Lily stifled her questions. She sensed explanations would come, and trusted Karla enough, since nothing untoward had happened to her in Berlin, even as she had lain helplessly bound at the mercy of the older woman. Lily forced herself to be patient and to watch where they were going, to actually take in some of this new world.

Karla, too, was in no hurry to unveil the plan for Lily's future, other than to say she would be staying in Kilburn with Karla for two nights, before starting her new job, which would include food and board.

'I'll give you this now, Lily, as a gesture of good faith. You need have no fears. We'll look after you.' She pulled a polaroid photo out of the pocket of her raincoat. For a moment Lily thought it might be the return of one of the dreaded incriminating photos of herself, but it was another of Aysha. Lily felt instantly guilty at her self-obsession at the expense of her friend, but recognised the rush of joy at the sight of Aysha – still in a hospital gown – sitting on the edge of the bed in what was obviously the same room in the Kiev hospital. She was looking straight into the camera, her expression neutral. Lily thought she looked a little better than her exhausted state two weeks previously. Tears welled in Lily's eyes and she stared out the window at the rain-sodden streets, determined not to cry in front of Karla.

In the welter of emotions and changing scenery, Lily had no idea where they were going. Signs for Kensington, Shepherd's Bush and Queen's Park registered like a new language – places she might once have seen or heard on an English television show. They were familiar from the past but she could not now place them in her present.

'This is Kilburn,' Karla told her, as they turned off a main road into a street lined with semi-detached houses – identical paired brick residences which were alien to the New Zealand girl. They drew up beside one and climbed out, with Meyer making no move to help Lily with her case after opening the boot. Karla and Lily walked up the path to the dark blue front door. The house was two storied, matching front doors and bay windows as though split by a mirror down the middle of the building. Meyer took the pathway to the other half of the building and disappeared inside.

'A woman lives there who is caretaker for the whole house,' Karla explained as she turned the key and they entered the hallway. 'She cooks and cleans this side of the house when necessary. Andreas will stay there for the moment, to give us some privacy.'

The place had an air of disuse. There were no smells of cooking, of pets, of smokers, or wet clothes or other indications of human habitation. Sterile. Lily was filled with questions, but her caution told her to be patient.

Immediately inside the front door a set of stairs led to the first floor, and here Karla showed her two large bedrooms and a small one, along with the bathroom.

'You have this room,' Karla told her, indicating one of the larger pair, facing the street. 'Put your case in here.'

The room had net curtains shielding a bay window – now misted with condensation. A large flower pattern in shades of beige adorned the walls, while the carpet was a stained caramel shag. The only furniture was a dark chest of drawers and a double bed with a burnt orange candlewick bedspread. Lily shivered.

'Only two nights,' Karla reminded her, as Lily dumped her case on the bed. 'I'll show you the rest of the house and we'll have some tea. I'll be sleeping in the room next door. It's just us, Lily,' she added, as though to put a touch of intimacy to their situation.

Like the apartment in West Berlin, the house was devoid of personal effects – photos, books or memorabilia. There was a living room downstairs, beneath Lily's bedroom, and a dining room looking out on to a small fenced back yard with a sparse lawn and a few shrubs. Beyond the fence lay the backyard of an identical house.

The house was cold and Karla elected to sit at the kitchen table over a pot of tea and some biscuits. She had shed her raincoat but not the boots, and wore a short white jerkin over a black blouse. Her fashion sense made Lily feel unsophisticated in her jeans and chambray shirt.

Everything had happened so quickly since she had stepped off the bus that Lily had barely had time to sort the questions from the input of new sights and sounds. Such was her nature, however, that she was prepared to trust Karla to explain things in due course.

Karla poured two cups of tea and placed a bowl of sugar and a small carton of long life milk on the table before sitting down opposite. From a packet labelled 'McVities Chocolate Digestives' she slid some biscuits on to a plate. She patted Lily's hand.

'I know you have a thousand questions, Lily. Let's start at the beginning. We've arranged a job for you. Can you cook?'

'Of course.' Lily was not sure what Karla meant by "cook", but she had grown up in a middle class family with a mother who produced regular meals of meat and three veg every night, with a traditional roast dinner and dessert every Sunday. She had shared a flat at university. Who did *not* cook? She wondered where this was going.

'Excellent. I thought as much. You look very capable,' Karla said warmly. 'You know what an *au pair* is, Lily?'

'No.'

'*Ach*, it's a European thing, I guess. An au pair is a live-in helper who helps out with the children of the family. Like a nanny. But in this instance there are no kids. You'll be looking after a professor – cooking and cleaning. Easy work. You will be paid by us.'

Lily could restrain herself no longer.

'You keep talking about "we" and "us". Who are you, Karla? Why are you doing this to me?'

Karla was silent for a short while. It was clear she knew the question was going to arise, and it was equally clear frustration was starting to emerge from beneath Lily's normally placid demeanour.

'I work for a government, Lily. No, not the Soviet government. We are not the KGB. You don't need to know the exact details – it is of no relevance to you.' Karla's expression suddenly became hard, almost predatory. 'What you need to remember is that we have those photos of you in such indecent and disgusting poses that your father will be the embarrassment of your country. *You* will be the downfall of your father's career, never mind your own, after the tabloids get hold of the pictures. Have you ever seen the Sun newspaper, Lily? No, of course not. It's a grubby tabloid here in London – the most popular amongst half a dozen newspapers, not least because of its page three topless models. It says something for the intellectualism of this country, don't you think? I'll buy you a copy when we go shopping.

'And as if that isn't enough, don't forget Aysha. Aysha might just have a relapse. Who knows?' Karla reached into a pocket of her jerkin and pulled out another photo and slid it across the table. Lily looked down and her blood ran cold. Aysha was curled up on a tiled floor, her expression blank, her eyes showing dark circles under them. She looked drugged and exhausted. 'Am I making myself clear enough?'

Lily nodded, her heart thumping in her chest at the awful picture of her lover. She pushed it back, unable to look further, nor to stop the tear sliding down her cheek.

'It doesn't matter who we are, Lily. You'll have a steady job, and you'll do as you're told. Common sense tells you there are no options if the people you love are to remain safe. It will not be hard. You're intelligent enough to realise that cooperation will see you though.   Any mention of this arrangement to anyone will end badly.   Most importantly – something to make the position a little easier – the professor has similar interests to you.'

'What do you mean?'   Lily's throat was dry, her voice was barely a whisper.

Karla continued as if Lily hadn't spoken.

'You'll be paid by us.'   Karla enumerated Lily's soon-to-be circumstances as if ticking off a mental list. 'There is a bank account which – while not exactly in your name – will be accessible to you.   You'll have a cheque book to take out money to purchase essentials.   Food and board will be part of the deal at the professor's house in Hampstead.   As I said, you will cook meals for him, clean the house, walk the dog, and do the shopping.   It isn't hard, Lily.   The professor knows you are contracted through what we will call "The Agency".   If you have to have a name for us, that will do.   It is a nice house; you will have your own room.   The professor is a nice man – a professor of economics and political studies.'

'And the "similar interests"?'   Lily persisted, trying not to let her resentment show.   She realised that whoever these people said they were, they held all the cards.   Karla's re-iteration of Aysha's position had been the final blow which snuffed out any defiance Lily had left and opened the tap for a chilling hopelessness to flood her stomach.   But there were many things Karla was still not telling her.

'Ah.'   Karla's rancour receded somewhat and a sly smile appeared. 'That, my dear Lily, is the little bonus you get for compliance here – as does our dear professor.   He, you understand, is a Dominant – a Dom.   You may find yourself asked to "participate" in some role play.'

'What?  You mean I have to sleep with him?' Lily was aghast.

'Oh, Lily, don't be so dramatic.   I seem to remember you hardly knew me before you were spreading your legs and begging for more.'   Lily felt her cheeks redden with the memory of the two days in West Berlin and how she had yielded to every glorious temptation which had been placed before her. 'No, you won't have to "sleep with him" as you so prudishly put it.   Don't be so outraged.   But the fact is, you're a bondage slut through and through.   I think we've established that beyond all doubt.'   Karla topped up her cup from the pot.   'The professor will likely offer you more of the same.   It will be entirely voluntary – the fellow is a thorough gentleman.   If you want to "sleep with him", that bit is up to you.   I suspect what he will suggest to you will be exactly the opposite of sleep.'   She grinned lasciviously.

'How do you know all of this?'

'We – the Agency – had another of our people working for him in the same role. She had to leave suddenly – an illness in the family, I believe. You are her replacement.'

Lily was still taking in this unforeseen aspect of her employment, and the coincidence of her arrival on the heels of a sudden departure did not immediately occur to her. The unexpected possibility of her barely-suppressed fantasies being catered for had turned the whole thing upside down and confused her emotions even further.

'And what's the catch, Karla?' Lily tried to assert herself, to gain back a little self-respect. 'This is all very good, but you've gone to a huge amount of trouble to get me this job which could mostly be done by anyone. You want me to believe you specialise in some sort of black market bondage agency masquerading as household help?'

'That's what the professor thinks. There are plenty of people out there with kinks, Lily. Matching them up is the hard part. Even in so-called swinging London, this is not something you advertise openly. Everything is word of mouth, under the table. You understand? You'd be surprised at what goes on in the stately homes of England and the posh apartments of Mayfair.'

'But you don't go to extremes of blackmail just to procure a housekeeper with a kink,' Lily retorted.

Karla sighed and eased herself back in her chair, clinking the cup down.

'No, Lily, you're quite right. I was getting round to this, believe it or not. Perhaps a little background. The truth is, Lily, what we're looking at here is far bigger than appearances, however bizarre those might be. Let's start at the beginning. You've been through Iran, yes?'

'Iran?' The puzzlement in Lily's voice at this apparent segue was obvious. 'Yes, we spent about a week there. What has this –?'

'You need to know a little Iranian history for the purposes of your mission.'

'My *mission*?'

'Hush, Lily, stop repeating things. Just stay quiet and listen to me. Some of this you may already know – or not. I don't know what you people learn in your schools in New Zealand. But we'll start at the turn of the century. Have you ever heard of the Great Game?' Lily shook her head. 'No? It was an on-going spat largely between Britain and Russia from the late 1800's up until the 20th century. Russia wanted a warm water port in the Persian Gulf, or even better – British India, the so-called Jewel of the British Empire. All sorts of... shenanigans, I think you say... went on in the area between India, Iran and Russia – Central Asia, to be precise. Back then, Iran was known as Persia, and both Russia and Britain were doing their best to manipulate the monarch. In 1908 the British discovered oil there, and got control of the country's oil industry until after the Second World War, when the Shah came to power.

'There was a popular movement in the 1950s which wanted the oil industry under control of the Iranians themselves, rather than the foreigners. There was a crisis, the prime minister was deposed at the direction of the CIA and MI6, and the Shah took on an autocratic role as the puppet of the United States. He did this by crushing all opposition groups through his secret police, called Savak. Have you heard of them?'

Lily told Karla of the night she and Aysha had been dining in Tehran, when the secret police had arrested the young couple trying to flee through the restaurant, and how nobody had dared interfere. Then came the encounter with the protest group and their rescue.

'So you've seen it with your own eyes, Lily! Opposition has been stifled, though there is a group called Tudeh Party of Iran, who want nationalisation of the oil industry, with the wealth to go to the Iranian people, not the Swiss accounts of the Shah and his family of parasites. Many of their supporters have been arrested, tortured and killed by Savak. The party has existed for many years, and though they're banned in Iran at present, they're operating underground. They're preparing to oust the Shah and bring back their current leader from his exile in Paris.

'Which brings in our quiet professor. His name is Aurelius Oliver Cole. He's thirty-nine, speaks Farsi fluently and has a long association with Iran.' Karla's delivery was precise and businesslike, as though she had presented this before. 'For a number of years he was based in Tehran in the British Embassy, ostensibly advising the Iranian Government on economic theory and the management of oil revenues – those revenues which hadn't already ended up in the Shah's piggy bank, that is. In reality Cole was – is – an analyst for MI6, and he was very close to the Shah himself. He was invalided out of Iran two years ago following an accident.

'Because of his fluency in the language and his contacts in the Shah's government and security forces, he is the conduit to MI6 for intelligence emanating from Iran.' Karla paused to take a bite of a digestive, and chewed reflectively.

'We need to know how much our professor – and presumably MI6 – know about this impending coup. Are they are aware of it at all? Do they have any estimates of numbers and people… anything relevant. If this coup fails, the people of Iran will remain under the yoke of the Americans and British for decades. They'll be unable to develop, and the wealth of the country will continue to be syphoned off to the Shah's family and the multinationals.

'Now you see why you're so important to us, Lily. You're an investment, so we're prepared to look after you and pay you. You'll find the bank account will be quite forthcoming. You'll be paid two hundred pounds a week, no tax, no questions. You understand that's about three times the average wage here?'

Lily had no idea of what wages were in London, never mind the cost of food, rent and utilities.

'And, of course, you'll be getting food and board at no cost.'

'What do I have to do?' Lily asked tentatively, still trying to take in what Karla was telling her.

'First and foremost, you do what Professor Cole requires you to do. You give him no cause to get rid of you. Become indispensable to him. Do your job. Make his meals, keep his house clean. Let him dominate you. From what Erika said, he's quite good.'

'Erika?'

'Your predecessor. The one who had to leave.'

'Oh.'

'When he's comfortable with you, that's when you start to look and listen. Who are his visitors? Names, car registrations. Nationalities. You'll get to dust in his study only when he's present. The rest of the time it's locked. When you're in there, see what's on his desk. Listen to any phone conversations. Oh, you'll also have to deal with his secretary, Farah Bakhtiari. She's Iranian and very protective of him. Erika reckoned Farah fancies him – she's about the same age. She may be trouble, so watch out for her. Apparently she and the professor converse mainly in Farsi, so you may not overhear too much, but who knows?

'And before you ask, we haven't bugged his house because it is swept at random times, and we don't have the manpower to monitor such things.' The thought had not even occurred to Lily. The scenario was becoming more and more murky. 'This is the spy game, Lily. In the spy game, nothing is what it seems, and is usually much worse.'

'So you see there's nothing routine about this. It's really important. If you can discover something that indicates they are aware of the coup attempt, we may have time to postpone it and prevent the participants walking into a trap. It would be a bloodbath.'

Lily's brain had little concept of such distant consequences, nor did she really care, in comparison to the reality of the consequences affecting her – and Aysha – directly.

'How long must I work there? When will you let Aysha go? When will you return those photos?'

'Not long, Lily. Not long. Trust me.'

\*   \*   \*

260

# CHAPTER 20 - Preparation

After Lily had unpacked her things, Karla decided they should go out for lunch. The rain had stopped but the trees lining the Kilburn streets still dripped on the wet footpaths. Karla wore her pvc raincoat again, Lily had pulled on her navy rain jacket, and now they walked together to the Underground. There were few people around on the wet Sunday, for most of the shops were closed. Karla pointed out a few features but there was mostly a silence between them. Lily was trying to understand what had been imposed on her.

They took the Underground three stops to Hampstead Heath and emerged to a more genteel environment than the ordered semi-detached rows of Kilburn. Close by to the tube station they found a corner table in the bar of The White Horse, where Karla ordered two ploughman's lunches. Lily found herself gazing round at the wood panelling and sensing the place's age and a heritage which was accepted as common. The clientele seemed normal – well-dressed folks out for a pie and a pint at their local before returning to watch Sunday League cricket on the telly.

Lily watched Karla go up to the bar to place their order. She was starting to see the German woman in a slightly different way, as the initial shock of the revelation in Berlin had settled, then had been eclipsed by the two days "imprisoned" by Karla. The whole had taken some time to sink in, to be processed by Lily, who had obsessed about it all the way from Berlin. Until Lily's actual arrival in London, Karla's very presence and Lily's recollection of her sexual manipulation and bondage had been foremost in her mind, even ahead of the terrible fate she had been threatened with. Being bound and chained in the Berlin cellar resonated with Lily in a way which had astonished her, and Karla's role in that was equally prominent. She wondered whether Aysha might reach such heights, then immediately felt guilty for comparing her friend so clinically.

Now she looked at the German woman – just another person at the counter, smiling at the bar keeper, counting out money and receiving change. Lily was torn between wanting to be rid of what Karla now stood for, weighed against what she had shown and done to her. Doors had opened in Lily's psyche in those German cellars – exciting doors which challenged Lily's sexuality, her physical being, and her imagination. The front door – large, grandiose and impressive – had opened on another, limitless world, though the promise of this world had been overshadowed that morning by the details of her "mission". Without realising the direction her thoughts had taken, Lily wondered what Karla would look like, naked. Her legs were slim above the boots and below the hem of her dress, which was tailored to show off a slender waist and gently swelling breasts. Lily licked her lips when she realised her train of thought.

Despite this, and after all that had been explained to her that morning, Lily found the normality of the pub scene reassuring, but noted the gaze of a number of patrons also following the statuesque figure of Karla Graf as she returned from the bar with two glasses of golden cider.

'What's this?' asked Lily.

'Sweet cider. You've never had cider before? Really?'

'I'm not much of a drinker back home,' Lily admitted. She tasted the liquid and decided she liked it.

They sat quietly watching the locals, and Lily realised she was hungry. In a bid to ease the tension, she asked:

'Do you have family, Karla?'

Karla seemed surprised by the question. 'No,' she said simply.

'You speak such good English, and you're now here and in West Berlin. How come?' Lily had decided at very least she could make her situation a little more tenable if she understood a little more about this woman who had such a hold over her.

Karla leaned back and crossed one leg over the other in a rustle of nylon and the slickness of pvc. 'Long story,' she said.

'Tell me.'

Karla sighed and pulled out a packet of cigarettes, going through the ritual of lighting one and exhaling a subdued plume of smoke away from Lily. Her ruby lips left a faint stain around the end of the cigarette, suggestive of a sultry 1940's movie star.

'I was born during the war, Lily. My father was in the army. He was killed in 1944, so I never really knew him. I was an only child, and somehow my mother scratched a living in the aftermath, during the occupation. It was a horrible time and I think my mother did some awful things just to keep me fed, though I still remember hunger and cold.

'Everything was in ruins. I remember American and English soldiers, and eventually I worked out that their presence came with money. The Americans were much better paid but for some reason I liked the English. By the time I was fifteen I was hanging out with the Brits, working for an "escort service". One thing led to another and I found myself doing things which were perhaps a bit more "specialised", if you know what I mean. I found I liked doing things to these people who were occupying our country, and for some reason they seemed to like what I did to them, and what I made them do. I moved from the lower ranks to senior staff. The English upper classes are all emotionally repressed and perverted. Too many boys-only schools, I think. Too much corporal punishment – they seem to thrive on it.' Karla was staring out the window. She seemed to have lapsed into a stream of consciousness, as though Lily was not present.

'My mother and I were caught in East Berlin when the wall went up in 1961. The East German authorities were just as morally bankrupt as the British, except they didn't pay as well. My mother died six months later. After two years I was smuggled across the wall in the boot of a British diplomat's car. I made my way here a few years later and have some well-paying clients. You know – aristocracy, politicians, businessmen. The usual suspects, as they say. They all have different perversions, and they appreciate my discretion. From time to time I do freelance work – like looking after Lily.' She smiled and stubbed out her cigarette as their food arrived.

Despite her best efforts, Lily could elicit very little further about Karla as they ate their lunch. Lily knew she was a trusting soul. She had grown up in a convivial household and social circles where lying and manipulation were rare, and she had little experience in detecting either. While the thought crossed her mind that the story told by Karla could be pure fiction, she had no yardstick with which to gauge it. She had met Karla's gaze during the narrative, but saw nothing to make her doubt the veracity of the tale.

With their lunch over, they left the pub heading north, walking along a road which seemed far from being part of a huge metropolis, lined as it was with bush and trees.

'That's Hampstead Heath on our right,' said Karla, gesturing through the trees. 'Massive area of parkland. You will go there each evening when you walk the dog. The place where you'll be living is not far from here – we'll go past it soon.'

They had walked half a kilometre from the pub and the first houses appeared on their left, beside an entrance to the Heath. Here they turned off the road and walked a hundred metres along a narrow gravelled path, to the first of several wooden benches spaced a few metres apart, looking out over a green swath sloping down to some large ponds.

'If you have something to communicate urgently to us, you will come here on your evening walk and sit down with the dog for a minute on one of these benches, then carry on with your walk. On the way back there will be someone in the same place waiting for you.'

'Someone? Who?'

'Maybe Andreas. Maybe me. You will use this entrance every time you come here. It doesn't matter where you go from this point on during your walk, but be aware that someone will be watching you. We will always be close by.'

'What if I need to talk to you urgently? What if it's at night time, or in the middle of a raging storm?'

Karla sat down on the first bench and patted the seat for Lily to sit beside her. 'I will give you a phone number, which you must memorise.' She gave Lily the number a few digits at a time, which Lily memorised and repeated fully to her until she could do it correctly. 'There is a public phone box a short way down the street from where you will live. I'll show you how to use it. Always have some small coins handy, just in case. Do not use the phone in the house, ever. You'll leave yourself open to questions you can't answer,' said Karla firmly. 'Is that clear?'

'Yes, Karla.'

They returned to the road and continued their walk, halting after five minutes.

'That's your new home, Lily,' said Karla, indicating a three-storied brick house across the road from them. 'Memorise the address Number 8, East Heath Road, London, NW3 1BN.'

'What?'

'Post code, Lily. Do you not have them in New Zealand?'

'Uh... no, we just have a suburb, like Auckland 9.'

'Must be difficult living in the last century,' Karla mused, her disparagement barely concealed. 'Here, everything has a London postcode. NW3 means Northwest 3. The remaining numbers indicate post office delivery points. It works very well if you get it right.'

Karla made Lily memorise the address as they stood opposite the house. It was a well-preserved three-storey residence, with white window surrounds against patterned brick walls. Surrounded by a high brick wall, it had wrought iron gates on the left, opening on to a concrete driveway which turned into a concealed garage at the rear of the building. Front and centre in the wall, a smaller gate led directly to the front door under a twin-columned porch. An oriole window protruded beside the entrance, with a further one above it on the first floor. The second floor looked as though it might be an attic, albeit a roomy one. The house looked at least fifty years old, matching its neighbours in an affluent little enclave, with mature trees and gardens visible beyond walls, fences and hedges. It had an aura of solidity and gentility – as English as cucumber sandwiches and Wimbledon. Lily felt that if she went and knocked at the door, a maid in a black and white uniform would open it and politely enquire as to her business. The thought occurred to her that *she* might well be that maid in two days' time.

But the look of the house was almost comforting. Lily wondered what her future employer might be like, and whether he was there, in the house, at that very moment.

They moved on, walking around the block and making their way back down the hill towards the tube station. Beyond this was the small shopping centre Lily would have to visit for her shopping.

264

'We'll come back here tomorrow to get any personal stuff you might need, and also to get your bank account activated.'

'What about my mail, Karla? I need to collect it from New Zealand House and to let my father know where I am.'

'The professor is happy for you to use his house as your address, but you must use the public phone box for any calls home. If you need time off to do anything personal, you will need to agree it with the professor, but you must keep it to an absolute minimum. You will not mention me, nor Aysha, nor your personal circumstances to the professor. You are a Kiwi girl newly arrived in London and – as will soon be evident – you have certain proclivities which will match those of the professor for mutual gratification and a satisfying employer-employee relationship. It's as simple as that. Don't over-think and don't make it complicated, Lily.'

Back at the Kilburn house there was a casserole in the oven, left by the caretaker. Lily was exhausted by the intensity of what had been thrown at her that day, and had no further strength to try to elicit further information from Karla. They had eaten the casserole off trays in the living room, watching television, then Lily had pleaded tiredness and sought an early escape to her bedroom.

It had barely begun to get dark, though the rain had returned and it drummed against the bedroom windows. The room was warm, for Lily had turned a small bar heater on during their meal. Even though it was summer, the room faced north and received little sun during the day. The heater had done its job but the bed sheets remained cold.

Lily wore satin pyjamas but in spite of her perceived tiredness, she could not fall asleep. Despite a succession of unfamiliar hotels and campsites for the last few months, the unfamiliar house gave off a different atmosphere. This was London, city of her dreams and vague expectations, but she was here alone.

A tear trickled down her cheek, and she turned to face the window. She had spent the last three months in the company of Aysha, then in the presence of her fellow travellers. Now, in the midst of one of the greatest cities in the world, she knew nobody except Karla and her sullen colleague, Meyer. Loneliness descended and suddenly everything in Lily's mind which had kept her together for the last week gave way. This was not Lily's world, not what she had imagined in coming to London. Many months previously it had once been a vague but alluring dream, which had turned into something more inviting and beautiful at the thought of sharing a house with Aysha, the pair of them finding work and exploring the history of a country so much older than the Antipodes. Lily sobbed into the pillow, finally succumbing to her inner self.

There was a tap at the door. Lily had had enough of Karla for the day, and tried to stifle her crying. She heard the door open, and sensed another person in the room. She did her best to stay still and feign sleep, but the covers were lifted and she felt a warm, naked female body slide in behind her. Karla's breasts pressed into her back and her arm slid under Lily's, the warm hand slipping under Lily's pyjama top to gently cup her breast. Lily let out a sniffle, but made no move to resist the other. Karla's body carried the scent of soap and shampoo, but not perfume. Comfort smells. She said nothing, but enveloped Lily in a way which again released the emotions, and the paused tears came once more, her body shaking in Karla's arms, until sleep finally overwhelmed her.

Lily awoke with the light of day peeking through the faded curtains, and for a few moments wondered where she was. It came back to her then, the torrent of developments from the previous day, culminating in her enforced presence in a house in Kilburn, London, and the journey that was being mapped out ahead of her. Her last memory was of a naked Karla enfolding her in a warm, secure embrace. The bed beside her was empty, though a faint fragrance lingered in the pillow indent. No, she hadn't been mistaken.

The door was ajar and the smell of coffee drifted up the stairs. Lily eased herself out of bed and opened the curtains, looking down on the neatly-ordered, tree-lined road now with a random scattering of commuters making their way to the tube station. It was Monday, Lily remembered. People were going to work. Tomorrow she would be reporting to this professor person. She tentatively opened the window. The rain had disappeared and the air was warm with the promise of a fine day. Lily at once felt a little better than she had done the day before.

She showered quickly in the claw-foot bath with the hand-held hose nozzle which had no hook to hang it on. The water was not very hot, and did not encourage lingering. She dressed in a denim skirt, mauve tee-shirt and sneakers, before going downstairs. Karla was sitting at the kitchen table perusing a newspaper. She looked up and smiled warmly.

'Hello Lily. Did you sleep all right?' Conscious of her state of mind when Karla had slid in beside her, Lily simply nodded. 'Coffee? Busy day today.'

Karla's idea of a busy day was to take Lily back to the Tube, this time to exit into Hampstead High Street, where Lily found a slightly village-like air and people going about their business. Karla took Lily to the local Barclay's Bank, where she was made a signatory to an account called Highgrove Services Agency, presented with a cheque book, and encouraged by Karla to withdraw fifty pounds in small notes, with the assurance that such a sum would likely cover her expenses for a little while. They visited the chemist, two doors down, where Lily bought some personal items as though to herald some form of normality in her life, at least as far as sleeping in the same bed each night.

Karla showed Lily the location of the supermarkets and greengrocers, and where to catch the bus that would take her closest to her employer's house. Lily felt herself slowly coming to terms with her circumstances, and the likely mundanity of her tasks.

They lunched at a small café, where Lily announced she would like to visit New Zealand House, to collect her mail. Fully expecting Karla to insist on accompanying her, Lily was surprised when Karla offered to take her purchases back to the Kilburn house and pulled out a London A-to-Z from her shoulderbag. The small book contained an Underground plan and street maps, easily sufficient for Lily to find her way to the High Commission building on the Strand, in central London. Karla showed her the Underground route to travel and soon Lily was strap-hanging, taking in the stifling mid-summer fug of the Northern Line carriages to Embankment.

She was in no hurry to get to New Zealand House, instead savouring the look and feel of one of the great capital cities of the world, its buildings reeking of history and import. She walked beside the Thames, then past Whitehall and Trafalgar Square, soaking up the views etched in her memory from long-ago Sunday dinner place mats. Now, finally, London was showing its character, its relevance to her and why she had come.

New Zealand House was a boxy modern 18-storey building on Pall Mall, and collecting her letters proved straightforward, as did leaving the Hampstead forwarding address, until such time as she had advised her parents and any others who had written to her. Lily then asked for directions to Australia House, determined to follow up on Aysha.

A short walk later, she found herself on the Strand, outside the Australian High Commission, housed in an imposing Edwardian edifice. It took her some time to find someone with whom to raise the matter of Aysha, but after some minutes while enquiries were made, Lily found herself in a meeting room across a large table from a middle-aged woman who introduced herself as Mrs Alison Thompson. She wore horn-rimmed glasses below short greying hair, and carried a brown manila folder with Aysha's name on a label in the top corner. Lily had no idea how many staff were in the High Commission, or where in the hierarchy Mrs Thompson ranked, but the woman seemed efficient, albeit a little intimidating when Lily explained that Aysha was her best friend, and how she had come to be left behind in the Soviet Union.

'I am aware of the case,' Alison said, indicating the folder now lying on the table. She opened the file and Lily could make out several pages of official looking documents and what might have been correspondence. 'We do keep track of such instances. Most unfortunate. But be assured our Moscow people have been advised and will be right on top of this.'

'Do you have any news of her?'

'I'm sorry, Miss Maddison, I can't give you that information, seeing as how you're not next of kin.'

Lily's shoulders slumped. Somehow this was what she had expected – the official sidestep and runaround. She hesitated, then decided she would leave nothing on the table. 'It's just that... I think they may detain her unnecessarily... or at least make medical excuses to do so, after she's well enough to travel.'

Alison Thompson eyed the young woman with a mixture of scepticism and interest.

'And why would they do that?'

'I... I can't really say. It's a feeling that something's not right...' Lily was flustered. She hadn't prepared a story, however contrived it might have sounded. 'Aysha has hepatitis, not bubonic plague. She'll be able to travel in a short time after rest and care. All I'm asking is for someone to take a specific interest. Get her test results, don't take excuses and prevarication from the hospital. Look, she's a foreigner, she doesn't speak Russian, and will probably be a pain in the bum to them. There's no reason they would want to delay her return beyond a certain point when she is able to travel.' The argument ran off Lily's lips as something she had thought about so many times.

'They'll want to return her as an example of the excellent health care in the workers' paradise. Perhaps it's too early yet. All I'm asking is for someone to keep an eye on her progress. When she ought to be ready to travel, and suddenly can't, you need to start asking questions and not accepting excuses. Can you convey that to your Moscow people? Please?'

The room lapsed into silence as the woman made some notes on a pad.

'And you can't tell me why they would detain her beyond her recovery?'

An idea occurred to Lily. 'Suppose she had forbidden materials – you know, books or photos – in her luggage, and they found them. Maybe after she was admitted to hospital.'

Alison Thompson looked at her sharply. 'You know that for a fact?'

'No. But what if... Suppose that was the case, or perhaps something of that nature. It would be enough reason for them to make an example of her.'

'This is a serious supposition, Miss Maddison.'

'It should be enough to make your people take more of an interest,' suggested Lily.

The woman sat back in her chair, as if considering the implications in Lily's words, then perhaps deciding that she could at least offer a placatory solution without commitment, an excuse that was better than nothing.

'Very well. I'll pass the information on, asking them to take a closer watching brief. But until such time as your friend ought to be well enough, we can do very little. Nobody will sanction her repatriation until such time as she is no longer contagious and is properly fit to travel.'

The absence of any news of Aysha weighed on Lily, but at least she had done her best to stir some interest in the case and given them cause to keep a closer eye on Aysha. Maybe even visit her in person. Back on the streets of historic London, she tried to cheer herself up by wandering through Covent Garden and Soho, unexpectedly finding herself drawn to the adult bookshops and their evocative plastic-wrapped magazines, whose covers of bound women made her stomach flip in excitement. It was at least a diversion for her brain from Aysha's plight.

After a first exploratory entry into one of the shops, she was embarrassed to go inside again. It was nothing like the bright *Fetischhaus* of Berlin. Bondage magazine were displayed beyond the fly-curtained doors in the stuffy back area where the male customers had leered at her. She tried to focus again on Aysha, and bought a bunch of post cards which she vowed to send regularly to Aysha, both to the address of the hospital and also care of the Australian Embassy in Moscow. She had given the High Commission what was to be her new address in Hampstead, in the event of any contact with Aysha, and figured she had now done all within her power.

She lingered in the city through the rush hour, buying a Sun newspaper and spending 30p on a magazine called Time Out, which provided details of attractions and events for the following week. Lily had no idea whether she would get the opportunity to partake in such things, but at least she would be informed. She sipped a coffee in a café while she read the Sun, now understanding what Karla had been talking about. Beyond the front page proclaiming "Werewolf Seized in Southend", page three provided a cheesy headline above a pair of perky breasts belonging to an eighteen-year-old wannabe. It was a sleazy publication, but one that would grab at a lurid sex scandal involving a politician's daughter and polaroids with the most intimate parts blacked out as "too rude".

Back at the Kilburn house, dinner was not dissimilar to the previous night, and Karla did not seem curious to learn how Lily had fared on her own. Lily was in a better frame of mind when she retired to bed, though nervous at her impending job the next day. It was a cloying evening and she opened the window sufficiently to let in the warm night air, leaving a gap in the curtains, heedless of the streetlight seeping into the room.  Again, she was awake when Karla slipped into the darkness of her room and under the sheets.

This time, Lily did not play dead when Karla's hand slipped under the satin to caress her breast.  She slowly turned towards Karla and met her gaze in the dim streetlight illumination.  She could just make out the shadowy outline of Karla's breasts as she lay on her side, watching Lily.

'Tell me, Lily,' said Karla, her voice low and husky.  'If I gave you a choice of making love freely, or taking your chances of not being satisfied in bondage, which would you opt for?'

Lily's thoughts leapt immediately to the magazine covers that afternoon, and the exciting helplessness Karla had engendered in Berlin.  Her stomach knotted and her heart beat faster as she whispered: 'Bondage, Ma'am…'

The German woman sighed.  'I knew you'd say that.  I don't know why I even doubted it.  You *are* a bondage slut, Lily.  The idea of being tied up is even more attractive than sex itself.  Am I right?'

Lily had never considered such a proposition before, and after some seconds thought, whispered: 'Yes.'  The prospect of being bound and helpless came with the Great Unknown – the likelihood that all manner of unforeseen things might then happen.  Sex was only one of those possibilities.  Bondage had the greater allure, for it encompassed so many subsets in its seduction.

Karla slid out of bed.  'I should not have to be doing this, Lily,' she said.  'You should be doing my bidding, not the other way around.  Still, I will make the best of it.  Unfortunately, this is not my house, and there's not much here with which to pursue our little game, but I think I saw some packing tape in the kitchen.  That will have to do.  Now get up, take off those pyjamas and wait for me.'

As Karla disappeared downstairs, Lily stood by the bed in the semi-darkness, her mouth dry and her heart thudding wildly.  Her brain had gone into overdrive, trying to imagine what Karla might now do to her, following the exertions in Berlin which had left her exhausted and incoherent.  She had learned this was the reaction of her body to the mere suggestion that some form of bondage was about to eventuate.  As dopamine, endorphins and oxytocin flooded her system, it was almost as exciting as the activities themselves.

Karla reappeared and turned on the small beside light.  Now Lily saw the svelte body without an ounce of spare flesh, belying her age, which Lily had worked out as at least 33 or 34, if her wartime birth story was correct.  Karla's thick blonde hair now spilled around her shoulders and Lily eyed the silhouetted breasts which still retained the firmness of youth.  She flourished a wide roll of brown packaging tape.

'Turn around, put your hands together behind you.'  Lily did as she was told.  'Bend forward and lift your hands.'  Lily did so, recalling the helplessness she had felt in the strappado in Berlin. The cold tightness of the tape began to wrap around Lily's wrists, and within only a few turns she knew she knew escape was impossible. There was a snip as the tape was cut. 'No – hold that pose until I tell you!' More tape was wrapped around her two thumbs, melding them together and removing any further movement of her hands.

Karla stood behind her and ran her hands over Lily's tautly displayed bottom, before delivering two hard open-handed slaps – one to each cheek. Lily gasped and bit her lip, instinctively holding the position. Karla pushed Lily's arms down and bent over her like a spoon, her breasts nuzzling Lily's back and her hands reaching down to cup and fondle Lily's breasts. A sudden warmth radiated up from Lily's groin as her heart-rate upped. Karla squeezed the nipples making Lily jerk and suck in a mouthful of air.

'I know you like the darkness, Lily. You're a child of the dark – a sucker for your own fantasies – so once again I'm prepared to oblige. Not all Dominants are so attentive to their submissive's fantasies. You do realise that, don't you? Don't count on so much consideration from the professor, when he has you bound and helpless.' Karla said this as she wound several turns of the tape around Lily's head, covering her eyes. At the mention of the professor and whatever proclivities he might have in store, Lily's breathing went up a notch, as though that situation had already arrived.

She found herself pushed on to the bed, forced on to her knees, head down almost to the sheets. Then Karla was with her, legs on either side, pulling Lily's face into the smooth, warm moistness of her sex. Karla smelt nice – the unadorned scent of soap and desire.

Lily needed no encouragement, dropping her mouth to engage with the wetness evident even before her nose touched the smoothness of Karla's pussy. Lily's instinct sensed no need for foreplay. Karla wanted this and wanted it quickly. The bound girl's ability was raw and enthusiastic, her tongue probing and licking, ears seeking responses in Karla's voice and breathing. She sensed a sudden tension in Karla's thighs as her tongue found a sensitive spot and she pursued it until Karla was panting and her hands grasped Lily's blindfolded head, forcing it down harder. The tension turned to a rhythmic bumping, as Karla's bottom began to add to the ministrations of the bound submissive.

When Karla climaxed, she was still gripping Lily's head, and came with a sudden shuddering that nearly pushed Lily over the edge as well. Then Lily was on her side, embraced by the older woman who now lay supine, letting her breathing and heartbeat slowly settle. Lily waited, wondering what was to happen next. Karla, it appeared, was in no hurry to progress, and Lily wondered if she was even going to do the clichéd post-coital cigarette thing. But no, Karla Graf was evidently satisfied. She climbed out of bed and unexpectedly Lily found her ankles taped together, before the bedclothes were pulled up over her.

'Good night, Lily. Thank you – that was quite something. I'm going to sleep now, with a smile on my face, as you can see. Oh, wait, no you can't. Too bad. I hope you get some sleep too, you deserve it. If things get a bit crampy for your arms, the scissors are on the floor somewhere. I'm sure you can undo yourself. Just do it quietly, please.' There was a soft kiss on her ear and Karla snuggled under the blankets again to spoon Lily, hands lingering over breasts and pussy, just enough to make Lily feel unfulfilled.

She lay there for a long time, listening to Karla's breathing settle, and the teasing hands finally dropping away from those places where Lily ached for more attention. When Karla finally turned on to her opposite side, Lily knew she was asleep, but found in her own bound world that she could not manage enough pressure on her pussy to gain any sort of relief. Frustrated, she tried several positions, including face down, trying to grind her mons into the mattress, but it was no use. Bitch, she thought unkindly of the woman sleeping soundly and contentedly next to her. Sleep eventually came to Lily, only for her to wake again with hands going numb and shoulders complaining.

Lily had no idea how long she had lain there – eyes closed under the tape but brain and body still unsatisfied, longing for the return of the queen who had imposed this punishment on her. Had she been inadequate to the royal demands? Would they send her to the dungeons where worse punishment would be imposed? She would have to escape before they came, but could she do so without triggering the lurking fires smouldering in her crotch?

Mindful of the advice given her, Lily slowly eased her legs over the side of the bed and slid awkwardly to the floor. The scissors were somewhere on the floor in the room, Karla had said. With her legs out in front of her, she swept the carpet in a series of semi-circles, seeking the scissors, and gradually shifting herself towards the foot of the bed. What if the queen was just teasing her, and the scissors were not here at all? Could she get back on to the bed again? Should she wake the sleeping form and complain? Should she just curl up and try to sleep on the floor? Would she be punished? Did she secretly want to be punished? Why did she have to overthink everything?

How much time did she have, before the forces of the queen came rushing in on her, foiling her escape attempt? Her foot struck something cold and metallic. She wormed her way to get her hands on the scissors, realising then that the tape deviously wrapped on her thumbs now made any cutting exercise a hundred times more difficult. She held the scissors in her fingers, lying on her side, trying to open the blades and slip them up under the tape securing her wrists. It took ages, but even when she had managed that, she found she could get almost no purchase to close the blades, and ended up forcing her hands against the wall to push down on the handles. It was exhausting and tedious, but Lily wanted to show her captor she was sufficiently inventive and determined to manage this difficult task. She paused to listen for running feet, for raised voices and cries of alarm, but there was no sound from the sleeping jailor.

Finally the blades sliced through the wrist tape, and she found she had enough wiggle room to slide her thumbs free of the remaining turns. Joyfully she brought her hands to the front and plunged them between her thighs, her fingers scrabbling to bring to fruition that which had threatened for hours. Lily sat propped against the wall, her fingers kneading and cajoling and finally unleashing the explosion she so desperately wanted. She found herself making stifled grunts of pleasure in the darkness beneath her blindfold in the depths of the prison to which she was confined.

Panting and drained, she located the scissors again and severed the tape at her ankles, then turned her attention to the last of the tape covering her eyes and adhering to her hair. It was two-forty-seven when she climbed under the covers again, wrung out but content, and whispered half to herself, 'Good night, Karla.'

'Good night Lily,' said Karla.

*　　*　　*

# CHAPTER 21 - Checks and Balances

It had taken Helen Feldman two days to obtain tickets and permissions for the flight to Kiev, and on the Monday morning following her discussion with Graham Parminter, she had turned up at Moscow's Sheremetyevo Airport prepared to spend most of her morning being delayed.

Helen Feldman had got used to flying in the USSR. Endless patience was required, along with a healthy dose of fatalism. She had this in abundance, figuring if the Tupolev Tu-134 was going to crash on approach to Kiev then there was nothing she could do about it, and hoped it would be quick. Word amongst the expat staff cocktail parties was that Aeroflot suffered up to three dozen crashes each year, from Vladivostok in the far east to Leningrad in the west, and all the subservient republics along the borders. Rarely were such failures publicly admitted, unless there were foreigners on board or the accident took place outside the USSR.

In this instance, the flight from Moscow to Kiev had been little more than an hour and a half, in a plane that reeked of cigarette smoke and strange mechanical smells that Helen tried not to think about. There had been a half-hour drive to the hospital in a beat-up Lada taxi before Helen announced her arrival at the main desk. Another hour had passed before she had met Doctor Fischer.

In a small, windowless interview room that smelled of disinfectant, the German doctor had been amenable at first, then had become less helpful under remorseless questioning by Helen as to the timing of the illness. At length, sensing the man was closing down, and she might risk his disengagement entirely, she had asked to see Aysha. This was accomplished only after gowns and surgical masks had been issued, and was carried out in the presence of Doctor Fischer. Helen had done such interviews many times, and knew how far she could push the authorities with her diplomatic credentials. In general, the medical profession were cooperative – more interested in the technicalities of their field than politics, though a number of times Helen had encountered KGB interference. This time, as well as being chaperoned by Fischer, there was a second man present for the visit to Aysha's room – a short man whose hairy brows were his most prominent feature above a mask, which remained in place for the entire time. The man was introduced simply as 'Petrov', and said nothing during the interview. Helen was in no doubt that he was KGB, but got the distinct feeling he was watching Fischer, rather than Helen or Aysha.

Aysha had been overjoyed to see Helen, to know that she was not forgotten, and that the Australian Embassy was aware of her presence. When Helen mentioned that they had been made aware of Aysha's presence through the Sundowners office via Australia House in London, Aysha had looked sharply at Fischer, as though to inquire why such news had not travelled directly, but then appeared to reconsider her situation and had said nothing.

Though she was not a doctor, nor had she seen Aysha's condition at the time of her admission, Helen thought the young Australian woman looked reasonably well. Helen had made detailed notes as to the emergence of Aysha's symptoms, to best establish when they had first appeared, with a view to narrowing down whether she was still contagious, and had also questioned her about her family and Lily as contacts. Again, Aysha had made it clear that her family was not to be contacted, and that Lily was the only one they were to talk to.

In Helen's presence Aysha had asked about her release – clearly a subject that she had regularly broached with Konrad Fischer – and had again received what Helen took as a standard, vague response involving further test results, monitoring, and observations. Helen had found this strange, for it had been her experience that Soviet medical institutions usually wished to discharge foreigners as early as possible, since they involved extra resources for supervision, paperwork and political correctness. To Helen, Aysha appeared bright and alert – "much better than when I was admitted", Aysha had said. Helen did not discuss options in front of Aysha, other than to reassure her that everyone was working hard to get her to London as soon as possible. She had left Aysha with three English novels, and the promise that things would begin to happen very soon.

Freed from the gowns and masks, as well as the presence of the mysterious and vaguely threatening 'Petrov', Helen had elicited the name of the senior hospital administrator responsible for Aysha, though had stopped short of threatening to call him when Fischer mentioned that the man was allegedly on leave. Helen doubted that this was the case, though resolved to follow it up. The Soviet passion for reporting upward as a means to avoid making decisions was well known, and Helen knew that if there was a deputy standing in for the man, no decision would be forthcoming on Aysha's release date. She left Kiev on the 9.25 flight to Moscow feeling she had made as much progress as could be expected, but also sure that something was out of the ordinary in the case of Aysha Newton.

When Helen reported to Graham Parminter the following morning, he told her of the phone call he had just received from Australia House in London, and the visit there of Lily Maddison.

'She spoke to Alison Thompson, and hinted that for some reason the Soviets might consider stalling on Aysha's release. Alison said Lily was cagey as to why this might be. She suggested there might be some dodgy photos in Aysha's luggage, but I just don't buy that. I think your nose is right, Helen. I think there's something going on here that we don't know about.'

'I'm going to go over Aysha's travel dates with the Brit's doctor, to see what he thinks about contagiousness, but by my reckoning she's past that. She doesn't look too bad, to be honest.'

'If he thinks the same, then we'll ramp it up, contact the hospital manager and start to put some pressure on.'

'Maybe discuss with the Ambassador?'

'Maybe.'

\*    \*    \*

# CHAPTER 22 – The House of Asha

Beside the front door of the East Heath Road house was a brass plaque with the word 'Asha' engraved, above a depiction of a stylized bearded king with broad wings spreading from the lower half of his body. Lily was sure she had seen something like it amongst the Persepolis friezes.

The front door of the house had four small bullion windows above a brass knocker which must have resounded through the house as Lily rapped. She shifted uneasily, like a pupil waiting outside the headmaster's office. She was not sure what she was expecting. The word 'professor' conjured up images of men with receding hairlines, spectacles and maybe a wispy beard. The man who opened the door had none of these.

As Karla had intimated, he was about forty, half a head taller than Lily, with thick greying hair swept back untidily to cover the tops of his ears. It was a patrician face, clean shaven with the first lines of age visible in the forehead and jaw. A thin scar ran from below his right ear along his jawline, disappearing level with his mouth, showing white against the darker skin. Blue eyes took in the young woman standing on his front doorstep, neatly dressed in blouse and dark skirt, suitcase and cello-case beside her.

He smiled easily, and looked her over for several seconds that almost made Lily wonder if she was at the right address, as though she was being assessed on the very doorstep. He wore dark trousers and a navy shirt with the sleeves rolled back along his forearms. Not the formal Oxford pedagogue she had been expecting.

'You must be Lily Maddison. I'm Professor Aurelius Cole.' His voice was smooth without being aristocratically plummy. Lily nodded. 'Come in, Lily.' He stood aside as she picked up her cases and entered the lobby.

The house was as Lily had envisaged from the outside. There was lots of dark wood – the panelling, a polished parquet floor and bannisters to the stairs leading to the floors above.

'I'm very glad to see you, Lily. Erika's departure was unexpected, and I'm pleased the agency managed to find a replacement so quickly. I hope you'll find this place to your liking.' He made it sound as though she was a hotel guest, rather than the hired help. Lily liked that.

'I'm afraid I'm rather busy at the moment, but I'll show you to your room, and you can get a feel for the house. Farah – my secretary – can fill in the details, when she comes tomorrow.'

'Thank you,' said Lily, then, not knowing the protocol for the household help in an affluent English residence: 'Um... what should I call you?'

'Oh, 'Sir' will do nicely, I think,' he said off handedly. 'Short and to the point. It'll become more appropriate as we get to know each other. This way.'

Cole led the way to the foot of the staircase which wound upwards to the right of the entrance. He made no move to help Lily with her cases, and Lily noticed he moved with a pronounced limp to his right leg. There was no small talk, no enquiry as to her trip, her origin or her background. He paused at the first step pointing to two doors opposite each other.

'That's the drawing room, and opposite is my study,' he said. 'Next to that is a bathroom, the dining room and kitchen. My study is locked except when I am working or Farah is in there. You will only clean when either of us is present. Clear?' The tone was now clipped and peremptory.

'Yes, Sir,' said Lily.

Cole nodded towards a door under the stairs. 'That leads to the cellar. I'll introduce you to it in due course,' he said. Karla had mentioned the cellar, and Lily was at once filled with an unexplained excitement and dread, for cellars of late had become synonymous with captivity and dungeons in her fixated mind. What was she picking up in his words?

They started up the stairs, the panels beside them decorated with Persian wall-hangings and rugs. At the top of the stairs were three doors.

'My bedroom and ensuite on the left. Spare room and bathroom on the right. Farah sometimes sleeps here if the need arises,' he said, before turning on to the last flight of stairs.

At the top of these Lily knew they were at attic level, with two doors either side of a short passage. 'Spare room on right, bathroom at the end, your room in here,' he said, opening the lefthand door and entering the room.

The cream-walled room had a sloping ceiling with two dormer windows looking down on the street. Beneath one window was a double iron bedstead with a bedside table and lamp while on the opposite wall stood a dark timber a chest of drawers and a chair. A thin Persian carpet covered most of the floor, and Lily found the room homely enough. She lifted her cases and dumped them on the bed, which squeaked faintly.

'Well, there we are,' said Cole, as though he had completed an exhaustive historical tour of a stately house. He eyed Lily up and down, as though appraising her for something specific. For the first time Lily felt uncomfortable, though she could not put her finger on why. There was a slight narrowing of the blue eyes that suggested his thoughts lay elsewhere, and that the introduction to the house was merely a step towards something more significant.

He turned at a scratching noise from the hall, as a golden cocker spaniel sauntered into the room, tail wagging effusively. It ignored the professor and conducted a detailed inspection of Lily's legs, before satisfying itself Lily was kosher, and that a scratch on the head was warranted.

'Oh, this is Charlie,' said Cole. 'He has no ability to discriminate amongst human beings. Pretty much anything on two legs is a meal ticket. And he's already given you the thumbs up. Charlie will be one of your responsibilities – feeding and walking each day. A good romp on the heath each evening is necessary.'

'Hello, Charlie,' said Lily warmly, squatting and rubbing the dog behind the ears.

'There you go. You now have a friend for life. Any questions?' His speech seemed to have slipped into abbreviated sentences, as though he had to be elsewhere.

'Uh... actually lots... What do you like to eat?'

'Plain stuff. Not fancy, me. What can you cook? You're a Kiwi, aren't you. Yes, thought so. Haven't lost your accent yet – we'll have to work on that. What do you Kiwis eat?'

'My mum brought us up on plain stuff – sausages, chops, potato pie, mince, roast on Sundays...'

'Splendid! You and I are going to get along just fine. Whatever works, my dear. Farah will fill you in on the details. Anything else?'

On a hunch Lily asked: 'Do I have a uniform or anything?'

'Oh my word! Yes, of course. Don't need you messing up your own clothes. In the wardrobe there.' He indicated a pair of mirrored doors in one wall. 'Now, I must be getting back. Farah's away today – back tomorrow. Just you and me today. Learn your way round. See what food we have, what we need, what Charlie needs. Breakfast at eight, lunch at noon, dinner at six. Charlie's walk after dinner. English breakfast, coffee, something light for lunch and you've got dinner covered. Oh, except that I'll be out until mid-afternoon. So it'll be just you. My food is your food – I don't suppose you eat much.' Cole's words seemed to have lapsed into a stream of consciousness, adding things as they flitted into his head. 'There are two telephone numbers, Lily. One rings in the study – my private phone. The other rings in the entry hall. You may answer it and take a message on the message pad, if there's nobody here. You are to answer it 'Hampstead 3576. Repeat.'

'Hampstead three-five-seven-six, Sir.'

'Very good. Oh yes, I have a bell system here. When I press a buzzer in my study, you'll hear it on each floor. Come find me. Dinner at six. Welcome, Lily.'

Then he was gone, Charlie tagging along behind him.

Lily looked around the room, then peered out the window, expecting to perhaps see Karla or Meyer lurking in a parked car, but the street was clear of traffic. It had all happened in such a rush. Cole seemed quite nice, though a bit distracted. Was he actually a Dominant? What did he really expect of her?

Lily looked around the room again. There was a heavy lock on the door but no key. So much for privacy. Some watercolours hung on the wall – landscapes which looked like Iran – mainly gardens with fountains..

She opened her case and took out those clothes suitable for the drawers, then turned her attention to the meagre selection of skirts, dresses, blouses and slacks she had brought from New Zealand. It would at least be nice to hang them up and finally not be living out of a suitcase.

She opened the wardrobe to find several articles of clothing already there, and after a moment of surprise she realised that these must be her uniforms. As they had passed the house yesterday, Lily had momentarily envisaged some sort of French maid opening the front door to greet visitors. Perhaps in her subconscious she had seen herself dressed as such, though she would not have admitted such. Now, however, she put down her own clothes and took the hanging clothes out of the wardrobe, laying them on the bed.

There were two sets, she saw. A skirt of soft, supple leather, and a silk blouse – one set white and one black. Not the sort of thing a housekeeper would wear, she registered, then saw the white and black PVC aprons obviously intended to prevent accidents. After this discovery, it came as no surprise to find four pairs of black stockings and a garter belt hanging up, along with two pairs of black pumps, one with one-inch heels and one twice that.

Lily sat on the bed and ran her fingers over the clothes. There was no mistaking the quality of them. They were expensive, but then the house – what she had seen of it – said 'expense' and 'style', even to Lily's untutored Antipodean tastes. The feel of the leather and the silk excited her, for she had rarely worn anything like them, but the plans Cole might have in store for her were still unknown. She admitted to herself that she was relieved at the demeanour of her employer, for he could have been an angry old man – or a hideous young one.

Steady, Lily, she thought. Don't get ahead of yourself.

She put the clothes aside and finished unpacking, putting the polaroid photos of herself and Aysha on the window sill with a pang of sadness and guilt, then placing her folding travel alarm clock on the nightstand. She carried her toiletries out into the hallway and into the bathroom, presuming she had it to herself. The room was small and poky, the plumbing ancient, with a chain-pull cistern and a hand-held shower which she now decided that the English liked, but the place was clean and had space for her things. She returned to her room, on the way turning the handle to the room opposite hers, but found it locked. So much for her exploration of the top floor.

She heard a car start somewhere in the distance and looked out the window to see a dark green Jaguar turn out of the driveway into the road. She now had the whole house to herself. How strange someone would just leave her to wander amongst their personal surroundings, with barely an introduction.

She put her suitcase in the bottom of the wardrobe and the cello case in the corner, and returned to the clothes on the bed, again fingering the soft leather and silk with rising anticipation. The provision of black and white versions was clever, allowing a number of combinations. Lily stripped down to her underwear, and held the black skirt against her body. She wondered about the waist size, but it looked as though it would fit.

She stepped into the garter belt and settled it snugly about her waist, before pulling on the sheer black stockings. The feel of the stockings sent a tiny shiver through her. She had not expected anything like this, nor was she used to wearing such garments. Self-consciously she sat on the bed and ran her fingers down her legs, enjoying the sensuality and closeness of the nylon over her thighs. Her hand lingered between her legs, before she decided guiltily that she should behave more responsibly in someone else's house.

She decided on the white blouse and skirt together, pairing the skirt with a thin black belt. They fitted perfectly, which surprised her. She tucked the blouse in and buckled the belt, then admired herself in the full-length wardrobe mirror. The blouse hugged her breasts but not so snugly as to be tight, while the skirt felt elegantly to mid-thigh, concealing any hint of garter and stocking top. Lily gave a little twirl in front of the mirror, pleased with the look and giving in to her own girlish vanity.

The correctness of fit bothered her, though. She wondered whether these were the clothes used by her predecessor, the girl called Erika. Was Erika the same size? Lily thought back to Berlin and her submission to Karla's control in the basement dungeon. Lily had been so out of it, so lost in her own fantasies that it would have been easy for Karla to take any measurements she needed, never mind noting the sizes on the labels of Lily's own clothes. Had they been planning this whole thing since that day? What had happened to Erika, then?

Lily realised she was over-thinking again, that she could answer none of those questions. Still pleased with her appearance, she tried on the higher-heeled shoes. They were new and fitted well, a strap buckling easily across the bridge of the foot. She stood up and moved cautiously to the mirror again. It had been a long time since she had worn such shoes, and after sneakers and sandals for the last few months the extra height and slight unsteadiness from the heels made her a little uncertain on her feet, but the look in the mirror brought a smile to her lips. Her dark-clad calves now stood out, leading up to the white leather skirt and blouse, showing off her waist and breasts. Yes, she did look good! She ran her hands under her hair, lifting it up in a mock bouffant style, then let it drop. She took two hair clips and pulled the auburn tresses back over her ears and pinned them there, turning her head left and right to admire the result.

This was ridiculous, Lily thought, as though her sensible side had suddenly woken from a coma. I can't cook and clean a house dressed like this. What was the man thinking? He was just playing out some absurd fantasy. But that very fantasy had triggered Lily's own pleasure centres, she admitted. All right, then. She'd compromise.

She replaced the high heels with the other pair of shoes. They had a practical heel, and Lily at once felt she could perform her duties in them. She pulled the black pvc apron over her head and tied it around her waist. It hung down to the hem of the skirt and would protect her clothes if she was careful. Another saunter to the mirror, and a little thrill at how different she looked from the bohemian who had travelled from Kathmandu to London on an overland bus full of unsophisticated Antipodeans.

Leaving her room, and as though expecting something different, she again tried the door opposite her bedroom, but it remained locked, making her wonder what lay beyond. Probably one less room to dust and clean, she thought, as she descended the stairs to the first floor, where all the doors were closed. She tried the centre door – a bathroom with a few female effects neatly placed on a shelf and in a vanity cupboard. It had the look of exclusive but infrequent use.

The large room next door had the same feel. This was Farah-the-secretary's home-from-home, it seemed. Lily wondered whether Farah and her boss had sex. Maybe she'd have a better idea when she met the woman. The queen bed, the two arm chairs and the furnishings were all tasteful and harmonious in what Lily thought to be Iranian style, with richly coloured rugs and wall hangings. Under half a dozen vibrant pillows, the bedspread was a complex pattern of reds matched by the floor-to-ceiling drapes. Lily wandered over to the window, which looked out over a similar brick mansion next door. She ran her fingers along the window sill and came away with a faint smear of dust. The place had been cleaned, though not for a little while. She peeked inside the big double doors of the built-in wardrobe and found a range of female clothes which suggested Farah was not averse to overnighting.

Opposite Farah's room was the master bedroom. Lily eased the door open, half expecting some rebuke from inside. It felt like she was an intruder, and she had to keep telling herself she would be expected to keep the place clean, so of course she had to have access. Aurelius Cole's bedroom was like Farah's, but the colours were a dark mix of maroon and navy. The room was three times the size of Lily's on the floor above. The bed was of dark carved wood, matched by night stands, a settee and a glory box. A mirrored wall opposite the windows seemed to make the place even larger, while providing concealed hanging space. Lily gently slid one of the mirrored doors aside, revealing a line of hanging clothes, black the predominant colour. There were built-in drawers and shelves, mostly full but organised. Lily was not quite sure what she expected to find. Karla had told her the man was a Dominant, but how did that translate to his everyday life? She had thought there might be something to be found in the private spaces of his wardrobe, but there was precious little to indicate that Professor Aurelius Oliver Cole was anything other than ordinary.

Still finding herself almost tiptoeing, Lily opened the door to the ensuite. It had obviously been refurbished, for the tiling and glass surround to the shower was modern and well-lit. Towels were folded neatly and hung on rails and racks. Minimal toiletries sat beside the large basin, and Lily could not resist a covert sniff at the cologne. It was subtle and masculine. She peeked behind the large mirrored vanity door. Several small bottles of pills clustered together on one shelf, amidst the usual bathroom and medicinal accoutrements. She looked at the names on the bottles, but gleaned nothing as to the nature of the tablets or the condition they treated.

She returned to the bedroom and on impulse, bounced on to the bed. Not surprisingly, the quilt was soft and giving, the bed much more enticing than her own. Then her sensible side asserted itself again and she stood up guiltily, smoothing away her imprint.

She paused on the stairs leading down to the entrance foyer. She had already decided she liked the house. The dark wall panelling gave it more warmth than she expected, with the oriole windows allowing light to filter down in a haze of sunlit motes.

For a brief daydreaming instant she pictured what the room must once have witnessed when perhaps a wealthy couple or family had lived there. She had no idea how old the place was, but to Lily it could have been a century ago that the lord and lady of the house had descended the stairs, arm in arm in their finery, before heading to a party or a function in the West End. Now, in her apron, she felt like a serving girl whose employers had done just that, leaving her in charge.

Taking the last steps to the polished parquet of the foyer, she noticed the door under the stairs, leading to the cellar. Lily's overactive imagination made her catch her breath in excitement, but – perhaps predictably – she found it locked. For the moment, whatever rooms lay beneath the house were to remain a mystery.

Disappointed, she moved across to Cole's study, and as she did so, a telephone shrilled beyond the door. Lily was unsurprised to find the door locked and the sound of the telephone continued to reverberate unanswered, finally dying as the caller lost patience.

The downstairs bathroom next to the study was more like Farah's, retaining the age and style of the house, but with a little more functionality, which was a description which equally suited the dining room. The eight-seater table protruded into the space created by a large bay window that looked out on to the back garden – an unremarkable square of manicured lawn surrounded by a high hedge. Lily guessed that if Cole ate by himself, this end of the table would be his domain. On the window seat were several newspapers and the first plants she had seen in the house. Lily could see this room as a focus in older times for stiff-collared men with cigars and port as the women retired to keep their own company.

She skipped the kitchen, intending to return to see what lay in the larder, and what she would need to purchase. The last room was what Cole had referred to as the drawing room. It was a large formal space but softened with the Persian décor. A big fireplace dominated the room, together with a bookcase which featured more records than books. The professor was evidently a musicophile, and had a stereo system to match. Lily gazed rapturously at the titles of the LPs, thumbing her way through them. They were mostly classical, though with some jazz and Middle Eastern amongst them.

Lily could not help herself when she discovered the du Pré version of Elgar's cello concerto, sliding it lovingly out of the row. The performance by Jaqueline du Pré in the 1960's, younger than Lily as she then was, had become an iconic recording that Lily's teachers had constantly referenced and Lily had never tired of hearing. Du Pré had succumbed to multiple sclerosis at the age of 42, and like the rest of the world, Lily saw it as a tragically unfulfilled talent.

Not for the first time that morning, Lily looked about her guiltily as she eyed the expensive stereo and pushed the 'on' button. Lights came on in the amplifier and turntable and two large speakers occupying the bookshelf. Slipping the record out of its sleeve she lifted the perspex cover of the turntable, placed the record carefully and lowered the needle. Moments later the first dramatic chords filled the room.

The quality of the record and the sound system were extraordinary and as always when she heard it, Lily was captivated. The music of Elgar, written at the end of the First World War, fitted perfectly with her surroundings in this aged brick house. Enfolded in an armchair, Lily found herself transported to a time of loss, of sadness that brought tears to her eyes as she opened herself to the strains of her beloved cello.

Abruptly, she started at a noise, and turned to see Charlie's nose appear around the door. He sidled up to the chair, sniffed her stockinged legs and collapsed on her feet. She patted his head and returned to another time.

By the time Cole returned in late afternoon, Lily had thoroughly investigated the kitchen, larder and laundry, and had made a decent attempt at a shepherd's pie with some mince she found in the fridge. She had investigated the mailbox beside the front gate and had collected the mail. If she did nothing else, she thought, she might at least learn who was writing to her employer. There were over a dozen letters, most with British stamps, but one Iranian and two from France, both with a Paris postmark. Lily remembered her nerdy childhood friend Imogen collecting stamps, and had admired the way she could identify obscure colonies from their stamps.

Looking at the overseas letters, Lily saw there were no return addresses, and decided they provided little information, other than that the professor was clearly still in contact with people in Paris and Iran. Hardly surprising, she thought. She left the letters on the telephone table in the foyer.

Aurelius Cole limped into the kitchen as she was cleaning up after making the pie. He saw her handiwork and smiled as she put the dish down on the kitchen table.

'Ah! So glad you've made yourself useful, Lily. I'm afraid this morning was a little rushed. I think we need to have a more extensive chat, yes? I'm looking forward to learning all about you. Come to my study in five minutes and we'll get to know each other.'

Cole's study was all Lily expected, and was sufficiently intimidating not to help her nerves. Despite the inevitable Persian rug on the floor, there was precious little space for much else of a decorative nature, for most of the walls were taken up by bookshelves filled to overflowing, with many books jammed horizontally on top of the vertical volumes. There was a huge map of the world and a small section of wall on which hung some framed photos. Opposite the door a large circular bay window looked on to the driveway, forming what was obviously a reading nook with a slew of newspapers on a small table beside an armchair.

A dark heavy desk under a mess of papers and books dominated the room which contained several chairs, none of which seemed to match, but all of which looked well used. In the corner, in a niche at the end of one of the book cases was an electronic machine Lily did not recognise, but which she thought might be a telex, though it showed no spool of tape running through it. Close beside the machine was a smaller, more compact desk with a typewriter, and beside it a metal filing cabinet. The room was a conflict of functionality, neatness and chaos, each having their sphere of influence within the four walls.

Cole was seated in a black leather chair behind his desk when Lily entered, and he gestured her to close the door. It was perhaps unnecessary as they were alone in the house, but it at once seemed to remove any external influences, blocking the outside world.

'Sit down, Lily,' said Cole. 'No – take that chair.'

Lily had been about to sit in one of the large wingback armchairs, but he gestured her to a small straight-backed wooden chair with brown buttoned upholstery. Lily sat, the chair obliging her to hold an upright, slightly unnatural position. She smoothed the white leather of her skirt over her thighs and again felt like a schoolgirl at an interview with the headmaster.

Cole was relaxed, and rose to cross to a small cupboard next to the strange machine. A small shelf opened downwards to reveal several bottles and glasses. He selected a bottle of Glenmorangie and poured himself a generous shot in a cut crystal tumbler. Lily waited for him to speak, feeling more nervous as he elected not to, but turned, glass in hand, to stroll around behind where she sat, then stopped a few feet to one side.

'Stand up for me, will you, Lily.' She stood, conscious that he was now inspecting her again, with the air of a farmer checking breeding stock. She caught a hint of cologne – musky, masculine, attractive. He put his hand on her shoulder, as though smoothing out a small wrinkle in the silk material. His touch surprised Lily, feeling warmth and undisputed strength. 'You look charming, Lily. The clothes suit you. You wear them well.'

'Thank you,' Lily murmured. She felt she should have been offended, but somehow his approval made her feel good, as though she had done something well. Then, summoning up courage, she asked: 'How do they fit so well? Were they Erika's?'

'What? No. They're brand new. They were delivered on Saturday by your agency. I don't know why they fit so well. Just be glad that somebody's done some homework. God knows things are shoddy enough in this country sometimes.'

'What happened to Erika, Sir?' Lily asked, recognising that her sudden placement in this position still bothered her.

'I have no idea, Lily. I was told she had to leave due to an illness in the family. She was German, you know. Spoke good English, but... well, she actually wasn't that efficient. The agency seem to have done well to find you at short notice. Mind you, they charge like a wounded bull, so a quick replacement was what I expected. No disrespect, Lily – about the charges, I mean. To be honest, I'm hoping you'll be an improvement over Erika – a win-win, as we say.'

He gave her a look which was both disarming and discomforting. 'Sit,' he said. Lily obeyed, sensing for the first time a power in his voice, and feeling that she had asked her questions before she had realised they might be considered impertinent. The hired help should not be asking about their predecessors, but Lily had never been hired help before, and Cole obviously knew this.

'What do your parents do, Lily?'

'My mum died; my dad's a Member of Parliament in New Zealand.'

'Brothers? Sisters?'

'No.'

Cole returned to his chair and slid into it with a whisper of leather. 'And what brings you to England's green and pleasant land?'

'I came overland from Kathmandu.'

'Ah yes, the hippy trail. Do you take drugs, Lily?'

'No.'

'Never?' His eyes narrowed slightly.

'Uh, I smoked some dodgy sheesha in Pakistan...'

'Did you like it?'

Lily thought back to the flimsy little bakery shop in Swat Valley, where she and Aysha had whiled away a morning, and a pang of guilt flitted through her.

'Yes,' she admitted. 'But there were circumstances...'

'There always are,' Cole agreed. Then: 'Did you visit Iran along the way?'

'Yes,' said Lily. 'I liked it.'

Cole took a sip of the whiskey and turned his chair to gaze out the bay window. Lily thought he would question her further, but such was not the case. After a long moment of reflection, he asked:

'What do you do for a crust, Lily?'

'I was trained on the cello.'

'You were "trained on the cello",' he repeated. 'Yes, I saw your case. It sounds to me like you have a passion, but not actually a paying profession. But well done, you. A musician! How wonderful!' There was no disguising Cole's enthusiasm. 'You've seen my collection in the drawing room?' Lily nodded, remembering her unauthorised impromptu concert with Charlie.

'Very impressive, Sir.'

'It is, isn't it.' He paused for a minute, glass on the desk, hands steepled to his lips as though considering and resolving an issue. 'Yes,' he said, half to himself. 'Let's do that... Good.' Lily did not understand what he was talking about, for it was almost as though he had forgotten she was there. Then he returned to the moment.

'You seem to have found your way around, Lily. I'm sorry I had to run out on you. I'm sure there are questions you have. Everything was rushed this morning. Now, while I remember...' He opened a drawer and took out a key, which he put on the far side of the desk. There you are – key to the front door. Take.' Lily stood up and retrieved it, then sat down again. 'You'll need that if you're going out and there's nobody home. So let's clarify a few things regarding your duties.

'Charlie needs to be walked twice a day. A short walk before breakfast and a longer one after dinner. You'll also need to go shopping. I have an account at Balsams the greengrocer and at Tate and Fordham, the grocer. They're both in Hampstead High Street and between them they'll have most of what you need. My dining requirements are not significant. I don't pretend to be a gourmand. I've advised both of those establishments that you'll be signing on my behalf.

'You'll be on duty Monday to Friday from eight until seven, plus cleaning-up time and walking-Charlie time. Charlie-time includes weekends, but between walks your weekend time is your own. You may eat what you like from the kitchen, when it suits you, as long as it doesn't affect my routine.

'The house needs to be dusted, polished, vacuumed. Sheets are to be changed fortnightly, the washing and ironing done weekly.' He sipped his drink again. 'Anything I'm saying that is strange or unfamiliar to you?'

'No, Sir.'

'Good. I thought not. You look as though your parents educated you enough in the management of your life. There's a man who does the garden occasionally, but apart from that you need not be concerned about having to interact with others. Oh, and tomorrow being Wednesday, a man named Newby will come to do a sweep.'

'A sweep?'

'For bugs. Electronic detection. Listening devices – that sort of thing,' he said casually.

'Listening devices? Really? What sort of work do you do, Sir?' Lily found she had little difficulty in sounding surprised, for the whole thing seemed quite surreal.

'I work for the government, Lily. I'm an analyst.'

'And you think people will bug this house?'

'It's happened before, Lily.' He gazed hard at her and she blushed. 'He'll check every room – including yours, so make sure there's nothing to be found.' For a moment she was not sure if he was joking or not, then she detected the glimmerings of a smile and tried to match it. 'That's why you're never to enter this room unless either Farah or myself is present. Is that absolutely clear?' The smile had disappeared and there was no mistaking the intent. Cole's expression had flipped to one of warning that made Lily quail inwardly.

'Yes, Sir.'

'Mister Newby will be here after breakfast. Said breakfast will be bacon, fried eggs, black pudding and french toast. Earl Grey, milk, one sugar, in the dining room with the newspapers. Any questions?'

'Um... about the uniform, Sir. It's very nice, but must I wear it outside while shopping or walking Charlie?'

Cole chuckled. 'No, you need not. It's too nice and you'll have all of Hampstead ogling at you. Too much beauty on display to peasants who don't deserve it. No, wear your own clothes when shopping, and when walking Charlie.' His gaze hardened a touch. 'But in here, in this house, the uniform goes, in whatever combination you see appropriate.'

'Yes, Sir.'

'Good. And let me ask this question, Lily.' His tone changed to something vaguely reflective. 'Why did you choose 'all white' today? Is that how you see yourself? Pure?'

'No, Sir. I... I don't know. I guess I'm a little more white than black...'

'Are you a virgin, Lily?'

Lily was vaguely shocked at the question, but Karla's preparation had suggested that such personal interrogation was likely.

'No, Sir.'

'I thought not. Boyfriend in New Zealand?'

'Not anymore,' said Lily, without thinking.

'Other boyfriends?'

'No.'

'Girlfriend?' It was evident Cole was merely fishing, and he looked surprised and amused when Lily answered in the affirmative.

'Really? Where is she now, letting you loose with an unrespectable fellow like myself in this house of evil repute?'

'She's... still travelling, Sir.' Lily had been on the verge of saying 'in the Soviet Union', then caught herself just in time. She did not know this man's politics but suspected that the mere sniff of a communist connection could be disaster for her. 'She'll be away for a little while.'

'Travelling without you?'

'I... needed the money, Sir.' Lily hoped her ad hoc story was not going to be pursued too earnestly, but she thought it sounded plausible. She wondered if – when – he was going to start on her other 'duties'. Part of her dreaded this, part of her could hardly wait. Her instinct told her she could manage this man – or at least cope with him. Whatever his agenda, she did not feel threatened. Rather, there was a hint of anticipation stirring the butterflies in her stomach.

'Good. All right, if there are no more questions, perhaps that pie needs some attention. Six o'clock. On the dot.'

Lily's nervousness in the study had eased, replaced by inexplicable pleasure at his assessment of her appearance. Her anxiety had returned at dinner, but Cole's praise for the shepherd's pie made her flush with pleasure. When he asked for a second helping she knew he was not merely being polite, and she felt ridiculously pleased with herself.

They spoke little during the course of dinner, Lily fussing in the kitchen, venturing into the dining room only when Cole – reading the evening newspaper – rang a small hand bell on the table. To Lily, raised in a middle class New Zealand household, the whole servant thing was a complete anachronism, and she thought she had every right to be offended at having to wear a uniform and wait on this man in such surroundings. It was the nineteen-seventies, for God's sake. Yet she discovered another part of her enjoyed it, and this conflict disconcerted her. Cole made the job simple : come when I call; bring what I want; don't try to second guess. It was evident to Lily that if she followed these simple rules, her employer would be happy with her and life would be uncomplicated.

Charlie the cocker spaniel seemed to sense Lily was to be an integral part of his life. He slept in a basket in the laundry, but had the run of the house and a small doggy trapdoor giving access to the back yard. As Lily cleared away and washed the dishes he was watching expectantly from the doorway to the laundry, where his basket lay and where his leash hung. Like Lily, he had attended his master during dinner, and had received appropriate head scratches, but clearly the routine walk after dinner was done by a different human – the one in charge of the kitchen.

Lily had changed into her denim skirt and a white tee-shirt and was led by Charlie down the driveway and out into the street, golden tail wagging from side to side, nose to the ground to check what had changed since his last inspection of local goings-on. Lily – now obliged to remind herself the reason she was there – looked around for any watchers who might be expecting her, uneasy in the sudden reality of this role outside of the house. She realised that even after only a day, she felt secure in the House of Asha, and that the foray on to the heath was literally taking her out of a new comfort zone.

It took only five minutes to reach the pathway leading on to the heath – five minutes for Lily to make a decision whether or not to sit down on one of the benches, to elicit a contact on the return. Would it be Karla? Lily was in two minds, for she really had nothing to tell, other than perhaps to update her handler on how her first day had gone. She finally decided this was reason enough, and figured Karla would likely attend a first meeting to ensure all was well.

It was a peaceful evening on the heath, the late August summer sun still with an hour until it would dip below the trees on the skyline. Runners and others walking their dogs were visible scattered across the pathways and grass amongst the trees, but nobody occupied the benches overlooking the ponds. Charlie paused at the first bench, and looked at Lily, as though expecting something to happen. Lily wondered how many times Erika had sat at this very spot, and what information she had passed on. Charlie appeared gratified when Lily sat down, as though he had correctly anticipated his human. He sat beside her, content, while Lily gazed about her, not knowing what she might see, but there was no sign of any watcher.

She waited a couple of minutes, then as she stood, Charlie was at once impatient, as though the obligation was now complete and they could have fun. Lily had had a dog when she was young – until she was thirteen and it had died. It was a breed her father called a 'Bitza' – bitza this and bitza that, resulting in a black and white mongrel who doted on the girls and whom they named Deefa Dog. Deefa was loyal and goofy, and taking Charlie for a walk brought back pleasant memories for Lily, temporarily suppressing her impending rendezvous. She let Charlie off the lead and watched the oscillating tail as it fossicked in the long grass, then charged vainly at a bird.

She let him have his way for fifteen minutes, then called him back. He came obediently, now content that this new human was adequately trained in providing him with food, pats and exercise, and allowed his leash to be reattached, before they turned back towards the entrance pathway.

Karla was waiting on the bench, her blonde hair in a long ponytail, wearing a green blouse and tan skirt and smoking a cigarette, as though simply admiring the view. Charlie recognised her and wagged a greeting, silently telling Lily that Karla had been Erika's handler as well. For some reason she felt a small pang of jealousy, as though suddenly she was not quite so special as she had imagined, but rather, was a replaceable part in an operating machine.

Karla patted Charlie as they sat down beside her.

'How's life in the big house?' Karla asked.

'Not what I'm used to,' Lily admitted.

'You'll cope, Lily.' Karla placed her hand on Lily's thigh. It was a gesture of reassurance, of confidence in her protégé. 'I think you'll start to enjoy it. Do you have anything to tell me?'

'Um… no. There were some letters today – two from Paris, one from Iran and the rest local. No return addresses other than on the bills. I have a key to the house; the sweeper man is coming tomorrow, the Professor was out all day today, and there are some locked rooms I can't enter. I have to go shopping tomorrow.'

'That's very good, Lily. Succinct and to the point. I can't ask more than that. Keep your eyes open when you clean the study. You will no doubt be closely watched, and things will probably be tidied before you do it, but still… Always watch the fax machine.'

'The fax machine?'

Karla sighed. 'There's a machine in the corner of the room, Lily. It's called a fax machine – short for facsimile. It allows documents to be transmitted electronically over the phone line. Scanned at one end and printed out at the other. New technology, but you can understand how this will revolutionise things. Imagine being able to send a ten-page plan of attack instantly from Paris to Tehran and London. Masses of information available at the touch of a button. It will be printed out in that study.'

'Oh,' said Lily.

'Tomorrow I'm going to give you a very small camera, Lily. It will sit in the palm of your hand, about the size of an elongated matchbox. You'll need to find somewhere to hide it. Maybe in the house, but perhaps better outside – maybe the garden, but somewhere it can be quickly and easily hidden. In case you get the opportunity to photograph anything.'

'But the only place likely will be in the study,' Lily said. 'I can't take photos when other people are there.'

'Just be patient, Lily. You can hide it in your pocket. It will be there if the opportunity presents itself. You've done well. I'll see you tomorrow evening. Goodbye Charlie.'

\*   \*   \*

# CHAPTER 23 – Upstairs, Downstairs

Lily awoke to the jangle of her little alarm clock at seven the next morning. For a moment she wondered where she was, gazing at the unfamiliar sloping ceiling and the sun streaming through a chink in the curtain. Then it came back to her. She had despaired of getting to sleep the night before, so crowded was her head with Karla and Aurelius Cole and their different agendas. More specifically, her own mission to spy on the professor niggled at her, for she liked the man, despite his somewhat patronising attitude towards a young woman from the colonies.

She had lain awake re-visiting her time in his study, his gaze and his touch, trying to reconcile Karla's demands and the realities of her duties in the big house. Lily had never experienced a master-servant relationship. Life was just not like that at home. The whole English upper class snobbery thing was looked on by Kiwis with faint amusement, the way one would look on a child's games. Now, faced with different society norms, Lily had to adapt.

Karla had briefed her on Cole's bondage proclivities, and had told her of the dungeon in the cellar, though not in detail. Lily's presence in the house was to gain intelligence for Karla, while Cole saw her as household help with benefits, for which he was evidently prepared to pay a premium. The presence of the cellar at once both excited Lily and made her anxious. Her first impression of Cole had alleviated her concerns, for she sensed in him a degree of respect, notwithstanding the power that he carried over her. Now that her initial introduction to him and to the house was over, she wondered when he would make the first move towards something other than housework.

Breakfast and the morning's papers proved uneventful, with Cole polite but otherwise engrossed in the day's headlines. Lily had made no major mistakes, while Cole had been gracious in pointing out small refinements to suit his tastes, which were only to be expected. She had suggested that she would like to go shopping that morning, and he was agreeable, after she had walked Charlie.

As she was clearing away the breakfast things, he told her: 'When you go shopping, you're to buy for a week. It saves distracting you and taking you away from your duties.'

'Yes Sir,' said Lily.

'So you must check and make sure you have everything you need until next Wednesday, which will be shopping day. You can buy bread today and put it in the freezer. Most other things will last a week in the fridge or freezer.

'Oh, and Lily, one more thing.' Lily poked her head around the door to the kitchen. He beckoned to her. 'Come, sit.' She entered the dining room and sat at the table where he indicated. 'Farah will be here around ten this morning, to deal with my correspondence. Before that, I'd like to introduce you to another part of the house.

'Now, not to beat about the bush, you're here in more than the obvious capacity of simple household help, or so I was given to understand by the Agency. Is that correct?'

'Yes, Sir,' said Lily, her mouth suddenly dry and her stomach doing a small backflip.

'So when I tell you of the existence of a dungeon below this house, you'll neither be surprised nor disappointed – is that the case?'

'Yes, Sir.' Her voice was unintendedly husky. She could suddenly hardly contain herself, taken aback by the excitement such a suggestion engendered.

'Excellent,' Cole said, his previously neutral expression now giving way to a smile. 'Now, a very relevant question, Lily: How long have you been into the sordid world of bondage?'

'I guess a few months, Sir. I was… um… introduced by my friend while we were travelling…'

'Oh. So you're quite the newcomer! Capital! I love a newby. Everything is exciting and new for you – at least that's what we'll try to achieve. I'll be asking you a lot of things, Lily – whether you enjoyed something, whether you wanted more of it – or harder. Bondage – and all its associated spinoffs – is a very individual thing. I'm sure you've already figured that out, if you haven't been actually told. It's important for me to understand your predilections and tolerances. It's a mental and emotional pursuit – every bit as much as a physical one. But one step at a time. Come.'

He led the way across the entry foyer to the small door under the stairs and unlocked it. It opened outward, revealing a short flight of steep stone steps, lit by a bare bulb that came on with the door opening.

'After you,' he said, standing aside and gesturing Lily inside. Lily's heart raced and her stomach tightened as she crossed the threshold and began to descend.

'Once upon a time this was the coal cellar, then a wine cellar, and now it's been adapted again,' he said, the note of pride and amusement in his voice. As she reached the bottom step, he snapped on another light and illuminated a large basement anteroom that was the size of the drawing room above. It's walls were of brick, the clear space achieved through the use of several load-bearing steel beams spanning between them. Around the walls were arrays of bondage equipment that rivalled those Karla had shown her in the Berlin dungeon. Like Berlin, these were ordered and neatly hung on hooks or placed on built-in shelves. The place smelt of leather and a dry odour of brick dust tinged with damp.

In the far wall, opposite the stairs, were two doorways – the first with a rusty solid steel door, the second with a steel grille. Cole watched as Lily ventured to the latter and gazed inside. It was a small, dimly-lit cell with a narrow steel-framed bed and plastic-covered foam mattress. Several anchor rings were embedded in the brickwork around the room. Lily felt herself become moist at the sight and the implications that it held. She gripped the bars of the door and stared for a whole minute, before moving to the second door. It was barely her width and height, made of solid steel plate with two large sliding bolts on the outside. It swung open with a creak when she pulled it.

The inside was small and dark, barely the size of the bed in the first cell. In this one there was nothing, just a concrete floor and the same assortment of anchor rings in the walls. Lily paused again, trying to get her excitement and her heart rate under control.

She turned to in the doorway face Cole, and found him in a corner of the anteroom beside a bench that she had barely noticed before. He beckoned her over. She saw that a variety of implements and devices had been laid out on the bench top. There was a pair of handcuffs, a flogger, a single-tail whip, a leather blindfold, a butt plug, a large pink dildo, a ballgag on a strap, a posture collar, a cane, and a stainless steel device that Lily didn't recognise but which she thought might be a chastity belt. Lily gaped, then looked questioningly at him.

'Lily, there are ten items here. I want you to select three of them. The basis of your choice will tell me most about you – what your preferences are, what your desires are, what might follow as a result. I get the impression that you're quite new to all this?'

Lily gulped. 'Yes, Sir.'

'Then we will have a little bit of getting to know each other. This is not something that happens like a one night stand, you know.' Cole's smooth voice was matter-of-fact, but reassuring. 'It's a complicated and very personal process to understand what works for both of us. Everybody in the business has their own favourites – their proclivities, as we call them. Some people like the punishment side, some the restraint side – long term or short term – and then there is always the pain or pleasure at the end of it. "It's better when you can't move", is a motto for many. These things apply equally to Dominants and submissives. Does that make sense?' Lily nodded, not trusting herself to speak. She was still coming to terms with the fact that this amazing toy store was in the house where she lived, and to which she would now have access to explore – albeit at the whim of Aurelius Cole.

'Very well. Pick three. Don't over-think – trust your gut.'

Lily ran her gaze over the table and picked without hesitation – the blindfold, the handcuffs and the ballgag. They felt important and weighty in her hands, as she held them out to Aurelius Cole.

'Are you sure?' he asked softly.

'Yes, Sir,' she whispered, unable to conceal her blush, and realising she was opening up both to this man and to her own self.

Cole left her holding the items while he replaced the others on their hooks and shelves, before taking the three things from her and putting them back on the table.

'We'll leave them for now,' he said. 'Plenty of time. You can ponder on what you've seen today. Life must always be anticipated, Lily. A happy life involves always having something to look forward to. Don't you agree?'

Lily had never considered living her life in such terms, but it made sense, especially after this gigantic carrot had been dangled in front of her. She nodded. When Cole's next pronouncement came, it hardly seemed to phase her, after what she had just seen.

'After you've walked Charlie, go shopping, Lily. That'll save you changing twice. But when you return after shopping, you will wear your uniform without underwear from now on. Do you understand?'

'Yes Sir.' Lily was too excited to reflect on the implications, other than to sense herself sailing down a set of metaphorical rapids that carried her along with no control, no turning back and no indication of what lay at the end.

It was late morning when Lily returned from shopping in Hampstead High Street. A minicab collected her and brought her back, and the expedition had gone off without hitch. Neither grocer nor greengrocer had been fazed at the new girl shopping for Professor Cole, and Lily had taken the opportunity to visit the bank and withdraw a further thirty pounds from the account set up by Karla. She did not know exactly what she might use the money for, but something told her it might be prudent to have a little money set aside for a rainy day, and she had wanted to make sure the process worked by herself.

As the minicab dropped her off at the front gate, she saw a white Morris 1100 parked outside. She figured it might belong to Cole's secretary. She had carried the bags into the kitchen and unloaded the frozen foods before going to her room to change. Voices were coming from the study, and she guessed that Farah Bakhtiari had arrived.

Lily had started to change into her uniform, this time picking the black skirt and blouse with the white apron, when she remembered Cole's instruction about underwear. It had not really registered at the time, but now, with only the garter belt and stockings beneath her skirt and with her nipples nuzzling the silk, she felt suddenly more vulnerable. Once again she stood in front of her mirror, twisting and turning, trying to see how much might be on display below her skirt hem.

Her state of undress did not seem overly obvious, though the unfamiliar airiness beneath her skirt made her flush as she descended the stairs. She was almost at the bottom when Cole emerged from the study.

'Ah, Lily. Come and meet Farah.'

Farah Bakhtiari was in her late thirties, her black wavy hair pulled into a bun, wearing a cream blouse, navy skirt and sensible shoes. The top button of the blouse was done up and the skirt fell past her knees, giving her the conservative appearance of an older woman. Farah stood up from her desk behind the typewriter, but made no effort to approach Lily or to shake hands. Lily thought that with a little effort and judicious make-up Farah could be quite attractive. Her grey eyes assessed Lily with the look of a competitor, and Lily's musings from the previous day returned, concerning whether Farah and Cole had ever shared a bed.

'Hello,' said Farah, her expression neutral.

Lily was not sure how to answer – not sure what role Farah Bakhtiari held in the house and how Lily was to address her.

Cole saw her confusion and stepped in.

'Farah will be here for a few days each week. Sometimes she will stay over; sometimes she will be here while I am out or possibly overseas. In my absence, Farah speaks on my behalf, and you will take orders from her. You may address her as "Ma'am" or Ms Bakhtiari.'

Well, that made things clear, thought Lily. She might have resented the "Ma'am" bit had Farah been any younger, but the woman carried the authority of someone more than a decade older than Lily, and there was no question that Lily would follow her orders. She did not warm to Farah Bakhtiari, and the fact Lily was standing in her uniform, naked underneath, made any residual conversation even less likely.

'Yes Sir,' said Lily, pointedly addressing Cole.

There was an awkward silence until the door knocker sounded. Lily looked at Cole.

'One of your duties,' he said, waving dismissively, then turning back to his own desk as Farah sat down at hers.

Lily trotted into the foyer and opened the front door, trying to ignore the breeze that slipped up her skirt, and found herself facing a man of around thirty in a suit and tie, carrying a metal briefcase.

'Hello. My name is Newby. Ministry of Defence. I'm here for the regular sweep.' Lily's uniform must have made her role in the household plain to the man, and she figured he had previously most likely met Erika. It appeared that the household help was all but invisible to those used to such routine, and Newby entered without being asked, comfortable in a familiar role, though not past ogling Lily's chest as he passed her. 'I know the way,' he said brusquely, heading for the open study door.

Lily saw Newby briefly a couple more times during the next hour, as he skulked about the house with a hand-held device that apparently could pick up the presence of recording devices. She noted that he went into her room, but not the dungeon nor the locked room opposite hers. Evidently these rooms were either sufficiently secure of their own accord, or else they were deemed out of bounds and in any case not subject to careless security talk inside.

After she had provided lunch for both Cole and Farah, Lily recalled Karla's instruction the evening before, and ventured into the small garden at the rear of the house to look for a hiding place for a camera. There was a washing line between two tee-shaped posts, a small shed and little else by way of cultivated garden. Lily thought about hiding the camera in the foliage, but was worried about the lawn guy finding it. She finally found a small spot under the eaves of the shed, where she reckoned that a small camera could be placed, but then made the startling realisation that with her 'new' uniform there were no pockets and she now had almost nowhere to hide such a camera if she was to take it into the study. She did not believe she would have the opportunity to photograph anything, but she had to go along with Karla's order.

She was allowed to clean and dust the study in the presence of both Farah and Cole, and she made a point of being as thorough as possible, for it allowed her to stay in their presence. She saw little of interest on the two desks, for she could not reasonably intrude on their work while they were sitting there, but it allowed her to gauge how much conversation they made. It was unfortunate for Lily that much of what was spoken between Farah and Cole was in Farsi – or so Lily presumed, for she could understand none of it. From the English conversation that did pass, Farah Bakhtiari spoke with the cultured English accent of a good education in an elite school.

In the course of twenty minutes dusting of bookshelves and picture frames, and polishing of bare surfaces, the telephone rang several times. There were two extensions, one on each desk, and the phone conversations frequently included both people. On one call, Cole answered and spoke briefly in French. Lily had done rudimentary French at high school before switching to German, but could make little of the rapid-fire exchange.

Twice the phone on the fax machine rang, evidently on the same line as the study phone. Each time there were vague buzzings and screeches audible before the machine seemed to connect with the sender, and a small needle like a seismograph zapped back and forth across special paper, filling the room with an faint burning smell as the paper rolled out bearing the visible imprint of the received document.

Lily watched it as innocently as she could, pretending fascination with the new technology, and ultimately giving it a dust after the paper had been retrieved by Cole, but she learned nothing. All in all, it had been a most interesting day, but for the purposes of reporting news to Karla, it was a bust.

That evening, Lily, Karla and Charlie sat on the park bench in the twilight, Lily wearing a green sleeveless shift that allowed the lingering sun to warm her exposed arms and legs. She explained her efforts to her handler.

'There were fifteen letters today. Nine were obvious bills, two I couldn't decide on, but they're local, and there were two from Iran and two from Paris. Why Paris?' she asked.

'The exiled leader of the Tudeh Party lives in Paris with some of his followers. They're waiting for the word that a coup has been successful, so that he can return in triumph. The Shah, in turn – and MI6 – has a watching brief over them. It's not surprising that Cole has his own spies there.'

'Why don't they just arrest the leader?'

'The French government is sympathetic to the Tudeh. Any strategy the French can use to upset the British – without it being overt – is usually followed. The French like to oppose the Brits – it took ages for them to agree to Britain joining the European Economic Community. Enmity runs deep, Lily. They may see an opportunity for France if the Tudeh become the government.'

'I think the professor may be planning to go to France in the near future. There's been talk of 'bookings' and I thought I saw an air ticket in the mess on his desk.' Lily was trying to sound useful, trying to give Karla something, but didn't know what she wanted.

'That's very good, Lily,' Karla told her. 'It'll take time to learn the way things run, although we may not have much time to play with. Don't be despondent.' Then her voice changed and a mischievous look appeared in her eyes. 'And what else happened? Have you been into the dungeon?'

'Yes,' admitted Lily.

'And?'

'Just had a look around... It's impressive.'

'As good as Berlin?' Lily reckoned Karla was sensing her reluctance, almost embarrassment in talking about it. She did not want to tell her about the three-item choice she had made. That belonged between her and the professor, she had decided, leading wherever it did.

'No, but he only has a house to work in, not a whole deserted factory,' she said, slightly defensively. Karla did not respond, instead glancing along the path in each direction, satisfying herself that there were no people nearby. She dug in her handbag, to produce the small camera about which she had forewarned Lily. She held it out to Lily in the palm of her hand. It was a tiny thing made of aluminium, not much longer and wider than Karla's middle finger.

'This is a Minox camera,' Karla told her. She held it between thumb and forefinger to allow Lily to see the little dials on the face. 'What do you know about cameras, Lily? Have you ever done any photography?'

'My boyfriend... uh, ex-boyfriend – had a Nikon. I messed around with it a bit.'

'Good. So when I tell you that this dial here is the focus and this one is the shutter speed, that means something to you.'

'I guess so.'

'This little window here is the frame counter – you can take up to fifty exposures. Amazing, huh? Such a small camera. German technology,' she added proudly. Sometimes Lily almost forgot that Karla was German, for her accent seemed less than when they had first met in Berlin. Karla seemed to be integrating more into her surroundings as she interacted with locals. She showed Lily how the camera opened and advanced the film, them made her practice for a minute, as though she was taking a photo of a document.

'You probably want about 25 ASA,' Karla said, 'but don't forget, if the opportunity arises, a photo of Cole's desk itself, with all the papers, and anything else in the room could be useful. The picture quality is good and can be enlarged. Have you found a place to hide it?'

Lily told her of the little spot she had found under the eaves of the garden shed.

'But there's a problem. I'm now not allowed any underwear.' She said it with slight embarrassment, like a child who has been punished for some mis-deed. Then an unsettling thought occurred to her. 'Do you think he's done it to stop something like this? Does that mean he might be expecting something like this?'

'No, Lily,' Karla said firmly. 'He's done it because he likes to see your tits pressed against your blouse, and he likes the idea of no knickers because it makes you uncomfortable and vulnerable. That's what Dominants do. I'm not averse to using such measures myself. It's human nature for a submissive to feel more insecure under such circumstances.'

'But I was going to hide the camera in my bra. Now I have nothing.'

'You still have the garter belt, yes? Slip it in the top of your stocking, on your inner thigh.'

Lily was dubious, but reluctantly resolved to try it out. She had not really considered the implications of getting caught, because up until that moment she had nothing that might incriminate her, other than deniable curiosity. Now, suddenly, this camera changed the whole game.

Lily returned to the house via the driveway, taking Charlie into the back garden and thence the laundry. She glanced furtively at the house and slunk to the shed to slip the camera into the spot she had chosen, feeling like an escapee waiting for a searchlight to expose her, but nothing happened. Relieved, she slipped inside again, passing through the kitchen to the foyer, ready to head to her bedroom. The Morris 1100 had gone and she assumed Farah had departed. The study door was open and Cole's voice called her name. She poked her head round the door. Cole was at his desk, his face illuminated by a small banker's desk lamp.

'Ah, Lily, come in. Sit.' Lily knew which chair to use, and placed herself on the uncomfortable one with the tall upright back. She wondered what he wanted, trying to gauge whether she had done something wrong by the tone of his voice, but could detect nothing untoward.

Cole seemed relaxed, and finished signing several documents with a fountain pen, before capping it and placing it in a drawer. He looked up at Lily as though deciding how to proceed with something he was about to convey.

'What did you think of my little cellar, Lily?' he asked. Lily swallowed the dryness in her throat and felt her heart begin to thump.

'It was very... impressive, Sir,' she said.

Cole stood up and walked to the window, gazing briefly over the darkening front garden, before drawing the drapes. The room immediately took on a more intimate feeling, lit only by the desk lamp and two wall sconces. Lily felt the masculinity of it, the purpose and functionality, subtly softened by the Persian decor.

He moved back to the desk and casually half-leaned on it.

'You picked three things out of the line-up this morning. The handcuffs, the gag and the blindfold. Do you know why you chose those items?'

In truth, Lily had acted on instinct, with little conscious thought behind her choices. The *entire* selection had excited her, displaying a world of possibilities, but these three items in particular had sent chills down her spine, in part because of what she had experienced in Berlin, and in part for the promise they conveyed. She was cautious in her reply, not wanting to show innocence or ignorance, though both had legitimate presence.

'Um... restraint?'

'Yes, Lily. You picked those items ahead of the pain, pleasure and appearance.'

'I could have picked more,' she said shyly, 'but you limited it to three.'

Cole smiled. 'Yes, I did – for the purpose of seeing where your proclivities lay, Lily. But on the basis of that statement, I think I'm right in saying that we may now proceed further with this side of the relationship, yes?'

'Yes, please Sir.'

'Good. Stand up, Lily.' She did so, smoothing down her dress over her thighs. Cole moved behind her, while Lily kept her gaze on the desk, deliberately not following his movement, her breathing becoming shallower. Again she smelt his cologne, which did nothing to calm her. 'Put your hands together behind you, Lily, palm to palm.'

She had no sooner complied when she felt a rope slip over her wrists and draw them together. It was sash cord – the white cord that she had experienced with Karla, that she knew was soft, smooth and unyielding. It was not tight, but was joined by further turns. Six...seven...eight... A voice counted them off in her head, feeling his strong fingers positioning the turns of cord snugly against each other. With each turn her insides also seemed to wind tighter, as she became more helpless yet more secure in that very helplessness. Then, abruptly, there was a cinch cord pulled between her wrists and wrapping around the loops, pulling everything tight and immovable, Cole's hands securing the bonds with a knot. He stepped back, and she felt the restraint on her wrists now transferred to an immovability in her arms and a rigidity in the top half of her body. Unbidden, she tested the rope but found it unyielding. Lily could only stand there, trying not to make her breathing sound like panting, suddenly conscious that her nipples had hardened and were straining inside her dress.

Cole came around in her field of vision again and paused, as though to admire his work. Lily blushed and looked at the ground, overwhelmed with both her captivity and the presence of her captor. He moved behind the desk and opened a drawer, removing a length of chain about two metres long. Lily's heart missed a beat in anticipation of something she could not really guess at. Just 'something' – some unknown fate that he had planned for her. She shivered when he wrapped the cold chain about her neck and clicked a padlock closed on it, securing it at her throat, leaving the remaining length as a leash. Without a word he tugged and she walked demurely beside him, out of the study and up the stairs of the silent house. Lily was in a dream, captured by forces far beyond her control, being led to a remote tower and an undetermined future. Whether in dream or reality, she did not know if pain or pleasure lay at the top of the stairs.

She had been surprised that they had not gone down into the cellar. Now she sensed that the room opposite her own bedroom was her destination, even before they had reached the first floor. Behind the now-unlocked door, the room was a twin of her own room, though devoid of furniture, carpet or decoration. Cole did not turn on the lights and Lily was disconcerted to find the walls, ceiling and floor all painted black, the impact only lessened by the receding daylight from the two dormer windows. Whatever expectations Lily's imagination might have been suggesting, nothing matched this.

Cole halted her in the middle of the room.

'Sit, Lily. Cross-legged.'

Awkwardly, her bound arms limiting her movements, Lily knelt then shuffled about to sit cross-legged, her green dress riding up over her thighs. No sooner had she settled than Cole had pulled a short strap from his pocket and wrapped it around her crossed ankles, before a further padlock appeared and the loose end of the leash chain was locked to a small U-shaped anchor screwed to the floor, which Lily had not noticed as black on black.

'I'm going to leave you here, Lily, in the company of your own imagination. Think on what you've seen in the cellar. Be aware that whatever daily routine I might have prescribed, it always remains subject to change – to the extent that I decide. Don't, therefore, assume you will need to prepare breakfast tomorrow morning.'

There was a pause as Lily tried to take in the implications of what he was saying, and Cole seemed to be daring her to respond.

'How long must I stay like this?' Lily asked, her voice barely above a whisper.

'Until you have learned your lessons, Lily,' said the man standing in front of her. 'One lesson is that you will never ask such a question again. You do not question my motives or my methods. If I even *considered* asking you how long you would like to stay there, Lily, your answer would be: "As long as it pleases you, Sir".'

'Yes Sir.'

'Indeed, you will remain here as long as it pleases me. You will think on your fate, on your expectations, on your fantasies, on the infinite possibilities that lie before you, and you will consider your good fortune in all of this.' Cole moved behind her, then squatted to run his hands over her shoulders, and down to her breasts, cupping them through the cotton of her dress. Lily could not suppress a little intake of breath, as a tiny shock of pleasure rippled through her and a warm jolt came from her groin, now open for all to see. His hands stayed there for a long minute, the fingers now gently kneading her nipples as they hardened further. Lily squirmed, all of a sudden wanting him to pull down her zipper and place his lips over those giveaway nubs.

But then he was gone - retreating footsteps behind her and a closing door, leaving her bound and impotent in the Black Tower.

\* \* \*

# CHAPTER 24 – The Black Tower

Lily watched the twilight fade into dusk and then into the black satin night beyond the windows. That she was horny did not begin to describe the feelings – both physical and emotional – now running amok. She tugged at her wrists, but they remained as fixed and confining as she had discovered on the long climb up the stairs. Her ankles were secured equally rigidly, crossed and strapped so she could not stretch out her legs.

She shuffled on her backside away from the anchor point, coming to a halt as the chain tugged at her neck, knowing finally the inescapability of her situation, the utter helplessness of her body and soul. The acceptance of this made the wetness between her legs almost palpable, but she could do nothing about it. The impressions of his hands and fingers on her breasts and nipples lingered in her mind, their strength, and the knowledge that should they choose, those hands could do anything they wanted to her – and she would surely respond.

How she wished he had stayed. She recognised her desire, though whether it was purely physical or something stronger and deeper, she did not trust herself to answer. Her body was playing tricks, making demands which her brain now turned to anger – anger at Aurelius Cole and his leaving her in this situation. She twisted herself, trying to get her hands to the front but it was futile. She was becoming wetter and more excited but frustrated at her inability to touch herself to ease or to stimulate the fires.

The blackness of the attic room merged into something more medieval over the course of the next hour, as Lily became more aroused but more frustrated. As her brain embroidered her circumstances and the terrible fate lying before her as a captive in this castle, the reality of her situation was left behind. She was bound and chained in a house in London and that should she never leave the premises again, only Karla Graf would know her whereabouts. But if something bad happened, Karla would not come knocking. Lily's body would be hidden in the cellar never to be found without just cause. Cole would simply say she had gone away… to visit a sick family relative of whom he had no knowledge…

A cold chill ran through Lily's body at the thought of Erika. She shook her head. No, she was now just making things up and taking her fantasies to ridiculous limits. She struggled furiously at her bonds, and considered yelling for help, but nobody would hear her in this attic room. Calm the fuck down, she thought, unknowingly echoing Aysha's words from long ago.

Yes, there she was, a prisoner in this old house, held captive by a mad professor intent on doing unspeakable things to her. Her imagination stepped in again, picking up the reins, then spoiling the fantasy with the realisation that she *wanted* him to do unspeakable things to her, if only to ease the ache in her loins.

The room was stuffy, touched by a faint lingering odour of potpourri. The windows had been closed all day and the sun had warmed the place, enough that Lily felt a bead of sweat rolling down her temple. Her armpits were damp and as she squirmed some more, her dress rode up around her backside and waist. So much for the glamourous captive princess. God, where *was* he? He had made suggestions that she might not need to prepare breakfast. Did he intend to leave her there all night? My God! He couldn't do such a thing! She'd go mad!

Should she call out to him? Beg for release, beg to please him in whatever way he wished, in return for the blessing of relief? Could he even hear her two floors below? Or was he already in bed, asleep, or listening for her movements on the floor above him? Either way, he could do what he wanted. How could she promise him the world when he could take that world in any way he wanted, without any requirement for cooperation by Lily.

Something slid down her cheek. Lily was not sure if it was sweat or a tear. She stifled a sob, pretty sure it was a sob of frustration. She had no idea how much time had passed. It had been light when she had been chained up; now it was dark and silent, no sound reaching her from the quiet streets of Hampstead. Once again her sight had been curtailed.

Then the door opened with a gentle movement of air. A beam of light illuminated the room and she felt his presence behind her. Again he was kneeling behind her, his arms enclosing her shoulders and cupping her breasts, his breath close beside her ear. He said nothing, and she willed herself not to break the silence with a plea for release – not of her bonds, but of the urgency now brewing again in her loins. He *must* finish what he had started hours ago. She realised how desperate she was for him, wanting him to take her now, hard, quickly.

She wriggled within his embrace, and his hands brushed her nipples as his touch dropped down her stomach, over the ruched dress to the wetness of her panties. She gasped at the contact, as though his fingers were on fire. They sensed the damp material and Cole made soft tut-tutting noises beside her. Then he was undoing the strap around her ankles and lifting her to her feet.

'There you go, Lily. Better? There's a key on the floor somewhere around here. When you've unlocked yourself, come down and see me. I'll be in the study.'

'Wha-? What? No-! Don't leave!'

There was a last, hard caress of her crotch before he was gone and the door closed on darkness again.

'Fuck,' Lily moaned, unsteady on her feet in the blackness. 'Bastard!' she muttered, trying to bring her breath under control as she came up against the end of the chain. She willed herself to stand still, to consider his words, but she could not shake off the last caress of his hand, the firmness just where she wanted it, but needed for longer than the two seconds he had lingered there.

She was wearing light sneakers and figured she would probably notice if she stood on a key. The trick was to make sure she covered all the circular area around the anchor point, and didn't kick the key away in the process.

Somewhere in her stumbled searching, Lily became entangled in the chain as it slid up her leg and caught her in the crotch, sparking a sudden blaze of pleasure as it grooved through her slit.

'Ohhhh...' she gasped, realising she had an outlet for her release and abruptly losing interest in the key to the chain padlock. She manoeuvred the chain so it ran from her neck down her stomach and between her legs, now able to lean on it, placing pressure just where she needed. So aroused was she it took only a few small movements to stoke the embers into a full blaze, and to cause her to hump the chain like an animal in heat, dimly grateful for the darkness of the Black Tower, and now thankful the neighbours hopefully *wouldn't* hear the barely contained cries of release.

Lily dared not consider the figure she cut when she finally reached the study a little while later. Her wrists were still bound behind, her hair was mussed, her dress rumpled, sweat-stained and dirty from sliding about on the floor. The chain dangled from her neck and had clunked down the stairs with her, announcing her approach to the figure sitting at the desk. Lily felt as wrecked as she no doubt looked, for the climax had drained her and left her legs rubbery.

Cole looked up as she entered, the thin smile on his face the expression of one whose grandiose plan has come to fruition exactly as he had anticipated. He made no objection as Lily collapsed over his desk to rest her torso on the mass of papers, presenting her bound wrists for release.

'Oh, had enough now?' he inquired.

'Please, Sir, yes Sir. Don't joke.'

'You realise I could just tie your ankles and leave you for the rest of the night?'

'Yes Sir. I realise you could do anything you want, but I'm so tired, Sir. If I have to beg, consider this begging. Please don't tease me further...'

Cole appeared to consider her plea, staring down at the sweaty face staring sideways at him from the desktop. If Lily had ever doubted the absolute power he held, that moment dispelled any such uncertainty, and her expression told him so. He stood up, and within a few seconds his fingers had untied the knot at her wrists. She heaved herself off the desk, massaging the deep imprints of the cord in her skin. The bindings had been tight and secure, yet her circulation had not been cut. Dimly, with her limited experience, she acknowledged this man knew what he was doing.

'Go to bed, Lily,' he said gently, and kissed her on the forehead.

Lily lay in the darkness, staring at the sloping roof vaguely defined by a streetlight through thin curtains. By rights she should have crashed into sleep, so exhausted was she after the hours in the Black Tower, as she had now formally named it. The Black Tower seemed destined to feature again in her future. It had been painted thus for some sort of psychological torture, she reckoned, designed to limit sensory perception and to stimulate the imagination – both of which had worked scarily well in her case.

She turned on to her side, pulling her legs up and slipping her hands into the sensitive triangle between them, again feeling the sensitivity which threatened to send her off the edge again in a new, self-inflicted round of gratification.

The physical satisfaction her awkward and carnal climax had delivered had been tempered by the fact that it was the result of her own weakness. Lily told herself she had become aroused and excited – and had climaxed – through her own deficiency, her love of bondage. Add to that a far-too-active imagination, and Cole had taken advantage of what was an open goal. It did not take much to score.

All of that annoyed her, but despite the outcome, she was angered by Cole's refusal to actually take the goal kick himself, whether by those roving hands and fingers, or something more significant. Instead, he had left her to the mercy of her own devices, turning her into a rutting animal intent on satisfying her needs by whatever means was at hand. He had out-thought her, had picked her for what she was, and the intensity of her reactions had unsettled her.

Were there other submissives just like her in the world? There surely must be, and this gave her hope that her penchants – while perhaps not normal – might at least be more commonplace than she supposed. Cole had alluded to many variants of her desires – variations on a theme, as the musical expression went. She took small solace in the conclusion that she was not alone in these perverted longings. The well-equipped dungeons in Berlin and now London confirmed that idea.

Yes, she was angry with him, angry with herself for having been outwitted and falling into a self-induced trap, when she actually wanted him to be a physical part of her satisfaction. There it was. She had articulated it and recognised that yes, she *fancied* her employer. He was calm and in control, but also clever and thoughtful, she thought. No, this could not happen. Not as long as Aysha was a part of her world.

Her final thought before sleep finally battered down her doors, was dim but scary – the question of what had happened to Erika.

'What's the matter, Lily?' Aurelius Cole asked, as she served coffee with his morning papers.

'Nothing, Sir,' said Lily, unable to keep the stiffness out of her response.

'Oh come on, tell me. You're like a bear with a sore head. Did you not enjoy last night? Did you not go to sleep with a smile on your face?' Cole ran a hand through his hair and leaned back in his chair beside the bay window, casually crossing one leg over the other.

Lily didn't know how to respond. She had finally gotten to sleep with her hands still nestled in the warm, satisfied place between her legs, though her brain insisted in asking questions and trying to over-think that very satisfaction.

'Yes Sir,' she said stiffly. 'Thank you for asking.'

'"Thank you for asking"? Not "thank you for bringing me gratification"?'

'That too, Sir,' Lily conceded.

'Good. What about "thank you for letting my head run amok and dragging my pussy with it"?'

Lily turned on her heel and headed for the kitchen, unwilling to follow the solo physical humiliation of the night before with a re-lived and shared version, where there would only be one winner.

'Lily!' She stopped, caught by the sharpness of the command. She turned, rebellion stifled, but still evident.

'I'm sorry,' he said. 'That was uncalled for. Forgive me?' His expression changed to that of a mischievous schoolboy caught smoking behind the bike sheds.

'You were mean to me last night,' Lily said in a small voice.

'Yes, I was, wasn't I,' Cole agreed, contrition in his tone. Then: 'In what way was I meanest?'

'You went away,' Lily said, then realised her own admission, and flushed.

Cole gazed at her for a long time, then said: 'Let's put that aside for the moment. It so happens I have a couple of tickets to this Saturday's Proms concert at the Albert. Would you like to join me, Lily?'

The sudden turn of conversation and the unexpected offer left Lily momentarily speechless.

'The Albert? You mean the Royal Albert Hall? God, yes!' Lily was familiar enough with the place, if only through having seen the Last Night at the Proms on New Zealand television, and her knowledge of famous performances having been recorded there.

Cole grinned at the change which had come over the girl, how the sullenness had been replaced by a radiant smile that toned down a moment after Lily remembered her position in the house.

'May I ask what the program is, Sir?' she ventured.

'Would that change your mind, Lily?'

'Of course not, Sir. I'd just like to know what to be looking forward to.'

Cole leaned forward and flipped a few pages in the paper to the entertainment section.

'Borodin, Kelly, Dvorak and Holst.'

The unexpectedness of the treat and the quality of the program left Lily grinning stupidly, until something female tugged at the logic of acceptance. This was the Royal Albert Hall, after all, in the middle of the exclusive district of Kensington, London SW7.

'But I've got nothing to wear.'

'Oh Lily, the promenade mob will turn up in jeans and tee-shirts. You'll look fine, whatever you wear.'

'But we won't be in the promenade pit, will we, Sir?' It was a hunch on Lily's part, and forced an admission from him.

'Well, no. We'll have a box.'

'A box? Then I have nothing to wear,' she reiterated flatly, as though there was no further progress to be made until the issue was resolved.

Cole sighed. 'Very well. Have a look through Farah's wardrobe when she's not around. She's about your size,' he said, with the look of a male on uncertain ground. 'You at least have some nice shoes and stockings,' he extemporized. 'Concert at 7.30, we'll go to my club for dinner afterwards. How does that sound?'

Lily's smile said it all.

Lily's time in the Black Tower was made less significant over the remainder of the day. When she did think of it, it was an experience that ultimately *did* leave her with a smile on her face. It would probably not be the first such capitulation on her part, and she really didn't mind that. It was just Cole's smugness which annoyed her – that and the fact he had not lifted a finger, literally, to assist in her loud finale. But that would assuredly come, she decided.

Of more import now was a concert in the Royal Albert Hall. Lily was beside herself, and was in the process of surreptitiously investigating Farah's wardrobe when she heard the front door opening and words exchanged in Farsi. Lily had decided that for some reason Farah Bakhtiari did not like her, and reckoned that Farah had proprietary intentions towards Cole. The woman was at very least in a position of influence within the house, and Lily did not want to cross her. A brief inspection of the clothes in Farah's wardrobe was sufficient to mollify Lily that she might come away from this engagement with something acceptable to the refined society of Kensington.

That evening, she had little intelligence to report to Karla, though she felt obliged to mention the Black Tower and the concert. She had not considered either event important in the bigger scheme of things, but Karla was enthusiastic.

'It shows you've gained his trust – much quicker than I expected. The 'Tower' as you call it – well, that was kind of expected. It's what he loves – messing with your mind. It's what he does.'

'He didn't do much last night,' Lily grumbled. 'Just left me to it to sort myself out.'

'And did you?' Karla asked tartly.

'Yes.'

'Was it good?'

'Yes.' Shit, yes, she had now concluded, looking back. She'd been as randy as a tom cat and felt pretty damned good at the end of it – aside from the over-analysis, that is.

'Then stop complaining, you ungrateful girl. But the Proms... That's something special, I think.'

'He said we're going to dinner afterwards at his club.'

Karla's smile ratcheted up a notch. 'This is where people talk, Lily. Aside from the fact he has already accepted you, he's prepared to show you off. You're arm candy to his friends. I'll bet you get to have a few conversations during the interval. Take note of who these people are and listen like the dumb trophy you will seem to be. Got it?'

'Yes Karla.'

Lily had wondered whether that evening would bring some kind of further initiation or whatever one might call the experience of the Black Tower, but nothing came about. Cole seemed pre-occupied and was still in the study when Lily went to bed, feeling vaguely miffed at being ignored, but banishing that thought with the expectation of the concert. She had already resolved to treat herself by having her hair done on Saturday morning, and had managed to make an appointment, after scouring the Yellow Pages and asking Cole's permission to use the phone. He seemed amused at the turmoil the invitation had caused for Lily – amused in the slightly condescending way only a male can manage for the female's preoccupation with appearance.

Again Lily slipped into over-think, unable to stop herself wondering what this meant – her boss asking her out to a concert. There had to be an ulterior motive... Or was he just being nice? He could virtually do what he wanted to her ... with her... as long as there was some form of restraint involved. Whatever happened, she admitted, just before she fell asleep, she would likely have no objection...

*    *    *

# CHAPTER 25 – Up the Line

The air-conditioning in Graham Parminter's office was playing up again. It was Friday morning and the chance of getting anything done about it before the following week was minimal. Against regulations, Parminter opened the window. The old wooden casement – repainted dozens of time in the life of the building – creaked and yielded. He doubted there were any high-powered directional microphones pointed at his window, though KGB-contrived air conditioning failures had occurred before now to initiate such a reaction. He poked his head out the window, but his side of the building had a limited outlook only on to neighbouring roofs.

Parminter returned to his seat and lit a cigarette. Helen Feldman was already halfway through hers. Parminter leaned back in his chair and crossed his legs.

'And how far up the chain did you get?'

'I spoke to Doctor Fischer again. Same story – more tests, observation. Don't want to discharge her prematurely, blah blah blah. Then I went to the Department head, the Director of Admissions and then the hospital manager. I suspect our Doctor Fischer had not communicated with some of these people, and I have a sneaking suspicion that our friends the KGB are somehow involved, though whether this is routine with a foreigner or something more insidious, I don't know. I told you there was a KGB goon present when I saw Aysha, didn't I?

'Suffice to say, I rattled a few cages, and I think there will be some words coming down to Doctor Fischer from on high. I suspect there will be some raised voices between comrades, because clearly they're not all on the same page, and that makes a few of them look even more stupid than usual. There's no doubt in my mind that Aysha is now non-contagious and she should have been able to travel by now.'

'Do you think there is anything to this suggestion that she is somehow being punished for some mis-deed? For maybe something found in her luggage?' Parminter asked.

'Well, if such *had* been the case, I'd expected Aysha to complain about it when I saw her. Of course it was a question I didn't know to ask, at the time.'

'So what's the plan?'

'I'll leave them to stew over their inability to coordinate with each other, and to decide who looks the biggest fool and who is going to start making the excuses, and I'll phone them again on Monday, but I won't be taking no for an answer. If there's no cooperation then, the Ambassador will be speaking to someone and there will be the threat of a bucket of shit descending from the heights of the Grand Kremlin Palace. Maybe that will move some arses.'

'You have a way with words, Helen. I hope you're right.'

# the submissive spy

* * *

# CHAPTER 26 – Collar and Tie

She had walked Charlie before breakfast the next morning – Friday. Tomorrow was the concert. Lily debated whether to try sneaking the camera into her stocking top, but decided against it. Instinct told her she needed to know more about the household routine before taking the risk, for that was what it would be – and a big one.

Cole appeared in a good mood over breakfast, and summoned her from the kitchen after she had cleared away the last of the dishes, leaving him with his coffee and the newspapers. She had been watching for routines, and had noticed Farah arrived around ten, which left the period immediately after breakfast as a time when he might provide any instructions to her for the day. It was evidently also a time in which to apologise for his actions or offer concert tickets.

This morning he beckoned her back into the dining room. Lily stood in front of him, deciding that this was like a morning meeting in the running of the household, and wondering whether she had done anything which might displease him. Today she had opted for the black skirt, the white top and the black apron, and stood before him, hands at her sides as he liked.

'How are you finding your duties, Lily? Not too onerous?'

'No, Sir.'

'Good. Let me know if there's anything you need or which could be improved upon, won't you?'

'Yes, Sir.'

Preliminaries were over, it seemed, for he shifted in his chair and dropped his hands to his lap, as though to make a more significant pronouncement.

'Lily, has anyone ever told you about the significance of the collar, to a submissive?'

Lily had not seen this question or subject coming, but her mind shot back to Istanbul, when Aysha had placed the thin leather band with the fleur-de-lys around her neck. Aysha… A wave of guilt flooded over her, for she had been so engrossed in her own situation and experiences in this house that she had barely thought of Aysha in the Kiev hospital. She still had the collar in a drawer in her bedroom. Then there was the heavy steel collar Karla had locked on her, in Berlin. It had been anchored to the floor with a heavy chain. The symbolism of each collar had been plain, though it had been Aysha's which came with the explanation and the deep emotion behind the gift.

'Yes, Sir. I've worn collars before.' She was about to elaborate but decided not to. She did not want to bring Karla into the picture with the need for awkward and possibly revealing commentary. But Cole did not appear

314

interested in her past encounters, only that it saved him some time in his own explanation.

'Good. Very good. Now, Lily, the thought occurred to me you might like a little jewellery to go with your outfit tomorrow. This is not actual jewellery, though it might pass as such.' He stood up and moved to the sideboard where he opened a drawer and returned with a cream-coloured square box about an inch thick. It looked as though it should contain chocolates, but had no markings. He put it on the table and removed the lid, standing back to let Lily see.

A stainless steel choker lay on tissue paper in the box. Lily looked closely and saw there were almost-invisible joints on the right and left sides, while at the front hung a small vertical ring.

'Go on, take it,' urged Cole.

Hesitantly, Lily reached out her hands and lifted the collar clear. It was surprisingly light, though clearly strong and exquisitely made. It was no wider than her finger, and opened up as she raised it, through a concealed hinge on the right hand side. Both edges had a slight outward roll, as though to protect the skin and sit more comfortably. She saw that where the two halves met there were interlocking teeth, through which a tiny hole was drilled, obviously to take a thin screw.

'Do you like it, Lily?'

'It's gorgeous, Sir.'

'Would you like to wear it?'

'Oh yes, Sir.'

'I don't mean just for a short while, or to the concert. I mean permanently – or at least until I decide otherwise.' Lily's heart fluttered. 'It is not a formal submission to me, Lily. It does not give me ownership or anything like that. But it will be there when you go shopping, when you take Charlie for a walk, or go and get your hair cut... Are you prepared for that?'

Lily had a brief realisation that if she thought about it for too long, reason might prevail. What harm could come of it? She followed her gut instinct – or was it simply loin lust?

'Yes, Sir,' she whispered, instinctively giving the collar back and holding up her hair, submitting the soft white skin of her neck for encirclement.

Cole took the collar and moved behind her, slipping the two halves around her neck. It closed with a finger-width clearance between metal and skin, and she felt his deft hands slide the screw into its hole and be wound into place with a tiny allen key. Then it was done. He turned it so the little ring sat in the front, at her throat, then gently removed her hands so her auburn tresses fell down over most of the shiny steel. It didn't feel so bad. Not uncomfortable, just a presence – a reminder. But that was part of its purpose, wasn't it? A reminder that whatever he might have said to the contrary, she was his...

He turned her to face him, examining her face closely and brushing some hair away from the collar. 'It suits you, Lily. You look very beautiful in it. You'll be the star of the concert – well, of the patrons, anyway.' Lily felt herself flush at the compliment, but her mouth was dry and she couldn't find any words. He seemed to sense this, almost with embarrassment himself, and said: 'Well, the dishes won't wash themselves, Lily.'

She turned to go, her jumbled thoughts an excited confusion. Then he added: 'Oh, since this is Friday, Farah usually leaves early, and if business permits, I open the cellar – you know, like other people open a bar. Kind of a Friday informal. I'll be away Monday and Tuesday, so things will be a little irregular.'

'Away, Sir?' Lily finally found her voice, and wondered whether the disappointment she felt was audible.

'Business. I have to go to Paris. I'll be flying out very early Monday morning and back Tuesday afternoon. Farah will be in charge.'

'Oh,' she said, still trying to take in everything which just had happened in five minutes, overturning any routine that might have been on offer.

Lily's mind was not on the job that morning, though she managed to hide it by doing the laundry with the distraction of Charlie in the back yard. As though the concert had not been enough, Cole had now given her this exotic collar which would go so well with the dress she had in mind from Farah's wardrobe. She didn't worry what the hairdresser would think. She could flaunt this. To the uneducated, it was an elegant shining choker, smooth and lustrous, though they might have wondered at which Hatton Garden jeweller she had purchased it. To those in the secret society of submissives, they would smile knowingly and be jealous in a different kind of way.

As she hung out the clothes, she smiled to herself, touching the hardness at her throat. Then had come that allusion to a 'Friday informal' and the opening of the cellar. What did that mean? It had overtones of the Black Tower about it, though she hoped she would not be left to her own devices again. Suddenly time could not pass quickly enough.

When Farah's car drove away at four-thirty, Lily pretended to be polishing some of the wooden panels in the foyer, where the study door remained open. She could hear the odd rustle of paper from inside, and jumped when the electric bell sounded high up on the wall above the stairs.

'Sir?' she asked, going to the doorway of the study.

'What's for dinner, Lily?'

'I've made some macaroni and cheese, if that's okay, Sir.'

'Excellent. Ready to heat up in the oven, is it?'

'Yes, Sir.'

'Good. I think I can manage that. It's Friday, Lily. POET'S Day.'

'Poet's Day?' she was genuinely puzzled.

'Piss Off Early, Tomorrow's Saturday, Lily.' He grinned, a boyish look which made her laugh. 'Which means your duties are ended for the day.'

'But I have to walk Charlie, and heat the dinner, and –'

'I'll walk Charlie, and – contrary to popular opinion – I'm capable of heating something by myself. Come over here, Lily.'

She ventured across the big Persian rug, to stand before his desk, again feeling just a little intimidated and not knowing what was coming next. He tapped the edge of the desk. 'Round here, next to me.' She did so, and Cole opened the bottom drawer on one side of the desk, pulling out a pair of wide black leather cuffs adorned with steel D-shaped rings and buckles, giving a look of toughness and permanence. 'Left hand out,' he ordered.

Lily did so, and he buckled the heavy cuff around her wrist. It was intended for a larger wrist, and he had to go to the end hole to achieve enough snugness. She looked closely as he tucked the loose end of the strap away, and she saw the strap holes were slightly elongated, and the buckle pin had a small eye at the end of it – requiring the elongated strap-hole – and through this eye Cole locked a small brass padlock. Lily held it up to examine the lock, and realised the strap could not now be unbuckled. She caught her breath and hoped he didn't notice, for it seemed to her the room must echo with her now rapidly beating heart.

She held out the other wrist, and a moment later that was similarly cuffed and locked in place.

Cole stood up and moved behind her, pulling the two cuffs together behind her and locking them together with a large padlock through the two D-rings. She tugged, knowing it was futile, but liking the resistance and the limitation now put on her movement.

He pulled out two more leather cuffs, adroitly fastening them about her stockinged ankles and locking them together with a short length of chain through the D-rings. Lily was already getting the warm fuzzies, though she couldn't tell if this was her over-active brain or over-active pussy.

'What are you going to do to me?' she whispered, realising as she said it that this was what she had been told not to do in the Black Tower. Cole eased himself half on to the desk, letting one leg idly swing.

'What *should* I do to you?' he retorted, his tone suddenly changed, becoming aggressive and harsh. 'You come into my house, under the pretence of doing housework, and you're now prepared to steal from under my nose.'

'What?' Lily was aghast. 'I haven't stolen anything! What are you talking about?'

'Don't try to deny it, you bitch!'

'But I –!' Lily's stomach dropped at the thought she had somehow slipped up, that he had overheard or seen something. Maybe the camera? Oh God!

'Shut up!' he ordered and she did so, cowed by the sudden change in him.

He grabbed her by the shoulders and spun her to face the door, propelling her towards it, making her take short, desperate, hobbled steps. They moved across the foyer, Lily just managing to stay upright with his strong hands still gripping her shoulders. Then, before she realised it, he had lifted and slung her over his shoulder. She gasped, surprised at the strength of the man, for he had not seemed to her excessively well built. But there was no mistaking his purposefulness as one arm gripped her round the thighs while her breasts bumped his back, and they descended the stairs into the cellar. She was still too overwhelmed by the sudden head-down view of the world to shout, to protest, as her breath came in bouncing gasps with each downward step.

Lily tried to struggle as soon as he put her down, but it was token resistance. She tried to plead her innocence, tried to avoid the leather hood forced over her head, blotting out her sight as it was buckled under her chin.

The loss of her sight calmed Lily, though only on the outside. The smell of the leather hood filled her nostrils in a strangely familiar way that reminded her of Karla and Berlin. The circumstances of this predicament now came home with a horrible realisation in the blackness, and she knew she couldn't fight, couldn't run. But she could still abuse him.

'I haven't done anything! Let me go, please Sir!' Then: 'Tell me what I've done! I don't understand!' In her darkened world she felt she had to make her demands felt, until his hands were on her head again and his fingers grasped her nose, shutting down her breathing and forcing her to open her mouth, in time for a rubber ball to be pushed into it and a strap buckled around her head. Lily was now silent, save for some hmmming protests which came to nothing. She stood there, in the large cellar, not sure which way she was facing, where Cole was, or what was happening next.

'I can't abide noisy women, Lily. I think it's time you learned that. Not that it matters. I'll let you settle down here, while I call the police. They're usually pretty prompt, but Friday night may be busy. Perhaps I'll wait a while until rush hour's over. Before you become a guest of Her Majesty, you can be my guest.' The hands on her shoulders pushed her forward and she heard the creak of the grille door opening and closing behind her, followed by the sound of a heavy padlock.

Lily stood there, disorientated, in darkness, tugging at the cuffs on her wrists and trying to push the ball out of her mouth with her tongue, but everything was tight and unmoving. She pictured the cell from her first visit, and knew there was a small bed to the left. Tentatively she shuffled until her knees bumped into the steel frame with its plastic-wrapped mattress, then turned around and eased herself down, feeling the cold plastic with her cuffed hands.

God! Had Cole been on to her all the way, but merely assumed she was a common thief, rather than a spy? But it must have been the camera – that was the only thing she could be at risk from. It occurred to her she was not going to be meeting Karla now. What would happen then? Would Karla abandon her?

Lily's over-active imagination began to run riot, as she wondered again what had happened to Erika. Had Lily's predecessor been similarly trapped? Was Cole really going to call the police... or did he have something more permanent in mind for meddlesome *au pairs*? And where was Cole now? Was he watching her through the grille or had he gone upstairs? Lily felt tears under the leather of the hood.

A voice came out of the darkness: 'Enjoy your Friday informal, Lily.' The voice was different, the harshness gone, replaced by a chuckle. 'Imaginative enough for you?'

Lily sat there, as the truth dawned on her. He had used her again, unconsciously homing in on her imagination which only needed a push-start in the right direction to take on its own momentum and direction. She was shaking from relief and realisation at the deception played on her. God! He had been so convincing! She had been totally suckered by his act.

Now she was a prisoner in the cellar, under the house that she – a long-time cat burglar – had made the mistake of trying to rob. Her fear was abruptly replaced by the warm flood of uncertainty as to what now lay ahead of her. The local constabulary was well-known for its unorthodox methods of interrogation, and for extracting the truth from its suspects. But would she even get to the police cells? She was captive in a cell already, and while she had admitted to nothing, this house owner seemed sufficiently motivated to extract a confession himself.

Lily sat on the bed for a short while, the excitement of her precarious situation and undetermined fate growing within her, feeding her arousal. She squirmed, rubbing her nyloned thighs together, but failing to achieve anything approaching relief. With her hands cuffed behind her, she was not going to get any help from her fingers. He had thought of this, for sure. Lily was now firmly of the view that Aurelius Cole did very little on the fly – that his actions were premeditated and aimed at the long game.

She stood up in her darkened world, her hearing – stifled by the hood – consisting largely of her exaggerated breathing and blood rushing somewhere in her ears. She again tested the rubber ball strapped in her mouth, but could only manage an incomprehensible mumble or a sort on humming through her nose. A runnel of saliva dripped on to her blouse and soaked through over her breasts. She must look a sight, even after just a few minutes. Again, she wondered if he was watching her, planning, scheming, deciding on her torture and punishment.

A faint rush of warmth ran upward from her crotch, and she involuntarily bent over, to try to savour it, to preserve the wonderful feeling and make it last. But it was gone, and she straightened, shuffling forward, trying to orient herself. She was astonished how the slightest turn seemed to destroy her sense of direction. She stumbled forward, heading for where she thought the iron grille was, pushing her breasts out to soften any contact before she did so with her nose, and was surprised to bump into solid wall.

She turned her back to the wall and edged along it, cuffed hands brushing the brickwork, until her left shoulder came up against the grille. Her hands explored the iron bars, feeling the latch plate and venturing between the bars to encounter the heavy padlock securing the bolt. Lily snorted, realising she was well and truly imprisoned. The solidity of the grille and the padlock inexplicably excited her, underlining the completeness of her captivity. She was utterly helpless.

Lily's small hobbled steps now took her on a blackened tour of the cell, establishing there was a bucket half-filled with water, with a lid, but precious little else. Perhaps she had to decide between how much she drank and how much she had to pee, although right then nothing was going to pass the ball in her mouth.

Lily sat down on the bed again, then flopped on her side, drawing her knees up and luxuriating in her restraints, and the dark, evocative smell of the leather hood. She wondered how long she would be left like this, how long she could endure it. The obvious answer was that she would endure it as long as she had to, because right then all choice had been taken away, and that did nothing to calm the warmth brewing between her legs.

She rolled on to her stomach, but that position gave no relief, and the frustration began to rival the excitement. This was going to be another Black Tower, she thought, already starting to wish for an intervention. How long would he leave her? All night? Oh dear God.

Maybe she dozed. Lily's thoughts were random, scrambled, though with a common theme of cuffs, restraints and warm fuzzies creeping up from her crotch which remained tantalisingly beyond fulfilment. She was drooling around the gag on to the plastic of the mattress when there was a sudden bang on the iron grille.

'Urgh?' If she had been half-asleep, she was awake in a second, wrestling against her bonds as the recollection of her predicament came back. She struggled to sit up, awkwardly sliding her legs over the side of the bed in time to hear the faint tinkle which might have been keys hitting concrete. She paused there, trying to detect any sound through the hood, listening for any instructions or anything which might have meant a change in her circumstances or a new phase in her incarceration.

Finally, as the silence remained, Lily got cautiously to her feet and found her way to the grille, her still-buckled shoes encountering what had to be a set of keys on the way. Cole's release *modus operandi*. She squatted, fingers on the dusty concrete, scrabbling for the prize – a steel ring with two keys on it, attached to some sort of plastic key tag that gave it enough substance not to be mislaid.

Grunting to herself, Lily stood up, fingers now assessing the prize. The keys were of medium size and seemed to be similar, if not identical. It took no time to establish they would not fit the small locks on her cuffs, and could only be the bigger padlock joining her wrists. Lily worked her way back to the bed and sat down, carefully hanging on to the key ring, before taking some deep breaths, telling herself to take her time. The padlock linking her wrist cuffs had its keyhole facing her fingers, and after some judicious manoeuvring of one of the keys, she felt it slide into the hole and turn, then her arms came free.

Lily sighed with her success, now able to remove the hood and the gag. She worked her jaw, revelling in its freedom again, though the lights remained out and the removal of the hood made no difference in the blackness. She confirmed that the keys were in fact identical, and that the cuffs on her wrists and ankles would remain locked in place, but it was still progress. On a hunch she hobbled to the grille, but the bolt was still firmly locked. Lily Maddison was still imprisoned in a dark cellar, but now had her hands free to alleviate her frustration.

Lily could resist no longer. The unknown length of her sentence was suddenly unimportant, for she was at least partly in control and could literally take matters into her own hands. In the inky blackness of her cell, Lily Maddison cried out with elation and delight, before curling up on the mattress, uncaring about the future. She fell asleep to the memory of the strong arms carrying her down the steps, and to the revelation that being a chained and confined prisoner was what she loved most of all.

When Lily awoke, the light in the room outside her cell was on, though the latter remained unlit. As her ordeal came flooding back, she realised she had no idea if it was day or night, or how long she had slept. She felt drained and weak, but somehow satisfied, now not sure whether the scenario was over or whether her jailor had planned something further.

Slowly she swung her legs off the bed, the tug between her ankles reminding her she had been unable to unlock the hobble nor remove any of the cuffs. When she reached the iron grille, she found the padlock had gone, and she was able to reach through the bars to slide the heavy bolt back. The grille creaked open and Lily stepped into the brightly-lit room with its smell of bricks and leather, and its arrays of devices for restraint and pain, but found she was alone. There was no Aurelius Cole waiting for her with a lascivious grin, intending to subject her to a new range of tortures.

Lily climbed the concrete steps, realising she was hungry and had not eaten dinner, but perhaps that was part of the rightful punishment she had endured, for her audacity in thinking she could rob this house...

When she emerged from under the stairs, an early morning sun was streaming through the oriole window. She had hoped the study door might have been open, with her captor available to unlock her cuffs, but such was not to be. Lily shuffled out to the kitchen, then the dining room, but there was no sign of Cole. It was gone six-thirty, and Charlie was ready for his walk, not appreciating why the female human was unable to take more than mincing steps. On the kitchen table was a prominent note stating: 'Morning paper and post, please.'

It was fine for Old King Cole to demand her servitude first thing on a Saturday morning, but had he forgotten her hobble and cuffs? She couldn't go outside like this. Except that she had to. With a sudden certainty that this was exactly what he intended, and that the intention was for a reason, Lily retraced her steps to the foyer and opened the front door a crack. She had chosen the black leather skirt and white silk top yesterday – something about as far from Hampstead Saturday attire as possible, unless one was doing some sort of bizarre morning-after walk of shame.

Cautiously Lily looked about, but nobody was in sight. She eased herself down the steps and along the short path to the iron gate, where the two morning papers lay close outside. She pulled the gate open and grabbed the papers – the Telegraph and the Times – before retreating and closing it gently. She didn't know what time the morning post came on Saturday, but nevertheless looked in the letter box set in the wall. There was no post, but a set of small keys with a red plastic tag lay inside. Lily grabbed them and shambled back to the front door, not looking to see who might have followed her ordeal as she shut it behind her.

\*     \*     \*

# CHAPTER 27 – The Albert

L ily! Taxi's here!'
When Lily descended the stairs, Aurelius Cole was standing in the foyer waiting for her, wearing a dark suit with a blue silk tie. He looked up as she reached the bottom flight.

'Oh my gosh! Lily, you look ravishing!'

Lily had settled on a bronze-coloured silk sheath she had found in Farah's wardrobe. It fastened at one shoulder, leaving the other bare, and fell just to her knees. It was not tailored to be figure hugging, but Lily's was on show anyway, in small, subtle glimpses. Her hair was pinned back behind her ears, dropping to her neck and showing off the gleaming steel collar. Cole looked truly impressed, and greeted her with a chaste kiss on the cheek. Lily felt exceptionally pleased with herself, acknowledging the hairdresser and manicure had been worth it.

She was unaccustomed to such treatment – not since a long time ago in New Zealand, when she and Robert occasionally went to a classical concert in the town hall. There had been nothing like that for months, and now this handsome gentleman – yes, she also decided that he scrubbed up well – was waiting to take her to the Royal Albert Hall. Lily was beside herself, but managed to suppress her excitement for the sake of decorum. This was England, after all.

'I have a little something for you,' said Cole. 'It's difficult to improve on perfection, but I feel there's something lacking in that collar, with the ring on the front. It's kind of there to take something more substantial, but may I present this to you, Miss Maddison…'

He pulled a small black velvet bag from his pocket and placed it in her palm. Intrigued, Lily undid the drawstring and a tiny silver padlock slid out. It was barely larger than her thumb nail – a padlock with a small clip through the shank which could be attached to the ring.

'Oh, it's gorgeous,' said Lily.

'Allow me,' he said, taking it from her fingers and moving in close. He smelled good, and she wished he would take his time, as his fingers fluttered at her throat before the little lock dangled free. Lily took a moment in the foyer mirror to admire the result, cocking her head to make it catch the light, then turning to smile her appreciation. Cole offered her his arm and they walked out to the waiting black cab.

The distance to the Albert Hall was not great, but by the time they had passed Regent's Park and Lords Cricket Ground, then driven through the green swathe of Kensington Gardens, Lily was entranced. As Cole paid off the cab, Lily stood transfixed by the great domed red brick building, with its cream-coloured window surrounds and the ornate terracotta frieze encircling the structure. This was her Mecca, where the great Jacqueline du Pré had played, where the greatest conductors and orchestras of the world had performed. This was The Albert, its picture gracing so many of her records back in New Zealand. It was on show every year in the Last Night of the Proms on television, where the patriotic crowds would sing *Rule Britannia*, *Jerusalem* and the orchestra played Elgar in a strange eccentric showing of Britishness that somehow Lily identified with.

Lily hung on to Cole's arm as they swept into the crowds milling in the foyers and corridors. She made no attempt to converse, but simply breathed in the atmosphere. Cole procured two glasses of champagne and had the awareness to let her absorb the buzz. It was hardly surprising the champagne went straight to her head, but it was pressed into submission by her awe at the occasion.

Their seats were in a 4-seater box on the second level, nearly central to the stage. They nodded politely to the other couple already seated. It seemed to Lily that the auditorium almost surrounded her. Cole finally decided to engage with his companion.

'See the statue just in front of the organ?' Lily could make out the bronze bust of a bearded man wearing a green wreath between two Union Jacks in front of the massive Grand Organ – at one time the largest in the world. 'Sir Henry Wood. The Proms were his idea. Now he's revered and his bust is placed there at the start of every Proms season.'

'And he introduced a Wagner Night on Mondays, and a Beethoven Night on Fridays,' Lily said.

'Oh. I see you're up with your musical history,' Cole said, slightly taken aback.

'Sorry. You learn all sorts of things studying music and its history,' Lily said. She tossed him a test. 'Fredrick Septimus Kelly. Born where?'

Cole smiled, giving a slight shrug – the admission of defeat concerning the composer of the first piece that evening.

'Sorry. He's not on my list of favourites.'

'Maybe he will be after tonight,' Lily suggested, 'even if he is Australian. You should know better... Sir.' She had wondered if she should call him 'Aurelius' under such outside-work circumstances, but somehow, between themselves, she liked the 'Sir' better. For now.

'What do you know that I don't?' he teased.

'Kelly was a friend of Rupert Brooke, the poet. We're going to hear the Elegy for String Orchestra, but it's subtitle is 'In Memorium Rupert Brooke'. Of course you'll know that Brooke wrote 'The Soldier'. Something we all had to learn at school - shows how tied we are to the motherland. "A corner of a foreign field that is forever England",' she quoted. Cole looked impressed. 'Yes, I know the words to "Jerusalem" as well,' she added. 'It's a pity we don't value our own Kiwi culture so much, but that'll change, I guess.' Cole was attentive. He had not seen Lily so talkative.

'So... Brooke and Kelly?' he prompted.

'Kelly was born in Sydney, though you Poms claim him for yourselves. They were heading for Gallipoli from England when Brooke developed sepsis and died on the ship near a Greek island, where he was buried by Kelly and some friends. When I hear this music I can almost see the grave overlooking a little bay, with the olive trees and wild flowers... I'm sorry, but you'll probably see me cry during this. Some music does that. I don't know why.'

Cole looked strangely moved at this admission, and laid his hand on her arm.

'Me too,' he said quietly.

Lily gave him a curious glance. 'Kelly made it through Gallipoli,' she said quietly, 'but was killed a year later at the Battle of the Somme...'

When the applause for the concert master and conductor had died away and the music had begun, the initial wonderment of the auditorium faded from Lily's mind with the dimming of the lights. She had read accounts of the burial of Brooke by the small shore party, how Kelly believed that no more fitting resting place for a poet could be found than the little grove, where it seemed as though the gods had jealously snatched him away to enrich the scented island.

She felt the first tear trickle down her cheek. She could not explain this, though it happened every time she heard the piece. This time, however, her thoughts took her to her own experience on the Gallipoli hillside and the grave of her great uncle – her own connection with the place. Arthur Buchanan's grave had been one of many, all perfectly maintained, and overlain with tragedy that made Lily weep. The loss of young men of the time had become personal, six decades later. The last chords faded slowly away and the audience sat in contemplative, rapt silence for several long seconds, before the applause began.

Lily sniffed and wiped her eyes, not trusting herself to speak. She looked at Cole, who also seemed to have something in his eye and avoided her gaze. Neither spoke as the orchestra adjusted their chairs and several players were added for the next piece.

The first notes of Borodin's "In the Steppes of Central Asia" transported Lily to another moment of the overland trip, as the dun and dusty mountains of Afghanistan came into her head. Aysha was beside her in the bus, as they crossed the endless spectacular landscape, following the routes which camel caravans had taken for millennia. It all came flooding back, not least the presence of her friend, and the plight that still lay heavily over both of them. Like the first piece, it had a quiet and reflective ending, and another long hesitation as though the audience searched for breath before the applause began.

Lily exhaled slowly, surprised by the intensity of the music and the memories of Afghanistan. Cole looked at her questioningly, but she ignored him and stared straight ahead, unmoving, not wanting to let Aysha go and not caring that more tears slid down her cheek. She refused to speak again before the soloist appeared for the last work of the first half – Dvorak's cello concerto. It was a work Lily knew well, had played many times, albeit without a world famous conductor and orchestra to back her up. It did not have the same emotional connections as the first two pieces, and she thought she could get through it dry-eyed, enjoying the music and the performance for its own sake.

The cellist was a young Swedish woman in her late twenties, and Lily was impressed by her performance. Playing at the Albert Hall had been the subject of her many girlish dreams at university, until the reality set in that she was not the prodigy she would need to be to scale such heights. It had been a slow and frustrating realisation, one softened by her teachers who did their best to convince her that there would remain plenty of openings within the orchestras of the world for which she was more than qualified. She had clung on to these hopes, deciding that the orchestras of Europe would be a good place to start – a vague strategy which had not developed during the overland journey, and had faded dramatically since her arrival in Berlin. Now she engrossed herself in the music, a piece written over eighty years previously, and as always, she marvelled at the familiarity and longevity of such a work of art – for the moment managing to forget the circumstances which she would return to in the House of Asha.

Cole had steered their way expertly to the bar during the interval, reappearing with more champagne and another couple in tow. The man was in his late forties, slightly balding behind horn-rimmed glasses and sporting a suit which was anything but off-the-rack. The woman was a little younger, blonde hair piled on her head, her trim figure fitted inside a long black dress with three rings of pearls at her throat.

Cole introduced them as Victor and Jennifer Hopkirk.

'Victor is the Permanent Under-Secretary for the FCO,' he said. Lily realised she must have looked blank. 'Foreign and Commonwealth Office,' he added quickly. Lily had little understanding of the functioning of the British Government and its departments, but managed to look suitably impressed. 'Kind of my boss, somewhere up the line,' Cole said with a modest cough, 'though we've known each other for a good many years.' It appeared Jennifer either did not have an occupation, or else it was irrelevant or insubstantial compared to her husband's. 'Lily's a cellist – just arrived from New Zealand,' Cole told them, making it sound as though she was merely waiting for her luggage to arrive before she, too, would be sitting in the orchestra pit with the LSO.

'Really?' said Jennifer, sounding genuinely impressed, though her eyes also made the assessment that Cole was running around with a woman nearly half his age.

'Look, at the risk of being terribly rude, would you mind if I had a private word, old boy?' said Victor. 'I'm most awfully sorry to do this in such a place, but it's a happy coincidence I'd rather not waste. We'll just be a few minutes...' He touched Cole on the shoulder as though to steer him to a quiet corner. Cole threw Lily a look of apology, but Jennifer picked up the slack, though not before Lily noticed a tall athletic-looking man with an ear-piece follow the two men away from the crowd.

'Victor can't let work go, sometimes,' said Jennifer. To Lily's untutored ears her accent sounded slightly forced, as though put on for the evening. 'But, well, Foreign Office never sleeps,' she sighed.

'Just what does the FCO do?' asked Lily. 'Sorry – excuse my ignorance...'

'Quite all right, darling. What does it do – everything, it seems. Opening international markets, furthering trade relations, providing all the consular services for British nationals, increasing exports, and looking after national security.'

'Don't you have a Ministry of Defence?'

'Of course, dear. But that's all the military forces and things. This is... sort of behind the scenes.'

'What – like spies?'

'Well, MI6, that sort of thing.'

'No! Really? Should you be telling me this?'

'Common knowledge,' said Jennifer, taking another gulp of champagne. 'But... New Zealand – tell me about it. God, I'd love to go there, get away from all the shit that goes down here – pardon my French.'

'You'd probably find it incredibly provincial,' Lily said.

'Have to be better than this awful place,' Jennifer observed. 'Labour government, miners' strikes, the IRA, the Yorkshire Ripper, the National Front... And frightful weather into the bargain. Honestly, I don't know why you colonials come here.' The patronising use of the word was clearly unintended, so focussed was Jennifer her own misfortune in having to live in such terrible surroundings.

'You'd miss the culture,' Lily said. 'We have nothing like this,' she gestured to the animated conversation going on around them. 'So cosmopolitan.'

Jennifer sniffed. 'Stuck up twats, most of them. Been to the right schools, lining up for a knighthood.' Then she changed subject unexpectedly. 'So... you and Aurelius, eh? How did you two get together? I *am* surprised. But you'll be so good for him, after all he's been through...'

'All he's been through?'

'Oh you know – all that Iranian thing. Just terrible... He really deserves someone nice...'

Just then the men returned to rescue Lily. She'd thought that if the Hopkirks had known Cole for a while, Jennifer would have had some dirt on Cole, though whatever Jennifer Hopkirk had been on about sounded anything but dirty. Lily grasped Cole's arm with more enthusiasm than was warranted, and observed the man with the ear-piece looking at her with an expression she could not make out. It was as though he was assessing her and mentally filing her in a box marked "okay", "acceptable", or "not a problem".

They had time for another champagne, and Lily was starting to feel the effects, magnified by the excitement of her surroundings. Strangely, the conversation turned to the Hopkirks, rather than the program.

'Who was the guy with the ear-piece?' Lily asked, *sotto voce*, glancing at the people milling around them.

'Oh, that was Reg. It means the Secretary's not far away. Reg is part of the detail.'

'The Secretary?'

'Secretary of State for Foreign and Commonwealth Affairs, to give him his full pompous title.'

'I wouldn't mind a nice foreign affair,' Lily giggled. 'Oh, wait – maybe I'm already having one! Am I? Are we having an affair?'

'You're having too much alcohol young lady. You're already ruining my reputation.'

'Ruining? Enhancing, probably.'

'Old man running around with young women? Hardly proper. Word's probably gone up the gossip ladder already, thanks to Jenny.'

'Old man's capable of *attracting* young women,' Lily corrected. 'Means you've still got it. It's a *good* thing.'

Cole laughed. 'I think you're good for me.'

'Is that what your mate will think?'

'Victor? He's insanely jealous already. Thank you for that.'

'Arm candy works well on testosterone,' she said. 'It's one of the reactions they *don't* teach in chemistry. But I bet you didn't discuss *me*.'

'Well, not all the time. Affairs of state, my dear.'

'To do with you going to Paris?' Lily asked on an innocent-sounding hunch.

'Perhaps. Ah – there's the gong. We must head back. Did you like the Dvorak?'

'No. Hated it. That Swedish chick is far too good a player and she's beautiful as well. Life is completely unfair... No, it was quite good... Excellent, really.'

'You're funny, Lily. You should've been a stand-up.'

'Thanks. I'll remember that when all the orchestras have turned me down.'

The Planets Suite was from the same vintage as the first piece – a product of the First World War and the fading dreams of British colonialism. Yet Lily, despite her New Zealand upbringing, still found a connection with this music, with her love of all things imperial. She listened enthralled through the sequence of the Planets, with their symbolism and significance, leading to Saturn, the Bringer of Old Age, Uranus the Magician, and finally Neptune the Mystic.

In the darkness of the auditorium, the eerie melody from the orchestra merged imperceptibly into an aethereal women's choir. Lily strained to see where this choir was located, but there was nothing to indicate that it was in the usual place behind the orchestra. Then she realised the singers were not near the orchestra at all, but must be high above her, in the unseen gallery – in the Gods, the highest balcony – their voices drifting down from the great dome.

This was what heaven must be like, Lily decided, her slightly befuddled thought processes ignoring a similar thought she'd had the previous night in utterly different circumstances. If at that moment she could have grown wings, she thought she would have floated over the edge of the balcony and simply kept going, some strange emotion welling up inside her that made her again want to cry. The voices began to fade, slowly, slowly, dying away into the distance until the conductor stood motionless, holding the last note before dropping into a silence that swamped the hall.

The Bellingham Club was ten minutes' walk from the Albert Hall, a dignified four-storey hotel-cum-private club matching the surrounding architecture to the point of understatement. A small brass plaque was the only advertising and as they neared it, the windows glowed warmly with unseen bustle. Lily noticed the short walk appeared to exacerbate Cole's limp, though she said nothing as they reached the entrance and were greeted by a uniformed doorman.

'Thank you, Harold,' said Cole as the man held the door open for them. 'All well with you?'

'Yes, thank you Mister Cole.'

Lily was impressed by the exchange, as she was when they entered the imposing foyer with its moulded ceilings and portraits of old England's explorer heroes. She barely had a chance to take in the sumptuous surrounds before Cole whisked them up the wide marble staircase to the restaurant on the first floor, where they were shown to a table by a waiter who was also on familiar terms with Cole. It was a small restaurant, but buzzing with clientele, many of whom were also the post-concert crowd.

'They stay open late for the likes of us hoi-polloi – those civilised people who like a leisurely meal *after* the event, rather than a rushed scoffure before opening.'

'Scoffure?'

'Something I just made up. You know – scoffing down your grub like at boarding school, in case the bloke next to you nicks your jam tart when you're not looking. 'Scoffure' – noun, a feeding frenzy; from boarding school English; first used September 1977. Satisfied?'

Lily laughed. The white linen and sparkling glasses were immaculate, and she looked around at her fellow diners in the discreet low lighting.

'Is this place a hotel as well? Are you a member... oh, probably a stupid question, yes?'

'No such thing, Lily – stupid question, I mean. Yes, it is a hotel, as well as a club. A lot of these people will probably stay the night, since by the time they've finished, British Rail and the Underground will have gone to bed. It's a nice little niche market and works well.'

He picked up the wine list.

'Are you a red or a white woman... Make any pun you like with that question, but you know what I mean. New Zealand does the odd good wine, so I'm told.'

Lily was embarrassed, since her student mates had usually imbibed nothing more sophisticated than cheap German *Black Tower* and *Blue Nun*.

'I'm white... so to speak.' She smiled at the double entendre. 'Rieslings are popular back home,' she added, trying to sound more confident.

'Good, then a bottle of the Hammerstein it is,' said Cole, giving his order to the waiter when he appeared with the menus.

With Lily's chicken and champagne pie and Cole's ballotine of rabbit ordered, Cole asked:

'So, you enjoyed the concert?'

'God, what was not to enjoy? Thank you so much! I've dreamed of the Albert Hall since I got my first LP with a picture of it on the cover. I actually think it was an organ piece. Ralph Davier playing Bach – there's a picture of him in front of the hall.'

'So it met your expectations?'

'And a lot of other people's, obviously. Your friends. How long have you known them – the Hopkirks?'

'Oh, we go back years. Victor and I were at Oxford together. Both went into the civil service.'

'Is that where you are now – the civil service?'

'What? Working from home? No – if I was in the civil service I'd be catching the 7.48 Northern Line from Edgeware each day, fighting the brown raincoats and rolled up newspapers. I like to consider myself a little more civilised than the so-called civil service.'

'Civil servants don't drive Jaguars, have private club memberships and a Hampstead House with a dungeon, where they lure innocent young women,' Lily observed dryly, locking gazes with him.

'Absolutely right,' he agreed. 'Did you enjoy your night underground? I didn't get the chance to ask you this morning.'

Lily blushed, her attempt to wheedle more information about his background deflected by the memory of her incarceration, and her ill-suppressed rapture at the experience. At once she was pushed back from an almost-equal in the conversation to the receiver of a gift so overwhelming she could hardly express the effect it had had on her.

'It was... very nice, thank you, Sir.'

'"Very nice?" It wasn't a bunch of flowers, Lily.' Cole was clearly amused.

Lily looked around at the other diners, deep in their low-lit conversations, the crisp-linened tables far enough away to promise privacy. 'It was all I could hope for, Sir. Well, almost all.'

'Almost?'

'You left me to my own devices again.'

'You're a very imaginative person, Lily. I suspect you manage very well on your own devices. That's kind of the point. The thing about our little scenario is that everybody is different. Let's face it, how many woman have so-called joyful sex with their partner, but secretly wish their partner would do it just a little bit differently, the way they *really* like it? Bondage is so much more than just a straight sex technique. I'm sure you've worked that out by now. All the fantasies you have, the nuances in your own head, the positions, the roles, the adventures, the different eras... Yes, dungeons are a common theme, from medieval to the Inquisition, to the Bastille, to the Resistance, to simply being wrongfully arrested by corrupt police. You know you'll be in for a bad time, in whatever place you find yourself, but each will have a hundred variations. Only *you* will know what these are in your own scene.'

'But it would be nice to have a little help with them,' said Lily, sounding just a little plaintive in her own ears.

'Then we must talk about it, Lily. You must tell me your fantasies if you want them to come true.'

Lily was silent for a long time. Cole topped up her glass with the translucent Riesling which slid down her throat with a smooth fruitiness and no apparent effect on her senses – except that talking became a little easier. And the talking was also made easier by the need for Lily to articulate in her *own* mind the needs she had, and the scenarios that satisfied these.

She did her best to describe the vague Middle Ages drama between her and the Queen, and how whatever she had done had displeased said queen, leading to incarceration. There was the instance in the village where she had been caught with the blacksmith's son, tied to a tree and whipped. Then there were cells, dungeons and torture chambers, where she refused to name the woman she had slept with, because of the shame it would bring on her family.

'A true submissive, Lily, is one who falls asleep each night in an imaginary dungeon, or wherever they secretly desire, in whatever bound position obsesses them on that night. They fall asleep because they are captured, because they have no control, but are at the same time safe. The ability to fret, to worry about their fate, about the problems of the outside world, has been taken away from them. They're chained or bound and are helpless until others decide otherwise. They can only surrender to their fate. So they fall asleep. Trust me, I've heard this many, many times.'

By the time the dessert had come and they were nearly through the second bottle of wine, Lily had surprised herself, not least for the range of fantasies which had tumbled from her lips, but from the articulate and concise way in which she had apparently described them. As a non-Catholic, it seemed to Lily that this was what confession must be like, but she hoped sharing these desires might make them actually come about, rather than be met with a prescription for avoiding them.

Cole had proven himself an exceptional listener, even if Lily did not notice it until it finally dawned on her she was monopolising the conversation, albeit at prodding from Cole. It was only when the dessert plates had been cleared and the cognac arrived, that Lily realised that in revealing her inner desires, she had learned nothing further about Cole.

'Can I ask you a question, Sir?' She hoped she was not slurring her words, but couldn't quite be sure.

'Of course.' He seemed composed and relaxed, mellowed by the wine and the surroundings.

'Why is your house called "Asha"? What's the thing on the brass plate by the front door?' The question surprised both Cole and Lily herself. Clearly it had been lurking in her brain and had surfaced out of the blue.

'Not what I was expecting,' he commented with a smile. 'You're full of surprises tonight.'

'So?'

'So... Asha is a Zoroastrian concept. You know about Zoroastrianism?'

'Sort of. Persian? To do with fire?'

'Yes. Asha has to do with "Truth" or "Righteousness". The figure on the plaque is called the Faravahar, which is like a personal spirit.'

'So it's the House of Asha, not the House of Usher,' Lily said with a giggle.

'Very droll, Lily. I wouldn't have picked you as an Edgar Allan Poe fan.'

'It's surprising what you'll read when you're young, and you only have a mobile library visiting once a week. I have a friend called Aysha. Asha, Usher and Aysha. Weird, huh?'

'Yes.'

'So why "Truth" and "Righteousness"? It's a bit... I don't know...'

'Pretentious?'

'Your friend Jennifer suggested a lot of the people at the concert were... 'twats' was the word she used.'

'With the word "pretentious" thrown in?'

'More implied than spoken.'

'Sounds like Jennifer. She's always looking out for me.'

'Why?'

'Oh... you know, women...'

'What happened in Iran?' Lily slid the question on to the table like a hand grenade. Cole stiffened, his easy manner disappearing. He avoided her gaze, and impulsively she put out her hand and covered his where it grasped the brandy balloon. 'Tell me, please,' she whispered, sensing she had poked a raw nerve, and that it was suddenly important to her, though she did not understand why.

He leaned back in his chair, though not pulling his hand away, as though considering whether to answer. Lily saw hurt, for the first time finding something beyond the confident and controlling façade. Cole turned his head as though to look for a waiter, but when he looked at her again his eyes were watery. She squeezed his hand.

'I used to work in Tehran,' he began, not looking at her. 'As a kind of private consultant to the Iranian Government. This was a couple of years ago. I'd been there a year. I speak Farsi, I know stuff about economics and politics and security. Kind of a jack of all trades. Maybe a jackal of all trades... I worked with the British Embassy, and I met this woman, at an embassy party. Her name was Leila. She was three years older than you, and we hit it off.

'Leila was a niece of the Shah – one of a few such nieces, but also one of his favourites. I was already on speaking terms with the Shah through the diplomatic help Britain was providing, and to be seeing his niece socially enhanced my standing even further. She was a beautiful woman, loved by the fashion magazines as much for her beauty as her intellect. She was one of the shining stars of the House of Pahlavi. Then she met me, and almost overnight she disappeared from the social scene.

'We'd found each other, found out our common love – she to the submission, me to the dominance. It was largely unheard of and frowned upon in Iran, though they're a very liberal society. But the secret culture was there – you just had to know where to look. She'd been to London, Paris, Berlin... Just like in those cities, the underground culture was there, the bondage, S and M, the private fantasies and release. We met as often as we could. We were in love – so much more than just pleasures of the flesh, though they were without a doubt a wonderful part of it. She was a true submissive, who loved the ropes, the pain, the pleasure that came with the subjugation...

'We moved in together – a lovely old colonial house on Fereshteh Street, overlooking the Turkish Embassy gardens. Then, one day...' He stopped and sipped from his glass of water. Lily saw his bottom lip quiver and the effort it took to control it. He took a deep breath.

'You have to understand the forces at work in Iran, Lily. The Shah has brought the place into the twentieth century at an astonishing rate. They have vast reserves of oil and gas, but not the expertise to properly utilise it. The Soviets have always been snooping about there, since the Great Game in the last century. They want the oil, and they also want access to the Persian Gulf. They'll try any means possible – diplomacy or by revolution. There's this organisation called the Tudeh, which the Soviets have infiltrated and manipulated, and which they're using to their own ends. The Tudeh are being groomed for revolution.

'One day, after we had been to a cocktail party at the palace, Leila and I were in our house, in what we called the play room, on the first floor... It was private and we used it for our...passions... Leila was naked... God she was so beautiful... She was standing there, wrists bound above her head, facing the french doors... I had turned my back to her, to retrieve the riding crop from the chest of drawers against the wall. The car bomb went off, demolishing the front of the house and killing Leila instantly. I was badly hurt...'

Lily was aghast. Her mouth opened but no words came. She caught her breath, now understanding the meaning behind Jennifer Hopkirk's words, but unable to comprehend the shock, the loss and suffering Cole had faced.

'They traced the car back to a Tudeh cell. The Cemtex came from behind the Iron Curtain – most likely Czechoslovakia. We never established whether the target was me, as a specialist adviser to the Shah, or Leila, as the Shah's niece, because the royal family were considered fair game for assassination.  Maybe it was both of us.  Don't think I didn't ponder it as I lay in hospital, while my leg healed.  I've thought of her - of that moment - every day.'

'Is this part of it?' she asked softly, moving her hand to touch the pale scar along his cheek.  He nodded.  'And the limp?  Does it still hurt?'

'Only when someone reminds me,' he said gravely.  'I'm sorry, Lily, I didn't mean that as being applicable to you.  I haven't talked about this with many people – especially our exact circumstances at the time of the explosion.  In fact I think you're the first…  You can understand why.  As a submissive, you can understand our relationship.  You're very special to have coaxed this out of me, Lily – and I'm grateful.  It's kind of nice to have someone to share the real truth, even if it hurts.'  He made a very visible effort to pull himself together.  'I think we should be getting going.  I'll get the bill.'

They hardly spoke on the way home in the black cab.  Lily knew she'd had too much to drink, and Cole's story had affected her deeply.  Her arm was locked in his and she leaned into him during the journey, deciding that a warm body and comforting touch was the best she could offer, for she could find no adequate words.

The house seemed cold when they entered.  Charlie appeared from the kitchen to greet them, then disappeared back to his bed after the ritual of pats was completed.  Before they had left the house, Lily had reflected on where the outing might take them by the end of the evening.  A concert and dinner, and…  Surely this would be the opening she was looking for?  She had recalled his strength in carrying her down to the cellar, and the confidence and sureness of his manner.  What would he be like in bed?  She had been sure she would find out – that she wanted to find out.  Memories of Aysha in a Kiev hospital had faded, and she'd decided she had to get close to this man, to make him lay his hands on her – and the rest of his body as well.

That was until the revelation over dinner.  Now, standing with him outside his bedroom door, she did not know what to expect…

'Thank you for tonight – and last night…' she said softly, waiting for him to make a move, for it was surely not her position as employee and after-hours submissive to be forward, especially in light of their last subject of conversation.  She did not know how deep was his hurt, nor what coping mechanisms he might use.

There was no resistance from Lily when Cole wrapped her in a hug which crushed her to him with surprising strength.  She yielded to the embrace, her breasts pressed against his chest.  He kissed her hard, as though to exorcise a passion which had been unrequited for a long time.  Her hands wrapped around him, and found their way into his hair, holding his mouth to her, tasting the aftermath of cognac and inhaling a lingering fragrance that she liked but could not identify.

She felt his hands in her own hair, as they held the clasp, she pushing her body against his, already feeling the warmth rising between her legs. They broke away, breathing heavily. Cole's hands fell to her breasts, caressing their outline under the silk of Farah's dress, making the nipples harden and fight against their containment. Lily's heart was pounding, wanting more, when suddenly his hands moved to her shoulders and he gently pushed her away. Her own arms dropped as she stared at him, not understanding. Tears were running down his cheeks.

'Lily... I'm sorry... This can't happen...'

'But... can I not sleep with you, Sir? Please?' She wanted him desperately now. The fuse had been lit, and she would settle for any sort of outcome if it meant waking up next to him. She wanted to comfort him, to heal him. She did not know exactly how that would happen, but it had suddenly become important to her, to the exclusion of the purpose for which she had been embedded in the house.

But his hands held her away, and she knew she could not force the issue. There would be time, something inside her reasoned – time to work through things. This could not be the end of it – whatever 'it' was.

Then with a kiss to her forehead, he was gone, the bedroom door closing and leaving her crestfallen in the hallway in the silent House of Asha.

\*    \*    \*

# CHAPTER 28 – Chaste

That Lily was not used to alcohol was evident to her when she awoke the next morning. It was Sunday, another fine English summer day, and Charlie was keen for his walk, but it took a cup of coffee and two aspirins before Lily was ready, telling herself the fresh air would help quell the dull headache.

There was no sign of Cole when she left, and the heath itself was still quiet while the local populace enjoyed the Sunday paper supplements in bed, before rising at a more civilised hour. Lily worried that she had not been to the park bench for the last two evenings, the first because she had been locked in the dungeon, and the second because of the concert. She did not know how much surveillance was kept, and whether they would be looking for her in the morning as well as the evening, so she dutifully sat for a couple of minutes on their way into the park, where she did her best to tire out Charlie with an old tennis ball she'd found in the garden shed. Charlie was his usual enthusiastic self, charging after the ball and then refusing to release the drool-covered object without a tussle.

They returned to the benches a half an hour later, but they were empty. There was no Karla, no Meyer, nobody on the lookout for her. Part of her was relieved, for she was not sure how to process the events of the previous two days. Both the dungeon and the concert had brought her closer to Cole, and she was starting to feel something far more intense than merely the fulfilment of her bondage fantasies. She dare not admit this to Karla, though she could at least report him taking her more into his confidence, along with the encounter with Victor Hopkirk and his wife at the concert.

That encounter intrigued her. Cole's demeanour had changed subtly after he and Hopkirk had gone into their side huddle during the interval. He had tried not to show it, but Lily sensed something had been imparted to Cole that made him the tiniest bit distracted – until Lily had taken the scalpel and opened up the old wound to bleed all over her. She could never tell Karla that, either.

Her headache was gone by the time they returned to the house, via a roundabout route. She was feeling better and was pleased to see Cole was reading the Sunday papers at the dining room table.

'Good morning, Sir,' she said cautiously, not sure what the aftermath of the evening was going to be. 'Is there something I can get you?'

'Oh, good morning Lily,' he smiled. 'No – thank you. Today's a day off for you, you know that. But Charlie clearly is in your debt.'

'We enjoyed the heath. I'm more than happy to take him out – gives us both fresh air. Thank you for the concert yesterday. It was wonderful.' The open ending to the night before hung between them, with Lily not willing to raise it again.  The alcohol had opened them up, and the night had just as efficiently closed the shutters again.

'You're welcome, Lily.  Oh, I have something else I want to... er.. give you.  Do you have anything planned for the rest of the day?'

Lily tried to interpret the tone of his voice, but it was casual and told her nothing.  Except that her senses tingled and the butterflies made her stomach turn over.

'No, Sir.'

'Very well, come.'  She followed him, and found herself descending the cellar steps with thumping heart and shallowed breathing.

In the bright light of the large anteroom at the foot of the steps, she stood still as he selected a coil of rope and turned to face her.

'I'd like you to undress, Lily.'

As with all his commands, there was no 'please', though it was polite and respectful.  But no amount of respect prepares you for getting naked for the first time, Lily thought.  Cole had seen her in her uniform with no underwear, and he had seen her bound and helpless in the cell.  In some ways those moments of helplessness and vulnerability were almost more significant than pure nakedness.  Partners saw each other naked all the time, but seeing someone captive and exposed to their captor's slightest whim... Wasn't that an even more significant moment?

Lily hardly thought twice.  After her come-on to him the previous night, a small part of her thought that perhaps the moment had now arrived, just in a different circumstance.  It was almost dreamlike, she thought, as she removed her sandals, pulled her tee-shirt over her head, and dropped her shorts, placing them neatly on a bench, followed by her underwear.

The cellar was a comfortable temperature, insulated as it was from the daily fluctuations outside.  Lily turned slowly to face Cole, who leaned against the brick wall watching her with an intensity she found at once both beguiling and disconcerting.  She took a deep breath and stood there, arms by her sides, as his eyes roved over her body.

She did not know what to expect – whether he was going to take her on the floor there and then, or something less direct, more devious.  She would not have cared, for she found herself turned on by his very gaze and tried – unsuccessfully – to meet it.  Instead, she was staring down at her pink-painted toenails, submitting her will to his.

'You're very beautiful, Lily.  You know that?'  She said nothing, not trusting her voice to not waver.  He moved in close, his hands – warm and gentle, but strong – slid over her breasts, barely touching the pink-brown nipples which seemed to take on a life of their own, becoming erect with a suddenness that made Lily catch her breath.  God, she was so sensitive there.

The nipples always gave her away, displaying her seemingly lustful thoughts and inability to resist.

Cole leaned closer. His eyes took in the birthmark teardrops on her left breast, and his fingertips touched them curiously, as though they might disappear.

Lily closed her eyes, anticipating a slight bend of his head and their lips meeting. His hands were stronger on her beasts, kneading them and extracting more stiffness from the nipples. One hand slid down her stomach to rest on her labia. Lily could not suppress a faint moan. Then the touching ceased.

'Put your hands out in front of you – palms together.'

There it was – another bondage session. God, please let him finish me off today, she willed. I'll take anything, but I want a happy ending.

Cole took a neatly-coiled length of sashcord, and Lily watched him wind the rope around her wrists, like a mouse watching a snake, feeling the slow tightening of the coils before the cinch loop went between her wrists and everything was pulled snug tight. There was always a moment when she found herself beyond escape, and that instant was it. Her wrists were bound immovably, the knots unreachable, and as she stood there, Cole pulled a cable and hook down through an overhead pully, and looped a chain between her wrists, dropping it over the hook. Before she had time to catch a breath, Lily found her arms being pulled upward as Cole turned the handle of the winch bolted to the wall.

A minute later Lily was standing with her arms raised above her head, wondering where this was going and how long she would have to hold this pose.

'Legs apart, Lily,' came the command.

Lily moved her legs apart as much as she could while keeping her soles flat on the concrete.

She was quite unprepared for what came next, as Cole briefly disappeared behind her and she then felt the coldness of a wide metal... belt around her waist. She looked down as best she could. The belt was made of stainless steel, about two or three millimetres thick and five centimetres wide – enough to follow a natural pre-formed metallic curve around her waist. Somewhere in the small of her back, the belt ends met, tugged into place by Cole's hands and clicking somehow into position.

Casting her eyes down, she could see three small protruding bolts at her stomach, and sensed the connection at her back must be something similar – holes in one end dropping over some bolts in the other. The belt had smooth rounded edges and felt quite comfortable – snug over her stomach, though she had not eaten lunch yet.

She felt his fingers on the belt doing up nuts, tightening the connection with some sort of small spanner, she imagined. Lily had no idea where this was going, until Cole appeared in front of her with a second metal part - another strap-like piece bent into a quarter circle which narrowed from a handspan width at the top end to a finger-breadth at the other. At the wide end of the piece were three rows of three holes, while halfway down were three vertical slits the length of her little finger, and the width of matchsticks. Dangling from the narrow end were two smooth flat-link chains.

Lily's curiosity was beginning to get the better of her – the nature of this new imposition now of more interest to her than the purpose and the end game. It was only when Cole aligned a row of holes with the three protruding bolts and began to screw it in place, did she realise how the carefully contrived piece of steel came to rest covering her pussy, with the two chains dangling between her legs.

'No!' she breathed. 'Please tell me this isn't…'

'A chastity belt? All right, I won't. You'll figure it out yourself. You're a smart girl.' There was no mistaking the smugness in his voice.

'Why?' Lily whispered. 'Why would you do this to me?'

'Simply because I can, Lily. Because it amuses me. Don't worry. This is just a little fitting exercise, to see how it sits, to ensure comfort and functionality.'

Lily was silent, as he left the connections loose then moved behind and reached between her legs to pull the chains up to connect somehow at the back of the belt. Returning to the front, he jiggled the crotch piece and re-adjusted the three-bolt connection to a different set of bolt holes which made it all snugger.

'How can I wear this?' Lily complained uneasily, not sure how much complaining would be allowed until she ended up gagged.

'It's very easy, my dear,' said Cole. 'Now close your legs.' She did so, feeling the pressure from the crotch piece around her pussy and between her legs, the chains tight up her butt crack. Surprisingly, the metal had been shaped well and there were no sharp edges. Even so… 'These slits in front allow you to pee, Lily,' said Cole, moving the metal to align with her labia. 'But the piece is wide enough and the slits narrow enough to prevent wandering fingers or other objects penetrating. When you want to take a dump – pardon my crudity – you need to pull the chains apart as you sit down and hold them there.'

'It sounds messy,' she ventured, not wanting to resist him.

'You'll work it out,' he said cheerfully, starting to unwind the winch. As her arms lowered in front of her, he untied the knot on her wrist ropes and headed up the stairs. 'You may get dressed now. Enjoy your Sunday afternoon.'

'How long must...?' came her voice, but the stairs were empty and there was the faint thump of the study door closing.

Lily stood there for a minute, still naked, trying to process how she was now wearing a steel belt around her waist and between her legs. It felt odd – restrictive, slightly uncomfortable, yet strangely exciting. Wasn't this what maidens of olde were imprisoned in, when their knights left with their armies to do battle? Clearly there wasn't a lot of trust in the olden days, or else everyone was just a randy lot, especially the women.

Lily looked down and examined the chastity belt. The crotch piece was positioned by holes over the three dome-headed bolts protruding slightly from the waist belt. She figured these could be undone with a spanner, but there was a small button-like lock in place right over her navel, and this would have to be overcome in any attempt at removal. She felt behind her, and found a similar button lock securing the two ends of the belt in the small of her back and the two chains in her butt crack.

She ran her fingers down the sides of the crotch strap, feeling the slight rolling of the edges, designed to prevent any rubbing or cutting into the skin. It was impressive craftsmanship, and not for the first time Lily wondered how they had got her measurements. It all harked back to Berlin, she concluded. There must have been some sort of deal where Lily – as an Agency resource – came with 'accessories' in her size. She was beginning to understand the investment made in her, and the expectations Cole would have in using her as a... submissive. The word 'plaything' had been momentarily forefront in her mind, and not for the first time she decided she was reading too much into their nascent relationship. Was there a change to this relationship after their conversations the previous night, or were they back at square one this morning?

She took a couple of tentative steps, bending her knees and squatting to test the device. It was unyielding, but it slid over her skin where necessary. It was then she realised the section over her labia was slightly dome-shaped, forming an elongated bubble around the three vertical slits, so there was no contact with her pussy beneath. The penny dropped that no contact meant no pressure, no entry, no penetration, no nothing. That was how it worked. She tried to wiggle her finger under the edge. It was awkward and painful – a solution worse than the problem. Dammit, how long would he put her through this? Messing with her body was messing with her mind!

Lily dressed again, conscious of the new confinement of her loins, and the absence of the steel restraint touching the most sensitive part. She climbed the steps from the cellar to see the study door closed, and she had no excuse to accost her employer. She did not dare ask how long she would have to wear this thing. Admitting defeat, she made herself some lunch and perused the Sunday papers which Cole had left on the table. She was clearing away the plates when the door knocker sounded and instinctively she hurried to answer it, with no idea whether Cole regularly expected visitors on a Sunday afternoon.

She was mildly surprised to find Victor Hopkirk on the doorstep and she smirked inwardly at the look of greater surprise on Hopkirk's face.

'Oh, hello... Lily, isn't it? How are you? Aurelius is expecting me.' He was unable to hide the start of a lascivious grin.

'Yes, Mr Hopkirk, I'll just see...'

'Victor!' Cole appeared behind her. 'You remember Lily? Yes? Good, please excuse us, Lily. I'll be closeted in the study for some time. Please see we're not disturbed.'

Lily nodded, her cheeks flushing, seeing the light of understanding dawn on Hopkirk's face and imagining the "randy old dog" exchange that would likely ensue beyond the study doors. That did not stop her wondering what was so important that a top civil servant would visit a private political analyst on a Sunday afternoon. She had to see Karla that afternoon. Something was going on. It had been almost three days since they had met. Now she distracted herself with some postcards to her father and a letter to Aysha.

Writing the letter brought back her love and guilt, and she thought very carefully about what to say, not sure at what point Soviet censorship might step in. She kept it as bland as she could – the new job, Charlie, Cole, the nice house with a 'cellar', the concert... Too much left unsaid, too much unknown, still waiting for more news from Aysha. It had been four days since she had spoken to that woman in Australia House...

Late in the afternoon she took Charlie and left by the front door, noting the study door remained shut. She posted her letter and postcards at a red post box a short distance down the road, before taking a longer route to the heath. Her body seemed to have settled around the chastity belt, and she'd had her first bathroom experience, which had not proven as awkward as she'd expected. She had applied some powder to the contact points with her skin and now it was not the hindrance she'd worried it might be.

It did not make things feel any less weird, though. Was she walking differently? Was it something someone might notice – the small protrusions under her shorts? And in the back of her fixation with whether it showed, lay the fact she was actually imprisoned, even though she was out in the open air. Nobody could see what lay beneath her shorts, but she had no *control* over the belt, other than to bow to the whims of Aurelius Cole and whenever – *if* – he decided to release her. The thought almost made her wet, but there was nothing she could do about it.

She sat edgily on the bench, the act making her belt press between her legs, making her more self-conscious. She tried to imagine binoculars trained on her from some nearby car or other observation spot, which just made things more uncomfortable.  At Charlie's insistence they moved away for a walk down to the ponds.  Karla was waiting on the bench when they returned.

They sat an arm's length apart, just two strollers passing the time, enjoying the last sunlight of a London weekend.  Lily recounted her experiences from Friday onwards, explaining that she could not make the Friday evening meeting because she was handcuffed in the cell, having been lured there by Cole under false pretences.  Karla smiled.  She was about to tell Karla about the device she was subsequently fitted with, but decided Karla would only tease her.

'It wasn't funny at the time,' Lily said defensively.  'I was about to crap myself!  I thought I'd been found out.'

'I understand, Lily,' said Karla.  'It must have been very frightening.'  Her words were serious but Lily thought she detected a continuing note of amusement, the way a parent pretends mock seriousness at a child's complaint.  'But did you have a good time when you found out the subterfuge?'

'Maybe...' Lily admitted.  'I woke up and the cell was unlocked.  So suddenly it was Saturday and I had to get my hair done and get ready for the concert, and then there was the concert, and dinner, and home... And that was Saturday gone.'

'That was all?  No 'dessert' afterwards?'  Lily shook her head, not smiling.  'So did you enjoy the concert?'

'It was wonderful,' Lily reluctantly enthused, the recollection of the emotions flowing from the music now rushing back to her.  She recalled something.  'Do you know of a Victor Hopkirk?  We bumped into him during the interval at the Albert Hall.  He and Aurelius went into a huddle about something.  It was very earnest and Aurelius was a bit distracted when he came back.'

'Really?'  Karla was thoughtful, staring off into the distance.  'Do you know who Hopkirk is?'

'Aurelius said he was the Undersecretary for the Foreign and Commonwealth Office.'

'That's correct, Lily.  He's the top civil servant for that section of government.  He reports to the Foreign Secretary, who is elected.  So your Mister Hopkirk is the top dog in his department.'

'Oh,' said Lily.

'Worth a lot more than 'oh', Lily.  Amongst the departments who report to the Foreign Secretary is MI6 – also known as the Secret Intelligence Service.  Rest assured that in reporting to the elected Foreign Secretary, MI6 will be keeping the top civil servant in the loop.  Your Mister Hopkirk is in something up to his eyeballs.'

'He's in the house now,' said Lily.

'What?'

'He came round to visit this afternoon and he's still there.'

'Something's brewing, Lily.' Karla was suddenly very focussed. 'And you said your man is off to Paris... when?'

'Sometime tomorrow.'

'Back?'

'Tuesday.'

Karla gave this some more thought, pausing in her reply for a long minute. 'Lily, just to put you in the picture a little bit, so you can see where these people are coming from... Back in the fifties, British Intelligence was instrumental – along with the CIA – in overthrowing the democratically elected Iranian government to prop up the Shah. It's all about controlling the oil. The Shah and his family have fed like parasites off the oil money, backed up by their Savak secret police. But all that is about to change. Do you remember what I told you about the Tudeh?'

'Yes.'

'There is going to be a coup *again*, Lily, but this time it'll be the Shah who is deposed. I'm only telling you this because you need to know what to look for. We suspect British Intelligence may have either infiltrated the Tudeh with an agent, or may possibly be tapping their communications. There will be a piece of disinformation planted within the organisation which will refer to a date for the coup. The date it will specify is 14 September – eleven days from now. This is a false date, and if it turns up anywhere in Cole's study, or if there's any talk that you hear, or any change in behaviour suggesting that this date is being acted on, you must get a message to me urgently. Use the number I gave you. Do you still remember it? Repeat it to me.'

Lily did so. 'And what will happen then?'

'The *real* coup will take place earlier – in the next week. If MI6 pick up the false information, and accept it as truth, firstly we will know that there is an agent within the organisation, but if they accept it as true, the real coup will take place a week earlier than they expect.'

'And if they know it's a plant?'

'That's the harder part of our mission, Lily. If the disinformation comes through to Cole, is it seen as real or a plant? That's the real question. That's where you'll have to make yourself indispensable.' Karla seemed to read the younger woman's expression and sensed the concern.

'How do I do that, Karla? I can only work in the study for a bit. There's only so much dusting, vacuuming and polishing you can do, especially if both Farah and Aurelius are there.'

Karla patted her hand. 'I know, Lily. Let me just say we do have other sources – you're not alone, though you're by far closest to the top. Let's just hope no false information comes through, that there's no infiltration and everything can go ahead as planned.'

'How close is it?  When should I have heard by?' Lily wanted to know.

'If you haven't heard by this time next weekend, you'll probably be reading about the coup in the Sunday papers, Lily.  And you'll be proud in returning to the Iranians what is rightfully theirs.'

\*   \*   \*

# FINALE - ENSEMBLE

## London, September 1977

*Prestissimo, agitato*

# CHAPTER 29 - Questions

When Lily returned to the house, the note she found was not what she wanted. Cole and Hopkirk had gone 'out', said the note – for dinner, it inferred. That they would likely be late was obvious. Lily ran her fingers under her waistband and felt the hard steel of the belt and crotch piece. She had hoped the wearing of the device would be merely a try-out for something further down the track and had not been at all prepared for any sort of over-night experience.

She made herself some dinner and watched television in the drawing room, with Charlie at her feet, until she found herself yawning. The intensity of the last two nights had caught up with her, and there was still no sign of Cole. Reluctantly she shooed Charlie out to the laundry and made her way upstairs, trying out the shower for the first time with the shiny belt locked between her legs. It was manageable, she decided, though far from ideal. Water seeped from crevices long after she had stepped out of the shower, and she returned to her room with a towel wrapped around her. Momentarily indecisive as to whether she was ready for bed, her gaze fell on the cello case in the corner, and she realised that in the flurry of astonishing new experiences over the last week, she had overlooked the purchase from Berlin.

With new excitement she set the case on the bed and opened it, removing the instrument and savouring the weight and feel of the polished wood. She examined it closely for signs of any damage since she had first placed it on the bus, but it was pristine. Sitting down near the open window she tweaked the pegs and bow until she was satisfied with the sound. She shed her towel, letting the air cool her skin, and experiencing the surreal sensation of sitting semi-naked in a chastity belt, with the cello between her legs, snuggling close to her chest.

The first notes of Bach's cello suite took Lily away from everything – the house in Hampstead, the dungeon below it, the stress from Karla, from Aysha's absence... Lily was off and drifting languidly into in another world where the only thing that mattered was the music and the genius of a man born nearly three centuries before. This was her refuge, her sanctuary that had become real to her since her mother had died. Had she been asked, this abstract world was not somewhere that she could describe in words. It was Lily's retreat in the same way that an addict sought a trip on LSD, a cognitive shift into a place of goodness and wellbeing. The notes soared up the sloping attic roof and seeped out into the silent Hampstead night, and Lily was finally content.

She resolved to wait up for Cole, but sometime soon afterwards, the effects of the hot shower, her immersion in her music and her tiredness overtook her. There was no sign of Cole returning, and reluctantly Lily put away the cello and fell into bed, electing to sleep naked in her new accessory.

She awoke to the sound of the front door shutting, sunlight streaming into her attic room, and a strange tightness around her lower body. It all came rushing back as she swung her legs on to the floor and looked down at the strange steel device still locked on her torso. She had been taunted by dreams centred on this thing which had stimulated her to arousal, and her awakening found her flushed with desire for... Lily was not quite sure what had been the focus of her lust, other than that she wanted gratification, right then, right there. She tried to wedge her finger underneath the steel, to grind her pelvis against it, but neither worked in a way that would take her where she wanted.

'Arrgh,' she grunted in utter frustration, then recalled the sound that had woken her. 'No!'

She sprang to her feet and stepped across to the dormer window in time to see Cole climbing into a black cab and closing the door, before it drove away.

'Shit,' said Lily. 'Shit-shit-shit!'

She was going to be wearing the belt for the next two days, unless Farah had a key. Farah was Cole's proxy, but Lily had no idea how much she was under his thumb. Their encounters had been frosty until then. What would it mean now Farah was in charge? Lily presumed Farah was at least familiar with the goings on in the dungeon, though whether she was an active practitioner, Lily figured she would find out soon enough.

The walk with Charlie did nothing to ease her imprisoned loins, and now back in her uniform of black leather skirt and black top, Lily began her chores despondent about her circumstances. The study was predictably locked until Farah appeared, so in his absence Lily elected to wash Cole's bed linen. She lingered in the room, relishing his scent amongst the sheets, and his cologne in the ensuite. She wiped and polished the shower tiles and tapware, and remade the bed with new sheets, bouncing on the bed just a little, until she found the motion transferred too easily into the belt. No good would come from that, she decided.

She heard Farah ascend the stairs and disappear into the bedroom opposite Cole's, then ten minutes later, with an armful of sheets, Lily encountered her in the foyer.

'Good morning Ma'am,' Lily said politely.

Farah's response was more an acknowledgement than a greeting. Lily suddenly had the feeling the next two days might not be as easy as she had hoped.

After washing and hanging the clothes out on the line, Lily decided she had better get the interaction with Farah over, and cautiously knocked on the open study door. Farah looked up from her desk where she was typing up a document.

'Yes? What is it?'

'Um... Ma'am...' There was no easy way to ask the question. 'Did Professor Cole leave any keys with you?'

'Keys? What sort of keys?' Farah's tone was clipped and brusque. If she was a Dominant, Lily thought, I don't want to be on the receiving end. The woman unnerved Lily. 'House keys? Car keys?'

'Um... keys to a chastity belt...'

'Oh – you're wearing it, are you?' She smiled, but it was a tight smile – amusement at the discomfort of someone else. 'Well, Lily, that's too bad. I know nothing of any keys. You should have thought of that before you flaunted yourself such that you have to be constrained.'

'But I never –'

'Not interested, Lily. Now while you're here you might as well do the study, since I won't be in tomorrow. You can also clean the house windows outside when you've finished. There are things for that in the garden shed. Now, go about your business.'

Lily obeyed, feeling the frostiness in the Iranian woman's voice. She decided not to vacuum, reckoning that the better chance to uncover anything would be after the bait of the disinformation date had been laid, when the longer she could spend in the study the better. She did a brief dust of the bookshelves, window sills and furniture, then was about to leave, when Farah called to her.

'Lily!'

Alarmed at the sharpness of the tone, Lily stopped in the doorway. Farah rose from her chair and approached Lily. She was the same height as Lily, dressed in her usual prim skirt and blouse, hair pulled back and grey eyes scrutinizing Lily.

'There was a mess made in the cell over the weekend. Was that you?'

'The cell?'

'Yes, girl, the one with the grille. Nobody else has used it, I think.'

'I don't know what you mean, Ma'am,' said Lily, taken aback but now worried that she had somehow disgraced herself in her unforeseen occupancy on Friday night.

'Come with me!' Farah strode briskly across the foyer, sensible heels clicking on the parquet floor. Lily hurried behind her, down the steps and across the antechamber with its displays of implements of impact and restraint. Farah stood aside at the entrance. 'See?' She pointed to the mattress.

The single light in the cell was not bright, but it gave sufficient illumination on closer examination for Lily to see the plastic-wrapped mattress was free of stain or damage. Too late, she turned as the grille clanged closed behind her, followed by the sound of the bolt sliding and a padlock clicking shut.

Farah was smiling malevolently through the grille door.

'Now, you little slut, you can have some time to consider what I might do to you before rescue arrives. I know you've been poking around in my wardrobe, and one of my dresses has gone missing. Got anything to tell me about that?'

'I… Professor Cole said I could wear it to the concert on Saturday night!' Lily blurted.

'Did he? I suppose it's got your wetness and smell all over it now, thanks for nothing.'

'I'm sorry – I was going to take it to the drycleaners today, truly. I didn't make it dirty, but I'm happy to get it cleaned for you,' Lily stammered, taken aback by the venom. 'Please let me out.'

'You seem in such a hurry to ingratiate yourself with him,' Farah said. 'Not even here a week and he's dressing you up first in my clothes and then in some fancy chastity belt – like *that's* important!'

Lily didn't know what to say, but it was again too late, for Farah had turned on her heel and stalked to the steps, moments later shutting off the lights and closing the door under the stairs.

'Oh fuck,' said Lily, finding herself shaking as her plans fell in a heap.

She felt for the edge of the bed and sat despondently in the pitch blackness, wondering yet again at her misfortune. Whatever else she was, Farah was now an enemy. Lily's intuition wavered between the just cause Karla had told her about the Tudeh, and the savageness Cole had experienced. If someone had told Lily Farah Bakhtiari was a representative of Savak, Lily would have had little trouble believing it.

Was Farah an Iranian government plant to keep an eye on Cole, to make sure he came through with whatever communications were running to British intelligence? Was she a short cut to the Iranian regime? Whatever the case, she seemed to have it in for Lily.

Lily brooded in the darkness, sitting on the bed with her back against the rough brick wall. She had found a bottle of water and an apple on the floor next to the bucket she had previously used to pee in, and concluded that Farah had had time to plan this incarceration. The woman seemed to be the epitome of the regime Karla had vented against, and Lily found it hard to see how Cole could align himself with such a person. Cole could surely not be linked to Savak. She understood any motive he might have had against the Tudeh – God, how she understood that and ached for him. But that did not make him devoid of humanity and focussed only on revenge. Her gut told her he was not like that. Whatever pain he had suffered, she could still see the compassion within him. It told her that given freedom of choice, she would ignore Karla's directions. But choice was denied her.

She thought of the possible outcomes, and hoped the disinformation would never come through. That would absolve her of any decision as to whether the coup went ahead or whether there might be a Savak ambush waiting for them.

A picture of Aysha floated before her, and again Lily tried to stifle her guilt when she thought of her best friend. She had heard nothing from the Australian High Commission nor had she received any direct word from Aysha since she had arrived in London. Here she was, trapped in a dungeon under an elegant Hampstead Heath house, but Aysha was at the mercy of the Soviet medical system in a hospital far away, where nobody even spoke English.

She wanted Aysha. She missed her female touch, her sensitive awareness of Lily's needs and moods, and the way she could arouse Lily which only a woman would know. Aysha and Lily were soul mates, she thought, casting her mind back to Srinagar, Swat, and all they had shared on the overland journey which had led to this debacle.

But the journey had also led to Aurelius Cole, her very-much-in-control employer, benefactor, and... what? Lily recalled the physical strength of the man and his confidence, but also the vulnerability he had exposed. It had been something which seemed to surprise Cole as much as Lily, and she could sense a catharsis had occurred – something she'd hoped would take them further. She had wanted to be led into his bedroom that night, to have him make love to her, to feel him inside, holding her close. Such imagining had taken place in a vacuum where Aysha did not exist, where the world was a more straightforward place and where the carnal lust of a woman for a man was acceptable and free of complications.

Lily drank some water and munched on the apple, feeling hugely sorry for herself. She tried once more to gain some solace in bypassing the imprisoning chastity belt, but to no avail. The tears finally started and Lily Maddison curled up on the mattress and sobbed. This time the captivity was real. There would be no Queen's vizier intervening at the last minute. She was at the utter mercy of the Iranian woman, and God help Lily if Cole was delayed.

The distortion of time brought on by the deprivation of sight and sound again messed with Lily's head. She thought she had dozed, but she wasn't sure. She didn't know whether it was late morning or even late afternoon. If the latter, someone would need to take Charlie for his walk.

When the antechamber light came on and Farah undid the padlock, there were no words exchanged. Farah gave her a look as though she was simply letting out a dog from its kennel, before she turned and started up the steps.

'Oh, by the way, get used to that belt of yours, because the Professor will be away until Friday.'

Lily stood, frozen by the words. All week? Her first thought was selfishly that she would be unsatisfied – even by her own hand – for another four days. The fact this was apparently now the most important thing to her was itself a shock. Then came the implication that if Cole was away, and if Farah was only here intermittently, she might be denied access to the study and to any other developments to report to Karla.

A further thought occurred – that Farah was lying, just to fuck with Lily.

She moved to the doorway and – putting her hand through the grille – pulled back the bolt with a sense of déjà vu. At the top of the steps the foyer was light – the low sun at the oriole window indicating the onset of evening. Lily saw the study door was closed, and heard Farah's Morris 1100 start up. The dark wood pendulum clock on the wall chimed seven.

Lily hurried upstairs and changed into her own clothes, hastening to the heath with Charlie as the sun dropped, but nobody was on the bench to meet her when they returned from their ball-chasing. Lily had an uneasy thought that if Farah was working for the Iranian government, Lily – and thus Karla – might just be under surveillance herself. Had Farah deliberately held her incommunicado long enough for her to miss the rendezvous?

No, Lily, don't be stupid. Now you're overthinking everything again and just getting paranoid.

Lily had lost a day with her chores. Tuesday dawned overcast, and a gusty morning heath walk with Charlie found them alone for most of the outing. Lily wore her jeans over the chastity belt, conscious now of the tightness around her crotch that kept precipitating unwanted fantasies in her head. These, in turn, stimulated her, though not to the extent she was aroused. Charlie sufficed as a distraction until she returned to her room, where she changed into her uniform. She dare not risk Cole's ire by not being dressed appropriately if he did return home early. That could lead to isolation punishment in the cell – just when she needed to be alert around the house. She had obsessed as to whether Farah was lying about his return, and concluded it was just as likely to be the case, and she should prepare for him to be back that day. On random impulse, she wore the white skirt and black blouse, determined to present a welcoming face on his return.

When the door knocker echoed through the house at a little after nine, she assumed it would be the man Newby, come to do his electronic sweep of the premises. She was surprised to see a short man of about sixty wearing a

352

dark sports jacket and tie over crumpled grey trousers. He had thin blond hair pushed to one side and cool brown eyes in a lined but pleasant face.

'Good morning,' said the man. He held out an open wallet with an ID photo of himself beneath the heading "Metropolitan Police". 'Detective Chief Superintendent George Burrows. I understand a Professor Cole lives here. May I speak with him, please.'

'I'm sorry, Professor Cole is overseas at the moment,' said Lily, slightly unnerved by the policeman.

'When is he due back?' The man's demeanour was easy, comfortable, but alert.

'I was expecting him sometime today, but now I'm not sure of his movements. It could be later in the week. Can I ask what this is about?'

Lily was slowly starting to gather her thoughts, realising her exposure on so many fronts.

'And you are...?'

'Lily Maddison. I'm Professor Cole's housekeeper.'

Burrows eyed her with a more than professional gaze, likely concluding that this was not the normal house-keeping attire.

'You live on the premises, Miss Maddison?'

'Yes.'

'How long have you worked for Professor Cole?'

'Only a week. Why?'

'May I come in? There are some questions I need to ask. You may be able to help us with our enquiries.'

Lily had no idea whether she was in trouble or what her rights might be, but the idea of refusing this man entry did not seem smart, nor the act of an innocent person with nothing to fear from the constabulary.

'Of course.' She stood aside and closed the door after him, leading the way into the kitchen, which she decided was appropriate for her status in Cole's house. She gestured to a chair at the kitchen table. 'Would you like a cup of tea...' She had forgotten his rank. 'Superintendent?'

He smiled, disarmingly. 'It's Detective Chief Superintendent, but Superintendent will do. Ranks are a bit of a mouthful in the police. Sorry – yes, a cuppa would be nice.'

Lily filled the kettle and put it on the gas stove, placing milk and sugar cubes on the table, before taking down two mugs from the cupboard and dropping teabags in them.

'Please Miss Maddison, sit down. I'm not here to arrest you.' Lily did so, conscious of the belt and her sudden uneasiness. 'I'm investigating the death of a woman called Erika Baumann.' He put a photo on the table.

It was a black and white passport photo of a young woman perhaps slightly older than Lily, long blonde hair tucked behind her ears, staring intensely at the camera. It put a face to the name Lily had heard several times since her arrival in London. 'Does that name mean anything to you?'

'Erika? She's dead?' The detective's question and the physical presence of the photo had come totally from left field. The name and the realisation that her predecessor was dead shocked her further.

'You knew her?'

'I... no, but I'm her replacement. But I was told she'd left due to an illness in the family.' The words came tumbling out before she realised what implications they might have. 'How... did she die?'

'Her body was found in Regent's Canal twelve days ago. It's taken this long to trace her,' said Burrows. 'She had a tattooed name on her arm – "Siegfried". A boyfriend, we found out. Figured she was likely German, and such was the case, as our West Berlin colleagues informed us. Had a record on file with a passport photo. Lady in a Hampstead chemist identified her as a regular customer for epilepsy-prevention medicine. Gave us this address.' Burrows laid out the chain of events crisply, as though reading bullet points.

Lily was stunned. She had never had dealings with the police before, let alone in connection with the death of somebody. The kettle began to whistle and she retrieved it and turned off the gas, pouring the boiling water into the mugs. Burrows had taken out a small notebook and began jotting notes.

'Lily... May I call you Lily?' She nodded. 'Lily, you said you were told Erika had left due to a family illness. Who told you this?'

'Professor Cole did – after I started work here... You didn't say how she died...'

'The jury is still out on that,' Burrows said non-committally. 'Maybe drowned. There are a number of other factors.' Burrows added milk and sugar to his tea and stirred it deliberately, as though looking to get the colour just right.

'Other factors?'

'Suggestions of rope marks on wrists.'

Despite her own proclivities, Lily could not suppress a small gasp.

'What are you saying? That she was murdered?'

'Waiting for the coroner's report. Not ruling anything out.' Burrows saw the pallor of Lily's face. 'You okay?' She nodded.

'I can tell you're not local. Australia? New Zealand?'

'New Zealand.'

'How old are you, Lily?'

'Twenty-two.'

'How long have you been in England?'

'Only a week and a bit. I came overland from Nepal with Sundowners.'

'Oh. Great. When exactly did you arrive?'

'The Sunday before last. We came in through Berlin to Dover to Earl's Court.' Burrows jotted in the notebook. 'Berlin? A little unusual, isn't it? How did you get to Berlin?'

'We went from Greece to Moscow, then back through Poland and East Germany.'

Burrows nodded, jotting. Then: 'How did you get this job?'

Lily realised she was on dangerous ground. Karla, the photos, Aysha... all were suddenly at risk.

'I... there was an ad in Time Out – you know, nannies, au pairs, that sort of thing. Professor Cole was obviously keen to get a replacement.' More jotting. Lily tried not to fidget, trying to decide whether her fictitious ad had been direct or through an agency – *The* Agency – and what giant hole might result for her to fall into.

'Where exactly is Professor Cole?' Burrows asked.

'Paris.'

'What's he doing there?'

'I have no idea.'

'He's a professor of what?'

'I'm not sure – economics, or something like that. He works for the government.'

'Really?' Burrows did not look up until Lily said:

'Yes, he's a private consultant – an analyst of some sort – for the Foreign Office.' She didn't think there was much harm in telling the man that, not least since it distracted from her employment route. Burrows stopped his writing and looked at her.

'The Foreign and Commonwealth Office? The FCO?'

'Yes.'

There was a long pause. 'And you think Professor Cole might be back today?'

'That was what he told me.'

Burrows was about to ask another question when the front door knocker sounded.

'Excuse me,' said Lily, glad of the excuse to gather her thoughts amid the crazy rush which had descended on her out of nowhere. Why had this happened when Cole had been out of town, leaving her to muddle her way through this interrogation? Had he been here, she could have safely watched from the sidelines.

Newby was standing on the doormat.

'Hello,' he said. 'Come to do the sweep.'

'Professor Cole's away at the moment,' said Lily, unsure whether this made a difference, but hoping it might deter the man. 'I can't get you into his study – I don't have a key.'

'That's all right. I'll log it as 'unavailable' but I need to do the rest of the house. Part of the routine, you know.' He sounded like an officious civil servant, Lily thought.

'I've got a visitor in the kitchen at the moment,' Lily added.

'No problem. I can work around you. Kitchen doesn't take long.' He did not wait for an invitation, but moved past her into the foyer and dumped his case on the telephone table, opening it and extracting several pieces of equipment. Lily watched him for a moment, then returned to the kitchen.

Burrows looked up inquiringly from his notes.

'A man from the Ministry of Defence – just doing the weekly electronic sweep.'

'Oh.' Burrows' brow furrowed. The news seemed somehow significant to him. He nodded. 'Are you and the Professor the only ones in the house, Lily?'

'Normally. He has an Iranian woman who works with him. She has a room here where she sometimes stays, though she hasn't done so since I've been here.'

'An Iranian woman? Does she have a name?'

'Farah Bakhtiari. I don't know how to spell that.'

The furrowed forehead did not lessen.

'Lily, I have to ask this. Have you ever felt unsafe with Professor Cole? Ever felt like you might be in danger, that your job might not be what it was intended to be?'

The implication behind the words shocked Lily. 'You're suggesting the Professor had something to do with Erika's death... No, I don't believe it. I've felt quite safe here. Farah comes and goes. He's far too busy to be bothered with me. He lets me get on with the cleaning and cooking and washing. He'd never hurt me.'

'You're very sure of him after only a week.'

'Yes. I am.'

Burrows pulled a card out of his wallet. 'If you ever need help – well, nine-nine-nine is the emergency number here in the UK. Normally I'm at New Scotland Yard, near Westminster, however you can contact me through West Hampstead station, where I've been liaising, since Erika was local to here. This is the number at West Hampstead station, in case there's anything you need to tell me. Anything at all.' He caught her gaze. 'Seriously.'

\*　　\*　　\*

356

# CHAPTER 30 – The Nineteenth Floor

Detective Chief Superintendent George Burrows had been only a month shy of retirement when the body of Erika Baumann had turned up, floating in Regent's Canal near the Kentish Town lock. There were no immediate clues as to the woman's identity, however a smart constable's observation of the name "Siegfried" tattooed on the inside of the woman's forearm had suggested a possible German connection. It had led to the case being directed to Burrows by his boss – aware of Burrows' past record in overseas police liaisons – as the police searched for a starting point in tracing the identity of the woman when fingerprints found nothing in the British system.

At fifty-nine, DCS Burrows had decided enough was enough, and was looking forward to some imminent golf and time with the grandkids. That, apparently, was what one did in retirement, though he was not wholly convinced. He had gradually been transferring cases and management to colleagues, in a planned effort to slip out the back door gracefully, and his office in 'C' Department of New Scotland Yard in Westminster was only gradually becoming less cluttered.

Burrows was not a flamboyant person, nor was he a rain-maker. His name was known in various circles, however, as a solid performer with a knack of seeing connections where others didn't. More specifically, he was known a man who – while he did not have all the answers – knew who might have. In the course of three decades as a detective in the Metropolitan Police – much of that time with the colloquially known 'Murder Squad' – following a post-war stint in the Royal Military Police, George Burrows had amassed an extraordinary network of contacts, on both sides of the fence that separated the forces of law from its *raison d'etre*.

He carried a pedigree which surprised many people, and it was something he did not bandy about. Coppers with a degree in mathematics from the Regent Street Polytechnic and who could speak at least one other European language were rare. Burrows had graduated just in time for World War Two, and had found a niche in Army Intelligence, and then the Royal Military Police in post-WW2 Germany and France. In that time of chaos, and the subsequent tensions with the Soviet Union, Burrows had forged many friendships which had been maintained even through the more formal organisations which had subsequently been established. At the end of a long period of laissez-faire Labour government, after the KGB had managed to create a relatively unmolested network of agents in key parts of the British economy, he had played an integral part in the operation to unmask the network. In September 1971, under a new Conservative government,

"Operation Foot" had uncovered and expelled over a hundred Soviet officials, dealing a massive blow to Soviet intelligence. George Burrows had been a key member of Special Branch responsible for intelligence gathering and coordinating the raids, and his name and experience had become low key legend.

In the Baumann case, it had been the German connection that had initially caused it to end up on his desk.

'Thought it might be a change for you, George,' his boss had said. 'A chance for a final hurrah on the streets – something a bit different before you get on the fairway.'

Burrows had appreciated the gesture, for it had been a long time since he'd had to do serious leg work, and this case had some strange feelings about it. Now, as he climbed into his car outside the Cole residence after the interview with the young New Zealand housekeeper, bells were ringing. She'd been hiding something, Burrows knew. She was more than a housekeeper, that was obvious. No housekeepers he knew wore a silk top and a leather skirt, never mind a steel collar which looked as though it would require a bolt-cutter for removal. He'd bought his fair share of jewellery for his wife and daughter over the years, but nothing like that had ever been on show. In his time on the force, George Burrows had seen enough kinksters and swingers, and blue-ribbon Hampstead was no less likely to have its own underground groups. More so, perhaps. It did not come as a surprise.

Not that he had anything against such proclivities. He was, if anything, a liberal-minded person, and had occasionally found himself at odds with some of his colleagues from the conservative side of the tracks. Lily Maddison's appearance told Burrows was that as she was a replacement for Erika Baumann, it was likely that Erika had been in the same role – that there had been a relationship way beyond house-keeping.

Burrows also knew the girl had lied to him. He was familiar enough with the Time Out magazine in the decade since it had first appeared to know it did not carry ads for the likes of housekeepers. There were other, more-targeted magazines, particularly for Antipodeans, which offered such fare, but not Time Out. Rookie error, he thought. This begged the question, who had hired Lily Maddison and why? Was this just a case of jolly old perversions in upper class Hampstead, or was it something more sinister? What had happened to Erika Baumann? How had she been replaced so quickly? Surely these B&D people were not that common on the ground, he mused.

The recollection of the rope marks on Erika's wrists came to mind. There were also several deep bruises on the woman's buttocks, which he had not mentioned to Lily. Perhaps it had been a bondage session that had gone wrong? Too many ifs and buts, he decided. He needed to get more out of forensics, now he had an idea what he might be looking at.

Then there was this Professor Cole, and the FCO. The man was well off, and was clearly valued in the private sector sufficiently for MoD to regularly check his house for electronic bugs. It told Burrows that Aurelius Cole was involved in some important things at a pretty high level – something that required Burrows to tread carefully. He would have to pay a call on a friend at Century House, the home of MI6.

His visit to the home of the Secret Intelligence Service that afternoon turned out both enlightening and frustrating. Burrows had operated as Special Branch liaison officer a number of times in the course of his career, for the Intelligence Services had no powers of arrest and often required close coordination with the Met.

Her Majesty's Government had long denied that the 22-storey glass block located at 100 Westminster Bridge Road was the headquarters of the Secret Intelligence Service, though as the Daily Telegraph had reported, this was London's worst-kept secret, known only to every taxi driver, tourist guide and KGB agent.

His contact was an old friend named Howard Westmoreland, and they had shared a number of undertakings over the years, including "Operation Foot".

Now, sitting on the nineteenth floor looking out over Waterloo Station and the Thames beyond, Westmoreland thoughtfully tamped tobacco into his pipe and managed to kindle a fire after several tries. He had a lined face showing the scars of many diplomatic battles, with brown eyes which disappeared into creases of amusement behind heavy black-rimmed glasses. Both men had a glass of sherry at hand, and both appeared as comfortable as if they were in a gentleman's club.

'And just how did you track down this Baumann woman, George?' Westmoreland asked.

'Well, technically I went through Interpol, as is only right and proper. *Our* people contacted *their* people in Bonn. I, on the other hand, spoke to a friend. The answer *was* there, and I got it faster by the back door. Turns out Miss Baumann's fingerprints were on their file, and we got a copy of her West German passport photo. She'd been booked for prostitution in West Berlin – though she was born in East Berlin.'

Westmoreland looked up from his pipe.

'Yes, I thought that might get your attention. She came through immigration a couple of months back, but we lost her at that point. After finding the body we put her passport photo in a couple of newspapers, asking for information. A Hampstead chemist recognised her, since she was a regular visitor for prescription medicine for epilepsy, and they had her address – namely that of Professor Cole.'

'And cause of death?'

'This is where it gets interesting. There was water in the lungs, but there was also a lot of alcohol in the stomach.'

'Drunk and drowned?'

'Maybe. Except that I'm told a drinking binge can bring on a seizure in some epileptics, so most epileptics know better than to take the risk. So if the alcohol was ingested *voluntarily*, an accidental seizure could have expedited the drowning.'

'Either way, a reasonable case for death.'

'Yes, except if the alcohol was forced. There were faint rope marks on the wrists.'

'So... bound, forced to ingest alcohol and then into the canal?'

'Yes. No personal effects, either. So you see, Howard, looking down from the helicopter, we have this German woman – East or West – with no identification but with suspicious circumstances, who was working for a highly placed private consultant to the FCO. The woman has now been replaced by another, who has lied to me already. So I ask the question, who is working behind the scenes, manipulating these young women, both of whom appear to be into bondage and discipline? You have as good a knowledge of the FCO's little overseas adventures as anyone. Is there a connection? Do you now see reasonable cause for my visit?' Burrows sat back and sipped at his sherry.

'You know I'm not supposed to tell you too much,' Westmoreland said. It was a casual observation, not an admonishment or rejection. Like Burrows, Westmoreland was close to retirement and to his pension, but they went back a long way, and had negotiated many comings and goings of the political bullring. Also like Burrows, Westmoreland was respected in the circles he moved, and had the ear of the Permanent Secretary and the Chief of MI6.

'I'm not asking for state secrets, Howard. I'm simply raising the issue that in the event this fellow Cole has done something criminal – and by that I mean possibly murder – are your chaps likely to cause me grief in the name of national security and the alleged 'common good'? Higher motives and all that. Look, this won't be the first time I've had my wrist slapped – or metaphorically handcuffed to a pole – when I've tried to bring a villain down. We both know this. But I'd rather know about it now, than to be taken out in a rugby tackle by one of your lads, just as my boys are going in with an arrest warrant.'

'Understand perfectly, old chap. Mind you, the mis-step may already have happened, what with your interview of this young lady – she of the steel collar.' Westmoreland smiled sanguinely. 'Cole will likely know of your visit when he returns, whether guilty of anything or not. Of course I have no knowledge of the man's kinks, though I can tell you he left our embassy in

Tehran under a tragic cloud a couple of years ago. Seems his girlfriend – a member of the royal family, no less – was killed in a bombing by the Tudeh. They're the organisation dedicated to overthrowing the Shah. Cole almost died himself. There were rumours he and the girlfriend were into some dodgy kink stuff, but the ambassador managed to suppress that, and the Shah certainly wasn't going to spread the word.'

'I'm told he has an Iranian woman working for him. Do I assume he's still heavily involved in that country's affairs?'

'Assume what you like, dear boy. Shouldn't affect your investigations, although… perhaps give it a day or two before pursuing too vigorously, what? Things are rumbling on the Middle Eastern front, if you get my drift.'

'That's all very well, Howard, but if this chap is a bit enthusiastic with the ropes and whips, and the Kiwi girl is on the receiving end, there'll be hell to pay, and I'll have my "ass in a sling", as our cousins over the pond are wont to say.'

'I'm sure it won't come to that, George. I suspect your man will be too busy to be distracted by fun and games – at least for the rest of this week. Things are brewing – big things.'

'From the look of Miss Maddison, I'm not so sure. She wouldn't have to do much to distract me.'

'Fresh meat?'

'Oh, very much so. Very fresh, very attractive, very innocent. I never ceased to be surprised at the human race and our perversions.'

'And in Hampstead of all places,' said Westmoreland with mock outrage. He crossed his legs in the armchair that came with the nineteenth floor and the accompanying seniority.

'You know, I think we're getting a little over-focussed here, George.' Westmoreland, like Burrows, loved a good puzzle, over and above the Times crossword. 'We're overlooking the fact that if Cole is innocent of our cruel aspersions, then *somebody else* may be in the picture. I think it was you who told me that for every accused person genuinely acquitted, the real culprit is still on the loose.'

'You're right,' Burrows agreed. 'I'd still like better forensics, but for my money I'd bet two things: Firstly, Erika Baumann's death wasn't an accident, though it may have been made to look that way, and secondly, she was killed by someone she knew. If it wasn't Cole, then who was it? Who else could be in the picture?'

'You mean, who else could have an interest on what's happening in the Cole household?'

'Ah,' said Burrows. 'That's it exactly. Well, *you* tell *me*, Howard. But here's a thought. Lily Maddison lied to me about who hired her. She said she got the job through an ad in Time Out. If it wasn't Cole who hired her, then somebody else did. That somebody might well have created the opening in the first place, by disposing of the incumbent.'

'So, George, the question then becomes – as well as 'who' – why? What does Miss Maddison have which Miss Baumann did not? Or had Miss Baumann upset the apple cart somehow, that she had to be replaced?' Westmoreland sipped his sherry with the expression of a chess player contemplating a particularly devious move. 'I wonder if this isn't something we can turn to our advantage, George.'

'You mean the royal "we", don't you Howard. And by "our", you mean "your" advantage.'

'Anything wrong with that?' Westmoreland's eyebrows raised and Burrows shook his head with a wry smile.

'I do love a good bit of intrigue, Howard…'

'It's the German connection which unsettles me, George. Ever since our masters gave official recognition to East Germany – and ever since Operation Foot – the Soviets have been using the East Germans to do more and more of their dirty work here.'

'Well here's a thought. The Kiwi girl arrived on an overland trip – via Soviet Union and Berlin.'

'Oh. My word. "Curiouser and curiouser, said Alice". I do believe we need to act on this now, George.' Westmoreland's tone – previously laissez faire – now took on a tone of urgency. 'Look, there *is* something afoot in the Middle East. I'm not telling tales out of school – not to you, anyway. It's imminent, and big. Very hush-hush and I won't say anything more, other than that we need to keep Cole in the clear and undistracted. I think we need to put a watch on the house – specifically, on this Lily person. She's the key to it all, that much is evident. I know there are protocols for this with you Special Branch boys, but frankly I don't think there's time for the paperwork.'

'My people or yours?'

'I think mine, at this stage. This German bit worries me, George. The East Germans have been stepping up their foreign intelligence work in the last year. They're being used in lieu of KGB – a lower profile, different mindset. You know the HVA – the Stasi Foreign Intelligence Service – are in town, in the new embassy. We're only now starting to spot some of their operatives about town. If there is some connection here, Six will be better positioned to spot it. We don't have much time. I'll get something organised – they can liaise with you?'

'Yes. No time for proper channels, if what you say is correct.'

'Done. Just like old times, George, yes?' There was no mistaking the enthusiasm.

*   *   *

# CHAPTER 31 – Taken

With the departure of Newby and Burrows, Lily sat for a while in the kitchen, going over in her mind the questions which had been asked and answered, and most significantly the fact that her predecessor might have been murdered. That both Karla and Cole had told her Erika had left "because of an illness in the family" made Lily's stomach tighten at the possibility that one or both might be lying, and that she might be in real danger.

Lily did not know what to do. She had now implicated herself with the story about answering an advertisement in Time Out, though the detective had not – as yet – pursued the veracity of that. Erika's body had been found in the canal twelve days ago, though of course that may not have been when she disappeared. That would make it a few days before Lily arrived in London – perhaps while she was in Berlin.

If Karla's hold over Lily had been serious before, it now ratcheted tighter. Lily decided she dare not tell Karla of Burrows' visit. Things were becoming complicated enough. Maybe if she could get through this coup thing and there was a successful outcome – whatever "successful" meant – she could maybe get out of the whole mess.

She thought of Karla and Andreas Meyer and whether they could have killed Erika. Lily was still uncertain who were Karla's masters, but she was now being forced to confront this question, and the awful potential which came with the answer. Karla's background was German – East German, most likely. The doctor in Kiev had been East German, and reluctantly Lily was forced to admit some element of Soviet Bloc power was behind her predicament. Karla could even be part of a diplomatic mission in London. Unloading a confession to Burrows was no guarantee her nightmare would go away.

Lily's mind went in unnerving circles for the rest of the day. She wished Cole was back, though she did not know what she was going to say to him. But just having him in the house would make her feel a little less alone and at the mercy of outside forces. She hoped Farah had been lying about his return. It would be par for the course, for everybody around her seemed to be lying, and Lily was not adept at dealing with it.

Though her instinct told her Cole wasn't involved in Erika's death, she had to admit he *could* have perpetrated such a thing. The very thought had come to her when he had handcuffed and carried her into the cellar. It would not have been hard to have subdued and killed a woman in that place, and the suggestion of rope marks on Erika's wrists made her uneasy, though such marks might have come from real restraint, not role-playing.

That evening on the heath, Lily had almost given herself away though her nervousness. Karla had asked what the matter was. Lily had equivocated about the chastity belt making her horny, which was in fact a half-truth. She was also nervous about the disinformation being planted, she'd said. She was not used to this sort of subterfuge and she told Karla it was making her anxious.

'You'll be fine, Lily,' Karla told her, fondling Charlie's ears as they sat on the bench. 'The information will be out there by now. Tomorrow or the next day it may make an appearance. Try to find some excuse to hang around the study. Listen for phone calls, conversations, watch the fax machine.'

'If the Professor isn't back, it won't be easy,' Lily said. 'Farah locked me in the cell today. Implied I had stolen – well, illegally used, I suppose – her dress when I went to the concert! Aurelius told me I could!' she said indignantly, like a five-year-old arguing to her mother that her father had given her permission for something now disputed.

'So it's 'Aurelius' now, is it? And then you had to sit in the dark and get all steamed up?' Karla's eyes sparkled with amusement.

'It's not funny,' Lily sulked. 'Things are very tense…'

'No, you're right,' Karla agreed. 'I'm sorry. We mustn't get on the wrong side of this woman. We need you flitting through their lives as though you were invisible. Just the hired help. Not the beautiful princess in disguise come to steal the prince's heart.'

'Not funny, Karla,' said Lily again, though she was surprised at how apt the analogy suddenly seemed in her mind. Did she really want to steal Cole's heart?

Lily was hovering on the verge of sleep that evening when she heard the front door open and close. Her heart leapt at the sound of footsteps ascending the stairs and entering the bedroom below hers. She imagined the suitcase being put down, the man walking into the ensuite. So Farah had been lying. She would surely have known of his impending return.

A few minutes later she heard the faint sound of water in the pipes, picturing then the naked figure in the shower and knowing she would never get to sleep unless she could gain resolution. She had not thought through her intention, other than she was now determined to have her way - whatever that actually was.

Lily climbed out of bed and pulled off her Mellow Cello tee shirt that she now habitually slept in, looking at herself briefly in the mirror, half-lit by the bedside lamp. The shiny surface of the chastity belt glittered at her waist and between her legs, and the thought of the man in the room below abruptly made the restriction as much emotionally painful as any physical tightness. She wanted the belt gone, and she wanted Cole.

When Lily knocked at Cole's bedroom door, the voice called her to "come" without hesitation. Cole was standing in front of his closet mirror, wearing only navy satin pyjama pants, his hair damp and tousled from the shower. In the mirror Lily could see white scars criss-crossing his back in a jagged pattern, some of which tracked down the side of his ribs. Her mouth opened in a small gasp at the sight, which not so much horrified her as made her want to touch him and explore the muscles that had overcome such carnage of the flesh.

On Cole's part, the sight of Lily in the doorway, clad only in the chastity belt, left him speechless. His arms dropped to his side as she walked into the room, suddenly feeling empowered enough to enunciate her request.

'Please Sir, I'd like this off...' Then, in a whisper: 'I'd like you to finish what you've started...'

'What I've started?' Cole's surprise changed to calm. 'What might that be, Lily?'

'I think you know, Sir. You've managed it from Day One.'

'Not sure I get you, Lily,' said Cole, feigning ignorance. 'Didn't you ask Farah for the keys? One set is in my desk drawer, a second in the dungeon.'

'She denied all knowledge, Sir,' Lily told him, unable to keep the resentment out of her voice. She reached him and took the plunge, shutting out all thought of consequences, embracing him, pressing herself against him. At once his arms were around her, enfolding her tightly and drawing her to him, crushing her breasts against his chest and forcing the hard steel of her belt into his groin. Lily gasped, sucking in the smell of soap and the touch of damp chest hair.

The kiss was long and languorous, Cole evidently accepting that the young woman was not to be denied, and that what had almost begun after the concert now constituted unfinished business. The fierceness of his mouth on her and the maddening presence of the belt made Lily's loins wet, and she squirmed to gain some sense of pressure on her pussy, realising now the true deviousness of the device.

'Oh...fuck...' she whispered. 'You've started it again, Sir... I really need this...thing... off... Please...'

She eased away from him, enough to run her nails down his chest, catching and tugging at the dark hair sprinkled with the first hints of silver. Her hands slid over little bumps and ridges on his ribs, and she broke the kiss to feel these strange but terrible wounds. For his part, Cole's hands held her head, her neck, then her breasts, with the inevitable sprouting of her nipples like springtime bulbs. He bent his head to envelop one with his lips, sucking and testing it with his teeth in a way that made Lily throw back her head in a sharp intake of breath. She groaned, wanting him to take her there and then, on the bed, on the floor, she didn't care. She dropped her hands further, now wanting to grasp his manhood and tease it to explosion, chastity belt or not, but he was faster, anticipating her want and flipping her face down on the bed.

Lily made barely a token resistance. Things were happening. Whatever she'd started, something was going to come of it, and she was happy for the outcome to be driven by this man who could to control her at every turn. Whatever followed, the belt had to come off – was *going to* come off. Then she would be at his mercy, would be finally satisfied. But the keys were downstairs…

Lily felt the weight of Cole on her, pressing her into the softness of the duvet, then his hands pulling her wrists behind her and securing them with a belt. Resistance was both futile and unwanted, for the bindings only pushed her arousal to new heights. The silk tie over her eyes confirmed she was indeed to be abducted and ravished by the handsome soldier who had stormed her stronghold and who now held her in his power.

Once again she found herself hoisted easily over Cole's shoulder and carried downstairs, though this time it was not accompanied by the terror of discovery. This time had to be the prelude to the real thing, in whatever form he saw fit for his helpless prisoner.

They reached the foyer, then down the steps into the anteroom of the cellar. Lily was put down, standing, feet apart, breathing heavily with anticipation and excitement, her legs trembling as she felt ropes secured around each ankle and attached to something so she was unable to draw them together. His hands were strong against her skin, sliding up the insides of her thighs and gently testing the edges of the belt. Someone was panting like a dog, and Lily swallowed as she realised it was her. God, she was horny! Please, Sir, just get the belt off and do it!

But for the moment it was not the belt but her wrists that were the objects of his attention, as sashcord was knotted around each before the belt was released. A minute later Lily found herself with her arms now raised in a star-pattern, pulled upwards and apart, unable to move anything save her head, which could only turn blindly in anticipation of she knew not what.

Finally - *finally*… came the fingers undoing the locks front and back and the removal of the stiff device which had imprisoned her for the last two days. She grunted with pleasure as Cole lifted the belt clear and the cool air of the cellar touched her loins.

'Better?' asked a voice close to her ear.

'Yes, Sir. Thank you, Sir,' she whispered, warmth flooding her crotch. His hand slid down between her legs, cupping her mons, and Lily groaned again, thrusting herself against the palm like a libidinous adolescent. The fingers lingered there, stroking and teasing as Lily's senses went wild and she pulled on the ropes restraining her wrists and ankles. Cole seemed in no hurry. Damn him!

'Please... Sir...' Lily begged the darkness. 'I need it now... I need *you* now...'

'Not so fast, Lily. You're not in a position to make demands.'

'But - Ow!' Something small and sharp fastened on to Lily's right nipple – something metallic which dangled and tinkled like a little bell. 'Ow!' The same happened on her right nipple and she felt the tie removed from her eyes.

Lily looked down to see two elaborate-looking steel pincers, each the size of her thumb, each sporting a small bell, dangling from her nipples.

'Mustn't rush into the pleasure,' Cole said casually. 'These things have to be earned, Lily. Instant gratification is bad for the soul. Does that lessen the urge?' he asked, with fake sympathy, as his hand slid between her legs again, stroking the flesh of her thighs.

'Yes... I mean, no, Sir...' she stammered as his touch ignited her momentarily halted ardour.

'Oh dear.' He tugged the clamps gently, making her catch her breath and stifle a little squeal, then moved out of eyeline to somewhere behind her. By now Lily's body had reached top gear. Everything seemed super sensitive and demanded satisfaction, despite the momentary distraction caused by the pain of the nipple clamps. Cole sensed this as well, acknowledging that the application of the clamps had been insufficient to stem Lily's raging passion.

'I need you to calm down a little, Lily,' he said, now standing beside her. 'Can you do that for me?'

'I... don't know, Sir...' said Lily through gritted teeth, staring at the blank wall a few yards away, as though it was five miles distant.

'Maybe something to help you focus,' Cole suggested. He reached down behind Lily and she felt something slippery and smooth slide wetly between her butt cheeks, then nuzzle at her anus.

'Ohhh!' she exclaimed, as the pressure of his hand behind the object began to force it into her, little by little. 'Oh - Sir! It hurts!'

'Relax, Lily,' his voice crooned beside her ear, and she tried to comply. The device eased out, then in again, widening her sphincter muscles, sending a small stab of pain through her insides, then it was retracted. 'Focus on those muscles. Push back!'

Then there was the pressure again, forcing her hole wider and wider, as though she was giving birth through her arse. She groaned, then cried out as the pain suddenly peaked, and the intruder was inside her, filling her, her sphincter closing around the narrow neck of the plug. 'Ohhhh....' The whine died away from Lily's lips. Cole grasped the protruding end of the butt plug and waggled it. Lily jerked and struggled, her breathing making a rasping sound at the unfamiliar fullness.

For the time it had taken to insert the plug, Lily had been distracted from her loin lust, but despite this intruder in her arse, her arousal now returned. She wondered briefly what it would be like to have his cock inside her as well as this seemingly enormous plug in her arse. It did *nothing* to calm her.

'Do you know what a pain slut is, Lily?'

'Yes, Sir,' said Lily, not liking this sudden change of conversation, her memory going back to Aysha's description of her submissive, Joanne, and to her own encounter with Liezel in Karla's dungeon.

'Are you a pain slut, Lily?'

'I… I don't know, Sir.' Lily had almost denied it outright, but somewhere inside her there was a doubt, and with that doubt came the realisation this was the moment to find out, unpleasant though it might be.

'Do you know what sub-space is, Lily?'

'Yes, Sir.'

'Ever been there, Lily?'

'Don't think so, Sir,' admitted Lily, biting her lip.

'Well,' said Cole cheerfully. 'This may be a new adventure for us all. You have a Safeword?'

'Happy Birthday, Sir.'

'Good. Excellent. Top hole!'

Lily was wondering what Cole meant by 'top hole' when the first bite of the flogger across her butt cheeks made her scream. It was not a top-of-the-range scream, merely an expression of surprise at the unexpected. Then came a second strike. The flogger was not the makeshift implement picked up by Aysha in the Istanbul Grand Bazaar, nor was it applied as one might do to an acolyte, a beginner in the arts of bondage and discipline. Lily had moved beyond that now, and Aurelius Cole knew this. The flogger was hand-crafted leather with fifty tails, now wielded by one with the dexterity of long practice. It smacked across the soft flesh of Lily's left buttock and she stifled a further scream, the pain abruptly suppressing her brain's need for sexual gratification.

A further blow landed on her right buttock, then a slow rhythm settled in, the flogger alternating – forehand, backhand, left, right… Lily bit her lip, trying to hold back the outburst building in her throat, knowing once she started she would probably be unable to stop. As though anticipating her need, Cole halted his assault, flourishing a black rubber ball on a strap in front of her face. Lily's eyes were watering, but something inside her head acknowledged the offering and she obediently opened her mouth to allow the ball to be lodged behind her teeth, wedging her mouth open and pressing down on her tongue. As the strap was buckled tightly at the back of her neck, she knew there was nothing else she could do in the face of whatever came next. Pain or pleasure, she was helpless, bound and silenced.

The flogging that followed ran down her buttocks and thighs, then up her back. All the while Lily Maddison jerked and thrashed in her bonds, the mantra bouncing around her head that "it's always better if you can't move". That was not from a lack of trying, as Lily threw herself against the ropes and did her best to articulate the agony through the rubber ball stretching her mouth wide. The antechamber echoed with the sound of leather on flesh, of garbled cries and the tinkle of two tiny bells as clamped nipples set them jangling.

For a moment there had been a respite when the heavy flogger had been replaced with a smaller one, but one now designed to stimulate and lash the flesh of Lily's breasts and the tender parts between her legs. Lily yowled into the gag, sweat streaming down her flanks and legs, making the thongs of the flogger heavier and the pain of each blow sharper as they absorbed the moisture. Lily's mind slipped somewhere, as her eyes closed with each strike, somewhere beyond the initial fantasy scenario to a place beyond. As her body was flooded with endorphins and adrenaline, Lily thought she was flying, but couldn't be sure. The blows seemed to merge, her surroundings now fuzzy and dreamlike. The introduction of a thin, whippy cane on her buttocks and legs took her higher, almost to an out-of-body experience. The idea of the Safeword could not find a place in Lily's overwhelmed mind.

Finally Cole stepped back, leaving Lily slumped in her bonds, snorting through her nose and making muted moans, her breasts heaving with the effort of futile resistance.

Then his hand was back between her legs, stroking her mons and insinuating his fingers deep inside her. Lily jerked as though struck with an electric prod, uttering a long 'Urrrrr...' as heat erupted hotter than before. Cole moved behind her and pushed his leg between hers, driving the plug deeper and letting one hand caress her breasts while the other engaged with her clitoris. Lily went wild as the three sensations hit simultaneously and she could do nothing to halt the sudden tidal wave rising out of nowhere. She whinnied into the gag, tossing her head, her hands clenching and unclenching as her crotch was overwhelmed and she forced herself hard against Cole's hand. He pushed back, grinding into her pussy and was rewarded with a series of thrusts, each accompanied by a long drawn-out cry, before Lily was spent, and hung there, the muscles of her thighs trembling and twitching. A vague, distant thought concluded that this total capitulation had outdone even Karla's outrageous torments in the Berlin dungeon.

For what seemed an infinity, Lily barely supported her weight, feeling every muscle quivering, the juices of her submission sliding down her legs. She was beyond humiliation or embarrassment, striving only to get her heartbeat and breathing back into normal range. The pain of her nipples had lessened to a dull ache, the fullness of her rectum now subsiding to something almost pleasant. Her cognisance of her surrounds slowly came back, and she knew that for all her exertions, she still had not achieved the one thing she wanted so desperately – to climax in the same way with him inside her, feeling his breath on her face, his lips on hers, hearing his own cries mingling with hers – gagged or ungagged.

She widened her eyes and tried to explain this around the ball in her mouth, making muted and garbled hmmming noises, but he either did not understand or chose not to. She was unprepared when he sank to his knees before her and fastened his lips around her labia, making her eyes widen with something which went beyond the mere word 'pleasure'. Lily was already stoked down there, and the presence of his lips, tongue and teeth in her most private of places sent her into a new shuddering round of ecstasy.

She tried to protest that she could not take much more of his attention, when the hardness of his teeth sent her over the edge again in a flood of impassioned struggles and muted pleas which went unanswered. All her strength against the ropes could not prevent the inevitable and she was again screaming over the waterfall, tumbling headlong down a dark tunnel of flashing lights going off in her crotch and in her brain.

Lily didn't know whether she actually fainted or not. Everything was hazy as an exhausted warmth swamped her body. She barely acknowledged something warm and full parting the slickness of her labia and sliding smoothly inside her with an accompanying sense of contentment, of happiness, of fulfilment. The leather belt and crotch strap which held the big dildo in place were hardly noticed by Lily, who could only just stand when her ankles and wrists were freed and the ball gag and clamps removed. She slumped into his arms and laid her head against his chest, beyond caring, as he carried her upstairs. He laid her under the sheets, arranging them over her, before she closed her eyes slipped into a far off world.

\*    \*    \*

# CHAPTER 32 – Threats

Lily Maddison was in a faraway place. It was warm, dark and safe. She lay in a cocoon which had provided her with more than mere comfort and security. She was awaking from dreams filled with blissful sensations arising from between her legs, sensations that made her roll on her side and squeeze her thighs together, thrusting her hands between them. She was naked, feeling the fullness inside her pussy and her arse, each sending wonderful waves of rapture through her body.

Lily did not know where she was, nor did she care. The ebb and flow of the delightful tides was all she wanted, just more, more. She was vaguely aware she was lying nestled in the crook of a bare arm, and that a body was pressed up behind her. The hand at the end of the arm was cupped around her left breast, idly playing with a flinty nipple in a way that sent connecting messages to her crotch.

Somewhere in the molten core of that very crotch another hand – not her own – was pressing and manipulating the hard fullness embedded between her labia, into her deepest and most sensitive parts. It had been this movement that had drawn her back from the warm darkness in which she had sought refuge. It was not refuge from something bad, merely respite from a passion that had drained her until she had nothing left to give – or so she thought.

Lily slowly surfaced as one rising from a deep warm pool, awakened by the incessant and unceasing vibrations in her crotch, a slow and subtle in-out, in-out, combined with a hardness against her clitoris. Eyes still closed, Lily grunted, mumbling a faint protest under her breath, her body making to deny further stimulation her brain insisted was acceptable.

'No…no…' Lily whispered. 'I can't…'

The continuing and rising vibrations did not acknowledge her half-hearted protest, and somewhere in her dreamlike state she realised that the big invader inside her was what she thought she had been searching for. It was as though such acknowledgement was what she needed, that it was acceptable, validating. Lily's last remaining reservations seemed to vanish and she committed herself to the stimulation without care as to the what or how. It just felt so gloriously *good*.

The act of acceptance brought down the last of her resistance and she surrendered to the increasing pounding of the intruder, her own hands unsure whether to resist or assist. Then there was no time for a decision because the tidal wave swept up from her pussy, making her flail about under the sheets, screaming into the pillow, before subsiding into a series on reflexive jerks and grunts.

The big prong inside her teased her gently, but she was adamant now.

'No more, please! Oh God!' The fact she had been backed into a corner where surrender and a plea for mercy were the only options was enough to make her eyes snap open. It took a while for her to focus on the armchair and the suitcase beside it, and to realise she was in Cole's bedroom, and by implication, his bed. Through the subsiding rapture she became aware of the lean body pressed up against her, and the arms enveloping her.

Lily sighed contentedly, overflowing with so many emotions. How many were merely physical passion, simply degenerate lust, kink or whatever was obsessing her body at that moment, Lily did not know or care. It was the culmination of a carnal desire she didn't think could be satisfied, but which she now simply wanted to go somewhere else so she could recover.

It was several minutes before Lily trusted herself to move. Cole lay quiescent behind her, refraining from any further stimulation, though she was aware of his warmth and the cosy scent of his body. But as her senses slowly came to order, Lily realised she was still impaled at pussy and arse – devices held there by a leather crotch strap – and that she had again been the victim of artificial stimulation.

The fact brought her back to the present with a jolt – the realisation that for all her elation, she had not experienced the true person that was Aurelius Cole.

She sat up abruptly and turned, ignoring the momentary dizziness that flashed through her brain, propping herself on the pillows to look at the figure beside her. Words failed to come for a moment, then she could only whisper:

'Why...?'

'I'm sorry, Lily,' he said quietly, not meeting her gaze. He pulled her down against his body, and she realised he still had his silk pyjama pants on. She lay against his chest, torn between the extraordinary and wonderful experience she had just had, and that after everything done to her, she was still yet to touch his penis.

As though to address this oversight, Cole took her hand and guided it down to his crotch. Her fingers felt his flaccid manhood, hanging limp between his legs.

'I didn't want things to go this far, Lily, but I had to respond to your insistence and desire in the only way I can.'

He closed his eyes, as though summoning up an explanation. 'When the bomb went off,' he said, his voice distant, 'I was standing with my back to the french windows and to Leila. The glass and shrapnel damaged many nerves, and have made it impossible for me to achieve an erection.' He paused, and his voice wavered. 'It was as though the universe decided that if I could no longer have Leila, then I had no need of other women.'

Lily's mouth dropped open at the awful reality. 'Oh God...' But after that she didn't know what to say.

372

'I'm so sorry…' she whispered, feeling the tears well then slide down her cheeks on to his chest. She was aghast at what she had done, guilt overwhelming whatever other feelings she might have been developing for him.

'Now you know the truth,' he said gently, still not looking at her. 'It's better this way.'

The bedroom was empty when Lily emerged from his ensuite, having showered and finally removed the plugs from her body. She realised she had arrived there naked, and was now without attire to return to her bedroom. She grabbed Cole's silk robe from a hook behind the door and exited to the hallway carrying the crotch strap and plugs, just as Farah emerged from the door to her bedroom opposite. Her spiteful look took in the robe and the devices which left no shred of doubt as to Lily's recent activities. She felt the heat rising in her cheeks, knowing that she had trespassed somewhere she shouldn't, despite the fact it had been Cole who had led all the way. Farah said nothing, but stood there as Lily hurried up the stairs to her own room, the Iranian woman's eyes burning into her back.

Lily resumed her morning duties with a bittersweet glow which made it difficult to concentrate. Things were happening so fast. She had gone shopping to the High Street, dropping off Farah's dress at the drycleaner, her intention noted by the Iranian woman as Lily had left the house carrying the dress in a clear plastic bag. Farah had shot her a look which boded no friendship.

It had been by chance that her route to the drycleaner took her past the West Hampstead Police Station – an old three storey brick building which looked more like a library or school than a police station. For a long moment Lily halted, wondering superstitiously if the universe had brought her here for a purpose. She had only to push through the double wooden doors and ask for George Burrows and blurt out the real truth – about the Agency, Karla, Aysha and the blackmail photos. Then what would happen? Likely something bad to Aysha. An accident, maybe? A relapse? Then the photos would hit the papers. She had seen the depths the Sun newspaper would sink to.

But her situation had worsened. Erika was dead, and likely it was not an accident, which meant Lily, too, was in danger, though she did not know who from. Blabbing to the police would be no guarantee of safety, and she had nowhere to hide. No, she would have to bluff this one out, just see things through another week, one day at a time. But there was one thing she had to do first, which might bring her some clarity…

After lunch, Lily had knocked on the open door of the study. She had made up her mind to tell Cole about the detective's visit, not least because the policeman would likely return to interview Cole in person. She would have no excuse for not having told her employer, but had needed time to get over her awful sexual faux pas that morning, and to recover from the emotional and physical experience.

Lily also saw that any conversation she had with Cole would be better conducted in the study, since it gave her a legitimate reason to be there, in the presence of phones, faxes and any loose conversation which might slip out.

'Come in, Lily,' said Cole, looking up from a pile of papers at his desk. Out of the corner of her eye, Lily saw Farah's head lift at her desk at the other end of the room.

'Sir - could I have a word, please?'

'Long word or short word, Lily?' Cole appeared his easy-going self, as though nothing at all strange had happened since his return.

'Long, Sir,' said Lily, sitting on the upright chair in response to his gesture.

'Sir, yesterday, while you and Ms Bakhtiari were not here, a policeman visited. His name is George Burrows. He's a detective from Scotland Yard.' It was immediately evident she had the attention of both of them. 'He was making enquiries about Erika Baumann – my predecessor?'

'That's right, Lily. What do you mean "enquiries"?'

'They found her body in Regent's Canal twelve days ago. It's taken them that long to track her back to here. Apparently she's German, so they had to go through the German police.'

'Erika? Dead?' To Lily's eyes, there was nothing false or affected about Cole's reaction. Unaccustomed as she was to spotting deceit, the man's shock was plain in her eyes. He sat back in his chair. 'My God! How did she die?'

'Maybe drowned. He says they're not sure. Apparently she had a condition – something to do with epilepsy – that she needed regular medicine for, and her photo was recognised by the local chemist where she went. That's how they traced her to this address. He said there was alcohol in her system.' Then, as though to not be overheard by Farah at the other end of the room, Lily added in a whisper: 'There were also some rope marks on her wrists, Sir…'

Cole ran his hand through his hair and stood up, slowly pacing the length of the room. The phone rang, and Farah answered, listening and talking in a low voice. She was speaking Farsi, Lily thought distractedly, though her focus remained on Cole. He seemed genuinely distraught.

'You… you don't think I had anything to do with this, Lily?' His tone was distressed.

'Of course not, Sir.' It was the truth, at least in Lily's mind. She could not picture Cole as a murderer – not after the vulnerability he had shown in bed that very morning. But rope marks? Were they just coincidence?

'What else did he ask, Lily?'

'Uh... he asked what I knew about her. I said I knew nothing. I told him I was just her replacement. I said I'd been told she'd had to leave due to a family illness.'

'Quite so.'

'He asked who told me that. I said you had.'

'That's correct. That was what the Agency said.'

'I didn't mention the Agency, Sir. I told him I got the job through an ad in Time Out. He didn't ask whether it was through an agency or directly to you. I'm sorry. I thought if I mentioned the Agency it was going to get very complicated, because I couldn't give any details. But he's sure to come back to speak to you in person.'

A long silence hung over the room. Farah had finished the phone call but made no move to continue with her typing or filing.

'How did she leave, Sir?' Lily wanted to know.

'I was out,' Cole said. 'We both were. I came home that evening and she was gone, with her things, leaving a note explaining the sudden departure. I got a call from a woman at the Agency the next morning, confirming the circumstances and advising they would have a replacement in a few days. That was you.'

'Oh.' Lily did not want to press the case further, afraid any questions about the Agency might go somewhere dangerous.

'Did the detective say when he was coming back?'

'No, Sir. I told him I thought you were back yesterday, but I couldn't be sure. Ms Bakhtiari told me she thought you might be away all week.' Lily was not sure why she said it, and wished she hadn't. Cole shot an odd look at his secretary, but said nothing. Lily could feel daggers lancing the back of her head.

'Very well, Lily. Thank you.'

'Shall I get the mail, Sir?'

'Farah has done that already, Lily. You were a little late in starting this morning,' Cole said with a faint smile. 'I need to discuss this with her. You may leave us for the moment.'

Karla was tense when Lily met her that evening, demanding to know what had transpired that day, and how much access Lily had managed in the study. Lily was not good under questioning, for she was a truthful girl, not skilled in fabricating stories. Karla's methodical interrogation – starting from the time of Cole's return – had elicited that Lily had now been relieved of the chastity belt, and had enjoyed a night in Cole's bed.

'And what did you learn in the course of the night, Lily?'

Lily had learned nothing she thought relevant to Karla and her plans, though she now had a deeper and more sympathetic understanding of Aurelius Cole.

Lily prevaricated, then on a sudden reckless spur, irritated by Karla's insistence on her having to be present in the study without adequate reason, she asked:

'Did you know Erika was dead?'

In Lily's mind, if Erika had been murdered, there were only two possibilities – Cole or Karla. Her gut told her Cole could not have done it, though the rope marks worried her. They could be from a previous session, but Cole had said he'd been away that day. Rope marks went away after a few hours unless they were actual bruises, Lily knew. Karla knew her way around ropes, too. Both Cole and Karla had told her Erika had gone to be with family. Somebody was lying.

'What?' Karla sat back at the question. 'Who told you that?'

There was no going back from it now.

'A policeman came round. They found her body and traced her to the house.'

'Did they interview Cole?'

'No, this was yesterday. He was away.'

'Yesterday? Why the fuck didn't you tell me last night, Lily?'

'Did you kill her, Karla?'

'Oh for fuck's sake, Lily! I don't go around killing people! Act your age! Fuck! This means the police will start digging around...'

It was the first time Lily had seen Karla flustered, not in control. She stood up and took several paces, then returned to the bench, gripping Lily by the shoulders.

'Lily, this is no time to lose your nerve. You have to make yourself indispensable in the study. Clean the windows, spill coffee all over the floor, vacuum, polish, do whatever you have to do. Probably tomorrow will be the last day we have. If the disinformation is to emerge in time, it will be tomorrow. If you learn something, find an excuse to leave the house and get to the phone box. You know the number. If anything out of the ordinary happens, do that. If word comes through that you've gone off script, I can't guarantee when Aysha will see the light of day, Lily.' Karla spoke low and fiercely. 'Do I make myself clear?'

There was no denying the vehemence in her voice and Lily recoiled from her grip, abruptly standing and jerking the leash to pull Charlie away from the bench. She did not look back as Karla called after her: 'I mean that, Lily! Don't risk your friend!'

Karla considered her harsh attitude justified if Lily was to realise the seriousness of the situation. Karla had done her best to pull Lily along through coercion, through the belief that there would be a good outcome at the end. Now time was running out. Lily had needed a kick up the bum. It was a trickle-down effect, not least because Andreas Meyer was becoming increasingly agitated and even more fixated than usual. It was clear his superiors were leaning on him – those in the upper floors of the HVA in Normannen Strasse, and conceivably those in the yellow brick building in Dzerzhinsky Square.

Karla knew of Meyer's time in Tehran, and of the debacle at Tehran Airport that had resulted in his sudden recall to Berlin. For those in the KGB, the "recall to Moscow" was almost always a one way ticket with a predestined outcome – a bullet in the back of the neck. Most HVA officers would likely not have survived such a failure, but such had been Meyer's reputation and his network, that certain benefactors had intervened, arguing that the long term strategy was too important to be set back by elimination of an officer whose detailed knowledge remained vital. This time, Meyer had been spared the last steps into a sound-proofed room beneath Hohenschönhausen prison. But it had been made clear to him that failure of Operation *Parthia* would mean a end to his career – in the most permanent of ways. There would be no excuses this time – for anybody.

\*　\*　\*

# CHAPTER 33 – Breaking Chains

The Vatutin Hospital manager, Vladimir Nemtsov, was a short, bespectacled, balding man in a white coat. Helen Feldman had him pegged as a doctor who had reluctantly wound up in an administration role, where others did much of the string-pulling. He had been forewarned of the arrival of the Australian Embassy woman from Moscow, and had been under instructions to delay Aysha's release as long as possible. It was not a task he relished, not least since medical reasons for keeping Aysha Newton in hospital were now tenuous at best. The embassy woman had implied that there would be diplomatic exchanges if the release did not happen, and Nemtsov had learned that the orders to delay had not come from his health superiors in Moscow. Rather, Konrad Fischer was behind it – something that did not surprise him, for it was common knowledge that the East German was a likely HVA informer.

Nemtsov's phone conversations with Helen Feldman had not gone well. She was a formidable woman who spoke Russian like a native, complete with an extensive range of raw colloquialisms. She had clearly schooled herself on the treatment of hepatitis and had was sufficiently familiar with names in the Moscow health hierarchy to imply that those people would be down on Nemtsov if he didn't come to the party. While health protocols were one thing, the KGB was something else entirely. Nemtsov's career could be ruined from either direction. On learning that this Feldman woman was on the way from Moscow again, this time with the express intention of collecting her countrywoman, Nemtsov had broken out in a sweat and had spent an hour chain smoking as he tried to figure out a solution. The normal plan was to stall, to prevaricate, to pass the decision to superiors. However his superiors in Moscow had no knowledge of any KGB agenda, nor could they see any reason to become involved – until the Australian Embassy started rattling their cages and asking embarrassing questions for which they had no answers. His head would be in the firing line.

When Aysha, dressed in her own clothes, was shown into the office of the hospital manager, Helen Feldman had been there to greet her, and after some discussion in Russian between Helen and the manager, there were some signed forms and Helen had escorted her into the lift down to the ground floor. Konrad Fischer was nowhere to be seen, though a man in a white coat – who might have been the masked KGB man Helen had known as Petrov in Aysha's room – had followed them into the lift. The hair on the back of Helen's neck had prickled. She was no stranger to the deviousness of these people. Their methods and ruthlessness were well known, especially so in the treatment of their own people.  In the course of her time with the embassy, through countless consular gatherings, Helen had heard all the stories of disappearances and "accidents".  Nothing surprised her any more, and the worrying would not stop until she received advice from London that Aysha had reached safety.  She had still not figured out what Aysha Newton had done, why she was of importance, or why the officials had finally capitulated. Not for the first time was she reminded of Churchill's words that Russia was "a riddle, wrapped in a mystery, inside an enigma".  It was something she saw every day.

Aysha was silent as they crossed the echoing foyer to the front doors under the gaze of Petrov, who had stopped beside the lift.  She held on to Helen's arm, not game to speak, for fear of upsetting a delicate tightrope walk that might at any moment prove to be an illusion.  There remained the flights to Moscow then London, still seeming impossibly far away.

It was a bright September afternoon and Helen found a taxi that would take them to the airport.  Only when they were on their way did both women relax a little, as they crossed the broad expanse of the Dnipro River.  Aysha's Kiev nightmare was almost over.

*

The news of the death of his mother in Rostock had taken a while to reach Konrad Fischer.  It transpired that Elke Fischer had taken her last breath over a week previously – a fact evidently known to Andreas Meyer and withheld from his step-brother in order to continue his leverage.

When Konrad had visited the hospital manager, Vladimir Nemtsov, and told him that the reason for continuing to delay Aysha Newton's release had ceased to be relevant, Nemtsov was so relieved that he did not question the cause of his good fortune.  He did not take in the ashen face of the East German doctor as Fischer informed the manager of the change in circumstances and the resolution to Nemtsov's dilemma, just in time to face the fearsome Australian Embassy woman.

It was only when they found the body of Doctor Konrad Fischer that evening, in the service alley beneath the open sixth-floor window, that Nemtsov connected some of the dots.  He would never know of the chain of events that would follow, like a butterfly shaking the world.

*

It was like a dream to Aysha, sitting beside Helen Feldman on the brief flight to Moscow, then the night in the accommodation quarters at the building they shared with the British Embassy single staff on Solyanka Street. Here the British doctor checked her over and pronounced her fully fit.

'Nothing that a few good meals won't set to rights,' he had declared.

Aysha had hardly slept, so excited was she to be heading for England. She felt like a spy on the run, striving to quell her fear that something would arise at the last minute, that the men in the grey uniforms at Domodedovo Airport would pull her from the boarding line. But again, Helen had seen her through, watching like a protective mother until the British Airways 747 lifted off.

Aysha had been met at Heathrow by a young woman from the Australian High Commission named Vanessa, who had accompanied her to a cheap hotel in Earl's Court. Aysha had immediately dumped her luggage and established the location of Lily's new place of work, as explained to her by Vanessa. Vanessa had shown her the best route on the Tube to get there, and Aysha had set out into the brave new world of the London Underground, her stomach a mass of excited butterflies at the prospect of surprising her love. She pictured the joyous look of amazement as she tried to imagine the house and Lily opening the door.

It was late afternoon. It had taken her an hour on the Tube, then walking down the well-heeled Hampstead streets, to reach the three-storied brick house that was Lily's new residence. In her postcards, Lily had told her of landing the housekeeping job, but other than that she had seemed deliberately vague about the duties. So typical of Lily, thought Aysha – more concerned with Aysha's welfare than revealing her own.

She pushed open the gate and walked the short distance to the front steps. She noted the odd brass plaque that reminded her of the Persepolis carvings, before she rapped on the brass knocker, the sound resonating through the house. There was no response for what seemed like an age. Had she come all this way to find that everybody had gone out? Was this even the right place?

Aysha retreated to the street and looked through the big wrought iron gates down the drive at the side of the house. She could make out the beginnings of a back lawn – a garden shed and the end of a clothes line. There, flapping like a tired flag in the evening breeze was a yellow tee-shirt with the words "Mellow Cello", and the outline of a musical instrument. Aysha stifled a cry of joy in her throat.

She returned to the front door and rapped again. This time, after a few seconds, the door opened. A severely-dressed woman with her black hair in a bun stood there, one hand on the door handle, the other hidden from view.

'Yes?' She looked foreign, but even in that single syllable the educated English accent was evident.

'Does Lily Maddison work here? My name is Aysha Newton. I'm a friend of hers.'

'There's nobody by that name here,' said the woman peremptorily, making to close the door. Aysha was having none of it, and put her foot firmly in the way.

'Don't bullshit me,' she hissed. 'I've seen her tee-shirt on the line. I know she's here!'

A fleeting expression crossed the woman's face that might have been surprise or shock. For a couple of seconds she appeared to be debating options. Then she said:

'Come in.' Only when the door closed behind them did Aysha see the pistol.

\*     \*     \*

# CHAPTER 34 - Sprung

Lily's night was sleepless until the small hours, and then was haunted by dreams of the small hospital room in which Aysha lay. Now there were manacles on her ankles, securing her to the bed, where she lay naked under the gaze of men dressed in army uniforms. Karla and the Kiev doctor, Konrad Fischer, were there, looking concerned as if discussing a course of treatment. There was a big hypodermic needle lying on the bedside table, and two soldiers grabbed Aysha's arms as Fischer took the hypodermic to administer it. Aysha was screaming, tossing her head from side to side as she fought weakly, but she was never going to win.

The screaming carried on, and Lily realised it was her, waking in a sheen of sweat soaking her Mellow Cello tee-shirt. She sat up and looked at her travel clock's luminous hands. Two-thirty-seven. Outside, the streets of Hampstead were silent. If only time could just jump ahead by twenty-four or forty-eight hours…

Lily knew something was wrong when she returned the next morning from her walk with Charlie. She did a load of washing and hung it out on the line, fretting about getting access to the study. On impulse she looked guiltily back at the house, then retrieved the tiny camera from under the eaves of the garden shed, tucking it into the top of her stocking on the inside of her thigh. Karla was in such a mood that Lily might have to grab any chance she could. Perhaps she could manufacture a diversion which would give her a chance to take some photos of the papers on Cole's desk or that of Farah. At least she could say she tried.

As she returned to the house, Farah's voice called out to her through the study door. Feeling like a naughty child, Lily entered the study, thinking at least she had penetrated the domain without needing an excuse.

'The Professor has been called into Whitehall,' said Farah peremptorily. 'You may dust in here while he is away. Go get your things.'

Lily retreated to the kitchen and returned to the study with the dusting cloths and polishing oil. She had barely begun to dust the window sills when Farah stood up from her desk and collected the cup and saucer from Cole's desk, as well as one from her own and left the study for the kitchen, leaving the door open. Lily could hear the sound of the cups going into the sink and the kettle being filled and placed on the stove.

Her heart pounding, she put down her duster and moved across to the fax machine, casting a furtive glance at the door. There were several faxes in a tray, where they had been cut from the roll of special paper used for the machine. She had barely had time to scan the top two when Farah's voice sounded from the doorway.

'I thought so!'

Lily spun round, her face a mixture of surprise and fear. 'What?'

'Find what you're looking for, Lily?'

'I... I was just... curious... I've never used a fax machine...'

'No, but you understand how to read the print out well enough!' Farah spat.

'I was just curious...' Lily repeated, sounding even less convincing.

'Who are you spying for, Lily Maddison?'

'What? I don't know what you're talking about...'

Farah advanced across the room while Lily retreated towards the window, as though putting distance between herself and the incriminating machine would somehow lessen her guilt.

Farah continued: 'He wouldn't listen to me. Too busy satisfying his little perversions to even think you might be something other than what you claimed.'

'I didn't claim anything,' Lily stammered.

Farah reached her desk and pulled out what looked like a post card from a pile of letters.

'Too bad you were so preoccupied fucking yourself silly that you didn't collect the post this morning, you little slut,' Farah taunted her, flapping the postcard at her. She tossed it on the floor at Lily's feet, close enough for Lily to see her name on it, and several large USSR stamps. Her mouth opened and she fell to her knees, grabbing the card and hardly understanding the significance of Aysha's handwriting. Her discovery by Farah was momentarily forgotten as she read the card with the fervour of a starving person thrown a cupcake. The message was brief and to the point:

'Awaiting final all clear! Maybe home next week - Inshallah! Love you so much; so sorry for everything!'

It was signed 'A', and followed by four kisses.

Lily's situation was forgotten in taking in the marvellous news, until she looked up to see the small pistol in Farah's hand.

'A bit obvious, a postcard from the Soviet Union as a code, I would have thought,' she said, 'but again, hiding in plain sight can often work.'

'What? No, it's from my girlfriend – she's been sick in Russia – she's been waiting for release from the hospital...' The words tumbled from Lily's lips, as though she barely believed them herself and had to hear them aloud for the news to sink in. Then the presence of the gun overcame the realization of the information and she froze. Lily had never seen a pistol at close quarters in her life, other than the holstered guns of border guards. The grey of the steel was unwavering in Farah's hand, matched by her gaze. Lily froze, stunned at the turn of events.

'Stand up, Lily!' Farah's voice sounded like an icy wind and sent a chill down her spine. Lily found herself shaking, as she got unsteadily to her feet. 'Go – to the cellar!'

Farah stood aside, out of reach, motioning Lily through the study door and across the foyer to the cellar door under the stairs. Lily opened it and descended, her brain trying to work but seemingly frozen at the incongruity of a handgun in posh residential Hampstead, though in truth it was no more bizarre than the dungeon itself. She dared not ask what Farah intended for her, for she did not now trust her voice to articulate words.

'Back against the post!' Farah commanded, indicating one of the solid six-inch square wooden posts supporting the floor bearers above. Farah grabbed a pair of handcuffs from a hook and moments later Lily found her wrists secured behind the post, clearly not going anywhere in the near future.

'I knew you were bad,' Farah snapped. 'I can tell these things. Right from when you came out with that concert stuff, and the submissive shit. All a bit coincidental. You're a commie plant, Lily – I can smell it!'

'No! I only arrived the weekend before last! How could I be a spy?' Lily's voice wavered between indignation and fear.

Farah was in her face. The gun was gone, but she slapped Lily hard across the cheek.

Something in Lily's normal demeanour snapped. Whether it was the feel of the cuffs anchoring her hands behind the post, or some deeper-seated rebellion, the stress of the past few days surfaced as she spat in Farah Bakhtiari's face.

Farah wiped the spittle and turned to the wall of implements hanging neatly on their hooks. She returned with a bright red rubber ball gag on a strap.

'Spit on me, would you...' The upper class accent was dripping with menace, borne by one who has all the control. 'Open wide, Lily...'

Lily clamped her mouth firmly closed, only for Farah to grasp her nose between thumb and forefinger and pull it roughly upwards, until the pain and the need to breathe made Lily open her mouth just a little. It was enough for the Iranian woman, who forced the ball hard between Lily's teeth, buckling the strap tightly behind Lily's neck.

'I was going to ask you a few questions, Lily – and I still will. But I don't want you spitting all over me. Do you understand?'

Lily glowered at her and grunted something which made no sense but was clearly uncomplimentary.

'I think there will have to be a lesson learnt, first, so when I remove that gag you will be compliant and cooperative. Does that seem reasonable?'

Lily mmphed through her nose - something which might have been 'fuck you'.

Farah went to the shelves and procured a coil of rope, with which she bound Lily's ankles to the post. Lily realised now that Farah was neither a stranger to bondage, nor stupid enough to allow any opportunity for her prisoner to lash out. Only then did Farah begin undoing the buttons of Lily's white silk blouse, pulling it open and tucking it in behind Lily's pulled-back arms. She stood back and appraised the helpless girl, as though deciding what to do next, but also enjoying what she was looking at.

Farah ran her fingers down Lily's neck, and over her breasts. Despite her likely treatment being anything but sensual, Lily's nipples again betrayed her, and she cursed her body's automatic response. Farah's carefully-manicured nails dawdled over the birthmark which always attracted attention, then traced Lily's areolae and played with the nipples.

Lily groaned under her breath and closed her eyes, snapping back to reality as Farah squeezed the nubs simultaneously between thumbs and forefingers, eliciting a gagged yelp. Farah's hands slipped under Lily's breasts, weighing them and pressing them hard.

When Lily's captor then undid the zipper to her skirt, Lily realised with horror what was about to happen. As the skirt dropped to the ground around her bound ankles, there was an exclamation from Farah and her hand reached between Lily's thighs to retrieve the small Minox camera from the top of her stocking.

Lily closed her eyes. Everything was turning to shit and no fabricated story was going to earn her a reprieve from this. Farah examined the device, pointed it at Lily and pressed the shutter button, sliding the mechanism back and forth to advance the film, giving the impression that she had done it before.

'Huh,' she muttered, as though there was nothing more to be said.

The first blow struck Lily across the breasts – the heavy thongs of a flogger that seared across Lily's nipples and made her bite down on the ball in her mouth. The impacts continued, Farah's face locked in an intense scowl as she put her weight into the beating.

'This is for spitting at me,' she told Lily. 'When I'm done with this, then I'll ask you some questions. Better start thinking of the answers – like who you're working for!'

Lily screwed her eyes shut against the pain, then slowly felt the fuzzy darkness approach, the sensation she had first encountered the night before, at the hands of Cole. Then it had been strange, uncertain... Now it was suddenly comforting, like an old friend offering her a place of refuge. Her mind gradually became oblivious to her struggles, to the arching of her body as she strained against the steel cuffs securing her wrists behind the post and her attempts to scream around the obstruction in her mouth. Lily's consciousness had crossed into sub-space again, her body becoming aroused in its temporary absence. Lily was away in a dark but protected zone, where the pain became pleasure and reality had vacated itself.

Lily had no idea how long she had stayed in her trance-like state. Her eyelids fluttered open to the sound of voices but she couldn't focus on sight or sound. The blows to her naked body had ceased, though she found herself still secured to the post, her mouth still distended by the ball. Her body was throbbing, glowing, on fire... All of the above... Warm, intense feelings radiated from her groin...

'...you fucking mad?' She recognised Cole's voice and slowly a shadowy figure became clearer. It was Cole, wearing a grey suit with the tie hanging at half-mast. It was the most dishevelled she had seen him. Farah came into focus. She was sporting the red imprint of a hand on her cheek and glared malevolently at her boss.

'This girl is a submissive – she's a fucking pain slut, woman!' shouted Cole. 'You're sending her off to sub-space to enjoy herself!'

'Okay, Mister Smart-arse – over to you, then. She's a spy!' Farah waved the tiny camera at him. 'She had this stuck in her stocking, and had decided to rummage through the fax printouts when I went out to make a cup of tea – or at least make the sounds of it. She grabbed the chance with both hands! She's a plant – sure as shit.' The expletives sounded strange, delivered with Farah's upper class accent, as though practised but still unfamiliar. 'Who else would be running around with a camera like this? It's the fucking Soviets. And all because of you and this perverted fucking dungeon of yours.'

Cole made a visible effort to control himself in the face of the provocation. He turned and strode to the grille of the cell in which Lily had previously been imprisoned and leaned against it, as though by turning his back on Farah he could regain his self-control. He took several deep breaths, after which his voice was calmer.

'Did she see it? The fax?' It was obvious they both knew which one he was talking about.

Farah shrugged. 'Doesn't matter. I got her down here before she could do any damage. I don't know if she got a shot of it, but she's had no chance to send any word outside.'

In Lily's dimly re-igniting brain, she recalled the message she had been told to look for, confirming a later date for the forthcoming coup. So something had come through. Which meant... what? Hauling her consciousness back to a functioning level, she remembered the discussion with Karla. The fact these two were talking about something as important as this meant the disinformation *had* come through. Which meant British Intelligence *did* have a source embedded in the Tudeh – most likely in Paris. But did these people recognise this as false information or not? The first question had been answered, but the second – and greater issue – was on the table.

Lily's body ached, now that she was becoming more *compos mentis*. Her skin felt like it had a bad case of sunburn, and she did not dare look down to see what weals and scars might have appeared.

'So what do we do with her?' Farah hissed. They were both behind her now, out of sight and discussing her fate as though she was not even in the same room.

'What do *you* think we should do? You brought her down here... We can't let her go now, not until everything dies down.'

'Then what? She'll be blabbing to the cops.'

'I think I can pull a few strings which will keep them out of our hair.'

'But longer term... We have to get rid of her...'

'No!'

'Then what? You want to keep her chained up down here till you tire of her as a plaything and she dies of old age?'

'Shut up, Farah! We do nothing for the moment! We think about it and come up with a plan.'

'She needs to have an accident,' the woman hissed again. 'An untraceable, unfortunate accident.' Lily froze in her bonds, staring wide-eyed at the brick wall opposite, shocked at the discussion on her fate.

'We wait,' Cole said firmly, though it was plain he had no Plan B.

'That's all very –' Farah started to respond when the sound of the door knocker carried down to the cellar. Everybody seemed to freeze. Farah and Cole looked at each other, raised eyebrows questioning whether anyone was expected but drawing only barely perceptible shrugs. Lily's mind lifted at the thought that a visitor might offer a distraction – something, anything that might ease the precarious situation she found herself in. They waited long, silent seconds, to see if the visitor would go away. After a long minute, no further sound came, and the protagonists looked to resume their argument, when there was a further hammering of the door knocker.

'Go and see who that is,' said Cole dismissively. 'I want some time with Lily.'

'Of course you do,' muttered Farah as she climbed the steps and vanished into the foyer. Cole moved around into Lily's line of vision. He put up his right hand and gripped her face in his thumb and fingers, the way doting aunts do with small children. Lily looked into his eyes and moaned softly behind the ball as she felt his other hand cup her crotch, now inexplicably wet with her juices.

'Oh Lily, what have you done?' he whispered.

There came the sound of voices from the foyer – Farah and another woman's. There was a brief conversation, then the voices – indistinct as they were, became raised. Both Lily and Cole involuntarily looked upwards, wondering what was going on, then shadows appeared on the steps as two figures came slowly down, the second holding a gun on the first.

Lily's eyes widened and she snorted into the gag, struggling against her bonds and making incomprehensible noises at the sight of Aysha Newton, hands half-raised ahead of Farah's weapon.

\* \* \*

# CHAPTER 32 – Reunion

Lily rolled her eyes and made garbled noises as Aysha was forced down the steps at gunpoint. She wore the emerald green salwar kameez Lily recognised from Pakistan, obviously intended as a reunion surprise. Aysha managed to keep her wits about her without abusing her captors or firing off questions which would not be answered. She reached the bottom step with Farah's gun in her back and took in the sight of her friend bound to the post, along with the wall rack of bondage impedimenta.

Cole looked at Lily theatrically.

'I'm guessing this is… what was her name? I don't think you ever told me. Your girlfriend who went off travelling by herself, Lily?' He looked at Aysha. 'Aurelius Cole at your service. And you are…?'

'Aysha.'

'Aysha. Nice name. I suspect you're the one who "converted" Lily, on your long overland journey. Must have been quite a trip,' he said conversationally. 'You don't appear at all surprised to find Lily here amongst all this.' He gestured to the display wall.

Aysha shrugged, showing self-control which amazed her friend.

Cole stood to one side, leaving Farah with a clear view of Aysha from behind.

'Aysha, please go to the bench and lean over it, face down and arms behind you,' he said. 'For the benefit of all doubt, the lady with the gun is a professional bodyguard – though she can also type at eighty words a minute, I might add. For some reason she also seems to have a chip on her shoulder concerning the young ladies who have frequented this room, so I'd suggest you do exactly as you're told.' He gestured towards the solid workbench on one wall. Aysha did so, bending so her cheek and breasts pressed on the benchtop.

It took Cole only a minute to tie Aysha's wrists and to loop the tail of the rope over a horizontal steel pipe running along the underside of the timber bearers above. He hauled on it so that Aysha's arms rose up behind her in a strappado, forcing her shoulders down harder on the bench. Cole tied the rope off to a cleat.

'What are you doing with her?' Farah demanded.

'I'm guessing you're the Domme of the partnership,' said Cole to Aysha, ignoring the Iranian woman. 'Am I right?'

'Fuck you,' murmured Aysha. Lily uttered a soft groan around the ball in her mouth.

'Oh yes, you're the Domme all right.' Cole smiled, like a child given an unexpected toy. 'You've done an excellent job on Lily, Aysha. You should be proud – although if I say so myself, Lily has progressed significantly since her arrival here. Shall we just say that she and I have shared several significant moments?' Aysha elected to be silent, while Lily had no choice.

'You see, Aysha, Lily appears to have been planted on me. By whom, I'm not sure, nor am I sure where *you* fit in, having just turned up out of the blue. In short, I intend to find out what's going on, and I intend to have a little fun in doing so.' Cole's voice was single-minded and calm, but had an underlying tone of one whose patience is on the verge of being tested.

He moved behind the bound figure and undid the drawstring tie at Aysha's waist, pulling the loose pants down along with Aysha's underwear, exposing her buttocks in the harsh fluorescent light of the dungeon antechamber. Aysha tried to kick backwards, but her foot got tangled in the clothing. Cole sidestepped the attempt and moments later Aysha's ankles were bound to the bench legs, her clothing kicked to one side.

'Farah! Put that fucking gun away and go upstairs. You're making me uncomfortable. This need not concern you.'

Farah shot Cole a venomous look and reluctantly went up the steps.

'Good,' said Cole, as though to himself. 'Now, Aysha, there have been developments since you last did rude things to young Lily. Lily knows things I want her to tell me, but I won't even attempt to beat them out of her, because dear Lily will likely head off into sub-space and have an orgasm or five on the way. She'll become exhausted and incoherent, which means she's the only winner. Did you know she was a pain slut? No? Well, we've figured that out even in the short time she and I have been bedfellows. And yes, she's found her route into sub-space. I don't think I've seen anybody go down that road so quickly. Quite remarkable.' Aysha remained silent, though Lily could see a flush in her cheeks. Cole turned to Lily.

'Lily, we've been very focussed on you, but you need to learn a little more about people you work with. Some Dominants are purely that, while some can switch to become submissives – at least temporarily for the purposes of some play. Did you know that? It's very rare a true Dominant will tolerate a submissive role, either through the requirement to submit to humiliation and command, or the punishment itself. Submissives typically have a high pain threshold, even if they can't all be pain sluts. Are you taking notes, Lily?'

He chuckled. 'I'm guessing Miss Aysha here is happy to dish out whip marks, but less happy to receive them.' He took down a springy cane from where it hung on a hook and swished it through the air. The sound cut through the silence of the dungeon with a frightening swish-swish.

Lily realised what was about to happen, and shook her head – no! No! Cole scrunched the jacket of the salwar kameez up around Aysha's waist, so it would present no obstacle to a clear strike on her buttocks. Aysha's breathing was now audible, her bound hands clenched into fists. Cole stood to one side and laid the cane purposefully and precisely against Aysha's cheeks. Lily saw the first trembling of the other girl's legs.

Cole made a practice swing, stopping just short of impact, as though testing his aim and distance. Then the first blow struck Aysha cleanly across the buttocks with a harsh crack. Aysha stiffened and stifled a cry, then shaking started in her arms and legs. Immediately a bright red weal sprang up across her skin. Cole paused, running his fingers over the welt, as though massaging it. Lily heard Aysha's breath now coming in a rapid panting.

Thwack! The second strike landed a finger's width below the first, perfectly parallel, creating an identical contusion on each cheek. Aysha jerked and almost screamed, but somehow managed to suppress it, while Lily tugged frantically at her bonds, striving to articulate her fear, and to plead for mercy.

When the third blow fell, Aysha's scream echoed around the room, bouncing off the dusty brickwork. In a moment of desperation, Lily began to hum 'Happy Birthday' as best she could.

Cole stopped, pausing with exaggerated surprise.

'What, Lily? The Safeword? You can't use a Safeword for someone else, Lily, though kudos for trying.' Tears were now streaming down Lily's cheeks, the saltiness seeping past the rubber ball on to Lily's tongue as she whined and mmphed for freedom of speech and for the torture of Aysha to cease.

'You have something to tell me, Lily?'

Miserably, Lily sniffled and nodded her head. Cole undid the buckle at the back of her neck and pulled the gag free. Lily gasped and tried to catch her breath in between trying to sniffle, cry and plead.

'Please stop! Please, Sir! I'll tell you what you want to know – if I can... Just don't hurt her any more...'

'Lily!' It was Aysha, through gritted teeth. 'I don't know what the fuck is going on, but don't let this bully make you do shit! I've had worse than this!'

'Oh shush!' said Cole, with the tone of a mother talking to a mildly grizzling child. Lily's dripping gag was now forced into Aysha's mouth with a minimum of effort and buckled at her neck. Aysha continued to make muffled protests.

Cole moved close to Lily, now trembling against the post. He pulled a handkerchief from his pocket and gently wiped the tears from her cheeks as they continued to well in her eyes.

'Shhhh...' he murmured, and Lily could have sworn his compassion and consideration for her was real. She did not understand how he could do what he had just done to Aysha. He stroked her hair and kissed her breasts. Lily's emotions went off the chart.

'Lily,' he whispered. 'It's all over. Everything will be finished very soon – whatever 'everything' might be. Now I just need some information – whatever you can tell me.' He spoke as though to a small child. 'Just tell me the truth and nothing will happen to your friend. You can both stay here for a bit longer, then you'll be free to go. Okay?' He lifted his hand under her chin. She saw him through a blur of tears and did her best to nod her head, trying to ignore the indignant grunting from the bench.

Cole pulled up a metal chair which looked as though it had once graced a 1960's kitchen table – all tubular chrome and padded plastic.

'Let's be friends, now, Lily. Whatever cover you had has been blown. This whole thing is over. You'll have nothing to gain by lying. The shit has hit the proverbial fan, made a big mess, now it's time to clean up. Do you agree?'

Lily nodded, barely processing the words. She now understood how a guilty man – once discovered – could seek solace in a confession, knowing there was no more hiding, no more pretending. The cards would fall and things would take their own course.

She had also seen her beloved Aysha return. Part of her registered that Karla had been bluffing the previous night, when she had threatened to harm Aysha. By whatever means, Aysha had returned. Her trip must have taken several days, and yet Karla had concealed it. Probably it had been out of her hands and she'd been hanging on to the deception until it was no longer possible. Whatever fate might have been threatened against Aysha in a distant country... that had ceased to be an option. But the threat was now new and different.

'Good,' said Cole, the epitome of reasonableness. 'Start at the beginning, Lily.'

Lily slowly let out her story, with prodding from Cole. She told him of the photos, realising as she did so that Aysha was hearing the story for the first time, too, and that the reason for them both being there lay with those photos. A sob escaped Aysha as she bent over the worktable – a sob that came from her mouth but then seemed to spread to her body, which began to convulse as much as her bonds permitted.

'Please... could you let her arms down, Sir?' Lily begged. 'This is the first she's known of any of this.'

Cole stood up and undid the rope from the cleat, dropping Aysha's arms and allowing her to lift her shoulders from the bench, though she could not wipe the tears now streaming down her face. The three lines of welts on her skin had now turned a deep blue-black.

Lily told Cole how she had been seduced by Karla in the Berlin dungeons on one hand, but threatened with harm to Aysha and exposure for the photos on the other.

'Mmm, very carrot-and-stick,' Cole commented. Then he was serious. 'So, that explains how you came to be here – in part. What we don't know is why they had to get rid of Erika. And let me tell you, Lily, I swear I had nothing to do with that. Erika was nice, but really not very bright. She liked the sex, liked the bondage, but that seemed to be the limit. She never asked questions, other than when next this dungeon might be used for her. If I had to speculate, I'd say the imminent attempt at Iranian regime change and your appearance with a ready-made big stick prompted them to... retire her. You're way smarter than she was, Lily. Not to speak ill of the dead... I'm sorry for her. I genuinely liked her... I like you even more, Lily...' Cole sat back in the chair and wiped the back of his hand across his forehead.

'Fuck me, what a mess. So what are your orders as of this moment? Or immediately prior to Farah running her own unauthorised sting operation?'

'They put out some disinformation through the organisation,' Lily said. 'I was supposed to look out for it, to see whether British Intelligence had a mole in place.'

'And have you seen that information?'

'Uh... no, sir. I didn't really get a look at your faxes.'

'And what then?'

'If the disinformation had come through, they need to understand whether you believe it or not.'

Cole nodded slowly. 'What was the disinformation, Lily?'

'That the coup was to take place on 14 September.'

'Uh-huh. That's a week from today. Looks like you might have a long time down here, Lily, but at least you'll have Aysha to keep you company.'

'But that was the *dis*-information, Sir! The real coup is happening today!'

'Yes, Lily. Ever heard of double-bluffs? Tell them the truth, but also provide a lie that is known to be a lie. Messes with people's minds.'

'But it *is* dis-information!' Lily insisted. Then she wondered, why was she trying to insist on her version of the truth? Was she even sure of what they'd told her? *"In the spy game, nothing is what it seems, and is usually much worse."* That was what Karla had told her. Karla's forces were backing a people's revolution against a tyrannical Shah, yet those same people had committed horrific acts themselves, including the damage they had done to Aurelius Cole. Lily was caught in the middle and was losing the will to fight for either side. She and Aysha were now prisoners in the dungeon, for however long that might be, but for all the bluster of Farah Bakhtiari, they would surely not die down here. They were likely safer in the Hampstead cellar than exposed to the killers of Erika Baumann.

Aysha and Lily leaned on each other in the darkened cell as the chill from the concrete floor and the brick wall slowly ate into them. The certainty that the whole mess might be over had been replaced by the possibility that 'over' might not be for days, yet. Lily was confused by Cole's reaction, by his apparent over-thinking of the bluff and double bluff. Did he believe the dis-information story? What date was he working to?

Her head throbbed. So much had happened in the last few hours – her discovery, Farah running around with a gun, Aysha's appearance, the beatings to both of them, Lily's confession… She tugged at the chain locked to her elegant but now highly functional steel collar. The chain was a couple of metres long, passing through a ringbolt embedded in the cell wall, with the other end locked around Aysha's neck. They now sat together in the second cell – the one with the solid steel door and nothing else by way of comfort or sustenance other than a bucket to pee in. They had been permitted to re-dress before Cole had secured them in the small dark room, lit only by a sliver of light from under the door – until the antechamber light had been extinguished. Each had her wrists handcuffed behind her, as if Cole had considered them a flight risk as he had secured them in the cell, or maybe he had merely wanted to make a point, to deliver an initial punishment. It was a harsh position, for the steel of the cuffs cut into their wrists, making it impossible to ease the discomfort.

They had talked in whispers, as though in fear of being overheard. There had been confessions and heartache but no recriminations. The tears came, the affirmations of forgiveness, the kisses and the slowly rising exhaustion as they awaited their unknown fate. There were the explanations from Aysha, the role of the Australian Embassy in Moscow, the passing on of Lily's new address, and the sighting of her Mellow Cello tee-shirt on the clothesline. At that point Aysha was not going to take any denial from the Iranian woman who answered the door.

Their experiences had tumbled back and forth.

'Looks like you'll miss your rendezvous with your friend Karla,' said Aysha at one point.

'She's not my friend.'

'Obviously not any more. What about your boss? Was it good for you? Did the earth move?' Lily knew Aysha was teasing her, but was there a little jealousy there as well? He had taken her to the next level from where Aysha had been obliged to abandon what Lily now looked on as "training". Each time she and Aysha had explored their relationship Lily had been taken a step further. Cole had continued that journey – from a male perspective – not that it really mattered. He had shown her the road into sub-space, and she had surprised herself at her own aptitude and willingness.

But it had been hastened by her own feelings for him, for the suffering and loss he had endured, and for his vulnerability, as well as for his dominance. Aysha had sensed this.

'How serious is it, Sweetie?' she asked softly.

'I'm sorry, Aysh... I was just so lonely... He sparked all sorts of things in me – things that you started...'

'I understand. And where has that taken you?'

'I thought I was falling in... falling for him... I thought there was something here... until you came back. Then it all returned... It's like you've never been gone...'

Aysha's lips touched Lily's face in the darkness, coming up against the warm salty tears on her cheeks.

'It's okay, Honey. You were seduced by an expert.'

'It wasn't just that, though. I still feel for him, Aysha.'

'Is it sympathy, or something more?'

She had seen the mess of scars on Cole's body, and understood the trauma he had seen in losing his love. She understood how he could hate those people. She also understood – or had thought she had – her feelings for him, and how they had been approaching something serious...

But Lily was troubled with what they had seen in Tehran, with the young couple taken in the restaurant, and being caught up in the protest. She had seen the Peacock Throne and the lavish wealth belonging to the royal family, and understood the oil revenue being syphoned from the Iranian people after the Brits and Americans had re-installed the Shah.

Now Aysha had returned, along with the rush of love, of memory of her body, her intelligence and her understanding, all overwhelmingly comforting.

'I... I don't know... But I do know I love *you*, and nothing's going to change that...'

'So how does it feel now, to be chained by the neck in a dark dungeon? Princess or slave?' There was no hiding the mockery in Aysha's soft teasing.

'It doesn't matter,' said Lily. 'You and I are chained *together*. *That's* all that matters.'

She was too tired, too exhausted from the stress of the last week eating away at her as she was forced into the new and deceptive role now tumbling down around her. She just wanted to cuddle up to Aysha and make the world go away.

Who would miss them, she wondered. Nobody knew they were here – nobody who might come looking, unless that detective returned, but he could be fobbed off. Could Cole – or British Intelligence – really afford to let them go? Whatever happened, it would surely be resolved by the end of the weekend. There would be a revolution in Iran, or it would be called off... or it would be a dramatic capture of the plotters...

That was the moment two shots came from upstairs.

\*   \*   \*

# CHAPTER 33 – Plans of Mice and Men

The clock on the wall showed three minutes past six in the evening. The room was in the basement of Century House, containing half a dozen cubicles with various items of telex, telephone, fax and radio equipment, while three large television sets were positioned on a wide shelf at one end of the room. Three of the cubicles were occupied by men wearing headphones or with them draped loosely around their necks, while three more men sat at a larger table close to the double entry doors, through which a fourth had just entered. On the big table was a base radio set with a microphone attached by a spiral cord, along with three telephones – black, white and red.

George Burrows, Howard Westmoreland and a man named Brian Carlisle had been at the table for several hours. Victor Hopkirk, the Permanent Undersecretary, had only just arrived.

Carlisle was an aristocratic-looking man in a well-fitting suit and public school tie. He was past fifty, had three decades of working in MI5, and knew the others in the room from previous occasions of collaboration between the security services.

Westmoreland acknowledged the Undersecretary and introduced George Burrows as the only person Hopkirk did not know. Burrows stood and the pair shook hands.

'Your reputation precedes you, Mr Burrows,' said Hopkirk. 'Hope you don't mind the 'Mister'. You chaps always have the longest titles.'

Burrows murmured a greeting and resumed his seat.

'I hope there's no objection if I bring the Undersecretary up to date,' said Westmoreland. The nearest thing providing a pecking order amongst the three security men was that Century House was the turf of MI6, and it had been Westmoreland who had been instrumental in bringing them together. He turned to Hopkirk.

'This circumstances are a little unusual, Undersecretary, and things have been thrown together in a bit of a rush. DCS Burrows was the one who initiated the action, and I've known him long enough to vouch for his security clearance, even if it is – for the purposes of tonight – unofficial.'

As Victor Hopkirk seated himself, Westmoreland continued the briefing, not directing it specifically to any of the others.

'We have a situation in Hampstead, where one of FCO's chief analysts – well, *the* chief analyst on Iran, Aurelius Cole – may have been compromised. The nature of his work for the FCO – and the nature of MI6's involvement in that country – account for myself and the Undersecretary being here. The fact we've now uncovered the presence of the East German Stasi looking to get their fingers in our pie on our soil, well that's Brian's – MI5's – bailiwick, and I thank them for their prompt assistance last night and today. George has been in it right from the start. We may need his chaps if arrests are to be made.

'For the benefit of perhaps George and Brian, the heart of the matter here is that there is an intended coup in Iran, scheduled for kick-off in a little less than four hours, by an organisation called the Tudeh, who've long been a thorn in the side of the Shah, and a tool for our friends in the Kremlin. Whether you call it a coup or the perhaps more appropriate term of "revolution", it's aimed at deposing the Shah, which of course will bring about enormous destabilisation of the Middle East, with the Soviet Union sure to be sneaking down both sides of the Caspian Sea to fill in the political void with their "advisers". Suffice to say, MI6 and the FCO have been... er... monitoring these developments, and we have sources inside the Tudeh which have kept us apprised.

'At the London end, a couple of weeks ago a female body was discovered in Regent's Canal. George has come up with an identity for her – a woman named Erika Baumann, supposedly from *West* Berlin – though more likely *East* Berlin. Suspects for killing her lie either with Aurelius Cole or "others" – possibly the HVA – that is, the *Hauptverwaltung Aufklärung,* the Stasi's Foreign Intelligence Service.'

'Are you serious about Cole?' asked Hopkirk. 'What's the connection? I've known him for years. Can't believe he'd be capable of murder. If that was the case, he'd be a suspect in something much bigger in this whole business. He'd be a possible traitor.' Hopkirk shook his head. 'I just can't believe it of him. His antipathy to the Tudeh runs far too deep, in light of his personal circumstances.'

'Let's not forget the Cambridge Five,' murmured Westmoreland, alluding to the senior British Intelligence officers who had flown under the radar for years before defecting to the USSR in the fifties and sixties.

'Yes, yes, I know all that,' Hopkirk said, irritated. 'I'd still back my reputation on Aurelius. Not a killer. Not a traitor. Let's stop this line right there.'

'You may be right, Undersecretary, but since we're unloading confidential secrets here,' Burrows began, 'it's my belief that Professor Cole is a little on the kinky side – bondage and discipline, if you know what I mean. We're pretty sure Ms Baumann was so inclined, and – lo and behold – her successor, Lily Maddison, is also into it.'

Victor Hopkirk knitted his eyebrows. 'Interesting. I met her at the Albert last weekend, then saw her again at Cole's the next day. Hardly surprising. There've been rumours, after the Tehran bombing, of course. Let's put personal judgements aside, gentlemen, and take it as read that Aurelius... goes down a road less travelled. Where does that lead us?'

# the submissive spy

'It leads us a little more to the "others" theory,' said Brian Carlisle, the MI5 man. 'I was contacted the night before last by Howard here, to see if Five could do some quick surveillance. And it *was* rushed. We got someone on the job on Tuesday afternoon, watching Cole's house, mainly looking for the Maddison girl. She's supposedly the "housekeeper", and one of her duties is evidently walking the dog. Seems they go to Hampstead Heath every night. On Tuesday evening she sat down at a bench for a minute, went on with her walk, and returned to the same bench half an hour later to have a chat with a blonde woman. Same thing happened last night.'

Carlisle reached down to a briefcase at his feet and extracted a large brown envelope, from which he pulled half a dozen black and white telephoto shots of Lily and Karla in earnest discussion, which he passed to the Undersecretary. 'The first few were taken Tuesday evening. The remainder – as you can see from the changed clothes – were taken last night. We did some digging and we believe we have an identity – Elsa Kruger, though she may be under an alias of Karla Graf, or so our immigration people tell us. West German passport, but likely East German ancestry. She was recognised by some of our surveillance people as meeting with one of the East German attaches during routine surveillance at a bar, a month or so ago. Our surveillance people are very good at recognising faces, and as you know, we keep a good watch on the East Germans out of Belgravia Square.

'This Graf woman is not attached diplomatically. Five has no previous record of her here. So I flip the ball back to you, Howard.'

Westmoreland, voicing the MI6 position, continued.

'We've been doing some digging since Tuesday, Undersecretary, primarily with our colleagues in the German BND in Bonn. This afternoon we got some background. Graf has been running bondage and discipline operations in West Berlin and Bonn for the last 3 years. No doubt there would be blackmail ops going on as a sideline.' He gave a tight smile. 'Hard to believe, but it seems people are a bit sensitive about their kinky predilections being public knowledge. Before that time, things are a bit murky. Her parents live in Rostock, up near the Baltic Sea. Now, here in the UK, there's this further kink connection. It seems probable she's Lily Maddison's handler, and if that's the case, she was likely handler for Erika Baumann.'

'Which puts her firmly in the frame in connection with her murder,' said Burrows.

'So, first photos were on Tuesday evening, on the heath.' Carlisle resumed. 'We only had one watcher. Graf wasn't alone. There was a chap in a car with binoculars watching the meeting, and she joined him afterwards. Our own watcher elected to stay watching the car, rather than Maddison, who he figured would return to the Cole house. He followed the car to a semi in

Kilburn. The man went into one residence, Graf into the other – in the same house. We've followed up on the ownership. Seems both sides of the house have been rented for some time – to the same shell company. We're still trying to dig through the paperwork, but sure as eggs is eggs, it will be dodgy. It looks like an HVA safe house. Which in itself is a pretty good find, given the Kremlin seems to be devolving a lot of their intelligence work to the Stasi. We need a wedge in this new door.'

'And the man?' asked Burrows.

'Goes by the name of Colonel Andreas Meyer. Supposedly a diplomatic attaché at Belgravia, but in fact is HVA up to his eyeballs.'

'Interestingly, it seems Cole and Meyer have crossed paths previously,' said Westmoreland. 'Meyer has connections to Iran, back in '74 – ended badly for him but was hushed up. Cole was working for us and was part of an op that caught Meyer red-handed at Tehran Airport, trying to smuggle armaments into Iran. We also suspect Meyer was involved with the later explosion that nearly killed Cole. He's been linked to the Graf woman – possibly her controller. We'll have a permanent watch put on the house.'

'That's all very well, gentlemen, and I'm happy for Five uncovering the house in our own backyard,' said Hopkirk. 'Likewise, this may lead us to solving a murder. But uppermost in my mind is this imminent Iranian thing. Where does this leave us right now, Howard?'

'Cole's our lead man watching and coordinating with the Iranians. We have a mole in the Tudeh, which the HVA likely know about, even if they can't finger him. They fed some false information through, giving a false date for the coup of next weekend. They likely know we have their planted information, but they won't be sure if we know it's false. That's the thing they'll be desperate to find out. If we accept the information at face value, we'll be expecting crowds in the street on Saturday week. If, on the other hand, the Tudeh realise we're on to them, they'll pull the pin and we'll be in the dark again. But if they think they're in the clear, they'll walk into a trap tonight – tomorrow, their time – that will set them back years and keep our mate the Shah on the Peacock Throne.'

'Under four hours to go,' said Hopkirk, looking up at the clock. 'I don't have to tell you, the PM will be watching the hours as well, not to mention our cousins in Washington. I know I speak for the PM when I say that nothing must happen which will allow these people to get the jump on us and pull that pin. What's the situation in Hampstead now?'

'We have two watchers, Undersecretary. One on the house and one on Graf and Meyer who are currently at the heath. Last I checked, just before you came in, there'd been no sign of Lily Maddison all afternoon. She walked the dog this morning, then did the washing, but there's been no sign of her since. There was one point of interest – another young woman approached the house recently and went inside. Tall, glasses, possibly Indian extraction. Hasn't come out.'

'So Maddison hasn't been to the rendezvous?' Burrows said.

'Correct. Our watcher there has reported no movement. Both Graf and Meyer were sitting in their car at last report.'

'What options have we got here then, gentlemen?' Hopkirk asked. 'If the proverbial hits the fan, what then? Suppose our friends decide to take matters into their own hands – to force the issue?'

'We've got taps on Cole's phones,' Carlisle told him. 'We can cut off the place if need be – phones and utilities. Those people are on standby. George has a small group of his Armed Response Unit people out of sight a couple of minutes away, if they're needed. And of course we're in radio contact from here with all of them, including the watchers. And there's the Iranian woman.'

'And she is…?' George Burrows asked. 'Don't tell me – Savak?'

'A member of the Iranian Ministry of Intelligence and Security,' said Westmoreland smoothly. 'Personal protection, supposedly. A condition of sharing information with them.'

'Good,' Hopkirk said. 'All things being equal, we should just have to wait it out. Now Brian, I know you MI5 chaps would like to keep the lid on this and see how much of the HVA network you can track, but understand this, if there's any threat to this Iranian op, I won't hesitate to order the arrest of this Graf woman and her friend, if it means preventing any warning getting out.'

'Understood, Sir. Meyer will likely pull diplomatic immunity, of course, but by the time we "verify" that, he'll be neutralised for a good while.'

'Any reason we shouldn't already have a protection detail at the house?' Westmoreland asked of nobody in particular.

'It *was* suggested,' Hopkirk said. 'But we daren't do anything which would tip them off that we're counting down to a very close deadline. We want them to think we believe the coup is still a week away.'

'Brian,' said a voice from one of the cubicles, 'Watcher One says Graf on the move. Seems like they've given up on the rendezvous. We're tracking.'

'Roger. Route? Direction?'

'The rendezvous on the heath is very close to the Cole house. Looks like they're doing a drive by.'

'What?' There was a sudden edgy note to Carlisle's voice. A silence descended on the room. 'Fuck! Something's up! Get those people of yours on the move, George! To the Cole house! Cut off the Graf woman!'

'No!' said Hopkirk sharply. 'Even if they're going there, we'll have them trapped. We can't scare them off before that! If they see the ARU people they'll head for the hills! Hold your positions!'

'But...!' Burrows was about to protest.

'I said no!' Hopkirk's icy voice cut off the discussion.

There was the urgent sound from another cubicle as the orders were relayed.

'Watcher Two reports the Graf car pulled up beside the house. He's a hundred yards away. Graf and accomplice are approaching the front door!'

'Fuck!' Carlisle swore.

'Door's opened – suspects gone in – Watcher Two reports shots fired!'

*   *   *

# CHAPTER 34 – Breach

The dark green Triumph 2000 was parked two hundred metres from the benches on the heath, down the road from the entrance Lily and Charlie normally took on their walk. In a casual blue and white shift dress, a fidgety Karla Graf sat in the passenger seat with the window down, as Colonel Andreas Meyer paced beside the car, chain smoking. He wore flared jeans and a wide-lapelled black shirt which looked too young for him. Impatience steamed off him like a bad smell. Beside the car were the butts from the last hour of watching the benches.

'She's not coming!' he snapped. 'Fuck! Something's happened!'

'She's missed meetings before,' Karla said, but there was an edge to her voice, acknowledging that this was not a routine meeting. 'Cole's probably got her in the dungeon.'

'This close to the kick-off? I don't think so! Something's going on. If the fucking pervert has got her there, it's to shut her up, not because she's flashed her pussy at him. Fuck, why do I have to work with deviants?'

Karla did not tell him to his face that it was because the Party deemed it a perfectly acceptable way to achieve its objectives. Every man had secrets, though she had still to find any dirt on Meyer that she herself could use. The man seemed devoid of any emotion which might suggest a meaningful relationship – past or present – with another human being. Andreas Meyer was his own best friend. This operation had been a long time in coming, and he would shortly be in the spotlight of its international success.

Karla Graf had been reluctant to finally admit she was in over her head, but the enormity of the project – designated *Parthia* in the Stasi play book – had slowly become apparent to her. The set up of Erika Baumann as a submissive to the Dominant Aurelius Cole had taken a lot of work, only to discover Erika was self-absorbed and would neither aspire to nor achieve top marks in any life class she might be bothered to attend. What had seemed like a subtle embedment plan had foundered on the rock of an operative's inadequate skillset.

Karla and Meyer had acknowledged the suitability of Lily Maddison early on her first day in Berlin. She was vulnerable and pliable, but also intelligent and with significantly more motivation than Erika Baumann ever had. Getting rid of Baumann had not proven difficult. Like an addict – for that was what she was – she would use any reason she could to ingratiate herself into a bondage scenario, and she'd needed no persuading by Meyer, that evening a couple of weeks ago.

It had been a quick flight for Meyer back to London from Berlin, where he and Karla had taken time out from their monitoring of Erika in London to meet the Maddison girl. Cole had been absent on one of his frequent trips to Paris, and it had been easy for Meyer to take Erika to the Kilburn house, bound and gagged in the boot of the Triumph, convinced it was a prelude to a reward kidnap role-play with Karla. At the house, strapped to a chair, she had been plied with alcohol. Realisation of her plight had come all too late, and Erika Baumann had been unable to resist, slumping into an alcoholic stupor. Meyer had driven to a quiet part of Regent's Canal in the small hours of the night, and the plan had been completed. It was all very simple.

Back in Berlin as she dealt with Lily on the second day, Karla Graf had tried not to think of the act, but had not been in a position to protest. As one of tens of thousands of *inoffizieller Mitarbeiter*, the unofficial collaborators for the Stasi, she remained in thrall to the State's control of her employment, family and friends. The health of her parents in Rostock remained conditional on her successful role for the State. Perception of her performance, in turn, was dependent on the reports prepared by Andreas Meyer in his obsessive involvement with *Parthia*.

Meyer had become increasingly stressed over the last week, and had communicated this unease to Karla, resulting in Karla's download on Lily. Meyer and Karla had learned of meddling by the Australian Embassy in Moscow, and they had received the news that no further reason could be found for the continued detention of Aysha Newton. The release of Aysha did not overly concern them, for it was almost zero hour, and Lily's motivation from any threat to Aysha was now academic. But the news of Aysha was accompanied by word of Konrad Fischer's death.

Though she had not seen Konrad for over three years, the time that they had spent together as nominal husband and wife, and the ruse that they had used to get out from the suburbs of Rostock into their own flat in East Berlin, had bonded them together as two good friends. While they had subsequently drifted apart, it had been Konrad's brother who had woven the sticky Stasi web around her. However Karla harboured no ill will towards Konrad, and his death shocked her more than she expected, though Meyer appeared to take it in his stride.

There had been a blazing row between the pair that had resulted in all manner of threats from Meyer to control his subordinate. Karla had accused Meyer of being uncaring at Konrad's death, at the same time as she wondered why Konrad had taken his own life. That was how the death of his mother had slipped out – along with the fact that Meyer had concealed it from Konrad, hoping to get through this most critical of times without Konrad becoming the weak link in the same web that held Karla. Karla seethed and could hardly bear to be in the same space as this man who dismissed his step-brother as though he was merely a passing acquaintance.

# the submissive spy

They had driven to the heath in an icy silence. The London rush hour was filtering through the suburbs, bars and pubs were filling up, and people were heading to the cinemas and theatres. In the refined and quiet streets bordering Hampstead Heath, a few evening walkers were out, enjoying the warmth of dusk, ignorant of the hovering cloud of tension at the green Triumph.

Andreas Meyer angrily stubbed out his cigarette, as though making up his mind. Time was running out – there were only a few hours until the operation began, with the word from Paris set to initiate a series of uprisings in Tehran, Mashad, Isfahan and Shiraz – provided there was nothing to indicate that British Intelligence or their American pimps knew more than they ought. He'd been pinning his hopes on the Maddison girl, relying on Karla to put the fear of God into her, but something had gone awry. Maybe Cole was on to her. Maybe Karla was right and the bitch was simply strung up in the bastard's basement as he flogged the crap out of her. On top of the news from Kiev, things were suddenly starting to go off script.

Instinct told Meyer that Lily was not delayed through more deviant games – not this close to the start of *Parthia*. You don't plan for a Grand Final then go sailing three hours before kick-off. Fuck! He had to know that there was no hiccough, that British Intelligence were not waiting in the wings with their puppet police, Savak. The time for subterfuge and secrecy was gone. If he was exposed now, but successfully clarified the situation, such exposure would not matter if the revolution was successful. Meyer was prepared to sacrifice his cover and that of Karla if it meant certainty for the State in this operation which would change the world.

If he had been honest with himself, Meyer might also have conceded that the presence of Aurelius Cole as the key player in the whole operation was disproportionately significant to him. The memory of the ignominious arms smuggling incident at Tehran Airport, four years previously, lurked in the recesses of Meyer's mind, however much he attempted to suppress it. He had avoided a bullet himself only through swift accusations of betrayal at the Berlin end, the result of which was the subsequent disappearance of the two pilots and several baggage loaders in the days following the debacle. But the personal humiliation remained like a bleeding ulcer. Meyer never found the true leak of the cargo information, but the presence of Aurelius Cole alongside the Iranian colonel on that night remained a cerebral wound that refused to heal.

When he had heard of the Englishman's severe injuries in the explosion that killed Leila Khatami, Meyer had exulted, then cursed that the man had survived. Now the prospect of attending to this last loose end beckoned more than he would admit to himself.

Meyer stalked round the front of the car and climbed in behind the wheel, leaning across to open the glove compartment. He withdrew two pistols and two spare magazines, handing one gun to Karla. She looked at him, the question unasked – and ignored. The weapon was an East German version of the Soviet Makarov PM, a small snub-nosed eight-shot pistol – standard issue in the East German forces. Both Karla and Meyer had been trained in weaponry, though Karla abhorred guns. Give her a whip and a compliant submissive... but guns... no, not if she could help it.

He started the engine.

'What are you going to do?' She finally asked the question, trying to hide the trepidation at whatever this sudden decision might be.

'*We* are going into that house to establish once and for all whether they have any knowledge of *Parthia*,' he hissed. 'We have three hours to make sure there's no leak, and if we have to beat the shit out of people in the process, then so be it! If there's collateral damage, too bad! If we're found out – as long as it's not until three hours have passed, then it doesn't matter. We'll make the sacrifice for the State, for a far greater good, and that greater good is massive. Remember that!'

Meyer pulled out into the quiet street, driving past the entrance to the heath and then turning into East Heath Road. There were few cars parked in the street – most houses were affluent enough for a couple of garages.

'Watch for anything unusual – anyone watching, and security on the house...'

Karla's stomach turned over, and she found her fingers tightening on the pistol in her lap which had suddenly become very heavy. This should not be happening. The man was going to blow everything in an impetuous rush.

'The moment we pull up, we head through the gate to the front door and bang the knocker. The second it's answered, we force our way in.'

'But this isn't what –'

'Karla! We are not letting something this big go down the toilet because we fucking well didn't check!' He braked to a halt outside the gate. 'Now go!'

The road seemed quiet but they exited the car at a run, through the iron gate and up the few paces to the front steps, then rapping sharply with the big knocker.

Karla glanced nervously back at the street, looking for any indication that they might be walking into a trap, that the house was under surveillance, but she saw nothing... Or was that someone further down the road, sitting in a brown Ford Cortina?

She spun round at the sound of the door opening. Gun drawn, Meyer already had his shoulder thrusting against the door, forcing it open. A woman had been on the other side. She stumbled back, losing her footing and falling backwards on to the parquet floor. Karla caught a glimpse of her hand bringing a small pistol up, attempting a shot while trying to recover from the fall, but she never made it. The two shots sounded loud in the panelled foyer and Farah Bakhtiari lay still, sprawled awkwardly, blood oozing from the two bullet holes in her chest.

*

The basement room held its breath as Watcher Two reported: 'Front door's closed.'

'Armed Response Unit still on hold.'

'Stand by,' Hopkirk said. 'Let's all take a breath. Whatever's just gone down, gentlemen, has hopefully done so in isolation. They've entered the house but are unaware we're watching. It was unfortunate, but it's happened. We can still use this to our advantage – remember that time is on our side now. Every passing minute gets us closer to the kick-off. Every minute that they don't try to call it off means they're either not sure if we're on to them, or else they definitely believe they're in the clear. If they reach a different conclusion from inside the house, they'll try to contact Paris or otherwise signal that the operation must abort. The moment they try to phone from there – as they surely will if they have an urgent message – then we cut the lines. That's when they'll know we're on to them. Until that time, as I said, every minute that passes is a win for us.'

'But the shots –' said Burrows.

'We don't know who was in the way of them,' said Hopkirk. 'We're not going in there until absolutely necessary. Is that clear, gentlemen?'

There were nods from the three men.

'We could cut the lines now, sir,' suggested Carlisle. Then he appeared to think the better of it. 'Or they may simply check to verify they're working. Maybe we hold off...'

'Do that.'

The black phone on the table began to ring with a soft buzz. A voice from one of the cubicles called out: 'Downing Street, Mr Hopkirk.'

Hopkirk picked up the receiver and listened briefly, then gave a succinct summary of the situation.

'Yes, Prime Minister,' he ended, putting the receiver back in its cradle.

'If you didn't appreciate the importance of this operation before, gentlemen, you should do now. The PM is right over this. Let's not stuff it up,' he said sharply. 'We watch, and wait. Nobody goes near the place. If they twig we're on to them – if we have to cut the phones, for instance – that's a new scenario and everything changes. We cross that bridge when we come to it.'

'There may be hostages involved,' said Carlisle.
'Agreed, so get your negotiators lined up. Worst case scenarios.'

*

Karla was stunned at the noise, the suddenness of death. Her heart beat as though the whole house could hear it, and she leaned back against the door for support, pushing it shut. She was aware of a door opening to her left – that must be the study – and a man was standing there, his face white with shock, staring at the tableau of a man and a woman with drawn guns standing over the still figure of Farah Bakhtiari.

'Mister Cole, please come out here!' Meyer ordered, his voice stressed, gesturing with his pistol. Cole did so, struggling to comprehend what had just taken place. 'Karla – where is this dungeon? I want this man secured while we search the place.'

Karla looked around and spotted the door under the stairs, just as Lily and Erika had told her.

'There,' she said, moving towards it.

'Who else is in the house?' Meyer demanded of Cole, recovering some composure.

'N-nobody...'

'Where's the Maddison girl?'

Cole figured the blonde woman in the blue and white shift with the nice legs – and the gun – had to be the Karla that Lily had described, though she hadn't mentioned anybody else. But now it all dropped into place. Andreas Meyer – he should have seen it earlier, should have made enquiries years ago, instead of assuming the guy had been given a bullet for the fuck-up at Tehran Airport. And with a gun in his hand he looked just a little unstable.

'She's... gone out for the evening,' Cole blurted.

'Liar,' said Karla. The shock of the shooting had dissipated a little, the adrenalin was flowing and her thought processes were returning. She took a deep breath, though her pulse barely slackened. 'She wouldn't have missed our rendezvous for an evening out. She's downstairs in your playroom.'

Meyer took three strides across the foyer and in a single motion pistol-whipped Cole hard across the side of the face, drawing a runnel of blood that began to drip onto Cole's shirt. Cole staggered back, hand to his head, but Meyer grabbed him by the arm and jerked him in the direction of Karla. Cole stumbled, his weakened leg nearly folding at the sudden load.

'Take this shit downstairs,' snarled Meyer to Karla, gesturing to the cellar door. 'Any funny stuff – blow his kneecap off!'

Karla motioned to Cole with the pistol, taking in his physique and trying to judge whether he presented a physical threat. Either way, she was careful not to get too close, allowing him to move three steps ahead, down the stairs into the dungeon. She noted the pronounced limp as he reached the floor of the antechamber.

She did her best to try to stay focussed amongst the sudden display of toys and implements that always stirred her loins – the desire to assess and compare someone else's collection and predilections with her own. A brief glance ascertained that there were no restrained prisoners nor other threats here, though there were two smaller cell doors off to one side.

'The handcuffs!' she barked, trying to get into Domme mode, to drive the sight of the dead woman from her head. 'The ones on the wall in front of you! Cuff your wrists behind your back!'

She saw Cole's hands shaking as he took the steel cuffs down from a hook. As soon as a real gun came on to the scene your thought processes were compromised, she thought. Cole tentatively fastened one cuff around his left wrist, then awkwardly managed the other around his right, behind him. The snicking of the ratchet notches was loud in the antechamber. When the man's wrists were secure Karla approached from behind and closed the cuffs a couple of further clicks. Only then did he appear to gather his courage to speak.

'What are you going to –'

'Shut up!' she snapped, pausing for a moment to look more closely at the collection of bondage apparel this man had collected for his recreation. Then she saw it – the winch with the thin cable that went over a pulley attached to a beam. Every dungeon worth its salt had such a device, the cable ending in a hook intended to elevate or suspend limbs or whole bodies. Karla flipped the ratchet lever off, allowing the hook and cable to unwind as she pulled down, before clipping the hook over the chain links connecting the two manacles locked on Cole's wrists. Cranking the hand lever on the winch saw Cole suddenly forced to bend over as his arms were pulled painfully up behind him.

Karla knew exactly what the human body could take and how it was obliged to move under such load. Cole was not one of her flexible twenty-something submissives, and inside ten seconds he was bent over, his breath rasping, staring at the floor.

'What –' he tried again, but Karla was intent on checking out the rest of the dungeon, then making sure that Meyer was still in the world of reason. She grabbed a ball gag from where it lay on a bench and jammed it into the man's mouth with the skill of a practiced professional, buckling it tightly at his neck, ignoring the feeble attempts to resist and the blood oozing over the strap from the pistol gash.

'Different when you're on the receiving end, huh?' she observed, now satisfied he was incapacitated and silent.

Though she had been aware of Meyer's heightened stress, his attack on Cole had taken her by surprise. She had previously heard about the failed Tehran operation, but had no knowledge that Cole was involved, and that there was unfinished business between her superior and the Englishman. It was not the first time she had seen the face of obsession, and the attack had done nothing to reassure her of Meyer's state of mind or his capacity for decision-making.

Karla looked around the room again, this time with more care. She moved to the small cell with the grille and turned on a light to illuminate it. A single mattress lay on the floor but the room was empty. No Lily Maddison.

The room next to it had a solid steel door and a lock that looked like it took an old-fashioned skeleton key, but it was missing. She tried the handle. Locked.

'Lily!' she called, hammering on the door. 'Answer me!' There was silence. 'Lily! Don't fuck about or it'll be the worse for you!' Nothing.

She turned and looked through the padlocks, chains and manacles on the wall, the work bench and in the drawers, but saw nothing which looked like what would be a very specific skeleton key.

'Where is it?' she hissed in Cole's ear, annoyed. The man mumbled something that might have been 'fuck you' or might have been something less provocative. She patted his pockets but found nothing.

'*Stay* there, then,' she snapped. 'Enjoy!' Then she turned and strode up the steps to the foyer. Meyer was in the study, searching through papers on Cole's desk.

'He's secured,' she said. 'I think Lily's in the cell but I can't find the key.'

'Go and check the rest of the house,' Meyer ordered. 'Make sure there's nobody else here, that the doors are locked and the curtains drawn. Check the street – see if there's anybody who might have heard the shots.'

It took only a few minutes to learn the layout and determine the security of the house. Karla had been alarmed at how loud the shots had sounded, but to any neighbours peering out and seeing a deserted street there would be no indications of anything amiss at Professor Cole's residence. Back in the study, Meyer flourished a fax sheet.

'Looks like we have our mole,' he said grimly, 'well, not by name, but the fact of their existence. The dis-information has made its way through.'

'But do they recognise it as such?' asked Karla.

'There's no evidence of what they did with this information. They've either destroyed any onward message, or it went by word of mouth. This is what we must find out!' He reached into his pocket and produced a skeleton key. 'This was in the desk drawer. It's probably what you're looking for.'

Karla took it and turned to go.

410

'Any activity outside?' Meyer demanded.

'No. All quiet.'

'Good. The phones are still working – we have some time to check this out. We need to persuade Professor Cole to assist us.'

As the sun disappeared they crossed the now-gloomy foyer. The body of Farah Bakhtiari continued to unnerve Karla, and she avoided looking at it and the blood congealing on the polished wood.

In the dungeon, the key fitted the lock to the cell and Karla swung the door open to reveal the two young women sitting side by side on the floor, handcuffed and chained to a ringbolt in the wall.

*    *    *

# CHAPTER 35 – Interrogation

My goodness,' Karla said, unlocking and entering the tiny cell, then surveying the two chained prisoners. 'Good evening, Lily. And Aysha.' Karla tried to put on a casual air, though she was unnerved at the alacrity with which Aysha had managed to arrive from Kiev with the assistance of the Australian Embassy.

Karla was now obliged to re-think any strategy she had. Presumably the pair had divulged the full stories of their time apart, and filled in any missing pieces. The fact Cole had imprisoned them here also suggested something was amiss, or was it simply precautionary? If he had done it because he thought Lily was meeting Karla, then possibly the game was already up... But did Lily even know about the fax they had just seen, never mind whether it was believed by British Intelligence? Karla recalled the last conversation she had with Lily, and the date she had told Lily for the true impending coup. It had been necessary so Lily could recognise and understand any disinformation, but had she now told Cole? And if so, had he believed it, and not suspected a double bluff? Had Karla herself blown this whole thing through mis-handling Lily? Dear God! What a possibility!

Karla did a quick assessment. Only Cole truly knew British Intelligence's understanding of the situation. Lily might, but it was doubtful. But it was time to have a little chat with the submissive. Ultimately they would have to get to Cole, and she reckoned he would be reluctant to part with the knowledge, but would be vulnerable if Lily's welfare was endangered. But she had to learn what Lily knew first

'What were those shots?' Aysha asked, trying to disguise the tremor in her voice.

'None of your business!' snapped Karla, and waved her pistol at them for effect. Despite her attempted bravado, Aysha recoiled at the sight of the weapon. 'Do as you're told and maybe you won't get the same treatment!'

Karla returned to the antechamber. One of the bench drawers was divided into small compartments with padlocks and keys in each. Some were empty, though there was an open box on the bench with several keys in it – obviously the "keys in use" receptacle. She smiled inwardly, recognising the obsessive and orderly mind that so often came with such territory. A place for everything, and everything in its place. Yes, Cole was as retentive and fixated as so many Dominants. She could spot the indications she knew so well herself.

She picked up the key to the neck chain joining the two women and returned to unlock the chain from Lily's collar, relocking it to the anchor ring. Aysha would be going nowhere.

'Get up!' she ordered Lily. With her wrists locked behind her, Lily struggled to her feet.

'What are you going to do with her?' Aysha demanded unconvincingly.

'I'd shut up if I were you,' Karla said, ' – unless you want something stuffed in that mouth of yours for the next few hours... or days...'

Aysha glared at her retreating back as Karla hustled Lily from the cell and locked the steel door behind them.

'What are you going to do...' Lily's version of the question was timidly put from someone who had no expectation of an answer. Karla took down a padded leather blindfold and tied it over Lily's eyes. It would help control her prisoner, but would also shield Lily from the body at the top of the stairs. Karla wanted to talk to Lily in private, away from Aysha and Cole, to keep their stories separate, and she did not need hysteria from the young woman at the sight of Farah Bakhtiari lying lifeless in the foyer.

Karla grabbed a couple of coils of rope and edged Lily up the stairs, into the foyer and across into the kitchen. Here she dropped Lily's arms over the back of a kitchen chair and tied the manacled wrists in place. Lily knew where she was and turned her blind head back and forth as though to detect whether anybody else was present. The arrival of Karla and sight of the chained figure of Cole in the cellar left her frightened. She was now a prisoner of other forces she did not understand.

Karla drew a chair up in front of the bound figure and seated herself, putting her gun on the kitchen table.

'Now, Lily, I want you to tell me what happened.' Karla's voice was measured and calm. With their entry into the house unnoticed and all the inhabitants taken care of, her own trepidation had eased, and she willed herself to breathe slowly. If she could communicate control and self-restraint to Lily, the answers would likely be more coherent. She could not afford Lily to have a panic attack.

'Why were you and Aysha chained up in the cell?'

'I... I was caught by Farah... looking through faxes while she was out of the room... I'm sorry, Karla, really... She pulled a gun and chained me up in the dungeon... and then found the camera on me...' Karla had not expected this. This explained a lot. 'Then Aysha appeared... You never told me she'd been released. You lied to me, Karla...' Lily now spoke in a whisper.

Karla thought for a minute, trying to make sense of things.

'So Cole now knows you're a spy. Does he know about me?'

'Yes. He started whipping Aysha...'

'Did you see any faxes – anything we talked about?'

'No. Farah caught me. I don't know if anything had come through...'

'Did you tell him about the dis-information, the dates?'

'Yes... yes, I'm sorry...'

'And what did he say? Did he believe you?'

'I don't know. It got confusing. He said it might be a bluff, or a double-bluff...'

'And I always thought *you* were the one who over-thought everything, Lily. Can't say I blame him for considering the possibility, though. So, what were his plans for you and your girlfriend?'

'He said we'd have to stay in the cell until things came to a head.'

'How long was that to be? The answer is critical, Lily!'

'I don't know,' Lily whimpered. 'One moment he talked about days, but everything happened very quickly. I told him about the dis-information date and the real one. I don't know which he believes.'

'Really, Lily?' Karla's voice was harsh as she pushed Lily's skirt up to expose the tops of her black stockings. She folded the remaining rope into a loop and slapped the bound girl hard across her thighs. Lily screamed and stamped her feet, kicking out, then pressing her thighs together.

Karla took the tail of the rope securing the handcuffs and bound Lily's ankles to the chair legs.

'No, please,' Lily moaned.

Thwack! Another scream as Lily writhed in her bonds, tugging against the chair. Then a rapid slashing across her exposed legs, sending hot fires from her skin to her groin.

'I don't know any more! Truly!'

Karla got up and stood beside Lily, bringing the loop of rope down in a fierce arc that struck Lily in the crotch.

'I'm sorry – I'm sorry – I'm sorry!' Lily howled. 'I don't know what he believes! Please, Karla!'

Karla could not help her instincts, for she had no doubt Lily was telling the truth. The young woman was too innocent to perpetrate a lie, and now she had Aysha alongside her, that particular hold was largely gone. Karla had a soft spot for Lily, despite everything the State held over herself. In another time, another place, Karla and Lily might have had an intense relationship, for Lily was a quick learner and had the potential to be a devoted submissive. There was a youthfulness and vigour in her nakedness that Karla had enjoyed, as well as her mental and emotional vulnerability to role play.

The whole situation had turned to shit. She finally decided that if *she* could plainly see Lily's ingenuousness, then so too could Cole. He would figure that the dates Karla had told Lily to watch for would be genuine, and that Cole had been messing with Lily when he pretended to disbelieve the real date. Yes, she thought – that was it. Lily's naivete was the giveaway. Cole was on to them. They *would* have reacted to the fax. British Intelligence would *know* what was about to unfold. Everything was about to go down the toilet with an almighty flush.

The leather blindfold was wet where tears were seeping from the bottom of it down Lily's cheeks.

'Ssshh, Lily,' whispered Karla, close beside the bound girl's head. She almost felt sorry for her, caught up way beyond her capabilities in this operation which was now turning into a debacle. Lily was snuffling and trying to catch her breath like a child in the midst of a crying jag. Karla slid her hand down between Lily's thighs and encountered wetness.

'Ohhh...' Lily groaned, suddenly distracted from her self-pity.

'My, Lily,' said Karla. 'It seems you can get aroused on more than just pleasurable stimulation...'

Lily said nothing, though her breathing changed, as Karla's fingers found her slit and wormed their way inside. Lily squirmed, suddenly gasping and sucking in a series of breaths as Karla's unerring touch alighted on her most sensitive spot and spurred a sudden flood of warmth.

'Oh-oh-oh...' The questioning had stopped, the pain of anticipation turning to pleasure, and now the boat was adrift on the river. Lily knew what lay around the bend and had no intention of falling overboard, as long as those fingers continued to do their work.

It took Karla barely half a minute, astonished how the bound submissive had progressed since her time in the Berlin cellar. Now Lily was throwing herself against her bonds, her thighs clamped together, trapping Karla's hand and willing it to continue its incitement, making incoherent grunts. Then she was there, in the white water, the cascades, the waterfall forming a light horizon against a black backdrop, and she was over the edge, falling, falling, crying out...

Karla stood up, wiping her hand on Lily's blouse as she now bent forward in the chair, her ragged breathing interspersed with moans of exhausted pleasure. Karla allowed herself a tight smile at the exhibition in selfish indulgence that had just occurred – gratification for both parties.

'What – the – fuck...!' Andreas Meyer was standing in the doorway, his expression incandescent.

\* \* \*

# CHAPTER 36 - Off Script

For a moment Karla thought the HVA Colonel would explode, such was his fury. He strode across to her and slapped her face hard, then gave a forehand-backhand to Lily, rocking her head sideways, though in her sated state she barely felt it. Karla, in contrast, put her hand to her stinging cheek and glared at the man.

'We have an operation hanging in the balance and I find you in here playing with your toy! You cunt! You were supposed to be interrogating her, not fucking her! What's the matter with you!' The man was almost incoherent, flecks of spittle flying in his rage. He was about to strike her again when Karla grabbed her pistol from the table and raised it.

'Don't you dare!' she hissed. 'Get a grip on yourself! You're acting like a madman!'

'Don't you threaten me! I'm your superior! You had a job to do!'

'And I've done it! They're on to us!'

'What?' The statement seemed to break through his umbrage. 'How do you know? Did this one tell you?' He indicated Lily with a dismissive wave.

'I deduced it,' Karla said icily. 'We saw the fax. They knew of the dates. I'm convinced they know today is real!'

The fire of anger seemed to go out of Meyer's eyes. His brow furrowed. 'Paris!'

They hastened to the study and Meyer picked up the phone, beginning dialling with the international code for Paris. Then he stopped, looked disbelievingly at the receiver, jiggling the connection buttons.

'It's gone dead!' he breathed, then rushed into the foyer to try the telephone there. From his expression, Karla saw that the result was the same. In the instant they caught each other's gaze, the house suddenly went dark as the power died.

'Fuck!' roared Meyer.

'We're gone...' Karla whispered. 'It's over...'

There was no noise from outside that they might have expected. No screeching tyres, no assault on the house. It was almost dark, the last of the grey evening light percolating through the curtained windows, just enough to dimly illuminate the foyer.

'They'll be out there,' muttered Meyer. 'They'll be sneaking up. Make sure all the curtains are closed. Find a torch while there's still enough light. Are the doors locked?'

'Yes, but that won't stop them. We should give up now.'

'No, we can make a run for it – get to one of the neighbour's houses – get to a phone...' Meyer declared.

'Have you seen the fence around this house? The back yard? If they're out there, they'll pick you off like a sideshow shooting alley.'

Meyer was thinking furiously. He moved to the study to peep between the drawn curtains.

'They're there. A vehicle has just pulled up! Armed Response Unit... *Sheisse!*'

In the gloom of the study Karla saw Meyer take out his pistol and, peering between the curtains, he fired. The noise was deafening, accompanied by the tinkle of the glass and shouts from outside.

'What in God's name are you doing? Are you mad? They'll kill us all!'

Meyer ignored her.

'We have four hostages!' he shouted through the broken window. 'Reconnect the phone or they will be shot!'

Karla put her palm to her head, not understanding how a barely tenable situation had turned to a nightmare in the space of a few seconds.

A minute passed. There were faint noises that might be made by people dispersing around the perimeter of the property. Karla and Meyer stood either side of the window, whose curtains now fluttered in a faint breeze through the broken pane. Then a voice came, amplified and metallic through a bullhorn.

'This is Commander Mason. We know who you are, Andreas Meyer and Karla Graf, and we know what you want. There is no chance of that happening. One of my men is approaching the front door with a walkie-talkie. He will leave it just outside. You may collect it and we can have a chat without the whole world having to listen.'

There was a pause as Karla and Meyer looked at each other.

'You can see the front door from the bay window next to it,' said Meyer tersely. 'Go! Don't open the door unless it's clear. We can use the radio to our advantage.'

Karla crossed the darkened foyer and peeked through the lace curtain in the oriole window, just in time to see a dark-uniformed figure retreating down the path. Something looking like a walkie-talkie lay on the doormat.

She gave the man time to pass beyond the gate then moved to the door, opening it a crack, just enough for her arm to reach out and grab the radio, before she shut it and turned the snib.

Meyer took the radio from her and moved into the kitchen. He pressed the button.

'Commander... what was your name?'

'Mason,' came the immediate reply.

'Commander Mason, I have four hostages here. I am prepared to kill them one by one. I am not a very good shot, either, so it may take several shots in each case. All I'm asking is the reconnection of the phone.'

There was silence on the other end.

417

'We need to make a point,' Meyer said urgently to Karla. Then, suddenly struck by an idea, he said: 'That woman will be the first example,' he said, indicating the body of Farah Bakhtiari. 'We'll toss her out of an upstairs window!'

Karla looked at him, astonished at the brazenness of the plan and the refusal of the man to back down. He thumbed the radio button again. 'I know you're going for orders from your bosses. You have two minutes before the first body comes out.'

Meyer turned to Karla. 'We don't have much time – we can't wait! They'll be getting into position. If they think we're going to start shooting, they'll try an assault if they're in place. Grab her feet! She can go out an upstairs window – no need to give them an opening on the ground floor.'

Unwillingly, Karla picked up Farah's ankles as Meyer hefted her shoulders and together they staggered up the stairs into Cole's bedroom. Their eyes had adjusted to the darkness sufficiently to see the window outlined beyond the lace curtains.

'This is obscene!' said Karla under her breath.

'Shut your face! We can do this! They won't want a bloodbath in Hampstead all over the front pages for the sake of a few Iranians. Won't look good for the government,' Meyer said, panting from the effort of carrying the body. 'Put her feet down at the base of the window...'

Karla braced the dead woman's feet against the wall below the window, while Meyer held the body upright and pulled his gun out. The deafening sound of two shots made Karla jump, even though she had been half expecting them. One went through the window and a moment later Meyer gave the body a shove. It leaned through the broken glass and received a further push, toppling through with a shattering of glass and tearing of curtain, tumbling to the grass below.

'Two minutes until the next one!' Meyer snarled into the walkie-talkie.

*

'A body's been thrown out of the upstairs window!' The voice of Commander Mason came through over the speakerphone in the basement of Century House. 'They're threatening to execute a further hostage in two minutes unless the phone connection is restored.'

Hopkirk looked at the three shocked men sitting round the table.

'Who was it?'

A pause.

'We think it's the Iranian woman.'

'What are the options, Commander?'

'First option, stall. Second option, give them what they want. Third option is an assault, but it's a big house and we've only five members of the team. It was short notice, we're undermanned and have no knowledge of the house or where the hostages are. My men are trained, but they're not the SAS, with their weapons, nor do we have a hostage negotiator yet. They want the phone line in a hurry. They've killed one person and seem prepared to kill more.'

'Then stall, ask for ten minutes to get the Post Office to restore communications.'

'Roger.'

'Fuck,' said Hopkirk. 'Somehow they've worked out we're on to their plan. They'll be desperate to get word to Paris by any means they can.'

'Do we have any knowledge of the others in the house? We know about Cole – what about the Maddison girl, and the other one who went inside but never came out?'

'I did some digging before,' Burrows said. 'I hoped this wouldn't be relevant, but suddenly everything's changed, so you ought to know. Lily Maddison is the daughter of the New Zealand Minister of Overseas Trade. It may be relevant to why she was working there – I don't know if blackmail was involved. In any case, it raises the stakes.'

'Oh for fuck's sake!' Hopkirk ran a hand through his hair. 'Anything else you want to dump on the table now, Mr Burrows? Any *good* news?'

'Sorry sir.'

Hopkirk pushed his chair back and paced the small distance the cramped room allowed.

'Second hostage at a window! It's Lily Maddison!'

'Oh fuck...' breathed Carlisle.

'Give them what they want!' Burrows insisted, against all his cop instincts not to yield to the villains. But he had seen Lily, had spoken to her, to the naïve but charming New Zealand girl, somehow caught up in something she could not understand. He saw support from Carlisle and Westmoreland, though neither would say so.

'No!' Hopkirk was adamant, though his voice contained no conviction. 'The PM said under no circumstances!'

'Then he'll have her blood on his hands,' Burrows said through gritted teeth. If this got out, the media would lap it up. The government – or at least the Prime Minister – would fall, unless the spin doctors got there first.

\*

They had dragged Lily – bound to the kitchen chair – across the foyer and into the study, trailing two chair-leg marks across the parquet floor. She had been positioned in front of the large broken study window facing the street, the curtains behind her. In her white skirt and top, Lily felt the rustle of the evening breeze. Still blindfolded, her other senses heightened by the loss of her sight, Lily heard the hushed murmur of voices somewhere out in the street. She had heard the two shots from upstairs and though she could not distinguish the words, she heard the urgent stressed exchanges between Karla and Meyer. Was there a third person... Aurelius?

Meyer: 'Put him in that chair! Tie him there!' A minute's silence, the sound of pacing, palpable tension. Then the sound of an impact – a human fist on another human. A grunt of pain – Cole! More impacts, more grunts, the noise made by a gagged man unable to resist or cry out.

'What the fuck?' – Karla.

'This bastard nearly cost me my life!' – Meyer through clenched teeth. 'Remember Tehran Airport, Mr Cole? It was a shame those Tudeh didn't finish you off with your girlfriend, though it looks like I get to do that, instead. Perhaps it did work out for the best!'

Now Lily twisted in the chair, tugging futilely at the handcuffs and at the ropes binding them and her ankles to the chair. She turned her head left and right as though the blindfold might come loose, but her world remained hopelessly dark. From the breeze through the window and the occasional fluttering of the curtains behind her, she had a sense of where she was, that she was visible from the street like a mannequin on display. The momentary silence that followed her placement in front of the window told her something was going to happen imminently – something bad. Her captors were somewhere in the room behind her, out of sight in the darkness back of the curtains, whispering. She began to shake.

'Karla? Karla, what's happening? What are you doing?'

The harsh voice of Meyer came from the room behind her, talking on a radio. 'You have two minutes, then the girl's dead. You want to watch her brains blown out?'

Lily gasped, the tremors in her body increasing as though she had contracted a palsy.

'No...' she whispered. 'No... please...'

There came the crackling response: 'Wait – we're getting the Post Office telecom guy – he's working on it!'

'Then he'd better work faster!' barked Meyer. 'One and a half minutes!'

'You can't do this!' Karla's voice, low and imperative.

'I fucking can, and I will! We can't give them any time to get their shit together!'

'She's a fucking innocent!' Karla again.

'She's collateral damage! Everybody knew that when they signed her up for this job!' Meyer's retort. Then into the radio: 'One minute!'

'Wait! We're on it!' Metallic voice, almost panicked.

'Andreas... do not do this...'

Sound of a phone receiver picked up. Meyer: 'Still dead!'

Karla: 'They'll assault the house!'

'Then more people will die.' The low voice of Meyer now sounding cold and resigned, the captain of a sinking ship. Timbre changed; on the radio: 'Time's up! You were warned! '

\*

'Shot fired!'

Hopkirk gripped the table to stop his hands shaking. Burrows put his head in his hands, while the other two seated looked at the ceiling and closed their eyes.

\*

The handcuffs on Lily's wrists were vibrating against the steel of the chair and the warmth of urine slid down her legs. The curtains behind her were now stained with blood and grey brain matter.

She heard Karla's voice, also shaky, speaking on the radio.

'Commander Mason - this is Karla Graf. Colonel Meyer is dead. I'm going to release Lily and we will come to the front door. We will be unarmed. Do not shoot. The other two are unharmed. I repeat, do not shoot.'

\* \* \*

# EPILOGUE

# London, January 1979

# the submissive spy

ere're your papers,' Lily said, presenting Aysha with the Sunday Telegraph and the Mail On Sunday. Aysha was sitting up in the queen bed enjoying the bacon and eggs Lily had cooked and presented on a tray with a small rose.

Aysha was naked under the satin robe draped around her shoulders, and looked fondly at Lily, who – even two years since they had met – managed to appear coy and embarrassed under Aysha's gaze. Lily wore a long-sleeved navy dress which reached her thighs and clung to the curves of her body. It was bitterly cold outside, but Lily had been made to wear the dress on her errand to fetch the papers from the newsagent at the end of the street. More significant was that she had been obliged to wear nothing underneath and her nipples now strained at the restriction as she waited to take the tray away.

'You look good enough to eat, my darling,' said Aysha. 'It must be cold out there – you could scratch glass with those nips of yours. Take off that dress and come back under.'

Lily put the tray aside and complied with enthusiasm, snuggling up to Aysha in the warmth under the duvet. It was a Sunday ritual that they followed, usually after an energetic Saturday night involving Lily's participation in the local amateur orchestra, then a more athletic performance in the spare room of the semi-detached Kilburn house. They had lived in it rent-free, in an informal *quid pro quo* that Her Majesty's government had arranged after declaring the previous occupants to be persona non-grata and quietly confiscating the place for purposes undisclosed. The spare room had held many happy hours for Lily, bound or chained at the whim of her adored mistress, who at other times was waited on or otherwise served by her submissive.

There had been some evidence of the former occupants when the MI5 and MI6 teams had scoured it, in the wake of the Hampstead siege. They had found a high frequency radio transmitter in a concealed cupboard, along with some polaroid photos which had been returned to their embarrassed owners, and nothing further had been said. Now the pair had made their mark on the house, with travel posters featuring the ancient sites of Turkey, India and Iran dominating the hallway. In the third and smallest bedroom was a desk and a second-hand electric typewriter, where sheaves of pages traced the evolution of a novel of overland travel and love from the mind of Aysha Newton.

'Oh my God,' murmured Aysha as she opened the paper and Lily's head surfaced from under the duvet beside her.

'What?'

'The Shah has fled Iran...'

Since the siege of Hampstead, they had followed the train of events which had begun on that night. A month after a dramatic round up of Tudeh supporters by the forces of the Shah, a cleric named Mostafa Khomeini had

423

died in custody of a heart attack, according to an official statement. The man was the eldest son of a religious leader named Ruhollah Khomeini, who had been exiled in France. Months of anti-Shah protests and the deaths of hundreds of demonstrators had followed through 1978, culminating in martial law being declared, and general strikes following. Throughout this, the Tudeh Party of Iran had continued to grow and encourage the rebellion.

In November 1978 the British Embassy in Tehran had been partially burned and vandalised. Now, in the first month of 1979, as the snow blanketed the Iranian capital, the paper reported that Mohammad Reza Shah, – *King of Kings* and *Light of the Aryans* – had flown with his family to Egypt.

*

After a series of temporary exiles in Egypt, the Bahamas, Mexico, Panama, being treated for leukaemia, the Shah of Iran died in Morocco, with a bag of Iranian soil under his bed. He was buried in Cairo at a ceremony attended by Anwar Sadat and Richard Nixon.

In the wake of the Shah's exile, Ayatollah Khomeini had returned to Iran to a hero's welcome, to become the nemesis of Jimmy Carter's America, following the takeover of the American Embassy in Tehran and the Iran hostage crisis in November 1979. A month later, the Soviet Union had occupied neighbouring Afghanistan and would remain there for the next decade. The USSR's search for a warm water port in the Persian Gulf was never achieved. The largely secular Tudeh Party of Iran slid into obscurity in the wake of the fundamentalist Islamic government that scorned the Soviet ideals.

# THE END

## Postscript

The 1977 global events around which this story is framed are mostly factual and I have endeavoured to adhere to the timing and outcomes of them. The executions described in Chapter 1 did indeed take place and the Tudeh Party of Iran continues to exist. With the success of the Islamic Revolution under Khomeini in 1979, the Tudeh Party was initially integrated within the Islamic Republican Party, even though links with the Soviets remained strong. In 1984, 18 Soviet diplomats were expelled from Iran and the Tudeh Party was banned, with many leaders and ordinary participants being imprisoned and tortured. Iran had become a one-party state.

Today the Tudeh barely survives, its leadership largely in exile, in France.

\*   \*   \*

## About the Author

The author was born in New Zealand and did the hippy trail from Kathmandu to London in 1977. As an engineer, the author has lived or worked in over a hundred countries, and has become fascinated with the Cold War and its effects on politics, geography and history. The author currently resides on the Sunshine Coast in Queensland, Australia.

For those who enjoyed this alternative sexuality theme, the author has produced a book series under the nom-de-plume Steven Z Reynolds, which may be found at Fiction4All:

https://fiction4all.com/ebooks/a2758.htm


The author may be contacted at bilboes1@gmail.com

## By the same author:

Fiction

# Axum

For half a millennium a secret has lain hidden in the highlands of Ethiopia – a legacy of the 1520 Portuguese expedition into the uncharted interior. The Portuguese had been searching for the fabled lands of Prester John of the Indies, but one of their number, Tristan Perreira, had found something far more momentous. In 1535 Tristan finds himself destined to lead the people of the city of Axum in a fight for survival against the invading Moors from the east, and most of all a fight to protect the Ark of the Covenant.

Nearly five hundred years later, the murder of a priest leads Tristan's descendant, Marco, on a desperate flight to save Tristan's journal and the explosive knowledge it contains. Marco is caught up with Claire McKinnon, a World Bank engineer, in an Ethiopia on the verge of war in the north and internal civil instability in the capital. In strange parallels with Marco's ancestor, they find themselves on the run from the police through the harsh landscape of the Simien Mountains and the Danakil Desert, as they gradually learn the fate that befell Marco's forebears.

Even as they do this, their lives are threatened by other ruthless forces with links to the British Embassy and a modern jihad resurgence from the east, threatening not just a diplomatic incident but something much more far-reaching.

# Land of Stone

It is 1918. In the Caucasus, the British Government is sending millions of pounds in gold coins by train to prop up the Armenian army against the rampant Turks, in a bid to protect Caspian Sea oil reserves at the end of World War 1. A small squad of British soldiers pulls off an audacious heist of a crate of gold, secreting it with every intention of recovering the treasure at the end of the war.

Fast forward a century to Philip Blake – a burned-out ex-journalist researching National Archive documents from the Caucasus campaign for a commemorative display of the British evacuation of Baku. Regimental and private diaries reveal the story of the missing gold – something that will draw

Blake to the hair-trigger border of Turkey and Armenia and the love of an Armenian woman.

While Philip Blake begins searching for an exclusive story, the Director of the National Archives – Cassandra Jennings – begins her own secret hunt for the gold, for much less altruistic reasons. Competitive, jealous, opportunist and kinky Cassie comes from a well-to-do family with a dubious past and few scruples.

The news of the surreptitious ventures in Armenia reach the ears of Iosif Kasharin, ex-Director of the Armenian National Security Service, whose intention for the gold is no less self-serving. Kasharin has local knowledge and resources that he can call on – until he learns the location of the gold, and the political ramifications that could result.

Against a background of the recent history of Armenia – the Land of Stone – through a century of misfortunes from the Genocide in 1915, then disease, famine, earthquake and political upheaval, the story twists and turns to a tense political climax.

## Trip Hazards (Non-fiction)

An account of the author's encounters around South America, from Katmandu to London, and crossing Africa, in the days before email, mobile phones and the Internet, when paper maps, hard copy guide books, and engaging with the locals were relied on to get from A to B.

Printed in Great Britain
by Amazon